Abducting
Arnold

Abducting Arnold

Becky Akers

Abducting Arnold
Copyright © 2013 Becky Akers

ISBN for paperback: 978-0-9882032-2-8
ISBN for eBook: 978-0-9882032-3-5

Cover design by Inkslinger Designs
Book design by the eBook Artisans

For Mark. Always Mark…

Prologue

It looked like all the other pouches that constantly arrived, its leather as dusty and scuffed as the man who brought it. Not a thing hinted at the horror and heartbreak inside. Still, when the courier handed it to me one hot afternoon a few months ago, I shook so bad I dropped it.

"Express for General Washington, ma'am," he croaked, scooping it from the floor as I wiped my sweaty hands on my skirts.

At last His Excellency would learn of the doom threatening him and our rebellion, would receive the warning I'd failed to deliver these last hours. So I trembled, yes, but I was mighty relieved, too. For out of the eighteen or twenty folks there that dreadful September day, I alone knew that our most astounding hero had turned traitor, that he'd sold General Washington and the fort a mile or two upriver at West Point to the British—and that his customers might appear at any moment to collect their purchases.

I was also the only one who understood that the papers within this weary case told the whole wicked plot. They'd sound the alarm I couldn't and save our Cause.

"Pray come in," I said to the thirsty messenger. "Can I get you a sup of something?"

"Be obliged for some kill-devil, you got any."

I led him toward the kitchen only to meet one of the general's aides in the hall. Colonel Hamilton grabbed the packet without a word and passed upstairs to His Excellency's chamber. Our guest stared after him, then glanced sideways at me. "There's some calls him King Alex, and I can see why."

He drank his rum, thanked me kindly, and returned to his horse.

I was laying the table for dinner some minutes later when a door over-head flew open. "La Fayette, attend us, please!" 'Twas Hamilton, voice quavering as though he were three years old instead of three-and-twenty.

Then General Washington's cry pierced us. "Oh, Father in Heaven!" I stood rooted, forks in one hand, a plate in the other. "'Tis Arnold! *Arnold* has betrayed us! Whom can we trust now?"

All these weeks later, I still hear the agony in those words, the despair, still feel our helpless fury. It's cold now, but that's not why I shiver as I scoot closer to the hearth in this house some fifty miles south of West Point and behind British lines, too.

I watch the man poking the logs to rouse the flames higher: Major General Benedict Arnold, formerly of the Continental Army, now with His Majesty's Land Forces in North America.

He looks up to catch my gaze on him. "That better, Clem?" He smiles, warm and welcoming as the fire. He forgets that a traitor has few friends, and they're mostly false.

Including me. I'm here to kidnap him.

General Washington himself asked me to do it, a fortnight after that packet had seared our souls and one conspirator—the wrong one, accord-ing to His Excellency—had already hanged. "He was more unfortunate than criminal," the general said, eyes grey as river ice. "'Tis Arnold I want. I want him brought back for trial and punishment. I swear I'll knot the noose myself."

What you've heard about General Washington's reserve is true. He's the most contained man I ever met. So for him to burst loose that way was a shock, like birds flying upside down or George III agreeing he's abused our liberties after all. Only shows how deep the general was hurt, that an officer he'd defended time and again, a hero he'd admired, a friend, would deliver him to the enemy.

"'Tis beyond me, this treason—it—it—I can't apprehend it. It's not within the compass of my reasoning." He stood staring out his headquarters' window, huge fists balled at his sides. Then he faced me. "It even baffles conjecture. But he'll answer for it yet. I'm sending an agent after him, Miss Shippen, but we need someone there with Arnold, in the house, who'll direct things. I thought of you, of course. You know him, and he trusts you." He added softly, "And so do I." That was a high honor then, when he suspected everyone, not knowing how far the treachery had spread.

And so I traveled to New York City, long since fallen to the Redcoats and Arnold's new home. I pushed my way to his door through the crowds out front. They'd watch the place for hours, curious to see the champion who defied tyrants and bullets and nature and death but who had now, in a move as fatal as any on the battlefield, turned his Cause's flank to sign with the enemy.

Still, he was a lonely newcomer and glad to have me, especially because I might bring news of his wife.

I told him she's fine, but he plied me with a hundred questions while his dog sniffed my skirts. Had she come to any harm because of the, ah, business at West Point? Had I seen her recently? Had she trusted me with any letters for him? Well, then, if not a letter, what about a message? Not even that I should give him her love?

I shook my head.

"Hmm." General Arnold clenched his jaw. "Reckon she's got a lot on her mind."

"She surely does." Once again, I'm the only person, other than the turncoat and his lady, who knows that she's in this even deeper than he. I've mentioned her part to General Washington, other officers, even—a measure of my desperation—King Alex. But her beauty blinds them, and they only laugh. So I look for evidence of his wife's guilt as I wait to abduct Arnold.

Meantime, he and I sit night after night at the hearth, cozy as an old married couple in December's storms. I've given my plans for the kidnapping to Washington's agent; all we need's his approval. Unsuspecting, Arnold tells me stories by the hour, his dog at his feet while my embroidery needle flashes in the firelight. I may be poor company, a homely woman, his cousin by marriage and servant to boot, but I'm all he's got. He talks of his days in the field, of the battles that made him a hero, second only to Dr. Franklin in worldwide fame. I hang on every word, charmed as the men who starved with him on the march to Quebec or followed his suicidal charge at Saratoga. But my heart breaks as I match what Arnold was with what he's become—

"Reckon I'll pop some corn," he says. "You want some?"

I shake my head and glance away quick to hide my sorrow at his ruin.

But he misses nothing. He was ever a smart-looking fellow and is so still, even with that mangled leg. Better than that, he commands your notice. "Here's a man," you think, "can do anything, doesn't matter how impossible." His blue eyes are pale yet bold as a lion's, and they crackle with an energy that keeps his whole body in motion, even when he's sitting still, or still as he can. Some part of him is always moving: fingers, feet, blackbird head. He's well muscled, though shorter than you'd expect after the tales you've heard, a hand's-breadth over five feet, middling size. Somehow, everyone expects him to be tall as Washington. His chin juts masterfully. He hardly laughs anymore, but he used to, loud and often. He used to joke and talk so witty, and then he'd point that chin skyward and let it peal.

He asks, "Something wrong?"

"No, sir." But my voice wobbles. The dog cocks an ear.

"Aw, Clem, I know the ladies too well for you to fool me. What's the matter? Maybe I can help." He can be kinder than you'd credit a rascal for.

"I was griev—I was just thinking about—about before the war."

He's surprised. We seldom talk on those years. For Arnold, there weren't any. He wasn't a hero then, fallen or otherwise, just a merchant with some ships and a reputation for such bravery as most would call foolhardiness.

"You were born here in New York, weren't you?" he asks.

I nod.

"But you removed to Philadelphia when you were fourteen. That's when you first met Peggy." For Benedict Arnold, everything circles back to his wife.

"Yes, sir," I say, "her father and mine were brothers, you see. 'Twas her family took me in."

"That's right, you went to Philadelphia without your parents, if I remember aright."

"Well, my father was dead by then, but my mother, um, she did what she thought was best, I guess."

"Lord preserve us from folks doing what's best." He pulls a face, making me smile.

"In a way, 'twas because of the king." I must be careful. Arnold's a friend of government now, so I can't let him see I blame it for Dad's death....

Chapter One

My father was a ship's captain who loved me as I did him. I suppose my mother cared for me, too, but she had a strange way of showing it. First, she saddled me with a name never heard in these parts, one I longed to swap for Anne or Molly or Sarah. "But Clementine's so unusual," she'd say, as though children want to be unusual.

Then, as I grew, she'd leave me home doing chores while she visited around town. She wasn't too chary about whose house she stayed at nor how late. With Dad at sea more than he was in port during the French War, gossip and everyone else had his way with her.

When Dad did spend a week or two at home, he spoiled me. He taught me my letters and read to me out of his logbooks, even rode me on his shoulders as he strolled about New York, calling on merchants, haggling over the goods for his next trip to the Indies. Because of the war, folks paid dear for things, and we prospered.

Peace came in 1763. Dad toasted it along with his mates and gave me a draught of rum, too. Never did he dream he'd survive a war that made him mount cannon on his decks only to die of peacetime regulations.

Like all kings in every season, ours wanted money. This time, George III used the excuse of his late war. The cargo my father carried had always been taxed, but that tax went uncollected while the troops were busy fighting the French. Peace let His Majesty turn that army on us.

Dad eluded them for three years, until one day a customs sloop fell in behind him off the Chesapeake and gave chase up the coast.

"Even pitched some of the goods overboard to lighten us and gain speed," Dad said when we visited him in gaol. "Didn't help. Time we reached New Jersey, king's men was close enough to fire on us."

Though mortally wounded, my father was spared a watery grave, alone of his crew. The customs men usually fished the captain out and hauled him aboard so he could stand trial.

Mother dabbed at her eyes, but I saw no tears. "We'll miss you, Robert, though you're going to a better place, I hope."

"No customs men there, neither." Dad squirmed on his bloody straw. "Devil take 'em all, thieves and robbers, every one. Bad as the Redcoats up to Boston, firing on folks. You hear about that? A massacre, that's what it was."

I'd heard something of those killed in Boston one snowy night last week, four or five men shot down after heckling a sentry. But Mother preferred living men, fluttering her handkerchief at the gaoler as he passed on his rounds. "When do you go to court, Robert?"

"I won't live long enough to see it." He grimaced, though I think 'twas meant for a smile. Sure enough, he died the night before his trial, so perhaps he had the last laugh.

Mother grieved but little before she took to playing the belle of New York. Soon a peck of swains was underfoot, snuffling after her and my father's small fortune.

That fortune gushed through Mother's hands. I longed for the last pound to be spent, for when the money went, her suitors would, too. Meanwhile, she found it bothersome to have a fourteen-year-old daughter about, especially one that was plain and clumsy. One evening I fell down the stairs and split my lip, scaring her caller so's he jumped out the window—or tried to, for it was closed. Next morning, tongue clamped 'twixt her teeth, Mother scrawled a letter. Some weeks later, brow furrowed, she ciphered out the answer. Then she packed me off to my father's brother in Philadelphia.

Dad had been a Shippen, one of Philadelphia's foremost families. They hobnobbed with the Penns, and one or another always ended up on the Governor's Council.

But my father loved the sea. He'd fled the respectable life of a Philadelphia Shippen for New York's docks. Soon he was master of his own ship, sailing from Newfoundland to the Indies and all ports in between. In one of them, at Norwich, Connecticut, he met my mother. Seems she'd have been happy to get any man, let alone a Shippen, coming from a waterfront family of drunks herself. But she scorned Dad and all his relatives, especially his brother, Judge Edward Shippen.

'Twas to the judge and his family that we sailed one spring day in 1771.

"He'll see to you, Clem. You need a man's guidance now that your father's dead and gone." Mother sounded as sincere as when she talked of missing Dad. "Time enough you'll be wanting a husband, and all the gentlemen the judge knows, why, he'll find you a good one, better than I could. You'll like it there in Phillydelphia, you'll see. Besides, the judge'll be pleased to get you. He never approved of me, you know."

I watched the stevedores load cargo and shut my ears to Mother's plaints against Uncle Shippen. I'd heard them all my life, especially when she argued with Dad. "Your brother told you not to marry me," she'd scream. "He was right, you shoulda listened." From this I pictured my uncle a sage, wise as Solomon.

Philadelphia seemed to stretch forever along the river when first I saw it, with a hundred wharves lining the waterfront until I couldn't have told afterward which one we used. 'Twas a grand city, the Empire's biggest after London and proud of it. Here were none of the cow-paths that passed for roads elsewhere. Instead, the streets were wide and straight, some running north-south, others crossing them regular. The goodly buildings lining them were of brick and stone, whether homes or shops. Over everything rose the bell-tower of what I later learned was Christ Church. All I knew then was that it must be the tallest thing in the world, taller even than Trinity Church up to home. 'Twas an edifying prospect, with only the flies and mosquitoes buzzing everywhere to mar it.

My uncle was there to greet us. He wasn't the confident man I expected but a nervous little rabbit, large nose twitching and hands wringing—Dad's opposite. He held out those hands to us as we stumbled down the gangway.

"Ah, Hepzibah," he said, face pinched with the effort to be cordial.

Mother endured his kiss, then pulled me forward. "Here's your niece, Judge. I'm obliged to you for taking her. You'll be a good parent to her." She hesitated. "There's that other favor I mentioned in my letter. Not a favor, really, because I'll repay it, with interest of course. Robert and I did that other time, you know, but I—"

"I thought Rob left you some money."

"It don't go far, Judge, with new gowns costing what they do, and the house falling down around my ears, and I thought mayhap I'd buy myself some stock, set up in trade. That way, I can send you somewhat for Clem's upkeep."

My uncle laughed. "You, Hepzibah, in trade?"

"I'll repay it. Don't you worry."

"You did before." My uncle pursed his lips. "All right, here's ten pounds sterling, same terms as last time." He pulled a wee sack from his pocket.

Mother's eyes lighted, and she snatched it from him. "Obliged," she murmured, then thrust me forward. "Now take my daughter, Judge. Maybe you'll do better by her than we did."

Mother strutted up the gangway, and my uncle turned to me with another sigh. Grey hair peeped from under his wig, and though he wasn't fat, his jaws hung heavy. His eyes as he studied me were sad but gentle—the only thing about him that reminded me of Dad. "Appears to me they've done pretty well by you," he said and patted my shoulder.

I didn't expect such sympathy from him after Mother's rudeness and ducked my head lest he see my tears.

"Where's your bags?" he asked. I had only one, and 'twas pitifully small. He tipped a stevedore to bring it to his carriage and, taking my arm, helped me to it as though I were a great lady.

"Your aunt and cousins are eager to meet you," he said once we were underway.

"I won't be a burden, sir, I promise. I can keep house, and do chores—"

"A burden?" He shook his head with a chuckle. "Truly, my dear, you're no burden. Nor do we look for you to be. We have four girls, you know. One more won't be any trouble."

The carriage stopped before a mansion grander than any I'd seen. A whole block of Philadelphia lay fenced and gated, with formal gardens around a double-bay palace of red and black brick. Pediments crowned the doors and windows.

But 'twas the girl standing before the mansion took my eye. She was delicate as a fairy. Her hair, the yellow of buttercups, hung below her

waist. The sun danced in that hair, filled it with light, until it was alive
in its glowing. Her eyes sparkled grey and wide. Her face was chiselled
fine as marble with translucent skin, a contrast to mine, now pocked
by my fourteenth year. She was the most winsome creature ever, I'd
warrant, though she was but eleven. With every year, she grew more so.
In truth, I don't think Peggy aged: she beautified. And as her loveliness
bewitched folks later, fooled the best men of our age, so it caught me
now. Staring, I forgot there was anything in the world but her. Never
saw my aunt and her children standing there, neither, till my uncle's
words startled me from my trance.

"This is our cousin Clem," he told them, and the fairy stuck out her
tongue at me.

He introduced his family, my aunt, and their daughters and son.
"And Peggy has a gift for you from all of us," he said, gesturing to
the fairy.

Innocent, dazzling, she stepped forward to hand me a package.

"Here," she said. "I picked it out myself."

"I helped, too," said the cousin who looked to be the eldest girl. Her
hair was Peggy's shade of gold, though it didn't gleam nor beckon.

"Yes," Peggy said, "but if I'd listened to you, Betsy, Clem'd have a
horrid old book now instead of—oops, almost spoiled your surprise.
Open it, Clem."

I untied the bundle to find a kerchief of grey cotton. 'Twas a costly
thing that matched Peggy's eyes, not my brown ones. I'd rather had
the book.

"Maybe I could borrow it sometime," Peggy said as I dutifully draped
it round my neck.

My aunt kissed me. "Come inside, dear. Let me show you
your chamber."

Uncle Shippen's house held everything mortal man could want, good
food and fine clothes, sets of sofas and wide hearths, shelves of books,
company bustling in and out, and my cousins always thinking on some
mischief or other. 'Twas a contrast, and no mistake, to what I'd known
in New York.

Yet I was homesick those first weeks. Servants attended to every
chore, and though I thought to enjoy such leisure, 'twas boring after a
day or two.

And so I busied myself with Peggy. I brushed her silky hair while her silky voice spun stories. Upstairs, we found a wardrobe that stood nigh empty and turned it into our private castle. 'Twas here we pricked our fingers with one of Peggy's embroidery pins and made ourselves blood sisters. "Same as if you'd been born to Mama," Peggy said. We threw tea parties for Peggy's dolls, though I was really too old for such things, with Peggy passing a plate of cookies pilfered from the kitchen. Even the needlework Aunt Shippen set us each afternoon was entertaining, so long as Peggy made her jokes.

I'd lived there but a fortnight when Peggy announced we'd give a real party in a few days, this one for her friends.

"It'll be so much fun!" Her eyes beamed. "Oh, I do love parties, don't you? I can't wait till we're old enough for courting. Just think, beaux lined up, and a different gown to wear every night, and the dancing—oh, Clem, won't it be heaven?" She leaned towards me, all sweet and confiding. 'Twas part of her charm that though she leaned towards everyone, in every conversation, you never noticed, but thought you alone had her favor. "Now, listen. For this party, we're all bringing our favorite doll and dressing to match her."

"But I—I don't have a doll. I mean, I—I do, but I didn't bring it with me. It's at home—"

"That's all right. You can have one of mine." We were sitting on Peggy's bed. She slid off it, skipped to the mahogany chest, and took a doll from the lowest drawer—the only tattered one she had, dressed in the fashion of ten years ago and the paint on its face rubbed away. But Peggy handed it to me as though 'twere a great gift. And what could I say? For a gift it was and generous of her to share with me, her poor relation.

Next morning, I hunted through some old sacques waiting to be turned into quilts for an outfit like the doll's. Though the clothes were wrinkled and patched, they were finer than anything Mother ever made me. I stared long at the mirror, hoping I was almost pretty.

That lasted until I stepped into the hall to see Betsy in her Sabbath best.

"Clem." She giggled. "Why're you dressed in those rags?"

"Well, I, um, my doll, see, it—"

"Where'd you get that old thing?"

"Peggy gave it to me."

"Goodness, I haven't seen that doll for years." Betsy wrinkled her nose. "Well, but Peggy didn't mean you couldn't change the clothes on her." The doorknocker thumped. "Too late now. Come on." Betsy grabbed my hand and pulled me downstairs as a servant hurried to the door.

"Peggy, look at her," Betsy whispered as we gained the parlor. A vase of flowers from the garden graced the mantel, and more posies peeped from the two earthenware cornucopia on the wall behind the settee and tea table. Beneath those blooms, and lovelier than any of them in her satin and lace, sat Peggy. "Why didn't you tell her she could dress her doll in new clothes?"

Peggy's eyes shaded, maybe with concern, but there was plenty of laughter, too. "Oh, Clem, I never thought you wouldn't realize—well, tell you what." She handed me an apron lying folded beside her. "I was going to wear this when I poured, but you go ahead. It'll cover you up."

Mayhap Peggy hoped to make things better with the apron, a workaday affair borrowed from the cook. But all it did was brand me a servant. While the others giggled and gossiped, I handed cups round and fetched more hot water, opened the window wider, and carried the slop jar outside.

I thought naught of it at the time. I was too thrilled that Peggy included me and shared her friends. It was enough to sip tea with her and Betsy after the party as we talked everything over.

"Wasn't that something that Becky Franks has her own carriage now?" Betsy said. "Just think, a pony of her very own, and a carriage built half-size so she can drive it herself. Wouldn't you love to have one?"

"I sure would." Peggy set aside her teacup and clapped her hands. "I know, tonight at supper, I'll ask Daddy to buy us one."

Betsy stared. "Are you touched? He'll never do that."

"Betsy." Peggy was as close to chiding as she came. "Daddy's so good, you know he'll give us anything we want. You wait and see."

Supper in my uncle's house was not so grand as dinner, but there was still more meat than Mother would have served in a week, and the wine poured free. In New York, I usually ate alone since Mother didn't come home until late; I'd grab some bread when I had anything at all. But now I feasted on roast beef and onion soup, with flummeries and syllabub for the asking. We dined off china, a different set than what we used at dinner. Enough candles shone to have done my mother's table for a month, and though 'twas late spring, and not so cold you shivered, a fire cheered us.

My uncle had barely said grace when Peggy mentioned Becky Franks' pony and carriage. "It's the cleverest thing, Daddy. The carriage was made just her size, she says. Now she can go all over, any place she wants to."

My uncle signaled for the beef as Peggy continued.

"I'd sure like it if we could have one, too. Becky and I could go driving together then. 'Twill pass the time until I'm older and my beaux drive me to all the parties."

"I'm sure 'twould." My uncle chewed his meat. "But you're too young for such folderol, go driving about Philadelphia wherever you want."

We ate in silence until Peggy put a hand to each side of her head and moaned.

Aunt Shippen dropped her fork. "Peggy?"

She moaned again, longer and louder. "Oh, my head!"

"Honey, what's wrong? Are you—"

"Oh, it hurts so bad!" Peggy was rocking in her chair now, clutching her hair as she groaned, "I'm gonna die. Make them stop!"

My aunt rushed to her while my uncle said, "Now, Peggy, we went over this last time you had one of these fits. There's no one here but us. No one's doing anything to you—"

"They're pulling a band around my head so tight! Oh, it hurts! Make them stop!" Eyes fluttering, she swooned.

My heart thumped as my aunt and uncle called her name. They rubbed her hands, then gathered her in their arms, my aunt in tears at her baby's pain. They hadn't even gained the stairs to Peggy's chamber afore Aunt Shippen convinced my uncle to bespeak the carriage after all, a small thing, really, and 'twould make Peggy so happy.

And so the months passed with Peggy always having her way. Even Ned, Uncle Shippen's nephew who was reading law with him and asked to court Betsy that November, fell under Peggy's spell. After she said how much fun his sleigh must be, he took her riding along with Betsy.

Meantime, I explored my uncle's library. I'd not read much before. Mother owned a Bible and a copy of Shakespeare, both handed down in her family and battered, with more pages missing than remained. But now I feasted on Scripture with every chapter in place, Aristotle, Cicero, Locke, Addison. This drew Uncle Shippen and me close, for no one else took the leather-bound books from their shelves. Then, too, in that dark and private library I could grieve for my father or re-read the letter my mother sent.

Soon almost two years had gone and with them my sixteenth birthday. Uncle Shippen came home the next week with a smile for me. "Well, Clem," he said at dinner, "Eli Belks asked leave to call on you. I thought you wouldn't mind, eh?"

A servant offered him the ham as I blushed.

Peggy clapped. "Oh, Clem, your first sweetheart! Maybe he'll ask you to a ball." She sighed. "Wish I was older."

I knew naught of Mr. Belks but that he was a wealthy man with at least ten more years to his credit than me and a Quaker-turned-Anglican, like my uncle and his family. Aside from his money, there's little to commend him. Likely 'twas the business my uncle could throw him more than me that interested him. Still, when I was plain as a hen's egg, especially beside Peggy, it was nice to have anyone come courting.

And so Mr. Belks called on me that winter. Actually, he called on me for the first month; after that, he came to see Peggy.

We had little to talk of anyway. Mr. Belks lived and breathed business. His family owned an iron plantation on the Schuylkill River, and its affairs consumed him. He'd stretch his legs before the fire and speak of the forge and blast furnace or his need of more timber to feed them. Then we'd sit staring at the hearth.

I tried discussing the books I read, but he yawned. "Miss Shippen, truth to tell, I never cared much about the Greeks and Romans. Waste of time, you ask me."

Even the Boston Tea Party that December gave us only a minute's worth of speech. "They're a lawless mob, violent ruffians," he said. "Just like those ones taunted the soldiers a while back and got themselves killed. They had it coming, don't you think, cursing at officers sent here to protect us. Heroes willing to give their lives for their country and—and serving the public, and those ingrates *threatened* them. A *course* they fired on 'em: that's what troops do! 'Twasn't any massacre way the Whigs up to Boston claimed. Now you got more of the same with these—these lunatics protesting tea. *Tea*, for God's sake! Next they'll riot over chocolate. Idiots!"

He laughed at the newspapers with their talk that the king didn't belong in the marketplace, selling tea and stealing trade from private merchants.

"But I been thinking," he said. "If that ship been fitted with iron bars, in the hold, see, like a cage, those vandals'd never have got their hands on the tea."

The next week, Peggy twinkled into the parlor on some errand. Mr. Belks couldn't take his eyes from her, and for good reason. Uncle Shippen spent enough on her clothes as would have fed most families for a year, yet Peggy always looked to be bursting the seams. However fine her dress, it emphasized the body beneath, every curve and dimple, and those curves were amazing for a girl so young.

She settled on the hearth with a dozen questions about the iron-works. Peggy could have no interest in the plodding Mr. Belks, but she must always be the center of things for every man. I didn't mind as it relieved the silence. At times, I even opened Livy or Euripides and stole a few paragraphs.

Then one day I returned from the necessary to hear their voices from the hall outside the parlor.

"—bore you to death with her books," Peggy was saying.

"Well, but Miss Shippen, every lady cannot be as delightful as you." Mr. Belks spoke in a daze, as men did with Peggy.

My cousin made a "tch" sound. "I suppose we should feel sorry for her, plain as she is."

"That's charitable of you, Miss Shippen."

Worse, my aunt slipped up behind me and heard this last. She patted my arm. I blushed at being caught eavesdropping, and on such insults, too.

Aunt Shippen drew me into the parlor after her. "Who were you speaking of, dear?"

"Oh, no one that signifies," Peggy said, "just old Widow Sterne."

But the Widow Sterne with her bad eyes never opened a book, not even the Bible. And Mr. Belks sat silent, nor looked at me the rest of his visit.

When he next appeared, my aunt told Peggy to leave us to our courting. Eli Belks showed up once more before taking his iron-stores elsewheres.

Only my pride was bruised, not my heart. Withal, the news distracted us. The government put Boston Town under martial law after the Tea Party, stirring up a hornet's nest as far away as Virginia and even Georgia.

Uncle Shippen's nose twitched as he mourned the perilous times and our threatened liberties. But for all his talk, he cared mostly for his estate, his business and posts. He loved sitting on the Governor's Council and conferring with the Penns. All he wanted from his country was safe, prestigious posts. So far, that's what he'd had; 'twas how he'd made his fortune. Supporting the king and Ministry was as natural for him as collecting his salaries. Indeed, 'twas the same.

But his friends differed. Some said the Bostonians were true defenders of liberty, that the British Empire was tyrannical. Others sided with Eli Belks and called them traitors.

'Twas hard to guess who'd prevail. More were cheering the rebellion than damning it, but that applause wouldn't mean much once it echoed off a battalion of Redcoats. So Uncle Shippen determined he'd show no favoritism. He continued to sit on the royal governor's Council, but when representatives from all the colonies came to Philadelphia that May for to air their grievances, he invited some to dinner.

My uncle passed over the lesser congressmen in favor of those most influential, so among our first guests were two cousins named Adams. I'd seen their names in the paper as leaders of the rebellion in Massachusetts.

And there was a colonel from Virginia's militia, said to be one of the wealthiest men this side of the Atlantic. Though I'd never heard of George Washington, Uncle Shippen claimed he'd distinguished himself during the French War.

The Adamses arrived first. They were small men, and dour, as New Englanders often are. We repaired to the front parlor, where my aunt served cider. This touch of home brought smiles from them.

"Lovely country you have here." Samuel Adams raised his mug in a palsied hand, and Aunt Shippen flinched lest the cider slop over to spot the carpet. "But I've missed my elixir."

His cousin John nodded. "I drink a quart every morning. I dasn't set foot out of bed otherwise. Now, if I may, a toast: let Britain be wise, and America be free!"

We'd barely sipped when the doorknocker banged, and the tallest man I'd ever seen joined us. Though he was wearing a blue velvet suit and not a uniform, you could see the warrior in him with the lift of his chin, his square shoulders, his back straight as a ramrod.

Colonel Washington bowed, murmuring, "Your servant, ladies." Then he asked leave to take the chair aside me. I nodded, too overwhelmed to speak, for men always flocked to Peggy. The colonel also sat silent, following the talk of my uncle and the Adamses.

"Now tell me, gentlemen," Uncle Shippen said, "what's your Congress been up to?"

"Declaring our allegiance to king and country," John Adams said.

"Excellent." My uncle rubbed his hands. "I commend you, sir. That was wise."

The cousins nodded. John continued, "We're loyal citizens, sir. All we want is our liberty restored to us, you know, the liberties Englishmen have cherished for centuries."

"Well..." My uncle waved that aside. "I hardly think—British citizens are the free—"

"That's why we've petitioned the king, sir," Sam Adams said.

"'Petitioned the king'?"

Both Adamses nodded. "We want him to repeal the Trade Acts. Let our commerce be free as it was ten, twelve years ago."

"But—but—" Uncle Shippen kept his smile, though you could tell he was only being polite. "The world isn't what it was then, gentlemen. We must protect British merchants. Why, where'd they be if merchants from all over the world could rob them of our business?"

"I know where *we'd* be, sir," Sam Adams said. "We'd be paying lower prices for our goods."

"Well, yes, but they'd go bankrupt! Shouldn't good Englishmen buy English?"

"Maybe they should find other work if they can't sell cheaper than the Dutch or Spanish." Sam Adams shrugged.

"And there's the taxes the king takes, too, for his ministers that set the tariffs and the officers enforcing them." 'Twas the first time Colonel Washington spoke. His voice was kindly, especially from such a large man.

My uncle's brows climbed to his wig. "But we have debts! From the French War, we must pay those debts. And funds to run the government, the army and navy that protect us—"

Sam Adams snorted. "You mean that spy on us and gaol us and kill anyone who protests."

My uncle didn't even glance at him. "Where's the king going to get that money if not from imposts and tariffs?"

"We've given him sixty days to repeal the trade acts." Sam Adams spoke blandly, as though colonists dictating to rulers was not the most unheard-of thing in the world, and revolutionary, so revolutionary it gets men dispossessed, imprisoned, even hanged. All us Shippens gasped.

"And if he doesn't?" my uncle asked at last.

John Adams smiled thinly. "Then we hit them in the purse. We won't buy any more goods from England. We'll do without rather than pay the tariff, and the government can whistle for its money."

It took my uncle several draughts of cider to recover from that one. Not my aunt, though. With cold courtesy she asked, "What do you mean, 'We'll do without'?"

For the first time, John Adams lost his fervor. "Well, madam, we—we—we'd all agree not to buy anything from, ah, England."

"Anything?" My aunt stared. "And what, sir, am I to do for clothing?"

"We, um, we'll make it here."

"'Make it here.'" Aunt Shippen was even more aghast. She looked down at her skirts, sumptuous with their yards of lace and furbelows. "There's no tailor here could make this. Nor that harpsichord over there." She gestured at the corner, then hefted the silver flagon of cider. "Nor this pitcher. Stop buying from England? Gentlemen, that's—I'd never you expect me to agree to such—such insanity?"

Sam Adams spoke as freezingly as my aunt. "'Tis an inconvenience, true—"

"'Inconvenience'?" She shook her head. "'Tis an impossibility, sir!"

My uncle cleared his throat. "King'll hardly capitulate, sir, way you've framed it. He can't back down—"

"He doesn't respond, we'll quit exporting to England, too."

My uncle sat flummoxed. "But—but how will you control such a thing? How will you prevent people—how will you prevent my wife from buying gowns and—and pitchers? Or farmers selling their tobacco to English customers?"

"The Ministry controls the ports now, doesn't it?" John Adams spread his hands. "They regulate them for the government's benefit, so why can't we? Why can't we regulate them for liberty's benefit?"

My uncle was too gracious to insult guests, but after they left, he told my aunt, "They're becoming the very thing they say they detest: tyrants dictating how the rest of us can buy and sell."

The Congress met at Carpenters' Hall for about seven weeks. In that time, we dined with delegates thrice, though Uncle Shippen was more and more unhappy with them.

"They want the militia to turn out!" he'd rant. "Militia! As though a bunch of farmers should stand against our troops, or even could. They're fools, all of them. And this non-import business. That's the end of your books, Clem. We do what the Congress wants, it's the end of all the things we don't make ourselves—as though Parliament'll listen if we starve the merchants over there. Ha!"

Winter closed around us, and Uncle Shippen bought madly against the day that the non-import agreement ("There's no agreement! I never agreed to anything") took effect. Everyone must have new wigs, clothes, saddles, fans. But contrary winds slowed the ship carrying our finery so it didn't arrive until April, which put it under the ban. The Whigs pacing the wharves allowed nothing to be unladed, not so much as a parcel, let alone the crates holding my uncle's order. Even presents must go back, like the port wine someone sent our neighbor. Took a while, then, for our vessel to spy out a cove down the Delaware deserted enough to unload, and another week afore someone could smuggle those crates into town to us. We got them on a Monday, April 24 'twas, the day of another dinner party.

I remember it well, for that afternoon I read in the paper of a Virginian who'd thundered in their assembly, "If we wish to be free, we must fight! An appeal to arms and to the God of Hosts is all that is left us!" The report called Patrick Henry a young farmer from the backcountry, with hair red as his face when he shouted, "Is life so dear, or peace so sweet, as to be purchased at the price of chains and slavery? Forbid it, almighty God. I know not what course others may take, but as for me, give me liberty, or give me death!" Peggy burst into the library then, and led me upstairs with giggles and jokes so's we could dress for our party.

We descended later in clouds of perfume and laughter, Peggy waving her fan, my aunt looking like a fashion doll. Excitement hung in the air, more than the new baubles should have caused. Seemed all Philadelphia was on the move, with people and carriages racing past the house. Then the door opened, and there's my uncle, a full hour early.

We hushed and stared at him, until Aunt Shippen found her voice. "Edward, what is it? Are you sick?"

"They fired on our troops."

This made no sense, and we continued staring. Finally, my aunt said, "Who? What are you talking about?"

"Some rabble up near Boston Town, they shot at the king's Regulars. That's treason, Margaret. It's war."

"War!" Peggy clapped. "Oh, Daddy, will soldiers be coming here? And officers in those gorgeous uniforms?"

My aunt stepped forward with hand outstretched. "No, Edward, it's a big thing, a war. Likely this is just a misunder—"

"No. It's war." My uncle wandered into the hall like a child, my aunt leading him and motioning for us to leave them. Still, as we rustled up the stairs, my uncle's shocked voice followed us. "Farmers, Margaret, they'd been stockpiling muskets for the damned militia—"

"Edward, I won't have cursing in this house."

"—for the militia, then, and the Regulars marched to get these muskets, but at some little town, Lexington I think they called it, farmers fired on them, Margaret, on our soldiers—"

The tale filled the newspapers and every conversation, so that only the blind and deaf wouldn't learn the whole story. The king's troops had indeed received fire, and not just at Lexington but at another village further down the road named Concord.

I'd seen Regulars as a child, when a troop would land in New York. They were fearsome men with their scarlet coats, muskets, and bayonets, one as alike as the next. I wouldn't want to be a farmer standing against them in homespun, clutching the old Brown Bess used to butcher hogs and then only.

No wonder the Redcoats killed a score of farmers and plundered the arsenal at Concord (though, hearing that the army planned a visit, folks there had moved most of their guns to safety). But when the Regulars turned around for to march back to Boston, the farmers and their neighbors lined the roads. Those men shot at them all the way, killed or wounded nigh half. Once they reached the city, the soldiers scurried within whilst the farmers settled down on guard outside. More folks joined them, until 10,000 or so was besieging 3000 troops.

As if that weren't enough, other men set off from Boston for the province of New York and a fort on Hudson's River called Ticonderoga.

Ticonderoga's left over from the French War. It had cannon, big ones and plenty of them, something the militia around Boston Town needed as much as muskets need powder. Seemed only sensible to surprise the handful of Regulars inside Ticonderoga's crumbling walls and take those guns. In truth, 'twas so sensible that several men thought of it.

One of them was Benedict Arnold.

Chapter Two

"Ticonderoga." Arnold hunches forward to shake a pan of corn over the fire. "That's Iroquois for 'Big pain in backside.'"

The rattle of popping kernels fills the room. Though we've eaten a bountiful supper—generals in His Majesty's army dine well no matter what—the corn smells delicious. I take another stitch on the pocketbook I'm embroidering and wonder if the aroma will rouse Peggy from her lair. She's a tiny thing, not much bigger than me, but she's got an appetite to match General Washington's.

She joined us a fortnight ago, fresh from her father's house, where she'd fled in the wake of the treason—until Philadelphia's rulers decreed that as the wife of an "attainted traitor," her "residence in this city has become dangerous to the public safety" and gave her fourteen days to get out. I wonder if the Arnolds' property there has anything to do with it, for they own a choice estate that now sits empty and ripe for confiscation. Regardless, packing Peggy off to us shows what cowards sit on the Council, to pick on a woman, and one defended only by my weak, nervous uncle. The husband who would have killed anyone offering such insolence was ninety miles away and behind the enemy's lines to boot.

But that husband's as happy she's here as if it's her own choice. Now he continues, "Only five years ago that we marched on Ticonderoga but seems like a hundred." He opens the pan, fills a bowl, and passes it to me. "Figured you'd want some, once it was popped."

As I said, he's kinder than a traitor should be—so kind I blush at plotting to kidnap him. I put aside the pocketbook. "Thank you."

He fills another bowl, sets it on the candle-stand between us. "Case Peggy comes down," he says, hopeful-like, and I pity this man who must bribe his beloved to sit with him.

The dog lumbers to his feet and lays his head on Arnold's thigh. "Beggar," Arnold says, but he rubs the dog's ears and holds out a kernel to him. "You don't even like this, Flash. We went through this last time I made it, remember?" Flash sniffs, loses interest, and sinks to the floor again at Arnold's feet.

We munch a couple of handfuls before I say, "So Ticonderoga, when you marched against it, that was your first, um, military—" I cast about for the right word.

"Campaign? Ah-yuh." He gives the grunt that means "yes" in New England. "'Course, even before that, when I was a merchant, I'd gone past the Ti dozens of times on my way to Canada, buying and selling, so I'd seen first-hand how strategic it was. Tremendous traffic coming down from Canada or up from New York, and there's the Ti, right where Lake Champlain and Lake George meet, right in the middle of that waterway where it controls all the shipping. And only a handful of soldiers garrisoned there 'cause it's twelve, thirteen years since the last war ended, and the Ti itself's crumbling."

"But they had cannon."

He smiles. "Ah-yuh, cannon galore. Used to see 'em fired when I was inside the fort, selling horses. Soon as I heard about Lexington and Concord, I knew we better get our hands on those guns, 'cause they were gonna be used one way or another, either by us or against us."

A log settles on the hearth, exhaling sparks. I pick up the pocketbook again. The diamonds I'm embroidering on it are the lopsidedest you ever saw, more like triangles or circles. I'm not much of a seamstress. Or mayhap it's Arnold's fault, distracting me with his talk.

He crunches a few kernels before saying, "So there I was, a merchant and horse-trader in Connecticut and married to the girl of my dreams, Margaret, you know, my first wife, the one before your cousin. Curious, both my wives were named Margaret, though I misdoubt anyone's called Peggy since her christening. Well, anyway, with affairs so strained back then, the spring of '75, they elected me Captain of the Second Company of the Governor's Foot Guard."

He settles back to tell Ticonderoga's tale, and I do, too, for I love his stories. There's a Patriot down to Philadelphia, a surgeon before the war, name of Benjamin Rush, one of those sour kinds that can't enjoy life and don't want anyone else to neither. He's called Arnold's conversation "uninteresting and sometimes indelicate." Well, of a time, the general forgets he's not in an army camp anymore, that it's just him and his female cousin by the fire, and lets slip a few words maybe he shouldn't. But "uninteresting"? Never.

Tomorrow I'll write everything down best as I remember. But for now, I just listen…

He was drilling the Foot Guard on New Haven's green, trees proud with new leaves and the fields beyond town plowed black, when word came that Redcoats had marched to confiscate the militia's arsenal at Concord and, while they were at it, arrest John Hancock and Sam Adams.

"But we chased them soldiers back to Boston Town!" The courier who brought the news grinned. "Killed some, winged a lot, too. Reckon they'll think twice afore they go roistering out into the country again."

The Foot Guard gathered round, brows puckered, mouths agape. Even the buildings bordering the green, the shops and offices and warehouses near the waterfront and the large, neat homes to the north, seemed shocked and frowning.

In the troubled silence, Arnold asked, "Redcoats get anything?"

The courier shrugged. "Nothing but a coupla flintlocks so old they wasn't no use to no one. They're holed up there in Boston now, the Redcoats are, don't look like they'll be busting out anytime soon. We need all you men that can to march up there, make sure they stay put."

They voted on it, as they did on all matters affecting the troop, though they could have saved themselves the trouble. They were nearly unanimous in agreeing to go, with only Luke Chappel and old Dr. Platts saying nay, and when Luke saw everyone glaring at him, he gave one of his crazy cackles and cried, "Aye! I meant 'Aye'!" Dr. Platts shook his head and muttered that they were fools, brave fools, but fools nonetheless.

"Look at us, Cap'n." The surgeon's voice grated in the twilight. "Haven't but ten or twelve of us got muskets, and the rest of us make do with scythes. What help we gonna be up to Boston?"

Arnold raised a hand as the others jeered. "There's plenty of muskets in the town magazine, weren't any of us thinking of marching without them, Doctor."

"Got bayonets, too? Remember, I was in the French War, and I'll never forget the sight of all them bayonets when the Regulars attacked—"

"I know."

"Well, if you know, then how you fixing to fight them, huh? How you fixing to defend yourself once you fire and there's no time to reload 'cause they're on you with them bayonets? You ever seen a man wounded by a bayonet? Well, I have, helped bandage more than my share, and—"

Josiah Wallet's arrival spared them the rest of the doctor's harangue. Arnold had dispatched Josiah to New Haven's selectmen when the courier galloped off.

"Selectmen are gathering now, sir," Josiah said. The youngest of the Guard, he would not turn sixteen for a month yet, and a flush colored his hairless cheeks at the importance of his news. "They're gonna discuss things, have a vote."

Arnold nodded. Confident that these friends and neighbors would stand behind the Foot Guard, provisioning and arming them, he sent Josiah back to the selectmen.

"You bring me word soon as they vote," he ordered. "Rest of you, you're dismissed until morning."

Anxious to tell Margaret, he loped for home, past houses and squares, elm trees and docks. He turned onto Water Street, and his heart swelled. New Haven boasted so many pretty homes and well-tended gardens that even visitors called it the most beautiful town in New England, perhaps all America. Yet his grounds were the loveliest.

Three acres of New Haven's finest land held stables and a coach house and an orchard of a hundred trees. The warm weather this last fortnight had most of the trees in leaf: apple and cherry, plum, pear, peach, apricot, and even a nectarine or two. The house—a mansion, really, folks judged it the grandest place for miles—boasted two chimneys, a gambrel roof, and pediments over the first-floor's windows in the latest style. Pillars framed the entry.

Only the exterior was finished at present, though one day a central passage would run its width and marble hearths grace the rooms. For now, a web of planks and banisters, barrels and sawhorses lurked inside, with carpenter's tools scattered between. Doors leaned against the walls, waiting to be hung. The aroma of beef and baking bread wafted across the threshold, transforming the mess into a home.

"Margaret!" He picked his way to the kitchen at the rear. "News, Margaret. Wait'll you hear! Where are you?"

"Here." She appeared at the entrance to the kitchen, between doors propped on either side, and his heart swelled again at sight of her. Blonde and delicate after a sickly childhood, barely reaching his shoulder, dainty as a kitten and playful as one, too—

Margaret gave a tight smile that dashed him. "We're waiting dinner for you, Benedict."

She swept past him to the mahogany table. Their two eldest sons stood behind Chippendale chairs, hands folded for grace, faces anxious as always when their mother was upset. His sister Hannah held their youngest, a three-year-old they called Hal. She did not meet Arnold's eyes, and he saw that Margaret had learned through her of the trip he planned next week.

Taking his place, Arnold bowed his head. "Father, for this and all other blessings, we give Thee thanks, amen. Margaret, Hannah, have you heard?"

Chairs scraped, and Margaret helped herself to bread as though he had not spoken. Only Hannah answered. "Heard what, Benny?"

"Redcoats fired on militia up near Boston Town, killed some of them."

Margaret busied herself serving the boys, but Hannah gasped. "You— you mean our soldiers fired on—on *people?* On *us?*"

"On folks up to Boston." He nodded.

"Dear Lord, *why?*" Hannah's eyes rounded with horror. "How many dead?"

"Don't rightly know, maybe ten or twenty." He speared some beef with his fork and spooned sauce over it. The beef was tender, the sauce tangy with spice, but he was too intent to notice. "Messenger says the army left Boston middle of the night last Monday, went marching for Concord where the militia's been stockpiling muskets and swords and stuff. But folks had warning from some fellas that work for Boston's Committee of Safety. So they were waiting at a little place called Lexington. Forced the Redcoats to fight their way through."

Margaret glanced at him from the corner of her eye, then lifted her chin. "Hannah," she said, "seems to me you're like those men who work for the Committee of—of Whatever."

"Safety," he said, while Hannah sipped her wine, refusing to be drawn into the battle.

Margaret inclined her head ever so slightly before continuing. "They warned the people in, um, Lexingville that the Regulars were leaving Boston Town, you see, and you warned me that a certain husband is leaving us."

His oldest child and namesake pushed his plate away. "Mama, can I go outside?"

"You haven't finished your beef, Ben," Margaret said. "Don't you want to grow up strong like your father so you can break some poor girl's heart?"

"Margaret, please," he said, "not in front of the boys. Go ahead, son, go on outside, and take your brother."

"That's right, Benny," she cried, "tell him he needn't obey me." She leaped from her chair, flushed cheeks making her more beautiful. "Then next week, after you've left us all, how am I supposed to get him to mind?" She fled the room with wrenching, hysterical sobs.

"Well." He smiled bravely at his youngest, sitting on Hannah's lap.

But Hal's lip quivered. "Mama!" he bleated, then, sliding from Hannah's lap, pattered after Margaret.

He and Hannah were alone. They avoided talk and each other's eyes until Hannah coughed. "I'm sorry, Benny, I—I said something this morning about your trip to the Indies. Forgot you hadn't told her yet."

"It's all right, Hannah."

He reached for the porringer doing duty as sauceboat. Made of pewter, it was dented and scratched but precious nonetheless for it bore their mother's initials. It had graced their table since his childhood, until he seldom noticed it. But tonight it seemed to gleam as it had thirty years ago, lighting the way to Mama's parlor. There sat his three sisters at table, whispering and giggling while his baby brother waved plump hands. His mother was laughing, too, as she sliced bread, while his father helped him to soup with a pat on the shoulder—

Hannah sneezed, and the vision fled. Those days were but a dream now, one that ended almost before it began. The baby died first. Then fever killed his sisters, except for Hannah. His mother waited for him to grow to manhood before she, too, succumbed, apparently of a broken heart. His father took three years to drink himself into the grave beside her.

Only he and Hannah had survived their doomed family. That endeared her to him, until even her carelessness in telling Margaret of his trip would earn no reprimand nor even a sigh...

Arnold leans forward, elbows resting on his knees. "Don't wanna give you the wrong idea about Margaret," he says. "She was, I don't know—" he pauses, hunting the right words—"she—she loved me deeply. We were so happy together." His voice sinks to a whisper.

I nod, but she reminds me of my mother, a troubled wife picking quarrels. "Why didn't she want you going to the Indies?" I ask.

He clears his throat. "There'd been talk, Clem, a few years before this, all of it false, but it hurt her badly. People were saying I'd hired a—a lady."

"A lad—? Oh!" I'm thankful for the shadows that hide my red face.

"They even said I fought a duel over her. I think that hurt Margaret the most, that anyone thought I cared so much about another woman I'd risk my life over her, especially one like that. Not an ounce of truth to any of it, though."

Which makes it like the other tales told now of Benedict Arnold. You can take your pick from a whole store-full, every one of them risen since the treason. Most of them have Arnold leagued with the Devil. Sold his soul a while ago, they say, that's why he does what no one else can, whether leading men to impossible victories or selling his country. Others claim it's worse than that: he's not leagued with the Devil, he *is* the Devil, or he's the Devil's son or brother or some other degree of kin, and they prove it by asking how a mortal man could travel to Quebec the way Arnold done. "You ever heard of anyone marching hundreds a miles on no victuals?" they'll say. "Or hunker under the trees while a hurricane blows and no more scared by it than them trees was? My cousin knows a man whose best friend's brother was on that march, and he says ever' night after dark, Arnold'd confabulate with a big old hairy fella that had cloven hoofs down where his feet shoulda been."

Such gossips don't stop with the march to Quebec or Arnold's other feats. They've gone clear back to his childhood to show how deep his wickedness runs. You've probably heard how he'd scatter broken glass around the schoolyard to slice the children's feet, or that he caught songbirds and cut out their tongues so as to laugh at their poor, gaping mouths, or how even then he was fearless, otherworldly fearless, as only a body leagued with Satan could be.

No truth to any of this either, except that last, for Arnold's brave as they come.

"Took me a while to scotch those rumors," the brave man says now, "but I did. I got depositions from other ships' captains and sent those around town until even the worst busybodies admitted their lies. But ever after, seemed Margaret could stand nigh anything but my leaving on another trip..."

Hannah reached for the porringer. "More sauce, Benny? I can fetch—"

"No, thanks." He fixed his eyes on the teapot, a stoneware monstrosity sprouting enameled flowers that Margaret had seen in his shop and coveted. "Hannah, I've been thinking I—maybe I should, well, give up the business, way it upsets Margaret and all."

Hannah sighed. "Maybe you should."

That shocked him. Though they endured one of Margaret's tantrums every time he departed, whether to the Indies for rum or just up Hudson's River selling horses, Hannah had never agreed that he ought to quit sailing. She was his partner, keeping the books and the store that sold the goods he imported. If he found a deal on barrel staves or tanned hides, Hannah would line up coopers or shoemakers to buy them, until he had only to anchor in New Haven's harbor to dispose of his cargo. She was good at what she did, the best he'd seen, and she relished her end of things as much as he did his. So he expected her to argue, not acquiesce, at relinquishing the business.

He pushed his plate aside. "'Course, we'll be paupers in a week. I don't know how to make a living any other way, not a good one, you understand."

"I know, Benny, but she—it's killing her, I think. She can't stand being away from you."

Something in him lifted and soared. For that was why Margaret enthralled him, never mind the scenes and sulks: she returned his love, steadfastly, worshipfully, completely. She cared naught for his money nor for what he could give her. She wanted only him, and his absence alone riled her. For such uncommon devotion, he would sacrifice everything, suffer anything.

He did not realize he was grinning, infatuated as any schoolboy, until Hannah sniffed. She had the spinster's impatience with romance.

"Anyway," he said hurriedly, "I may, that is, with this news and all, I'll probably cancel this trip I'm planning. Foot Guard's voted to march on Massachusetts, what with Redcoats murdering folks up there. Selectmen'll probably want us to leave first thing in the morning."

"I—I just can't believe—it's so—so—I mean, our soldiers, firing on us..." Hannah poured them both more wine. "You gonna tell Margaret?"

"Think I'll wait till I hear from the selectmen. One of my boys in the Guard's over there now. He'll bring us word."

"Maybe the militias from other towns'll march too."

"Ah-yuh, soon as old Sam Parsons over to New London hears, he'll have every man who can walk hoofing it to Boston Town."

"Maybe they'll want you to command *all* the militias." She beamed with a younger sister's admiration.

He laughed. "More likely, I'll be marching under Parsons, Hannah, since he's a colonel."

A door slammed, and Ben stood before them, breathless with excitement. "Father, a man's here from your troop to see you."

Arnold hid a smile. Josiah was a man only to six-year-old Ben. "Well, show him in, son."

Josiah clattered through the barrels and crates, scarlet uniform and black boots of the Foot Guard glowing in the lamplight until he looked at least seventeen. "Sir, I got word from the selectmen."

Suddenly, Arnold wanted only to postpone leaving Margaret. "You eaten yet, Josiah? Want some supper?"

"No, sir. Mother'll have my hide, I don't eat when I get home."

"All right, then." He steeled himself. "When do we march?"

"We—we don't, sir." The starch seemed to leave Josiah, his uniform sagging before their eyes. "Selectmen voted against it, sir. They don't want us helping Boston Town. They won't provision us nor arm us, neither."

Arnold staggered to his feet, his jaw in spasms.

It spasmed throughout the evening as he stewed about the vote. Redcoats blasting their neighbors to kingdom come, yet New Haven content to sit back and twiddle its thumbs. But not Benedict Arnold, nor his Foot Guards.

He put his sons to bed. Then he stepped over the casks of paint and linseed oil in the upstairs hall to his chamber. It alone had a door in place, though he had hung it himself. He opened it, stuck his head in. A fire burned on the hearth, flickering on a slight lump in the bed.

"Margaret."

The only answer was a muffled sob.

He shut the door behind him. "Margaret, honey, please, you know how I love you." He seated himself on the bed and patted the lump. "I love you with all my being, forever."

The lump moved then and tossed aside some pillows. Finally a tearful voice said, "Oh, Benny, I love you with all of me, forever, too." The next moment, she was in his arms, smothering him with kisses. "Please don't go. Stay here with me, Benny, please. I just can't stand it anymore, really. I need you here."

"But how would we live?"

"We could farm, Benny."

"Farm!" He kissed her hair. "Live hand to mouth, you mean. You'd be wearing old patched rags and taking in boarders. Then we'd be in trouble. They'd probably want doors on their rooms—"

"I don't care, Benny. We'd be *together*. I can't bear to have you gone for months on end. I love you too much. Besides, you can't sail if they're firing on people. That—that's war, isn't it?"

War. Strange, the word had not occurred to him. A skirmish, yes. Even murder, with trained professionals killing farmers. But *war?* Here and now, in peaceful, prosperous America? There'd been trouble the last years, disputes with the administration, too many edicts from the Ministry for sure. But war?

"You can't go," she whispered as he held her. "Too dangerous, Benny. They'll seize your ship, won't they? Isn't that what they do in war?"

"Likely they would." He laid her on the bed. She was as light in his arms as little Ben. "No, you're right. I'll need to cancel the trip."

She clapped and giggled...

〰

"My poor girl," he murmurs. "She was so happy, thinking I'd stay home with her because of the war, and instead, we marched off the very next morning."

"What'd you do for guns, though?" I lean to pet Flash, not from affection—he's Arnold's dog nor ever lets me forget that—but because my hands are so cold they're numb. "I thought the selectmen voted against you."

"Ah-yuh, they did." Flash cocks an ear at the amusement in Arnold's voice. "We had our own little rebellion right there in New Haven before joining the real one. I told the selectmen, 'None but Almighty God shall prevent my marching,' and they could either give us the key to the magazine so we could arm ourselves or we'd break into it. They saw sense pretty quick..."

〰

Waving his sword as the Foot Guard hoisted their new muskets, Arnold started them north to Cambridge, headquarters for the militia besieging Boston and the Redcoats there. But it was Margaret he spoke to when he joked with his lieutenant, and Margaret's laughter he heard in the birdsong along the road. Dandelions there reminded him of her hair, and a lone tree in a field with its branches reaching skyward was Margaret, arms spread to hug him.

At the tavern where they stopped for the night—a tavern Margaret would have scorned with its yard unkempt and littered and two broken windows—he met Sam Parsons. Arnold had seldom known a man whose name so suited his appearance, for Parsons' face was as friendly as any preacher's, nor one who better proved how deceptive appearances can be. The colonel was returning from Cambridge to recruit more troops—or so he said.

Over roast chicken and cherry bounce, Arnold asked, "What's the situation now up to Boston Town?"

"Long on spirit, short on most everything else 'cepting flies and dung, sir, to put it plain."

"No provisions, then?"

"Provisions?" Parsons shook his head. "That's the least of it. They haven't got arms, Captain, nor ammunition if they did. The few that's got muskets don't know how to use them without they're killing hogs."

"Muskets alone won't work anyway." Arnold drained his bounce and signaled the serving maid for more.

"You're right about that. We want cannon, too."

"I know where we can get all we need."

"Oh?" Parsons' shrug was innocent, though his features tightened.

"Plenty of 'em in the old French forts to the west."

Parsons chuckled. "Plenty over to England, too, sir, but that don't do us any good, neither."

"That's where you're wrong, Colonel. Those cannon up on Champlain, in Fort Ticonderoga, they're ripe for the taking."

"Only a fool would—"

"Ticonderoga's naught but a ruin now, easy to capture. I been there dozens of times."

"Ah-yuh, but they still got a garrison there."

"Government pulled most of it back to Boston long ago, what with all the unrest. Hardly any Redcoats left to guard the place, let alone make repairs."

But Parsons continued to argue, insisting ever more strongly on the fort's impregnability. At last, Arnold shrugged—from courtesy, not agreement—wondering why the man cared so deeply about Ticonderoga's artillery.

It was midnight when Arnold sought the necessary. Then he climbed the stairs to the biggest bed in the tavern, where Parsons and one of the Foot Guard's lieutenants already snored. He eased himself in, pulling his share of the quilt from them and enduring louder snores for his trouble.

Even if such noise had not kept him from sleep, his desire for Margaret would have. He longed for her warmth and softness under his arm. Besides, he was too excited at the idea of taking Ticonderoga, whatever Parsons thought of it, to close his eyes. And he was the man to do it: not only had he commanded, both aboard ship and as a captain of militia, but he also knew the fort's terrain.

He spent the rest of the trip to Boston puzzling out the details of the raid and how he could convince someone with authority to issue him orders for seizing Ticonderoga. When they arrived, he sought the Massachusetts Committee of Safety, then sat with a dozen others waiting their turn: he wasn't the only one with advice on the rebellion.

"...they oughta do, see," a man with a bedraggled periwig was saying as Arnold found a perch on the windowsill, "they oughta carve a big old horse outa wood, hollow, see, and hide a set of our boys inside, and leave it there in sight of the Redcoats, and they'll be so curious, see—"

"Been done." A blacksmith still wearing his apron cleared his throat.

"Well, a course it's been done, and it worked, didn't it? Them Trojans took that horse right inside their walls, didn't they?"

At last a committeeman summoned Arnold.

There was no need to argue the beauty of his scheme, especially after the projects that had wasted the Committee's morning. As Arnold described the ordnance at Ticonderoga, his hearers lost their bored expressions, straightened in their chairs, asked questions. They studied the plans of the fort he had sketched the night before, when he must do something to pry his thoughts from Margaret or go mad.

"The place could not hold out an hour against a vigorous onset," he said.

One of them nodded. "Ah-yuh, that's what that John Brown's been telling us, you know, from over in Pittsfield. He just come back from out there."

Arnold almost said, "Bah, don't listen to him." Brown was a cousin by marriage who had been nothing but trouble since joining Rhode Island's branch of the family. First, he finagled a post as clerk in Oliver Arnold's law office. Then, despite his diploma from Yale College, he made so many mistakes that Oliver discharged him, relative or not. That had been six years ago, a month or two before Oliver died, but Brown still ranted about his hatred for all Arnolds when he had hunched too long over his rum.

At least Brown's report agreed with his this time—though perhaps Arnold was wrong after all if a fellow as crazed as Brown concurred. Nonetheless, he continued, "Now's the best time to seize the fort, what with the Redcoats penned up here in Boston, all worried and distracted. Ti's the furthest thing from their minds. And even if it weren't, they can't reinforce it, any reinforcements must come from England. Let's attack now, before they get here."

They assented, objecting only that Ticonderoga lay in New York.

"'Tis a sister-colony, sir." The Committee's chairman grimaced charmingly. "We can't very well invade them, not when we want their help fighting Redcoats."

"Say, Dr. Warren." A delegate to the chairman's right laid a hand on his arm. "Whyn't we tell them to grab Ticonderoga themselves, you know, the Committee of Safety there? We could send 'em the captain's plan, maybe even you yourself, there, Captain Arnold, you'd consent to go."

"No." 'Twas abrupt, but Arnold had no stomach for wrangling with committees, seeking this one's nod and that one's license for what plainly needed doing. "Dr. Warren, gentlemen, the matter wants haste, and surprise, too. We can't take time to run all over Creation for permission."

"New York'll decline, anyway," another said. "Mostly Tories down there, scared of their own shadows let alone the king."

They compromised. They would advise New York to seize Ticonderoga before the Redcoats could strengthen it. Meantime...

"We're raising Captain Arnold here to Colonel," Warren said. "And since New York won't do aught about the Ti, sir, you go take it, and bring us its cannon and stores. You're authorized to raise 400 men. No more than 400, sir, and for no purpose beyond capturing that fort and the lake, too, if possible. You understand."

He did. Armies were dangerous things, prone to spilling off the field and turning swords wielded against the enemy on their own people.

Arnold rose to leave, their gratitude sounding in his ears, his commission and the hundred pounds they had advanced in his pocket, when a man entered the room.

He had the air of one whose talents are remarked and appreciated. He was wealthy, too, his burgundy velvet coat adorned with silver buttons. But something in his smile narrowed Arnold's eyes. "I pray your indulgence, gentlemen, for my tardiness. Anything of moment been decided?"

Warren returned his bow. "We've commissioned Colonel Arnold here to secure the Ti for us."

"Ticonderoga?" The newcomer's brows rose. "Good Lord, Warren, that's a bit reckless, don't you think?"

"No, sir. Colonel Arnold says—"

"Now, Doctor." The newcomer sighed, then smiled patiently. "We've already been over this. No matter what anyone says, attacking the king's property, it's—it's nonsense. Our quarrel's with Parliament and the Ministry, remember, not the king."

Dr. Warren stared, nonplussed at this parsing of tyranny, and Arnold said, "Excuse me, sir. I don't believe I've had the honor."

"Dr. Benjamin Church, sir, at your service."

Arnold bowed, wondering whether anyone but surgeons sat on the committee. Where were the warriors?

"The doctor's also a poet, sir," Warren said. "You've probably read some of his work. He writes songs to liberty, good ones, too."

Arnold folded his arms. Poets, surgeons: how skilled were they at strategy?

"Gentlemen, let's keep calm." Church seated himself and crossed silk-clad legs. "Taking Ticonderoga will only anger the king, and for what?"

"For guns, sir. Cannon." Arnold wondered whether the man were daft. "There's powder there, too, and muskets."

"We'll never be able to hold it even if you do capture it." Church stifled a yawn. "As a member of this Committee, I can't give my consent to this—this harebrained scheme."

No matter how Arnold talked, how he proved by his maps and drawings that capturing Ticonderoga was possible, Church shook his head. Finally, worn out, Arnold said, "I'd almost think the administration's paying you, Doctor, way you're gainsaying this thing."

Church shed his pose of bored sophisticate coaxing fanatics from their folly. He leaped to his feet, eyes blazing, and hissed, "I beg your pardon!"

Arnold was surprised at such vehemence, but he was never one to back down. "Your opposition, sir—it's beyond what's reasonable."

"Revere says the same thing," someone murmured.

Arnold did not take his eyes from Church. "Who?"

"Paul Revere, one of the Sons of Liberty here, does some work for us from time to time. He thinks the good doctor there is spying on us for the government."

"I'm not gonna listen to this." Church grabbed his gold-capped walking stick and stalked from the room.

Dr. Warren's laugh broke the tension. "Pay him no heed, Colonel. He's a poet, and you know they're prone to melancholy."

Chapter Three

S o there I was, commissioned to take the Ti," Arnold says. He crunches the last fistful of popcorn, which sets Flash's tail wagging. "You want more? I can make another batch."

"No, sir, thank you."

He reaches for Peggy's bowl with a glance at the stairs. "Don't reckon she'll be coming down for any now."

"Nobody knew Dr. Church was working for the king then, did they?"

"A few suspected, but we didn't know for sure, no. Explained a lot, when we found it out later that year, showed why Church always stalled anything that woulda helped." He sighs. "But, Clem, he's the least of it. I thought all I was doing was grabbing us a fort away from the enemy, getting us some cannon. Turns out instead I'm offending New York and Congress and all the damned cow—beg pardon, all the cowards still thinking the war'd just blow over. And then, the few who're ready for war don't wanna fight Redcoats. They wanna fight *me*."

'Tis the same today, though there's reason for it now. But what did they have against Benedict Arnold back in '75, when he was naught but a merchant and West Point's just a bend in Hudson's River?

When I ask, his eyes go hard.

"No government anymore, remember? Look, we don't need a king, nor Congress, neither—all they do is muck about in a man's affairs and then charge him for the pleasure. But there's not too many see it that way. Most folks want someone ruling, don't matter how corrupt or cruel. So soon as we said king's got no more authority, everyone wants to know who does. And a good many think it oughta be them. There's the boys in Massachusetts calling themselves a Committee and claiming they're in charge, but here's Parsons in Connecticut hollering the same thing. Only way to prove who's boss, only way it's ever been proved, is to see who's got the most power, who can kill the most and survive the longest to lord it over everyone else."

"See who's the most ruthless." I say it sadly, and he smiles just as sadly.

"There's all of history in a nutshell for you, Clem. Every battle, every war that's ever been fought—it's all about who's gonna order everyone else around once the dust settles. Me, I was too stupid to have anything in mind beyond what I'd told Massachusetts' Committee: I wanted the Ti's guns to use against the Redcoats. But back in Connecticut, Parsons is raising an army so he can 'save' us from the British. That's why he tried to discourage me on Ticonderoga, so's he could get there first. Reckon he figured his grateful countrymen'd crown him King Sam. Him and his cronies controlled Connecticut's treasury for years, which was real convenient now, seeing as how he needed money to hire soldiers."

"You mean he borrowed money from Connecti—"

"'Borrowed'?" Flash's tail thumps the floor at the disdain in Arnold's voice. "That's a charitable term for it, Clem. 'Stole's' more like it, way he helped himself. Then he hired the Green Mountain Boys, you know, those farmers up in the Hampshire Grants, as his army."

I squint, trying to remember. "They had some kind of fight over that land they settled, didn't they?"

"Right. The Boys bought their land from the governor of New Hampshire, got it all cleared and improved. But then once the work's done, along comes New York, claiming the Grants belonged to it, not New Hampshire. So the Boys must either pay for it all over again or give it back."

"Good Lord!"

"Boys hated New York and all affairs Yorkish after that, and can't say as I blame them. What New York did there was robbery. 'Course, that's what New Hampshire'd done, too. Governor there didn't own that land, didn't have any more right to sell it than you or I do. Mark me, those Boys were good shots, always had their muskets with them case any Yorker set foot on their farms."

In a trice, I understand. "So Parsons from Connecticut hires the Green Mountain Boys, sort of an instant army that already hates New

York. That way, he can beat you and Massachusetts at taking the Ti and
set up as king. But the Boys got no interest in making him king. They
just wanna go into New York—"

"*Invade* New York."

"They wanna invade New York because of the fight over their lands.
And of course, the Yorkers'd shoot back." I close my eyes, sick at how
our rebellion was nigh finished before it began. "We'd been fighting
each other 'stead of the Redcoats."

"Ah-yuh," says the traitor who kept that from happening. "Now the
Boys, most of 'em, were good men. All they want is to farm land they
bought and paid for. But commanding them was a rascal named Ethan
Allen…"

Arnold left Massachusetts' hundred pounds and another hundred of
his own with the officers he appointed. They would recruit his regiment
while he galloped hard and northwesterly.

He collided with Parsons' mob on a cold and rainy day at Bennington,
a miserable village with a miserable tavern anchoring one end and
an equally miserable meetinghouse at the other. A dozen shacks shivered between. The ordinary was the worst of its species, planks nailed
together for scant shelter from the elements, a mud-daubed hearth, and
a slattern waiting on a mob of brawling backwoodsmen—Parsons' army,
undisciplined but ready, while Arnold's officers had yet to raise his.

When he appeared in the doorway, uniform of the Foot Guards
glowing red, back stiff in military posture, the room hushed. Men who
had fought in the French War stared with slitted eyes: officers in similar
dress had cursed, bullied, and whipped them. Some produced knives,
slanting them towards the hearth until the blades gleamed in the light.

The serving maid hobbled over, and he said for them to hear, "I'll
have whatever they're drinking."

Whoops and oaths against tyrants were roiling the air when he got
to his feet, mug raised in a toast. "Gentlemen."

Some paid heed, but most continued their banter. Still, he knew
how to win them. He had experience with this sort when he sailed from
New Haven and hired their Connecticut counterparts to swab his decks

and caulk his seams. He'd never known such men to decline more rum.

He leaped atop the one table in the room, so rickety he prayed it would hold his weight, and shouted, "Gentlemen! Let's drink to your health in capturing the Ti."

This time, more of them listened, especially when he added, "Another round for everyone, madam, if you please."

There were cheers, then, and a toast to him. Their fellowship continued until he mentioned his commission and his pleasure at commanding such likely troops.

Silence fell.

His new friends shuffled their feet, looked at each other, the walls, the rafters. In a dark corner to his right, a knot of men he took for officers—providing this mob had officers—stood muttering. One of them stepped forward into the firelight.

"Arnold." John Brown sneered up at him. He was a long way from Cousin Oliver's law office—and sanity, too, judging by his rage. "You're not wanted here, can't you see that? Get out."

A grizzled man said mildly, "Now, hold on there, Brown. He done right kindly by us with the drink and all—"

"You don't wanna let him fool you, Isaiah." Brown's eyes were slits of hatred. "He's one of them that'll march you to your death whilst he hogs the glor—"

"See, mister," Isaiah said, "we already gots us a leader and don't look for none other. Ethan Allen, that's who we signed on with. He's bold and tough and prideful."

Arnold said, "You're Green Mountain Boys, aren't you? Feuding with New York over your lands?"

"Damn the Yorkers!" someone shouted.

"Damn you, Arnold!" Brown said.

"Aw, shut your phiz, Brown," a third man bellowed. "Let him talk. He's right. We paid good money for them lands, and now the Yorkers wanna steal 'em from us!"

Arnold waited for their hubbub to fade. "Now, how's it gonna look, you go over into New York and attack their fort? Nobody's gonna credit it, that you done it against the government back home in England. They're gonna say you're warring on New York. That's why you need someone's been authorized leading you."

They weighed his words, nodding. Even the officers, except Brown, were agreeing that Arnold and his commission from Massachusetts could turn their revenge against New York into something official. It might even save their necks if things went sour.

And so they offered to take him to Ethan Allen. "We's supposed to all of us gather here, then meet him up north, on the lake," Isaiah said. "You and him can fight it out there. 'Course, you're a city boy, and I never seen one yet can lick Allen. He talks fancy like you, plenty of staunch, blunt, fearless words, but watch out he don't punch you or nothing." He lowered his voice. "Best keep clear of Brown, too."

Collecting Boys along the way, they caught up with Allen after midnight. He stood knee-deep in the lake, surrounded by boats moored to trees on shore. He counted off a dozen men to scavenge more vessels, then leaned an arm against a birch arching overhead, so tall and substantial he might have been a tree himself. Allen was the largest of the Boys, though none were small. Arnold remembered a book about an Englishman who lost his way and found himself among a race of giants. He felt a sudden sympathy with Gulliver.

Especially when Allen's eye fastened on him. "Who's this?" Allen roared.

One of the Boys muttered something in Allen's ear. Allen glowered. "*Colonel* Arnold, huh? What's wrong, they run short of full-grown hogs for officers? Using the runts now?"

"Better runts than asses." Arnold returned the Brobdingnag's glare as he pulled his commission from a pocket and proffered it. The wind had kicked up until it nearly whipped the paper from his hand.

Arnold had supposed Allen illiterate, so he was surprised when the giant beckoned for a torch. He grasped the paper with hands big as twelve-pound cannonballs, then studied it without even moving his lips before thrusting it back at Arnold. "You got your orders, fine, but the Boys won't march with no one but me. Isn't that right?" He raised a fist above his head, and the answering huzzah must have been heard at Ticonderoga, still a mile away.

Arnold had lost whatever goodwill his largess in the tavern had bought. He tried reasoning as thunder cracked, insisting that Allen's expedition was outside the law, while Massachusetts' Committee of Safety had empowered his.

"Committee?" Allen guffawed. "Oh, that's real legal, king chartered 'em just the other day. Listen, us here, we're legal as they are. Only way the Boys agreed to be an army was they get to choose their own officers so's they don't get whipped they forget to say 'sir' or some such, like happened the last war. They elected me to lead 'em, and I won't never turn 'em over to a stranger, especially one dresses like a damned Redcoat'd sooner whip a man as look at him." He sneered at Arnold's uniform as rain pelted them.

"My officers been recruiting. They'll have hundreds of men in a few days—"

"Well, you wait here for 'em, *Colonel*." Allen's contempt turned "Colonel" into an imprecation. "Meantime me and the Boys got us a fort to capture."

"Listen, Allen, I'm gonna have 400 troops next couple of days. You got what, a hundred, hundred ten men here?"

"Hunnert seventeen." Allen's voice was as sulky as the rain spattering them.

"You take the fort, sir, without proper orders—" Arnold shrugged. "You're as much an enemy as the Redcoats. I'll march my men against you."

Moonlight dimly filtered through the clouds and branches thick with new leaves. Still, it showed Allen staring in wonder—and suddenly grinning. "You're a damned rascal, Arnold, but don't nobody march with us who isn't. So you come on along until your own army gets here."

The Boys seeking boats had still not returned. With a glance skyward, Allen boomed, "Come on. We'll pile as many as we can into these tubs here. Rest of you foller across if them laggards ever get back with something that'll float."

His ship-captain's eye told Arnold these barges were unserviceable even if the lake had been calm instead of choppy. But he scrambled aboard with Allen right behind. Their race to reach Ticonderoga first continued when they landed, both leaping ashore and running from the lake up the road.

The last of the rain fell as they crested the hill.

There sat the fort: star-shaped, one side and two of its points overhanging the river, impervious to an assault by water. Massive stone walls protected the rest. The cannon Arnold had come to collect poked through slits in those walls along the top. Behind them rose the roofs, chimneys, and flags of barracks.

The place was invulnerable, but for one mistake: the wicket gate stood wide as the road to Hell.

The most crucial fort in the colonies, three weeks after the shooting at Lexington and Concord, lay slumbering with its wicket open. Arnold saw the dark hump of the sentry leaning against the gatepost, even thought he heard snores, impossible at that distance.

So easy! All Arnold could think was how proud Margaret would be. Unless—

"Come on, boys!" Allen yelled and blundered towards the fort, likely alerted by his bluster. He would not stop to wonder at a gate left open, perhaps deliberately. His only concern was gaining it first.

Arnold leaped forward and, in two bounds, was beside Allen. "You considered the possibility this might be an ambush?"

"Aw, Arnold, you're scared, go home." Allen boomed down at him for the whole army to hear. "Didn't nobody want you along on this anyway."

His bellows wakened the sentry and set him scrabbling for the musket at his feet.

"Leave it, you damned rascal," Allen shouted as Arnold cried, "Surrender, soldier!"

The sentry squeezed the trigger, but the rain had wet his powder. Shouting alarm, he dashed into the fort with Allen on his heels and Arnold's legs pumping to keep pace. Behind them streamed the Boys, howling like savages. "No quarter, no quarter! Kill everybody!"

They had reached the parade ground now, with faces inside the barracks pressed to the windows and another sentry leveling a musket from the far end. "Halt!"

Allen leaped the parade in two bounds to confront this second sentry. He swept the musket aside with his sword, slashing the boy's arm. "Hush your blubbering!" he bawled over his victim's screams. "Where's the damned rat in charge here?"

The sentry writhed on the ground while the Boys milled aimlessly and whooped. Allen's glittering gaze roved the fort. For the first time, he stood silent, uncertain what came next. He seemed almost grateful when Arnold began issuing orders.

"You men to my left," Arnold said, "go secure the cannon. Don't let any Redcoats near them. Rest of you, get in the barracks, soldiers're still in bed. Hold 'em there 'til we get their arms to the other side of the fort."

They scattered to obey, leaving Allen on the parade, alone and absurd.

Arnold raced for the stairs and the commanding officer's quarters on the upper level.

A sleepy voice challenged him from the landing. "What's the meaning of this? Who are you?"

"Surrender the fort, sir. We've invested it entirely."

"Surren—? Pray tell me, sir, in whose authority you demand this?"

Arnold had supposed Allen still downstairs until he thundered from directly behind him, "In the name of the great Jehovah and the Continental Congress!"

"I see." Moonlight struck the speaker, showed him struggling into his waistcoat and jacket without a scrap of linen beneath. He stooped for his breeches, trying to shield his nakedness with them. Over the screams of "No quarter!" from below, he shouted, "Well, I, ah, I'm Lieutenant Feltham of His Majesty's Twenty-Sixth Foot—"

"Don't give us all your titles, you damned Redcoat. Don't none of us care," Allen hollered. "'Tis the fort we want, damn it, and all the effects of George the Third."

The lieutenant's brows lifted at this bald mention of the king.

"You go firing a single gun," Allen continued, "and my Boys won't leave anyone alive, nor man, woman, nor child."

Arnold's head was aching. Allen roared continually, as if he owned no regular voice. Now he waved a sword over Feltham as would an actor in a farce.

"Sir." Feltham's tone dripped disdain. "The men here, most of them, are old, wore out, and unserviceable, I assure you."

Arnold scowled at Allen. "Put your sword away. We're not on stage, after all." To Feltham he said, "Colonel Benedict Arnold presenting his compliments. The colony of Massachusetts commissioned me to seize this fort. Any officers who surrender may expect to be treated as gentlemen. You commanding here?"

"No, sir, that would be Captain De la Place."

"Frog-eater." Allen spat. His gob glistened as it slid down the wall. "Isn't that just like the damned government, put a Papist at the head of things?"

The lieutenant tore his gaze from the spittle to address Arnold. "The captain should attend us presently, sir. May I inquire how many men—"

"Quit delaying!" Allen cried. "You think we're fools? Dammit, git your frog-eatin' captain out here or I'll run you through."

The door behind the lieutenant opened. Inside stood a man, wig askew, buttoning his uniform. "Thank you, Lieutenant. I'll take over."

Allen shouted, "Come out here, you damned old rat..."

"The negotiations for surrender went downhill from there, Clem." Arnold kneads Flash's neck. The dog's eyes are closed. If he were a cat, he'd be purring. "I was just praying I'd get out of it with a few shreds of honor. I suppose Allen's a proper man to head his own wild people, but he's entirely unacquainted with military service. Knew nothing of protocol—couldn't even treat the women and children decently."

"What women—oh, families of the soldiers, you mean?"

He nods. "Probably a coupla dozen of 'em living there. I told the lieutenant they'd be safe—we weren't barbarians, after all—but hard for him to believe that what with Allen's Boys bellowing 'No quarter' every two seconds. Withal, I'm the one authorized to take possession of Ticonderoga, Clem, so that made me responsible for whatever happened. And then, when Allen took to plundering and looting, I thought it my duty to remain there against all opposition until I had further orders, keep it at every hazard..."

Alone on Ticonderoga's bastion after Captain De la Place relinquished his sword, Arnold inspected the cannon, so scarce, so precious, and now in colonial hands. Neither Allen nor his men could be bothered with such mundane concerns as munitions after they broke into the fort's supply of rum. Arnold stilled his protests, thinking the day's salvation lay in the Boys' drinking themselves senseless.

He bent to examine the largest cannon. He knew little of artillery, only what any merchant who armed his ships against pirates and customs officers would. Still, this one was a beauty. It ought to blow the Redcoats back to England while it put his name on the lips of every Patriot. He pictured Margaret in their parlor, wearing the sprigged muslin whose yellow flowers matched her hair, face aglow as neighbors praised his victory.

Commotion beyond that of the drinking, whooping Boys roused him from his reverie. He glanced over the parapet and then catapulted down the stairs, drawing his sword as he went.

Ticonderoga's fifty Redcoats, shorn of their weapons and officers, still stood under guard on the parade. Their families cowered in the barracks. A few wives were plastered to the windows, watching their husbands. Now Allen's men, soaked with rum, were looting those barracks, preying on the women as they went.

Arnold reached the first Boy, lugging a deerhide trunk out the barrack's door while its owner clawed at him and shrieked, "'Tis mine! Give it back!" Her voice was high and girlish, like Margaret's. Arnold smashed the flat of his sword across the man's back. The Boy collapsed in the dirt.

Arnold worked his way through the melee, slashing, whipping, knocking heads as he went. "No looting! It's against military law!"

Then Allen was towering over him, immovable as an oak.

"Allen, restrain your men!" he shouted. "This plundering, it's inhuman! No civilized—"

"What the hell you talking about?" Allen aimed Captain De la Place's pistol at him while John Brown sidled up to peer over Allen's shoulder. "What you think my Boys come along for, huh? Hey, Brown," he bellowed, and Brown stepped from behind him. "He thinks we're here for a little frolic with the Redcoats."

Brown cackled. "He's a fool, Colonel, I been telling you. All them Arnolds are."

Allen shook his monstrous head. "A damned fool, you mean. Mark me, Arnold, my Boys come for the loot. Gimme them orders of yours."

Arnold stared down the pistol's barrel and gripped the hilt of his sword.

Allen moved the pistol closer. "Gimme 'em, Arnold, or I'll let some daylight into you."

Someone grabbed him from behind. Brown ripped his sword from him and thrust hands into his pockets while Allen shoved the pistol in his face. "You're starting to annoy me, *Colonel*."

Brown found Arnold's commission and tore it to shreds before Allen signalled the Boys to release him. "Now get out, Arnold. You hear me?

You haven't got a commission no more, so get outa here and leave us be. I got a lot riding on this. I'm not gonna let you ruin things." Allen stomped back to the looting, Brown chasing after.

Arnold waded into it, too, determined to protect the women. But the Boys, though thieves, weren't sinful enough to rape.

He came on one of them rifling a pocketbook. "Put it down!" he shouted.

Almost magically, a musket appeared in the man's hands. He tapped the barrel against Arnold's chest in time to his words. "I takes my orders from Allen, not you. Now get on back to your dung-pile afore I blow you to bits."

Arnold slept poorly that night, a sword from the fort's armory in one hand and a pistol in the other, longing for Margaret. For the next few days, he barricaded himself in his quarters. He emerged only to check the guns or some fact for his report to Dr. Warren in Massachusetts, until he saw that Allen's mob was thinning. With the fort stripped of its valuables and the last of the rum guzzled, there was nothing to keep them. Whatever plans Allen had to swap Ticonderoga for the Hampshire Grants would wane with his Boys slipping away...

The wind whistles down the chimney, laying the flames horizontal and pricking Flash's ears. I pull my shawl tighter around me.

"Remember that memoir Allen published in the *Packet* coupla years ago?" Arnold asks. "Issue after issue?"

"Yes, sir. Made me laugh, that part about his men 'tossing about the flowing bowl' after they conquered Ticonderoga. Reckon that was true, but not the rest, was it?"

"Ah-yuh, that 'flowing bowl' was the only truth in the whole thing, Clem, except those parts about liberty and us being 'a scourge and terror to arbitrary power.' Allen can turn a phrase, that's certain." He shakes his head. "'Course, what do you think folks will remember years from now? That Allen was a liar, or that he and his Boys took the Ti all by themselves the way his damn—his memoir says?"

"Maybe you should write an account too, sir, set things straight? The story of your life."

"Well…" He lobs kernels into his mouth one after another like a *feu de joie*. "Wouldn't do any good. Folks generally believe what they want to believe…"

As his war with Allen and the Boys ended and his recruits arrived, Arnold could prepare to fight the enemy rather than fellow Patriots. He detailed two men to clean the commanding officer's quarters of Allen's filth, then moved his baggage, orderly book and maps into the room. From it, he surveyed the fort and the lake beyond.

There he held his first council of war—indeed, the first of the campaign, for Allen and his troops had ever been too drunk when assembled to discuss strategy. As it was, his own officers sat wide-eyed in the legendary Ti, so awed by its capture that none had thought beyond that stupendous feat. They could offer no advice on the next step.

Fortunately, Arnold needed none. He had long since determined to seize the fortifications at Crown Point, ten miles north, and now sought only their agreement. They were already nodding as he spread the map before them to demonstrate that Crown Point guarded the lake as did the Ti, and so they must conquer it, too. And then it would be on to Canada, that vast province with its oppressed people and wealth of resources.

"Recruits coming in by the dozens, sir," a captain said. "Reckon we oughter send some of them up there, get that fort for you."

By Sunday, his army was nearly complete, enough to secure not only Crown Point but also the lone warship assigned the lake.

The *George* was anchored at St. Johns on the Canadian border, according to his scouts. But soon it would sail south and disgorge Redcoats to recapture Ticonderoga and Crown Point—unless the rebels seized it. And so Arnold issued orders and bought supplies for the trip up Lake Champlain. This time, no one contested his command—he was the only one who knew how to sail—but his officers did object that to attack the *George*, they must first invade the province of Canada…

"That was the grand objective, a course." Arnold leans back to trickle Peggy's corn into his mouth. "Anyway, my orders from Massachusetts said I was to capture the Ti and 'the vessel'—the *George*, you understand— 'and other cannon and stores on the lake.'"

But he'd gone far beyond those orders. What he'd done was nigh miraculous, astonishing, heroic, and all within a couple of weeks. Not only did he take Ti, he planned our first naval attack that netted us the *George*, too. That forced the Continental Congress to think beyond the here and now. They must ponder strategy, decide whether they wanted vast Canada in the war with us—or against us.

They were meeting again across town, styling themselves the Second Continental Congress and buzzing with all Philadelphia over Arnold's exploits. Not that they knew they were Arnold's: John Brown brought them the news of Ticonderoga, and 'twas a dozen to a shilling his version glorified himself and Ethan Allen.

More than ever, my uncle disagreed with the Congress, but he was determined that none outside the family should suspect. And so the Adams cousins and Colonel Washington again came to dinner.

Over the soup and meat, John Adams mentioned the doings up north. "Some of the delegates are worried, if you can credit it, that our capture of Ticonderoga has angered His Majesty." He threw up his hands. "*Angered* him! After Lexington and Concord, where we killed his soldiers, and a good number of 'em, too. How many dead were there, Sam?"

Sam Adams had been there that wild night, lodged with a family in Lexington while the Redcoats hunted him as chief among the trouble-makers. Even Peggy, bored by talk that didn't center on her, listened with sparkling eyes to his account.

"Near 300 casualties, John, on the march back to Boston. Upwards of seventy killed that day, the rest wounded or missing. Loads of 'em go missing, you know, decide they'd rather live free than be flogged like beasts and bend the knee to the king's officers."

"'Twould seem there's no turning back after such a day. But they like to dilly-dally in Congress. We daren't upset the king." Disgust twisted John Adams' voice. "We got fire-breathers like Ethan Allen, after what he's done up on Lake Champlain, I'd wager he could defeat the whole British Army, and the Congress wants to—to—"

When words failed him, Colonel Washington said quietly, "I think we might better credit Benedict Arnold with the victory."

"What?" John Adams flushed. "Oh, you mean at Ticonderoga? Well, of course, Colonel, you should know since you're head of the Committee on New York Military Affairs."

"Ethan Allen may be as good as he says he is." Washington's eyes twinkled. "But he hasn't Arnold's genius."

As the colonel recited Arnold's conquests, Uncle Shippen and the other men shook their heads. Aunt Shippen sighed. Peggy and I looked at each other. Arnold was a hero, for certain sure. No matter where your loyalty lay, you couldn't help but admire him.

While the Continental Congress debated and Benedict Arnold raked up hornets' nests to the north, men continued gathering around Boston Town to keep the Redcoats penned inside.

"That's a tinder-box waiting to explode," Uncle Shippen said, and one evening in June it did. The Patriots filed onto a couple of hills overlooking the city and dug fortifications all night. By dawn, they were waving to the Regulars from Bunker's Hill, laughing at them from Breed's.

No commander could ignore such a challenge, least of all His Majesty's general, William Howe. He choked down his surprise at seeing breastworks where none had sprouted twelve hours before and led his troops to the attack. Eventually, he chased the rebels off their hills, but he lost near half his men and officers.

Until Bunker's Hill, our talk of the Patriots and Regulars was something to pass the time around the hearth, something Uncle Shippen could worry over. But now things came close to home. Saturday at supper, while Neddy Burd smiled at my cousin Betsy from his usual place, Uncle Shippen mourned how America's best days were past.

"I must disagree, sir," Neddy said. "About time we stood up for our liberties as Englishmen."

"Neddy, I'm surprised at you." My uncle gave him an indulgent smile, then motioned for more bread. "Don't you see that all liberty means to these—these *Patriots* is that they don't pay their fair share of taxes?"

"But you're too interested to speak of it, aren't you, sir?" Though Neddy said it respectful, my uncle flushed. "You've made your fortune on taxes. All those salaries you collected from offices, sir, that you got from the king, those were all paid with taxes."

It was a sore subject now, what with those offices fast disappearing, one after the other. New men were grabbing power in Philadelphia, the sort that would have appeared before my uncle's bench in the old days as bankrupts and thieves, and 'twas them abolishing the king's offices. Quick as they got rid of one, they set up three more, with themselves and their friends rather than my uncle as place-holders.

Uncle Shippen carefully set his fork beside his plate. When he spoke, he sounded judicial, same as if Neddy'd blasphemed and stood before him for sentencing. "Those were lawful taxes, Neddy, lawfully collected—"

"Sir." Neddy held up a hand with a look at Betsy. "I've got somewhat to say, might as well say it now."

My uncle leaned forward, anxious as us. We'd been expecting Neddy to ask for Betsy's hand, though he'd picked a strange time for it.

Neddy's eyes never left Betsy's as he got to his feet. "I got the honor to announce I been commissioned a lieutenant in the Lancaster Rifle Company. For the, um, defence of America's liberties from the, ah, the government, the—the king and Ministry."

Betsy glowed. Aunt Shippen gasped. My uncle fell back in his chair, speechless.

"Well," my cousin Edward drawled, "that oughta sink the rebels once and for all."

"Shut your mouth, Edward," Betsy said.

"Lancaster," my uncle spluttered at last. "That's the—well, it's the backcountry, Neddy. You can't—a lieutenant, you say? Those are rough men out there. You'll never command them. They won't take orders from the likes of you."

And in truth, Neddy was biting his lip and looking ready to cry.

Uncle Shippen continued. "You're not used to the woods or hunting, Ned. You don't know how to use a rifle. You'll be deemed a very unfit person for such service."

"I can learn, sir."

My uncle spread his hands. "'Twill appear to all the world a ridiculous thing for a young man bred in an office to command riflemen."

Neddy sank back into his seat, miserably silent.

"This rebellion," Uncle Shippen continued, "it's just farmers and shopkeepers against the best army in the world. It'll soon be over. And then those who sided with the rebels'll be cooling their tempers in London's Tower, waiting to hang at Tyburn."

"But, sir, our liberty—"

My uncle's tone softened. "Son, you got a good head for the law. You'll have a comfortable life here, in the city, not the backcountry. You and Betsy, once you marry, I'll settle an estate on you, mayhap even get you named to some of those offices I held, when government's restored. Believe me, 'tis easier making money in Philadelphia than farming or—or—or whatever it is they do out there in Lancaster." He forced a chuckle. "There's no cause for you to go off hasty and—and reckless with these rebels—"

"Sir, no, it's not reckless. It's a decision I've struggled over—"

"Well, it's a bad decision, struggled over or not. Don't be a fool, Ned, and let a bunch of—of idiots and—and traitors call themselves Congress and lead you around by the nose."

Uncle Shippen paused to mop his face, and Edward whistled a few notes of the ditty that was amusing all Philadelphia. Then he warbled, "'These hardy knaves and stupid fools—'"

"Stop it, Edward!" Betsy cried.

He took no heed, beating time with his hand. "'—Some apish and pragmatic mules, Some servile acquiescing tools, These, these compose the Congress!'"

"Make him stop, Daddy," Betsy pled.

"Why? It's the truth." Then, incredibly, Uncle Shippen joined Edward for the second verse, as though they were two tipplers in a tavern. "'When Jove resolved to send a curse, And all the woes of life rehearse, Not plague, not famine, but much worse—He cursed us with a Congress!'"

Neddy was on his feet again before they could sing more. And so the argument ended as such things do when a young man favors an ideal and an older one urges prudence. Neddy's voice rose, my uncle pounded the table, Betsy cringed. Neddy called for his hat, my uncle forbid him the house until he came to his senses, Betsy fled the parlor in tears.

For the next week, we spoke aught of politics or war. Then came a message from the Patriots around Boston, wanting the Congress to adopt them as its army to protect the liberties not just of Massachusetts but the whole continent. I expected Uncle Shippen to be apoplectic at that, but after so many disasters, he was numb. He shrugged and hoped that someone who could control "that mob of lousy farmers" would assume command before they took to looting.

Someone did: Colonel Washington, now made General of the Continental Army. He nor any of the Congress dined with us again.

Tensions climbed with the heat of summer, among us and Arnold's men up north, too…

"'Twas Church's doing, Clem, I see that now," Arnold says. The popcorn's gone, and he reaches for his pipe. Flash, sound asleep, doesn't even lift an ear. "Dr. Warren, God rest him, was already dead at Bunker's Hill, though none of us yet had the word, and Church become chairman of the committee in his stead. That's before we knew Church was spying on us for the Redcoats."

"That fellow the committee used for a messenger suspected him, though, didn't he?"

"Revere, you mean? Ah-yuh. Anyway, Church was probably supposed to stop us, keep the Massachusetts Congress from doing anything more than talking, but here they'd gone and told me to take the Ti, and I'd done it, too, done far too good a job to suit Church." Arnold laughs, but it's bitter, not the hearty, happy peal I remember from before.

"That's why he kept harassing you, isn't it, after you took Ticonderoga, so's you'd quit the Continental Army?"

"Especially after I said we oughta take Montreal next."

"Montreal?" I gape.

"Remember, the point's to bring Canada into the rebellion with us. And it was possible then. Indians wouldn't have fought for the Redcoats against us, and Carleton couldn't have recruit—"

"Carleton?" Of course I know who Guy Carleton is, but 'tis wiser to act ignorant.

"Military governor up there. Anyway, he couldn't have found a dozen Canadians willing to fight. There's about 600 Regulars throughout Canada, split among five forts. I told the Congress 1700 men could take the whole province, and if no person appeared who'd undertake to carry the plan into execution, I'd do it and answer for the success of it."

"So what'd they say?"

"Nothing. Never got an answer, except from Church." He snorts. "*He* kept after me day and night, trying to thwart me and confusing things, too. Even sent three men up to see me, three"—he frowns—"committeemen…"

The committeemen, come all the way from Massachusetts, arrived one stormy Saturday in June to stand before Arnold in his cabin aboard the *George*, now called the *Enterprise*. He set aside his letter to Margaret and smiled, thinking they brought money. "Ah, gentlemen, we've been waiting for you, all my unpaid, hungry soldiers."

But two of them examined their knuckles while the third glared at him.

"Been trying to get them to fight for free," Arnold continued, "but they insist on being paid, and they wanna eat, too. They're particular about that—"

"Colonel Arnold." The middle one cleared his throat. "'Tis to relieve you of command that we've come, not give you more money."

Arnold fell back in his chair to sit staring at Jedediah Foster, the trio's spokesman.

"Opinion of the Committee," Foster continued, "is that this here operation is getting too bothersome. It's—"

"Bothersome?"

"Dr. Church says it's gonna hamper us, sir, when we go to His Majesty to negotiate."

"*Hamper* you?" They must have heard his roar in Boston. "Men have fought and suffered and held on here. We've taken two of the enemy's forts, captured their warship. We've neutralized the savages so they won't go scalping along New York's frontier. Now we're ready to take Canada, march on Montreal, and you tell me we're *bothersome*, sir? God help me, I—"

"I don't know anything about Canada nor Montreal, neither, Colonel. All I can say is, you're relieved of command."

"Gentlemen." Arnold scowled at each in turn. "You're being a tad ungrateful here, and I don't like ingratitude. Makes me itch." He got to his feet, eyes fixed on Foster. "Makes me itch to kick something, say, committeemen, right off my ship."

"Sir, you forget, you're under our authority—"

"Get out!"

"You'll do what we say, sir!"

Arnold leaned over the desk, his jaw a foot from Foster's. "Get off my ship now, sir, before I send your sorry ass back to Boston Town by express."

After they had gone, Arnold sat pondering. The committee lacked military men, so its members didn't realize how egregious, how unprecedented, this was, to dismiss an officer who had achieved the victories he had.

Worse, he still had no money to pay his troops. He'd long ago spent every pound from Massachusetts and much of his own fortune too, nearly ruining himself in the process. And for what? So a bunch of surgeons could sip their punch and criticize him? Too late he saw that he had made the thing look so easy they neither appreciated it nor realized what it cost in discipline and leadership. They did not understand what molding an army from raw, homesick, scared recruits required.

He grabbed a sheet of paper and began a letter to the Congress, not the craven one in Massachusetts, but the one for all the colonies, in Philadelphia, the one where justice prevailed while they debated lofty concerns like liberty.

He reached for a second sheet. He would resign his commission (though, in truth, he had none left to resign). Let them find somebody else to win their battles for them.

And then—

He smiled. The only bright spot in the whole mess was Margaret. He saw the joy on her face at his homecoming, tasted her kiss, felt her arms tighten around him and his knees go weak with love for her.

He would never leave her again, certainly not to fight for ingrates.

He returned to his resignation. He was too engrossed to hear the knocking at his door, scarcely realized his aide had opened it and stuck his head in. He started as the boy said, "Letter from home for you, Colonel."

Thank God, word from Margaret at last! That was just what he needed now, encouragement from her, assurance of her adoration and pride in him. He snatched the packet from the aide, gabbled his thanks, closed the door. He stood against it, gasping, hugging the paper to him.

Only when he glanced down to open it did he see that it bore his sister's script, not Margaret's.

Disappointment knifed him, and then terror. Something must be wrong. He had received Hannah's report on the business just yesterday—

His hands shook until he could hardly still the page to read it. The words leaped at him. "Dear Brother, I am so Sory to tell You this, but Margaret took sick after Supper & died last Night in her Slepe..."

Chapter Four

The boys are in school, Benny. I thought it best."

Hannah stood with hands folded before her, the black ribbon around her arm paining him until he could not look at her. He hitched his chair closer to the window and stared at New Haven's harbor. A fleet had arrived from the Indies that morning, and all was bustling. Sailors and stevedores swarmed, with merchants elbowing through the jumble to inspect the barrels of molasses, pinch the tropical fruits, and heft the cones of sugar before joining the knots of bantering, bartering buyers crowding the captains. A breeze wafted the scent of lemons and limes, tar and saltwater through the window.

"The school's not far from here, Benny. I'm hoping it'll take their minds off—off matters, you know."

And how many, how tragic, were those matters! Their mother's death had not ended it. Grandfather Mansfield had barely staggered away from his daughter's deathbed before slumping to the floor as though turned to stone. Three days later, he, too, was dead, doubtless of a broken heart. Arnold wondered how the old man had done it. It hadn't come from wishing, else he would expire, too: all week, he had wished, hoped, prayed for his own swollen heart to quit.

Hannah sniffled. "They'll be home for dinner, Benny. But of course, if you think I did wrong, you—"

"No, Hannah, it's—I think—don't—" He shook his head, ashamed to cry before her. "It's fine," he said at last. "And Hal, where's he?" Poor Hal, the baby of the family, motherless at three. What devastation Margaret had left them, what wretched lives and misery.

"I put him down for his nap, Benny."

He started from his chair, the desire to hold his son suffocating him. But Hannah was beside him in a moment, restraining him with her words more than her hands.

"Let him be, Benny. I—I had a hard time getting him to sleep. He cries and frets so for Marg—his mother."

He sat back, closed his eyes. It had begun already, the shunning of the word "Margaret," as though to say it would make her deader than she already was. He must live the rest of his life with people afraid to speak her name when it was the only one he wanted to hear. A sob escaped him. Hannah hugged him, her face against his hair.

"Benny, I'm so sorry, I know how you loved her. I'll do whatever I can to help. You know I will."

He patted her shoulder. Such small effort wearied him beyond belief. "Thanks, Hannah. I just want to rest now."

"The chills again?"

He was shaking with malaria but had not noticed. He nodded, too broken to care.

"Let me fetch some rum." Hannah withdrew, and his tears for Margaret came in force.

He had met Margaret during his first days in New Haven, when he and Hannah removed there from Norwich Town, eager to escape the place that had taken their brother and sisters and parents, too. He was twenty years old, his apprenticeship as an apothecary complete and fresh from his first trip abroad to London for stock. He was becoming a man of the world, a born leader whom the ladies adored, too.

He'd mapped his route to success by the time he arrived in New Haven. He would establish himself as an apothecary, save his money, then set up as a merchant with ships sailing the world. He would enjoy such adventures, reap such riches. Not for him the cramped lives of most folks, the petty struggle to survive. Life was short, uncertain, as his family's deaths proved. He meant to live before he died.

He gave little thought to marriage beyond knowing he must do it at some point. Most likely, he would hunt a wealthy girl, perhaps a rich widow, who would wed her fortune to his.

But his first glimpse of Margaret Mansfield shattered such plans. There she sat in her pew at First Church, her grey eyes sparkling as his mother's, blond hair curling down her back. Just sixteen, she was not yet binding that glory atop her head. Her father, the high sheriff of New Haven County, frowned as Arnold stared.

It took him five years to win Margaret. Part of that was due to Mr. Mansfield's insistence they wait until she turned twenty-one to marry. Part was due to Margaret herself, as timid as he was bold. She seldom spoke, even when directly addressed, blushing and stammering instead. She was scared of everything, while he who had braved the sea and his family's deaths feared nothing. Margaret was kind, sweet, sensitive. Best of all, she idolized him.

And now his shy, loving girl lay under the churchyard's dirt.

He took to his bed with the malaria, not as ill as he sometimes was but able to shut his door and be alone with his memories. He thought of his voyage to the Indies after their marriage and how he hated to leave Margaret, expecting the first of their three sons. Weak with worry, he had contracted the malaria, a usual hazard in that part of the world. And now the wife who so hated his journeys had turned the tables, taking the longest trip of all, whatever he thought of it, no matter his rages and protests.

He rose from his sickbed after a week, still feverish but able to face his sons. He found them subdued and anxious that he was about to die, too.

"'Twas only the chills, boys. I've had it before." He tried to smile at dinner that afternoon, but it was more of a grimace. Ben and Richard watched with unblinking eyes, while Hal, sitting in Hannah's lap, hid his face against her.

"How's school?" Arnold asked.

"Fine, sir." Ben was seven now and trying to be a man through all the changes in his world. Still, his voice quavered.

Arnold saw he was a stranger to them, and a scary one, too. He had been away at Ticonderoga for three months, and before that, at sea. Now here he was again, returned once their mother was dead but lying abed all day with Hannah hushing them. The greatest kindness he could render was to let them eat in peace. He said nothing more, not even when Richard upset his buttermilk. Gradually, they relaxed, talking with each other and Hannah, though not him.

He spent another week in New Haven, answering Hannah's questions about the business, writing letters of introduction for her. He thought he would need to persuade her, for it was one thing to act as his agent, and another to have the whole affair handed to her, but she cut him off.

"Benny, I've done it right along. There's not much will bother me now, long as you don't want me out there sailing the ships. You know how seasick I get."

"What about the boys, Hannah? They gonna be too much on you?"

"I love those boys as if they were my own, Benny, always have since I helped birth them. Just wish you could stay longer. You sure you need to go?"

He nodded. Capturing Ft. Ticonderoga was not an end in itself, nor ever meant to be; rather, it was the first step in the grand project of enlisting the Canadians in their rebellion. Yet no one in the army or Congress seemed inclined to march beyond Ti's high, stone walls. He'd written the delegates urging a Canadian campaign, but though the summer was fleeing, he had received no satisfaction. And action must commence before the northern winter sealed trails and lamed horses. Waiting until next year—or next century, as the Congress seemed content to do—allowed the Redcoats to regroup. Last spring's victories would go to waste unless he goaded someone with authority to order a march on Canada.

And so he said, "They don't read my letters there in Congress, Hannah. Reckon I better call on them in person."

His sister's smile said she understood him thoroughly and cherished him anyway. "Oh, Benny, you know that's just an excuse. You want to get back to all the excitement."

He blinked against his tears. 'Twas true, but not for the reasons Hannah thought. Instead, he must get out of New Haven, away from the town where Margaret had been born, where every street and alley cried how much he'd lost.

Next morning, he left for Boston and the war.

He went first to Massachusetts' Provincial Congress and submitted his claims for reimbursement. How he loathed these politicians, from Church to the lowliest of his henchmen! While they sat dry and comfortable, endlessly talking, he had wrested Ticonderoga and Lake Champlain

from the government. Then they squabbled over his accounts, questioning this expense and second-guessing that, as though they could have
worked miracles on a budget. He stood it as long as he could before
telling Church they could fight it out among themselves, after which he
would return for his money.

Then he rode to Continental headquarters. Perhaps in exchanging
the Provincial Congress for the Continental Army, he could leave behind
the bickering over pounds and shillings, the incessant politics.

Withal, he was anxious to meet the Virginian appointed Commander-
in-Chief. Not only had this George Washington distinguished himself
in the French War, but he prized his honor, too: folks still spoke of
how he resigned his commission in Virginia's militia rather than serve
under a British officer he outranked. Surely such a man would resent
and rectify the insults Arnold had suffered.

The camp around Boston amazed him with its changes. All had been
chaos during his meeting last spring with Dr. Warren and the Provincial
Congress, when volunteers had converged to confine the Redcoats in
Boston. Though a few came prepared, most had walked away from the
plow with only the clothes they were wearing. Lacking tents, they felled
trees and tore fences apart for their lumber or scratched holes in the
dirt like groundhogs. Men and officers wallowed together in the muck,
while horses and pigs wandered at will and sutlers sold rum.

But now, four months later, Arnold scarcely believed he was in the
same place. His horse carried him past soldiers digging fortifications and
along neat rows of tents and lean-tos. There were parade grounds and
flogging posts and necessaries in proper military order. Headquarters
was a building that had formerly housed Harvard College, complete
with sentries guarding it. They ushered him into the front hall where
sat Horatio Gates, veteran of His Majesty's forces but now Adjutant
General of the new Continental Army.

Gates was nearly old enough to be Arnold's father, with the squint
and nervousness to match. 'Twas plain why some called him Granny.

Arnold bowed, then complimented the camp's orderliness.

"Oh, yes." Granny Gates peered at him over the spectacles at the end
of his nose. "It's been a job getting the men into some semblance of an
army, but General Washington's good at taking advice, and I tell him
every day, I say, 'General, we must work with what we have, sir, make

them into soldiers.' Those whipping posts out there, that was a direct result of my advice." Gates nodded until the wispy grey hair combed over his pate flopped onto his shoulder. "And good advice it was, too. Got rid of all the laggards and the drunkards and thieves, chased 'em out of camp."

Arnold whistled. "Maybe we oughta turn you loose on the Massachusetts Congress."

Gates guffawed, and Arnold asked, "General Washington took command when? Coupla months ago?"

"Just a month now. He's not had much experience, you know—only served a few years in the French War. Truth to tell," Gates lowered his voice, "I don't know why the Congress down there in Philadelphia wants him. Plenty of us are better versed in the martial arts." He shrugged. "Now, tell me, Colonel, what brings you here?"

"Canada, sir. I'd like another shot at it."

Gates shuffled some papers, then shook his head. "We haven't got the troops to fight here and take Canada, too."

"My plan relies on surprise, not numbers."

"Anyway, they're saying, sir, now mark me, 'tisn't my opinion, but they're saying you failed before, sir, so how could I jus—how could we justify giving you another army?"

"Failed?" Arnold blinked. "I captured the strongest fort in America without losing a man."

"But I thought—didn't Ethan Allen capture Ticon—"

"Ethan Allen *looted* Ticonderoga, sir."

"Uh-huh. Well, but the Massachusetts Congress relieved you of command. Dr. Church says you exceeded your authority."

"And I didn't even charge them extra for it."

Gates stared, nonplussed, then settled back in his chair with a laugh. "'Didn't charge 'em extra,' that's a good one! And now you want to invade Canada, huh?"

"Not invade, General, liberate. Government's trampling their liberties up there same as ours."

"Invade, liberate, call it what you want, how you gonna do it?"

Arnold hesitated, then noticed the genuine interest behind Gates' spectacles. "Quebec, that's the key to the whole—"

A door to Arnold's left opened, with half a dozen general officers filing into the hall.

"Excellency." Gates was on his feet, saluting, whatever he thought of George Washington's experience.

Arnold instantly picked out Washington. The Virginian towered above the rest, pleasant but aloof. The others stepped outside as Washington strode towards them.

"General." Washington handed Gates a sheaf of papers. "If you please, will you see that these are copied for the brigadiers?" He nodded to Arnold. "Pardon the interruption, sir."

"Certainly." He bowed. "May I have the honor, sir? I'm Colonel Benedict Arnold of—"

"Ah, the hero of Ticonderoga." Warmth flooded Washington's face. "A pleasure to meet you, sir. I'm a great admirer of your feats up north."

"Thank you, Excellency."

"Fact, Colonel, I'd like to talk to you about Canada at some point."

"Absolutely, sir! Send for me at your convenience."

Arnold had imagined an audience that afternoon, next day at the latest. He never thought that nearly two excruciating weeks of mourning Margaret would fly before Washington's invitation arrived. But one summer day melted into another, disappearing forever and pulling the northern winter closer, as though men marching to Quebec need not be snug inside its warm, stone buildings before snow fell. No plan, however brilliant, could succeed against Canada's blizzards—and such weather drew nearer each day. Surely Washington understood that.

Then, as Arnold's patience neared exhaustion, word came from headquarters. He hurried through camp, hoping for immediate commissioning, hoping for *any* commission, immediate or not. Please God, the long, frustrating fortnight had not condemned the whole enterprise before it began.

He found Washington seated behind a desk buried beneath papers weighted with rocks and horseshoes. The general apologized for the delay, but with no more time to waste, Arnold waved aside his words.

"Please, General, you're busy, I know. Thing is, I've got a plan for liberating Quebec that should get us the whole of Canada. Whether we want it or not."

Washington smiled. "Well, sir, Congress has finally approved taking Canada, so we've been working night and day, now that we've got authorization, outfitting an army for Montreal. 'Twas planning that, issuing orders for it, that's kept me so occupied I couldn't see you until now."

Arnold nodded. Camp sizzled with rumors about an army marching along Lake Champlain under General Philip Schuyler, rumors that had stoked his impatience.

Washington unrolled a map. "Governor Carleton up there's doing his part, too. Last few months he's been emptying his garrison, shipping his Redcoats down here to fight us."

"When I left Lake Champlain in June, he only had about 600 troops left."

"And that's for all Canada."

"Ah-yuh. Just two cities in the whole province, and he hasn't got men enough to fortify them both. He must needs decide between defending *either* Quebec *or* Montreal."

Washington grinned. "So far he's choosing Montreal, I make no doubt because of Schuyler's troops. Carleton sent half his Redcoats to fortify St. Johns, south of Montreal there, near the border, and Carleton himself took another couple of hundred to Montreal and its forts. He's only left about a hundred Redcoats in Quebec, even though that's his capital."

"Big mistake, and I want to attack before he figures that out."

"Whoever holds Quebec holds Canada." Washington rubbed his chin.

"Even if Schuyler takes Montreal tomorrow, we can't keep it without we take Quebec, too."

"Not with Quebec commanding the approach down the St. Lawrence to Montreal the way it does. I take it that's where your plan comes in?"

"Yes, sir. I want to march on Quebec secretly, from a direction no one'd ever expect." Arnold paused, fairly quivering with the ingenuity of his proposal. "There's an old Indian route through Maine, up the Kennebec River and then down the Chaudiere, that lands you within a coupla miles of Quebec." He traced the rivers on the map.

Washington stared, as baffled as Gates. "But that—that's tough going up there, Colonel. I don't see how—you can't move troops over that route. It—"

"Yes, sir, that's the beauty of it. They'll never expect it, not on top of worrying over Montreal. A whole army, coming over a route that could kill a man? 'Tis too impossible, or so they'll think. We'll surprise 'em."

"If the route doesn't defeat you first." Washington snorted. "That's providing you can even get to the Kennebec, what with the blockade the enemy's mounted all along the coast here. Be hard outrunning their men-o'-war."

Arnold shook his head. "We'll march to Newbury Port, board ship there."

"You'd need to move fast, too, Colonel—"

"I couldn't agree more, sir!"

Washington's brows lifted at such fervency. "—before Carleton's reinforced with troops from London or calls back the ones he's sent here." The commander rubbed his jaw. "So you'd make Carleton fight on two fronts at once, Quebec and Montreal, when he hasn't enough troops for even one. If he hears you're marching on Quebec, and he believes it, fine—he'll shift troops from Montreal to Quebec, let Schuyler take Montreal. But if he stays in Montreal—"

Washington's lips pursed in a soundless whistle as Arnold grinned. "It leaves Quebec defenseless. We'd slip in easy as pie."

"How many troops would that require, Colonel? How many we need for this plan of yours?"

Arnold's stomach tightened now that the moment was at hand. But he answered with only a slight emphasis on the first word. "I'd need about a thousand men, sir. That way, we'd outnumber the Redcoats in Quebec ten to one and maybe not even fire a shot, freeing it."

They had been leaning over the map. Washington straightened, then stood looking out the window while Arnold shifted from foot to foot. Every moment spent in this room subtracted one from the march and handed winter that much more potency.

"Think of it, sir." Arnold tried to keep the desperation from his voice. He must have this assignment. He could not return to New Haven and sit alone, Margaret-less, in the town where she had been his bride. "A thousand soldiers suddenly appear outside Quebec with only a hundred Redcoats there to hold it. Merchants and French folks'll welcome us. Canada'll join with us. Fourteen colonies fighting for liberty!"

"'Tis late in the season, sir. Winters come early there. They're brutal, too."

In Washington's voice was the note that said a customer would buy after posing one last objection. Harking back to his days as a merchant, Arnold turned the objection into a benefit.

"We'll need three, maybe four weeks to reach Quebec, and then let the St. Lawrence freeze. Let it freeze solid! Government can't get transports up it with reinforcements or supply the regiments already there."

Washington flexed his hands, then turned to stare intently. "All right. I'm commissioning you a colonel in the Continental Army, sir, to liberate Quebec. Though if General Schuyler takes Montreal and then joins you at Quebec, your command is, of course, subordinate to his."

"Of course." But he was thinking, Oh, Margaret, wait'll you hear! Then the grief stabbed him anew. How her eyes would have shone, how many questions she would have asked! He nearly cried aloud at his desolation, with the person he most wanted to tell deaf to every word.

Washington continued, "I hope that by commissioning you in the Continental Army, we can avoid some of the politicking that's plagued you so far. Though I doubt it, sir. Seems that men who want to fight for liberty are few and far between in this army, with stockjobbers and men jockeying for position prevailing. Those kind are always jealous of anyone with ability, Colonel, so watch yourself."

"Thank you, sir."

"You choose a thousand troops, even twelve hundred if you see fit, from camp here. Let me know when you're ready to march."

"This afternoon, tomorrow at the latest," he longed to say, though assembling supplies for a column that large would require several days.

"I'll write a draft for you. There's $100,000 in gold and silver just arrived from the Congress. You can have two-thirds of it." Then came an unexpected blow. "I'll write Schuyler, too, ask his approval."

"But—but, sir, that'll take—it could take weeks!"

Washington studied him, an expression Arnold couldn't read on his face. At last, Washington said sharply, "That's the chain of command, Colonel, like it or not."

Arnold swallowed his protests. No telling how many tales from John Brown or Ethan Allen had reached His Excellency's ears. Or perhaps Church's complaint about exceeded authority had reverberated beyond Granny Gates. If so, however pure his intentions, however he sought to shield his army from the approaching winter and secure the best chance for success, further objections to notifying Schuyler would seem fractious.

The second blow followed closely on the first. "Just one more thing, Colonel," Washington said.

Arnold hardly listened, expecting the usual good wishes and trying to calculate the march's schedule. It was already August 20; snow fell up north by late October in a good year, though he'd known it by the middle of the month and heard of it as early as the first. That left only five weeks to select and outfit an army, then march it, what, two, three hundred miles?

The general had finished speaking and stood awaiting his reply. Arnold gulped, realizing no wishes had been offered. "Sorry, Excellency. What'd you say?"

"I said, why don't you visit Dr. Church's committee, smooth things over with them. We must keep Massachusetts agreeable, Colonel. We don't want to fight them along with the Redcoats…"

"A lot of good that did." Arnold's mouth twists with disgust. "'Twas as bitter as the other session, Clem. No money at the end of it, either. But that was the last I ever saw of Church, thank God. They found him out for a traitor not long after that," says the traitor I'll kidnap.

The shakes quiver me anew each time I think on my task. So I push away the vision of Arnold bound and awaiting the hangman to say, "General Schuyler favored your expedition, though, didn't he?"

"Still, time the express got to him and back again with his answer, there's another whole fortnight gone."

"So what'd you do 'til you heard from General Schuyler?"

Above us, a baby cries, and we hear Peggy step from bed to cradle. Arnold gets that grin he ever does when Peggy moves or speaks or even breathes.

After a few moments, a log pops in the fire and I say, "Sir?"

He starts. "Oh, I spent the time redding things up. 'Tis daunting, when you think of it, finding enough food and supplies for a thousand men marching through wilderness. And I contracted for the bateaux, too, with—"

"The what?" Just as I know who Carleton is, so I know what bateaux are. Even rode in one once. But I want Arnold to suppose that, like other ladies, I'm ignorant of such things.

"Bateaux, they're these huge boats, Clem, with flat bottoms, unwieldy as the devil's own wheelbarrow, use them for transporting troops and supplies. We'd be needing 'em, and plenty of 'em, say 200 or there-abouts, once we started up the Kennebec. Anyway, there's a fella owned a shipyard on the Kennebec, right where I'd be loading my troops into bateaux, name of Colburn, Major Reuben Colburn. He's an officer in the militia, so you'd think he's a Patriot, but his real interest was him-self. He'd never shoulder a musket when there were ships to build and corners to cut, not Colburn. Only reason I ordered from him was the press of time. Shipyard sat right where we needed it, wouldn't be wast-ing another week or two transporting the things once they're done. But those bateaux—" He shakes his head. "I've seen barrels more seaworthy."

"Then, at long last, we heard from Schuyler. Next day, 16,000 Continental troops stood forth for my inspection..."

Washington mopped his brow. "They're eager to go, Colonel. I think guarding the Redcoats in Boston Town has lost its appeal."

"Hard to believe they'd rather stroll through cool woods than walk picket here in the heat."

Washington's eyes roved the lines. "There's another matter, sir, some troops that, well, they're from the frontier back home in Virginia, under command of a Captain Morgan. Marched all the way here in three weeks. Stout men."

"If there's anything left of them after a pace that quick."

Washington smiled, but Arnold was worried. He and everyone else had heard much of Daniel Morgan's company by now. Since their arrival, they had caused more mischief than a doxy in a barracks. He suspected Washington of foisting those troublesome troops on him, and His Excellency's next words confirmed it.

"Good with a rifle, too. Might be they'll help feed your men out there in the wilderness."

Arnold had planned carefully for the march, with provisions for six weeks, though the trip should take only three—God knew it couldn't take more than that, or the northern winter would finish them before scant meals could. So he doubted they'd need game what with his salt beef, biscuit, and dried peas. He started to protest, but Washington halted and faced him.

"Now, sir, you are entrusted with a command of the utmost conse-quences to the interests and liberties of America."

"Yes, sir, and it's an honor, but Morgan—"

"I rest easy in giving you this command. You're the best officer in this war, on either side, and I don't exaggerate. You fight and win on land or water. You understand strategy and logistics better than anyone I've seen. You're a master at gathering intelligence."

Arnold was speechless under such praise, and this from the reserved Washington.

"Upon your conduct and courage," His Excellency continued, solemn as a preacher in the pulpit, "and that of the officers and soldiers detached on this expedition, not only the success of the present enterprise, and your own honor, but the safety and welfare of the whole continent may depend."

Chapter Five

I shiver, either because of General Washington's words or the dying fire. "Getting cold in here, sir, don't you think?"

Arnold glances up with distant eyes. He's said nothing since reciting Washington's charge to him—has instead chewed his lip and stared at the hearth.

"Shall I add some wood?" I ask. "Closer to me and all." 'Tis a game we play, where I pretend it's only convenience has me doing a man's work, that, like anyone else, Arnold can jump from his chair and squat before the hearth, both legs supple and working. I reach for a log with Flash sitting up to watch. "So," I say, "you and your army traveled north."

"Ah-yuh, into such horror and disaster—" He closes his eyes. "I was so worried about the snow, turned out that's the least of our problems. There's a coupla women following us, three or four dogs, too, and thank Providence they did, for that saved us."

I glance at Flash. "The dogs did? How?" Then I understand. "You mean you—?" But I'm too sickened to finish…

Eleven hundred volunteers marched from Cambridge to Newbury Port, then crowded aboard eleven ships and sailed along the coast to the Kennebec River. This was the fastest of routes. Still, Arnold would not have chosen it had he owned more time because it was also the most dangerous: the Redcoats blockading Boston's harbor and patrolling the coast might capture his army before it left Massachusetts.

When they reached the Kennebec with only the usual disasters of seasick men and boats grounded on sandbars, he slumped with relief. God willing, they would beat the snow after all.

They poled up the Kennebec, to the falls near a trading post called Fort Western. There they clambered ashore, glad to leave ships that kept farmers who'd sworn they were sailors bent over the sides, vomiting...

"We were supposed to board Colburn's bateaux there, his yard was nigh Fort Western." Arnold rolls his eyes. "Boys thought they were queasy aboard good sturdy craft sailing the coast, wait until they're riding Colburn's buckets through whitewater. Then Colburn asks if I need maps, sends me to his wife's cousin. Cousin's a Loyalist, so those maps are bad as could be. Showed swamps where there weren't any and none where they were, and every river run straight when they were crooked as Colburn. And the distances! Those maps made it look as if Quebec's only a hop and a holler away, and here it was almost 400 miles." He sighs, then brightens. "Next morning, though, I met Dan Morgan..."

Arnold and his aides were chewing beefsteak at a table in the Spread Eagle as crowded as the tavern itself when someone yanked the door open with such force that he and the hundred other customers stared. Filling the portal until the rising sun behind him shrank to pinpoints was a giant of a man. "Arnold?" he roared, loud as Ethan Allen and as gargantuan, too.

Arnold wiped his mouth and got to his feet. "Ah-yuh."

In two strides the giant was before him, bending over the table, one fist planted next to his plate—and about the same size—the other waggling in his face.

"What's this I hear," the newcomer shouted, "you assigning my men out as goddam scouts? Got me marching under some blockhead of a lieutenant colonel, damn it, none of my troops with me—"

Arnold knew from the accent that this was Dan Morgan, captain of the notorious riflemen from Virginia, whose troops he had indeed divided in hopes of preventing mischief and mutiny. But he meant to put Morgan in his place, and so, while his aides stared, he said, "I've not had the honor, sir. Who are you?"

The man blinked. When he spoke, his voice was a few tones lower. "Name's Morgan, I—"

"Captain Morgan, isn't it? Well, Captain, the honor's mine, I assure you, having such men as you in my column."

Again Morgan blinked. This time his voice was soft, almost courteous. "I, uh, thank you, Colonel, but—"

"Have you eaten, Captain? Will you join us? Burr here was just finishing."

"I was?" Aaron Burr was a pipsqueak of a boy, about half Morgan's size. He stumbled to his feet. "Oh, certainly, I—ah, excuse me."

Morgan straddled Burr's chair, the other patrons staring. "Don't you got business of your own?" he bellowed. "What you tending to mine for?"

He ordered meat and biscuits and rum, scorning the coffee the serving girl brought, roaring he weren't no weakling, damn it, nor lawyer. He'd take kill-devil like a man or nothing.

But when he turned to Arnold, his tone was respectful. "Didn't none of my men enlist so's to march under strangers. They's used to their own officers, see, don't like this being farmed out to other regiments like a set of damned orphans."

"And their captain doesn't like taking orders." Arnold spoke lightly and smiled as he did.

An answering gleam lit Morgan's eyes. "His Excellency told me hisself I was reporting only to you."

"Washington did?" Arnold exchanged glances with his aides. Unlikely that Washington had encouraged Morgan to ignore the chain of command.

Morgan saw his skepticism, and the pleading expression of a boy caught hunting when he should have been hoeing flickered across his face. "Dammit, now, look ye here—"

Arnold had come to see Washington's wisdom in assigning the riflemen to his expedition: he would need their skills in the wilderness. And so he held up a hand. "I expect officers who report to me to obey every order immediately, sir, is that clear? My officers don't cuss me out, neither."

Morgan's scowl faded as he took Arnold's measure. When he spoke, it was in a quiet, reasoning voice. "I hate the damned government, Arnold. All I want's a chance to pay them back."

Arnold waited, but Morgan said nothing more. He didn't need to: the scars ridging his back were almost as famous as his ability with a rifle. Nor was Morgan shy about showing his wounds. He seldom changed his linen privately, preferring to strip before his quarters so that the whole camp could see. Morgan had worked as a teamster for the British Army during the last war, young and proud and resenting the insults English officers heaped on colonial troops. After he punched an especially obnoxious commander, they tied him to the whipping post for the standard 500 lashes...

Short, angry puffs burst from Arnold's pipe. "There's some say Morgan liked to joke he'd cheated the army, because he counted and they only lashed him 499 times, but I never heard him laugh about it in any way. Whipping men like that, well, it kills some of them, and the ones it don't kill, like Morgan..." His teeth grind the pipestem. "For sure, they don't laugh about it. I never heard Morgan mention it at all. He let the scars do the talking for him."

We sit quiet awhile. Finally, Arnold says, "About three days later, we left Fort Western and shoved those bateaux back into the Kennebec..."

The river seethed with rocks, ripples, and falls. Worse, its current was the swiftest Arnold had seen—in the wrong direction. Oars and paddles were poor weapons to fight such a river, however furiously the troops rowed. And when they finally reached a calm stretch, sandbars lurked to snag them.

The Kennebec was bitterly cold as they waded to free grounded bateaux. Even Dan Morgan admitted 'twas the hardest, meanest work he'd done, meaner than loping from Virginia to Boston in twenty-one days. Arnold kept his eyes on the sky, gauging the weather, praying it would hold until they reached Quebec.

The men swallowed gallons of water, nearly drowned, then crawled onto the banks, cramped with dysentery, racked with coughs. Injuries felled anyone who escaped sickness. Fingers and toes were stoved, gouged, smashed, knees and ankles twisted and bruised. The few women with them, soldiers' wives who were as banged up as their husbands after working alongside them, ran out of salves and bandages.

Between coughs, the troops wondered if they ought not dispense with the bateaux. "Keep the supplies drier if we just let them bob in the river, Colonel," a captain said. "Cleaner, too." And in truth, by day's end, each boat held a broth of trampled food, vomit, and other substances too foul to think on, smeared over the baggage and passengers too ill to march.

They were only twenty miles from Fort Western when they encountered their first portage. A cliff loomed overhead, the river churning down it in white fury. They must unload the bateaux, heave the ton of soaked wood onto their shoulders, and struggle half a mile through undergrowth to navigable water.

After such brutal work, they found the current so strengthened by the waterfall behind them they could not row against it. Finally, they harnessed the boats to men on shore who pulled them like mules. Progress slowed, from seven miles a day, to three, to one.

Arnold despaired at such delay. Catastrophe awaited if they could not beat the snow: men would freeze to death, the drifts silently settling over them while Quebec sat warm, unattainable, invincible.

Then again, if the weather held, if they could add a few more miles to each day's march—. Arnold laughed and joked, hiding his fears, until everyone not coughing laughed with him. He whistled as they stumbled along, turned cartwheels among the trees, grabbed low branches with one arm and chinned himself, walked on his hands when anyone complained about blistered feet, all to take their minds from the forbidding forest. Trees hemmed them in, dark, menacing, the sun never penetrating. Already, the air beneath those boughs set a man shivering. Animal cries echoed eerily, while trunks stretched eternally on every side. No sign of human habitation or comfort relieved the dreary monotony.

The end of each exhausting day brought them only chilled, wet ground for a bed. Arnold would lie coughing, shaking with cold, and watch the stars. Though thankful no clouds obscured them, he marvelled that what had seemed so enchanting when he sailed the Caribbean's warm waters, now glittered malevolently. By the first of October, it was so cold and wet that, come morning, their clothes were frozen a pane of glass thick. Still, no flakes swirled around them, no lowering skies threatened a blizzard.

Then the troubles spread to their food.

Arnold had just detailed eleven scouts to spy out a frightful riverless stretch on his map labelled The Great Carrying Place when a coughing aide approached. "Sir, there's a problem."

He steeled himself. The morning not an hour old yet and already a crisis. "Only one, Oswald?"

"The provisions, sir, we're down to the last few barrels. The rest are soaked. And that's on top of losing all the cod." The fish, dried and salted and stowed wherever a bateau would hold it, had been cleaned of its salt, waterlogged, and washed overboard during their first hours on the Kennebec.

Arnold stalked to the riverbank where the men had stacked the barrels. With the trip consuming more time than reckoned, supplies were perilously low. If these last few stores were ruined—

He pried the lid off the first and swore at the stench of rotting beef.

"Just like the cod, all the salt's washed off." Oswald sneezed.

"What about the peas? They gone, too?" He spat the words, so that the aide, coughing again, only nodded with an injured air.

The next barrel held flour, or so Arnold assumed from the pasty mess oozing between the staves. No need to open the third: the wet bread it held had swollen until the container burst.

Arnold squared his shoulders, strained his entire being to hide his desperation. He reminded himself that the weather still held, and with it their chances.

Then they reached the Great Carry, and that made spoiled food and burst barrels seem petty.

The map showed forty miles of portage to the Dead River, the next link in the waterway to Canada. But Arnold was suspicious of the map now. Stretches of the Kennebec that showed straight had been snarled and treacherous. Worse, a mile on the map turned into three or even four in travel.

And the scouts were back with tales that shook the soul. The Great Carry was eighty miles, not forty, and nigh impassible. It began by winding uphill through deep forest. Then the forest gave way to marshes.

"And them marshes, Colonel." The scouts' lieutenant turned aside and spat. "They's covered over with moss. Can't see a damned thing, not a rock or a stump, nothing in the water under that moss. We like to killed ourselves stumbling around in there. And cold." The lieutenant shivered. "Makes the Kennybec look like a summer bath in front of the fire. But mark me, Colonel, we make it to the Dead River, there's trout big as whales. Best eating I done in a long time." His eyes gleamed, and Arnold's gut growled.

He bantered with the men, laughed and praised them as they struggled through the marshes. "Just think, it'll all be worth it when we spend the winter in joy and festivity among the sweet nuns of Quebec," Arnold told one company, boys they were, really, some of them but ten years older than his son Ben, warm and safe in Connecticut.

"They cook pretty good, Colonel, those nuns?"

"Best cooks in the world, Wheeler."

"Won't turn us Papist to eat their victuals, will it, sir?"

Though Wheeler was serious, Arnold couldn't suppress a laugh. "Long as you stay away from their bread and wine."

"Brown bread's my pick of things, sir," Wheeler said, earnest as a philosopher. "There's some want Indian bread with their victuals, but me, I'll take brown bread any day."

"I hear them Papists eat bread with oil, not butter," another said, equally grave.

"My ma makes the best butter." Even Wheeler's cough was wistful. "Sweet as sugar, like eating honey on your bread. Now you want good eating, you get yourself a piece of my ma's brown bread and some of her butter."

Arnold hated such talk yet heard it often as provisions diminished. The hungrier his troops went, the more they spoke of food, forsaking even the discussions of ladies and their delectable attributes that had sounded all the way up the Kennebec. Now they debated whether apple butter or maple sugar better complemented johnnycake as passionately as they had once discussed female anatomy.

To distract them, Arnold said, "I wrote Washington about you."

"What'd you tell him, Colonel?" It was the boy beside Wheeler, voice cracked and hoarse, either from adolescence or the river he'd swallowed.

"Told him he'd take you for amphibious animals, all the time you spend underwater."

They hooted and coughed, calling each other Frogface and Tadpole.

"Hey, Colonel," another said, "speaking of animals, don't you think we much resemble those ones down in New Spain they call the Ourang-Outang?"

This time, they were laughing at Arnold more than themselves, for his beard hung thick while theirs, young and scraggly, barely shielded them from the cold. But he guffawed and then, at their request, turned a somersault in mid-air before helping them right their capsized bateau.

And the weather held.

Arnold carried supplies beside them, stumbled against submerged stumps, smashed his shins against rocks as often as they did. When they halted at night, he waited with them beside the fires until his skin thawed enough to bleed, to show him where the rocks and stumps had gouged him, where his boots had chafed wet flesh.

The time spent in freezing water was taking its toll. Every hand and foot among them was chilblained, puffy, streaked with angry red. Only a few noticed now when the screams of men bathing ulcerated legs with urine pierced the evening's talk around the fire.

Trying to drown those cries, Arnold spoke of the stars overhead, called their names and told how they guided navigation while the boys' eyes sparkled with respect. Invariably, someone asked about Ticonderoga, and again Arnold would describe taking it, first from the Redcoats and then from Ethan Allen. They had come this far on his heroism and charm, but sooner or later, they must see through both. They would realize neither could fill their bellies, would decide that warm beds and regular meals beat slogging through wilderness, however they idolized him.

After Arnold bandaged his cuts with moss and bade the troops good night, he would repair to his tent and write the American merchants in Quebec, those likely to sympathize with the rebellion. He boasted that his army had double its actual numbers and that they were fast approaching to liberate the city. The merchants should open Quebec's gates in welcome, not fear his army as plundering invaders.

But inside he was numb. They had covered ninety miles in sixteen days and were nowhere near Quebec. Now he reckoned it lay 160 miles ahead, almost as far as he had estimated their whole trip, though God alone knew. Today was the eighteenth—nineteenth?—of October. Sooner or later, snow would end their race in defeat.

Their provisions were nearly gone, with the last two oxen slaughtered that noon. Spooked by the column's noise and smell, game fled. However skilled Morgan's riflemen, they seldom spotted, much less shot, any moose or deer.

That forced them to distribute the remnants of the flour. Some troops, overcome with hunger, tried to eat it dry, out of hand, only to spew it in a cough, wasting it. Others mixed it with water, formed it into a tiny cake, and baked it. They called the resulting mess "lillipu," for the unappetizing, blackened crackers were so small only Swift's Lilliputians could have survived on them. Lillipu nearly broke a man's teeth on its way to the stomach and cramped the gut once it arrived. It embodied that torturous proverb, "For dying, too much; for strengthening, too little."

And still the weather held.

When at last they emerged from the marshes, legs and feet frozen, they stared dully at the Dead River. It seemed a long, placid lake, so still were its waters. But its trout would save them, and soon hundreds of cookfires lined the shore.

The fish were barely roasted before the rain began.

Rain, not snow, Arnold reminded himself as the needle-sharp drops pelted him. Besides, the troops needed a rest, even one imposed by bad weather, after the agony of the marshes. But this was no ordinary storm. The wind nearly blew a man from his feet, while the screech of falling trees deafened him.

"Puts me in mind of the hurricanes I saw in the Indies," he shouted to Oswald.

The storm's fury increased that night until it drowned the men's coughing. Though Arnold had thought to sleep well without that cacophony, the wind and thunderous rain kept him awake and watchful. Next day was worse. Arnold fretted at the delay, snapping at Oswald until the aide betook himself to the sopping woods.

The rain poured, the hours dragged. Arnold was amazed at each minute's eternity as he huddled, shivering, coughing, stomach cramped and rumbling for food—good food, too, something warm and soothing and delicious, not cold, soured meat or raw fish and lillipu. He would take his watch from a pocket, be astounded that only three minutes had passed since his last glance at it.

Then again, he was surprised time moved at all. It seemed he had endured forever in this freezing torment, that his feet had always squelched in his boots, his soaked clothes had always irritated and chilled, his ears had ever ached from the storm's din, head and chest so sore from coughing that breathing hurt. And yet, paradoxically, the days were fleeing, with Quebec distant and tantalizing, like the land a crew would swear lay just over the horizon after too long a spell at sea.

At least his grief over Margaret had lost its power to prostrate him. Either the physical misery had displaced it, or his obsession with survival, his own and that of an army, kept him too busy to mourn. Or perhaps her death, like everything but this direful wilderness, had receded as does the shoreline for a departing ship. Margaret herself, his sons, Hannah, his business, the Continental camp in Cambridge, Washington, Ticonderoga—none of it was real, all had been a bright and happy dream, now vanished. Perhaps the war, too, was but a fancy that his imagination had concocted in this dread and howling wasteland. Often he struggled to remember what had actually happened in that other world and what had been mere talk. Had Margaret really died, or had it only been his most horrible nightmare? Surely she was at home in New Haven, lighting the lamps against his return, lovely, happy, alive.

On the third day of noise and rain, Arnold forced his way over tangled windfalls to the head of the column. The storm battered him and the few others moving through it with implacable, icy gusts. Even those soldiers who had given up and sought shelter under downed trees huddled miserably, fire-less, all kindling drenched.

That night, Arnold camped with his aides a mile ahead of the foremost troops. Oswald worked for an hour to start a fire. As they settled around the little blaze—it was no longer a cookfire, for they had nothing to cook—the stench of burning hair assailed them. Arnold glanced up to see Oswald roasting a piece of rawhide over the flame.

"You mind?" Arnold coughed, waving away the smoke.

"No, sir, but see, I'm making broth."

"Broth." He had been expecting this—that the hunger would drive some of them mad.

"Yes, sir." Sneezing overcame Oswald so that he said nothing more, only devoted himself to singeing the hair from the hide.

Arnold was too exhausted, too lightheaded, to order Oswald to desist. He lay with eyes half-closed, so hungry sleep would not come while the others talked of roasted beef and ham, and whether turkeys hand-raised on corn were tastier than wild ones, and how eggs were best eaten. One of them nearly came to blows with Oswald over the proper way to bake beans, with maple sugar or syrup. Then Oswald slipped the blackened rawhide, floating until now in the bottom of their bateau and intended for making boots, into some boiling water, as delicately as though it were the finest of meats. Insisting that maple syrup toughened beans, Oswald dipped some of the steaming, stinking water into his canteen.

Arnold rose unsteadily and sought his tent. There he slept fitfully, dreaming of a walled city with real beds, plenty to eat, warm hearths. He was leading his men through it to welcoming cheers. Suddenly, the street became an everlasting river, raging like the Kennebec, threatening to drown his column. It was freezing his ankles, however he jumped to escape, and climbing his legs—

He woke with icy water lapping him, though his tent had been pitched far from the bank lest the river swell with the rain. Crawling through the flap, he found the wilderness turned to an ocean. But for the trees poking through the water, he would have supposed himself on Lake Champlain.

A figure emerged from the forest to his right. "That you, Colonel?" Oswald's sleepy voice asked.

"Rouse the men!" he shouted, or tried to shout. He was too hoarse to do more than whisper. "It's a flood!"

More figures staggered from the trees. They scrambled for their belongings, now bobbing on the water. Arnold splashed after his camp desk and worried about the rest of the army, strung out downriver where the flood was probably worse.

With dawn, they saw the full disaster. The river, their road to Canada, had disappeared. In its place was a boundless, unmapped lake, deep enough to obscure landmarks, too shallow to float bateaux. They could only hope they were going in the right direction as they waded through it to find the river's course again.

The flood ruined the fishing and drove away the squirrels and rabbits that the men occasionally caught. Only the provisions, rotten and nearly gone, stood between them and starvation. And though Arnold slashed the amount dispensed, and slashed it again as they wasted hours and then days fighting the water to hunt the route north, every meal consumed more precious food.

Still the weather held. But he was no longer sure that was enough. The treacherous map, the rushing Kennebec, the lost provisions and hunger, the mossy Carrying Place, the injuries and illness, and now this flood—he had always feared a blizzard would end their march, not these assorted miseries. And he might have contended with them, even triumphed over them, had they come in twos or threes. But heaped up and running over as they were—

Oswald touched his elbow. "Excuse me, sir, there's—ah—there's a—um—another problem."

Arnold set his jaw. "Go on."

"Seven bateaux wrecked in the rapids."

He blinked. "How many dead?"

"It's—it's worse than that, sir." Oswald gulped. "Most of the rest of our barrels was on those boats. Near all our food's gone."

That night, the weather broke.

It was only the twenty-fifth of October, but they woke to a forest ankle-deep in snow. Grimly, Arnold wondered whether the storm had waited for the moment when it could most harm them as he eyed the glittering jackets the branches wore, the white drifts against black trunks, the countless flakes transforming the hostile wilderness into an alluring beauty. But this was no gay and harmless portent of a winter passed before a warm hearth, house snug and cellar full. It was instead a harbinger of blizzards, of defeat, starvation and death for him and his men.

He had invested every shred of himself in this march, putting one chilblained, blistered foot ahead of the other, struggling to rise each time he fell, kicking aching limbs for the surface when the river claimed him, gagging on lillipu and rotten beef. But his enemies were right. He had failed at Ticonderoga last spring, and he would fail again. How they would laugh when word of this horror reached them! Sam Parsons and

John Brown and Dr. Church would elbow each other and smirk, though not one of them had ever imagined, much less attempted, a feat like this.

And Washington, his lone defender, with his fine words about honor and the welfare of the continent—Washington would be so disappointed. Arnold remembered their introduction in Cambridge that summer, Washington speaking his admiration while Granny Gates stared—

No longer could Arnold concern himself with victory or freeing the oppressed Quebecois. The snow had reduced this to a march for survival as he and the fifteen men of his advanced party pushed onward to the suburbs of Quebec and food.

He was helping salvage a swamped canoe, snow swirling around his head and shoulders while icy water clutched his chest, when Oswald appeared on the riverbank. "Sir?"

Arnold stepped towards shore. One moment he was watching Oswald's beard whip in the wind and the next he was spluttering and gasping as water closed over his head. Another sinkhole, his second in as many days. He kicked his legs and shot to the surface, so cold he was sure he must die. The air as he struggled from the river was warm by comparison though the wind instantly froze his clothes.

"You—you—" Oswald sneezed, "—all right, sir?"

He could tell from Oswald's face the news was bad. "What is it?"

"Word's come that Colonel Enos, sir, at the rear, ah, he and his officers held a council of war. They, ah—"

"A council? Enterprising of them, but I already sent them my orders. They can't—"

"They voted to turn back, sir."

Arnold digested that, then said, "Tell Enos I want to see him. I'll kick his worthless carcass to Boston myself, he wants to go back so much."

"That won't be necessary, sir. He, ah, he's already left."

Arnold stared, speechless. Oswald staggered back a pace before adding, "Took the whole rear guard with him, too, three companies."

A black mist engulfed him. That left only 700 men out of the original 1,000 to conquer Quebec. Seven hundred to take a city set on a bluff above a river, as naturally fortified as could be. If the merchants didn't cooperate and open those gates—

Arnold swam up from the mist as he had the sinkhole, squaring his shoulders. "Well, Captain," he said for the rest to hear, "that leaves more food for the rest of us, then, doesn't it?"

"Well, ah, not exactly, sir. They—they took what's left with them. They, ah, they claimed, sir, since they been bringing up the rear the whole march, and they're the ones been carrying the barrels, working to bring them along, you see, that they, ah, that the food belongs to them."

It took almost a week for the advanced party to reach the first farms, a week in which Arnold scarcely paused since every delay kept provisions from his men. Reports came of the army's privations, such reports as choked him with tears. Men chewed leggings, boots, cartridge pouches, anything made of leather. They ate pomatum and shaving soap and lip-salve for the tallow they contained. One company likewise boiled their candles in water and drank the broth.

Arnold was so hungry that night he tried the same thing, though between them, he and Oswald had but three stubby tapers. He'd rather have eaten soap and pomatum and saved the candles for writing letters and his journal at night while the others slept, but they had long ago exhausted both.

He ladled the greasy, dirty candle-soup into cups, his stomach growling at the steam. Oswald warmed his hands around his before handing it back. "You can have mine, sir."

He grunted his thanks and guzzled it. Empty as he was, he nearly gagged.

"Heard the men of Goodrich's company had a feast coupla nights ago, sir." Oswald sneezed twice, then blew his nose.

"They finally sight some game?"

"No, sir, they ate Captain Dearborn's dog."

Arnold sat dumb with regret that they hadn't sent a haunch forward to him while the candle cramped his gut. Then, eager for every delicious detail, he asked, "How? They roast it or boil it?"

"Don't know, sir, but dumplings, that's the way I'd go. Nice, thick dumplings with a rich gravy, that kind where the fat bubbles to the top."

"And some wheat bread, so fresh it's steaming, to sop up the dribbles."

"Yes, sir." Oswald sighed. "Apple pie afterwards, with plenty of nut-meg and cream."

"Speaking of dumplings, I'm partial to apple dumplings instead of pie, myself."

"Not as much fruit, though."

"If it's fruit you want, go to an orchard." Arnold coughed irritably, about to argue the merits of dumplings when he caught himself, horrified. *Like a couple of fishwives with naught concerning us beyond the next meal.*

Finally, they emerged from the wilderness as the first French farms greeted them. But for the smoke rising from chimneys, Arnold would have missed them: the houses and attached stables were whitewashed into invisibility against the snowy expanse. He counted a dozen barns filled with grain in the foreground, while cattle dotted the hillsides all the way to the horizon like brown sugar on cream.

"Aren't they beautiful?" Oswald whispered. "Just about hear 'em sizzling on the spit, can't you? Some onions, and a thick gravy—"

"Let's go find the owner and get ourselves some dinner."

The farmer and his family were startled to see them, though once Arnold explained who they were, with Oswald fetching Aaron Burr to translate, they smiled and nodded. The lady of the house showed them to a table drawn close to the fire and set bread and roasted chicken before them.

"Say they're ready to supply us, sir. They heard we're coming for weeks," Burr told Arnold after the farmer loosed a volley of French at them. Arnold was too busy cramming bread into his mouth to care that all surprise was gone from his attack. What he asked now was survival for those men and boys who had marched so far, suffered so much.

He bought everything the farmer would sell and what the farmer's neighbors would, too. Cattle and sheep, sacks of oatmeal, horses to carry the sick and lame, even tobacco—he started all of it on its way to his men...

The fire crackles, making Arnold's story a witch's tale, told to scare children safe and warm.

"'Course," he says, "once we thawed out there, got something warm in our bellies, matters begin to assume a different aspect. We'd survived what would have felled most men, not once, but over and over again. Made me think Providence must have a reason for it."

Arnold's march held Philadelphia spellbound that winter. 'Twas as signal as Hannibal's over the Alps, the newspapers claimed, or Xenophon's retreat. Folks called it the greatest action of the war and Arnold a modern Alexander. Oh, the praise flew thick and fast, even in my uncle's house, until Arnold seemed immortal, scarcely bound by the concerns that hamstring the rest of us. We'd no sooner reckon on walking to Canada than the moon, but he had, and he persuaded a thousand men to go with him. We needed food thrice in a day, yet he ate nothing but snow after trudging dawn to dusk. We wanted thick quilts and featherbeds at night, and as winter closed down around us, we scarce stirred from the hearth. Arnold spent all day outside in the cold and no comfort from a fire at the end of it either, with only his cloak for blanket and mattress.

"He's so heroic." Peggy would smile, infatuated as a fly in October.

My uncle sighed. "Thank God the rebels haven't more like him."

"How'd you do it?" I whisper now. And how will we ever kidnap a man this electrifying and determined?

His eyes twinkle. "Man does what he has to."

"But—but—seems impossible that you could do all that, march without food, through floods and hurricanes—"

"I'll admit, 'twas attended by a thousand difficulties I never apprehended, which accounts for the coupla dozen boys fell out along the way. Starved or lost or just too beat out to take another step." Sorrow crumples his face. "And those that survived—" He shakes his head. "Nothing but beards and scabs and rags. And they were sick, so many of my boys were sicker than dogs. Once they were out of the wilderness and started reaching the settlements there, they'd just collapse alongside the road…"

"Here, Henry, what's the matter?" Arnold drew rein before a filthy, hairy, angular heap lying under the bare branches of an oak. Not even London's beggars were as dirty and emaciated as this soldier entrusted to his care.

He had first seen Henry, dressed in a fringed hunting shirt and leggings, two months ago in Cambridge while inspecting a company of Pennsylvania's riflemen.

"How old are you, son?" he'd asked then, pausing before a lanky boy draped around a rifle.

Henry straightened and said in his deepest voice, "Eighteen, sir," even as those around him, most no older than he, jeered, "Isn't either. He's sixteen!"

But the frontier bred strong, eager youths, and Arnold was glad to have them.

Now he battled despair as he gazed at Henry. No trace remained of that sprightly boy, only an old man's wizened face on an old man's beaten body.

Snow sifted from the leaden sky as he dismounted and put a hand on Henry's shoulder. It was naked but for the scratches and grime covering it—Henry had bound rags around his middle, but both shoulders were bare—and he would have felt the fever burning the lad if his own hands, gloveless and calloused, had not been numb. As it was, he shook him and called his name until Henry's eyes opened, watery and unfocused.

"Why aren't you with your company, Henry? Captain'll be looking for you."

"Colonel?" The boy swallowed, squinting at him. "Colonel *Arnold*?" He made as if to stand but got no further than heaving a sigh, blowing snow from his scant beard.

Understanding at last, Arnold said, "That's all right, Henry. Let's get you some help."

"Tarnation, how you know my name, Colonel?"

"You know mine, don't you?" He got to his feet. That soldier would starve to death if the fever didn't kill him first, and all because he had volunteered to march under the hero of Ticonderoga. *God in Heaven, what have I done to them?*

Henry raised a wasted hand. "Colonel, wait. Don't leave me—"

But Arnold was already dashing for the riverbank and the glistening white house on its shore. He cupped his hands around his mouth and soon had the farmer and his family out in the yard, one daughter wrapping bread in a napkin and another trailing a blanket, while a boy led an ox from the barn. Two minutes later, a girl squatted on either side of Henry, their mother clucking over him and the farmer promising to care for the poor sick thing as though he were their own. Then he and Arnold lifted Henry onto the ox.

"They'll take care of you, son, don't worry," Arnold said as he tucked the blanket around him. "Here." He reached into his pocket, pressed two silver coins into Henry's blackened palm. "God be with you, son…"

"I confess, I thought that'd pay for his burial, he was that far gone." Arnold sighs. "But the farmer's lady, she got Henry back on his feet again."

"John Henry, right?"

He glances at me and away again, then reaches for his pipe. We're both remembering a piece in last week's paper, reprinted from one in Pennsylvania. Its author was a rifleman, John Henry by name, who claimed he marched with the "sordidly avaricious" Arnold to Quebec. I doubted his boast, one that loads who've never stepped north of Boston like to make, for the account was full of skimble-skamble stuff, let alone calling Arnold greedy. "Sordidly avaricious" indeed!—and that for the man who saved his life.

"But you're right, Clem," Arnold's saying. "Does seem impossible when I look back on it. In about eight weeks, we completed a march of near 600 miles, not to be parelleled in history, with the greatest fortitude and perseverance." He smiles, proud, and he has a right to be. "The men hauled their bateaux up rapid streams, obliged to wade almost the whole way, near 180 miles, carried them on their shoulders near forty miles over hills, swamps, and bogs almost impenetrable, to their knees in mire. Short of provisions, part of the detachment disheartened and gone back, famine staring us in the face, an enemy's country and uncertainty ahead—" He shakes his head, eyes glinting as a mother's do when her baby takes its first step.

Most amazing part is that Arnold had any men left when he reached Canada. 'Tis a marvel not that some deserted but that all did not. Here were volunteers in a new army that couldn't supply them, let alone force them to complete their service. Yet despite starvation, hurricanes, and swamps, they followed Arnold.

Arnold. It was this man, his courage and indomitable will, that kept 700 folks as skeptical and frail as you and me marching through Hell's parlor.

But he doesn't see it that way. "My brave men," he says wonderingly, "were in want of everything but stout hearts."

Chapter Six

*A*rnold sighs. "So there we are. It's early in November 1775, and finally, only thing between us and Quebec is the St. Lawrence Riv—"

Flash leaps to his feet, barking, and runs to the hall. Someone pounds at the front door, startling me, annoying Arnold. The clock has just finished chiming. "After eleven," Arnold says. "Used to be folks with insomnia stayed home and read the king's latest speech to Parliament. No, keep your seat, Clem. This late I'd better get it."

He stumps to the hall. I hear the door open, then the rumble of male voices.

"'Tis the indefatigable Sergeant Champe," Arnold says, leading him into the room. Flash quits barking to growl, ears back, until Arnold says, "Aw, Flash, stop it, now."

Champe nods to me, bumbling and confused as always when I'm around, the image of a shy suitor. So far, his act has Arnold fooled. Sometimes, it even fools me, so that I begin to wonder what marriage to Champe would be. Then I remember 'tis only a game, and a deadly one if Arnold sees through it.

Champe is Washington's agent. 'Twill be him does the kidnapping, once the plan's approved.

But for now, with his red cheeks and bashfulness, it's hard to see Champe as anything beyond what he says he is, not only my suitor but a convert to the Redcoats. He "deserted" the Continentals at the end of October, made his way to New York, and volunteered for the corps of "returned Loyalists" Arnold's raising. It's a wonder the government wants a whole regiment of traitors, but it does, 648 men who, like their general, have traded one uniform for another. Recruitment's been slow. Besides Champe, there's only twenty-eight men and some officers enlisted so far.

"Begging your pardon, Miss Clem," Champe mumbles. "Didn't realize it was so late, or I'd'a waited till morning."

"Ah, Love. It knows no times nor seasons." Arnold claps his favorite recruit's shoulder while I study Champe, trying to figure whether the word he brings is good. For a Virginian, though, he's saturnine, and I'll likely learn nothing just looking. "Well, Sergeant, now that you're here, take a glass with us."

Champe shifts from foot to foot, wafting the smell of rum to us. I'd wager he's soaked his clothes and not himself in it, grave and careful as he is.

"Well, sir, truth to tell, 'twas Miss Clem I come to see."

Arnold looks even more pleased, if that's possible. He follows our courtship sympathetically, however his wife laughs.

"Couldn't wait, eh, Champe?" He adds something in a low tone that I don't catch, but Champe grins. "I'll check on my wife and son, then, if you two'll excuse me."

"Thank you, sir," Champe takes the footstool beside me and my hand for Arnold to see as the general calls Flash and makes for the stairs. Flash bares his teeth with another snarl before following.

Champe shakes his head. "What's that beast got against me?" He waits until we hear Arnold clumping overhead to drop my hand and whisper, "Sorry it took so long. I think Baldwin went to His Excellency hisself—"

"It's all right. Just tell me, are we going ahead?"

He nods, and something inside me rises triumphant. "We're gonna use your plan. Even Baldwin likes it."

"He does?" I flush with pleasure. Mr. Baldwin's remote and disapproving and a cipher to me. All I know is he's from Newark and Baldwin likely isn't his name. Champe reports to him every second day, either in person or by letter. We've come up with plans galore afore this, a whole month's worth, but Mr. Baldwin disdained them all. "Too complicated," he'd tell Champe, "too many if's, too many things to go wrong." I'm near dizzy with pride that it's my idea finally won his approval.

"Baldwin says it's simple and direct," Champe whispers. "Catches him at a time when he's alone and got his guard down, so to speak, or at least his breeches."

My face burns as Champe continues. "So, without something comes up, Baldwin says week from today's fine, that'd be the eleventh."

My stomach knots. "Then we'll snatch him next Monday—"

"At midnight." Champe nods. "He goes out to the necessary, we'll grab him, get him across the Hudson to Bergen Woods. Baldwin'll have the patrol meet us there and take us to headquarters."

"Let's not wait any longer than Monday. Every day we wait's a risk."

"Yes'm, Baldwin told me the same thing, said even sooner'd suit him, but I misdoubted we'd be ready afore that. Here, here's an account of what we're gonna need." From his pocket he takes a paper close written on both sides. "Didn't want anyone overhearing what we're saying. I'll talk, make The Traitor think we're wooing, and you read. Just throw it in the fire when you're done. I got another copy t'home. He coming back down?"

I nod. "Still an hour to bedtime for him. He'll go out to the garden first, to the, ah—" I blush again, though I know Champe well enough to say the word and it's in the line of duty anyway.

"Necessary," he supplies. Champe doesn't waste words, and he don't mince them, neither. "He'll go piss about midnight, and then up to bed like always."

"Right on schedule."

"Yes'm, that's what Baldwin liked about your plan, relying on his normal schedule. Oughter work. Well, go ahead, read and see if I've forgot anything, and I'll talk."

He begins reciting softly, something from Cato, I think, while I study the paper. 'Tis a fearful long list, and I wonder can it all be done in a week. I only hope Peggy will be out of the house.

The hardest task comes last: "Silence dog." Flash is Arnold's dog, through and through. He won't cotton to seeing Arnold attacked and trussed, so I'll need to restrain him that night. But Flash pays me no heed at all, and it won't be different then. How'll I tackle such a big, unwilling animal? Champe won't be any help, either. If I ask his advice, he'll say, "Shoot him. Want me to do it?"

I read the list three or four times, memorizing as much as I can. Then I throw it in the fire.

Champe glances at the stairs. "All right," he mutters, "I better go. Sorry to make it so late. I rode clear out to Oyster Bay afore I could get the rope we're gonna need. Army's contracted for all of it here in the city. Goodnight, then."

The door's hardly closed behind him when Arnold clatters downstairs, Flash at his heels.

"Well?" He settles into his chair. "Am I invited to the wedding?"

"What wed—? Oh!" I marvel again that a rascal like Arnold overflows with such concern for me, and kindness. "No, General, he, ah, he didn't propose." I pick up the pocketbook with its lopsided diamonds and try to look disappointed.

Arnold genuinely is. "Well, it's none of my business, Clem. You'll forgive an old man like me taking an interest, but you're my cousin by marriage after all, and he's a fine boy. You don't wanna let him get away."

"No, sir."

"Can't you hurry him along, use some feminine wiles or something?"

"Well, I—"

"What's he doing here so late if he's not proposing, anyway?" Arnold's as offended as if Champe had been stringing him along, not me. "Want me to talk to him, Clem, take my horsewhip to him if he's trifling with your affections?"

I laugh. "No, sir, thank you anyway." I cast about for something to pull his mind from Champe. "But you were telling me about Quebec. I'd like to hear the rest."

He reaches beneath him, takes a bedraggled ball of yarn from where it's wedged in the corner of his chair. "Here, boy," he says and pitches it into the hall. Flash is after it like a—well, that's how he earned his name.

Arnold shakes his head. "I remember how glad we were to see Canada. That oughta tell you the desperate pass we'd reached." He grins before shaking his head again. "Oh, and on top of everything else, we'd already been betrayed."

"Betrayed?"

"Ah-yuh." Flash is back with the yarn. Arnold wrestles it from him and throws it again. "Been sending messages right along, like the one to the merchants where I told 'em we had a few thousand brave lads of pure heart and matchless aim marching to evict the Redcoats. Well, fella running them up to Quebec for me was an Indian, knew the forest trails. Thought he was trustworthy and all, but here he was selling every letter

I gave him to the government in Quebec. Probably made a fortune off them and not even the decency to give me, the author, a share."

I chuckle.

"So instead of the merchants looking for us so's they can open the gates, 'twas the Redcoats that're ready for us when we reached the St. Lawrence..."

Along the bank across the river stretched Quebec's Lower Town of docks and warehouses, blockhouses and palisades. From there, steep streets climbed to the Upper Town, with its rich homes and businesses, Mass-houses, a convent or two, the Place D'Armes. As if its escarpment on the river weren't protection enough, a wall thirty feet high, with six bastions and mounted cannon, ran behind the city where the bluffs gave way to plains. Those plains had seen Quebec's only defeat sixteen years ago, when General James Wolfe enticed the French into leaving their city to do battle.

Arnold turned to the aide awaiting orders beside him. "Think they'll open to us?" Oswald asked.

"Captain, way our luck's going, I'll be happy if they're not boiling oil to pour down on us."

"You said they've only got a handful of Regulars in there, sir."

"Did I? Well, I said it'd only take us three weeks to get here, too. When you gonna quit listening to me, Captain?"

"Yes, sir. But still, Regulars can't do much if the merchants welcome us."

Arnold pointed to the closed gates. "That look like a welcome to you?"

Flash growls playfully as Arnold grasps the ball between the dog's teeth to wrestle it from him. "Storm come up then. We waited five nights to cross the St. Lawrence, reinforcements marching into Quebec the whole time. So when the skies finally clear, there's about 1700 Regulars inside the walls, militia too, against the 450 of us fit to fight. All those Redcoats meant no one's gonna open any gate to us, that's sure."

"Too late by then, wasn't it?"

"Ah-yuh. If we'd'a left Massachusetts a week earlier, or not lost so much time on the march up, things'd been a lot different. We'd'a reached Quebec before that storm, see, crossed the river ahead of those reinforcements. Time the Redcoats got there, we'd'a owned the town, coulda laughed at them from behind that wall 'stead of them laughing at us. It'd'a been fourteen colonies against His Majesty, all Canada'd been ours."

Arnold sighs. "Instead, we mounted a siege. It was foolish, stupid, really, to say it plain, but I didn't wanna storm Quebec, and neither did General Montgomery. He arrived around then with his troops—they'd taken Montreal—so it's even more essential for us to grab Quebec since that's the only spot in all Canada the Redcoats still owned. But remember, we're there to free people from the British Empire, not subjugate 'em or kill 'em while attacking the city and plundering their homes. So a siege made sense from that angle. Problem was, there's plenty of water inside Quebec's walls—"

I try but fail to hide a yawn.

"'Tis late, Clem," Arnold says. "You oughta know not to start an old man talking about his war days."

I shake my head. "You'll never be old." I speak not from courtesy but truth. Arnold overflows with vitality. Even now, though 'tis almost midnight and I heard him moving through the house this morning before dawn, he's as fresh as though 'twere noon. He's not yawned once. I don't know that he ever does.

"Time for bed," he says.

"But you were going to tell me about Quebec, about how you almost—"

"It'll wait for another day, Clem. Doesn't do to keep the cook up 'til she's too tired to make breakfast of a morning."

I'll say it again: he's kinder than you'd think a rascal could be. And I am tired—too tired to record what he's told me tonight. It must needs tarry until tomorrow.

I wind my thread around the pocketbook as Arnold struggles to his feet, favoring his crippled leg. "Good night, my dear."

"Good night, sir." I turn for the stairs while he and Flash amble outside. I embarrassed us both the first time I sat up late with him, offering to fetch whatever he wanted in the garden, not realizing he sought the necessary. But he's like that, a man whose energies and ambitions rise so high you forget he's beholden to the same concerns as anyone else.

He's gone the next morning when I wake, though 'tisn't yet seven by the clock. There's a note saying I may have the day to myself, he and Peggy will dine with friends and require no meals. This is a lie he sometimes hands me. He and Peggy have no friends, none that'll be seen dining with them, anyway, and they'll either snatch a meal in a tavern or raid the pantry tonight, when they think I'm asleep. I take care at such times to leave a chicken or some ham and roasted potatoes under a cloth on the sideboard, not for Peggy's sake but his.

I eat no breakfast, writing so furiously instead that my quill nigh scratches holes in the foolscap. Finished, I go straight to the parlor's mantel. I'm too short to see the top, so I run my hand along it until I feel a key. Then I climb the stairs to Arnold's office. I'll spend the day here, reading his papers, as I do whenever I'm alone in the house.

I'm working my way through them, looking for anything about the treason and my cousin's part in it. Seems to be a lifelong habit that Arnold keeps a copy of everything he writes and the letters he receives, too. So it should be easy to learn exactly how he and Peggy sold us out, to find the evidence that'll convince General Washington of my cousin's complicity, that'll prove she's a traitor worse than Arnold.

Much of what I read is dull, the minutiae of this campaign or that, requisitions for supplies, copies of orders sent to colonels and captains. 'Tis easy then to keep an ear out, for sometimes they return afore Arnold says they will.

But now and then I find more interesting things, letters from Arnold to Peggy, or she to him, notation in a ledger for purchase of "one notebook, Leather bound." This last has me agog. 'Tis dated a month before Arnold married my cousin, and if he used it for a journal, that alone could convict her.

But though I've searched every cranny of the office, I've found no journal, leather-bound or otherwise.

It's after noon when I finish a stack of letters from the Massachusetts Provincial Congress. More letters lie scattered around my chair. I get to my feet, stretch, wonder if I've checked atop the tallest chest for the journal. I drag my chair to it, but I'm nowhere near the top. I pile books on the chair and try again. This time, my hand brushes cool, smooth leather—

The front door bangs open.

I stand stupefied. Arnold will find me here, searching his office. He'll know me for a spy and haul me to British headquarters next door. No, he will throttle me himself—

"Clem?" Arnold calls. "You home?"

His voice snaps me from my terror, and I scramble from the chair to the mess on the floor as he clatters up the stairs. "Clem?"

I grab papers, slap ribbons around them. Fool, to have taken so many out, nor replace the ones I'd finished—

The door opens.

Time stops, and we stare at each other, Arnold with one hand on the latch and startled to see me, I elbow-deep in his papers, fear twisting my face.

He says, "This is my office."

I nod, tongue stuck to the roof of my mouth.

"What're you doing in here, Clem? I thought when you didn't answer me you weren't home. Didn't you hear me calling?"

"I, uh, I—" My voice is a mouse's squeak.

His glance moves around the room. "Interesting reading, huh?"

"No, sir, I, um, I wasn't reading, just cleaning—"

He snorts. "Come on, Clem. You can do better than that. 'Tis a zealous housekeeper will invade a locked office to clean."

Flash pokes his head between Arnold's right leg and the door. Maybe I imagine it, but I swear the dog glares at me, scandalized. Then Peggy comes up behind, baby in arms, to peer over her husband's shoulder. She's too alluring to be a mother, and I'm always surprised to see her with a child. She holds her son awkwardly, as though motherhood surprises her, too.

My eyes go back to Arnold as he continues. "Don't lie to me, Clem. How'd you know where the key was?"

I open my mouth, but nothing comes out.

"I'd thought better of you, Clem," Peggy says, sweetly sorrowful.

"Know what?" Arnold says. "It doesn't matter. I don't even want to hear your excuses. Just get your things together and get out. I can't stand prying. Got no patience for it. Go on. Didn't you hear me? Get out."

Flash barks as I sidle past.

It takes half a minute to pack my duds, but I stretch it out long as I can and try to think how to salvage things. 'Tis heartbreaking that

I've been here so long, nigh two months, only to ruin it now that the end's near.

Arnold is still stomping around his office, replacing papers, when I return to stand in the doorway. I button my cloak with one hand and clutch my bundle in the other.

"Sir."

He turns with a scowl, papers in hand. "What?"

"I, ah, 'tisn't what you think, sir. I wasn't prying—"

"Right." He starts to turn away.

I say quickly, "It's just that you—you're my hero, General. I—I feel so honored to know you, and, um, well, I've had it in mind to write a book about the war—"

Though he yet glowers, he's listening.

"You can ask your wife, sir, if you don't believe me. She knows about my book."

"A history, you mean?"

"Yes, sir. Though," I add with sudden inspiration, "after all your stories, and—and what I've seen in your papers, begging your pardon, sir, I'm thinking I'll write about *you*. A—a life, you know, like Plutarch, and his *Lives of the Noble Romans*."

He's losing his frown, praise be, as curiosity battles outrage.

And triumphs. "Really? Hmm. Not a common thing for a lady, writing a book." And here's another sample of his goodness: he doesn't laugh, as would most gentlemen. Though I almost wish he had when he says instead, "Tell me more."

"More? Um, well, um, I, ah, I—I'll need to give it some thought, sir. I'm, ah, this changing it to a—a life from a history—" I put my free hand to my cheek helplessly.

But it works, thank Heaven, and he nods. "Perhaps I was too—too hasty, Clem, though you must admit, it did look like prying."

"Of course, sir, and I apologize. I should have asked you first, but when I woke and found you gone this morning, and the whole day before me, well, I thought I'd just come in and read about Ticonderoga and Quebec and—"

"How'd you find the key?"

"You've come down a few times of an evening, and taken something from the mantel, and then I'll hear you unlocking the door up here."

He grins in spite of himself. "You're a sharp one, Clem, and when you come to marry, you'll do well to hide that. Man doesn't like to be outsmarted by a lady."

"I can stay, then, General?"

"But I don't want you in here, all right? You need papers on something, you tell me, and I'll fetch them." He ducks his head. "I got letters here from Peggy, a wife's letters to her husband, you understand."

Or a traitor's letters to her partner. But I nod innocently, and we smooth things over. He says he'll help any way he can with my book.

I thank him and ask if he'll take dinner after all.

He waves a hand, and Flash's head jerks. No, he's just stopped to write a note of introduction for a deserter from the Patri—rebels looking to join Tarleton's dragoons. Then he's off to meet some friends. But Mrs. Arnold will be staying and need a bite this evening.

After he leaves, Peggy closets herself in her room. No matter: I don't go near his office. I've not yet recovered from my fright, and Arnold changed the key's hiding place anyway.

I eat a solitary supper. Then as I settle into my chair with Adam Smith's *Wealth of Nations*, the door opens and a blast of icy wind circles my feet.

"Clem." Arnold's voice is hearty, happy, as though he's just come from a party at his favorite ordinary. But there's no odor of tobacco about him. He smells fresh as snow, and I know he's done nothing but gallop up and down the empty, hostile streets.

Flash hurtles into the parlor as Arnold stumps to his seat. I don't ask about his evening; I, too, can be kind. Instead I trade the book for my stitchery as I say, "Now, sir, you promised to tell me about the assault on Quebec."

"Did I?" He looks over the bowl of apples on the table beside his chair. There's some chocolate, too, but I set it there over an hour ago.

"Yes, sir. The siege didn't work, so what'd you do? I need to know for the, um, book."

No matter that the chocolate's cold. He drains the cup, then glances sideways at me. "Well, with the siege a failure, time was running out, too, because most all the troops had enlisted through December 31st. Montgomery and I knew we'd be lucky if even a couple of 'em stayed beyond that, they were all so discouraged and homesick and tired of suffering. So whatever we're gonna do must happen before year's end. Only thing left to try in such a short time is storming the city. But you can't storm a place like Quebec, with those stout walls and sitting high above a river; it's suicide even if you outnumber the defenders three or four to one. Only way you stand a chance against a fortress that strong is if you can surprise 'em. So our plan was to attack during the next blizzard, when men of any sense are hunkered down next to a good fire."

"A blizzard?" I'm stunned. "But your muskets, they wouldn't work, would they? Wouldn't the snow wet the powder? And how would you see where you're marching, or who you're firing at, and—"

He holds up a hand, smiling and ironic. "Ah-yuh, sitting here, sounds as if blockheads came up with this idea, it's so silly. Shows how much Montgomery and I were still hoping to take Quebec peacefully..."

The American troops shivered on the Plains of Abraham, awaiting the stormy night required for their attack. But the skies that had dumped snow on them as they fought Maine's wilderness perversely cleared. Arnold's men grew bolder as they spoke of leaving. He overheard one soldier greeting another with, "Just six more days to go, friend," and that one replying, "Lieutenant says that's 144 hours. Probably less now, he told me that this morning. Home! We're goin' home!"

Montgomery delivered the only good news Arnold received during those weeks. "I'm putting you in for promotion," the general said as they leaned over their dog-eared maps of Quebec one evening, "to brigadier general. Oughta've come your way long before this. Congress is blind not to have rewarded you after Ticonderoga and your march up here."

The penultimate morning of 1775 dawned through heavy clouds. By noon, the first flakes were falling; by four, the blizzard they required raged, turning the day dark as midnight and obliterating the sunset.

Drums beat that night, the last before the men would start home, to assemble them on parade.

"All right, listen up," Arnold shouted, excited as a boy at this, his first battle. "General Montgomery's gonna attack Lower Town from the south. We're going in from the north, meet up with him and climb to Upper Town. Meantime, remember why we're here: we're *liberators*, not conquerors. That means no looting or pillaging, no breaking into houses or other buildings. We're kicking out the Redcoats, freeing the town from them, and that's all."

The snow was so thick Arnold could see only a few feet ahead. It turned the drums' noise to tinkling and nearly smothered the fifes. His troops stumbled after him over ridged drifts and ice, muskets held under their coats lest the powder become wet and useless.

They slipped and slid single-file towards the Palace Gate. A cannon boomed, though the storm muffled it. Bells tolled in the town above, alarming Arnold more than they did the Quebecois. If Carleton had already discovered their attack, or worse, had expected it—

He squinted against the driving snow to look up at Quebec's walls, where fire flashed from muzzles. Impossible to shoot uphill, at an enemy they could not even see. Still, he ordered the drums and fifes to signal "Forward." A fusillade and then screams from the men behind him drowned the music.

A barricade loomed ahead, ghostly in the snow. Arnold ran towards it and steadied his pistol on its logs. One moment he was pulling the trigger. The next he had collapsed in a drift, pain searing his leg. A part of him thought, So this is what it is to be wounded, while another answered, A wonder you haven't been long before this, and a third cried, Margaret! Then someone was kneeling beside him saying, "Yes, sir," and he knew he had spoken aloud.

"Help me up."

A soldier whose face was as white as the snow pulled him to his feet.

He stepped forward only to fall again. Again the soldier helped him stand. This time he hopped towards the barricade, leaning there as his column surged over it. Few of his troops had seen bloodshed: they would panic if he didn't show them a bullet was nothing to fear. Or was it? A quivering had begun somewhere deep within that shook his hands and made mush of his knees. He waved his sword to urge the rest forward.

"Hurry on, boys!" But his voice was ragged with pain. Men stared as they passed, eyes ghastly, some splattered with the blood of friends shot down beside them, thinking their last hope gone with their commander wounded.

Then big, brawny Dan Morgan lumbered towards him out of the swirling snow.

"Hey, Arnold, our damned cannon's stuck in the snow back—Hell, you're bleeding."

He'd felt the blood oozing in his boot, thawing his frozen foot, then warming his ankle and calf. Now a black stream trickled down the leather to puddle in the snow. The quiver within him roared from its hiding place to ambush his words and wring them hollow. "Took a ball in the leg."

"Best get you some help."

"Not yet." His cry seemed to come from the bottom of a well.

Morgan glanced at the scared faces passing them, then whispered hoarsely, "Right now, we should get you away from here, not let any more of 'em see you. Montgomery's coming up soon, anyway. He'll be taking command."

"Help me to the front, Captain. That's an order," he said, or thought he said. Instead, Morgan told Chaplain Spring to take one arm and gestured at a rifleman to grab the other. Then the Virginian vanished into the storm.

The snow hid Arnold as they half-carried him from the city towards a northern suburb and the *Hopital General*. The shaking and pain grew worse, if that were possible. "One minute," he tried to say. Suddenly, in the dizzying eddies ahead, he saw a woman wearing a sprigged muslin gown. Margaret!

She turned, smiling all her love, just as she used to. "Benny, my darling! Oh, I *miss* you, nigh as much as I love you! How are the boys?" But she was gone before he could answer, as was the snow and the pain, and all he knew was black peacefulness.

A shriek woke him, a shriek he didn't know for his own until a tired voice snapped, "More brandy!" and someone thrust a mug, sticky with blood, against his lips.

"Drink it down, Colonel," the same voice ordered.

"Wait, my troops, where are—" But the mug tilted, spilled brandy into his mouth, making him gulp and splutter. Then they pushed a wooden rod between his teeth.

"My tro—" he began, but hands gripped his shoulders, held them and his arms, while pain ripped his leg, such pain as turned his world whiter than snow while stars crazily sparked. He chomped the wood, determined to deny his torturers the satisfaction of hearing him scream again.

The rod cracked. An odor of wood and blood reached him, and the agony faded from excruciating to mere throbs. He lay gasping while the voice said, "That's it, Colonel. We got the ball, but it tore your leg up pretty bad. Passed between your tibia and fibula and lodged in the muscle there." The words washed over him, meaningless as pain. "Gonna bandage it now. You'll wanna change this dressing every coupla days. And stay off it for a while, sir, you understand? It'll need a good month, maybe more, to heal."

Arnold forced his eyes open with as much effort as fording the Kennebec required. He saw a room whose walls were lost in shadows. His left foot lay propped on the shoulder of a young man bloody as a butcher who was winding a bandage around his ankle and calf. He sensed someone at the head of the table, and nuns moving at the sides of the room.

"My troops," he croaked, "where are they? Montgomery meet up with them?"

"Sir?" The young man—Senter, wasn't that his name?—leaned over him, ear almost touching his lips. "Speak up, Colonel, sir. I can't hear you."

"Troops, my troops, where—"

"Sure, drink your fill, Colonel." Dr. Senter straightened, beckoning. "He wants more brandy."

A boy held the mug to his lips again. Arnold drank until blankness claimed him.

When he next woke, he lay in a bed with nuns again rustling about. His shaking had wakened him, but it was an honest trembling this time rather than the battlefield's hollowness, due to the cold his single blanket could not conquer.

Suddenly, Oswald was leaning over him. Montgomery must have sent him. "Sir, Colonel Arnold, wake up."

He blinked, then struggled to sit. "Ah, Captain, missed me, did you?"

Oswald wet lips blue with cold. "Yes, sir," he said, but he would not meet Arnold's eyes.

"The battle, Captain, we take the town?"

"No, sir, no, we—we didn't, at least not yet—"

"Ah, God." He turned his head to catch a nun's reproving glare.

"Sir, you need to get up—"

"Where're my troops?"

"I—I don't know, we've heard naught of them. Sir, we need to move you—"

"What do you mean, you don't know? How'd you lose half an army? Where's Montgomery?"

Again Oswald's gaze faltered, and he muttered something.

"What's that, Captain?"

"He's dead, sir, killed early on in the assault."

A disbelieving laugh welled at the general's fine joke: Montgomery had been more friend than commander these last weeks.

"Can you put your arm around my neck, sir?" Oswald's face was pinched. "We need to move you, you're commander now that the—the general's gone. You can't stay here, sir, too risky."

He swallowed his tears for Montgomery. "Where's here, Captain? Where am I? Where are my troops, damn it?"

"I don't know, sir, I told you. You're in the hospital, and Carleton's sending a force to attack here."

"He—what? Attack? He's going to attack a hospital?" Arnold wiped a hand over his jaw. "What's he gonna do, wound us? My pistols, Captain."

"Sir—"

"My pistols!" he roared. He propped himself on an elbow. The daylight flooding the room showed him nuns helping patients hobble for the doors. The less wounded and surgeon's mates were carrying anyone unconscious. At his shout, they halted, turned to look at him. "Every man of you, back to bed. Good Lord, you're all wounded. You can't run away—you belong in bed. That's an order."

"But, sir," Oswald said, "Carleton's coming. He—"

"We'll give him a rousing welcome, Captain. Hand me my sword, there, will you? Have the ladies fetch us muskets, pistols, whatever. I want every man armed."

Through the windows, he saw fieldpieces drawn up like forlorn widows in front of the hospital. "Captain, get those cannon out there loaded and ready to fire soon as Carleton's in range. And after you're finished, you've got one task and one task only, understand? I want you to find out where my troops are." He squinted, trying to make Oswald quit wavering, then muttered, "Mayhap we can still take the town..."

"Snarleton never did attack the hospital, though," Arnold says.

"Who?" I smile. "Snarleton?"

"Well, he snarled a ton, especially at us."

I take another stitch on the pocketbook, then snip my thread. "So why didn't Car—Snarleton attack? Were your troops keeping him too busy? Where were they?"

"Captured or killed like Montgomery." Arnold's voice doesn't quaver, but Flash leaves the hearth to stand with sympathetic eyes and tail a-wag.

I thread the needle, this time with blue. I'm making the purse double-sided, with two pouches, not one, but maybe I got too ambitious. Seems even one side's beyond my skill.

"Mark me," he continues, "the attack'd been disastrous for us, and not just because we lost Montgomery. Every field officer but two was killed or wounded or captured, and there's near a hundred troops dead, too. Redcoats got 500 prisoners off us, including most all the boys who marched up the Kennebec with me. Only men left were the ones that come with Montgomery, on account of after he fell, wasn't anyone to lead them into the city so's they could be captured, too. Lost all our cannon and 500 muskets." He cups Flash's face in his hands, rubs his thumbs down either side of the dog's nose. "So half my army's gone, no artillery, only a few muskets, ammunition near exhausted, food's low again, and the wind's howling. It got down to twenty-eight below that winter."

"Why didn't you just go home?" Seems an obvious question, one most folks wouldn't have thought about twice, but Arnold stops cleaning the sleep from Flash's eyes to stare, nonplussed.

"Go home? You mean quit?"

"Sure. You tried to take Quebec, and you, ah, you couldn't. Seems like fortune and the country was jointly against you from the start. So when the assault didn't work, and you're wounded and hungry and freezing, reckon I'd have called it quits and gone home."

His bewilderment fades until, to my surprise, he nods. "Looking back on it now, you're right, Clem. But I kept thinking we'd try again soon as we're reinforced." He stretches his good leg. "Ah, well, 'twas never meant to be, I reckon. Canada's never meant to join us."

The fire pops; my needle echoes it with a tiny hiss as I pull it through the cloth; Flash scratches and then shakes himself. But the general sits silent. Finally, he asks, "And what of you the winter of '75, Clem? You still in Philadelphia then?"

I nod, remembering that year of troubled and mighty changes. 'Twas a worrisome time, not so much from the war but because Patriots were still shoving the king's men out of office. Usually, they kept shoving until they ran them clear out of Philadelphia. No one takes kindly to eviction from his post and home, least of all rulers, and they put up an ugly fuss. But what else could we expect from tyrants, the Patriots cried, from men who loved controlling us? Odd thing was, once the Patriots put themselves in those offices, they loved controlling us, too—loved it so much they dreamed up more offices for their friends, and new laws as well.

"There were fights and mobs all that winter," I say.

"I'll wager that kept your uncle watching things with a wary eye."

"Yes, sir, sure did, because he's rich, see, and seems the only people Patriots hated more than Loyalists was rich Loyalists…"

Came a pounding at the door one evening whilst we sat at table. Then some men who only lacked tattoos to have come from the waterfront burst in on us, a servant protesting the intrusion at their heels.

"Who—what is this?" My uncle struggled to his feet. "You can't just walk in here. This is our home—"

The roughest one spoke. "We been author—aufer—we been sent by the Committee of Safety, you damned Tory. We're gonna take whatever guns you got here, afore you turns 'em against honest Patriots."

My uncle stood stuttering, and then Peggy was on her feet beside him. "There are no Tories here. You've been misinformed." Her eyes and hair gleamed against her sacque of grey velvet, and though she'd ordered the gown a month previous, its bodice fit tight as a second skin.

Our four visitors nigh licked their lips. Their leader put some courtesy in his voice. "Isn't this Judge Shippen?"

"It is." Peggy dazzled them further with a smile. "But we're no Tories. My sister's betrothed, why, he's a lieutenant with the Lancaster Rifle Company."

"That so? Well, haven't you never doubted the Congress?"

"Who could doubt the Congress?" Edward drawled while my uncle gabbled, "Never! Never!"

"You haven't never spoke a word agin 'em? Never cursed 'em or nothing?"

Peggy's laugh tinkled. "There's no cursing in this house, sir. My mother doesn't allow it."

They might have left, then, if my uncle'd kept quiet. But he quavered, "Besides, only guns I keep are a set of duelling pistols. They're set with silver and not too practical. Haven't fired them for years—"

'Twas those silver mountings that guaranteed they'd not only seize the pistols but search the house. Edward and my uncle followed them from room to room. Still, expensive baubles turned up missing for days afterwards.

"War!" Peggy sniffed as she hunted her silver-handled hairbrush. "Well, I guess they took that too. I hate this war. I thought there'd be officers and parties and dances, and I'm going to be sixteen this summer, too, old enough to finally have some beaux, and what happens? This horrid old war comes along, and there's no parties, and men come steal from us. It's so unfair."

The next week, gentlemen from the committee itself called on us for to hear my uncle's promise that he'd have no truck with Tories nor the government's agents. They even made him sign a statement, as though his word wasn't good.

And so men who argued for liberty forbid my uncle to think or speak what he pleased about the king. He couldn't keep his own pistols, neither, inherited from his grandfather. They claimed 'twas necessary, for the Tories would otherwise scotch the rebellion. But they seemed hypocrites as they hired toughs to bully us.

Maybe that's why I fell in love with one of the king's officers.

'Twas the beginning of 1776. The Continental Army under General Washington still circled Boston while the Redcoats huddled inside. Nothing much was happening except for the skirmishes that break out when too many armed men with too little to do face each other across a small bay.

We hadn't yet heard of Arnold's defeat before Quebec, nor his wounding. All we knew was that the Northern Army under his command had suffered terribly, trying to convince the Canadians to defy an empire with us.

Meanwhile, General Montgomery's half of the Northern Army had captured Redcoats at Montreal. Those disarmed prisoners were now arriving in Philadelphia. The men were quartered in barns, churches, the hospital, while officers had the run of the city on their honor that they'd not leave town. So long as they didn't try to escape, they could flirt at dinners and parties, bespeak a suit of clothes or visit the bookshops, squire young ladies to church or theater—and often did, for Philadelphia's mothers coveted these captains and majors, all aglitter in their ribbons and scarlet uniforms, for their daughters. Eventually Congress would send the captives further inland, where the enemy's warships couldn't penetrate to redeem them nor Philadelphia lose her belles to them. But not yet; this day, the city's arteries pulsed with red. Peggy and I were returning from a New Year's visit to Becky Franks when we first saw him.

He was one of a group of lieutenants, standing in the snow outside the hospital, playing to the applause of the soldiers inside and the crowd collecting in the road. 'Twas a farce that they must have memorized from the stage in London, but I thought at the time they were inventing it as they went, and I was lost in wonder. Four of them tossed the lines about, but 'twas the youngest caught my eye. He was more dapper than handsome, and exotic, with olive skin and black hair, though his confidence and playfulness were what you noticed first. His every gesture, every smile, said, "See what fun I'm having? Join me! Laugh!" And there were the winks he was throwing the ladies—even the married ones, some with their husbands at their sides, but who could object? As easily tell the sun not to shine his rays on you.

Before we left, we discovered his name was John Andre. I floated home. He'd winked at me once and maybe even twice, though the second time had more likely been for Peggy and her pert bodice beside me.

For certain sure, if any man snared my interest, he'd taken Peggy's, too. But she said little about it, only, "That young lieutenant'll know you the next time he sees you, all the looks he gave you. Did you notice?"

And when, like a fool, I prattled about his quick wit, Peggy smiled. "Why don't you have Daddy ask him to dinner?"

"Oh, goodness, I—I couldn't, I—I—"

"Oh, you could so. Daddy'd be glad. He'd think you're finally over Eli Belks."

I shot her a look, but she was busy admiring her reflection in a shop-window.

So it was that I asked my uncle, chin tucked to my chest lest I see his amusement, if he would invite a man who didn't know me from Queen Charlotte to dine with us. All so Peggy, whose father decreed that she was too young to have beaux come calling, could sit across from Lieutenant Andre at table the next week and bewitch him.

The lieutenant was even more charming at close quarters and careful not to mention politics. He discussed history with me, the stage with my aunt, and business with Uncle Shippen. Peggy listened with shining eyes, then smiled coquettishly.

"Lieutenant Andre," I said, beginning to see what Peggy was about and determined to fight for him, "I've heard you held them off so valiantly they were hardly able to capture you." I'd heard nothing of the kind—we'd been avoiding his distressing status of prisoner—but it was the only flirtatious thing I could think to say.

He bowed. "I'd have saved myself the trouble had I known what lovely company awaited me." He gave me the same smile he'd bestowed on Peggy, the one that said I was the most enchanting girl in the world.

"You were born and raised in London, Lieutenant. Isn't that right?" my aunt said.

"Born there, madam, but I was educated at the Academy in Geneva."

Peggy trilled a laugh. "Do the ladies there love war as much as the princes do?"

The lieutenant was puzzled at this, as was I. Then I realized, and I think he did, too, that Peggy was confusing Geneva with one of the German principalities. I wondered whether he could correct her and keep his charm.

He reached for a biscuit. "Only a war of words, Miss Shippen. The Swiss prize culture, you know. I was able to learn much of dancing and music and sketching while I was there. Indeed, 'twould flatter me if you'd sit for a portrait."

"I'd be delighted, sir." Peggy snuggled into the fur at her collar.

Over the next weeks, the lieutenant accepted every invitation we offered that didn't conflict with the many others he received. He showed no partiality to Peggy or me, bantering with either or both of us and with my aunt, too. By the time Congress ordered him and the other prisoners to Lancaster, I'd given up. The lieutenant cared naught for me nor anyone else that I could see, unless there was a girl in England.

But Peggy was heels-over-head in love. As the line of prisoners marched off towards Lancaster and the backcountry in the snow, her brilliant eyes filled with tears and shadows.

Lieutenant Andre left town a month after a new pamphlet appeared in the shops. *Common Sense* shook Philadelphia to its foundations with its refusal to look at folks in government as a breed apart and divinely appointed to lord it over the rest of us.

I bought a copy, eager to see what had the whole city talking. Then, at dinner the next week, I showed it to my uncle and asked did he want to read it. But he turned as red as the apple he was paring.

"'Tis a stupid lie, written by a stupid man, read by stupid people," he thundered. "I'll not have it in my house, Clem. 'Tis a shame you paid good money for it."

I sat confounded at his violent passion. He lifted the book by one corner and, wrinkling his nose, carried it to the hearth. 'Twas then I recovered both wits and voice.

"Uncle, no, wait—"

But he tossed it into the flames, and, when I ran to snatch it out, caught and held me fast. "Clem, I have been ever generous with you and lenient. This is a poor way to repay me, filling your head with trash those rebels—"

"'Tisn't trash!" But tears muffled my voice as *Common Sense* burned.

So when word came from my mother, it was easier to leave than I'd thought. Peggy had stolen John Andre from me; my uncle made tinder of my property and called me stupid in front of everyone. 'Twould be good to return to my mother, no matter that she'd never been one to me. Something about resentment makes us cherish it, hug it to us as a child does a toy, fearful that it may be taken away. So it was now. I wanted to think myself injured, with my uncle's family the culprit.

"Clem," Aunt Shippen said a fortnight after my uncle burned *Common Sense*, "here's a letter for you from home." She handed me a packet.

Mother never was much for writing, but I usually received a note from her around this time each February with belated New Year's wishes, or when something of moment occurred, such as her remarriage a year ago.

I repaired to the front parlor before breaking the seal.

New York Jan'y 13th 1776

Deer Dahter,

I hoap this Findes Yu Well I am a Wido agin My Husban dide of plurisy the DoktoR said i think it was just mean-esS. He was a baD Man worse then mos he left Me his bisnus which was a tavern an I neede HelP manjanin it if Yuv a min to Help. Remimber ME to YuR Uncle an Ant if you furgit, i writ them sepratly, sew dont wury.

Yur muther

It was as nigh an invitation to come home as Mother would give. I sat thinking it over as my uncle entered the room.

"Ah, Clem." He settled into the chair before the fire, newspaper in hand. "Time to see what miracles Arnold's wrought."

I continued musing as he read his paper.

"Lord help me," he said presently. "He's done it again. Look at this: wounded in the assault and taken to the hospital, he had everyone there armed so they could fight off the Redcoats if they attacked." He glanced over his spectacles at me. "'Course, that's just rebel lies. The king's officers don't make war on wounded men. Oh, by the way, your mother wrote to me."

I nodded. "She told me."

"She says she wants you to come home."

He sat watching me, but I made no answer.

Finally, he said, "You're old enough to make your own decisions, Clem." He studied me another few moments before adding, "Just let me know what you decide. I'm lending Hepzibah some money, and if you're going to New York, you can carry it."

He said nothing more—not that he wanted me to stay, nor how he'd miss me. My uncle was too fair to try to influence me, but I thought instead he was glad to be rid of me.

And so a week later, I tied my mother's loan in a kerchief around my waist beneath my clothes. Then I rode in the Shippens' carriage to the docks, found a vessel bound for York Island, and paid my passage with the money my uncle'd given me in farewell. I had enough left over for dinner and another copy of *Common Sense*.

We came in sight of the city the next afternoon, its rocky hills and outcroppings frosted with snow, and anchored at one of the wharves. Of these there were aplenty. The shore fairly bristled with them, boathouses moored alongside. Over everything rose the church spires. Seemed there was one every block, with Trinity Church's weathercock swinging from north to east this windy day.

I lurched down the gangway, wobbly from sea legs, to stand staring. The streets were as I remembered, running down to the river and chock-a-block with buildings. Lining them were trees, leafless and icy. After Philadelphia, where the only trees to be found were cut up and piled out back for the hearth, these bare, brown trunks struck me mightily. Most of them were beeches and locusts, but here and there twined an elm's crooked Y. How cool they kept us in summer's heat, when the great avenues were like gardens, and smelled as good, too, from the locust flowers.

The houses boasted two or three stories and pitched roofs such as the Dutch use on their barns. My favorites had crow-stepped gables. The biggest were all of brick, save white-painted wood round the windows and doors. The ones that weren't so large had their fronts of brick and the rest of wood. Their stoops and sometimes their trim were made of brownstone dug from northern York Island.

I'd gawked long enough that my legs had quit trembling. With the last of my money, I hired a horse to carry me through the city and north, to the Post Road, where lay my mother's tavern.

It was a large place needful of paint, its front door hanging crooked, the hitching rail before it cracked and warped. But there were plenty of beds for travelers, judging from its size, and orchards and gardens lay to either side.

My mother had grown old in the five years I'd been gone, face haggard, the hair stringing from her mobcap grey and coarse. She hugged me joyously, so that I never thought to ask why she hadn't fetched me before.

"'Tis good you're back, Clem," she said, "though I'd druther you'd'a caught a rich one down there in Phillydelphia so's I could make my home with you. This place's more than I can handle."

I saw that from the tavern's back room, where piles of dirty crockery towered. A fire spluttered on the hearth so feebly it would never raise the dough set before it, and the stench of rotting food hung everywhere.

I worked hard over the next weeks. Fortunately, with the tavern lying north of the city and a muddy spring keeping folks to home, there were few enough customers that I could learn the business. My favorite part was cookery. Though I didn't know a trivet from a warming pan at first, I soon took to setting such feasts before us that our few guests and even my mother lauded me. Without the beauty girls are praised for, I'd seldom heard such, and 'twas a heady thing to have our board resounding it. Seemed the more they applauded, the better my meals grew.

I washed dishes and swept floors while Mother rested in the chimney corner. There she cajoled me to find a wealthy husband and complained of her aches between reading aloud from the newspaper she took for sake of our guests. I'd as lief she hadn't read, for the variety of reports kept our minds in agitation.

"Says here that Washington's drove the Regulars out of Boston," she told me one day in March. "Some fellas went over to that fort in New York, that Tiderconda one that Ethan Aaron captured, and hauled all them cannons back to Boston. Says Washington pushed 'em up to the siege lines, and all it needed was the Redcoats getting a good look afore they took to nimble heels."

I leaned on my broom. "I met him in Philadelphia."

"Did you now? Washington? They say he's rich as Croesus—"

"He's married, Mother."

"Married one day, widowed the next. Just lookit me, two husbands dead and gone. You oughter write him, Clem, sweet and respectful-like, see. How'd you meet him, did you say?"

I counted ten and swept furiously. "Uncle Shippen invited him to dinner a few times."

"The judge'd invite the devil himself if he thought it'd grow his fortune. But I feel sorry for the rebels. Sooner or later, the king'll win. Probably sooner. Then your poor Washington'll hang higher than

Haman, mark my words. He'll leave a rich widow, that's certain, and might as well be you."

I couldn't answer, so sickened was I at the thought of that fine gentleman dancing on a rope.

Mother gave a strangled sound as though a noose had tightened around her own neck. "Says here the Redcoats'll be invading us next, and the Continentals, too."

"Well, of course, Mother." Not only was our city America's largest after Philadelphia, but it also sat at the mouth of Hudson's River, the waterway to New York and New England. Whoever controlled the river controlled all that land, so 'twas certain the government would invest us, whether they fled here from Boston or sent another army from London. "But that'll be good, Mother. Think of the extra business it'll bring."

"Extry business? Don't be silly, Clem. Soldiers don't pay for what they want—they just take it. 'Course, they'll have officers with them, and those officers is rich, I heard tell, loads of 'em lords and such." Her eyes glinted as I swept hard again, but then she sighed and rubbed her temples. "Truth to tell, I wish they'd just leave us alone."

Chapter Seven

Champe's hand wobbles as he holds a pistol on Arnold. "I'll shoot, Clem, I swear it! Now go on, get out! You don't wanna see this."

Snow swirls blindingly, hiding the walls of Quebec behind us. I can scarce see Arnold, sitting in full British uniform between Champe and me, right in the middle of a huge drift. Flash crouches before him, trying to wrest a ball from between Arnold's jaws. Dog and man are playful and unconcerned as can be.

Champe's finger tightens on the trigger.

"No!" I scream and wake to lie with pounding heart.

It takes me a few minutes to realize 'twas but a nightmare, like the others that've plagued me since I turned kidnapper. Finally, I stagger to the washstand and splash my face. The water's cold, but there's no ice, not even around the rim, so the weather must have warmed. Outside, a dreary dawn's trying to break through cloudy skies.

By breakfast time, it's raining. Arnold drains his tea as drops splatter the windows. "Maybe I'll stick around home today," he murmurs.

"Nothing to what you had on the march to Quebec, though, huh, sir?" I ask. We usually take our breakfast together, Peggy lying abed till noon.

He carves a chunk from the ham. "Not even close, Clem, you're right. Here, boy, give Daddy a kiss." He holds the meat arm's length above his head. Flash sits beneath, intent on the prize, tongue out and tail wagging so fast it's a blur. He's supposed to rear up on his hind legs and nuzzle Arnold's cheek for his reward. But he barks with excitement, which ends the game. "Hush, now," Arnold says. "You'll wake Peggy."

He feeds Flash the ham, but you can tell the dog's disappointed. He's more playful than hungry, as playful as in my nightmare.

I shudder and pour us more tea. "Wonder if it's raining all the way up to Quebec."

"Snowing, more like it." He plunks a knob of butter atop his griddle-cakes. "Snow never quit all that winter I was there. Then when it's spring, and the St. Lawrence thaws, there come the Redcoats sailing down it to reinforce Quebec, right on schedule. That ended things, once those reinforcements routed us. Half our boys sick with smallpox, the other half's sick for home and wanting an excuse to leave. Nine hundred bayonets of the enemy's advanced guard coming against 'em gives 'em a da—pretty good excuse."

I remember the Tories in New York laughing that neither smallpox nor wounds left any rebel too far gone for flight. Men recovering from inoculation, men nearly dead from the pox, wounded men, men missing arms or even legs—all of them staggered from their pallets and lurched westward, away from the Redcoats. And if the sick made swift tracks, that was nothing to what the healthy done. Headquarters' aides abandoned records and orderly books to flee. Commissaries turned their backs on a hundred barrels of scarce flour, two tons of scarcer gunpowder, and never mind the prodigious effort that assembled all those supplies in the first place. Soldiers ran so fast their dinners still hung over the cookfire, which give the Redcoats a feast of fresh beef after weeks of salt meat aboard ship.

The Regulars wouldn't stay in Quebec; the Ministry hadn't shipped 15,000 of them from England to enjoy the views from those fabled walls. No, they'd sweep down the St. Lawrence to Montreal, proudly held since Montgomery took it six months before in November, and on to the border until every last American was chased from Canada and the way down Champlain and Hudson's River to New York lay clear.

"A rout," Arnold murmurs and sighs...

"Our troops, they're not even an army anymore, sir." The messenger bringing word of the Americans' retreat from Quebec towards Montreal stood before Arnold and an aide, hands twisting the rag that passed for a hat, skin red with barely healed smallpox pustules. "Just a mob of men, General, scarecrows, more like it, walking skeletons, and you don't want to get between them and a crust of bread, no, sir. You'll lose a hand if you do. They're hungry and starving, and they're sick. But don't matter how sick a man is, he's fleeing along with the rest. Worst part is, they got no heart left to them, none at all. They're beat and they know it, and they aren't willing to suffer a blessed thing more when defeat's at the end of it…"

"A rout." Arnold sighs again. He chews the last bite of griddlecake. "But we kept the way south open until every man of us got out of there, and then we fell back, all the way south to St. Johns, kept requisitioning and burning everything as we went, and the Redcoats following behind so close I swear I could smell the bear's grease on their Indians."

Must have been bitter evacuating what he'd struggled so hard to gain. Maybe that bitterness made easier the burning and looting his army did, for he didn't leave the Redcoats so much as a shed to sleep in, a chicken for their kettles, nor a blade of grass to feed their horses. If you owned a farm, a barn full of crops, cattle, warm clothing, or even a rind of cheese, Continental troops nabbed it or set fire to it. Arnold handed receipts around, but slips of paper don't feed families left destitute.

We heard rumors that spring of 1776 about the disasters tormenting Arnold and the Northern Army. But, at least in New York, we didn't have sympathy to spare, facing our own calamities as we were. For one thing, the Continentals under General Washington had arrived. For another, we none of us knew for certain where Howe and his army had gone from Boston Town—all the way up to Halifax trying to recover, Patriots crowed. But everyone agreed their next stop was New York.

The Continentals planned a rousing welcome for them. They built breastworks along the wharves and at the end of every street. Bayard's Mound, covered with cedars, commanded a prospect very extensive, so they cut its top away and erected a fort. Round the hospital went more fortifications. You hardly ever saw a soldier, or any man, without a shovel in his hands, for they pressed all able bodies into service. By the time they finished digging their ditches and sharpening their abatis, I scarce knew whether I was on Water Street or the Broadway, though I'd grown up there. Then, as though York Island lacked dirt enough to occupy them, they spread across the East River, to Brooklyn, and scooped its sandy earth into forts and breastworks, too.

More houses and businesses went vacant each week. At first, only wealthy folks with country estates further up York Island left. But when the New York Provincial Congress laid restrictions on Tories, other people disappeared, too. The property they abandoned sat defenseless, and the Continentals, desperate for ammunition, sent troops after any lead they could find, even from around windowpanes. Tory houses stared blankly or had paper tacked over the holes, and Patriot houses did too as the summer wore on. Then the soldiers took to using them for barracks, and you didn't want to see the insides after that. If the owners ever got possession again, they must be years in cleaning them, unless they laid new floors and new-plastered the walls.

New York wasn't any longer the gay, polite place it used to be esteemed but was become almost a desert, except for the troops.

One hot day in July, they toppled the gilded lead statue of King George down at the southernmost tip of the city. I remembered that monument from my tenth summer or thereabouts, when my father walked me to the Bowling Green to watch them raise it. 'Twas in honor of the king for repealing the Stamp Act and fitted him out as a Roman emperor right down to the toga, which, considering how he spurns freedom, is about right. But the Continental Congress had issued a declaration on the rebellion and why 'twas necessary, and after the army heard it read, they tumbled that statue. The head they sent to a tavern ten miles or so to the north for erecting on a pole. Turn-about's fair play, the troops chuckled, for hadn't kings done that to our heads for centuries, and that when we're footing their bills? The rest of George, they said with another laugh, they'd cook and pour as musket balls so they could fire melted Majesty at his own troops.

Once they finished with the statue, those soldiers ripped down every sign that spoke of the king. Thanks be, our tavern was called The Cat and Dogs ("After me and my late husbands," Mother cackled), so our board still swung from its pole.

I first read the Congress' declaration in the paper over Mother's shoulder. "All men are created equal," it said, even the king of England.

And none of those equal men had the right to force his opinion on us, to tell us we must hearken because that opinion was law. Those who did were tyrants, and then it was our right and even "duty to throw off such government."

They'd scarce published their Declaration of Independence before the enemy, missing all these months, sailed into sight. I threaded my way through soldiers' huts towards the fort atop Bayard's Mound for a better look. Sails filled the horizon far as I could see, the ships under those sails so cheerful with their blue and yellow paint 'twas hard to believe they meant us harm. Seemed the whole city of London was afloat in the waters south of New York, with a fleet bigger than any since the one last century that crushed the Spanish Armada. They'd smash the Continentals, for certain sure.

I wasn't the only one affrighted. Overnight, the soldiers went from cocky to cowering, especially when they heard that the Ministry had hired troops from the prince of Hesse and other German rulers. Those Hessians were terrifying men, with their devilish mustaches and thigh-high boots.

As I mixed punch and served flip that burning August, patrons talked of naught but the invasion. Thirty thousand Redcoats and Hessians had stepped ashore onto Staten Island, but they traded it for Long Island before the month was up, landing at the village of Gravesend just twenty miles from us. General Washington sent half his army to meet them, leaving the other half in the city to defend us.

"No commander knows what he's doing would split his troops that way," one customer said, "not when the enemy's stronger than he is. Washington's got, what, 20,000 men or thereabouts? And now there's that fever spreading, taking more of his boys out of action. Though you can't expect nothing else, what with twice as many people crowding the city as usual and the weather the hottest I ever seen. You haven't had the fever up here yet, have ye, Miss?"

I wiped my sweaty forehead. "No, sir."

"Well, you're pretty far north, must be a mile or so from the city, aren't ye? That oughter protect you for a while. But Washington, he oughter keep 'em all here, or send 'em all over there to Long Island."

Others praised Washington's courage. One of our regulars said, "He'll show the government that free men, fighting for their homes and families and liberties, can prevail against mercenaries ever' time. Mark me, he'll send them Hessians and Regulars flying."

One sizzling morning at the end of August, we woke to cannon firing across the river.

They boomed all day, while Mother and I pumped everyone who entered our taproom for news. By evening, we knew the worst. The Redcoats had pushed the Continentals into Brooklyn, into their forts right across the East River from us here on York Island, and pinned them there. Rumor had His Majesty's forces building siege tunnels.

"That'll finish us," said a dusty, weary colonel. "Regulars outnumber us three times over. They aren't shaking with fear and fever, neither. Don't see that we'll survive this one."

It stormed that night. I stood on the porch with Mother, watching the downpour. "Always liked the rain," she said.

"It's as if the Lord's crying for the Continentals, isn't it?" My voice trembled.

"Aw, Clem, you take things too serious." Mother put an arm around my shoulders while rain drummed the roof and splashed in the garden. "The rebels aren't angels, you know."

True enough. "Who's ever in power, they find a way to separate us from our money."

Mother nodded. "Don't matter if it's Parliament or the Congress. Even if the rebels won, they'd'a been taxing us all soon anyway. You got no call to grieve for them."

I held out a hand to the cooling rain as I murmured, "'Government, even in its best state, is but a necessary evil; in its worst state, an intolerable one.'"

"What'd you say?"

"Nothing, Mother. Just something I read one time."

"Well, I'm a-going up to bed. Don't fret yourself. It isn't us that's gonna hang."

The rain continued next day, and day after, too, drenching fields, miring horses and men who ventured into the roads, drowning the Continentals in their forts and the Redcoats in their siege tunnels. The third day, we woke to fog so dense you'd scarce discern a man at six yards' distance, such a surprise and so beautiful I nigh forgot the disaster in Brooklyn.

Our first customers appeared about an hour after it burned off. I saw by the cockade in one man's hat that he was a Continental major. "Some weather out there, isn't it?" he said, settling into a chair. "You get this kinda pea-soup here often?"

"No, sir, only tell me, what'll happen to General Washington?" I poured his rum. "Will they hang him, do you think?"

"Well, darlin', only if they catch him first."

I set the glass before him, saw the twinkle in his eyes. "Is there news? Have you come from Brooklyn?"

"I surely did, along with the rest of the army."

I could but stare.

He lifted his rum and grinned. "Last night, soon as it got dark, His Excellency sent word we should be ready to march. Didn't know where to or why, but that's our orders. Well, he brought us out of our lines there in Brooklyn, down to the riverbank, and rowed us across, company by company, all night long."

More officers were arriving, and I toted orders as their talk swirled around me. "Never saw nothing like it…thought the game was up for sure, but lookit things now…like to see them Redcoats' faces when they seen we're gone…a miracle straight from the hand of the Lord, I'm telling you. First that rain kept the Regulars from attacking, finishing us off, and then the river smooth as cream so we could row across it with the boats burdened and low as they was, and then that fog this morning, so's they couldn't see us even after dawn…A miracle, I'm telling you, just like when He delivered the Israelites out of Egypt…"

Now the waiting began. The Redcoats and Hessians, all 35,000 of them, still sat across the East River on Long Island. Sooner or later, they'd leap that river, fight those 20,000 sick, ragged Continentals who'd retreated here, and finish the war. All Washington's brilliance done was set things back a week or two. And so the farmers and shopkeepers of the Continental Army took to slipping away, sometimes one man alone, sometimes whole companies, until less than 8000 was left holding the city. Most all the citizens went with them, and the town was nigh empty, one person left where there's five before. Our tavern alone was full, as full as our till, what with all the traffic.

One Sunday a fortnight later, with the Redcoats still perched across the river and none of us hardly breathing from the suspense, I started from my sleep with a mighty headache and thirst. I downed some wine, then retched it up and staggered back to bed. I wakened again a few hours later to booming cannon, so loud I wondered if they were outside my window, or even in my head.

'Twas the last I knew before a blackness broken by nightmares felled me. I burned with fever while eighty-four boats ferried the Regulars from Brooklyn to York Island; knew naught as they chased the Continentals still in New York City out of it to set up lines and pickets and camps; raved and tossed when a dozen British officers pounded at the tavern's door to tell my mother, herself swaying with ague, that they were claiming the rooms abovestairs for quarters.

By week's end, I shook off the fever and tottered from bed. My chamber was a tiny one, no bigger than a wardrobe, really, and set so close under the eaves that I near bumped my head, small as I am, which is why no Redcoat coveted the place for himself. I stood and swayed and swayed and stood.

My ears finally quit their roaring to hear the commotion outside: whips snapping; the thud of hooves; screaming, bellowing stock; the squeaks overloaded wagons make; dogs barking and little ones hollering at them; babies crying; mothers calling, pleading, scolding children while fathers shouted. Sounded like whoever's left in New York was passing by.

I wrapped myself in a blanket and staggered to the window. Straggling along the road were folks of all ages and conditions, families fleeing north with whatever they could carry, whatever they'd tossed into a cart or barrow. I tried to open the window for to stick my head out and see what they were running from, but that window'd been shut all week to keep out the miasmas such as poison the night air, and the heat had stuck it fast. I settled for pressing up against the pane and peering south. Wasn't any sky there, just clouds so dirty they were almost black, swelling and boiling. Lord have mercy, the whole city must be afire.

Came a banging downstairs. I wasn't steady on my feet, clinging to the wall all the way to the door, and the knocking stopped long before I reached it. I waited for my breath to slow, then tugged open that heavy door to watch New York City flying past. A soot-stained man saw me. He turned in at the gate, trotting up our path. "You got any—"

"Fever!" I cried. "We got the fever here! You keep on your way."

"Had it our own selves," he said. Behind him came a girl my age, carrying a boy maybe two years old, and both of them grey from smoke. "But what we haven't got is milk for the little'un. You got any? I'll pay you good."

"Cow's out back," I said. "We got Redcoats quartered on us. Reckon they've been milking her while I was sick, and I miss my guess if they've left you a drop." Then, like a thunderclap, I thought, The till! Likely they'd emptied it, too. The horror drove me dizzier.

"Mind if I try her?" He produced a flask from somewhere, and I shook my head. If he could get anything from the cow, maybe I'd set him to work on the till.

"You all right?" the girl said as her husband disappeared round the corner.

"I will be, soon enough." Soon as I'd checked our till and found it undisturbed. Even Redcoats weren't wicked enough to steal from a sick widow and her daughter. I clutched the doorframe, willing strength into my legs so as to walk to the taproom. Meantime, I asked, "Whole city's burning, huh?"

"Rebels started it." Her jaw showed hard.

"What for? Where are they?"

"Rebels? They run out of town like rabbits when the Regulars landed coupla weeks—no, wait, I guess 'twas just last Sunday. Seems like longer." She gave a tired smile, joggling the boy on her hip.

I closed my eyes, bid adieu to our gold. 'Twas impossible it had survived nigh a week with Redcoats in the house.

"Rebels're up north of here," she continued. "Silas wants to try and find them. He's talking crazy. Says he's gonna enlist." She rolled her eyes. "Leaving me with Punkin here to go throw in his lot with them as burn folks' homes right over their heads, just so the Redcoats won't have no place to live this winter, if the war even lasts that long, which I doubt. Well, none of us will, either, have a place to live, I mean."

"You wouldn't even if they didn't burn you out—not with Redcoats needing shelter. They'll shove you out of your own home."

"Don't I know it. Happened to us during the ruckus over the stamps, remember, 'bout ten year ago? We had a captain and lieutenant put on us, and it near starved us out, feeding them."

Her husband returned, scowling. "Come on, Molly. Lady's right. Damned Redcoats took every sip of milk in that cow." He raised his hat to me. "Obliged all the same."

I could probably have stood there all day, telling folks we didn't have milk, nor bread, nor rope, nor blankets, nor any of the other thousand things you need when you're running ahead of the flames, a child's hand in each of yours and praying you'll find safe haven by nightfall. But I didn't. I stumbled to the taproom. Usually, the money-drawer was closed tight, but now it gaped, the wood gouged around the lock. I was too weak to cry, or the tears would have scalded me. All that work the last month, all the cooking and serving and cleaning, for naught. Worse than naught: all so a Redcoat could buy himself doxies and cozy suppers, a gleaming black horse and saddle of softest leather, maybe a new sword and pistols, too.

Next day saw me a marvel better in the flesh, well enough for church that Sunday morning, though my spirit still ached at our loss. And there wasn't a blessed thing to be done about it. If I accused the officers quartered on us, they'd only laugh—or worse. So I moped in my chamber till the house had emptied but for Mother and me. Didn't want to bump into a thieving Redcoat, for certain sure. I might have killed him, Sabbath or no, I was that angry.

Finally, I crawled from bed to see Mother tossing with fever. No doctors were to be had, else I would have fetched one. The best I could do was the Reverend Dunker, though he'd be more comfort to me than to Mother. I'd ask him back after church for to read the Scriptures and pray with me in my trials.

I stepped outside into a morning hot for the end of September and choked on air heavy with the odor of charred wood. Church lay half a mile north, but the smell stayed strong all that way.

'Twas a walk in vain, for the meeting-house was deserted. Seems Reverend Dunker had fled north with the Continental Army to the Dutch village of Harlem this last week.

Loath to go home, longing for Christian comfort, I trudged north towards Harlem on the Post Road, smelling smoke the whole way. The East River sparkled through the trees on my right, and I lost count of the government's warships anchored there, cannon poking black and menacing from every deck, shot piled beside them. Put me in mind of that Latin the French write on their cannon, *Ultima ratio regum*, though it didn't seem so witty now the king had his ultimate arguments aimed at us. Those ships and their guns set me wondering if this wasn't the end of the rebels, what with their sick, hungry, panicked army crumbling like last week's biscuit and only one rusty old gun for every twenty new ones the Redcoats had. The longer I thought on it, the more I saw the war must end, and soon. Strange that the return of peace and normal days, with the Redcoats back where they belonged nor stealing from us, didn't set me smiling. Instead, I felt hollow inside, worse than from the fever.

Then I chanced upon a sight chased such worries from me.

I had reached a field of barley near the Dove Tavern, about two miles north of ours. But like everything else in the hands of Redcoats, that field had changed and now become an artillery park. I was shielding my eyes against the sun on the brass cannon, and pausing for breath, when my gaze lit on the handsomest man ever I saw.

He stood on a ladder beneath a tree, hands behind him and a noose hugging his neck. One eye was swelled, and there was a reddish brown streak down his sleeve, so they hadn't taken him easy. He was thin, too, and his good eye had the same hollowness to it that I'd seen this morning in my mirror. He must've had the fever and, from his looks, wasn't over it yet.

Still, he stood calm and indomitable. A clutch of Redcoats had gathered round with a drummer beating the "Rogue's March," but he paid them no heed as his blue eyes swept beyond us to the river. There's a pride about him, in the tilt of his head and the way he held himself, which was odd, considering he's dying the shamefullest death, one saved for thieves and murderers.

"Please, sir, what are they hanging him for?" I whispered to a Redcoat. He was an enlisted man, not an officer. The officers are arrogant and rude, but the soldiers, if you call them "sir," will sometimes answer, so starved are they for respect. Their commanders treat them worse than dogs.

Sure enough, this one whispered back, "Caught spying for the rebels, he was."

"Him?" It couldn't have shocked me more if his crime was robbing graves or killing children for to drink their blood. "Must be some mistake. He's too—too—"

"Fine? Aye, but he's a wicked spy all the same."

Near the ladder stood an officer gulping rum from a canteen. This was Billy Cunningham, provost marshal and terrible cruel. Later, I heard that in the week the Regulars had occupied New York, Cunningham got drunk and destructive in half the ordinaries. After he demolished his fourth taproom, word spread among the tavern-masters, and the next ordinary he visited, belonging to Abel Wittinger, served him watered rum. Cunningham caught on quick, though. He called Mr. Wittinger a damned rebel cheating the king's officer and had two Redcoats tie him to one of his own tables, face down. Then he whipped him. He kept on whipping even after Mr. Wittinger passed out, till his back was jelly with the bones poking through. That was Wednesday, and here it was Sunday, and no one yet knew whether Mr. Wittinger would live or die.

Let me tell you, everyone was living in fear of Cunningham—all, it seemed, but this boy he was about to hang.

Cunningham took a paper from his pocket. "Heh, you damned rebel, get ready to die."

Why? I wanted to cry. You've already won. They're beaten, all of them. You've got thousands of the world's best troops chasing Washington and his handful. A month, maybe just a week, that's all that's left 'til government's restored. You don't need to hang anyone, and for sure not this boy.

And I wanted to tell the boy the same thing, how the rebellion's finished, and he might as well admit it and save his neck. You're too young and beautiful to die, I'd say, especially now, it's the eleventh hour, can't you see? Just tell them you beg the king's mercy, and you'll sign a parole, or join their forces, whatever, long as they get you down off that ladder.

But the boy's proud blue gaze stayed on the river while Cunningham stuttered through the words on the paper. "'September 22, in the year of our Lord 1776. By order of His Gracious Majesty, King George III, Nathan Hale is condemned to hang by the neck until dead for high treason against king and country. God Save the King.'" He wadded the paper and lifted his canteen again. "Ho, Yankee Doodle, give us your last words, there, but be quick about it."

Nathan Hale's eyes came back to us, and we all crowded close, though the marshal glared. "Shut your damned bawling, the lot of yous," he roared, and I realized I was crying. Though I'd seen but twenty years,

I'd known my share of sorrow, and it took much to make me weep. But the boy's grace brought it on me unawares.

We hushed, not agreeable to his order, but so's to hear what this condemned spy would say. Those eyes, sparkling and brilliant as the East River in the sun, again looked beyond us to the water. His musical voice never trembled.

"I only regret that I have but one life to lose for my country."

I gasped, for in that moment, seemed that all I'd ever heard or read about liberty, whether *Common Sense* or the newspapers, the Declaration or John Locke—all of it in that moment flowed into me, and came alive, vibrant as this brave, unbending boy.

His words were still exalting the air when his glance rested on me. Then they pulled the cloth over his face. I was his last sight on this earth, and I wished more than ever that I were pretty, that he'd have had that as comfort afore he stepped into eternity. I watched them pull the noose tight and kick the ladder from beneath him. And I cried.

I stumbled home, Reverend Dunker forgotten with my troubles. That day, I thought of little but the hero who had died with such courage and dignity, for all he was a dirty spy.

The Redcoats who'd taken our rooms said somewhat about him next evening. I was mixing punch, for they were thirsty after marching north from their duties in the city. As I scraped sugar from the loaf into a bowl, a captain said to the rest, "I say, 'tis a bloody good wager we'll have no more damned rebels following his lead."

"Come, Finch." One of the others snorted. "They're a damned impudent lot. It'll take more than hanging one or two of them to scotch their nonsense. 'Tis Washington and Arnold and those Adams boys I want to see hang. B'God, I'd knot the noose myself."

They laughed, and I measured the spices into their punch with a shaking hand. I didn't yet realize they were speaking of Nathan Hale. Just their mention of hanging had done it, for the horror was fresh on me.

"I hear he died brave," another said, and then I knew.

"He did," Finch said, "I'll give him that, though he's a rebel and a spy. A spy!" He shook his head. "Astounding, isn't it? Here we are, trying to restore these provincials to the empire and all its benefits, and they *fight* us! Shoot at us, and—and wound us, and now they're *spying* on us.

You'd think we're trying to infect 'em with the pox 'stead of bringing order and—and the king's peace."

"Gratitude, that's what I'd like," growled the officer to Finch's right.

"It's the least they owe us," another agreed. "What, they think we wanted to leave London for this stink-hole?"

"They oughta thank us. I'd thank us, were I in their shoes."

"They haven't got shoes for you to be in, Finch."

They laughed until Finch added, "Tell you what I wouldn't do, though. I wouldn't go behind their lines and get all cozy with 'em—"

"You'd better not, unless you're wanting more lice than you've already got."

They laughed again, even Finch. But when he said, "I wouldn't pretend I'm their friend, and lie myself black in the face so I could turn about and betray them," he quivered with anger.

"Hear, hear." The major to Finch's left pounded the table in agreement. "Now that boy yesterday, what's he doing spying? They say he's a spirited sort, fought hard when they took him, smarter than your average rebel—"

Finch nodded. "So young, too, about twenty or so, I heard. And a captain, though you know these Yankees promote anyone, they're so pinched for officers." He took a draught of punch and passed the bowl. "They named Lee a general, b'God."

There followed obscene remarks on General Charles Lee, a strange man who'd served in the British and Polish armies before his generalship in ours. He was even uglier than me and except for his prodigious nose, about as scrawny, too, so that I felt a kinship with him.

They fell to discussing how few of the Continental officers were educated, which led back to Nathan Hale. I learned he'd graduated from the college in New Haven.

"Pity his father wasted all that money only to see him turn spy a few years later," the major said, and my heart broke for his family. Likely they hadn't heard yet of his death.

Mother lay weak and wan from the fever and left the tavern's duties to me. I set large breakfasts out each morning at eight, when the Redcoats stumbled from bed nursing sore heads and cottony mouths. I waited on them while they ate. They ambled back upstairs by ten, then reappeared in their uniforms to clatter out the door, seldom returning until midnight or later. I spent that time cleaning and shopping and caring for Mother. But back of it all, I was dreaming of Nathan Hale, imagining what he'd been like, grieving that I'd never know him in this world, wishing I had done something, anything, to save him, even if 'twas only kicking a Redcoat's shins.

Some say 'tis impossible to love a man you never knew, that you only glimpsed in the last minutes of his life, and that from a distance. They say you cannot love without you live with him and bear his children and cook his meals and talk and laugh together once the candles are douted. But I answer this, that never have I met anyone who could match Nathan Hale, just the bit I saw of him, and what I found out afterwards.

And I'll say one more piece: all the strange and wonderful things that've happened to me since, that I never imagined while mourning him then—all of it was because of him.

Weather cooled by the third week in October, and Mother took a turn for the worse. Once again, sure she was about to die, I wanted to fetch the Reverend Dunker. The major wrote me a pass in exchange for a bottle of wine.

I found the reverend had removed from York Island to near the river Bronx, so I stayed the night with a farmer and his wife off the Old York Road. 'Twasn't yet dawn next morning when I crossed in pursuit.

The river through there is treacherous enough in peacetime, for it's plagued with beavers, and their dams catch all the leaves and branches and whatever else falls in. Most folks go all the way to White Plains to ford it. It was even worse now, with fortifications dug this last fortnight as the Continentals retreated north from York Island rending the banks.

So all I thought about the men splashing across the river was that they'd help me if my mare lost her footing. Never occurred to me I'd wandered into a skirmish.

If I hadn't been so worried for Mother, I might've sensed something. There were Continentals, which wasn't unusual, but there were too many of them this far from their lines in White Plains. Muskets were popping, too, nothing new by now, but again too many. I sat my horse a dozen feet from a gristmill on the high west bank and watched men in the rags that passed for Continental uniforms flailing the water as if the devil himself was after them. A horseman galloped up to the other shore.

"Sirs!" I called, but they paid no heed.

The horseman wheeled, unholstered his carbine, and fired back towards the east. Coming over a rise not a hundred yards off were the bearskin hats and fearsome blue uniforms of Hessians.

I sat stupefied until my horse screamed and stumbled down the bank, dumping me in the river. The water was only neck deep, but the current runs swift through there, and it dragged me under.

I was fearful it'd sweep me into the gristmill's wooden wheel, but instead, I bumped a boulder. I hugged it and spluttered and heaved while Hessian muskets popped and the horseman shouted at his troops.

The shock of that frosty water made me realize that my horse had been wounded, and if I didn't want to be, too, I better run. I splashed for shore as another tattered Continental ran before the Hessians. He lunged for the horseman, I reckon so he could cadge a ride. The horse was a big bay, but the man already atop her was pretty large and powerful himself. Besides that, she was overloaded with saddlebags and holsters and a big thick blanket-roll across her rump. Now here came more weight swinging at her, though where he thought he'd find a perch I don't know, and that made her stumble. Men and mare slid into the river.

The troops who'd reached my shore were pouring fire at the Hessians. One of the men in the river, the one who'd leaped at the mare, was wading for the bank under that fire. But her rider rushed with the current towards the rock that had snagged me.

"Sir!" I dove back into the river and let it carry me to him. "The Hessians, they're coming! Get up!"

Mud covered him until I could see nothing clearly, even if the rising sun hadn't been in my eyes nor my hair streaming water—neither his features, whether they're pleasing or not, nor how many years he had, let alone whether he was wounded. I tugged at him while he clutched the boulder in a daze and the cold turned our lips blue. From the corner of my eye, I saw his horse scramble from the water and disappear into the trees with mine. And I kept shrieking about the Hessians.

He shook his head, then grabbed my hand. We paddled as had our horses for the western bank, with him hauling me up it.

Muskets exploded before and behind.

Powder smoke choked me.

Men shouted and cried and cursed as I struggled to keep pace with the soldier's long legs.

The Hessians reached the river as we reached the Americans. "Retreat, retreat!" my escort shouted. A Continental had stopped to reload, and we veered close enough that my companion could knock the ramrod from his hand. "Retreat, Cooper!" he cried.

"But, Major—"

"Retreat!"

We were still running. The major hadn't broken stride to holler his orders nor loosed his grip on me. We ran through fields of shocked corn and hay, dead brown vines twisting along the ground with pumpkins orange and cheery smiling up at us. We ran until I swore my lungs would burst, though the popping behind us spurred me on.

I was near beat out when the major called a halt, thanks be. We took another step into some trees lining a field, alone, the Continentals scattering. He held up a hand for silence, and I tried to quiet my gasps.

At last he nodded. "Good. I knew we'd lose them. Those packs on their backs weigh so much, they can't keep up with us, not when we're retreating." He grinned down at me through his mud and led me from the trees. "We're masters of retreating."

I smiled weakly. Though the danger had passed, I couldn't think of much beyond how close we'd come to dying.

"I owe you my life and my thanks," he said. We'd come to a well behind a farmhouse that, to judge from the weeds nigh hiding it, had been abandoned when the war first moved to New York. He pushed the bucket over the rim and flashed another smile as he hauled it up. "Kinda knocked the sense out of me when I went under, but you tugging at me, that did it—let me find my feet again." He cupped his hands around some water and sluiced the mud from his face to show features so resembling General Washington's he might've been a younger brother. About as tall, too. "You'll pardon my washing, I hope. I figure we're already beyond that in our acquaintance."

"Certainly." My voice was as faint as during the fever. I should have been on my way, but the thought of venturing out alone, without his protection, made me shake anew.

He seemed to read my mind as he poured the rest of the bucket over himself. "I'm going to headquarters up near the courthouse, report on all this, but permit me the honor of accompanying you that far. 'Tisn't too safe in these parts, you may have noticed." Again, there was the smile, as if 'twas all a game. There was no flinch in him, not anywhere.

"Thank you, sir. I'd welcome it." I took a breath to strengthen my voice. "And who do I have the honor of addressing?" I asked, expecting him to say, "So-and-so Washington."

"Benjamin Tallmadge, Brigade Major to General Wadsworth's Connecticut regiment." He was dripping water and had lost his hat to the river. Still, he pantomimed a flourish while he bowed. "And may I inquire as to the lady's name?"

"Clem Shippen," I said but thought, Connecticut! And he was young, about Nathan Hale's age. "You're from Connecticut?"

"No, actually, I was born here in New York, out on Long Island."

I must have looked disappointed, for he added, "But I've lived in Connecticut for the last, let's see, seven years or so. Went to college there, and when I graduated, taught school."

I knew of only one college in Connecticut. "The one at New Haven?"

He seemed startled. "Well, yes, I graduated from Yale, in New Haven, but I taught school in Hadley." He smiled. "That a mark against me?"

"Then you knew Nathan Hale."

Sadness chased the surprise from his face. He nodded. "We were both studying for the Gospel's ministry."

A preacher! My heart leaped. I knew he'd been too much a gentleman to spy.

Major Tallmadge whispered, "He was very—a very good friend of mine." He bowed his head. The water dripping down his cheeks wasn't from the well.

"Can you tell me about him?" I asked.

With a sigh, he took my elbow and guided me towards the road. We walked a ways before he spoke again.

"I never knew anyone like him. Things came so easy to him, seemed like he could do anything. That's why, when we heard they'd hanged him, we couldn't believe it. Just didn't seem possible because he always won at everything. Except checkers." He smiled. "I beat him every time. But otherwise... If they sent him to spy, well, he'd bring back everything they wanted to know, and—"

My heart quit its leaping to reel. "They said he was spying, hanged him for it, I know, but—"

"He was spying." He spoke so sure I stood bereft.

"But—but how could he? How do you know?"

He swallowed. "They found papers on him, from what I heard, in his shoe, notes on their fortifications and troop numbers and plans."

"Why'd he do it? Musta been a reason, something that wicked—"

"General Washington himself asked him to."

That knocked me back. I remembered the dinner at my uncle's, and the tall, straight, upright officer who'd sat beside me, talking liberty. How could a man that honorable send another honorable man to spy?

"Did you know him?" the major asked.

"I saw him die."

His eyes never left mine. "Tell me."

So I did. And he said, "Someday, I'll make them pay for what they did to him."

"How long you been in the army?"

"Long enough." He spoke so brusque, he apologized. "I was in the battle out on Long Island, saw things there I'd as lief forget. My—my brother Will—" His voice wavered. "He was with some of the militia there. Haven't heard from him since."

"I'm sorry." Likely the government had captured Will and clapped him in prison, mayhap that ship, the *Whitby*, they'd anchored down in the bay this last fortnight for a gaol. They'd filled the enormous Sugar House and the churches, dank and cold because they were built of stone, and that with winter coming on, and now must use the wide ocean to hold all the boys fighting to live free. Gaolers so indifferent to warming their prisoners didn't care about feeding them, neither. Poor Will had probably starved to death by now.

We'd reached the pickets before headquarters, and Major Tallmadge took my hand. "I hope we'll meet again soon."

'Twasn't likely, though. Shortly after, the Regulars chased our boys further into Westchester, with General Washington losing battle after battle. Seemed as though our victory up to Boston was the last we'd have this war. Especially now that the Redcoats held New York City and Canada, the ends of the waterway carrying our supplies and letters and troops. Only a matter of time, the Tories gloated, till His Majesty's army took the forts between and controlled all of Hudson's River and Lake Champlain. Folks quit saying, "If the government prevails" in favor of "When it does," and our taproom echoed with toasts to the king.

Even Benedict Arnold and his famine-proof army up north couldn't win. While Washington was losing New York City, Arnold built a navy on Lake Champlain. There were no shipyards; few workers, and almost none of them skilled; no cordwainers nor ropewalks; no oakum; no canvas nor needles to sew sails. What carpenters there were had nothing more than a forest to cut trees from, a couple of axes—and Benedict Arnold's determination. They cobbled together sixteen ships, mounted cannon, and cruised to battle. But even Arnold couldn't stop the government from sinking our navy soon as it hoisted anchor.

Chapter Eight

It rains all this Wednesday, sometimes sprinkling, other times pouring. Arnold spends the morning in his office, which keeps me at a desk writing instead of searching for the key. But by dinnertime, he's restless. "Be back in time for supper," he says before I've even served the pie.

I wait until he's clomped out into the drenched streets and Peggy's retired upstairs before I repair to the back parlor. It's a small chamber, little used. That's why I think the key's hidden here.

Between trying to be quiet and listening for Peggy's footfall, it takes an hour to search the room, and for nothing. Discouraged, I repair to the front parlor where the dinner dishes still sit, dirty and depressing. I'm scraping and stacking and wondering where on earth he's put that key when Peggy appears in the doorway, dressed to a fare-thee-well and so comely I can't help staring. Even Neddy, draped over her shoulder, seems happy just to nuzzle her graceful throat.

"We're going out, Clem," she says. "Miranda Jones's got a good nurse, and I want to see about hiring her. I may take supper over there, so tell the general, won't you?"

I carry plates to the kitchen, stunned by such good fortune.

Only when Peggy's long gone do I venture upstairs to their bedroom. Mayhap he hid the key here, though I still think the back parlor's more likely. Here, he'd risk waking Peggy or the baby.

Fifteen minutes' looking doesn't yield the key, but I do find some letters. One's from General Gates, dated the second week of October 1776. "It has pleased Providence to preserve General Arnold. Few men ever met with so many hair-breadth escapes in so short a space of time." I suspect he's talking about Valcour Island, where Arnold's navy fought the government's on Lake Champlain. I can't wait to ask about Providential preservation and hair-breadth escapes.

I hunt all afternoon. Finally, getting on to suppertime, I meet with success. The key's tucked under the carpet in front of the office, such an obvious spot I'd disdained to look there before. It's too late now to fetch the leather-bound notebook, so I replace the key, just as I found it, even make sure the teeth on it face the office, case Arnold's keeping track that way. Then I scamper to my kettles.

Arnold comes home, shakes the rain from his greatcoat, hangs his head when I tell him Peggy's dining with Miranda Jones, eats his meal. Afterwards, we take our chairs by the fire, full of fricasseed chicken and turtle soup. Flash gnaws a bone at Arnold's feet.

"Tell me about Valcour Island," I say.

His eyes fix on me but look beyond, into a past achingly glorious.

"Valcour Island." He smiles. "You know, my boy Hal always calls it Valor Island, seems strange to hear it said right." He takes an apple from his pocket, wipes it on his sleeve. I pick up my needlework. "Well, Clem, 'twas a rough time of it, after we left Canada in the summer of '76. Troops were desperate and dispirited, you know, way they are any time you must retreat. And the smallpox! Time we got everyone out of Canada, half the boys had it. I remember how quiet they were, Schuyler and Gates and the others, when they first saw the army, or what was left of it, that summer after I got it back to New York, quiet as folks round a death-bed…"

The officers said nothing as their horses picked their way through what had been the outlying works at Crown Point, 100 miles south of Canada on Lake Champlain. Arnold could read their faces, though, sweaty and red in July's heat. Schuyler's was a polite mask hiding despair, while Granny Gates chewed a fingernail and looked ready to cry. Generals Sullivan and de Woedtke were thunderclouds waiting to burst, most likely on Arnold's head. And they hadn't seen the worst yet.

Three weeks had passed since the Continentals withdrew from Canada, weeks of terror and confusion, hunger, exhaustion, disease, death.

The death never ended. Young men, healthy, brawny, proud at their enlistment a few months before, were now sick and starving rats, slinking about when they could move at all, eyes squeezed against the sun's glare, scrabbling for food, rags flapping with every motion, suppurating sores contorting their bodies. Each night the rats collapsed in their filth, defenseless in the war against death, lacking food, medicine, or even rum. By morning dozens had surrendered. This obscenity of young men dying, this perversion of nature, racked Arnold until sometimes he could not remember who he was, or where, or why. And was glad not to.

If only they had doctors, provisions—and, most essential, liquor. Oh, for some good New England rum, to soothe the dying and comfort the sick! What they needed even more than kill-devil, though, was time. Time for the sick to recover, time for recruits to fill the decimated regiments, time to train them, time for muskets and shot to arrive.

They dismounted, and Arnold led the four generals up the bluff to the fort itself. They had not even entered the iron gates before their shoulders sagged. Only one rebuilt barracks stood inside the stockade: a kitchen fire three years ago had left nothing beyond charred stone and chimney-holes silted with leaves and mud. But the destruction of Crown Point was old news now. What caught their breath were the rows of rats-who-had-once-been-men lying under the broiling sun, moans rising in an ominous hum, faces angry with smallpox pustules, some thrashing, others too still.

The officers stared silently until Gates spoke. "Has more the look—the appearance of a general, ah, hospital than a force, you know, an army formed to oppose the invasion of a successful and—and enterprising enemy, don't you think?"

De Woedtke pulled a flask from inside his uniform and gulped half before offering it to Gates. "'S not an army but a mob," he muttered, "the shattered remains of twelve or fifteen very fine battalions, ruined, gentlemen, *ruined* by sickness, fatigue, desertion—ah, Gott." He accepted the flask from Gates and again drank deeply before capping it.

A filthy heap of rags at their feet propped itself on an elbow. "The hell you say, you damned Yorker?"

For a moment, Arnold thought the man was addressing Schuyler, the only Yorker among them. Then a blackened foot poked from the rags to kick the ulcerated shin of what had been a soldier lying next to him. "I said, you damned Yorker, speak up. What'd you say?"

Years before, on his first trip to London, Arnold had gone ratting. He remembered the pit in the floor, lit bright as day lest patrons miss any of the bloody action, and the rats, horrifying, writhing, biting each other as much as they did the dog snapping their necks in his jaws. That night came back to him now as these dying soldiers fought each other.

The rat with the oozing leg turned on his tormentor. "I said, you damned Yankee, 'twas you as got us into this, you blockheads up there in Massachusetts Bay. And I'm a captain, damn it. Call me 'sir' when you curse me."

Schuyler gaped, either at the rats' words or their filth. "Void of every idea of discipline or subordination," he murmured incredulously, "the officers as well as men of one colony insulting another."

They climbed the steps into the cool darkness of the barracks housing Arnold's headquarters and seated themselves around a rickety table. After prayer, Schuyler nodded to Arnold. "General, if you please, favor us with your assessment."

Assessment? They needed an assessment?

But before he could answer, Gates cleared his throat. His cheeks burned red in the barrack's twilight. "General Schuyler, with all respect, sir, I don't think you—that is, you'll recall the Congress appointed me supreme commander of the Northern Army, sir, and as such, it'd be better—that is, I should conduct this meeting."

Arnold nearly laughed. "Mayhap you didn't notice," he wanted to say, "but there's no Northern Army anymore, just some corpses to bury. No need to fight over who's in charge of digging the graves."

Schuyler waited for Gates' querulous tones to fade before his own cultured voice flowed over them, smooth as new snow. "Certainly, sir, you command the Northern Army. I regret any impression that I'm disputing that."

"No offense meant or taken, General, I'm sure." Gates pushed at his spectacles. "Now, I think—"

"But of course," Schuyler continued, "you were commander of the Northern Army whilst it was in Canada, General, were you not? That army has retreated here, sir, into the theater I've had the honor to direct these last months, so the command rightfully reverts to me."

Arnold was not the only one to grin at this clever extrication. Gates, catching their amusement, flushed. "I—ah, that is, hey, wait a—"

Schuyler nodded to Arnold. "Now, General, your assessment, please."

Arnold pulled his eyes from a Gates scarlet with rage as Schuyler added, "Appears that you've collected our forces here, you're—"

"*Our* forces, sir?" Gates tried to chuckle, but his anger turned it into a squawk. "I saw precious few Yorkers out there. 'Course, this colony's mostly Loyalist, isn't that right?"

Schuyler's gaze swept Gates with the distaste reserved for a brimming chamberpot. "Sir?"

"Loyalists all around here, aren't there? Colony's rotten with them."

"That's unjust, sir, we—"

"I mean, those folks up there in Lexington and Boston, they're brave as lions, wouldn't expect most men to match 'em." Gates' mouth pursed. "But you'd think *somebody* hereabouts'd show a bit of courage, wouldn't you?"

"I assure you, sir, they'll turn out once the planting's done, and the harvest."

"The *planting?*" Gates squeaked. "*Harvest?* Well, sir, why don't we ask the enemy can they delay their invasion till it suits the farmers of New York?"

Delay their invasion. Arnold started as though he had touched Dr. Franklin's electrified key. "That's it! We—"

Schuyler leaped to his feet. "Perhaps you can ask them for us, General Gates," he hissed. "I understand you've a lot of friends over there."

Sullivan rapped the table. "Gentlemen." He too tried for a chuckle, but he was as unsuccessful as Gates. "It's the Redcoats we're fighting, remember?"

"I oughta challenge him for that," Gates sputtered as Schuyler filled a pipe with trembling hands and de Woedtke reached for his flask. Arnold sat jubilant at the idea unfurling within him. Then he remembered that he must depend on the rats for its execution—after he persuaded the antagonists in this room.

On the parade, a drum beat for dinner, a cruel joke. Sucking angrily at the unlit pipe, Schuyler motioned to him. "Please, General Arnold, do try again to give us your assessment. The men are regrouping. You're giving them time to recuperate, and stragglers can catch up."

"Giving them time." Arnold nodded as he repeated the magical words. Time. Delay. Winter came early here. Once snow flew, the invaders must scramble back to Canada, battle fought or unfought: lakes and rivers choked with ice would choke their supply lines, too.

Schuyler took the pipe from his mouth, jabbing it to emphasize his words. "Make no doubt of it, gentlemen. Enemy's halted at the Canadian border, but only temporarily. Thousands of reinforcements, spies are saying as many as 15,000, will join General Carleton there any day now."

Arnold tried to catch his glance, but Schuyler continued unheeding.

"We're all that stands between him and Washington's army in New York, and word is that General Howe down there's also receiving more troops. Then Howe and Carleton'll march towards each other, crushing Washington and us between them." Schuyler spoke calmly, as though discussing the weather, not his own death as well as that of every man in the room, let alone the thousands of rats outside, the war, liberty.

Arnold seized his chance. "Well, gentlemen, you know what that means." Sullivan and de Woedtke looked at him expectantly, and even Gates and Schuyler left their sparring to eye him. "We must attack."

"Attack?" They gasped as one, united at last.

"Absolutely!" How better to strike back at the misery? It would encourage those dying men outside, lend them hope that something could be done, that annihilation alone did not await. And it would surprise the Redcoats, converging so confidently for the kill, might confuse them enough, throw them enough off balance, to gain the time so desperately needed. It would buy the Continentals a few precious weeks, maybe even months, if Heaven smiled on them. Much could happen in a few months.

He saw disagreement replace the sulkiness on Gates' face—Granny ever favored a defensive stance—and amazement on Schuyler's. Sullivan looked ready to dart for the door. De Woedtke uncorked his flask.

Arnold added, "And, of course, best place to attack is on the lake."

This time, all four faces held only shock.

Finally, Schuyler said, "The—the lake, sir? I—I, ah—that would take a navy when we've barely got an army. You can't be serious."

"He's off his head." Sullivan sighed.

Gates grumbled something, provoking Schuyler to thunder, "He did *not* lose us Canada, sir! He saved our army from the Redcoats."

"Sure," Gates bawled, "saved 'em so the smallpox could get 'em."

Arnold longed to punch the fool, but instead he forced another laugh. The lives of his rats rode on his persuading these men. "Really, General, you do me too much honor, crediting me for the acts of Providence. Only He can afflict an army with smallpox or not, as He chooses."

De Woedtke chuckled as Gates glowered, and Arnold continued. "Now, what's our objective here?"

They fidgeted, impatient again, until Sullivan said, "Keep Carleton from capturing Lake Champlain and Hudson's River so he can't force a juncture with Howe."

"Right. But what if Carleton never starts down the lake at all? What if we keep him so busy *preparing* to invade he never actually does? Winter hits early up here. Usually snows by October or even September, and once it does, Carleton'll turn tail for Canada. October's just three months away. So let's keep him occupied until then, keep him so busy he can't invade."

Gates snorted, but Arnold plunged ahead heedlessly. "Carleton's cautious as an old lady on steep stairs. He hears we're building a navy, he'll—"

"What navy?" De Woedtke shook his head. "Is crazy."

"—he'll want one, too. Take him a coupla months to build some ships, probably the rest of the summer. Time he's ready to invade, won't be but a week or so left until snow flies. We'll sail out to meet him, eat up more time with a battle. But here's the beauty of it, gentlemen: doesn't matter who wins that battle because we'll have kept him *here*, building boats instead of forts, wasting time instead of invading and conquering. They'll have used up the whole season and leave us all winter to recover and recruit."

"Clever," Sullivan said at last while Schuyler murmured, "*Brilliant.*"

"Too clever by half." Gates' eyes narrowed. "Never work."

"Yes, it will." Schuyler scowled at Gates before adding, "I congratulate you, General Arnold. You're a genius…"

"Gates hated Schuyler and me ever after that, and probably de Woedtke and Sullivan, too." Arnold twirls his apple by its stem. Though after Gates' flight last August, when he turned tail at the Battle of Camden and ran so fast his army didn't know where he was for three days, Arnold's not the only one thinks Granny covered himself with indelible infamy. These days you'll look far to find anyone taking up for him.

Arnold asks, "You ever met him, Clem, Gates?"

I finish knotting my thread as I say, "No, but I oughta've, all the time he spent in Philadelphia pestering Congress for a promotion."

Arnold smiles. "He's annoying, Gates is, pesky old annoying granny. Made the summer there on Champlain that much more miserable, what with him being my immediate commander."

"But they liked your plan, didn't they, that Council of War?"

"Ah-yuh, by the time we adjourned they were downright enthusiastic."

And that after beginning the meeting in despair, defeated and knowing it.

"Tried to spread that enthusiasm to the rats," Arnold says, "but they were too—too—"

"Rat-like?"

He nods. "Man can get to the point where he's so beat, you can't do anything with him. Those troops cared about naught but going home, and if they couldn't do that, they didn't wanna do anything. Scared of the government and what it does to rebels, scared of fighting, scared of dying. And then we got reports…"

…that 12,000 Redcoats were assembling at Quebec, as were 5000 militia and Indians. Seventeen thousand healthy, well-fed enemies marching south against 3000 farmboys-turned-rats. Rats he had tried to fashion into an army but must now remake into sailors.

"They're gonna thrash us, General Arnold, sir," he heard time and again from the haggard faces surrounding him when he rode through camp.

"Naw." Arnold waved a hand. "They got Snarleton leading 'em. That's worse'n anything we could do."

They were beyond laughter, but a few smiled.

Arnold hired a commissary named Richard Varick, a capable man and cousin to General Schuyler. Then he fired off letters to Congress, Schuyler, Gates. He even wrote Washington, beset with his own devils in New York City where 35,000 Redcoats and mercenaries had arrived to defeat 20,000 Continentals. Arnold pleaded for food and medicine, for sailors, carpenters, rope, sailcloth, oakum, for gunpowder and shot. Ammunition was so scarce that they could do little more than fire a signal—and a feeble one at that—should they sight the enemy's ships. And that was frighteningly possible. His plan relied on Snarleton's keeping to the northern end of Champlain, amassing a navy of his own—but what if he didn't? What if he suddenly realized he needn't defend the lake, that he must merely transport troops over it to invade New York and New England? The rats could not stop him. Yet Arnold must teach boys who had never seen a cannon how to load, aim, and fire one aboard a rolling deck without powder to practice.

Many of his letters went unanswered. The responses he did receive repeated one another ad nauseam: "…regret We are unable to Help, General, by supplying your Request…" He would never float a navy at this rate, and if by some miracle he did, how could he intimidate Snarleton in boats lacking sails and cannon without shot?

And then, in the middle of it, as he was showing rats who were not carpenters how to build a row galley without plans to guide them, using green wood instead of seasoned planks, Gates summoned him to Fort Ticonderoga. An inquiry into the American withdrawal from Canada, and the troops' plundering on their way south, was convening…

"An inquiry of who?" I ask.

"Wondered that myself, after the thing got underway." Arnold tosses his apple core into the fire. "Supposed to be an inquiry of Colonel Moses Hazen's conduct when we retreated from Canada, his refusal to obey orders and his looting, which I'd tried to stop, but turns out instead it's an attack on me by Hazen and his friends, all the scoundrels and rascals in the Northern Army. Gates was probably in on it, too. Couldn't have come at a worse time, either, 'cause I was too busy to realize what was going on." He rolls his eyes. "Here I was, slapping ships together fast as I could and training men, had no supplies or tools, and the provisions—! We got enough there at first that the starving stopped and the dying. But most days that summer we went to bed hungry." Arnold stares at his apple, shrivelling black in the fire. "I'd'a bought what we needed, but I didn't have any money left, and Congress hadn't paid me a penny of my salary."

And still hasn't. 'Tisn't likely it ever will, either. "Well, even so, you built those ships, didn't you, sir?"

"And it worked! Snarleton wasted the summer building boats too, 'stead of ferrying his troops south and invading. We'd won the thing right there; after that, battle was just a formality. That give me time to train those poor sorry louts I had for crews, and I could scout the lake, too, find the best place to pit my little fleet against his. Always remember, thing to do when the enemy has all the advantages is attack, not cower and let him set the terms of battle, too."

"That how you wound up at Valcour Island, looking for a good place to fight?"

"Ah-yuh. There's a bay there, with narrow shores. It'd protect my small boats and keep the enemy's large warships out, force them to battle me one at a time. That went a long way towards balancing the odds in our favor."

I take some stitches, trying to imagine it all: a "navy" built and sailed by landlubbers, not enough shot for the cannon nor enough of anything else, either, and Arnold enjoying himself, guffawing at the joke on Carleton.

"'Course," he says, sobering, "if we couldn't stop Snarleton, well, we'd be facing disaster."

Disaster enough to kill our Cause. Courageous and sparkling as the march on Quebec was, it didn't finish the war when it blundered. Failure now would.

Arnold clears his throat. "After building all summer, we had sixteen boats, mounting thirty-two cannon, strung across the bay at Valor Island. 'Twas October 11, 1776..."

◦◦◦

...and not even eight o'clock that morning, with his officers at breakfast aboard his flagship, when a signal cannon boomed. They were laughing at Varick's joke as Arnold stepped to the porthole. All he saw was his spanking new fleet with the last of the morning's fog wreathing masts and sails and the new flag, the one with a rattlesnake and the legend, "Don't Tread on Me." The craft that usually plied the lake, the merchant ships and fishing boats, the occasional Indian canoe or farmer's dory, had vanished to leave the water eerily empty. Snow frosted the mountains rimming the lake as it had the last fortnight.

Arnold had sent Captain Premier north to the guard boats with the day's countersign. That signal meant Premier was back, and with news of the enemy: they must prepare for battle. Arnold ordered the white pennant hoisted to summon his captains for a council of war.

Steps pounded overhead on deck, and Premier burst into his cabin, silencing Varick and the rest. "Sir, enemy's seven mile north. Four big warships, whole fleet of gunboats, I'd say maybe twenty-five of them. Got a hundred, hundred-ten canoes packed with Indians, my mate lost count, sir. Ten Indians to a canoe."

Arnold nodded. "Have a seat, Captain."

"Even if you don't count the canoes, sir, their fleet's more'n double ours, nigh thirty ships, and all them ships loaded with cannon, sir. I saw dozens of 24-pounders—"

Arnold's four biggest guns fired 18-pound balls. A quartet of 18-pounders against God-knew-how-many 24-pounders.

"—and sailors, sir, professionals, the best of the king's navy."

The door opened again to General Waterbury, Arnold's second-in-command, and the other captains.

Arnold waited for them to find perches along the walls and on his bed. Despite his preparation and the surprises he would unleash this day—surprises planned in such secrecy, he had confided to no one, not even his officers, lest a spy carry word to Snarleton—despite that, obliteration awaited. And his officers knew it, judging by their hang-dog faces. They couldn't survive this thing, let alone win it; he and they were dead men. Yet the determination to triumph, to do what no one else could, sang in him so loudly he wondered the others could not hear it.

"Gentlemen." He stood before them in a new uniform, the dark blue coat highlighted by a buff sword sash and gold epaulette on his right shoulder.

Waterbury stared sourly. "You letting us in on the big mystery now, General?"

Arnold winked. Waterbury had begun asking months before about his intentions, offering observations and advice. At first, Arnold fobbed him off by listening, letting him talk but sharing nothing in return. Waterbury caught on, though. Then he became incredulous. What kind of officer kept his strategy from his own generals? Another fortnight, and he turned bitter. As second-in-command, he had a *right* to know. Now he sat scowling.

Arnold looked around the circle, eyeing each captain intently. "Here's my plan, gentlemen, and if none of you know it, no spies do, either, nor Carleton." He paused as though everyone in the room were not already on the edge of his seat. "Now, they think they're coming after us this morning, but in reality, we're going after them. We're gonna ambush them."

In the dumfounded silence, he unrolled the map of Lake Champlain and pointed to Valcour Island. His ships were anchored in a crescent between there and the mainland, in a channel filled with shoals that he alone had sounded, that would ground the enemy's men-o'-war.

"Most maps don't even show this island. I only know about it because I scouted the lake. Valcour hides us from ships sailing from the north. Snarleton won't see us till he's beyond us."

Arnold stumped to the porthole, gesturing to the lake beyond. "We'll sit tight awhile yet, let them get well past, then come out and fire on them from behind. We'll lure them in here one at a time. They can't fit more than a single ship in this channel—and that's providing they can tack around in the first place. That wind today's good as if I'd bespoke it for us, speeding them south. Let them try turning into it." Only a few tentative nods answered his grin.

"And they *must* turn and fight," Arnold continued. "Or so Carleton'll think. He's too cautious to leave us in his rear, threatening his supply lines."

Waterbury took his pipe from his mouth. He was the sort to gainsay anything planned without him. "General, you can't be serious, sir! An ambush, why, that'll be turned against us in a minute. Enemy could trap us here in the channel—"

"Oh, they'll think we're trapped, all right, Waterbury. That makes it even better, see: they'll be arrogant and cocksure."

Waterbury glanced upward, then spoke in the patronizing tone reserved for children and idiots. "Yes, well, General, we could actually *be* trapped, you know. It'd be better, much better, for us immediately to come to sail and fight them on a retreat on the main lake. Let's get out of here, now, before they come any closer. It's suicide otherwise, you—"

"Retreat?" Arnold shook his head. "*Where?* Ticonderoga? They haven't got enough shot down there to protect themselves, let alone us."

"'Tis suicide, your plan," Waterbury repeated emphatically. "Enemy with all those boats they got, they'll surround us on every side. Yes, sir, let's sail for Ticonderoga, quick as we can, forget this whole idea. Those men there—what've they got at the Ti now? Nine, ten thousand?—get them to fight this battle with us."

Waterbury had worked hard all summer at the shipyard, so Arnold did not begrudge an explanation. "Thought the same thing myself for a while, General." He did not add that he had conceived such a plan in July, before exploring the lake, but dismissed it within the day as hopelessly impractical. "Problem is, with these farmers we got for marines, we can't sail for the Ti in defensive formation because they can't hold the ships in place. Another reason my ambush'll work: ships are anchored. Boys won't need to sail, just fight."

Waterbury drew breath, and Arnold hurried on. "Besides, Redcoats are sailing men-o'-war. Big ships, right?"

"Yes, sir," Waterbury roared, patience gone, "they're big, all right, designed for fighting at sea—"

"They're big and unwieldy, can't tack on a lake, can't maneuver." Captain Premier chuckled. "That's brilliant, sir, absolutely brilliant. You're gonna use that like a weapon against them."

"We sure are." Arnold glowed. "Especially with that wind blowing like the devil from the north. Once they've passed Valcour, they'll never be able to tack into this channel against us. Now, on the open water, they could. They'd blow us into the hereafter. But not here in the channel. Here, the fact that they've got such huge ships," his smile widened, "it'll defeat 'em."

Captain Hawley cleared his throat. He was an old friend from Connecticut who had arrived the night before. "General Arnold's the best sailor I've seen, sir," he told Waterbury. "If he says this is our only chance, it is."

Arnold nodded at him. "You're a wise man, Captain, so I'm putting you in command of the *Royal Savage*."

Hawley bowed and came up grinning. "Great name, General."

"Accurate, too." Arnold smiled in turn. He pointed at the porthole again. White sails filled it. "There they go. Let's give it a few more minutes, then we'll lure 'em back here. We'll sally out, act like we're aiming north, for their supply line. To your stations, gentlemen."

Arnold limped on deck ahead of the rest and stood under the rattlesnake flag. The foliage ashore blazed in autumnal glory as his ships formed for battle.

His first command sent *Congress* skimming from the channel. Sails snapped; soldiers-turned-seamen moved as though knowing what they were about when drums and fifes sounded his orders; the crisp autumn wind whipped his hair and stung his eyes. Arnold welcomed each gust, knowing it for Snarleton's enemy. Before him lay the sapphire lake, trees of red and gold and deep green lining the shores, white sails on the southern horizon. He saw those sails furl. The enemy had swallowed the bait. They turned to attack, the northwest wind fighting the maneuver.

"All right, boys," Arnold cried, "make for the channel!"

Shouting orders for the drummers to relay, manning the sails beside his men, Arnold maneuvered *Congress* back into the line. Heart pounding, he watched through his spyglass as HMS *Carleton* came for them, with *Maria* and *Inflexible* close behind. The three warships gleamed with fresh paint, upper works of blue and bright yellow sides going to black at the water.

Arnold waited until his unaided eye could discern the officers' uniforms, vivid with professional dyes, a contrast to the drab colors his soldiers wore, the browns and faded blues and greens of homespun boiled with herbs and onion-skins. *Carleton's* guns loomed overhead, bigger and blacker than he had supposed guns could be.

His men stood silent but for nervous coughing here and there. This was the hardest part, the delay while ships were positioned, the wait for chaos to descend, for agony and death to sweep the deck. Even veterans could scarcely withstand these moments, let alone Arnold's green troops. A sob reached him, and then a lieutenant's voice, high with fear, "Dammit, Hutchings, get back to your station!"

"I'm not a-going to!" There was madness in Hutchings' cry, and that madness would spread. Already men were dropping their linstocks and cutlasses, ready to clamber over the sides.

"Twenty-five pounds!" Arnold bellowed, and they froze. "No, *fifty* pounds to the first crew that fires!" Men scurried to their cannon while Arnold prodded the boy nearest him. "Fire!"

The *Carleton* vanished in clouds of smoke. Arnold's ears nearly burst as the cannons' roaring echoed off the cliffs lining the channel.

Thereafter, the world was only screams and booms, shot and terror, confusion, and endless effort not to slip in the blood pooling on deck nor trip over bodies lying mangled and motionless. Cannonballs pounded the ship, so that anyone still on his feet went flying. Splinters and debris, flesh and blood rained on them as balls smashed the masts, rigging, decks, and Continentals. The stench of scorched hair sickened Arnold when men with but a few days' training in artillery stood too near active cannon. Their faces plainly cried that neither the instruction nor their worst nightmares had prepared them for this.

Arnold raced from cannon to cannon, sponging, ramming, firing, the implements hot and tacky with blood. A breeze lifted the smoke, enough to aim another blast at *Carleton* and to see *Royal Savage* with Hawley in command cruising straight for the shoals near Valcour's tip. "Fire!" Arnold cried, and both ships disappeared in smoke. Then, above the cannons' roar, came the screech of *Savage's* wooden hull across rock. His largest vessel was now disabled.

Another breeze cleared the air, and Arnold lifted his glass. Into view came Snarleton the Haughty aboard his most powerful ship, the one named for his wife, HMS *Maria*. An officer stood beside Carleton, a younger version of the governor who must have been his brother. And how would the Family Snarleton react if a cannonball came winging at them? Arnold dodged fallen rigging and corpses to run for the crew loading the 18-pounder. Gasping as acrid smoke billowed over the deck, he thrust aside the boy trying to aim the gun and grabbed the linstock. He put it to the touchhole; the cannon belched smoke and shot at *Maria*. "Snarleton!" he cried, ducking as a splintered beam flew past.

The ball plowed between the two men to knock Snarleton the Younger senseless. Snarleton himself stood pale and trembling, staring at his brother as other officers rushed to him.

"He's calling his shots!" The boy whom Arnold had shoved aside danced a gleeful jig. He was a small, skinny figure with no brows or lashes left. "Do another one, General!"

The crew sponged the cannon and rammed a load down the barrel while Arnold scanned *Maria's* deck. Another fit of coughing seized him. Finally, he gasped, "That knot of officers up there near the mizzenmast. See them?"

"There's four, no, five." The boy nodded.

Arnold sighted down the barrel. "Fire!"

Maria again disappeared in a cloud of smoke, but when the haze lifted, the boy whooped. "Bull's eye, General! There's three of 'em down, and the other two's wounded."

Arnold slid in a puddle of blood as the deck rocked under another cannonball. "You, sailor," he shouted at a man so blackened by powder he could not identify him, "shovel more sand around."

Then the *Carleton* hove to. Again and again, Arnold ordered, "Fire!" He coughed, calling more shots, while the crews sponged and loaded. "That tall fellow there with the long queue. Fire! Those two sailors there in the rigging. Fire!"

Like *Maria* before her, the *Carleton* was inching from the channel in a hail of shot, hull more hole than whole and taking on water. In her place came HMS *Inflexible*.

Arnold's ship, too, was taking on water and riding low. He glanced at the sky. Thank God, the sun was setting. It would soon be too dark to battle.

He drew a deep breath. The four-hundred-ton *Inflexible* had watched from outside the channel, unable to help *Carleton*, as Arnold had foreseen, and her crew must be bent on revenge. She dropped anchor to rake them with 24-pounders, flames spurting in the dusk. Still, the government's grand invasion had diminished to one warship battling the fifteen remaining members of the American fleet.

Half an hour after the echoes of the final fusillade had died against Valcour's cliffs, Arnold's captains once again crowded his cabin, lately doing duty as the surgeon's room. An amputated leg oozed blood under his bunk while gory handprints covered the table where lay the map. Odors of suffering and death oppressed the air. The lantern swinging overhead did little to light the dark and less to dispel their gloom. Silence held them, all the more profound after the battle's cacophony.

Arnold stood before them, ears ringing. "What's your casualties?"

He glanced around the circle of faces darkened from gunpowder and smoke. Their bloodshot eyes were huge with fear, dirty cheeks streaked with perspiration and tears. Here and there, a tricorn had survived, and three men still sported wigs, though the puffs and curls had lost their pins and the straggling hair was stained a dirty grey. So were their uniforms, except where they were caked with blood. A stench rose from them, compounded of burnt hair, sweat, and terror.

"Reckon about sixty dead, sir, and wounded," one of them whispered.

Another added, "Run through more'n half our powder."

"Half?" Waterbury snorted. "More like three-quarters. Not enough left for another battle like this one today. And every ship's taking on water. The *Philadelphia's* sinking—won't be but another turn of the glass before she's all the way under."

"They hit the mainmast on *Providence*. It can't sail for a while."

"Every officer on the *Lee's* dead."

"So's the ones on the *Washington*, and anyone isn't dead's wounded."

Arnold lifted a hand to halt the litany. "Captain Hawley," he said, "you're aboard the *Washington*, now, under General Waterbury." Hawley glanced at him with surprised gratitude at being given another ship after losing *Royal Savage*.

Waterbury snorted again. "Lotta good that'll do him, General. We're finished, as I told you this morning. Can't you see that?"

"No, Waterbury, we—"

"Sir." Another captain, features so filthy Arnold wasn't sure which one, spoke in quiet defeat. "They say Carleton's a gentleman, sir, humane and merciful."

"What?" Arnold stared, baffled. Seemed an odd time to be praising the enemy.

"He, ah, he'll give us easy terms, sir."

"You—you mean—*surrender?*" Arnold's voice cracked in disbelief. Though they nodded, none would meet his stare. "Gentlemen." He paused, willing himself to sound congratulatory, not angry. "You made me so damned proud out there I could cry. And now you're talking sur-render? Come on, you're better'n that. We're out-gunned, out-manned, but we gave as good as we got. And we're alive! We damn near defeated the government here, thanks to you, and that when we suffered much from want of seamen and gunners. During the action, I swear it, no slaughter-house could present so bad a sight with blood and entrails lying about, as our ships, but none of you flinched, not a one. *Surrender?* No, sir, never, not after all that."

Pride lit a few faces, sagging shoulders squared. Then Waterbury spoke.

"'Twas suicide, this ambush, I tried to tell you. Come morning, they'll finish us. And if the Redcoats don't, their savages will. They got them surrounding us ashore, General, on Valcour Island and the mainland. They're collecting canoes, gonna board us tomorrow at first light. I don't know about any of you," Waterbury glanced around the shadowed circle, "but I got no hankering to lose my hair to them. I say we surrender."

"No!" Arnold barked it, then strove for calm. Finally, he gave what he hoped was a playful smile. "I got another plan."

"Thought so," Waterbury muttered.

Arnold glanced from officer to officer. "I say we give them the slip as Washington did down on Long Island. There's a fog comes up here the equal of any they got there."

They sat gaping, and he continued. "Everybody hang a lantern over your stern rail, make sure you shield it so the light can't be seen from the front or sides. Only the ship behind you should see it so she can follow you."

He stepped to the porthole, pointed to the mist rising thick and comforting over the lake. "We're gonna row past them, quiet and fast as we can, shoot through their lines and make for Crown Point. Issue orders—I want every man still as a mouse once we cast off. Gag any of the wounded who're moaning. Wrap your oars in sailcloth or something to muffle it in the water."

An hour later, he stood on deck, the fog a wet salvation on his face. They slid past faint, ethereal warships while disembodied sounds carried across the water: the hammering of British carpenters repairing his damage, groans from the maimed, a fifer blowing sad notes, laughter from an officer's cabin.

Arnold cocked his head. They'd be laughing out the other sides of their mouths come morning.

Chapter Nine

Rowed all that night and the next day, Clem." Arnold leans to pet Flash. The dog rolls over, paws up, eyes closed. "And that's after fighting a battle. But we outfoxed 'em, that's sure. Should make a fine chapter for your book."

"Maybe the best one of all, sir!" I imagine Snarleton's ire the next morning, with the fleet gone he'd thought to smash. Here he'd brought invincible ships of the line, manned by marines from the world's best navy, against farmers in buckets, and the farmers had out-fought, out-sailed, and out-witted him. I see the rage twisting his face, scattering officers and men before him.

"What made it even better," Arnold says, "is that he thought we'd gone north after his garrisons and supplies. Never figured we'd got through his line. Fact, he tacked north all that morning. 'Twas noon before his lookouts sighted our sails to the south. Made him a laughingstock…"

…but a laughingstock bent on revenge. So were his officers and crews. How dare this upstart Arnold, with his makeshift tubs and volunteers, challenge the greatest navy on earth? And not only challenge it, but fight bravely and well when the only sensible course was surrender. Then, saved by nightfall, the rebels fled rather than await daybreak and the destruction they deserved.

Still, American luck was waning. In their crippled, leaking vessels, the Continentals gained only twelve miles the next night, fighting wind and current. Worse, the breeze shifted at sunrise to push Carleton after them. He caught up a few hours later.

This time, there was no protective channel to keep the enemy's fleet distant while Arnold fought them one at a time. And Carleton would smash their poor little boats, fitted for battle between Valcour's sheltering cliffs, to kindling on the open lake. Only *Congress* and *Washington* were large enough to withstand the Redcoats' fire. From aboard *Congress*, Arnold issued orders that sent the others whisking south. Then he and *Washington* braced for catastrophe.

HMS *Inflexible* bore down on *Washington*, and Arnold's stomach clenched as Waterbury hoisted the flag of surrender. "Not already!" he cried. "To your stations, boys, and fight!"

Arnold manned two of *Congress*' guns himself, cannonading the brace of ships under his stern and the one broadside. At first, only those three battled him. Then there were five, and, finally, seven of His Majesty's vessels surrounding him. For over two hours, his lone craft dueled the government, coming hard against him with an incessant fire of round and grape shot. And all the while Arnold inched *Congress* towards the eastern shore with its shallow Buttonmold Bay.

Suddenly his ammunition was gone.

He blinked at the deafening silence, noticed for the first time that the sails, rigging, and hull of *Congress* had been shredded. He turned to the lieutenant beside him. "How many men still fit for duty?"

Two balls smashed the deck. When they regained their feet, the lieutenant said, "Well, sir, before that last, there were twenty-seven casualties out of seventy officers and crew, so that leaves, ah—"

"Forty-three, Lieutenant." Arnold jerked his head windward, not daring to point lest a British spyglass see him. "That gap there between those two ships, order the men to their sweeps and get us through there. Then bend every oar for Buttonmold Bay."

That indent, already sheltering what was left of his fleet, would protect them from the government's ships with their deep drafts. "Lieutenant," he called after the man, "we get there, tell the captains to put their crews ashore and then fire their ships. They can scatter whatever gunpowder they've got left on deck."

"Yes, sir."

"And the flags, Lieutenant, the rattlesnake flags, burn those too."

Cannonballs chased them. But fired in anger at this second escape and increasingly out of range, they seldom found a mark. As Arnold's shattered vessel cruised into the bay, he dumped his guns overboard while the lieutenant relayed his orders and ships around him took flame. Overhead, *Congress'* colors whipped in the draft, proud, unconquerable...

The fire sizzles as rain pelts down the chimney. "Once we landed, Clem, 'twasn't that far a march to Crown Point," Arnold says, "only nine miles or so and then across the lake. We looked twice at every shadow, though, what with Snarleton's Indians all through those woods. And we're keeping one eye on the lake, too, 'cause Snarleton coulda sailed south any time he wanted."

"But he didn't, did he?"

His eyes twinkle. "Well, we couldn't have stopped him, but Providence did. Storms and gales riled that lake the next three weeks, and time things calmed down, 'twas too late, snow threatening every day. Snarleton flew back to Canada, the season was already turning severe and so far advanced." The twinkle becomes a gleam. "Meantime, Snarleton's spies told him there's 20,000 rebels with all the powder they could want at Ticonderoga."

Reckon Arnold had somewhat to do with those spies and their lies.

His smile fades. He's probably remembering how Valor Island, all his sweat and worry and grief, bought him what the retreat from Canada did: criticism, loud and merciless, and then, to pound the insults a little deeper, an inquiry. Didn't matter that the Redcoats wasted a summer, a fortune, an army and its stores thanks to Benedict Arnold.

Now, mayhap you're one of those as listened to Gates, or John Brown, or Arnold's other enemies risen since the treason. Or maybe you'd never trust such fools, but you don't know much about strategy and such. So here 'tis, plain and simple, what Arnold done up there on the lake:

He *won*.

I don't mean the battles at Valcour and Buttonmould Bay. No, he lost both, if by losing you mean one side gets beat, most of their ships sunk and men killed, whilst the enemy sails away, able and anxious to fight some other day.

No, what Arnold won there, on that frigid, stormy lake, was a campaign and, God willing, this war. See, everything Arnold set out to do—delay Carleton, convince him to waste time and energy assembling a fleet instead of invading New England, hold him at the north end of the lake so's he couldn't be building forts to the south where they'd count, nor capture the all-important Ti, neither—Arnold done *all* of that. Next summer, when Redcoats under Gentleman Johnny Burgoyne come down the lake again for to conquer us, they must start over, with Carleton's victory at Valcour helping them about as much as Gentleman Johnny's champagne. There was nary a fort to supply them, no troops in garrison to guard their rear, no reinforcements waiting and ready. 'Twas that as much as the fighting that finished Burgoyne at Saratoga. And it's Saratoga that turned things around and give us hope we'll beat the government someday. Valcour Island, and Arnold's defeat there, made sure we'd win at Saratoga.

But you'd'a needed to been a prophet, or a tactician good as Arnold, to see all that back in October of 1776. We got very few prophets and fewer tacticians. So 'twasn't long afore the talk about Arnold's courage, his gallant loss and magnanimous behavior, well, it fell quiet. "Wasn't it that same fella lost us an army trying to take Canada?" folks asked instead. "Now here he's gone and lost us a navy, too, which of course means there's nobody defending Ticonderoga and Lake Champlain, nothing to stop Carleton coming against us next spring."

All that criticism finally settled down to calls for an inquiry into just what Arnold had been about up there.

"Ah-yuh," he says. "Men that couldn't float a twig in a puddle wanted to hear how it was I'd lost all those ships. Well, guess what, I mighta lost 'em—and believe me, if anyone was grieving their loss, 'twas me, for I was father to every one of those boats, birthed 'em and raised 'em and was prouder'n hell—ah, heck of 'em. So maybe I lost them, but we kicked the enemy off Lake Champlain. Didn't matter, though. Most everybody thought it was the fleet we were trying to save, not the lake and New England and the war.

"So maybe they beat us," Arnold shrugs, "but we won. 'Course, only Washington and maybe a coupla others understood that…"

"Fine work up north, sir, extraordinary." Washington's beaming face disguised his weariness. "You've set back their invasion of New England by a year at the least. These reinforcements you've brought me couldn't have come at a better time, either. I thank you."

Arnold bowed, trying to hide his dismay. During the northern campaign, with men starving, naked, and diseased, and the march afterwards to join Washington's army through winter-blasted New York and New Jersey, he had thought his boys the most battered and pitiful in America. He had rejoiced in their union with the main body of Continentals as a panacea while assuming that the Continental Army was indeed an army, with soldiers, muskets, uniforms.

But he had seen neither those soldiers nor their commander for more than a year, since the September day when he and 1100 troops left for Quebec. Nor had he heard much from them. So he was shocked to find Washington's men as dispirited, tattered, and hungry as his own. No wonder the Redcoats had chased them from New York City to Pennsylvania.

They were melting away, too. Those troops whose enlistments had expired only laughed at requests to reenlist as they clutched their rags and started home. Others disappeared each night, willing to hazard a whipping for desertion to escape the hell that soldiering had become. Now, in December of 1776, Washington and the 5000 scarecrows left him huddled on the western bank of the Delaware River, confiscating all boats for seventy miles lest the Redcoats follow and finish them.

Washington indicated a stool. Arnold seated himself and said, "Not a cheering prospect, is it? But between the reinforcements and the field guns I brought, maybe we can attack their outposts."

"Perhaps." Washington's red-rimmed eyes circled the room like a cornered fox's. "Every bit helps, though I'm afraid, sir, the game is pretty well up."

"'Tis in our power to be free, Excellency, or nobly die in defense of liberty."

The bloodshot gaze rested on him, despair turning to confidence. At length, Washington nodded. "Let me show you the plan I have for taking back New Jersey."

The two bent over a map for the next half hour, Arnold reporting what he had seen on his journey south and discussing a raid His Excellency would spring on a Hessian outpost at Trenton.

"So you'd say it's feasible, this plan?" Washington asked.

"Eminently so, Excellency. They'll never be expecting it, not in the middle of winter when campaigning's over for the season. Yes, sir, I'd say it's not just feasible, but necessary. Your back's against the wall here. You'll soon be surrounded—you got no choice but to attack."

"They're planning an invasion of Rhode Island, too, sir, as I wrote you." Washington sighed. "A large fleet's anchored off the coast there. I need someone to command. What say you? Will you go raise some militia and take such measures as in your opinion will be most likely to frustrate them?"

Arnold hesitated. He had hoped to continue to Philadelphia and clear his name before Congress. Even Washington's letter about the doom awaiting Rhode Island, received as Arnold rushed south through December's flurries, had not altered his intentions. For thanks to John Brown, the rumors of Arnold's looting in Canada had only grown uglier with his defeat at Valcour.

Brown had not scrupled to kick a downed man. He had written a screed attacking Brigadier General Arnold's martial ability and integrity. Worse, he had turned his rant into a petition to Congress.

There were thirteen charges in all. Some were petty: Arnold had stripped Brown of rank during the Canadian campaign (indeed he had, and gladly, too), hurting his feelings. Others were ludicrous: the general had deliberately starved his own army, then infected the troops with smallpox. But tucked among these lunacies were dangerous libels. Arnold had "plundered the inhabitants of Montreal," had issued "cruel and bloody orders, directing whole villages to be destroyed," and that "without any distinctions to friend or foe, age or sex." If Brown hadn't pestered the Congress, Arnold would have laughed at the man, so obsessed, so eager to paint him a villain. As it was, he must defend himself.

"Excellency," he said, "there's been a petition to Congress, aspersing my character. Mayhap you've seen it?"

"Petition? No, I—oh, that one by, what's his name, Black or something?"

"I need to go defend myself, sir. No telling what harm—"

"General." Washington straightened to his full, impressive height. "The government's invading, man. They must be stopped. Don't speak to me of petitions written by madmen that only fools'll believe."

"Sir, I–"

"This is no time to be thinking of reputation, by Heaven, our freedom's at stake here. Now I need a fighter of your capabilities—I need *you* up there in Rhode Island, you understand?"

Arnold glanced away, chewing his lip. Whatever Washington said, that petition was rife with poison and the Congress with ninnies who would swallow it. He must counter it, must ensure that Brown's lies didn't obscure all his starving and bleeding and freezing. What good was fighting valiantly while a coward reviled him to those who controlled promotions, congressmen with the power to transform the lowest curs into champions while ignoring a worthy officer, however many bullets he dodged or campaigns he won?

Arnold looked back to find Washington's eyes on him, one massive hand tugging at the noose around his neck. Arnold blinked. The noose disappeared to leave Washington absently rubbing his jaw while awaiting his answer. "General Arnold, sir? Will you accept the command?"

"I–I–Your pardon, sir." He swallowed. If victorious, the enemy would strip life and liberty from them. Arguing his merits before Congress did nothing towards defeating the invaders. "I'd be honored, Excellency…"

"So you went to Rhode Island?"

"Had no choice, Clem. I'm not one for visions and premonitions, but I saw that noose sure as I see you sitting there. I hurried north, just stopped on the way to visit my family. Hadn't seen my sons for a year and a half."

"Reckon they were happy as pie to have you home."

"Oh, I was their hero and no mistake." He grins, and I fix my eyes on my stitchery. What will become of those boys when the father I kidnap hangs for his treason? Sometimes, I wish I were anywhere but this house, doing anything but spying on this man. "One morning, I slept later than usual, must have been about six of the clock, when all of a sudden, little

Hal jumps up on the bed, he was near five years old by then, and says, all disappointed-like, 'Daddy, are you going to sleep *all day?*'"

He chuckles; I try to. Flash lifts his head to eye us.

"I only stayed a week," he continues. "Just about killed me to leave them. But by then I'd raised 6000 militia, and 'twas time to go. 'Course, there wasn't much we could do, in any event. Redcoats had something like 15,000 men opposing us. Don't know why they finally withdrew, but it wasn't on account of us." He falls silent, stares into the flames.

He doesn't mention John Lamb, neither his chat with him then nor his generosity to that sore wounded officer. Still, I know about both because I had the story from Lamb himself one evening a few months ago when I was still at West Point, before His Excellency sent me here to New York. Lamb was artillery commander of the main works there, known as Fort Arnold till then. Now it's named for someone else.

It was five years before that Lamb, an old man of forty, attacked Quebec with Arnold.

"If you'd'a seen him then, you'd understand," Lamb told me and the officers gathered round. "Heard he had so many men wanting to march north with him, he turned 'em away by the thousands. And why do you think that was, if 'twasn't that he's the best?"

This was the day after we'd discovered the treason, when no one could yet believe that General Benedict Arnold had turned traitor. Especially not the veterans of Quebec. Especially not John Lamb.

"He's our fighting general," Lamb continued, "as brave a man as ever lived, a fine spirited fellow and active general, not like them others that talk so big and tell you all the congressmen they know, but you needa light a bonfire under 'em afore they'll shuffle onto a battlefield. He's so strong and confident and—and, I don't know, seems like he can work miracles. You feel better just being near him. Feel like you could do miracles, too. He can get more out of troops, don't matter how worthless they are, than anyone I ever saw."

"He's a filthy traitor," an officer said.

Lamb turned his mangled half-a-face on the man and swept him a look from his right eye. 'Twas the only one left him: the other was shot off with his cheek and left jaw during the assault on Quebec, when Lamb and most of his fellows wound up prisoners. "He's no traitor, sir, I'd stake my life on it. There's some other explanation, you'll see.

He's the best man I ever knew, however you go to measure it: bravest, smartest, kindest—"

"Stinking traitor."

Through his teeth, Lamb said, "Know what he done for me? First, 'twas him as asked Washington to get me exchanged out of that damned Canadian prison after I'm captured at Quebec. Then, he come to visit me in Connecticut couple of months later, after Valcour Island, when he was coming home a hero—he visited *me*, made time to see *me* when everybody and his brother was wanting to see him. And you know what he said? He says, 'Lamb, you're going back into action, aren't you?' He says, 'You're too good an officer to sit out the war.' Give me back all my sap that the Redcoats took away when they took my face. And then he got me appointed to head a new regiment, and never mind that I was all shot up like this. Loads of commanders woulda said, 'Sorry about your face, Lamb, thanks, but we don't need you anymore.' Not Arnold. Well, Congress was slow about finding the money for my regiment—I expect them politicians down there didn't think a man wounded bad as me was worth much. So Arnold wrote out a note for a thousand pounds, from his own pocket, see. Told me to go ahead and raise and equip a regiment." Lamb's voice caught. He blinked his eye. "He made that note payable to *Colonel* Lamb when I wasn't nothing but a captain before. I'm telling you, he's no traitor."

I still hear the heartbreak and conviction in Lamb's voice across the nine weeks since he told this story. Now I sit watching the traitor guilty of such goodness.

Arnold glances up to catch my gaze on him. "And you, Clem? What were you doing then, in '76?"

I shrug. "Nothing much, sir." I take another stitch on the pocketbook. "Nothing as exciting as that, just tending my mother's tavern. 'Twas there I met up with John Andre again."

The name slips out before I think. In truth, I mention him only as you do a mutual acquaintance, not intending to be cruel, only forgetting. Arnold despises Andre, though, in view of Andre's fate, he settles for rolling his eyes...

I was mixing punch one evening early in December when a whoosh of cold air had me looking over my shoulder at an elegant figure stamping snow from his boots in the doorway. "Lieutenant Andre!"

The officer I'd last seen marching out of Philadelphia as a prisoner bowed to me. He was as debonair as ever but otherwise changed. His face was stern now, not boyish, and there's a firmness to his eyes. His smile was still gracious, but it wasn't quick, nor easy, neither.

Reckon I'd changed, too. I'd grown up enough that last winter's infatuation with Andre made me squirm. I only hoped he'd never suspected. Withal, I'd seen Nathan Hale die, and beside him, Andre was a popinjay.

The popinjay's smile widened. "Miss Shippen, 'tis ever a pleasure to see you, specially when you have a reputation as York Island's best cook. May I ask, have you an extra room?"

"Lieutenant, I—I—it's not a question of extra rooms, sir, these officers are quartered on us against our will."

His brows lifted. "Are you a rebel then, Miss Shippen?"

For a moment, Nathan stood before me, hands bound behind, proud and indomitable. "I'm a friend of liberty, sir."

"Aren't we all?" He smiled again, but his eyes were dead. "Not a wise time to cast your sympathies to the rebels, Miss Shippen. Their troops are having a hard time of it."

'Twas true. After chasing our boys through New Jersey all the way to Philadelphia, the Redcoats were sprinkling outposts across the country whose purpose, other than keeping the Continentals at bay, was pillaging the country folk. You'd think those farmers would run far as they could from such oppression, but instead, they were swearing their loyalty, I guess to save what little property the Redcoats left them.

"Though, to be just," Andre continued, "perhaps I err, calling them troops. 'Tis a curious masquerade scene to see grave, sober citizens, barbers and tailors who never looked fierce before, strutting about in their Sunday wigs with muskets on their shoulders. If ever you saw a goose assume an air of consequence, you may catch some faint idea."

He waited for me to laugh at his wit. Instead, I asked, "Can I get you something, Lieutenant?"

"Wine, please. And tell me, how's the family in Philadelphia?"

"I—I don't know, what with the fighting coming almost to their door-step and all." I set a glass before him. "Madeira?"

"Thank you. And what brings you here to New York, Miss Shippen?"

I took a breath. I must speak of my mother sometime, maybe even introduce her, but at the moment, she was snoring off the afternoon's rum.

I pushed a strand of hair back under my cap. "Work. So you're no longer a prisoner?"

"Exchanged." But he lost his smile. He sipped his wine before continuing. "You been to the backcountry, Miss Shippen?"

"The backcountry? They sent you to Lancaster, didn't they? 'Tis a rough town, I warrant you, least that's what I've heard, but it's not backcoun—"

"We stayed in Lancaster just a few months before they ordered us to Carlisle, a front-row seat to the backcountry."

"I've lived only in New York and Philadelphia, sir. The backcountry's foreign to me as China."

"You have much to be grateful for, then." Quiet fury shook his voice. "'Tis inhabited by a stubborn, illiberal crew called the Scotch-Irish, sticklers for the Covenant, and utter enemies to the abomination of curled hair, regal government, minced pies and other heathenish vanities."

This time, I wanted to laugh, for he'd limned the pious Scotch-Irish perfectly. But his rage stopped me. "I'm sorry, Lieutenant." I wiped dribbles of wine from the table. "But you were a prisoner, sir, after all."

"Even prisoners are treated with courtesy by civilized nations, Miss Shippen." He lifted his glass with a trembling hand as I glared. But before I could mention the men starving aboard the prison-ships in the harbor, or a young spy who hanged without a trial, he rolled on. "We were every day pelted and reviled in the streets—" Suddenly his anger left him, and he tried for a smile. "Philadelphia may rest easy as the city of brotherly love, for Carlisle threatens no competition."

"Now, Lieutenant, surely you didn't expect love." 'Twas spoke lightly to make him laugh.

But his smile disappeared again. "I—I didn't—I played at love once, long ago, stupid of me..." He turned to stare at the hearth. When he spoke again, he had himself in hand. "No such thing as love, Miss Shippen. 'Tis only a conceit with which we amuse ourselves."

Andre drank wine with me a few times over the next weeks. We spoke no more of playing at love, nor of his months in Carlisle. Instead, he told about visiting Europe two years before, and Gottingen, where he had fallen in with some poets, or so Andre called them. They sounded more like ne'er-do-wells to me, young men who hadn't a penny among them but spent their days, and their nights, too, mooning after love—not of a wife or sweetheart or parents but just Love, which made about as much sense as cooking a meal and never eating it. They scorned the cold, cruel world that slept and worked and profited instead of sitting and moaning for Love as they did. Seems this was the kind of affection Andre preferred to the flesh-and-blood variety. He showed me some of their poetry, all of it bad though perhaps that was just his translation.

Most of it was addressed to a Cher Jean.

"'Dear John'?" I asked.

He shrugged. "My sobriquet." But from the way his eyes lighted, I suspected his lost lady named him that, not the poets. Still, I must remember to tell Peggy, for she'd be fascinated.

We seldom spoke of the war, not even when the government seemed certain to sweep aside Washington's rabble and take Philadelphia. 'Twas the Delaware River, and the boats the Continentals had pulled from it, not those pitiful troops themselves, kept the Redcoats plundering in New Jersey. Once the river froze, nothing would stop the king's forces marching down Walnut Street. That sent the Continental Congress fleeing to Baltimore.

Then Washington's stunning victories at Trenton and Princeton set us buzzing.

Christmas night of '76, the Continentals trudged from near Philadelphia and crossed the Delaware. Never mind that campaigning's done for the year, with soldiers holed up in winter quarters against the blizzards that render guns wet and useless—blizzards like the one icing the roads and rivers that very night, and the troops so ragged most didn't wear shoes.

"Makes it easier to foller the tracks of the man ahead of you when he's leaving blood in the snow," one of our customers told us. He was a sutler caught selling more rum to the soldiers than Headquarters permitted and so run out of camp. Fresh from the army, he was full of details we hadn't yet heard. "Storm was blowing so hard they couldn't see two feet in front of them. And the river so chunky with ice they thought they'd never get the cannon across. But they did, though they lost three or four hours.

"'Course, that ruined the plan to reach Trenton afore dawn. Hunnerds and hunnerds of Hessians garrisoned there, you know. His Excellency's figuring they'll be disguised with liquor after celebrating Christmas all night long."

I'd seen enough of the Dutch near Philadelphia to marvel at how they kept Christmas, a Popish holiday, and them Lutherans. They set out a feast and visited one another with gifts, as though they were Papists born. Such customs sat ill with Philadelphia's Quakers and us Protestants, too. 'Twas a grand joke on the Hessians that His Excellency used their holiday and drunkenness against them.

"Our troops was naked and freezing," the sutler continued, "but no matter, they attacked at eight that morning. 'Course, that's well after dawn, and no darkness to hide us, but them Hessians was too groggy to do much in the way of defense. We felled their commanding officer right off, and about forty others, too, and rounded up maybe a thousand prisoners."

Then Washington struck a week later at Princeton, after the year had turned. Again he hit an outpost, but this time 'twas Redcoats, not just Hessians. He hoped to march another dozen miles for New Brunswick, where sat supplies for the government's troops and £70,000 in gold and silver to pay them, but our boys were too beat out.

Still, they had turned New Jersey from a sanctuary for the enemy into a shambles.

Chapter Ten

Yesterday's rain gave way to a clear dawn this Thursday, clear but cold, with clouds pressing in. They begin dropping their snow this afternoon as I sit writing. It's too soon to cook dinner, and I can't peruse Arnold's papers since Peggy's upstairs even if her husband isn't. Can't say as I mind, though, reading over my notes from our conversations and adding more details as they come to mind.

I've just finished with the siege of Quebec when the front door opens and Arnold stomps the slush from his boots. Flash's nails click against the floor as he bounds to greet his friend.

"Clem." Arnold limps into the parlor with Flash cavorting after. "Regular blizzard out there."

It sure is. Flakes hiss down the chimney. I used to love the snow, its soft silence, how sparkling and fresh it made the world. Now I hate it. I see instead the agony it brings our troops, their struggle to keep warm, how they fight the frostbite for their fingers and toes. I see Arnold's men ducking their heads against it to attack Quebec, and the Continentals following bloody footprints through the drifts to Trenton. I pray God to comfort our poor, shivering heroes this day.

Arnold sinks into his chair and, as though reading my thoughts, murmurs, "Hard weather for the boys."

More flakes splutter in the fire, and the wind moans around the house. Flash moans, too, probably fearful of the storm, though seems he's mocking it. I smile, stack my pages and stow them in the drawer Arnold cleared for me. Then I trade my seat at the desk for one aside

that gracious turncoat. I pick up the pocketbook. I've finished one side
and want a rest before sewing more diamonds on the other. So I'll set
a legend in it, along the top where the thing folds over. The first letter
doesn't take too long. Neither does the second, a "G." Only problem is,
when I finish, you can't tell it from a "C."

"You know, snow reminds me," Arnold says, "that night in 1777, 'twas
storming when I learned about it, one of those ferocious blizzards you
get in February. I was in a tavern—"

"Learned about what, sir?" I ask out of courtesy, really, for I'm busy
with my "G." I add more thread to the little tail on it so there's no mis-
taking it for a "C." Only problem now is, it's crooked.

"Oh, that Congress wanted my resignation."

I drop both needle and jaw. "They—*what?* After all you'd done?"

"Made me read it in the newspaper like anybody else. Congress didn't
even have the courtesy to inform me directly. There's a list of the new
major generals, see, and my name wasn't on it..."

It was doubly humiliating because he was with a few dozen men, the leading citizens of Providence, Rhode Island, turned out to drink his and the
militia's health and to cheer him as the Revolution's most legendary warrior.

"'Tis you ought to be Commander-in-Chief," one man said, eyes shining from too much mimbo. "Never had much faith in that Virginian they
got. Man like that's used to ordering slaves about, not leading free men."

"You're very kind, Mr. Withers," Arnold said, "but we had the honor
of starting things here in New England, so better have a Virginian leading the war or folks down south'll say it's just New England's affair and
pull out. Besides, General Washington, you mark my words, he'll win
things for us yet."

"Well, by Heaven, sir, least they might make you a major general," said
the fellow to Withers' right. The others nodded agreement.

"Oh, they will." Arnold smiled, touched by their concern. "I'm first
in line for promotion."

"You sure?"

"Certainly. I'm the most senior brigadier general. Next promotion
goes to me by rights."

"Somebody oughta tell the Congress, then. They named four or five new major generals, says here in the paper. I didn't see you in the list, General."

Somehow the tavern's newspaper, stained and crumpled after passing from patron to patron all evening, was in his hand, with half a dozen fingers and pipe-stems pointing to the list of new major generals. The paragraph blurred as Arnold's eyes dilated with anger. Still, squint though he might, his name was missing.

"An insult," they were murmuring. "No man should stand for it... Not when he's done all the general there's done... Will he resign, do you think?... What'll become of us if he does?... Lookit him tremble... An insult, through and through..."

"Must be a mistake," he said faintly.

"I wager there's no mistake." Abram Collins, the town's justice of the peace and his host that evening, shook his head. "No, sir, tell you what, I been reading every piece in that paper about the Congress, and this fits right in. There's some of them Congressmen afraid of Washington, see. Think he has too much power, scared of him and his army. And it makes sense, sir, you can't fault them. What's to keep Washington from turning his boys against us if he wins the war, like you say he will? And even if he don't win, he could always use the army to bargain for hisself. He could say to the king and Ministry, 'Here now, I'll have my troops lay down their arms if you make me vice-regent of America and give me lands in every state'—or colony, I guess we'd be again, then."

Arnold hated politics, had no head for it. He barely listened as Collins continued.

"So you see, General, 'tisn't personal. It's just there's Congressmen there determined to rein in Washington. One way's to keep any of his friends from getting promoted, especially if Washington recommends them, which he done you, hasn't he?"

Arnold was too sunk in thought to answer.

They could not want him to resign, could they? Yet what other conclusion was there? Congress had denied promotions since the start of the war. Usually, victims took the hint and retired. It was a courteous system all the way around, saving Congress the embarrassment of discharging officers and officers the humiliation of being discharged.

If only Ethan Allen had not ruined things at Ticonderoga, if Arnold had taken Quebec, if even a single ship had survived Valor Island—

And then there was John Brown's pamphlet.

Not content with petitioning Congress, Brown had recently published his thirteen charges. Anyone willing to pay tuppence for trash could read of Brigadier General Arnold's depravity. One line was especially unfair after the fortune Arnold had exhausted on the war: "Money is this man's god and to get enough of it he would sacrifice his country."

True, Congress had given him a hearing that cleared him of Brown's calumnies while Philadelphians lined the streets to cheer. The delegates even presented him with a caparisoned horse and a panegyric. Now he flushed at the affront: flattery instead of a promotion, earned and bled for...

"They made you a major general later, didn't they?" I ask.

"Three months later. It took Washington's hounding them before they would. I've still got his letter that he wrote. Remind me, I'll show it to you for your book."

I don't tell him I've already seen it, that I read it when I was searching his office. I can see why he kept it. Washington had written the Congress, "Surely a more active, a more spirited, and sensible officer, fills no department in your army. Not seeing him then in the list of major generals, and no mention made of him, has given me uneasiness, as it is not to be presumed (being the oldest brigadier) that he will continue in service under such a slight."

Arnold sighs. "But they never did restore my seniority. See, I shoulda been made the first major general, ahead of the four or five others promoted before me. But Congress refused. We wrangled back and forth for a while. 'Twas a simple point of logic, Clem, and no earthly reason for refusing to make me in name what I was in fact, the major general with the longest service in the Continental Army. I told them honor is a sacrifice no man ought to make, and that as I received mine inviolate so I wanted to transmit it to posterity."

"Eloquent, sir."

He sighs again. "Ah, well, 'tis of no moment."

We listen to the fire spit as snow sifts down the chimney. I remember how it snowed the night my mother died, right after Brigadier General Benedict Arnold chased the Redcoats from Connecticut.

"Sir," I say, but he only sits, chin sunk to chest, fighting old battles with Congress, I reckon. So I sit silent, too, stitching, remembering...

New Year's of 1777, and Mother had still not recovered from last fall's fever. Also distressing her was the tavern, which, whilst it sheltered us, worried us, too. Twice, the officers held drunken parties in the taproom and nigh destroyed it. The first time, replacing what they broke took our profits for two months. I wanted to ask the major, the highest rank boarding with us, if he couldn't just return the money stolen from our till one hot August day, and we'd call it even. Instead, I suggested that he and his fellows might want to, ah, contribute, 'tis expensive for a widow to, um, you know, buy new, ah—

The major raised bloodshot eyes heavenward and reminded me that a couple of captains could better employ the beds my mother and I occupied.

After their second party, a celebration of Twelfth Night, we abandoned our tavern.

"Let 'em have it, Clem," Mother said as we rattled up the Bloomingdale Road in a public coach. "They'll con—confi—conscifate it sooner or later anyway. 'Tisn't making us enough money to blink at, and the joke of it is—"

She grinned, and I shuddered at the death's head she seemed.

"—it belongs to your uncle, really, all the money I owe him. Withal, I want my last days to be peaceful-like, not pothering about whether some high and mighty major's gonna turn me out of my own—er, your uncle's house."

Mother was dying, and we both knew it from the blood she coughed up to stain her chamberpot. She'd set her heart on going home to Connecticut, though only one sister still lived there, in a town twenty miles from their birthplace, and so cantankerous no man would have her.

"'Tisn't that I look for her to welcome us, Clem," Mother said, "but it'd be nice to get away from this war, wake up in the morning and see normal people, not soldiers everywheres I look. I don't care if I never hear another cannon, neither. I had me enough shooting and shouting to last me."

My aunt greeted us with the warning we must pay our way what with everything so dear. Still, Mother seemed to improve, and we stayed the rest of the winter. The war faded into the background. We mentioned it only when someone brought news.

But we couldn't escape for long. At the end of April, the fighting invaded Connecticut, at Danbury.

I'd gone to town to trade our eggs for some sugar. 'Twas a balmy day, the sort convinces folks winter is finally over, and they can carry the hay piled against the north wall of the house back to the barn. Away from the sharp tongues of my mother and aunt, and a warm sun overhead, my spirits lifted, until I reached the main street where sat Blackwell's Tavern and General Merchandise. There I saw horses and wagons spilling out the yard with folks crowding the door, and my stomach clenched.

"What is it?" I asked Mrs. Hayley, whose pew sat two ahead of ours at church.

She shrugged. "Haven't been able to hear, but bad news, whatever it is, most likely from the war."

"You think we got beat again?"

She shook her head. "Too early for battles yet. The troops aren't hardly out of winter quarters. I know, my husband's still home, nor joining his company till next week. There's Reverend Peters now." She pointed to the preacher squeezing through the crowd. "Let's ask him what's happened. Reverend Peters!"

"Terrible news, ladies, have you heard?" He bowed. "Redcoats come ashore down to Norwalk and marched up Danbury-way."

"Danbury!" Mrs. Hayley staggered back a step. "But there's supplies there! We been sending supplies for the army there all winter."

Reverend Peters nodded. "Coupla thousand barrels of meat, and another thousand or so of flour, and some hogsheads of rum and wine, all set to ship to our poor starving troops. But the Redcoats got it, burnt it all up."

"Dear God." Mrs. Hayley clapped a hand to her mouth. I stood speechless.

"They burnt the town, too," Reverend Peters continued. "Killed some of the people there, some old folks who couldn't run." He shook his head. "Lord forgive me, but after the way they starved your brother, Mrs. Hayley, and now this, I tell you, I hate government, I truly do. Nothing but murderers and thieves."

Mrs. Hayley sniffled. "David was too good for this world, Reverend. If he hadn't died on that prison ship, Lord'a taken him some other way."

Reverend Peters patted her arm. After a moment, he said, "But thank God for Benedict Arnold."

"The one that marched to Quebec?" I asked.

The preacher nodded. "He's a Connecticut man, you know, passed through here on his way to Rhode Island, earlier this winter. Got a hero's welcome, too. But nothing came of that campaign in Rhode Island, so he's back home in New Haven now. Thank Heaven, someone had the sense to alert him soon as the Redcoats landed, and he collected the militia together"—he said it "milishee," as New Englanders do—"and marched them off to meet the king's men."

"Militia!" Mrs. Hayley shook her head. "My husband don't think much of militia. Says only thing it's good for is running away."

"Mayhap he's right, except when Arnold's leading them. Man's a genius at getting militia to fight like Regulars. They were too late to save Danbury, and anyway, there's only 500 of them against a coupla thousand Regulars, but they harassed the Redcoats all the way back to the Sound, where their ships were waiting to sail to New York."

"Or, more likely, Hell," Mrs. Hayley said.

Reverend Peters' brows rose at that. "They killed a coupla hundred soldiers, got a few officers, too, shooting at them from behind fences and trees."

"Militia done all that?" Mrs. Hayley said.

"Puts me in mind of Lexington and Concord," I said.

"Does me too." Reverend Peters nodded. "The Lord knew what He was about when He give us General Arnold."

'Twasn't long after Arnold's defense of Danbury that the season's last snow fell.

Mother had gained strength lately, enough to quarrel on me, and as the snow swirled outside, she grew nasty, especially when we talked of my father. I don't remember who mentioned Dad first nor much of that night save the truth she told me after years of lies.

I do remember her bedgown flecked with blood from her coughing, and her hair, wispy and grey, standing up all over her head to throw monstrous shadows. Through the window beside her bed, I could see snowflakes dancing on a gentle breeze, melting before they hit ground. Come morning, there'd be only frost.

Mother said, "You always loved your dad more'n you done me."

'Twas true, but nothing I'd own with Mother on her deathbed and me having to live with the guilt. "I did not, Mother. It's just that he was at sea all the time, and when he was home—"

"I could tell you something about your dad would make you love him less." She chuckled, then fell to coughing, and her shadow jumped on the wall.

"Mother, be quiet, please. You're fretting yourself—"

"He wasn't really your dad, you know." Her eyes glittered in the lamplight.

It was only more of her meanness, or so I thought, and gave no answer.

"He wasn't," she insisted. "You was already in my belly when I married him."

"You—I don't believe you."

"It's the truth, Clem. Ask your aunt if you don't believe me. There! I wager you love him less, now, don't you?"

"He was my father. He loved me—"

"Oh, he loved you, that's certain sure, more than he ever done me. But he knew you wasn't his. He weren't as dumb as I hoped."

"He—he knew?"

"Think he'd'a let you know, somehow or other, not lie to you all those years, wouldn't you?"

"But he still loved me." I sat wondering at a man who had cherished another's child as his own, who never let me suspect I wasn't his flesh and blood but threw me high in the air and rode me on his shoulders.

"'Twas a lie, Clem," she said as though hers weren't the greater wrong.

"'Twas kindness, Mother."

"Aw, don't go getting all teary over it. Maybe I never told him you weren't his. I forget." She took to coughing again.

A new thought rooted me to my chair. Somewhere, perhaps, I had another father, though it was expecting much that he'd come close to Dad.

"So, if Dad wasn't my father, who was?"

Her face closed. "You'll never meet up with him, so won't do you any good to know his name. He's dead, anyway, the damned rascal, get a lady with child and leave her alone and adrift in the world."

"Well, mayhap he had family I could visit, or—"

"His family weren't no one you'd wanna know, Clem. They said I wasn't good enough for him." She snorted, which brought more coughing as she spluttered, "Can you imagine? Me not good enough for him when I turned around and married a Phillydelphia Shippen the next month."

Though I pleaded until she threw a hairbrush at me so I'd hush and let her sleep, she told me aught of my father, not what he'd looked like, nor what work he'd done, nor where his people hailed from. "He's a rascal," she shouted. "Now leave me be!"

Those were her last words to me, for when I woke next morning, she was dead.

'Tis wicked, but I grieved more that my father's name had died with her than that she was gone. I would have tended his grave and met his family, and never mind Mother's opinion of them.

Reverend Peters recited a psalm over Mother's body. Then he and his wife, the only mourners but for my aunt and me, went home. They'd barely gone before I tried to wheedle my father's name from my aunt, but she claimed to have forgotten it, if she'd ever known. Which she doubted. "Had enough problems of my own without worrying over hers." She drew her shawl tight to her bony shoulders. "Least she had a daughter to help her in this evil world, which is more'n I ever had. And husbands, too, how many times she marry?"

I bade her farewell soon as I packed my things, tired of her stingy ways and hot words. She made Uncle Shippen's house seem a paradise, Peggy and all. I thought long on my uncle's goodness to me.

The woods wore the green buds and the fields the green stubble of May as I meandered through Connecticut. But spring's beauty couldn't hide the ruin of last fall's battles when I reached New York. The Continentals' flight through Westchester lay spread before me.

At White Plains, the fog that named the place was lifting to show fields churned and muddy and littered with the bones of horses and men, wagons, broken muskets and traces, knapsacks. Bits of red wool fluttered here and there, as though to mock the wildflowers blooming among the trenches and mounds of the defensive works circling the hills and crowning their summits.

Two kids played on the far side of a meadow, and a man I took for their father squatted before a knapsack, rifling it. He watched me pick my way through the trash, then returned to his task. A woman travelling on her own wasn't a sight to turn heads anymore—not when whole towns of them was on the move, most times with children in arms and at their skirts.

New Jersey was even worse, for the devastation spread beyond battle-fields. Militia had nipped at the government's army all winter, and when the Redcoats couldn't catch those men on their fast horses, they burned farms sitting still and prosperous instead. Now the fields lay deserted, and the houses were only blackened chimneys and foundations. Same for most taverns and shops belonging to Patriots. Even the copper mines and furnaces at Middle Brook stood silent, ghostly. Anything still sur-viving catered to Redcoats. I continued south through a country barely able to feed the few farmers left there, let alone the troops.

I had crossed the Delaware River into Philadelphia before it came to me that Uncle Shippen wasn't really my uncle. And what if he knew he wasn't but never breathed a word, so that I lived unawares on his charity? I shrank from the shame. What if he'd said somewhat to Peggy, and she to Becky Franks... Had everyone but me known?

Continental troops thronged Philadelphia's streets—or men I assumed were troops. Few wore uniforms, and those mostly just a waistcoat here or breeches there, so telling soldiers from citizens wasn't easy. 'Twas simpler to see which buildings belonged to Loyalists: they stared with broken windows, or Patriots had seized them and turned them into something else. One man sold bread under a sign for "Josiah Abingdon, hatmaker," and another fixed muskets in the doorway of a tea shop where Peggy and I had eaten scones. I wondered how my uncle's—I mean, Judge Shippen's house had fared.

Scarcely breathing, I turned up Fourth Street. There stood the Shippens' mansion, substantial, secure, built to withstand the ages, never mind armies and wars. But its shuttered windows were lifeless. My stomach fluttered. A year and a half had passed, with mighty changes.

The judge himself answered my knock. His face was puckered, though, when he saw 'twas me, he relaxed a bit.

"Clem," he said, voice reedy and worried. He kissed me with the dry lips of an old man. "Your aunt and I were speaking of you just this morning. How good to see you. Please, come in."

I stepped into a hall that reminded me of the battlefields I'd passed, so littered was it with broken packing crates and straw. The house smelled of ashes and parties long done, and it was cold after the balmy air outside. When I shivered, my uncle drew me into the front parlor where a fire blazed. He settled himself before it, picking up a sheaf of papers. This he fed sheet by sheet to the flames, which give me a chance to study him.

He was nigh as changed as Philadelphia. He'd ever been careful and grave, but now he was aged and careful and grave, and anxious, too, anxious as a sentry in the woods on a moonless night.

"Uncle Shippen, how—what is this?" I sank down beside him. "Where's the family? Are they—is everyone well?"

"They're safe, Clem, and have somewhat to eat, which is more than most Loyalists can claim."

That nigh felled me. "Are you a Loyalist, then?" I could hardly credit his abandoning the fortress of expediency for the battlefield of principle.

He said nothing as he watched his paper burn. Then he sighed. "I favor the king, Clem. What sensible man doesn't? Especially after the murder and mayhem these rebels bring." He glanced at me over his spectacles. "If that's what you mean by 'Loyalist,' I guess I'm one. But I'm not about to take to arms. All I want is to be left alone. You'd think the rebels, with all their prattle about liberty, would respect that. What is liberty but the right to live without other men forcing opinions on you? 'Tis their opinion government ought to be overthrown. Fine, do so, but leave me out of it. But they won't. They say anyone not for them is against them, and if I don't run into the streets and find me a Redcoat to murder, I'm an enemy, too, as much as the king or Ministry."

We sat silent as he crumpled papers and hurled them at the fire.

When he spoke again, it was with his usual calm. "You know, when things first began up there in Massachusetts coupla years ago, there's all sorts of notions here. Some said it's justified, others said it's a lot of fuss over nothing, ill-advised, too, throwing off the best government in the world over a few misunderstandings. But we thought and spoke as we pleased. Only thing to worry about was spouting off in the wrong tavern. You daren't toast His Majesty where the Patriots gathered, and likewise, none of them drank at the King's Arms. But not anymore, Clem. Now there's new men in power."

"New men? What do you mean?"

He peered out the window, then spoke so soft I scarce heard. "Tyrants, Clem, to put it plain, men more drunk on power than His Majesty ever was, and they've got more power than he ever had, too."

"But who, Uncle? What are you talking about?"

"The men in charge of this city now."

I sat bewildered. In charge of *Philadelphia*? The biggest city in all America, with thousands and thousands of folks going about their business, birthing and burying, buying and selling? Who could take charge of such a place, unless he's God Almighty? I would have scoffed but for my uncle's fury.

"You know," he continued, "that Declaration last summer ended government here, or so they say, and that's when these men, these Patriots, came forward. They said they'd be ruling us now, so—"

"*Patriots* said that?"

"Not plain like that, no. But what they did was they held a convention and wrote out a new constitution for us, though we'd never asked for one. And what it says is—'course, I haven't read it, no man of sound mind can. I tried, but your aunt begged me to stop for fear I'd take a fever. The men behind it, very few of them can read, and even the ones that can don't know law. And they're proud of that, Clem, proud of such ignorance! But the worst is, that constitution lets them do things His Majesty never would have dared."

I felt sick. "Like what?"

"Well, just last Friday, their Assembly passed a 'Test Act,' and now anyone who won't sign an oath of allegiance to their Patriot government, well, we're traitors. We can't travel without their permission—"

I felt sicker. "No!"

He nodded grimly. "Not unless you want to be considered a spy, and hang for it."

"But that's tyranny!"

"Ah, but wait, there's more. Unless you sign, you can't hold office, or vote, or sue for debts, though we can still be sued, I'll warrant you. You tell me when His Majesty ever stole our liberties like that."

Again, I sat silent, head swimming. This couldn't be the work of Patriots. We were fighting for freedom. Men weren't starving and freezing and dying, weren't hanging with brave regrets for having only one life to give, so's new tyrants could take over where the old ones left off.

I looked up. "But, Uncle, if you can't travel without their say-so, then how—I mean, you're here—"

"Damned right I am! I've come here, to my house from my farm, as Englishmen have for centuries, and by God, I've asked no one's permission!" He nigh roared it, then added, with another glance at the window, "I guess that makes me a spy. That's why I'm burning my papers. No telling how they'd interpret letters to my agent in London ordering a pianoforte for your aunt." He snorted. "The more they order me to swear allegiance to them, the harder I'll fight. 'Tis not a matter to force a man to."

"But where's the family?"

"They are northeast of here, at a farm I—"

"Oh, no!"

"—I rented." He smiled bitterly. "You underestimate us, Clem. We're getting used to the rural life. You know, Mr. Washington—"

"General," I said.

He gave me another look. "Only government can grant commissions, Clem, not that collection of—of oafs they call Congress." He paused, still studying me. "Unless, of course, you're siding with them now, the rebels. If you are—" He eyed me hard.

There are moments that decide things for life. Sometimes you know such moments for what they are: the day you marry, or the hours you spend reading a book you'll never forget, or mayhap you see a young hero hang. Then there are other moments just as important, but they come disguised. One of those had sneaked up on me now. If I'd answered truly, if I'd talked of Nathan Hale and how he'd convinced me the fight for liberty was worth everything—and believe me, I wanted to, the urge to spew the truth burned my insides—all would have been different.

But something stopped me. I thought at the time 'twas cowardice, for if I spoke my Patriotism, and the judge forbid me his house, where would I go? How would I live, a girl with no prospects, no husband nor parents? I remembered the creatures who sometimes sauntered into our tavern before Mother chased them out lest they set the drunken, jealous Redcoats to brawling, smashing our crockery and tables. Those girls always looked ancient, faces lined and dirty, teeth missing, shoulders stooped. But they weren't old, not really: they all died afore that, of disease or childbirth.

And that was to say nothing of how they spent the days—or should I say nights—of their short lives. I shuddered, seeing the same fate for me, without the judge's sheltering home.

And so I said, voice squeaky with fear and deceit, "I—I'm no rebel, not me," and cursed myself for a weakling, never dreaming how my cowardice would serve liberty.

"Thought you were too sensible to swallow their nonsense." He turned towards the window, fist raised, and shouted, "Hear that? Nonsense, all your stinking laws and resolutions, damn your nonsense!"

I stood silent. Nor did my uncle glance at me as he poked up the fire with shaking hands. "Might as well be hanged for a sheep as a lamb," he muttered.

"Uncle," I said timidly, "you were going to tell me about the, um, farm and living there."

He crumpled the last of his papers into the flames. Then he said in tones more like his customary ones, "It's an hour's ride from here. I come back most days to check the house, seeing as how the rebels think they'll persuade with arson those unmoved by their ideals." He settled back in his chair, hands on knees. "But where's my manners? How's your mother, poor thing?"

"My mother—" I hesitated, and my uncle knew immediately, or thought he did. But her death was the least of it.

"I'm so sorry, Clem." He murmured the things folks do when someone unlovable has died: how sad her life had been, what a fine thing she'd done birthing me. If he knew the truth about that birth, he gave no sign, so that I wondered how to ask.

When he paused, I said, "Uncle Shippen, there's something I—well, that my mother, ah, said—"

A clock chimed eleven. My uncle rose. "Excuse me, my dear. There's a man I must see." He hurried to the window, yanked its sash up, and banged open the shutters. Then he peered down the street, alert as a hound awaiting the fox.

I joined him at the sill. "Who is it, Uncle?"

"Arnold," he said, "Major General Arnold. They promoted him last week."

"But what's he doing here? I thought he's up in Connecticut, fighting the king's—"

"Who knows? I've got enough problems without worrying over where rebel officers are. All I can tell you is, he's here seeing the Congress about something or other. He takes a walk every day about now, he and I—There he is. Now, Clem, smile at him, and make like I've been living here, not out at the farm. General!" He waved, but his gaiety was so forced, I thought 'twould fool no one, least of all the redoubtable Benedict Arnold.

I was eager to meet a man I'd heard so much about. He was the stuff of legend, for certain sure.

I caught sight of him then, a major general's purple sash, brilliantly new, across his chest, black cockade on his tricorn. Then I noticed his walk. It wasn't just that he limped. More and more men did: we'd grown used to limps that said a man had bled for liberty. But Arnold's limp was tragic. Until it broke his gait, you could see he had the sort of grace few folks do, that perfect balance and control that meant he'd run faster, jump higher, and do any trick you can think of, do it so much better than anyone else you stand awed. And here such grace was ruined. That ball that smashed his leg at Quebec, 'twas like having a town's best fiddler wounded in the hand or if one of those painters from Italy was to lose his sight. I felt such sorrow at his crippling my eyes stung.

"Well, Esquire." Arnold smiled, then looked past my uncle to me. Most men, when they see a plain woman, their gaze wanders on, and quick. Not Arnold's. He stared, shaming me. Dear God, my soul cried, Thou needn't make me beautiful as Peggy, but couldn't Thou have fashioned me so folks wouldn't drop their jaws looking?

"General?" my uncle asked. "You all right?"

"Fine, Judge, thank you." His blue eyes snapped back to Uncle Shippen. "And you, sir? How you keeping this fine day?"

"About the same, sir, though my niece has just returned. General Arnold, may I present Miss Clementine Shippen? Miss Shippen, Major General Benedict Arnold."

Arnold bowed. This time, his eyes crinkled at the corners, as though I were pretty, or at least interesting. "An honor, Miss Shippen."

"And how's the leg, General?" my uncle said.

"Improving, sir, thank you." They spoke of the weather and how fast prices were rising now that Congress was printing money, until Arnold lifted his hat. "My compliments to your lady, sir, and to you, Miss Shippen."

My uncle closed shutter and sash, though I longed for more warming wind. "Well, Clem," he said, taking his seat at the fire, "how are you getting along without your mother?"

"But, Uncle, what was all that about?"

He shrugged. "He's the highest ranking rebel who'll talk with me. I curry his favor to have a friend in the enemy's court, so to speak."

I was nigh tearful. This was not what our Cause was about, changing one set of masters for another. Nathan Hale had not died so we could bow and scrape to Patriots instead of His Majesty's minions.

"Now, Clem, tell me, are you here to stay or just visiting?"

"I, ah—" Again, my stomach fluttered. "I had thought to come back, Uncle, to—to live with you and work off my mother's debt, if you'll have me. And there's something else, something she told me before she died." The world seemed to stop, leaving us as we were, my uncle's legs crossed at the knees, shoes scuffed as they'd never been before the war, waistcoat patched and stained, me standing near the window with a fly buzzing about.

"What was it?" my uncle said at last, and I saw he had no inkling. "Something important?"

"She said—she said—" My heart pounded until I hardly knew what words I mouthed. "Dad wasn't really my father, you see, so you're not really my uncle." And then I burst out crying.

I cried as I had the day Nathan hanged, perhaps because life was turned upside down, perhaps because I was alone, truly alone, with no parents, no husband, and the only folks who cared about me, my uncle and aunt, no kin after all.

Uncle Shippen waited until my sobs subsided to sniffles.

"Clem." He offered his handkerchief. "Start from the beginning and tell me exactly what your mother said."

I repeated her words near as I could remember.

"And you believe her?" he asked.

"I—I—why wouldn't I?"

"Your mother, God rest her, often stretched the truth." He spoke judiciously, as though this were a case at trial. "She's not a reliable witness,

Clem. I don't say that to hurt you or dishonor her memory, but she was a—a troubled lady."

I blew my nose. 'Twas true.

My uncle continued. "Curious that she wouldn't tell you the name of this, what was her word, rascal. As though she didn't want you looking for him and finding he never existed or, if he did, never laid a hand on her."

"Well, but he's dead—"

"Also very convenient, isn't it?"

"So you think it's all a falsehood?"

"I'd say the evidence is weak."

"But I don't look anything like Dad—I mean, your brother. 'Course, I always favored Mother, but—"

"Not every child resembles its father, Clem. Mayhap your mother told you the truth, being on her deathbed and all. But more likely she didn't. Now, why don't we keep this betwixt us? It's nothing anyone else need know."

Such sense comforted me, and I sniffled with a lighter heart. "I was wondering, too—I had thought I could work for you, you know, pay off Mother's debt, live with you again."

"Hmm." He pursed his lips.

"That is," I added hurriedly, "I'd only thought of it, you see—not planned on it. But I haven't any cash money, so I—"

"Clem, 'tis fine that you want to work the loan off. It's just, ah, well, to tell you the truth, we're hard-pressed to feed ourselves, let alone anyone else." He took off his spectacles and rubbed his eyes. "I've even let the servants go."

"I could cook for you." I tried to keep the pleading from my voice. "I've learned much of cookery this year—"

"There's nothing for you to cook, Clem. One army or the other swoops down and steals everything edible. We been living on berries the girls pick in the woods and fish we catch in the streams. And there's little enough of that. No, best I can do is have you looking after things for us here."

"You mean stay here, in this house?"

He nodded. "You want to stay here and watch things for us, it'd ease my mind. Worries me to death, way the Continentals seize abandoned properties."

Living alone in such a huge place scared me at first. I jumped every time a shutter banged or a floorboard settled. 'Twas amazing how many noises that house made I hadn't noticed before. More than ever, I wished I knew whether Mother spoke the truth and who my father was. If he still lived, I would fly to him and beg protection.

But eventually I grew used to doing what I pleased when I wanted to, and to my solitude, so that my uncle's visits, though growing scarce, grated on me. I spent my days in the garden, both to escape his fawning over General Arnold and to put the time to good use planting onions and cucumbers, beans and corn and lettuce. Thus would I keep from starving, for food in Philadelphia was scarce as in the country.

Once the garden started coming in, my worst trial wasn't hunger but boredom. I stayed close to home lest I encounter those men my uncle mentioned, or their rules and regulations. That kept my days running together with aught to distinguish them, except for the flights of Congress. Anytime the king's forces, or rumors of them, drew close, the delegates packed up and fled. When they'd confirmed General Howe and his Redcoats was some miles distant, they'd slink back to the jeers of Loyalists.

Then it was July 4, 1777—the anniversary of Congress' declaring us independent.

So many times we'd thought that paper'd be nothing more than a footnote in a history book, with our rebellion scotched and its leaders following poor Nathan to the gallows. To think our fight for freedom had survived another year—well, it made us happy as folks can be who aren't sure they'll live out the season. Ministers preached sermons on the Almighty's watchcare over us, and we prayed our thanks and raised hymns. Patriots around the city gave parties, even if they only raised a glass of callibogus—and that mostly beer with the tiniest touch of rum— and whistled "Yankee Doodle."

I attended no parties, but I did light candles in every window of my uncle's house. So did hundreds of others until we had us a Grand Illumination.

'Course, some candles burned not to celebrate but to protect: the men my uncle'd mentioned prowled the streets that night, making free with any place lacking bright windows, and, once they'd finished there, the ones not bright enough to suit them. The reason didn't matter, not whether folks were too poor to waste candles all night, or mayhap too tired or sick to sit up and tend them, or even, like my uncle, whether they'd fled Philadelphia for peace in the country. Those thieves helped themselves to whatever they wanted if a house went dark, for such must belong to Loyalists, they cried, and who could object to taxing Loyalists?

Chapter Eleven

Hard on the anniversary of our Declaration came news of Continental defeats up north as the Redcoats pushed down from Canada again. This time, there was no Benedict Arnold to stop them.

That made me long to do something, anything, for the Cause. I heard of a group of ladies who gathered weekly to knit mittens and mufflers for the troops, and though they gossiped more than they worked, I joined them.

'Twas on my way to their second meeting that I caught sight of Nathan Hale's friend. He was marching alongside his men, shouting orders, using a spontoon for a walking stick. He'd lost flesh since our flight from the Hessians last year. For that matter, most of our boys were skin and bones. Still, he was alive with the enthusiasm of defending ideals held dearer than life.

I didn't call to him, nor to General Arnold, also with a set of men, who passed soon after. But I saw Ben Tallmadge in my dreams that night, saw and coveted his purpose. And I determined to join the army. I wasn't much of a hand at sewing or laundering or doctoring, like the other ladies who followed the troops, but mayhap they'd want a cook.

Next afternoon, I set out for the Continental camp. Finding it was easy if you looked for churned fields and rutted roads. I lugged a kettle with me, filled with soap, bread, and sass from my garden.

First picket I come to was a boy who should have been home learning his ABC's. Reckon he thought meanness would add some years, for he scowled while barking questions.

The lieutenant he took me to was older and polite, though just as ragged. He peered into my kettle, tucked the bunch of scallions I offered into his pocket and nodded when I told how I wanted to cook for the army.

"What regiment's your husband with?" he asked.

"I'm not married, Lieutenant. But I'm a good cook, they say."

"Ma'am, if you haven't got a husband in this army, can't enroll you nohow. Can't even have you fetching firewood or water. Don't need cooks. Men all do their own cooking."

"But don't you want everyone to come out and fight?"

"Sure." He waved at the camp around us. "But we got boys here away from their wives and families. Wouldn't be right, have you sleeping close by, you see what I mean. Don't imagine the wives back home'd like it much either. You got a brother with us?"

I shook my head.

"Too bad. Sometimes colonel'll bend the rules, seeing as how a brother'll watch out for you."

"I might have a father." 'Twas true as far as it went. I'd begun speculating about every man over a certain age.

"Father, huh?" He chewed his lip. "I dunno, probably too old, but I can ask the captain."

I shrugged, then thanked him for his time.

"Ma'am, if you don't mind—" He gestured at my kettle. "Sure could use that soap, if you're agreeable to leave it. I haven't had any in so long even the fleas won't 'sociate with me."

At the knitters' next meeting, I found them cackling over a report in the newspaper one member's sister had sent her from London.

"Just read this, Miss Shippen, if you please," that lady said as I took my seat.

"Our valiant Troops," it ran, "used to the smiles & Approval of English Ladies, must rid themselves of all expectation of such Blandishments in America. For there the women ('tis a disservice to call them Ladies), are as rough as any able Seaman, & take up guns to fight, alongside the rebel Men. A True & certain source reports, that a trusty Sergeant, of the king's Own, was Killed in battle when he discovered one of these harridans, giving Birth on the Field, & Withheld his bayonet from its deadly Work, only to receive a Thrust from behind for his Pains."

We had fun with this all afternoon, wondering whether the baby was even now toddling about with a musket. But my thoughts flew with my needles. That night, I dreamed Ben Tallmadge handed me a spontoon while Nathan Hale bowed to us.

I woke before dawn and went to my cousin Edward's room for breeches, linen, and a waistcoat. I posed long before the mirror, pulling and gathering. I'd never had much of a figure, and even less after this hungry summer; what's left I could hide with bands wound tight. But there's nothing to be done about my height, and I seemed a child playing dress-up in daddy's clothes. The best they'd take me for would be a drummer boy, for some were young as thirteen.

Over the next fortnight, I cut the duds to size when my uncle wasn't there and studied him when he was. I noticed how he plopped onto his chair rather than easing himself as ladies do. He strode across a room: no mincing for him. In fact, all his movements were free. Nor did he stifle sneezes and coughs. When I tired of tailoring Edward's duds, I practiced his father's mannerisms.

On the morning when the knitters next gathered, I cut a hand's breadth off my hair and clubbed it. Then I donned my breeches, left my uncle a note, and set off for New Jersey, where the army's supposed to be. Took me the best part of a day to find it, though, walking lanes lined with wildflowers and berries, chasing through fields and forest. After seven miles' foot-padding in two hours, I was beat out. I rested a spell, but even so, my feet began to be very sensible of my undertaking.

'Twas evening before I stumbled across some pickets.

They were sitting under the trees lining the path, the light so far gone I never saw them until they slipped out to surround me. Two carried spears; the third had a hatchet at his waist. I swallowed my scream and gave them back their stares, bold as a boy.

"Who're you? What's your business?" The one standing afore me seemed in charge, though he couldn't have been twenty.

"I'm here to enlist," I said and spit for good measure. I'd practiced spitting in the garden all last week, but my aim was still bad, and I nigh splattered the toes of the fellow to my right.

"Watch it, boy," he said, hand going towards his hatchet. "I want a bath, I'll make for the river. Anyways, you can't enlist. You's too young."

From what I could tell in the dark, he must have been all of seven-teen. Hungry and tired and grumpy from sore feet, I found it easy show-ing my anger instead of hiding it as girls are taught. "I'm older'n I look."

"Aw, you's no more'n fifteen."

Their leader said, "That's only a year less than you, Willis. Where you from, boy?"

"Philadelphia."

"Can't even shoot, I wager," Willis said. "None of them city boys can."

I ducked my head before remembering that a man stares down his enemies. "Sure, and they trusted you with a gun so much they give you that hatchet."

"No call to get riled," the first one said. "Can you shoot or not?"

I folded my arms. "I didn't know the army'd got so particular. They're saying in town you want all the men you can find to stand against Howe. Now," I tried for indifference, though my heart was pounding, "you wanna turn away someone that hates politicians and ministers and all their laws, why, I'll find somewhere else to sign up."

"Go on, Billy," the leader said to the third one, standing silent all this time behind me. "Take him up to Cadwalader's regiment. They's from Philadelphia, I think, and if they aren't, they'll send him on to one that is."

Billy was as quiet walking through camp as when he was standing behind me. That left me at liberty to gaze at men, tents, stacks of arms. The light from cookfires and the rising moon showed me tattered troops in tattered togs, filled me with pity more than confidence. They were the most miserably looking creatures that ever bore the name of soldiers, covered with nothing but rags and vermin. No wonder we're losing.

The tents were no better, though pitched in rows, officers' spontoons planted before them, and colors hanging limp in the humid night. The ladies I'd thought to join were scattered about, washing clothes, dress-ing wounds. After we'd passed the fourth man being bandaged, I asked, "Been a battle lately?"

Billy shook his head. "Naw. Just takes a long time to heal, is all."

We reached a cluster of tents, ripped and faded even by torchlight. The dozen spontoons before them had mostly plain iron heads, but there's a couple with such delicate scrolls and flourishes they'd comple-ment the fanciest parlor.

"Here, this here's Cadwalader's." Billy glanced at the colors. "You wanna see one of the captains." He left, and I remembered not to call my thanks after him.

The first captain I found answered all my hopes. He was eager as me to sign me up, for his company had shrunk to half its number.

"Tell you what, son." He twined himself around one of the spontoons. "We're kinda short on pay day, and seems like two or three men disappear ever' time we can't give 'em their whole wage. But long as you aren't looking to get rich, this here's the place."

"Helps if you don't care none about eating, neither," said a soldier passing by.

"That's enough, Guttman." But the captain's stomach betrayed him, rumbling long and loud. "'Course, sometimes we're short on provisions, too. Now here, son, come on into my quarters and make your mark and you'll be a soldier in the Continental Army of the United States."

"A starving soldier in the Continental Army," said Guttman, passing by again and dodging a thwack from the captain's spontoon.

I followed the captain into a tent where two men, officers I reckoned, though they're ragged as everyone else, sat cleaning pistols. A lamp burned between them. The captain fished a book and pen and ink from a haversack. He opened the book, dipped the quill, and pointed a dirty finger at line No. 53. "Sign here."

I wrote the name I'd had in mind all week, Nathan Hail. Captain held it towards the lamp and squinted, first at it, then at me, but all he said was, "Can you shoot, son? Now, most of us can't, coming from the city, so don't be shy about saying the truth."

I'd never held a gun, not even the little pistols some ladies carry, and shook my head. One of the officers shook his, too, muttering, "Figures."

"Never rolled cartridges either, has ya?" The captain stuck his head out the tent's flap. "Guttman!" he called. "Hey, come here. Tomorrow, I want you to show Hail how to load a musket and fire her. Fill him up a cartridge box, too."

Guttman worked with me a few days. I learned slow because I was nervous, scared someone'd see through me.

But on some counts, 'twas easier fooling folks than I'd thought. The five men in my tent missed their wives, so there's little talk of other women. I didn't need to pretend I lusted after the laundress, for 'twould offend them, pining for their Mollies and Sarahs.

Then there's answering nature. Plenty of soldiers, especially if they're farmers or backcountry-men, eased themselves where they pleased, though General Washington had made such license a whipping offense. My companions, hailing from America's largest city, sought the necessary and didn't marvel when I did, too.

At night, there's no bedclothes to change into, and what with the light fingers in camp, hardly anyone stripped to his linen to sleep. For sure, I didn't.

But here and there I made mistakes that set them wondering. I never whittled, didn't carry me a favorite jack-knife, and couldn't tell which woods were best for carving, whereas they all reached for their knives soon as they sat down to turn out spoons and noggins and buttons.

Worse, first time one of them tossed a chicken he'd foraged into the tent, I scooped it up for gutting.

Eliphalet, the man who'd fetched it, glared. "What you doing with my bird?"

I stood dumfounded, for no man would jump to cook for others.

Praise Heaven, Eliphalet misunderstood. They always called him "Lif" instead of that big long name, for he was a skinny little thing, nigh as small as me, and that made a bond betwixt us. "You can have some, Hail, don't worry, long as you share whatever you forage with me."

Another time, one of them got a bottle of kill-devil, 'twas better not to ask how. I didn't drink, afraid the stuff would addle my wits and they'd discover what I was. But I should have faked a swig.

"Too good to drink with us, Hail?" asked the oldest one. He was also the biggest, and though he'd scared me at first, I soon saw that Asa's muscles hid a soft heart. Fact, I came to like him so well that I asked, casual-like, had he ever been to Connecticut or known a lady called Hepzibah Heyes. He laughed and wanted to know was she pretty, but turned out the answer to both was no. Asa wasn't my father, much as I wished he could be.

Now I shook my head and uttered what was blasphemy up to New England. "Naw, just never liked rum."

Asa sat thunderstruck. I'd forgot he's from Charlestown, or leastways was until the Redcoats burned it that day, back at the start of things, when they attacked Bunker's Hill. He'd enlisted that afternoon, flames still curling round the beams of his house. Now he said, slow and disbelieving, "Don't like rum?"

Eliphalet distracted him. "Say, Asa, tell us about that march you went on, that one where you ate shoe-leather."

Asa raised the bottle in a toast. "Perpetual itching without benefit of scratching to the enemies of America." He drank deep, then sighed. "Aw, boys, that march, that's something that'll never be forgot, for certain sure. Men starving and freezing and naked and sick, and still we marched hundreds a miles through wilderness for to free Quebec."

"You were with Arnold?" I knew my eyes were wide as a girl's, but I couldn't keep the wonderment from them.

"Sure was, and that man, I swear to you, boys, that man's no more human than—than, well, I don't know what." Asa swallowed more rum. "There we was, struggling to put one foot in front of the other, and there's Arnold, running along aside of us, joking and praising us. And he's hungrier than us, because he never et unless we all had something first. Once, he give his boots to the boy behind me whose own was wore down with his feet sticking through. 'Course, that's pretty regular now, marching barefoot—we don't think nothing of it. But back in '75, 'twasn't normal yet. So Arnold goes and pulls his own boots off and said he'd just double up on his stockings." Asa shook his head. "And him a colonel, leastways he was then. It's like I told my wife when I got home, 'Sally,' I says, 'there isn't but one such man born every 500 years or so.'" He hushed, and we looked away. 'Twas Sally's name had done it. He was devoted to her as a husband could be, until sometimes at night we'd hear sobs from his bedroll.

Then he begin humming a melody we called "Sally's Song." It was a haunting thing, without words, that I still hear across the years. Asa'd only shrug when we asked its name. "Some ditty Sally sings."

I'd been in the army about a month, had learned to load and shoot my musket enough that I wouldn't embarrass myself, was growing used to the sameness of the days and the wretchedness of the food when there was any. I'd heard plenty speeches along the lines of, "For your honor's sake, never let it be said that an army of six-penny soldiers, picked up from prisons and dungeons, freed from transportation, the whipping post, and the gallows, fighting in the worst of causes and for the worst of kings, bore the fatigues of war with stouter hearts than you," and I'd cheered such talk, too. Then came word we'd soon fight those six-penny troops. Sure enough, we packed up and marched to Philadelphia, right through it, so's everyone could have a good look, on our way to meet Howe and his Redcoats.

The whole town turned out to gawk at us. I swear I even spied John Adams, haggard after all these months away from home, and since I heard later that the Congress stood in the crowds lining the streets, perhaps 'twas really he.

We'd been made to appear as decent as possible, no easy thing when the best-dressed among us had patches on his patches. For uniforms, we stuck hemlock sprigs in our hats, or for those without hats, in our hair. But we hadn't quite the air of soldiers. We weren't stepping exactly in time. We didn't hold up our heads erect, nor turn out our toes exactly as we ought.

I was sweating bullets and not just from the heat that August Sunday: someone might recognize me. It'd been simple enough to gull the men of my company, who'd always known me for a boy. But if Becky Franks spied me, or the ladies from the knitters' circle, they'd surely see 'twas only me, playing a part. For aught I knew, my uncle and cousins might have returned from the farm, might be watching and wondering and pointing, even now.

We paraded, twelve abreast, down Front Street to where it meets Chestnut and then across Chestnut. Drums and fifes played a tune for the quick step. I kept to the middle of the file, scarcely dared look right or left case a neighbor was in the crowd lining the street. I skulked behind Asa, kept so close I trod his heels, till he hissed there wasn't gonna be nothing left of me for the Redcoats, time he got done, if I didn't quit pestering him.

Finally, we cleared Philadelphia, and I breathed easier.

We camped at Darby that day, the next at Naaman's Creek twelve miles south, just over into Delaware. I was too tired from marching all that way in the heat to look around much, but when I finally did, seemed Delaware didn't differ from Pennsylvania, least not the farms I saw.

The general officers were scurrying around, pothering about Howe, and as Asa said, "Let 'em. That's what your general officer was made for. I'm taking me a nap, and then how 'bout you and me go scouting a nice little shoat or maybe a coupla geese for dinner, Hail?"

That's how it went for the next fortnight or so, though everyone was wondering where and when we'd meet the Redcoats. We joked about it, but there's a hollow inside us.

Then, on a Wednesday, second week of September, come the "General" on the drums at three o'clock in the morning. We rolled out and shouldered our muskets to stand ranks in the black night.

'Tisn't ladylike to say, but now that I would fight my first battle, the sweat poured down me. It wet my linen clear through, collected in a puddle at my waist, left me ashiver in the night air. No such worries troubled Asa, standing beside me and snoring. I waited for him to fall over and his musket to fire when he did. But soldiering had taught him to sleep any time, anywhere.

We waited till the sun rose, then watched it climb the sky. Asa woke with a start about eight, near as I could figure, and blinked at me.

"What's happening, Hail?"

"Still waiting on orders." My voice was high with fright, but he took no notice and was soon snoring again.

An hour later, drums beat a march. We plodded towards Red Clay Creek for to establish a line of battle. 'Tis a fancy phrase meaning you dig and dig in the sun until your blisters have blisters and there isn't another drop of water left in your hot, sore body. Then you drop into the ditch you dug and pray the earth will fall in atop you and kill you before the Redcoats do—or the bugs, because whole time you're working, fleas and other Tory insects have been making free with your property.

I struggled to keep pace, shoveling until my arms nigh fell from their sockets, but even Eliphalet out-dug me. He was too busy complaining to Asa to notice, though. A man nearby was swinging a pick, and when he left to answer nature, I changed my shovel for it, thinking it'd be easier. First swing into the bank shuddered me from head to toe. I went back to digging in a hurry.

The drums finally beat for a halt, and I can't say I'd ever heard more blessed music. We waited all day in the heat and the flies, but there's nary a sign of Howe or his Redcoats.

"Oh, he's probably somewhere out there in front of us," Asa said, "thinking he's just the cleverest general ever, keep us standing here all day."

Eliphalet swatted a mosquito. "Mark me, he's gonna try coming around our sides, close us in like a jaw on a big old hog. That's what all them generals like to do. That way, he'll have a clear shot at Philadelphia and the Congress."

Minding their flights this summer, I swallowed my fear to say, "He'll need to run pretty fast to catch the Congress."

His Excellency, too, knew what Howe's about, and that night, he roused us again and set us marching towards a creek called Brandywine. There we dug another line of battle by moonlight. I was so sore I could hardly move, let alone shovel, and I prayed the dark would hide my shirking.

Morning dawned with northern lights still winking and a cool fog rising from the Brandywine. But when it burned away, the sun was a brass cannon in a molten sky, shooting deadly heat at us, blinding us bad as flashing powder.

'Twas a strange morning in camp. Rumors flowed thick and sticky as molasses. King's men were just a mile off... No, they weren't, that was only a scouting party, old Billy Howe don't like this heat anymore than you do. He won't attack when he can sit in the shade and have one of his lackeys fan him some... You're wrong, you fool. He's coming around our rear and gonna hem us in, just as he done on Long Island last year...

Now and then, we'd hear gunfire, even a few cannon, which set tongues wagging all over again.

Then, round about eleven, things quieted. Dinner was a long time off, but breakfast had been thin, and there was a cornfield across the road. We pulled the sweet, fat ears from their husks, then stretched out there among the stalks, at the roots, where it's cooler.

'Twas too hot to sleep, but I dozed a while, visions and voices tumbling through my head the way they will when you're not awake but not sleeping, neither. Leaves were ripping and feet pounding as I, a child of eight or nine, played hide-and-go-seek with my father in the rustling corn. "To arms! To arms!" Dad cried. "Redcoats, they're coming up the road!"

I sprung to my feet as a sergeant raced past me down the next row, still shouting. Drums banged, fifes screamed. We scrambled back to camp for our muskets. Asa nodded at the west bank of the creek. "Look ye there," he said, and I espied the green uniforms of Loyalist rangers and riflemen coming for us while their band shrilled "The British Grenadier."

Now that the moment was on me, when I might kill or be killed, I wasn't as panicked as I'd thought. Things were too confused for that.

Men screamed while our captain shouted orders I scarce heard, let alone understood.

Cannon roared.

Balls sung like bees around me.

Powder smoke drifted so thick that, but for the noise, I'd have figured myself alone in the world. Then a breeze would scatter the smoke, though it still burned my eyes and nose.

I was standing bewildered when out of the chaos loomed a colonel on horseback. "Soldier," he shouted, "stay by your officer!"

I stumbled through the gloom, trying to find the captain or lieutenant. Best I did was Asa.

"Come on, Hail," he yelled, "hear that drum? Company's running for the center!"

Then, not fifteen feet ahead, I saw a red coat, ghostly through the haze. Weak sun glinted on a bayonet, raised to stab me. Mayhap you've heard somebody's never been in battle moan that he couldn't kill, he just couldn't. But that foot and a half of steel coming at you, ready to drain your blood, makes killing seem natural as breathing. I raised my musket and fired. Shoulda used my bayonet, if I'd had one, because now I was left defenseless without I reloaded, which I couldn't until we reached our troop, shooting from behind a stone fence. Once again, the sweat drenched me, left me shaking, until you'd swear I had the ague.

"Run, Hail!" Asa cried again, and never knowing if I'd found my mark, I staggered after him.

The Loyalists were still too far away to be much threat. Withal, they'd engaged another company.

We leaped the fence and slid into place on our bellies. "Any luck, they'll send the Loyalists packing," Asa said between gasps, "and we'll live to fight another day. But maybe not," he added as the green line pushed through the ragged brown one.

They come running towards us as our captain called the orders for aiming and firing while a drum rattled and the notes of a fife soared eagle-like above the noise and confusion. I paid no heed to captain or music nor did anyone else. One boy slumped against a tree, sobbing, but we didn't heed him, neither. Another, a lieutenant from the ribbon in his hat, rushed from man to man, begging forgiveness for any insult or injury he'd done with death coming fast upon us. Mostly, we shoved him away, though here and there, a few cursed him for his pains. Some stood with muskets leveled while the rest of us who'd already shot tried to reload. My hand shook so much I poured more powder on the ground than down my barrel. No matter how I pulled the trigger, no matter how the muskets around me popped, my gun stayed silent.

I'm gonna die, I thought as the green line advanced through the smoke. They'd got close enough to distinguish faces. The men around me jeered as they recognized neighbors.

"Rotten Tories!" a soldier to my right shouted. "What you shooting at us for, huh? 'Tis the government ye oughter be after!" He rammed home another charge as one of the green-coated men called, "Holt? Be that you?"

"Aye, 'tis me, Miller." Holt smiled, cordial as if he'd met a friend at Sunday worship back in Philadelphia. The Loyalists halted while their drummer banged away and we peppered them.

"What're you doing here, Miller, warring on your neighbors?"

"You're the damned rebel, Holt, not me."

"Damned rebel, am I?" Holt raised his musket and fired, but he missed, and Miller gave a mocking bow before the drummer pounded retreat.

We stayed behind our fence the rest of the evening, untroubled but for booming artillery somewhere to our right. I soon grew accustomed to it, and even to the heat and smoke and tearing eyes. 'Tis true, as my experience proves, that we get used to just about anything.

Time wore on. The action had passed us by, so that we were left with our hunger and thirst and no Redcoats to distract us. Cards and dice came out. Men lounged in the slanting sun and carved on their muskets' stocks. A fifer sent "My Days Have Been So Wondrous Free" floating around us. Many slept, and never mind the cannon.

Near sunset, when I was thinking I might die of my thirst, a messenger brought orders. Captain flourished his sword towards the southeast as a drum rattled. "Retreat!" he cried.

"Retreat?" Asa woke with a sneeze. "But I haven't got me a Redcoat yet, Captain, have you?"

Strange that though we'd been safe enough during battle, our withdrawal was hazardous. First sign of danger was the shrieking of bagpipes. We'd hardly begun marching before limbs overhead were cracking and leaves falling thick as autumn. Few of the balls found us, though they plowed the ground at our feet. And still the bagpipes cried their odd, pleasing music.

"'Tis the Highlanders!" flankers shouted as they galloped around us and another company forming up to fight the Scots.

I'd nearly passed them when a dog pushed at my right thigh with a very hot nose, until he clear knocked me off my feet. I glanced about but no dog's in sight. My leg was burning, and as I struggled to my knees, something grated inside. I cried aloud, and Asa turned to look. The sun was behind, shooting its last rays around him so that all I saw was a silhouette. He seemed to take a long time to say, "They got you, Hail."

"Got me?"

"Come on, lemme help." He bent over me and hooked my arm around his neck.

My leg was warm and wet. When I saw 'twas from my own blood, all strength left me, and my gorge rose. I managed naught but dry heaves as Asa limped along with me.

"We're falling behind," he grunted. "Don't know why, you're light as a girl. Can't straggle, not with Redcoats running everywhere."

We both knew what happened to rebels the government caught. With a wound, I wouldn't last a week on a prison ship, while Asa's worst terror was winding up captured, so fearsome were the tales he'd heard. And that was saying much after the march to Quebec.

"Think we'd make better time if I carried you like a sack of meal," he said and tossed me over his shoulder. The thing in my leg grated again, until the pain shook the tears from me. I sobbed for my father, a strong man if he yet lived, I was sure, who would spirit me away and soothe me with his laugh. I even longed for my mother, God help me, until blackness blotted the coming night.

I woke to screams of such agony I was sure the Redcoats had taken us. I looked about careful-like, saw men lying around me and others stepping among us by torchlight. Somewhere, a fife played "Chester," just the lines that go, "Let tyrants shake their iron rod/And slav'ry clank her galling chains/We fear them not, we trust in God," over and over.

"Rum," the boy aside me gasped, though a bloodcurdling shriek cut him off.

"Dear Lord," I said without knowing I spoke aloud, "what is this place?"

"Hospital, friend. You're at the hospital." One of the surgeon's mates walking about squatted next to me, holding a bowl to the boy's lips. "We're outa rum. All's I got is water." He spoke with a Yankee accent, so that I asked if I were among Continentals and not a prisoner.

He eased the boy back to the ground. "You're wounded, friend, that's all. You're no prisoner. We'll redd you up and send you back to your regiment right quick."

"But who's screaming?" Surely the Redcoats or their Indians were torturing some poor devil.

"We're out of brandy, friend. Rum too, like I said. Should be some coming in soon, but there's still plenty cutting needs doing, so there'll be screaming all night, and that's the fact."

He moved on, and I lay with thoughts swooping at me like swallows in a barn. Gradually, my head cleared. I realized that if I didn't want the surgeon's saw hacking at me, I'd best get back to my regiment.

I felt at my thigh, found a sticky hole in the back of it but little pain. No bone poking through, neither. I'd heard enough about balls shattering bones and how those bones pierced the skin to know 'twas a flesh wound only.

I sat up, gave the dizziness time to pass, then took my time standing. The howls continued, filling the world. However used I'd gotten to battle, here was something would never grow old.

"Ho, what you doing, friend?" Here came the surgeon's mate, stepping over the men between us. "Lie down and wait your turn—"

"No, see, I'm fine. I—"

"You're wounded, friend." He said it gentle, but his hands as he gripped my arm were strong, far stronger than me. He'd soon have me back on the ground I'd left with such effort.

I tried to shake him off. "Lemme be. I'm gonna find my company."

"Let him go, Red," said another mate with a water bowl. "We got enough that's wanting help not to trouble about the ones as don't."

Red released me, and I lurched across the groaning, writhing forms to the torches ringing the yard. The thing inside my thigh grated at every step, but the screams drove me on.

Once clear of the yard, I stumbled down a hill. A stream ran black at the bottom, and I fell into it gratefully. I could no longer see the torches nor hear the fife, but the screaming followed me. I sipped at the water, so good, so cool, then lay with it bathing my leg.

When next I woke, sunlight weighed heavy on me. I was far from my usual standards but gaining strength, and thirsty, so thirsty seemed I'd never get my fill from the stream. At last I left off drinking and got to my feet, and, praise be, there's no dizziness. But when I stepped forward, the grating started again.

I hobbled along all morning, trying to catch the army while it retreated north. About two that afternoon, the first stragglers come in sight. Then I reached the Schuylkill across from Philadelphia. There was a boat there, one of those big Durhams they use mostly down on the Delaware, I'd reckon fifty feet long or thereabouts, eight or ten feet wide, so it held plenty of men. Still, looked to be a whole brigade waiting to board. Some troops, the cowardly ones, were elbowing their way up the line, sure the Redcoats would catch them if they didn't cross next. I couldn't have held my ground against them if I'd been well, let alone now, so I collapsed against a tree and waited till that boat made three trips. I embarked then only because some soldiers saw my problem and helped me.

Next day, I reached the main army around Germantown. I asked everywhere for my company. Took until sunset to chance upon them, following Asa's whistle of Sally's song right into our tent. That stopped Asa mid-note and set him and Eliphalet staring as though I was a ghost.

"Nathan." Eliphalet stretched a hand to me.

Seemed I reached from a good ways off to grasp it.

"You back from the surgeons already?"

I nodded, tried to tell him how fearful tired I was, thirsty again, too, when Asa said, "Better lie down, Hail, afore you fall down."

I bit my tongue against the pain as they lowered me onto a pallet.

"Why didn't they bandage you?" Asa asked.

I was too breathless to answer, and by the time I could, Asa was saying, "You never saw a surgeon, did you? Better fetch the captain." He was gone, then, leaving Eliphalet shaking his head over me.

"Pretty bad at the hospital, huh?"

'Twas taking long to catch my breath, so I spoke in gasps. "Lif, when he—he comes back, don't let them take me back there, even if the captain says so."

"Well..." He chewed his lip. "Took a friend to them after Long Island, and they cut off his foot. He's never forgive me for it."

The flap opened to Asa, captain in tow.

Captain knelt beside me. "Son, you spoiled our record. I was about to send in a return of no casualties." He smiled, but he was staring hard.

"Tisn't nothing but a scratch, sir."

"Let's have a look. Here, help me get his breeches off him, and Lif, you fetch a lantern, dark as Hades in here."

I'd been so worried about losing my leg, I never thought about being discovered. My heart nigh stopped as the captain reached for my buttons, and I wriggled aside fast as I could.

"He's a shy one, Captain," Asa said. "Didn't bathe with us in the river last week, neither."

"Captain." I tried to speak steady. "My dad used to hurt me worse than this when he'd catch me shirking chores."

He smiled again. "Keep your breeches then, Hail. Don't know that I'd want to show my hindquarters off, neither. Just roll over."

Before I could resist, he'd pushed me onto my side. His fingers brushed the wound while Lif held the lantern high. I tried to squirm away, but he had a firm hold on me, and I was atremble lest he figure me out.

"Well," he said at last, "you're a brave one, that's certain. But we better fetch a surgeon."

"No!" I clutched at him. "Please, sir, no—no surgeon. My father, he—he died because of a surgeon, my brother, too, and an uncle—I don't want a surgeon."

He rubbed his chin. "I can see why. All those dead men in your family, you must be the last survivor."

I didn't know how to take that. "Yes, well, my mother made me promise—"

"Son, you can't walk around with a ball in your leg. It needs to come out. Now we'll get you good and drunk, and I'll stay here beside you, make certain that surgeon treats you better than your father and your brother and who else was it? Your cousin?" He shook off my hands and ducked from the tent with Asa and Eliphalet.

I struggled to sit, then tried to stand. Things were spinning, and even if they'd stayed still, my leg was hurting bad. First step I took sprawled me headlong.

I'd picked myself up and was limping away fast as I could when they returned, a surgeon in bloody apron with them. Asa scooped me up and carried me back to the tent, though I yelled and beat at him.

He and Eliphalet held me to the pallet while the surgeon laid a hand over my mouth. "Son, hush your noise, now. I've lanced boils on hogs didn't carry on the way you're doing. Hush now, you hear me?"

"That's an order, Hail," the captain said.

The surgeon moved his hand from my mouth to my breeches. I started to speak, but he said, "Not a-gonna hurt you, son, I promise. All I wanna do is have a look, all right?" He was unbuttoning my breeches as he spoke. Another moment and no modesty would be left me.

"Stop it!" I hollered. "I'm a girl!"

They couldn't have been more thunderstruck if I'd said I was His Excellency himself. The surgeon's eyes left my breeches for my face and chest. Asa bawled a word he shouldn't as he and Eliphalet let go, and if I hadn't been afraid of losing my breeches, I could have jumped up and run. Captain stared, face reddening, then stomped from the tent.

The surgeon slipped a hand under his wig and scratched. "So that's what all the caterwauling was about. You didn't want us finding out."

I sighed miserably.

"Well," he said, "don't matter whether you're a cock or a hen, you got a ball in that thigh, and it must needs come out. And I need to look at it, too. There's no way I can do that without you take them breeches off."

I turned as red as the captain.

"It's all right, honey," he said. "I'm married, I know what a woman looks like. I won't stare more'n I must. I'll wait outside, you get them breeches off and wrap 'em around your, um, you know, high up, above the wound. Call me when you're ready. Hey, you two." He turned to Eliphalet and Asa. "Here, gimme that light. Now, one of you fetch me some brandy or rum—don't matter which, whatever come in this morning. The other one of yas gonna stand outside there, make sure don't no one come in." He glanced back at me. "Best I can do, honey."

After I'd diapered myself with my breeches, he returned to inspect the wound and asked how long ago I'd joined and why.

I answered free, having naught further to lose. "Don't suppose they'll let me stay on?" I said it hopeful, but he shook his head.

"Though I'll tell you, honey, aren't too many soldiers so anxious to get back to their company they'll pad, what, ten, fifteen miles with a wound? That was a fool thing to do. Gonna take you twice as long to heal. Least the ball didn't touch the bone, so you'll keep your leg, even with all that walking. Best thing for you to do is sleep much as you can the next week or so—"

Asa called from before the tent with the brandy, and next moment the surgeon was holding a bottle to my lips. "Here, honey, drink it down. I'll need to dig to get that ball."

I've never liked brandy and only sipped it.

"Better take more'n that," he said, opening his kit.

The case was stained a deeper red than any cherry wood with a war's worth of blood. But I had eyes only for the big, curved saws he lifted from it, blades so rusty with dried gore they showed dull in the lantern's light but scary enough for all that. I closed my eyes and guzzled more brandy, then opened them to see him leaning over me. I'd likely fainted dead away if he'd been wielding one of those saws. Instead, he held what seemed a long pair of scissors, or maybe tongs, for they had no point to them. After the saws, they appeared downright friendly. I nigh smiled with relief, or mayhap 'twas the brandy.

"'S that?" I asked.

"Bullet extractor. Now you roll over again, and lemme at that wound."

First nip of those tongs, though, showed they weren't as innocent as they looked, and I discovered a new taste for brandy. Still, however much I drank, next touch of that extractor sobered me so that I'd plead for a respite, please, and another swig. Finally, I swooned.

When I next woke, I was in a real bed, with curtains and covers, in a small, sunny room. I slitted my eyes against the brightness. My head ached to splitting, and the light made it worse. Bandages swathed my thigh, throbbing to beat my head, and my arm, too, where they'd bled me, I reckon. I wore a bedgown with sleeves rolled up.

At the window sat a lady who might've come from the knitters' club in Philadelphia. Only difference was, her hands were busier than her tongue. A basket of rolled bandages was at her feet, and she held scissors and a length of fabric. She was young and small, not much bigger nor older than me, but prettier for certain. She had brown hair and eyes that darted from window to cloth.

"Excuse me," I whispered and winced. "Where am I?"

She put her bandages aside. "You're at headquarters."

"Headquarters? Why, whatever—oh!" They must be going to court-martial me. But surely they wouldn't waste their time when the Redcoats needed licking. Wouldn't they just drum me out of the army? Then I attended to what she was saying.

"The fellows in your, ah, mess, they were pretty angry, so my husband thought we best move you. Besides, you'll get more rest here. The whole regiment was flocking round to see you."

"Who's your husband?" I asked, expecting the worst.

And getting it. "General Greene." She flashed a smile. "He wants to meet you. I think he's about the only one in the whole army who isn't angry with you."

I winced again. "What're they angry for?"

"People don't like to be fooled, I guess. Besides, how are men who, ah, slept beside you going to explain that to their wives?"

I hadn't considered that.

"And your captain—" But she stopped and glanced out the window.

"What about him?"

She looked back, eyes mirthful. "He'd recommended you be raised to sergeant. The paper reached my husband just yesterday. Nathanael's been laughing about it ever since." She pushed her voice deep like a man's. "'Bravest soldier in the company—resourceful—a credit to our Cause—'"

"And now those things aren't true because I—I'm—?"

"It's because you lied."

"I just wanted to fight for liberty. I tried to join as a cook and washer-woman, but they wouldn't have me."

"Most times, folks have reasons for lying." She smiled to soften her words. "But it's still a lie."

I flinched at how right she was, and at how Dad, and Nathan, too, had he heard of this, would be shamed, and she asked, "Your leg paining you? Nathanael sent over a bottle of brandy, said I should dose you good if you—"

"No." My head pounded. "I'd had enough brandy to last me a good while. "I—I just want to rest, if that's all right."

I slept as much of that week as I could, which wasn't easy, for the army was on the march and the surgeon wouldn't let me alone. I'd no sooner burrow into my blanket than he'd be carving another notch in my arm, or trying to pour a tartar emetic down me for to purge whatever the bloodletting didn't get. Once I'd puked to satisfy him, he'd leave, but then Caty Greene would wake me. She'd have me up and into a wagon, or sitting a horse in front of her, holding me tight, for I was so weak I'd slide right off otherwise. Seemed we always moved at night, and in the rain. Later, I learned that Washington shifted the army time and again, determined to keep his beaten, shoeless troops between the king's forces and Philadelphia, so's to offer battle—and win this time.

But the best we did was stay near the government's men. When they marched, we marched; when they stopped, we stopped. Our guide was the beating of drums. I remember shivering, and damp clothes chafing me, but not much else of that week for I was burning with fever, brought on, the surgeon said, by chasing after the army with a ball in my thigh.

Finally, I woke in my right mind. I was in another bed and another room. Caty Greene was still there, this time darning socks.

"Ma'am?" I croaked.

She dropped her yarn to help me sit and sip rum. I pulled a face and begged some milk, forgetting that this was an army camp.

"Or syllabub," I added wistfully.

"You find some, you share it with me, won't you?" she said tartly.

Then I recalled that I was with the troops somewhere, and such a simple thing as milk, let alone syllabub, belonged to another life.

I nodded. "I surely will, Mrs. Greene. You've been more than kind, caring for me like this. What is today? Where are we?"

"It's Wednesday, the, ah, let's see, seventeenth of September. You've been sleeping nigh a week."

"But we're not at the Brandywine anymore, are we, or close by? I remember we were riding all night, I think."

"That's right." She held the rum to my lips again, and to be agreeable, I drank some. "Thunderstorm ruined our ammunition, so we're at Reading Furnace, waiting for more to come."

She helped me change my dressings, then asked if I could sit at table and eat. I answered without realizing what she meant. "I'm hungry as a soldier."

"Good. His Excellency's been requesting the honor of our presence with his family. I think you're well enough to attend him now, don't you?"

I gulped. To face a man of such integrity after the lie I'd lived, not to mention all his aides—

"Surely the girl brave enough to fight Redcoats isn't afraid to go to dinner," Mrs. Greene murmured. She was all pert and eager, and I was minded of her reputation as a lively lady who loved dancing and men about equally.

"'Course not. 'Tis my pleasure." Then inspiration struck. "But I have naught to wear."

"You'll look a proper Continental, then, won't you?" She bustled away to return carrying a dress such as I'd not donned for two months. "'Tis an old one of mine, and nigh threadbare," she said as she laid it across the bed. "I was going to rip it up for bandages, but I patched it for you instead."

"You're very kind." But I was thinking otherwise, what with her destroying my excuse that way.

"I knew you'd need clothes for when you go home, but it'll serve now, too. Hurry, 'tis past three of the clock, and you have but half an hour to dinner."

His Excellency's face bore more lines than I remembered, and his gravity seemed more severe. But his eyes sparkled at sight of Caty Greene, and he smiled graciously as ever. I sheltered behind her until she curtsied. His Excellency caught sight of me then as he straightened from his bow. I will always love General Washington for what he did next.

"Miss Shippen." He spoke quietly so that only Mrs. Greene and I could hear. "I understand from your captain's commendation that if all our soldiers were of your quality, we'd have secured our freedom long ago." Taking my hand, he turned to the rest. "Gentlemen," he continued, "we are graced this day by two delightful ladies, Mrs. Greene and Miss Shippen." His warm smile wrapped me in respectability.

His Excellency seldom acted as host, preferring to eat in peace while an aide did that duty, which, this day, was Alex Hamilton. As the only women, we were seated to King Alex's left and right. I was doubly honored when His Excellency took the place on my other side, with the Greenes across from us.

Caty's husband grinned each time I caught his gaze. He seemed to think I'd pulled a grand joke and laughed at all my witticisms when he wasn't laughing at his wife's.

But not Hamilton. His nose stuck so high in the air I wondered he didn't drown in the rain that spoiled our ammunition. Whether he disapproved more of my escapade or my ugliness, I knew not, for he was the sort dismisses any lady not pretty and pleasing.

Then King Alex defended government when General Greene mentioned our losses from the Brandywine.

"Final returns showing near a thousand troops killed, wounded or captured," Greene said. "That's ten percent of our forces."

"Against only 600 British casualties." Hamilton wiped his mouth. "Another battle like that…" He shrugged. "We took a beating, but what can we expect? They're the finest army in the world, brave, spirited men and good officers."

I was fidgeting in my chair, trying to ease my wound, so perhaps I misheard. Such speech was surprising, even if true. But his next words shocked me. "A clear proof of government's superiority." Hamilton raised his glass. "And a rebuke to those claiming 'tis government itself that's the trouble, that it can't do anything right. We finally win this war and establish our own nation, we'd do worse than have a system designed along the British Empire's lines."

I was astonished that any man fighting for freedom, especially in Washington's own family, would say such. But the others must have been used to it, for they continued eating. My head pounded.

"Colonel," I began, "that government you admire stole taxes from us so its soldiers can kill folks and burn their homes. I saw them hang a captain of this army as though he were a dog, and—"

"Indeed." Hamilton sniffed. "We've all seen such things, madam. You're not the only soldier in this army."

"No," I said deliberately, "but I pray God you're its only slave."

I had the satisfaction of seeing him flush before General Greene changed the subject.

I limped to my chamber shortly after. That I'd been permitted a retort to Hamilton, and him a colonel, proved I was no longer a soldier, that I'd bled in vain. By week's end, I'd be well enough for the journey to Philadelphia, where one day was pretty much like another and I could do nothing for the Cause. I stifled my sobs in my pillows and slept late the next morning.

When I finally left my bed, I chanced upon Caty Greene rolling bandages. "His Excellency asks you to attend him," she said, pointing to the house's front parlor.

Light flooded the room. All its tables had been pushed to the center to make one surface, and this covered with maps. These His Excellency studied with Nathanael Greene while Hamilton scribbled notes. King Alex didn't even bow before he left. General Greene lingered, but his banter was what he'd exchange with any lady, not the talk of battle soldiers share.

Then His Excellency and I were alone. I stood dreading whatever punishment King Alex had persuaded him to wreak on me.

"Miss Shippen." He hesitated. But his next words were not the condemnation I feared. "I said last night, and I meant it, you made a fine soldier."

"Thank you, sir."

"If it wouldn't entirely destroy discipline, I'd commission you myself."

I could hardly credit my ears. "I'll serve in the ranks, sir! I—"

He held up a hand to stanch my words, though with a kindly chuckle. "There's something else, another favor you can perform, Miss Shippen, if you're willing."

I nodded, but sadly, thinking he'd send me home with gratitude for how the ladies' mittens helped the Cause.

"You're still living in Philadelphia? With the Edward Shippen family?"

"Yes, sir."

"Your uncle must be unhappy with your, ah, service to us. His sympathies are Loyalist, aren't they?"

"Not so much as you may think, sir. He really only cares for his family and business. Besides, I—I didn't tell him where I was going." The note I'd left said only that I'd soon return and not to worry.

His brows quirked. "He has no idea you're here?"

I explained that neither my uncle nor anyone in his family knew of my Patriotism. "Anyway," I added, "he's fled Philadelphia."

"But he'll be going back?" Washington asked.

"Well, sir, he's got property to protect." I shifted uncomfortably. 'Twas strange, this interest in my uncle.

"Good." He tapped the map spread before him. "Miss Shippen, Philadelphia's going to fall before the campaign ends, but there's naught to be done. Howe has too many troops, and they're too well armed for us to hold them off any longer."

"But what's he want with it?"

His eyes glinted. "With Philadelphia?"

"Yes, sir, I mean, it's where the Congress sits, but they'll just pick up and run, first Redcoat that's sighted, as they been doing all summer. And there's no buildings for them to capture neither, 'cause Congress rents a hall to sit in. Don't seem there's much point to taking Philadelphia. It'll do nothing to defeat us."

I was only repeating what we'd argued around the cookfire the last weeks, whilst we waited for our stew, when we had any, to simmer. Lif was sure the king's forces would take Philadelphia, and that it'd be a mortal blow, but Asa was just as sure 'twouldn't matter, for the reasons I'd just said. I agreed with Asa, especially when he added, "Be a regular blessing them Redcoats take Philadelphia, 'cause mayhap this time they won't be too bumbleheaded to get the Congress, too. Be a whole lot easier to fight without them blockheads interfering all the time. Bunch of speechifying lawyers down there, happy to tell the rest of us how to live and die and asking us, please, can we give them our money. I just hope the Redcoats get 'em afore the war's over and they take to laying taxes on us."

"Taxes?" Lif nigh dropped his spoon. "What taxes? What we fighting for then, huh? Gonna pay taxes anyway, what's it matter if it's Congress or George III taking our money?" He shook his head. "Just can't believe—Congress'd never steal taxes. Why, they're Americans, same as us."

"Huh! You don't know nothing. Anytime you get a bunch of lawyers together, or even normal men, don't matter, and you call them Parliament or Congress or whatever, why, next thing you know, they're thinking they got a right to your money and laying all kinds of schemes and plans to get it. Let's just hope them Redcoats grab Philadelphia and the Congress and welcome to them."

Remembering Asa's words, I smiled, and His Excellency did, too. "Well, Miss Shippen, I devoutly hope General Howe's not as astute as you. Let him waste his time and supplies capturing something 'twill do him little good."

"Absolutely, sir."

"We'll go into winter quarters somewhere nearby and pray Heaven we're stronger in the spring. Meanwhile, we've been working on an intelligence network for Philadelphia for a while." He looked sorrowful, as though begging pardon for speaking such wickedness. "There's some folks in place there who'll report to us on enemy movements and plans, couple of bakers and booksellers and others who'll have concourse with the Redcoats." He studied me. "They're good, honorable people, Miss Shippen."

Once, I wouldn't have believed a spy could be good or honorable. But that was before Nathan.

The general cleared his throat. "I could find great use for a lady who lives with one of the leading families, who'll be attending parties and dinners with the king's officers, and who's got such a grasp of military matters as you just demonstrated, Miss Shippen. 'Tis as good as having someone at enemy headquarters, beyond my fondest hopes."

I stood stunned. "You—you want me to—to—"

"To spy, Miss Shippen, yes."

There 'twas, as gross an insult as could be, asking me to lie and betray for the best of Causes. "Like Captain Hale," I said softly.

"Though I pray you'll meet a less severe fate. You'll have this in your favor, at least: ladies usually don't arouse the suspicion male intelligencers do."

"I'd be a spy." I repeated it wonderingly, and he nodded.

"And on your own family, too, Miss Shippen, or rather by using them, for which I apologize, of course. I apologize for all of this, but the war—we speak and act in ways we never imagined. If you decline—"

"Decline, sir?" I shook my head. "No, sir, I accept, and I thank you for it."

Now it was his turn to stare wonderingly. "You won't thank me should they find you out. They hang women in London. I doubt they'll use better manners here."

"What sort of information you want, sir?"

"Anything pertaining to troop movements, plans for attack, numbers present and fit for duty, things like that. I daresay most of what you hear will be gossip, but officers at parties say things to make a lady laugh that they'd be court-martialled for anywhere else. So you'll need to be critical in your observations rather than a mere retailer of vulgar reports. Combine the best information you can get with attentive observation. That'll prove the most likely means to obtain something useful."

"And then what? Do I write it, or—"

"Write down what you can and send it along to me. Major John Clark's overseeing things there. I'll have him meet with you, tell you how to pass along what you've got. If it's something monumental, something you shouldn't commit to paper, contrive to see me yourself, or General Greene. Or," his eyes twinkled, "King Alex."

Chapter Twelve

I never breathe a word to Arnold about my time with the Continentals. Far as he knows, I'm lukewarm to the Cause. 'Tis true I admire him enough to write his life, but he understands you can marvel at the cabinetmaker's skill whilst shrugging at the chair he fashioned. Still, it's hard, acting as though I care naught for what means the world to me. But then I remember a certain blue-eyed hero depending from a noose, and I swallow and say nothing.

Brandywine will always stir me because I fought in it. Following after was the massacre at Paoli, where a detachment of Howe's army bayonetted our boys as they lay sleeping. Then come the battle in Germantown a few weeks later.

Our troops fought and suffered and died at all these, and Redcoats did too. Pity, then, that none of the three decided anything, that all they did was separate husbands from wives and sons from parents and steal the breath from boys who might have lived to be men.

But seemed that didn't grieve such Loyalists as Becky Franks. She joked to Peggy that a rebel, "one of their mangy officers, you know, the kind could give a dog fleas" had asked her if the Continental arms had not been crowned with great success since the commencement of the war.

"Well." Becky glanced sideways, wickedly witty. "I said I knew nothing as to their arms, but their legs were surprisingly successful—in running away."

Yet our boys hadn't run. Instead, they danced with Howe and accomplished nothing. At least they amused him enough that he didn't march north, up Hudson's River, to help General Johnny Burgoyne.

Poor Burgoyne with his 7000 professional soldiers, his supplies so abundant it took 500 carts to haul them through New York's wilderness, his gleaming cannon that needed 1400 horses to pull them—1400 horses, mind you, he must pry from sullen farmers—poor Burgoyne, I say, and all his troops who were marching towards the ragged, hungry, sickly Northern Department of the Continental Army—and Benedict Arnold.

When I ask about the summer and fall of 1777 at breakfast next morning, Arnold eases his leg with a grimace. "'Twas their Grand Strategy, you know. Ever since the war begun, they been trying to, ah, hmm—"

He stops, for his betrayal of West Point was the Grand Strategy's latest manifestation. But I know what he was going to say. Since the war begun, the government's thought cutting New England off from the rest of us would scotch our rebellion. As though only folks born east of Hudson's River want to live free.

Arnold coughs, and Flash, dreaming at his feet, wakes with a bark. "Anyway, in '77, enemy—ah, I mean, the Redcoats came up with this foolproof plan. They'd have an army under Burgoyne start down from Canada towards Albany, like Snarleton the year before, secure Lake Champlain and Hudson's River as they went. Another army'd sail down the St. Lawrence to the backcountry in New York and then march east, towards Albany, subduing us—I mean, the rebels in the Mohawk Valley along the way. Then a third army under Howe's gonna sally up from the City here, crush the rebellion along Hudson's River and meet the other two at Albany. Three arrows, you see, all aiming at the same heart."

Flash sniffs Arnold's hand, hoping for a pat. Arnold obliges. "Trouble was, nobody ordered Howe up to Albany until it's too late. So instead he fought at the Brandywine Creek and Germantown. Maybe you remember hearing about those battles, Clem?"

"Think I do."

"Well, anyway, Washington was wise to British plans even if Howe wasn't. He knew exactly what they're trying to do and what a fatal blow it'd be. So he asked me if I'd raise some militia, which was damn— ah, very clever because this way I'm not under Congress' authority. They can't criticize and second-guess me anymore—well, actually, they could, but so what? I'm commanding *militia*, not Congress' Continental troops. Withal, Washington didn't have enough regiments to defend

Philadelphia, let alone giving me a couple of 'em. So he told me to collect every man I could on my way north…"

"All Burgoyne must do is sail down Lake George, push through some woods to Hudson's River, and ride it to Albany. And the war's over." General Schuyler folded his hands and gazed calmly at Arnold. "That is, unless we stop him."

They were sitting in Schuyler's temporary quarters at Fort Edward, a small enclave chopped from the wilderness, surrounded by forests and swamps brooding breathlessly in the heat. A whine rose from those swamps. Merely thinking on the swarms of mosquitoes producing such din made a man itch. Outside Schuyler's office, troops drilled on the parade. Their officers' commands droned on July's somnolence.

Arnold waved away a cloud of gnats to study the map spread before them. It showed Burgoyne's progress, with the posts that had fallen to him crosshatched: Ticonderoga, Skenesborough, Fort Anne. Directly in his path lay Fort Edward and the Continentals quartered there. And like a rattler coiled to strike a man battling brigands for his life came another force, half Redcoat, half Iroquois, under Colonel Barry St. Leger from the west. The two armies planned to rendezvous at Albany and await Howe's march north from New York. Once he joined them, the government would fully control the Hudson Valley and geographically divide the colonies. The war would indeed be over.

"Burgoyne must be stopped." Schuyler smashed a mosquito biting his neck.

"My recommendation, too, sir," Arnold said.

"Country's in a panic, and I confess to my surprise at how fast panic turns a man into a Tory."

"Crawling out from under the rocks, are they?"

"And signing up with Burgoyne." Schuyler put his fingertips together and rested his chin on them. "He's got all the cannon he could want, thousands of soldiers. He's got the Iroquois scouting for him, petrifying folks—" Schuyler shook his head. "'Tis discouraging, General."

"More so for him than us, though, sir."

"That's what I'm hoping, too." Schuyler smiled wistfully. "All those cannon, all those troops, they're slowing him down. And then his baggage train, spies say it's a couple of miles long. Burgoyne doesn't leave comfort behind when he campaigns in the wilderness."

"They don't call him 'Gentleman Johnny' for nothing." Arnold barely resisted rubbing his hands with glee. Turning an enemy's advantages against him was a favorite ploy, one that had yet to fail him. "Roads up there aren't any too easy, neither."

"No, sir, mostly they're just a mule track through the forest that won't even take an ox, let alone the teams and wagons Burgoyne's trying to shove through. He's got his engineers laying out lines for his advanced units to clear. Then they put down logs as a road for the wagons."

"Be a pity if some of those logs went missing after the Redcoats worked so hard to lay them. I don't know about you, General, but I can always use good firewood."

Schuyler's smile grew to a grin. "I'm glad you're here, General Arnold. Something told me a man of your determination wouldn't sit back and wring his hands. Tell you what, I'm dividing my army and giving you command of half. Think that'll be enough men for you to stop Burgoyne?"

Arnold set his troops to chopping trees against the Redcoats' momentum, damming streams to flood the country, felling trunks in heaps across the path so that the enemy must work twice as hard to clear it. "They'll have a surprise waiting for them, hey, boys?" he said, for no sooner had the trees settled in tangled piles than rattlesnakes and copperheads slithered under them to make their dens.

Sometimes, Arnold insinuated his troops between the government's advanced team and its army. The road that team had laid stretched raw and ugly through the wilderness, stumps marching along either side. Between them moldered the ashes of old cookfires, rusty kettles, beef bones, peach pits, and the shallow holes of hastily dug privies. His men harnessed the logs to winches and oxen. Then, winches groaning and oxen straining, they pried those logs from their mud. Drovers cursed and whips snapped, but at last the road disappeared. In its place lay a bog the oxen churned to black muck.

They slowed the enemy's advance to a crawl. Still, Burgoyne was chopping his way through a mile of forest each day, a mile closer to Albany...

⌒≈⌒

The clock chimes, and Arnold comes back from Saratoga with a start. "Ten already!" he exclaims. "Clem, I swear, I don't know whether you're a better conversationist or cook."

Once again, guilt keeps my eyes from meeting his. Nor can I even mutter my thanks for such kind words. The best I manage is a nod as he drains his tea.

"There's a gentleman I'm meeting today, talk over a few deals," he says. "Won't be back until dinner."

I want to ask can he take his wife with him so's I have another chance to search his papers. Instead, I say, "But you'll tell me the rest about Saratoga tonight then, right? For the book."

"Absolutely," he says. "Fine breakfast, Clem, thanks."

I clean the kitchen, then settle down with paper and quill. Recording what Arnold told me this morning takes several hours. I read it over, add a comment here or there, and then it's time to start cooking again.

Arnold doesn't say much about Saratoga over our mutton for fear of boring Peggy. But at last, she retires upstairs and we settle into our chairs.

It's prodigiously cold this afternoon as the sun sets. Seems no matter how close I scoot to the fire, I'm still shaking and coughing. And that after a hot dinner and a pot of tea. The hall clock shows half past four, but it's dark as midnight with a storm howling outside.

"Have a seat there on the hearth, Clem." Arnold points to its warm, red bricks. "Maybe Flash'll lie next to you. He's as good as a foot warmer, all the heat he throws off."

I sit down, Indian-fashion. "Here, boy."

Flash, standing aside Arnold's chair, cocks his head, then lays it on his master's thigh.

I hold my hands to the fire. They're so stiff they won't even clutch my embroidery needle. "Burgoyne never did reach Albany, did he, sir?"

He smiles, but he's far away, lost in the wilderness and glory of Saratoga. "Too many of us between him and it, Clem. There's militia pouring into our camp every day, and Washington'd sent some reinforcements north." He scowls. "New commander, too."

I stay silent, for what is there to say? Granny Gates was the new commander, and if the enemy had picked him, they couldn't have served themselves better than the blockheads in Congress did. Never mind that Schuyler's strategy of slowing the Redcoats, wearing them down mile by mile, was working: Congress replaced him with Gates.

Not because Gates had a better plan, or was braver, or even that he'd inspire the farmers thereabouts to come fight. No, 'twas politics, pure and simple. Gates had gone to Philadelphia time and again, feasting and flattering the delegates, turning the heads of men who hadn't any more sense than a hungry Esau sniffing Jacob's stew. By now Granny had plenty of friends in Congress. And they made him a general, though they shouldn't have, any more than you'd fashion muskets from dough.

Seems some folks seize on the thing they haven't any bent for and turn that into their life's dream. With Gates, 'twas the military. He figured himself for the greatest warrior of our age, shrewd as that Prussian fellow Frederick the Great, or—don't laugh now—General Washington.

Now here come Gates up to Saratoga, no more a hero than you or me, but wanting to be, wanting it fierce as a man can. So far, he's not lifted his sword against the government, nor sent even one ball into its soldiers' ranks, much less won a victory, for in this contest he's not yet stepped onto a battlefield. And there goes Benedict Arnold, hero of half a dozen actions. Strategy and tactics, leadership and courage were natural to him as breathing. Gates would never learn half as much about war as Arnold was born knowing. You better believe Gates was jealous. And still fuming over Valcour Island, too.

"Pity about Schuyler," Arnold's saying. "They wronged him and that's the fact. But I wanted to get off on the right foot with Gates, hoped he'd let bygones be bygones. So I reported to him. We even shared some beer his scouts captured from a Hessian supply line…"

"To you, Arnold." Gates raised his mug, sloshing beer over the rim. "Good job out there. You've secured the whole Mohawk Valley to us, though I guess that's just a day's work to a hero like you." Though Granny's smile was innocuous, and had been all evening, malevolence lurked there. He belched, then continued. "And a course, 'cause of you, Burgoyne's got no reinforcements marching to meet him, nothing but his 5000 men. Whole camp's singing your praises, just like after you took the Ti, and Danbury, too."

Arnold nodded his thanks. "I'm hoping for a vigorous assault against them, sir. Got a score to settle."

Again, Gates smiled, but his bleary eyes narrowed. "Fought them hard up here the last two years, haven't you?"

"At Quebec and Valc—uh, Ticonderoga. Even got me a lame leg out of it, General, but no victories, at least not yet. I'm hoping to change that."

"Don't forget Valcour Island." Gates reached for the dipper on the barrel's edge but knocked it into the beer. He peered after it, muttered, "Aw, hell," then plunged his cup into the barrel and raised it, dripping. "This isn't gonna be any Valcour Island up here, is it, General?"

What did the old fool mean by that? Was he taunting Arnold with his defeat? Somehow, Arnold squeezed a "Sir?" past his fury, but Gates, savoring the beer, seemed not to hear. Shrugging, he said, "I could use a hero on my left wing. Whaddaya say?"

With an effort, Arnold calmed himself enough to accept.

He dined with Richard Varick the next evening. Now muster-master general of the army, Varick had recently left the staff of his cousin, General Schuyler. He relayed Schuyler's greetings, then reminisced about the previous summer, when he had worked tirelessly to secure provisions and ammunition at Valcour Island—only to find that his efforts would clothe or arm but half the troops. "Here's to more guns and uniforms this year, sir." Varick raised his glass. "And more brilliant victories like yours."

Arnold lifted his cup in turn. "I need another aide, Varick, and you're just the man I want, what with your spirit and diligence." Never realizing that Gates considered Varick a partisan of Schuyler, a spy the displaced general had sent to thwart his successor, Arnold said with a grin, "If you're good enough for Schuyler, you're good enough for me."

"I'm honored, sir."

Gates wasn't. When Arnold reported to headquarters the following day, Granny was sober but scowling and silent, refusing to divulge when the field officers would meet. Arnold shrugged and blamed Gates' usual prickliness. But it was still worrying him that evening, when a friendly voice hailed him.

"Arnold, they made you a general, huh?"

He turned to see Dan Morgan striding towards him, grinning.

"Proves them boys in the Congress don't know what they're about no more'n the king does." Morgan clapped his shoulder.

"Morgan!" Arnold's discouragement fled. Big, brash, inspiring, the Virginian was a tonic at any time, but especially now, with the officers at headquarters whispering while Granny Gates glared. He asked, "You here to fight?" and nearly added "the Redcoats," so bitter was the enmity among the American command.

"Me and the boys are here straight from His Excellency. He's been sparing all the reinforcements he can. But tell me something." Morgan flapped a hand at the gnats overhead. That scattered the insects but not the men gathering to gawk at two of the Continental Army's most legendary officers. "I asked for you up to headquarters, and you'd'a thought old Gates got a draught of vinegar, he screwed up his face so much. There bad blood atween you two? You been outshining him again?"

"Strangest thing, Morgan." Arnold spoke softly lest the swelling crowd hear, though that was unlikely. They were too busy calling to each other, "Look ye there...Morgan and Arnold...See, no waste timber in them, and bloody fellows they are... They don't care for nothing, they'll ride right in. It'll be 'Come on, boys,' 'twon't be, 'Go, boys'... Arnold's as brave a man as ever lived... Morgan, too, I was with 'em up to Quebec... Lobsterbacks don't stand a chance against us, now, what with them two here..."

Arnold tried to ignore the clamor, but such worship was distracting. "I, ah, never liked Gates over much, especially after all the trouble he give me last year on Champlain."

Morgan nodded. The hubbub around them grew louder.

"Then, this morning, I report to him—and I'm his second in command, remember. He put me in charge of the left wing, but you'd think I'm a leper, way he acts. He's holding meetings without me, orders me around as though I'm a sergeant, and a dumb one, too. Meanwhile, he's made John Brown a lieutenant colonel and inviting him to every meeting there is."

Morgan whistled. "Brown's up here? You two face off yet?"

"You think that coward'd face me? He knows I'll challenge him on sight, all the lies he's put out about me. No, he'll keep his distance."

"You all got duties to tend or not?" Morgan shouted at their admirers. "Go on, git back to what you were doing." As they drifted away, Morgan squinted at Arnold. "Gates is too mealy-mouthed to suit me."

"He wants to fight defensive all the time—don't matter how the odds are stacked in our favor."

"We got men pouring in every day, reinforcements thicker than fat on a hog. Now, Burgoyne, he must be careful. Every man he loses, new one's coming all the way from England or Canada. But you'd think it's the other end around, way Gates acts. Just dig in and sit it out, that's his take on things."

"That'll give Burgoyne the advantage then, from what our spies are saying. He figures we haven't the gumption to attack Regulars, so he's worked out a three-pronged strategy that oughta succeed, long as we fight defensive the way Gates wants."

"No gumption, huh?" Morgan's eyes went past him to the forest. "There's gonna be a big one, here, Arnold. I can feel it as I do when a storm's coming. Wind strips the leaves off the trees, they fall to the ground by the thousands, and that's what men hereabouts are doing, gathering by the thousands. Another couple of days, we'll outnumber the Redcoats."

"But that's militia against trained Regulars."

Morgan's gaze came back to him. "You're letting Gates sour you. Back home in the woods, we got us a kinda bee makes a nest in the ground. Maybe you got them here, too."

"Don't doubt it." Arnold slapped something stinging his hand. "They got every kind of insect in all creation here."

"Well, these nests I'm talking about look puny, like a 6-pounder ball made out of that brown paper them shopkeepers in Phillydelphia are always wrapping things in. Figure you could smash it under your boot, nice and easy. But them bees'll swarm out and sting you afore you're halfway done. Sting you to death."

"You got a point there, friend, or you just wagging your jaw?"

Morgan grinned, threw an arm around his shoulders. "Any grub in this camp, or is it like the ones you set up on the way to Quebec where a man boils his candles if he wants victuals?"

"Hear they slaughtered a dog this afternoon. Stew was kinda thin, but maybe you can mop it up with lillipu. Then, afterwards, what do you say to some reconnoitering? I been working with an engineer, looking for ground to fortify. Think we found some. It's square in the middle of Burgoyne's path to Albany. He'll need to fight us if he wants to get past us—'defensive,' see."

Snakes slithered before them as the two friends scaled the bluff above Hudson's River an hour later. More bluffs lay to the west, and hills dropped into ravines to the north.

Morgan surveyed the area, scratching insect bites the while, full face breaking into a grin. "About perfect, I'd say. We get us some redoubts and fortifications built, we'll have us a battlefield to be proud of. What's Gates say about it?"

Arnold shrugged. "What can he say? It's defensible, so he's happy, but it's far better'n that."

"Sure is." Morgan revolved slowly. "Redcoats can't get around us on the west, and we put some cannon up here on this bluff, they can't sail down the river, neither. All these hills and trees, they can't fight in ranks. They must fight our way, through the forest, and every time they do that, we beat 'em." His grin threatened to split his face. "I like it, Arnold, by gum. Better get the boys up here with their shovels. What they call this place?"

"See that tavern down there? That's Bemis' Tavern, and this here's Bemis Heights."

"Bemis Heights." Morgan savored the name as though it were wine. "Gonna have us a victory here, my friend. Gonna be limning that name Bemis Heights to our grandkids."

The leaves were reddening and, though it was only the eighteenth of September, the afternoon was cool when Arnold trudged north with his staff to check on the government's advance.

"Sir!" an aide named Clarkson cried. "Enemy on that hill yonder, I see them!"

Arnold peered through his spyglass. "So there are." The famous scarlet coats were faded and patched, and cut short to yield the material for patching. Word was an American privateer had captured the ship bearing new uniforms for Burgoyne's army.

Even better, the government's forces were mounted. They lay along their horses' necks, picking their way through the undergrowth, hacking at the brush with their swords. New York's wilderness was no place for riding. But Burgoyne, a cavalry officer from his first days with the royal forces, could imagine no other tactics.

"Well, gentlemen, I estimate they'll be here tomorrow, probably afternoon, if they move with their usual speed." He got a few nervous chuckles before turning towards camp.

"We gonna attack, sir?" Clarkson asked.

"When we spent all that time digging up Bemis Heights for their reception?" Again they twittered. In truth, Arnold hesitated to order out his troops lest Gates publicly countermand him.

The next morning dawned cold and foggy. Arnold dressed with care, brushing his uniform himself and endlessly straightening his epaulettes. He could only gulp coffee at breakfast, the steam rising from his mug indistinguishable from the misty air, but he made a show of eating so his aides would not think he dreaded the coming battle. He did, but it was the one he would have with Gates, not Burgoyne. So far, though the enemy had camped two miles from them last night, Gates had issued no orders nor prepared the troops.

The fog took its time lifting, but once it did, scouts reported that the Redcoats were marching in three columns, directly towards them.

Arnold ordered his division to arms. Men grabbed muskets, ammunition, bayonets, then stood on parade as drums rattled and the sun climbed the sky. After half an hour, guns trailed; after an hour, the troops talked, joked, lounged, while Arnold fumed. Still no orders, still no indication that Gates knew Redcoats were in the area, let alone moving. What was going on at headquarters?

"Here." He scribbled a note and handed it to Clarkson. "Take this to Gates. Tell him I'm requesting permission for Morgan and Dearborn to advance."

The lounging men had barely shifted position before Clarkson was back. "Permission denied, sir."

Arnold fumed for the next hour. Most of the militia dozed under the noon sun, while the rest muttered they hadn't turned out to fight Redcoats only to sit like idlers round a checkerboard and wait for Burgoyne to come kill them.

"What's Gates thinking of?" Arnold complained when Morgan rode up for orders.

"Defensive, like you said."

"Enemy's probably outflanked us by now, we—"

Cannon boomed. Trees and brush flew into the air to their left, and the men sleeping there leaped to their feet, yowling.

"Damn Gates," Arnold cried, "they're in range! Clarkson, hey, get to headquarters. Tell Gates I've sent Morgan and Dearborn to attack!"

Arnold watched through his glass as Morgan's riflemen pushed south towards a house at the edge of a meadow, where Regulars had fallen out while their officers surveyed the countryside from its roof. Rifles smoked, he thought he heard their popping, and officers in scarlet and white fell. The Redcoats scrambled for cover, reformed their lines. Then, fifes shrilling, they advanced. Bayonets flashed, men in buckskin and linen fell.

The hours seemed minutes as Arnold led troops into battle. All he knew of the passing time was that the sun, which had flashed on cannon and bayonets, now skulked behind clouds of powder smoke, while dead and mangled men littered the ground.

He jotted another order, thrust it at Clarkson. "Take this to the Hampshire colonels!" he shouted. "Get their brigades in there!"

But Clarkson shook his head. "Can't, sir. You—"

"Forgot! I sent them in already, didn't I? I'm going for reinforcements."

Arnold galloped hard for headquarters. When he reached the small, ramshackle cabin, he marched past an aide into Gates' office. The aide lunged, but Arnold neatly sidestepped him so that the boy hit the door-post with an "Ooof."

"More troops, Gates," Arnold shouted. "I need more troops!"

Ashen, face sunken as an old man's, Gates rose as though dazed from behind a table covered with maps and muster rolls.

"General Gates!" What was wrong with him? "I need troops, sir, and any orders you have for me!"

Gates shook his head, then muttered, "Defend, defend."

"General, I need ord—"

"I—I have no orders, sir, beyond—remember, we're defending." Both tone and gaze were vague.

"I'm taking more regiments into battle, then, General."

At this, a spark fired in Gates' eye. "Leave me Scammel's brigade, sir. Somebody needs to protect headquarters."

For a moment, Arnold was too stunned to reply. Then, voice dripping contempt, he said, "I shouldn't worry, sir. You're two miles from the field, safe as a baby in its mother's arms."

Returning to battle, Arnold spotted a gap in the enemy's line. He rallied his troops and charged, but Regulars rushed forward to throw him back. He reformed his line to try again, and again. Each time, they poured more Redcoats at him; each time, he led more men to the assault, until he had engaged all 3000 troops under his command. The scarlet line wavered, stunned and disheartened. Morgan's riflemen aimed at the officers, leaving soldiers to mill about, leaderless.

Then, from the right, Arnold heard voices rise in a hymn. Hessians! *Burgoyne's used up all his Regulars and now he's throwing in the Hessians! Way he despises them, he must be desperate.*

"Come on, my brave boys!" He spurred his horse for another charge.

"By God," Morgan shouted after their sixth assault, "once more oughta do her!"

"I'm gonna go wring more reinforcements outa Gates." Arnold wheeled his horse close to Morgan. "Get 'em formed up and ready for another try. We'll attack soon as I'm back."

"Arnold, the day's ours!" Morgan grinned like a boy about to trounce the schoolyard's bully.

Once again, Arnold galloped the two miles to headquarters, ears ringing from the cannon, the screaming horses and men. He found Gates, red with fury, on the porch with his aides. Clearly, the gibe about a baby in its mother's arms had found its mark. "Arnold, damn you—"

"I need more troops, Gates, order out reinforc—"

"Like hell I will! I gave orders—"

"The victory's ours! We're gonna drive them from the field! Their whole line's giving way!"

Instead of softening, Gates grew angrier. "I gave orders at the start of this. Defensive, sir, I told you *defensive*. I didn't want to commit the whole army, not when—"

"Gimme more men, *now*, or we're gonna lose our advantage. Burgoyne's using *Hessians*! You know what that means."

Gates spluttered as an aide blurted, "The baggage! He left the Hessians guarding his baggage."

Arnold nodded eagerly. "Gates, get some troops down there and capture his baggage, all his stores, his food, he must needs surrender or starve. I'll keep him busy on the field. Just gimme more regiments!"

"I'm not ordering any more troops out, raw militia against Regulars." Gates was shaking, in body and voice. "Damn it, I gave you permission for a reconnoitering force, Arnold, and that's all. You're not getting a damned thing beyond that."

Arnold stared, almost deaf from battle and supposing he had misheard. "You're gonna cost us the victory!"

"Gonna cost *you* the victory, you mean." A sly smile broke through Gates' rage before his face contorted again. "No glory for you, Arnold, what do you—"

"There's glory a-plenty for both of us! Get down there to the riverside and capture their baggage, Gates. It's—"

"You giving me orders, Arnold?" Gates hissed. "I don't need you to teach me war. Now get outa here, back to your reconnoitering. Reconnoitering *only*, remember."

Disbelieving, numb, Arnold mounted his horse. Somehow he found himself at the battle, leading troops towards the enemy's center.

"Sir!" An aide galloped from the flank. "Hessians, sir, attacking on our right. We're falling back."

Damn Gates! Hessians attacking instead of guarding baggage, and Gates too petty to improve on that. "We need more men!" Arnold wheeled his horse for another dash to headquarters.

Gates and his aides still clustered on the porch, stiff and hostile. Arnold reined to a stop before them. "Sir, I need one more regiment!"

"You're in direct violation of orders, sir!" Gates nearly hopped up and down. "I'll have you cashiered if it's the last thing I do!"

"Sir, please." Arnold was as close to begging as he came. "Order out more troops! We can still carry the day. Learned's regiment, General— have them circle around behind the Hessians."

Gates studied him, then turned to an aide. "Colonel Lewis, order out the rest of Learned's brigade."

Arnold wheeled his horse.

"Colonel Lewis," Gates continued, "tell Learned *he* is to lead the attack." He paused, then snarled, "General Arnold!"

Arnold threw Gates a glance over his shoulder. "Sir?"

"You'll await further orders." Gates gave a small, triumphant smile. "Here, sir, with us."

Arnold had already touched his spurs to his horse and must saw at the reins to pull the animal back, amusing Gates and his family. He dismounted as creakily as in a nightmare.

His weary mount nosed the grass while the sound of musketry teased Arnold. The enemy would be pummelling his boys, the victory once so close now receding. Then again, Learned's troops could reinforce them and win the thing if led effectively. Arnold reached for his spyglass as Learned's men began their march. He watched until they strayed into the woods, lost and floundering, then lowered the glass, unable to witness such disaster.

Lewis had returned. "Fighting's still indecisive, sir," he told Gates, while Arnold's gut roiled.

Inside him, something snapped. "By God, I will soon put an end to it!" Arnold vaulted into his saddle.

He was halfway to the field before he realized one of Gates' aides was neck and neck with him. "Sir!"

Arnold ignored him, leaning over his mare until foam flew up and nearly blinded him.

"General Arnold, you're to return to headquarters, sir, by direct command of General Gates. General Arnold, sir!"

The aide, on a fresh mount that had not galloped between headquarters and battle a half-dozen times, was in front of Arnold now. It was no use. Arnold let his heaving horse slow to a stop, then sat staring towards the battle as the sun set.

"General Arnold—"

"I heard you! Now leave me the hell alone!"

The Redcoats claimed the field that night, giving them the victory. The "if only's" banged in Arnold's head and knotted his stomach. Had headquarters reinforced him, had he met with even a dram of cooperation from Gates instead of resistance as fierce as Burgoyne's, he would have broken the enemy's center to win the day.

At least the government paid dearly for its victory. Returns showed 600 British casualties, against half that many American. Arnold held Gates responsible for the deaths and defeat.

The Redcoats would be shaken after so many losses, confused and vulnerable. Arnold eagerly awaited the next morning when battle would resume, God and Gates willing.

But whatever Granny wanted, Providence decided against more fighting. A cold, dense fog, worse than yesterday's, blanketed both armies. Water dripped from tents, dampening muskets and powder horns. Soldiers vainly tried to heat coffee over drenched wood as Arnold rode through camp to headquarters.

Outside Gates' hovel, he looped his reins around the soaked hitching post. Then he marched into the commander's office.

He did not even bother with a salutation before saying. "We need to attack, sir, immediately, soon as this fog lifts and we can dry out our powder. They'll be reeling, all the punishment we gave them yesterday."

"Hmmm." Gates did not lift his eyes from the letter he was writing.

"We need to attack, sir, now, before they dig in and entrench."

Gates dipped his quill, signed his name with a flourish. Still, he said nothing.

"General, look." Arnold leaned on his fists over the desk. "More time we give them, the more works they'll build. We've got mostly militia out there. They're good at forest fighting, but I lead them against entrenched Regulars, gonna be twice as hard to win."

"Wilky, here." Gates beckoned to the aide hovering behind him, one who had attended Arnold at Quebec. Wilkinson did not so much as glance at Arnold now. "Copy this over for the file, will you? Now, General Arnold." Gates tipped back in his chair and waved at the window with his sly smile. "There'll be no fighting today, sir. I'm afraid Heaven itself is against you."

"Tomorrow, then," Arnold said through clenched teeth. "I just want orders to attack as soon as—"

Gates let his chair drop on its four feet. "You must excuse me." The smile gave way to a scowl of freezing hate. "I very much assure you, I can manage my affairs without your assistance."

Arnold approached Gates several more times, urging an attack, suggesting postings for various regiments. Gates either insulted or ignored him.

Came the day Wilkinson barred the door. Perhaps it was just as well: Arnold had heard that Gates' report on the battle to Congress mentioned neither him nor his troops. Had he set eyes on Granny, he would have horsewhipped him.

"Might as well curse a hound for baying," Morgan said over their salt pork and Indian meal that evening. "'Tis his nature, no more'n what I looked for. He can't tell his friends in Congress what really happened, now, can he? Tell them he hid back there, miles away, while we were fighting and dying? Soon as Congress heard that, he'd be out of a command, friends or no."

Arnold snorted. "You got a lotta faith in Congress."

Gates' next affront came the third morning after the battle. Arnold read the day's General Orders with bile souring his mouth: "Colonel Morgan's corps not being attached to any brigade or division of the army, he is to make returns and reports to headquarters only, from whence alone he is to receive orders."

Arnold waited until evening lest he throttle Gates. Still, he arrived at headquarters breathing fire. Once again, he brushed past Wilkinson to burst into the office and find Granny at his desk.

Gates knocked over a mug of coffee leaping to his feet. "I thought I told Wilky you're not—"

"Why'd you do it, Gates?" He smashed a fist on Gates' desk, splashing coffee. "Whaddaya mean, Morgan's not attached to any division of the army? He's with *my* division, the left wing, you can't just go—"

"*Your* division, sir? In *my* army? You carry no commission from Congress, do you? So you have no authority but what I choose to give you!"

"You—you—Morgan marched with me to Quebec—" Arnold broke off. He had not meant to whine.

Triumph shone in Gates' eyes. "Anyway, I've recalled General Lincoln, sir, from Ticonderoga. Just wait till he gets here. He's twice the soldier you ever were."

Arnold stood speechless. Fat Benjamin Lincoln, a plodding and unimaginative officer Congress had promoted over him, was a menace to nobody but chickens pecking in a barnyard when they could be frying in a skillet. To compare Arnold with a man more adept at wielding a fork than a sword stung beyond bearing.

"Respectful to his commander, too," Gates hissed. "You could take a lesson from him—"

What did that signify? Was Gates threatening to replace him as the left wing's commander with *Lincoln*?

"—he oughta be here soon. And, even better, the whole army's not in love with him. Oh, you're the big hero now, way you almost broke the enemy's line, just like Valcour, but, damn it, I'm the commander here. I was commander at Valcour. The credit's mine."

"You wanna be a hero, Gates, then quit hiding back here two miles from the fighting—"

"You fool, I—"

"—letting brave boys die, refusing the reinforcements that coulda saved them!"

Gates stuttered incoherently, red as any British uniform.

"You're a jealous old biddy, Gates!" Arnold shouted, ragged and shrill. He paused for breath, heard only silence, realized the whole house was listening. "You'd rather lose than have me win it for us!"

"We got no more call for you here anymore, Arnold. Whaddaya think of that?" Gates shook a fist, voice as shrill as Arnold's. "Get your bags packed and get out. I'll write you a pass—"

"Get out? General, if I hadn't led the troops, you'd be dining with Burgoyne today. 'Course, maybe that's what you're after, a Tory like you—"

"Get out, I said!"

"Go to hell." Arnold whirled and yanked open the door, sent the aides huddled there flying in all directions. "Eavesdropping asses!" he howled. "You're all damned cowards on a damned Tory's staff!"

Arnold stewed over their encounter the rest of the day, especially while writing a memorandum. Much as he hated to admit it, Gates was right: he must leave. Arnold added a postscript to his report, asking permission to travel to Philadelphia and join General Washington.

He occupied himself with paperwork and packing for the journey as he awaited Gates' pass. He was scribbling a note to Hannah when General Enoch Poor entered his office. Arnold poured them each some kill-devil.

"Thank you, sir." Poor raised the rum to his lips, then handed him a sheet of foolscap. "General Arnold, we're all of us, the whole army, sir, we, ah, we're grateful for what you did the other day."

"What I did?"

Poor nodded. "Yes, sir, in battle. We're mighty glad you were leading us—been a lot more casualties and prisoners otherwise. Redcoats would have taken the field early on."

Arnold had seldom been more surprised. Poor had presided over the court-martial last summer that interrupted preparations for Valcour, with sympathies obviously slanted against Arnold. "That—that's kind of you, General."

"Not kind, sir, accurate. And now, well, with us surrounding the enemy, sooner or later they're gonna move. They must break through our lines. All them Redcoats can't just while away the rest of the campaign here in the wilderness. When Burgoyne decides what he's doing, whether he's going back to Canada or trying for Albany, either way he'll fight us. We're gonna need you again, then." He pointed to the paper. "That's a petition, General. Heard you're thinking of leaving us here at the mercy of Gates, no disrespect to him or anything, but enemy'll flog us good if he's leading us. Half my regiment's threatening to desert if you leave, and it's that way all up and down the line. That petition's signed by my colonels and generals, asking you to stay. General Learned's division woulda signed, too, sir, but they's afraid of offending Gates." Poor added under his breath, "Man takes offense at everything nowadays."

The signatures swam beneath Arnold's gaze. Granny Gates might spurn his services, but others esteemed them.

Over the next fortnight, with no official duties or councils of war to attend, Arnold visited around camp. Everywhere, men clustered to talk with him, clap his shoulder, offer him a drink or some tobacco. Some sidled up merely to stand beside him, scuffing a toe in the dirt, grinning or, occasionally, turning away to wipe their eyes. Thus did he learn the army's capabilities and weaknesses in a way that Gates, entombed at headquarters, never would.

Arnold spent most evenings with Dan Morgan, listening to tales his riflemen brought of the enemy's encampment less than a mile away. The Redcoats had dropped in exhaustion there after the battle, and Gentleman Johnny had no more sense than to entrench within reach of American rifles. They were deep in the wilderness, true, but besieged as tightly as any city, with Morgan's men sighting through the falling leaves to pick off anyone who strayed and sometimes even those in camp.

Suffering most were the cavalry's horses, for they had grazed the place clean within a day. High-spirited and glossy, the beautiful animals belonged in English pastures, not American forests. Now, after two weeks without forage, they were dying under the crisp autumn sky.

"They're a sad sight to see." Morgan poked at the fire burning before his tent. "All them starving beasts, it just breaks your heart."

Arnold poured more coffee. "Supply lines are cut, too. We've got them surrounded. Can't nobody get through."

"The scene thickens fast." Morgan spit into the embers. Night was settling around them, with the first stars glittering. "Redcoats been on half-rations a week now."

"Let's take care nobody slips them our recipe for candle-soup. Nourishing as that is, they'll rise up and fight like demons."

Morgan bellowed a laugh.

Arnold asked, "You get any reports on that council of war Burgoyne held last night?"

Morgan nodded. "Same as the one he held coupla days ago, and the one afore that. They're still digging in, building redoubts, and old Gentleman Johnny's still saying he'll work his way around us. That Hessian fella, Rye Hazel Whoever—"

"Von Riedesel."

"He keeps saying they better retreat—"

Arnold snorted. He could see that council plain as though he were sitting in it: Burgoyne desperate in his gold braid and plumes, his worried officers drab as hens around a rooster—especially that no-nonsense von Riedesel, whom Burgoyne had belittled throughout the campaign. Arnold pictured Riedesel, sympathized with him, as the German's blue eyes unflinchingly met Burgoyne's. "I think," he would say in his guttural French, "*Herr* General, we take the retreat and—"

"*Battre en retraite?*" Burgoyne's lip would have curled. Only Anglo-Saxon curses could convey his disgust, and he would have lashed Riedesel with a few. Riedesel spoke English anyway, better than the other Hessians, so that Burgoyne added through his teeth, "I tell you for the last time, sir, this army must not retreat!"

"—but you know old 'Must-Not-Retreat' Burgoyne," Morgan was saying, "stubborn as my mule back home. He wants to wait for reinforcements. He's still thinking the Redcoats way down to New York City's gonna sail up Hudson's River, cut through our lines, and rescue him. You hear what Gates said about Burgoyne?"

"How he's an old gamester?"

Morgan nodded. "And likely to risk all upon one throw. Must admit Old Granny's spoke that right. That throw's coming up tomorrow, or I

miss my guess. Gentleman Johnny's planning to ride out on reconnaissance. Gonna take a coupla thousand troops with him."

"Coupla *thousand*? For reconnaissance?"

"He says they're gonna forage and probe our flanks." Morgan winked.

"Uh-huh." Arnold grinned. "Well, I got ten pounds here says he's
gonna make a break for it."

"Foraging, probing, running for safety, it don't matter." Morgan
smiled in turn. "Me and the boys'll be waiting for him. They'll get a
chokey mouthful of us."

"What will be the event, time must discover." Arnold tried for nonchalance, but his hand trembled as he flung the dregs of his coffee into
the fire. The longing to ride with Morgan, to drive the enemy back to
Canada, to triumph, was so overwhelming his eyes prickled. He had
worked hard for victory. It was unbearable not to see it realized.

Arnold waited the next day as long as he could. He heard a pop
from the advanced guard on the American center, signalling that the
enemy had been sighted, and watched troops forming for the march
to the front. They stood in silent ranks, nervously fingering muskets
and hatchets. Some stared at him as though begging for his presence
at their head. Others seemed accusing: "We may die out there whilst
you sit here, safe and secure." Then a man and boy, whom he took for
father and son, walked by, the man's hand on the boy's shoulder, the
boy gulping as he looked into his father's face. That decided Arnold:
he swung into his saddle for the gallop to Gates' headquarters. Surely
Granny was over his pique.

Arnold reined in just after Wilkinson, who raced past without even
a nod. Judging from the aide's excitement, he had returned from reconnaissance. Arnold could see Gates through the window, leaning back in
his chair, hands folded across his belly, bantering with his officers over
a dinner of ox's heart. His troops were about to tangle with the enemy,
men would be wounded and dying, yet Gates sat with a glass of wine
as though at leisure.

A mist danced before Arnold's eyes.

He wheeled his horse as Wilkinson sauntered out of the house and
insultingly called, "Morning, Mr. Arnold. Where are you going, sir?"

He streaked through the trees for the battle, hoping to outrun whom-
ever Gates sent to order him back. In a clearing rimmed with red and

gold trees, he found stragglers drinking at a stream. "Come on, brave boys! Come on!" he cried and dashed ahead of them towards the center of the line.

There stood Ebenezer Learned and his men with muskets dangling. "General Learned, sir, let's go!"

"But, sir, I—I—my orders are to defend, sir. Gates was—"

"Gates isn't here, General. I am, and I'm ordering you forward to victory. Follow me!" Arnold galloped towards the Hessians in their blue uniforms.

This first clear glimpse of the Germans showed him fearsome men huge as giants, one as alike as the next. Their yellow mustaches made them appear as animals, shaggy and untamed, while their muskets and swords seemed too big for mortal men to heft.

It took two charges to capture their hill, with Morgan appearing out of the dust to cheer Arnold's men, but finally, the Hessians fled.

Arnold galloped for Freeman's meadow, beyond which lay the British camp. The Americans' furious fire was forcing the Redcoats towards it from the field. In another moment, the Continentals would hold the ground. They would be the day's victors, and, according to Gates' defensive orders, the battle would be over.

But that's not enough, Arnold told himself. I want a victory that'll end the campaign, hell, that'll end the war. I want to finish it here and now, not just push them back into their tents so they can fight again tomorrow while Gates moans and sighs and digs more entrenchments.

Cannonballs bounded among his boys from one of the log redoubts guarding either end of the camp. The Redcoats were forming in ranks near that redoubt, firing volleys, desperate to defend the only bit of earth left them. His men returned shot, the trees particolored witnesses. Their duel would continue all afternoon, unless the Americans captured a redoubt. With his men firing into the camp from even one of them, the enemy must surrender.

Arnold flourished his sword. Hurrahing madly, the troops surged after him through rustling leaves, over the writhing wounded and the dead.

The redoubt's wall exploded in flame and smoke. Men fell, screamed, cursed. "General, that's their strongest point!" an aide yelled but Arnold never heard, for he was shouting encouragement, urging them to smash through the red lines, to take the camp beyond.

Arnold's horse galloped for the thicket of cut trees barricading the redoubt's front. Cannon roared, bayonets flashed, and he realized that he alone of the charging Patriots was still upright, still driving onward.

He wheeled his mare for the race back to his lines. Even now, he could see officers in scarlet coats reforming troops, ready to loose another volley at him. But the second redoubt... He sat his gasping horse and studied the log fort at the other end of the camp and meadow. Compared to this one, it was tranquil and unprepared—only a few cannon and none of them firing while Hessians milled inside, singing their hymns, no doubt.

His eye caught movement halfway between him and the redoubt. Filing into the meadow from the brilliant trees came Learned's troops.

Arnold looked back to the Hessian redoubt. With Learned's regiment, they could win it—and the campaign, maybe even the war. But to command Learned's men, he must first reach them, and that meant crossing the meadow, under fire of both armies.

He leaned low over his mount's neck. "Lord, help me."

Men were yelling at him to get down—for God's sake, come back. Balls whistled everywhere. The golds and reds and oranges of the surrounding trees to either side blurred. He floated above it all, the only reality the pounding horseflesh between his thighs. Then he drew rein before the astonished Learned, safe, not so much as scratched, laughing, shouting orders to follow him.

On they came, whooping, while Arnold galloped around the redoubt, its several hundred Hessians fleeing, scrambling for position, firing wildly because they were cornered.

He reached the sally port at the redoubt's rear. A wall of frantic, shoving Germans smashed into his troops, swarming around him. A cannonball whizzed past to hit a Continental to his left. It clipped the man's head from his shoulders, sent his skull flying at the soldier beside him. Both victims fell, the dead man's trunk spurting blood, the other twitching atop him. Then Arnold's horse yelped and bucked him to the ground.

He lay for a moment, the breath knocked from him, then scrambled to his feet and found his sword. He lifted it while his eyes locked with a Hessian's. Time halted, and the same unreality from his dash across the meadow returned. He saw red rivulets coursing from a hole in the

Hessian's huge neck, saw the man's chest rise as he struggled for air, the stubble of beard on his vast jowls. The sun glinted on something in the Hessian's hand.

A pistol, and a fine make, too

Then came the shock. It jolted Arnold from his daze and pushed his leg from beneath him.

He was on the ground, thigh throbbing in the way that heralds agony. "No!" he shrieked, more from frustration than panic or pain. He could not be wounded, not when victory, his victory, the one tantalizing him for three years, was moments away. "Oh, God in Heaven, please! Just gimme this battle!"

His horse stamped and screamed above him, its bulk black and monstrous against the sun. Something warm splashed his arm. Blood. He must have taken a ball in the face. But why wasn't it paining him? More drops fell. They became a stream, and Arnold glanced up to see a scarlet cascade pulsing from the mare. She gave a final whinny as her legs buckled. Deliberately, as if she had all eternity, she sank to the ground.

It was ridiculous, really: she fell slowly enough that he should have had time to roll aside, or so it seemed. But the horse crashed down on him, full on his wounded leg, and he screeched as bones snapped. What had been mere agony became torture.

Time speeded up, as though compensating for its tardiness. Morgan was there, shoving the horse off him while someone pulled him free and the Hessian he thought too big to disappear vanished behind Americans with upraised bayonets.

Leaves whirled on the smoky breeze as his men seized the cannon and fired at the Redcoats from within their own camp. Other troops fought the Hessians hand-to-hand while Morgan squatted beside him. "Well, Arnold, you done it again."

"We winning?" he gasped. All he could see were booted Hessian legs and buckskin American ones clenched in a macabre dance.

Morgan pulled the major general's sash from around Arnold's waist. Though his friend's touch was gentle as a woman's, Arnold fought nausea. "Reckon we'll win, sooner or later. Burgoyne's a stubborn one. Takes a heap of licking." Morgan squinted at the sky. "Gonna be dark soon, anyway. They won't have time to mount another charge. That redoubt's ourn. Reckon their camp is, too." He spread the sash on the ground as Wilkinson reined in beside them.

"Mr. Arnold, sir," Wilkinson called, "I'm here to arrest you. General Gates' orders."

Arnold's tongue was clamped between his teeth against the pain, so Morgan answered for him. The Virginian slowly rose until his face was almost level with Wilkinson's, though the aide yet sat his horse. Then Morgan said something. His tone was so low Arnold could not hear and so menacing that Wilkinson blanched.

Without a word, Wilkinson wheeled and galloped away.

Morgan knelt and rolled Arnold onto the sash. "Come on, brother. Let's get you to a surgeon. Soldier, here, take that end there. Help me carry him..."

"The same leg," Arnold says, still marveling at it, still tortured after three years. "Ball smashed the femur in that same leg wounded at Quebec, and whatever bones it didn't smash got broke by the horse." He hitches closer to the fire, shifts the leg on its stool. It's shorter than the right one by a couple of inches, and the foot lies at an odd angle. He uses it, stumping along without a cane, but it pains him, frequently, relentlessly, until he must wonder whether he should have let the surgeon cut it off after all...

"Don't know that I can reach that ball, sir, it—"

"Damn you!" Arnold roared, or tried to roar. His voice was so weak it scared him. "You're not taking my leg, you understand? Rather die. Just get the ball out, you damned butcher."

"But, General, it's in there pretty deep, and besides that, and that's enough, sir, but besides that, the bones are broke all to kindling. Good chance the leg'll putrefy—"

If Arnold were not crazed with pain, he would feel badly bullying a man weary and patient as this surgeon. As it was, he hissed, "Dammit, I come out of this short a leg, and I'll make you wish you'd cut your own off, not mine." He glared with every bit of strength and venom left him until the doctor's tired gaze dropped and he muttered, "Hold him," to the surgeon's mates gripping Arnold's arms and hips and legs.

After every drop of water had been wrung from him in tears and sweat and piss, with more of his blood soaking the doctor's apron and the table beneath him than remained in his veins, he lay in bed, gasping, undone, immobilized from hips to ankles in a wooden box—a casket, he told himself morbidly.

And now what? he wondered between surges of excruciating torment. No place in the war for a cripple, and Gates, damn him, Redcoats'll give him the slip. That's all I am now, a cripple. Without me there to put some spunk in him, Gates'll let them get away. 'Twas bad enough when only one wound hindered me, but two, two in the same leg, and the leg smashed, too, 'tis more than anyone can overlook. They'll never give me another command. If that stupid old Granny ruins it now, ruins the victory, it's what I traded my leg for, no troops'll have confidence in me now, a cripple, and worthless—

He was back in the redoubt again, the moment of his wounding stopped and spread for him to examine like the most detailed canvas. He smelled the dirt and powder and fear, heard the screams and curses, the cannon and muskets, felt the heat of so many bodies packed inside a fort in the afternoon sun. He saw the Hessian with his mustaches and golden hair pulled into a queue, his bearskin helmet askew, the hole in his neck spouting blood, his right eye blacked and front teeth missing. And his gun, the pistol that had turned Arnold from hero to cripple.

Never again to run through the morning dew and mount his horse with a flying leap. Never again to lope through the woods on reconnaissance or just for the thrill of movement, muscles and sinews and bones working perfectly together. Never again to walk miles without tiring, to stride across a rolling deck effortlessly while all around him faltered, to jump, to dance until the lady was breathless, until she begged with a laugh, "Oh, General Arnold, do stop, please! I can't keep up."

It could be worse. He could have taken a shot through both legs like that poor British officer, Major Acland, and lain helpless on the field until carried off as a prisoner of war. He didn't know what happened to Acland, whether the surgeons took one leg or two, but what impressed everyone was Acland's concern for his wife, not his limbs. Mrs. Acland was heavy with child—a child with a cripple for a father. Yes, things could be worse.

Or that other poor devil he'd heard about, also British, stretched out to have his shattered leg sawed off a week after the battle, when the Redcoats were finally retreating—but too late, oh, far too late: get them, boys, *get them!*—with the Americans chasing them joyous as hounds running a fox to earth. Before the surgeon could start cutting, a cannonball bounced through the window and sheared off the patient's other leg at the knee. Rotten luck, awful irony, the sort to make a man say, "What sin did I commit that I should suffer so?"

And all the Regulars too wounded to crawl off the field on their own, left there perforce because the Continentals shot at anyone coming to help. At night, while captured Irish prisoners sent their haunting, tearful music over the battlefield, the smell of the corpses lying among the wounded drew the wolves. Those still alive must fend the animals off until, weakened and dying, they could only scream as the predators tore their flesh.

Yes, things could be a lot worse, he repeated endlessly, vainly.

Then came word of Burgoyne's surrender.

Relief flooded Arnold until it seemed that even his leg quit throbbing. The victory was secure! Not even Gates' cowardice had undone it.

But his satisfaction fled when the king's men grounded their arms. There he lay, mangled and forgotten, shut away in the hospital, in a casket, while Gates' army—no, *his* army, by Heaven, the one that had petitioned him not to abandon them to Granny—assembled in two ranks, drums tapping, fifes proudly tooting "Yankee Doodle." Morning's sun glinted on muskets and bayonets as, company by sulking company, humiliated Redcoats stacked their weapons. In truth, they did not stack so much as hurl the muskets, throwing them on the piles with enough force to snap stocks and dent barrels lest Continentals bear them against other British regiments in the next battle. Defeated drummers beat the "Grenadiers March," but it was a last, feeble effort, dismal as the stench of dead horses binding the meadow.

Then came Gates' acceptance of Burgoyne's sword. That was Arnold's sword, by rights, his and Morgan's and Learned's and Dearborn's and all those who fought while Granny lolled at headquarters. Arnold should have been there to take it from Gentleman Johnny, should have been sitting his horse proud, erect, indomitable. Instead, he thrashed in pain while competing drums banged their rival rhythms and the two generals, aides flanking them, rode towards each other. Arnold would have dressed in his best uniform if he must send to New Haven for it, would have turned out in such splendor that even Gentleman Johnny in his scarlet and plumes would envy him. But not Granny. No, he had shrugged into an old blue coat, not so much as a scrap of lace or an epaulette about it, and flashed his sly smile, and pushed his spectacles up his nose. Not even the decency to dress for the victory, *his* victory, Major General Benedict Arnold's.

Arnold had called a surgeon's mate and begged for something, anything, to dull the agony as Burgoyne bowed and offered his sword. "Nothing left, General. We're plumb out," the mate said while Burgoyne announced, "The fortune of war, General Gates, has made me your prisoner."

"I shall always be ready to testify that it was not through any fault of your Excellency," Gates simpered, though Arnold would have nipped such nonsense in the bud.

"'Fortune of war'?" he would have roared. "General Burgoyne, 'tis all these boys here who've made you a prisoner. Though I admit, we had a lot of help from your arrogance."

Instead, he roared at the surgeon's mate to get out, damn it, lest the man see him burrow into his pillows and sob with the pain, the loneliness, the devastation.

Now he was the weakling that others coddled, as his strength had once protected the ladies and the infirm and elderly. His soul shrivelled. Dear God, to be the protected instead of the protector.

They moved him to the military hospital at Albany. There the days of his convalescence passed, one more painful than the next, each with its own humiliation. The worst was when he read in General Orders that the Congress was striking a medal in Gates' honor—and this after their months of refusing to restore his own seniority. He wept at that, but quietly, blanket pulled high lest anyone suspect, and then badgered the surgeon and his mate when they came to change his dressing.

"My leg's not healing, Thacher."

"Don't doubt but what it won't heal, sir, long as you fret and worry the way you do." Dr. Thacher lifted the mutilated limb while the mate slipped a bandage under it, and Arnold nearly bit his tongue in half, holding back his howl. "'Tis likely it'll putrefy, sir. A wonder it hasn't already. Most wounds this bad do, and then we'll need to amputate—"

"You're not turning me into a cripple, Thacher. I didn't let them up at Saratoga, and you're not gonna, either."

"Don't wanna turn you into a corpse, though, sir, and that's what you'll be if putrefaction sets in and that leg don't come off." Thacher knotted the bandage. "It's fortunate you're the only one of our officers wounded this bad. We can take all the time we need treating you. And it's an honor, sir, a hero like you."

"Goes for me, too, General," the mate said.

Their eyes shone with the adulation of the boys who had marched to Quebec, the militia at Danbury, the farmboys-turned-sailors at Valcour Island. But such respect would grow scarce now that the brave, the daring, the invulnerable General Arnold couldn't even sit his horse. Arnold fixed his stare on the ceiling that he might not see such devotion and measure anew his loss.

Thacher continued softly, "There's only so much we can do, General. Rest is up to the Almighty. They set the bones good as they could up to Saratoga, and I'll change your dressing and watch for signs of putrefaction, but this fretting, sir,"—he strapped the casket around Arnold again, then turned to the mate for his fleam and bowl—"it's doing you harm."

"Aw, you ever been wounded? What do you know about it?"

"I know General Lincoln next door, his wound's not near as bad as yours, of course—"

"Lincoln? Bah!" Lincoln was about as competent as the Congress that had promoted him.

"Yes, sir, and he's bearing his affliction patiently, sir, like a Christian and a gentleman, and he's healing faster than you, too. You keep on like this, sir, you'll never walk again."

"I got a good leg left, haven't I? I'll walk. You'll see."

"You keep it up, sir," Thacher reached for Arnold's arm, began pushing up his sleeve, "and you won't."

He jerked away. "No more blood-letting, Thacher."

"But, General, when you're this choleric, 'tis a symptom of too much blood—"

"Lost blood by the gallon when I was wounded. That's enough bleeding for any man."

"General, it's for your own good, you—"

"Get out! You're all a set of ignorant pretenders and empirics! Get out!" Arnold threw his pipe at them, but Thacher and the mate ducked, and his petulance did naught but burn holes in the blanket where ashes fell.

If only the pain would leave him! But it gnawed him day and night and never let him catch his breath, merciless as the battlefield's wolves. He scarcely remembered what it was like to be free of anguish. He longed for the medicines he had handled without appreciation as a young apothecary, when he was healthy and as much a stranger to pain as he was to despair. There was James' Fever Powder, nothing more than sugar and some herbs to flavor it, and Spirits of Scurvy Grass, a vile concoction that was mostly rum. But there had been other mixtures, too, something the Indians made from willow-bark that cured every headache.

As it was, he must content himself with brandy and rum—poor anodynes unless he drank himself into insensibility. He asked for laudanum, but Thacher shook his head. "Used up all I had, General. I've written for more, but it'll be a while coming if it comes at all."

The only bright spot was Varick's news of another resolution from the Congress.

"Guess what, sir." A beaming Varick waved the paper. "You're such a hero, they're naming that new fort down there at West Point after you."

Arnold grunted. His mind played tricks on him now, made him remember things of no importance and forget what mattered. So he knew exactly how many geese had flown past his window this morning, but news of the world outside that window, and its war, was gone as soon as its bearer ceased speaking. Seemed someone had told him a fortress was a-building on Hudson's River, but he couldn't swear to it. He squirmed in his casket. "West Point?"

Varick gave a pitying look, and Arnold thought, You wait, Colonel, till you're wounded one day, and you need to study on just getting your food down, and we'll see how good your memory is.

"Well, General, as I told you couple of days ago, they're building redoubts at West Point, with a main fort right atop that bluff that sticks out into the river there, to control all the shipping. Claim it'll be impregnable, sir, that you'd need to try hard to lose it to the Redcoats, and that's a blessing, some of the officers we've got." Varick chuckled. "Speaking of which, remember what I told you about Gates?"

Gates? He was commander-in-chief, wasn't he? No, that was Washington. Poor, long-suffering Washington. He'd not even received Gates' report on the victory at Saratoga, for Granny sent it directly to Congress, over His Excellency's head. Probably Old Granny was hoping Congress would compare Washington's defeats at the Brandywine and Germantown with Gates' success. Probably hoping Congress'd get rid of Washington, elevate Granny to Commander-in-Chief—

"Sir? You remember?" Impatience tinged Varick's voice.

"Of course, Colonel. My leg's wounded, not my head."

"Gates praised you in his report to Congress rather than just ignore you like after the last battle. Called you 'the gallant Major General Arnold.'"

Certainly, Gates would praise him now, when he was no longer a threat to him, only a cripple, a useless cripple in a casket—

"Anyway, General, Congress got that report, and now they're naming that main fort there at West Point after you, sir. Fort Arnold."

He hugged the knowledge to him, used it to salve his pride for Gates' medal or when he must have help to bathe or dress or, worst of all, use the chamberpot. He who had sailed the Indies and swaggered through London, wed Margaret Mansfield, sired three boys, and survived her death, captured Ticonderoga, and led the march on Quebec, now must call the surgeon's mate when his bowels wanted emptying. A fort named for him, but still he was a cripple, a useless cripple...

"I knew soon as I went down I'd be ruined for life," Arnold whispers. "I wish that bullet had found my heart 'stead of my leg."

I say nothing, but there's plenty of others share that wish. For certain, if he'd died there in that Hessian redoubt, he'd have been a hero, honored ever after for Ticonderoga and Quebec, Danbury and Valcour Island. Not to mention Saratoga. Saratoga scared the enemy so bad that to this day they haven't campaigned again up north. They left their Indians and Loyalists to fight us and sailed south, thanks to the fear Arnold taught them at Saratoga.

He broods, staring at his leg. "And Gates—" He sighs then mutters so soft I scarce hear. "He's the greatest poltroon in the world."

'Tis true. Most folks says it's Gates won Saratoga, though why anyone would believe it of Old Granny is a cipher. But they were crediting Gates for the victory even before Congress voted him a medal, the newspapers were, and the politicians, and just about everybody who didn't fight that day and can't tell bullets from barrels. Gates' friends in Congress made sure of that. And of course, Gates never had the mettle to set them straight. He's the worst sort of coward, the kind that never blushes to claim another man's victory.

Wounded and crippled and cheated of his due—all that started Arnold's life spiralling downward. Everything since then's pushed him to treason, same as a beautiful birchbark canoe trapped by a whirlpool. The water rushes and foams and pulls the boat into it regardless, smashing it on its rocks till it's nothing but trash.

He clears his throat. "And that wasn't the end of the evil that came from that battle."

"No, sir," I say. "It brought the Papists in on our side."

Chapter Thirteen

'Twill one day be the fashion, I suppose, to pretend that wicked ideas are as good as any others. We already hear such from the Quakers. And while you daren't say a man's free to live as he likes but then clap him in gaol when he doesn't pray the way you do, all the same, you needn't pretend that his notions make sense.

So it is with the Papists. Here are people so beholden to their priest they think he can send them to Hell if they stint on the money they give the Mass-house. Folks that careless of their souls aren't likely to trouble much about earthly freedom. 'Tis for that reason, and not that we're narrow as the Quakers say, that we despise the Roman Church.

I have nightmares sometimes that my father, if ever I find him, might be a Papist. For Arnold, it's worse. That our victory at Saratoga—the victory he won with his blood and crippling—brought King Louis XVI of Papist France into the war, openly, on our side, well, that irony festers in Arnold's soul.

King Louie loathes the British as his ancestors did, so all along he'd been helping us, sending us arms and ammunition, even an advisor or two. But secretly, you understand: he daren't risk war with England, as his grandfather done fifteen years ago, without he can win. So he'd been biding his time to see could we whip the Redcoats. Saratoga showed him we could. Now he's our ally.

Curious thing, though. Louie and his grandfather tried all this century to defeat England. Last time was when I was a child, with the French and Indian War. Hard as we're fighting Britain now, 'twas our savior then, battling to protect us from a Papist king, from his persecution and taxes. Seems the world's turned upside down, now that we're running to a Papist ruler for protection from a Protestant one.

A hard question, this. We need more men and money, a whole treasury of money, to win. And the only ones offering that are the French. There's folks urging that we take it, otherwise we'll lose this war, and others saying what's the use of fighting if we're only going to trade masters, be subject to Louie's priests instead of George's ministers.

Arnold's with that second set.

"Big mistake," he says tonight. He and Peggy have just finished the supper I served. Flash is in the yard out back, barking, instead of in here begging food, as he done earlier. Begged so hard that Peggy frowned, and Arnold asked me to put him out. The storm's ended, or I reckon Flash's exile would have been to the parlor only. I know how the poor dog feels, though. Used to be, when I first arrived and Peggy was still in Philadelphia, Arnold and I sat at table together. Peggy put a stop to that, too, with her sighs and glances.

"Can't see why the Congress ever signed that alliance," Arnold continues as I clear his place. "If the French wanted to help us, why didn't they up to Quebec? All it needed was a word to the priests, telling them to side with us and open the gates. But taking Quebec, that woulda made us stronger than Louie likes. That's why they didn't lift a finger then: 'tis to their interest to keep us weak. They want us dependent on them 'stead of London, and the first step's their infernal alliance, which of course, that fool Congress snapped up. Sign away our souls, and what'd we—I mean, the rebels, get? Grief, and a set of French officers wringing their hands any time a cannon booms, and no cooperation at all. None."

He's right. Since we signed that treaty, our allies done nothing but second-guess Washington and refuse to attack. They outrank him, they say, aren't subject to his orders. Folks who cheered the alliance three years ago, thinking victory was just a Hail Mary away, aren't so sure anymore.

Peggy smiles cloyingly. "Now, Benny, we agreed not to talk about this. It upsets you so."

"You're right, my love, it's just—"

"Stop, *ma cheri*, I can't bear to hear you blame yourself again."

"Blame myself? For what?" Arnold's puzzled as me.

"It wasn't your fault that the French signed with the rebels, Benny. Really, it wasn't." She sips her glass of raspberry shrub. "If you hadn't beat the Redcoats at Saratoga, well, they, um—"

Arnold stares like a drowning man whose rope is snatched from him.

"Mr. Washington might have won a battle sooner or later, don't you think?" Peggy's laugh tinkles. "The French would have signed an alliance then, I'm sure."

"You think it—it's *my* fault?"

Peggy sighs. "No, *ma cheri*, didn't I just say it wasn't? You oughta listen better." She slaps his bad leg. Even I, standing well back from the table, hear his groan. Instantly, Peggy is all contrition. "Oh, Benny, I forgot. I'm so sorry. I didn't mean to hurt you." She turns helplessly towards me. "Clem, would you be so kind?"

I step forward, wondering what Peggy thinks I can do, but he waves me away. "I—I'm all right. It just—just startled me." Arnold's brow puckers again. "But I can't believe—it's not my fault the French—is that what everyone's saying?"

"Benny." Peggy's heavenly bosom lifts in another sigh, and I remember a girl so beautiful she seemed a fairy sticking out her tongue when first we met. "No one's saying that. It's not your fault any more than your wound is. I'm sure you weren't doing anything that wasn't, um, *needful* when you charged that redoubt, were you?" Her eyes widen innocently. "They couldn't have won that battle if you hadn't sacrificed yourself, could they?"

Arnold winces, for that's exactly what's been said since his treason. Folks who can't leave him one shred of glory say, "Oh, we'd have won at Bemis Heights, no matter what. That dash he made against the Hessians, that's just Arnold showing off like always."

"I only wish," Peggy's voice trembles, "for my sake, I know I'm selfish here, but I can't help it—" She bites her lip, and then the words burst from her. "I wish you'd never been at Saratoga, Benny. 'Tis hard seeing a husband crippled."

He winces again. We seldom speak that word.

"But it wasn't your fault, *ma cheri*, any more than West Point was. No one could think for a moment you bungled that or that it's your fault poor John—" Peggy's voice breaks as a new note enters it. She buries her face in her hands before struggling to her feet and sweeping from the room.

I carry plates to the kitchen and leave the general to recover.

By the time I finish tidying up, he's settled in his chair by the hearth in the front parlor.

"May I sit with you, sir?" I ask.

He looks up. I'd swear his cheeks are wet. But with nary a quaver, he says, "I'd be honored, Clem. Just let Flash in first, will you?"

Flash streaks for the parlor soon as I open the door to sit gazing at Arnold, reproachful but adoring. I follow him and take my needlework from the basket. Tonight's task is frustrating: I had three words of the legend sewn, only to find I skipped a letter in the second word. So I'm ripping out yesterday's work and starting over.

We sit silent until, to heal the general's hurt, I say, "You couldn't have known the French would sign a treaty with the—the rebels. It doesn't take away from what you did at Saratoga."

"Thank you, Clem." He smiles, the way a brave man does when he's mortally wounded. "But I'm a bore with all my stories. Tell me, what were you about in the fall of 1777? Still living in Philadelphia?"

My nerves are tightening with the kidnapping only four days off. So I almost blurt about spying before I recollect myself…

I'd thought myself a failure, pushed out of the army and going home as I was. But my assignment from His Excellency raised my spirits, and never mind how wicked it might be.

When I reached Philadelphia that Wednesday morning, so altered was it that I wondered if I'd been gone years, not months. I was hot and dusty and tired, and my leg was paining me, though a farmer and his wife drove me the last few miles in their wagon among the cabbages and carrots. They were making for the South Market, praise be, and would let me out near my uncle's.

There were already changes as we clip-clopped down Pine Street, past the Third Presbyterian Church and then St. Peter's Episcopal. The sun shone right through their steeples, no bells hanging there to block it. Later, I noticed that no church anywhere still had a bell, and the big one that rung last year for the Declaration was gone, too. It'd have been fair game for invading Redcoats, and Patriots had probably hidden it.

But why the church bells disappeared, too, I never heard. Probably so the government wouldn't melt them for ammunition.

At Fourth Street, I made my thanks and hopped off the cabbages. Walking, then, I felt more than saw another difference. The town was full and stinking with suspicion. Folks eyed each other without the usual pleasantries.

"Clem Shippen, I declare!"

There came Becky Franks down the dark and humming street towards me, her grin brilliant in the midday gloom. "Here." She opened her sack of gingerbread to me. "I've just been to Ludwig's shop. Haven't seen you for a while. I thought you were probably still at the farm."

"With my uncle? No, I—" Someone bumped me from behind. I turned as a Quakeress, clutching bundles in one hand and a child in the other, gathered the clothes spilling from her arms. I bent to help, but instead of thanks, she gave me a look that could have killed and snatched a waistcoat from me. 'Twas violently done, more than I'd ever seen from Quakers. I stood bemused as the lady hurried from us.

"What's she so angry about?" I asked Becky.

She bit a cookie. "Oh, last month, the rebel Congress locked a couple of dozen Quakers in the Freemason's Hall for questioning."

"They *what?* Why?"

"They claim they're Loyalists," she said, as though that explained it.

"But—but why are—"

"Though, I must say, I hope there's more martial people than Quakers with us." She laughed loud enough that a man passing us scowled. "Anyway, last I heard, they're exiling them to Virginia. Everybody's in an uproar because these men are wealthy and prominent, you see, and even they aren't safe from the Congress."

"But—they don't—they can't—how can they do that?" The Congress' own Declaration had charged the government with such crimes, listing them as reasons to revolt.

Becky shrugged. "Who knows? Thank Heaven, Congress itself is fleeing to Lancaster. So it seems we're about to enjoy His Majesty's government once more. They'll restore the Quakers and everyone else the rebels condemned."

She hadn't lowered her voice, and those walking by scowled again. One man muttered something I didn't hear and was glad not to.

"Well, Clem," she said with a wave, "I must go or Mother'll worry the Congress got me too. Remember me to Peggy."

I wasn't surprised to find the Shippens at home and the house echoing with them as though they'd never left. They weren't surprised to see me neither. The war stole our amazement, I think. People died or fled, were wounded or heard from no more, and we only tried to keep up with the news: we didn't expect to understand it.

Nor did we apologize, I for disappearing on my uncle, he for leaving me in Philadelphia. Though he did ask how I came to limp.

"I went looking for my father." I gave him the story I'd invented on my way home. "Heard there was a man with the Continentals from Mother's town, thought he might know something one way or the other. But there's a runaway horse, and I fell trying to get out of its path." As I'd hoped, he set himself to disprove Mother's tale rather than wonder what I'd been about.

We were too anxious to enjoy our dinner that afternoon. The fear from the streets seeped inside to silence us. Then, over our pudding, we heard a roar from down the road, the sort a mob makes.

"Oh, Edward, what is it now?" my aunt cried.

"I don't know, my dear. I'll go see."

"No, don't leave us!" She clutched his arm.

"My dear, 'twill only be for a moment. I'm just going to the gate. Peter." He beckoned the servant he'd hired in my absence. "Come with me, if you will."

It seemed they were gone a fearful long time as our hearts pounded and the din grew louder, with glass shattering now and then. Still, I'd barely tasted the pudding when Uncle Shippen returned to say that some of Philadelphia's Patriots were searching house to house for Quakers and other disaffected folks.

"They're kicking doors in and looting as they go," he said. "Come on. We're going down cellar till this is over."

"That won't do any good. We're not even Quakers anymore." Aunt Shippen wrung her hands hysterically. "They'll find us there, Edward. They'll drag us out—"

"Ssshh, now, darling, I've posted Peter at the door. He'll tell them we're not back from the farm yet. Come on, all of you."

And so we cowered in the cellar, dreading every moment to hear the mahogany door overhead splinter and Peter yell that we were downstairs instead of the lie my uncle had given him.

Wagons rumbled past the cellar's windows, the neighbors trussed inside shrieking and groaning. Papers ransacked from cubbyholes and ledgers somersaulted down the street like leaves on September's wind, while legs bowed under the weight of plunder staggered past.

"Liberty." My uncle snorted over my aunt's head while she sobbed in his arms. "They say they're fighting for liberty, but, damn them, 'tis just an excuse to steal from people and lock up anyone who calls them on it."

At last, the cries faded, the clink of breaking glass ceased, and we crept upstairs. When two delegates from the Committee of Safety appeared at the door next morning, my uncle dared no protest. Instead, he scratched his name across the parole they presented, promising not to leave Pennsylvania nor involve himself in politics, and thanked them for the privilege. 'Twas useless, and stupid, the sort of thing desperate men do, for the government's troops were already marching towards Philadelphia and most Patriots were flying before them.

Uncle Shippen also discharged Peter, after paying him handsomely, for fear he would spy on us to the Committee. Again I offered to make good my mother's debt by cooking for them.

"Fine, Clem, and I thank you." Uncle Shippen lowered his voice. "Your aunt, Lord bless her, tried to cook for us at the farm, but she can't even boil water. And with His Majesty's army here this winter, we'll be having guests in three or four nights a week."

The Redcoats invaded Philadelphia that Friday, the last in September, though since there's no one left to oppose them, mayhap "invade" isn't the right word. They never fired a shot, what with the Congress gone and most Patriots with it. We watched for hours as thousands of troops in red uniforms or the blue coats of hired Hessians swung down Market Street. "Look at them!" Peggy said as they stepped in unison. "Aren't they gorgeous?"

For certain sure, they were a contrast to us scarecrow Continentals that had marched the next block over a month past. They glowed with all the right accouterments. Their hats sat their heads at the proper angle, without the hemlock we'd worn, and each shouldered a musket and bayonet. Fifes shrilled "God Save the King" as drums beat time. I stood silent while Peggy cheered as much as my uncle allowed.

"See, there's Cher Jean!" Peggy pointed to an officer with his back to us. He was as slight and jaunty as Andre, but when he turned, Peggy sighed. "Maybe not."

Caparisoned horses were prancing past now, pulling artillery wagons. The brass cannon gleamed cheerful in the sun, as though innocent of killing. Then came a marching band and more Hessians, each man stepping so precise they appeared to move as one, mustaches and queues waxed to the same sheen. Baggage wagons, horses, cows, goats, and asses brought up the rear with the Hessian women. Those ladies looked fierce as their men, or what I could see of them through their smoke did, for they were all puffing at pipes. None of the livestock they were herding ever dared balk, not even the donkeys, and the children clutching mama's skirts marched along quiet and purposeful, like little soldiers.

Thus did the Regulars and Hessians infest Philadelphia.

But the Continentals hung onto the Delaware River. There were a couple of forts out there, nothing more than mud-pies with cannon atop them, really, but our boys fought hard for them. Kept them, too, long after Philadelphia was a-swarm with Redcoats. That made life tough for everyone, because as long as those forts blockaded the river, none of the government's supply ships could sail up and anchor at Philadelphia's wharves. Meaning the soldiers and us all fought over the same food, and you can guess who won, especially when the Redcoats were armed and the rest of us had lost our guns to the Patriots' committees.

The government shelled those forts, kept up a cannonade so constant that after a while, we ignored it, even forgot that there was such a thing as silence, or birdsong, or laughter and psalms floating out a neighbor's window. My memories that fall have a rumbling thunder behind them.

Overnight, Philadelphia's population doubled, with 50,000 soldiers, officers, and frightened citizens needing shelter. Soon the city echoed to hammers and saws as its conquerors built barracks.

All those soldiers needed cookfires, too. And so our wood began disappearing. What's stacked out back for the winter went first. Then it was the fences surrounding those yards. Folks took the shutters from their windows lest those go to warm a Redcoat's dinner, too, and stored them down cellar along with the hay from their carriage-houses that the troops coveted for insulating their new barracks. So much fuel hid where a spark could easier find it kept us mortally fearful.

Come Saturday, I elbowed my way through the crowds to market. I tried to watch the Redcoats' quartermasters scouting rooms for the officers so's I could report it to Major Clark, but I was too nervous over this first meeting to notice much.

When I finally arrived, I wondered if 'twas Philadelphia's market after all. Used to be, you could buy just about anything you wanted, eggs or beef brought across the Delaware from New Jersey's farms or pelts and rifles and strange Indian medicines from the settlements to the west or sugarcane and rum and even stranger medicines from the Indies. But now, with the Continentals controlling the river and Redcoats taking first pick of what could still get through, the stalls had emptied out. I wandered among them, nose pinched against the stench of spoiling meat, to count only half a dozen traders trying to unload wormy flour and sour pork. Later, we were glad to get whatever they had, though meat cost half a dollar a pound, and butter went to over a dollar.

Later, too, there'd be no more rum nor liquor of any sort by order of my uncle's relation and good friend, Joseph Galloway. Once he'd been a delegate to the Continental Congress—until the government arrested him. When they finally let him go, Galloway'd become a Loyalist's Loyalist and Superintendent General of Philadelphia, which meant he lorded it over us. If we thought to visit relatives in the country, we must apply to Galloway's office for a permit, and if we wanted some rum, or an herb a Lenape medicine-man swore would cure the gout, or even, God help us, salt, we must ask Joseph Galloway, please, could we have some. He'd confiscated all these, to be doled out at his pleasure—and high prices. Doled out to everyone else, that is. His friendship with my uncle meant we had all we wanted of salt and rum.

I returned to the market's entrance, where the Conestogas that brought the farmers and their bounty to Philadelphia used to gather. Today, I saw nary a one of those blue wagons with their huge red wheels and the canvas billowing overhead.

I pushed my hair, worn down my back as His Excellency and I had agreed, from my eyes and shifted the basket lined with blue calico, also as agreed, from hand to hand. Soon a man with a straw hat pulled low sauntered towards me. He took my arm in his, as though we were brother and sister.

"Divine gift," he whispered.

"Liberty," I whispered back and felt him relax. "You Major Clark?"

He gave me a glance. He wasn't that much older than me, so I never asked had he been to Connecticut or known a lady named Hepzibah Heyes. He guided me towards the meat-sellers' stalls, stinking and therefore pretty much deserted. "Call me John. After all, I'm your brother."

"Sorry."

"That's all right. Besides, 'tisn't every day I get a sister recommended by His Excellency himself." His voice had sunk to a whisper. "I'm meeting you now, but our other brother's gonna do it after this. You wear your hair like that again Wednesday and carry that basket, meet him here this same time. His name's Micah."

I nodded.

"Now, what've you got?"

I told about the quartering of troops among us, how they took the houses of Patriots who'd fled, while officers and their mistresses forced Patriots too old to run, or too sick or poor, into one room of their homes so they could have the rest. Whole streets of buildings bore chalked numbers on their doors to show how many officers from which regiments would be living there.

He asked, "You hear anything about redoubts going up north of the city?"

"They're building them now, case His Excellency attacks. But those fortifications, they aren't only to keep the Continentals out—they're to keep us in."

"Word is they're arresting anyone wealthy."

My uncle hadn't waited for a knock at his door. He'd visited General Cornwallis' headquarters only a week after signing the Patriots' parole. "That's right," I said. "Anyone they think's a Patriot, they're arresting him and confiscating his estate—"

"Mama says for you to read your chapter and say your prayers ever' night." He spoke so loud I started. "Don't forget just a-cause you're living in Phillydelphia."

A sergeant in scarlet uniform strolled past. I said faintly, "No, I—I won't."

Major Clark asked a few more questions, what regiments were
stationed where, how many cannon had come into the city with the
Redcoats, whether I knew any servants at Howe's headquarters. Then
he kissed my forehead, as brothers do, murmured an apology for taking
such liberty, and was gone.

With the enemy came a new freedom in Philadelphia. 'Twasn't the
freedom from government's force and corruption that most Patriots
sought, but a freedom from decency, as the army turned Philadelphia
into London. Soldiers paced off fields for cricket, dug pits for cockfights.
They even set up eating clubs and named them after ones in England:
the Yorkshire Club, the Friendly Brothers, the London Association. But
what with the blockade, there must have been precious little chewing
going on in them.

The rest of us weren't eating much, neither. So I rejoiced when the
corn I'd planted last spring was ready to harvest. Uncle Shippen and
Edward went to strip it from the stalks, only for some Hessians to mate-
rialize beside them. At first my uncle thought they'd come compliments
of the British command. But when he'd filled his basket and started
indoors with it, the biggest soldier gave him to understand that all but
a handful of the ears was going with them.

And so I trudged to market, to report to my contact and buy what
I'd thought to raise myself. But here, too, the army took first pick, so
we were getting what even a Redcoat wouldn't eat. There's hardly any
vegetables or meat. I was lucky if I found flour, and the cheese was so
bad I wouldn't have fed it to a dog. By the end of October, butter couldn't
be had, not even the rancid stuff lately sold. One night, despairing, I
added a line to the report I would next day hand my contact for General
Washington: "Everyday increases the Price and Scarcity of Provision.
Heaven only knows what will Become of us, if you do not soon relieve
us by Routing them."

I finally quit going to market for anything other than meeting my
contact. Food I bought off the farmers who smuggled it from Delaware or
New Jersey. There's always folks willing to supply what politicians won't
let you have, men so desperate they'd brave Joseph Galloway's wrath to
bring in a barrel of rum and sell it for double its worth to pay for their
risk. We hadn't many of these intrepid souls: Howe threatened terrible
revenge on any he caught, for they were supposed to sell their goods to

the quartermasters, not us, and never mind that the army paid less than we would. Nor could they carry much even when they got through. But their eggs and milk were fresh and their butter sweet. It took Galloway till January to fix this. Anyone tattling on such transactions would get half the value of the goods involved. So did he turn us against each other.

Uncle Shippen gave me a fortnight as cook before he invited guests. Perhaps he was waiting to see what kind of food I served and whether I'd shame him. And once, the dinners I concocted would have done just that, the meat spoiling and scanty and not even stretched by sass from our garden.

'Twas a wonder I could cook at all that first time. Couple of hours before the officers were due, the house shook to its foundation. The loudest thunder ever deafened me, and the window where I was sitting to pluck the chicken shattered.

"What on earth—?" I set the pan aside and stood. My head rang as I looked through the gaping window at a cloudless sky. Then I fell back in my chair as the house shook again and more windows tinkled to the floor.

Outside, ladies were crying. Someone shouted "Earthquake!"

I hurried to my aunt and cousins and collided with them in the hall. "Oh, what is it?" my aunt cried.

"Betsy's hurt," Peggy said.

Blood dripped from Betsy's cheek. Aunt Shippen reached a shaking hand towards her. "Darling, what happened?"

"I don't know. I was standing at the window. Becky Franks had come up the walk, and we were talking, and all of a sudden, there's that lightning, and the window just—just *exploded*, Mama. I thought someone threw a rock at it."

We cleaned Betsy and bandaged her, and I was setting some water over the fire for to brew the last of our tea when another clap sounded. We scrambled shrieking into each others' arms.

That afternoon we learned from our guests 'twas no earthquake but the explosion of two warships down on the Delaware, fighting our boys in the forts. "Damn rebels," one of the two colonels said, "they caught the *Augusta* on fire with all their shot, and she blew up. Killed more than sixty of the crew. Then we fired the *Merlin* on purpose. Didn't want the rebels claiming victory over her too."

You'd think the Continentals would slink away from those forts after their defeats at Brandywine and Germantown, leave nothing betwixt us and the Redcoats. And they might have, except word was trickling in about a grand battle at a place called Saratoga, where Arnold trounced the government. Soon as our boys heard that, they perked up and fought like winners instead of losers.

Our guests, too, had heard of Saratoga and Burgoyne's surrender.

"He's a fool, is Burgoyne," one of them raged, shivering. The blockade not only kept food but warm clothing from the British Army, too, though frost traced the garden this last week of October. "Always been a fool, since the day he joined the army. Plays around with poetry, for God's sake, and writes for the stage. The stage, by God, when he ought to be plotting strategy and securing his supply lines. Too busy mooning to win, damn him, but not too busy to surrender."

"What are the particulars?" Uncle Shippen asked as I toted in the chicken.

"Who can tell?" The colonel scowled. "His dispatches are so puffed, the man can't just say 'We fought a battle and lost.' It must be—wait, I've got it here." He pulled a paper from his waistcoat and unfolded it. "One of the captains at headquarters copied this when it arrived the other day, we were passing it around for laughs. Here we are, friends: Burgoyne's 'Proclamation.'" His voice went high and mincing in mockery. "'For the glory of Britannia and His Gracious Majesty, the forces entrusted to my Command are designed to act in concert, and upon a common Principle, with the numerous Armies and Fleets which already display, in every Quarter of America, the Power, the Justice and, when properly sought, the Mercy of the King.' Now you tell me, sir: will we ever learn from such bombast what actually happened?"

My uncle was too prudent to criticize one of the king's officers to another, so he only smiled.

The colonel continued. "All we know is he was up there in York somewhere—"

"In the backcountry." My uncle pulled his greatcoat tighter.

"Right. And the fool took so much baggage with him, he couldn't move fast enough. Couldn't find fodder for his teams. So that shopkeeper the rebels have for a general, that Arnold, surrounded him and cut his supply lines. Those shirt-tail men Arnold leads, with their cursed, twisted guns, I swear they're the most fatal widow- and orphan-makers in the world."

"How many prisoners Arnold take?"

"The whole army, Judge. Burgoyne had what, five, six thousand troops with him?"

Six thousand Redcoats taken out of the war, no longer killing and plundering us! I breathed a prayer of thanks for General Arnold as my uncle's eyes rounded with shock.

"'Tis said this Arnold fights like the devil." It was the other colonel, silent till now. "Even after being wounded, they say he rallied his men and attacked."

"Yes, well, he hadn't much of an opponent in Burgoyne, now, had he, Riley?"

"Still, Crocker, 'tis three or four times now that this Arnold has led men brilliantly against us." Colonel Riley lifted his wine to lips blue with cold as the other stared.

"What are you saying, Riley?" A vein beat in Colonel Crocker's forehead. "That a shopkeeper, a—a—a colonial is our equal, no, our superior, on the battlefield?"

I glanced at my uncle to see what he made of such insult as Peggy said, "Perhaps, Colonel, you should talk to Mr. Arnold about switching sides." Her twinkling laugh broke the tension. The jewels at her ears sparkled in the candlelight, while her fur hat and collar made her even more alluring. "Now tell me, do you know a John Andre? He's a lieutenant, I believe."

"Andre, hmmm." Colonel Riley spoke around a leg of the chicken. "At Paoli, wasn't he? Brilliant action there, the way our boys fell on the rebels while they were sleeping. Paid them back for the way they hide behind trees like savages and pick us off."

There was naught brilliant in slaughtering sleeping men that I could see, but then maybe I hadn't been a soldier long enough.

"Andre was there, I'm fairly sure," the colonel continued. "But he's a captain, now, I think, Miss Shippen, and a fortunate young man to have such a lady inquiring after him." The colonel bowed at Peggy's smile. "He's in General Grey's family. They're quartered at Mr. Franklin's place."

"Franklin." My uncle rolled his eyes. "There's an ingrate for you. Enjoyed all sorts of offices and emoluments under the king, and who does he side with?" He lowered his voice. "They say he'll be negotiating the alliance with the French, if it comes to that."

Colonel Crocker pounded the table until the hen near leaped from her bowl. "And that's another thing. We capture the rebels' capital, held it for a month now, and what's it get us? Rebels just packed up their papers and removed, little inconvenient for them but no harm done. But Burgoyne! He loses a campaign, one campaign, mind you, and the French want to fight us."

I was busy all that fall cooking and spying. I worried at first that someone would find me out and I'd hang like Nathan Hale. Many nights, I woke the house with my screams. I excused it by saying I dreamt of the Continental prisoners, for truly their plight would give anyone nightmares.

The Redcoats had taken the gaol at Sixth and Walnut Streets, built only a few years before, and into it they crammed the men captured at Brandywine and Germantown. I heard a rumble coming from it when I passed on my way to market, the cries of hundreds of men for food and mercy. The tales told of it raised my hair. Government's surgeons were working into the night over their own troops, with no time to spare for rebels, so every sort of contagion rioted among the prisoners, from measles and prison fever to smallpox. Seemed these always felled the good but never touched the rascals, the men who'd run away from apprenticeships or enlisted in Connecticut for the bounty she offered, then deserted to Massachusetts for hers. 'Twas them as did the nursing, not out of charity but so that they might rob patients too sick to fight them off.

Worse than the disease was the starving and thirst. Men were so hungry they'd eat clay and lime scraped from the walls, leaves and bark, shoe leather. They sucked stones to keep their spit flowing. The prisoner who caught a rat for supper was blessed indeed.

"It's true," Dr. Wahl said when he visited my aunt over some indisposition. He went on a charitable mission to the gaol two or three times each week. "I can't tell you how many twigs and pebbles I've taken from the mouths of the dead."

I shivered. Was my father one of those famished Continentals dining on rat? I put Dr. Wahl's words in my notes to His Excellency and asked my uncle if I might knead extra bread for the prisoners.

Those unfortunates weren't the only ones starving. Food was so scarce that when the enemy finally destroyed the Continentals' forts and broke the blockade in November, even we Patriots breathed easier. Now children wouldn't wake crying with hunger, nor our cheated stomachs constantly growl. Goods and food flooded into town. Merchants in New York packed up their wares and shipped them to us, sure to sell even their oldest inventory where everything had been so scarce for so long. But General Howe soon prohibited such trade. He made some excuse, I don't remember what, as to why 'twas necessary. The abundance fled, prices climbed, and I hated government's meddling more with every scrawny chicken and withered apple.

One morning after a breakfast of gruel that was mostly water, the house emptied, with everyone but me visiting friends or running errands. I sat at a table in the side parlor and stared at the paper before me. I must write a report for His Excellency, for tomorrow was Wednesday, and I was to meet my contact.

Last time, Micah'd given me some special ink, sympathetic medium, he'd called it. "'Twill disappear a few moments after you set it down on paper," he said, "leave the paper blank and innocent and save us if we're caught. Just be sparing with it. I haven't got much on hand."

I hadn't tried the ink yet, so I opened the vial and dipped my quill. "Philadelphia, December 14th, 1777," I wrote only to see the words disappear. A novelty and no mistake.

I began recording the plans some of our guests had mentioned for the redoubts circling Philadelphia. I was hunched over the paper, tongue clamped between my teeth, when someone poked me in the ribs and shouted "Ho!"

Mayhap Adam jumped higher in the garden when the Lord asked about his dinner, but I doubt it. I started so that I upset the ink, sent it running over the table to stain the paper brown. Behind my chair, Peggy bent double, laughing.

"Clem, that was so funny! You should see your face. You look like"—she took to laughing again—"like I'm a ghost or something."

"Yes, well, I—I—you shouldn't sneak up on a body that way."

"Oh, for pity's sake, it was a joke. Don't be so horrid all the time." She started to take the hat from her head, but then, with a shiver, left it. "So what were you writing, anyway? A note to your lover?" She laughed again, until she glanced at the table. There sat my paper, blotting ink, turning from brown to yellow.

The yellow faded with Peggy's smile. When the paper was once again white, she turned her stare on me. "What is that?"

"I, um, it—it's none of your concern, Peggy, you come in here and scare me half to death, and now I must explain my—my—what I'm doing to you?"

She shook a head piled high with curls in the British fashion. "Daddy won't like to hear—"

"It's just ink, Peggy, but there's something wrong with it. I need to take it back to the bookseller." 'Twas a paltry lie, one I was sure she'd see through.

Instead, she pressed on. "So what were you writing?"

"It occurred to me—" I stopped, waiting for inspiration.

"Yes?"

"That—that I—that we're all watching, ah, hearing history every night, and—and I thought I might one day write a book."

"A book." She repeated it as though 'twere nonsense.

"Yes, a—a history of the war, you see. We're listening to firsthand accounts of it all the time."

She rolled eyes emphasized by a tiny patch on her cheek, another style she'd copied from our conquerors. "Well, I don't think it'll get you many beaux—"

"No, I—I shouldn't think so."

"Just be careful," she said. "The way they're reading people's mail and papers, believe me, we don't want anyone searching the house again."

My book became the joke of the family, though my uncle called me aside to repeat Peggy's warning, especially with regard to our guests. Many might take it amiss to find their comments written down.

"I don't even answer letters anymore," he told me, tugging at his neck-cloth. "Too easy for those reading the mail to—to misunderstand, you see. What if some of these papers of yours got out, Clem, what if Redcoats should search the house? Doesn't suit to be, ah, indiscreet nowadays."

The next week John Andre visited.

Peggy doted on him when we gathered round the tea table. He was bonny as ever in his scarlet uniform, powdered and perfumed, and charming, too, but there's no conviction or character behind it. He could talk on art and poetry, in French or German if English didn't suit, but if I'd asked him, "Tell me, Captain, why are you here, fighting strangers who never hurt you?" he'd answer with naught beyond, "The glory, of course." There'd be no thought of principle, no idea that killing and plundering were still sins even if the king no longer called them crimes.

"Well, Judge, Mrs. Shippen, you're very kind to invite me," Andre said over cake.

They pronounced him an ornament to our table and hoped he'd dine with us often.

"As often as you'll have me." Andre bowed.

Sometimes, his superior officers came with him to our parlor. This delighted my uncle and me, for I hoarded every word they spoke. But it flustered my aunt, embarrassed by our scanty table.

"The carrots are old, sir, and mushy." Aunt Shippen looked indignantly at the major who had accompanied Andre. "I told my niece not to serve them tonight, we'll eat them *en famille*. And this beef, sir, I would once have blushed to set such before a guest, but what are we to do? Surely you gentlemen can procure us better food."

The major smiled politely. "You must blame Mr. Washington, madam. He threatens the farmers hereabouts that he'll hang them if they sell to us."

I almost smiled myself—not from courtesy but amusement that the government's officers had fallen for His Excellency's ruse. *Of course* he promised to hang anyone selling to the Redcoats. That gave men helpless against government's vengeance an excuse for feeding Washington's desperate troops as they'd retreated north of Philadelphia, looking for a snug, safe spot to build winter quarters—which they finally found at a place called Valley Forge. But though the Forge was long on natural defenses, it was powerfully short of food. The Continentals would starve without the farmers' sustenance. You'd be a bigger fool than Granny Gates not to protect the country folks who were helping rebels.

"Why doesn't General Howe attack?" my uncle asked piteously. "He outnumbers Washington two to one. Surely he could hit that rabble up at the Valley Forge. Why, they've got less meat than we do, and they're freezing to death in those huts. They're in no condition to fight off Regulars. Why doesn't he attack?"

Not only my uncle but all Philadelphia wondered that.

Andre and his general dined with us in February, as did a merchant whose wares not only pleased my aunt but whose conversation did, too, when we heard France had signed an alliance with the United States. The general was furious, and that made the merchant nervous.

"Have the rebels lost their minds?" General Grey, the same as murdered our boys whilst they slept at Paoli, was a lean man with eyes that seemed dead and a taste for rich clothing. Though all the government's officers were colorful as peacocks, nigh as vain, too, Grey topped everyone. Now he pulled his greatcoat about him. Outside, a freezing rain was falling, and inside, though dry, was no warmer, with the poplar logs on the hearth refusing to burn. "They object that His Majesty and the Ministry is too tyrannical for them, but now they're welcoming the French. They prattle about liberty morning, noon, and night, till you'd swear it's all they think about, and now they're allying themselves with a country never yet's heard the word. Amazing, Captain, wouldn't you agree?"

"Yes, sir." Andre lifted his glass, a gift he'd brought my aunt from Dr. Franklin's house, not only home to Grey and his staff but favorite shop too, though they paid for none of the goods they took. The glass was fine enough to catch the merchant's eye. "I do wish I could see all those good Congregationalists in New England, when their own Congress tells them they're allied with a Papist country."

"Now, gentlemen, what's this I hear about a theatrical troupe you've started?" Peggy smiled at Grey and Andre, but her gaze lingered on Andre.

"I wish you luck." The merchant sighed. He'd been born in London, and though he'd lived in Philadelphia the last dozen years, his accent was as thick as Andre's. "'Tis hard for those of us who love the arts here. Few people have an appreciation for the muses, not at all like London."

"I'd be delighted to escort you to a performance, Miss Shippen," Grey murmured.

"I turn my hand to music now and again," the merchant continued, "when business permits, writing songs, madrigals, that sort of thing."

"Lyrics, do you mean?" Andre's eyes sparkled more than usual. "I quite enjoy music, Mr. Stansbury. Can I prevail on you to favor us with a selection?"

The merchant politely demurred, and Andre politely insisted, and before long we had a ditty mocking the Continental Army along the lines of "Yankee Doodle." Though the melody was prettier, the words weren't nigh as witty, for Stansbury hated Patriots too much to write anything but pure poison meanness. Seems he'd warbled "God Save the King" one evening a few years ago, and though 'twas in his own home at a supper party for his friends, someone reported him. Patriots confined him to his rooms for months. Then came the royal army, and Stansbury went from imprisonment to rewards. He reaped one office—and pension—after another, not to mention invitations to dinner from such as my uncle.

Stansbury bowed as everyone but my uncle and me applauded his song. Andre clapped him on the shoulder. "Mayhap we could use your talents, sir, for Howe's Thespians, that's our theater company—"

Peggy clapped. "Such fun!"

"—we're always looking for good farce."

"I'd be honored, sir." Stansbury bowed again.

"They've had a few productions already, haven't you, Captain?" Peggy said.

Andre nodded. "And *Constant Couple* went so well, we're performing it again this Monday, if anyone cares to attend."

"What role do you play?" Stansbury asked.

"Afraid I'm not a very good player." Andre grimaced charmingly.

"Couldn't act to save his life." Though Grey was answering Stansbury's question, he raised his wine to Peggy. "So they've got him writing verse for it and painting scenery, didn't you tell me, Captain? First-rate artist, he is. I saw a curtain he did with mountains and a river. I swear I felt water lapping my ankles."

Through February and March, folks argued over the French alliance. I listened to every comment any officer spoke, scribbling late each night in my chamber, taking the notes to market, where I handed them to my contact.

But I learned nothing from our most frequent visitor. When I tried to draw Andre out, all he said was, "Ah, Miss Shippen, I like to forget there is any war, save at times it makes a capital joke."

Instead, he and Peggy warmed themselves before the hearth while Andre sketched her likeness and shared the gossip of Howe's Thespians. He so dazzled my aunt and uncle that whenever he asked if their daughter might accompany him somewhere, they always said yes. Courting couples couldn't do much, which may be why Peggy's parents were so willing. The army's commanders had increased the night watchmen from about a dozen to six-score, thanks to the soldiers' thefts and rapine. With a guard on every corner, a man thought twice before stealing a kiss. They couldn't go far, either. Pickets patrolled a tight ring around Philadelphia, and the Continentals would have picked up an officer passing their limits faster than you could say "Liberty or death."

'Twas a rainy day a fortnight later when General Grey and Andre again dined with us. My uncle had hardly muttered grace before the general gave me fodder for my notes.

"I suppose you've heard the news." Grey signaled with a glittering hand for roasted beef. "Howe leaves for home next month." I was glad enough to serve him and so not miss a word, for here was news indeed.

"General Howe's sailing for England?" Uncle Shippen beckoned for some meat as well.

"Soon as General Clinton gets here from New York. He's replacing Howe."

My uncle spoke mildly lest he give offense. "And do you think, sir, he'll enjoy more success than Sir William has?"

Grey drained his wine. "Hard to say. One thing's sure—no love's lost between him and Howe. Strange, that, for they're both Whigs and wedded to a system of politics that favors the rebellion. Though I must say, Andre's about convinced me the Whigs are right on one point."

"Which is?" My uncle smiled, expecting a joke.

Grey sipped soup and gestured at Andre.

"I was telling the general last night," Andre said, "I'm inclined to think this war is futile after all, as the Whigs back home claim."

My uncle's smile faded. "Futile, sir?"

"Yes, sir. Whigs in Parliament, some of the newspapers, too, have said all along we've got no business fighting here against our own citizens."

"But—but, sir—" Uncle Shippen looked as lost as the Children of Israel in the wilderness. "We aren't—*they* started it, the rebels did. *They* took arms against the king and Ministry."

Andre nodded. "Crazy, aren't they, hating government, thinking it's set on destroying them and their liberty. They see a minister behind every tree, just waiting to order them about and regulate their affairs." He dismissed such concerns with a wave of his hand.

"We have the best government on earth. It's there to help us, not hurt us. Yet these rebels damn our sovereign George as if he's the devil himself. They think they're liberty's last defenders, and so to win, the Whigs back home say, we Tories must convince folks we care about liberty, too."

"But we do!" my uncle cried as Grey glanced up from his bowl to say, "That's the part stuck in my throat, having to convince rebels about anything. Damned waste of time. Rather just hunt 'em down and hang 'em."

Andre nodded. "But we've all seen how hard that is, harder than we thought, conquering the rebels. They fight, get beat, rise, and fight again."

"Still, we—we can't quit. We must keep fighting them!" Uncle Shippen gulped. "They're nothing but tyrants, these Patriots, the new men who've come to power."

"Of course they are, sir," Andre said. "That's why we're fighting, to restore the king's easy rule. Only question is how. And the longer things drag on, the more I'm inclined to agree with the Whigs: this war can't be won in the field."

"So what are you saying?" My uncle's voice cracked. "We should settle back and let them work their wickedness?"

"No, sir, not at all, just that maybe we ought to attack the matter from a new angle. This rebellion's being led by a handful of men, isn't it, a few rabble-rousers?"

"Washington, those Adams boys, Arnold, the Congress," Grey murmured.

"The Congress." Uncle Shippen might as well have said, "Dung and pus," he was that disgusted. "Bunch of upstarts no one ever heard of before. Bad as that new Council here, with all their infernal committees, out to make their name and fortune on the country's ruin."

"Absolutely, leading the common folk around by the nose." Andre paused as I set a plate of gingerbread on the table. "For all their talk of liberty, things are the same the world over: a few men at the top do the thinking, and the rest follow along like sheep." He reached for the gingerbread. Taking three cookies, he laid one on the tablecloth and leaned the remaining two against each other atop it. Then, with more cookies, he added another storey. We none of us dared breathe lest the little house come tumbling down.

"Now," Andre's voice was a theatrical whisper, "what happens if those leaders, the foundation of the rebellion, so to speak, were to pull out of the thing?"

Spellbound, we stared at the sweet structure. A draft caught the candles to set them flickering while branches beat against the window.

Then, at Andre's nod, Peggy stretched out a hand. She had only to touch the base for the whole to collapse.

"You see?" Andre shrugged. "Once the foundation's gone, the thing's undone."

Crumbs and cookies littered the table. "Good strategy, don't you think?" Grey said and clapped Andre on the shoulder. "Specially now, with the French involved. They'll turn this little skirmish into a war. We'll be fighting them all over the world. Won't have the men and materiel to do things here the way we should."

"All the more reason to center our efforts on the leaders," Andre said.

My uncle asked, "But how, sir? I mean, short of hanging them, and God knows, you'd need to catch them first, how do you, ah, convince the leaders to—to—"

"To pull out?" General Grey leered a smile that was no smile at all. "It's simple, sir, really. You offer them money, or lands, titles, whatever it takes. And contracts! Back home, men of industry want contracts with government even more than they do titles. Larger profits, I warrant."

"You ladies have your part to do, too." Andre bowed to Peggy. "If you insinuate yourselves into the hearts of the rebels as you have ours, and ask them to lay down their arms, well, the war's over."

"Hear, hear." General Grey's dead eyes rested on Peggy. "You alone, my dear Miss Shippen, could persuade the whole Congress, and probably Washington and Arnold, too, to come to their senses."

"Arnold!" Andre raised his wine. "All the king's army would love you then, Miss Shippen, if you'd take that devilish fighting fellow out of action."

"But hasn't General Howe already tried this, sir, bribing the chief men?" my uncle asked.

Andre shook his head. "He only tried a few times, and then he didn't offer nearly enough. It ought to be the main strategy, take the money we're spending on provisioning the troops and give it to Washington and Arnold and Greene, throw in all the business they could want from government, give 'em contracts and more contracts. Every man has his price."

"True enough." My uncle speared some beef with his fork. "Perhaps you can persuade General Clinton to attempt it."

"You'll have plenty of time to try, Captain." Grey grinned, ghastly as a corpse. "It's a long march back to New York."

"You're abandoning Philadelphia?" My uncle sat bolt upright, and Peggy gasped. I nearly did, too.

"No point to our being here, sir," Grey said. "Mr. Washington's sitting tight at the Valley Forge, refuses to come out and fight. Why should he? It's a strong defensive position. He leaves it and we've got him."

"But—but—"

"And there's the French to consider, too, now that they've joined the damned affair. What if their fleet sails into your bay here? We don't want to get caught between Washington behind us and French warships in the bay. That's why Clinton's coming down here, to march the army back to New York."

"But we've had such fun." Peggy's voice wobbled with tears.

"You—but you can't leave us, sir, at the rebels' mercy—" My uncle's nose twitched like a rabbit's. "What will happen to us and—and our property, sir? Even the rebels admit government should protect our property, but—"

"Pity they don't practice what they preach, then," Grey said.

"Yes, indeed, I couldn't agree more, sir. But still, you leave us here, without protection for our homes and estates, they'll rob us, sir, mayhap even murder us!"

I nigh chuckled at my uncle's fears. 'Twas true Patriots had put themselves into office last year, then made room for their friends at the public's expense. 'Twas also true they'd passed a blessed set of laws, none of them good, against Loyalists and the rest of us, too, what with their searches and censors. But they weren't the king's troops, after all. They wouldn't plunder and kill.

Or so I thought.

Grey murmured something about "the empire's aegis" and "protection, don't worry." But my uncle's face stayed anxious.

Andre deftly changed the subject. "We'll be throwing a farewell party for Sir William," he said. "Something quite grand, it must be, to stand out after all the parties this winter. We were thinking along the lines of a festival from the Middle Ages, a banquet and some minstrels, perhaps a bit of jousting." He bowed to Peggy, a hand at his throat keeping his lace from his soup. "I think we can promise you an unforgettable event, Miss Shippen."

Turned out it was an unforgettable event for me, too.

Chapter Fourteen

Last time I'd met my contact, he'd told me he was ordered to the Valley Forge and henceforth I'd meet someone else. That person would see me tomorrow at four, in a tavern outside the city, the password "French alliance."

"Don't worry," Micah said. "They're friendly to us, the tavern-master is, and I told him you're coming, so they won't think nothing of it, a girl on her own shows up there."

I'd already asked my uncle could I have the next day free for errands. So everything was set—until that afternoon, when I opened the door to find Captain Andre and two grenadiers towering behind. My heart thudded. They'd discovered my spying; Peggy must have told about the invisible ink; they would haul me to gaol—

Andre swept me a glance. "The judge at home?"

"I, um, I'll see." I nearly sagged with relief, until I imagined my uncle's fear when I told him that a British captain, even if it was Andre, and two Redcoats were asking for him.

As though reading my mind, Andre beamed his beguiling smile. "We've a boon to request."

I found my uncle hunched over his papers. "Captain Andre's here, sir."

He started, then tried for nonchalance. "Oh? Have you told Peggy?"

"No, sir, 'tis you he wants to see. He, ah, he has some Redcoats, two of them, with him."

"They here on business or—or socially, do you know?"

"He says he wants a favor."

He capped his ink. "Clem, if you don't mind, bring us coffee and tea—"

"There's no more coffee, sir."

"All right, then, tea and some of the pie from last night."

When I carried a tray into the parlor ten minutes later, 'twas obvious that Andre's request was beyond my uncle's nerves. "—understand the position it puts me in, Captain," he was saying.

"It's not our intention to discommode you, sir." Andre's tone was soothing as the tea I poured. "I only thought you'd want to show your gratitude to Sir William for saving your city from the rebels this winter."

"Well, of course, I'm grateful, sir, but what happens when he goes back to England? The army's moving to New York, you're leaving us at the rebels' mercy here in Philadelphia, and then, sir, those of us who lent our mirrors and servants and—and—what else was it you wanted?—our china and daughters to your party will pay the price, Captain. Let me tell you, there's no one good as rebels at taking vengeance—"

"A miserable rabble, sir, 'tis true, and all the more reason why good men should render His Majesty's troops whatever service they can."

"Begging your pardon, sir," my uncle said timidly, "but how does this party help the troops?"

I handed Andre his dish of tea as the red stained his cheeks beneath their rouge. He made a show of cooling his drink before answering. "You're aware, sir, that Sir William has met with censure for his conduct here in America. The newspapers and Parliament and even some of the king's own ministers, they all criticize his actions in the field while they sit safe beside their fires. 'Twas our hope to send him back in triumph, with the full endorsement of the troops. This ball we're planning will be the most elaborate Philadelphia's ever seen, indeed, 'tis safe to say, 'twill be the most elaborate in all North America. Knights and jousting, fireworks, dancing and a mix of entertainments—you'll want to be a part of it, sir, mark me."

I offered pie to Andre. He took a bite, then held a forkful aloft as though 'twere a marvel. "Now here's an example of why your cook is thought Philadelphia's best and why we want him for our Meschianza. That's the most delicious pastry ever."

"Careful, sir." My uncle nodded proudly at me. "The cook stands yonder. You'll ruin her with such praise."

Andre knew I cooked, had known since he begged a room in my mother's tavern, so this was no surprise, though he acted otherwise. "Methought you only served at table, Miss Shippen. You're entirely too winsome for such wizardry with apples and crust."

"You're too kind, sir." But I knew 'twas only flattery to gain what he wanted.

"Miss Shippen, I was telling the judge we'd like to borrow you next week for the fete we're holding in Sir William's honor. There'll be about a thousand guests, and we'll want every kind of course and sweetmeat—"

"Really, sir!" The thought of cooking for Nathan Hale's murderers, let alone Andre's commandeering me, had me quivering with anger. Not to mention the back-breaking, endless labor, and all within a few days.

Unless… Would I overhear things, learn secrets Washington needed to know? But how would I, stuck in the kitchen? I scowled. "I can't, Captain, I—"

"Forgive me, Judge. I've taken too much of your time." Andre sprang to his feet, brass buttons glinting against his scarlet uniform. "If you'll allow us to take the mirror, we'll leave you to enjoy your day. I'll send someone round later for the china."

"Captain Andre." My uncle mustered all his resistance. "I'm afraid, that is—"

"I trust, sir,"—Andre's tone was still soothing, charming—"I needn't remind you how much you owe to Sir William's protection."

My uncle collapsed like raised dough. He led Andre and his grenadiers to the back parlor where hung the pier glass they wanted.

I tried again as Andre watched the Redcoats take the mirror from the wall and wrap it in blankets, my uncle fluttering nervously the while. "Sir," I said, "I will not cook for you."

"Careful with the doorjamb there, boys. I don't want any scratches." Andre didn't even glance at me as he said, "You mistake me, Miss Shippen. I did not ask you if you would. I have ordered you to do so. Please to present yourself at the Wharton house tomorrow afternoon, around one or so, and we'll discuss the fare." Now he did look at me, arrogant and commanding. "Shall I send an escort of Regulars for you?"

I felt myself flushing. I was about to plead that I already had plans, but that would bring questions I'd rather not answer. I shook my head.

"Good. You'll excuse me, please."

When they'd gone, my uncle stood silent, rubbing his chin. I cleared the cups and saucers and was about to carry my tray to the kitchen when he spoke. "Times like this I think the rebels are right, Clem. Anyway, 'twill make an interesting chapter for your book."

I disagreed. 'Twould be a waste of my time, shut up in a hot kitchen, worked to a frazzle for the enemy's benefit but hearing naught of their conversation since Andre would doubtless draft servants to wait table.

The next day dawned with grey skies. By noon, rain was falling, wetting me through as I picked my way towards the Schuylkill through streets littered with horses dead from starvation, the houses lining them without gates or fences, sheds, or anything wooden that could be chopped down and carted away to warm a Redcoat.

The Whartons' mansion overlooked the river, the trees that named it Walnut Grove surrounding the place. Poor Mr. Wharton, a Patriot, had fled the Redcoats two years ago, whereupon they took his large, square home with its pediment, gables, and out-buildings for officers' quarters. Many of its residents had already removed to New York, where the army under Clinton would soon join them, and the mansion was now hosting a colossal waste of energy, money, and effort. Thank Heaven they'd not worked half this hard at routing our boys from the Valley Forge.

I walked a path bordered with flowers and paused at the door as the sun broke through the clouds. Scattered among the trees and gardens were triumphal arches and, so help me, a tournament ground. Carpenters and engineers swarmed, while merchants demanding payment mobbed any officer who showed his face. But then the wind shifted to blow from the north, from Philadelphia, and the stench of dead horses and of the prison where Patriots rotted nigh smothered me.

I was glad to step indoors. There I saw rooms turned into something from a fairy tale. They had painted the panelled walls to resemble marble, with niches to shelter grenadiers. A multitude of mirrors, some hanging, others leaning against the walls, would reflect the candlelight a thousandfold. Green silk, paper flowers, and ribbons garlanded the mirrors and the branches holding the candles. Carpenters were framing another wing for the place, with the canvas for stretching over it lying heaped in the hall.

I found Andre, coat off and hair unpowdered, perched on a ladder. He was painting a cornucopia exuberantly filled with flowers of the richest colors on a panel over a fireplace. Below him stood a lady with a handful of brushes and a bodice displaying more of her bosom than it covered. She looked me over and smirked when I called to Andre. The smirk vanished as he dismounted.

"Mrs. Smalley," he said, "be a dear and find me more red paint, will you?" Then he turned to me. Someone must have reminded him that cooks can spit in the food, for he smiled flirtatiously, as though I were Peggy.

"Miss Shippen, we have a lot of work to do, I know, so I hope we can at least be civil. 'Twill make things pleasanter."

I counted ten flowers in his cornucopia before I spoke. "Sir, you have commanded my presence, so here I am. Can we get to business?"

The light on his face died. I wager his charm had never failed him before. "I—um, I see. Well, here are the dishes I was thinking of." He reached for his coat and took a paper from its pocket. "If anything cannot be had, or it's out of season, you'll advise me, please."

I looked over the list. I was ever hungry then, and my stomach growled as I read the names of dish after dish. Aside from puddings, it was mostly meat, roasts that could be cooked ahead. A note said a British fleet was rushing fruit up from the West Indies, but I'd be foolish to count on that. Cakes, syllabub, jellies, and sweets would finish things. The only hot item was Yorkshire pie, to be served at the start.

"You don't want anyone going away hungry, that's certain," I said.

"General Howe enjoys a good meal, as do we all."

I nodded. "Even the men starving in your gaols like to eat now and again." Andre flushed, and I hurried on. "I'm sure, sir, you won't object to the scraps from this dinner feeding them."

He worried a chunk of lumber on the floor with his foot, then glanced at me. "And will that make you more amenable, Miss Shippen? Will that guarantee nothing comes to the table burned that night, or spoiled?"

"Fine. I give you my word."

"We have a deal, then. Truth to tell, those prisons bother me, too. I told General Grey—" Then he remembered himself. "I've set aside only £900 for food, Miss Shippen. Don't steal me blind feeding prisoners."

Nine hundred pounds for food! When a carpenter or miller made do on £50 a year! But all I said was, "And there's how many guests?"

"We've invited 400 officers and their ladies and a hundred citizens, or thereabouts. Plan on an even thousand, that should cover it."

"I'd like to see the kitchen."

Andre pointed towards the rear of the house. "Out there, the one on the right."

I threaded my way through the ladders and lumber, paint and casks of nails for the outbuildings flanking the mansion. Each was large enough to house a family by itself, so at least I wouldn't want for space while I cooked. After looking over the fireplace and ovens, pans and crockery, I set off for the tavern.

It was a rickety building far smaller than Mother's ordinary in New York. From its looks, it might have served the first settlers, mayhap with the same loaf of moldy bread the serving maid set before me. The cider wasn't much better, though, from the dead flies in it, 'twas a favorite of winged creatures at least.

But for me, the taproom was deserted. Then the door opened, and a familiar voice called for callibogus.

I twisted and with vast surprise watched Nathan Hale's friend stride from the door to the table beside mine. "Major Tallmadge!"

He was even thinner than before and in uniform, or what passed for one up to the Forge. After the painted, powdered British officers, he was terribly plain—and masculine. And not nearly as surprised as me. "My savior from New York! So good to see you again, Miss Shippen!"

"Likewise, Major."

"I thought—well, don't you hail from York Island? How are you?"

"I'm well, sir. Thank you. But aren't you taking a big risk?" I nodded at his uniform. "You're behind their lines, you know."

"Riskier if I wasn't wearing it." He slid into the chair opposite mine. "I left a couple of pickets outside. They'll holler, they sight any Redcoats. You living here now?"

"In Philadelphia."

The servant brought his tankard. Tallmadge raised it in the Patriots' favorite toast: "May the collision of British flint and American steel produce that spark of liberty which shall illuminate the latest posterity!" He quaffed the callibogus before I could warn him only to set it aside with a splutter.

When the girl was out of earshot, he said, "'Tis good to see you, Miss Shippen. I was thinking about you the other day, how you saved my life that time."

"Oh, I didn't, either."

"Say, will you have dinner with me?"

"Well, I'm meeting a—a friend."

"What's this friend think of the French alliance?"

I grinned. "You? Since when?"

"Just a few weeks, though I've been an intelligencer for, let's see, nigh six months now, since December last while I was training dragoons."

"Intelligencer, huh?"

"Sounds better'n *spy*, don't you think?" He near hissed the word, mocking its horror, then glanced away. "You know, after Nathan—after what they did to him…"

I nodded.

He said softly, "Thought I owed it to him when it cost him his life. 'Sides, easy to pick things up when you're riding around the country on patrol." The hands cupping his tankard were hard with calluses, nails broken and lined with dirt, nothing like the soft, white fingers of Captain Andre and his fellows.

"I saw you once last summer, when the troops were in Philadelphia," I said. "You at Brandywine River or Germantown?"

"After our adventure in the Bronx River, I steered clear of the Brandywine." He smiled and sipped warily at the callibogus. "So you're living in Philadelphia now."

"With my uncle. I cook for them, earn my board." I shrugged. "My uncle's a good man, but my cousin, Peggy, thinks she's the belle of the ball—"

"Peggy? Peggy *Shippen*?" His eyes were sharp as the cider. "You mean your uncle's *Judge* Shippen?"

He broke a piece from the loaf as the girl appeared with some stew. When she'd retreated to the kitchen and the plates before us were sickening me with their odor, he said, "They told me you were well-placed, but it didn't occur to me, just didn't connect your name with his, I guess."

We returned thanks, and he tucked into the stew, downing half of his while I left mine untouched. He speared a piece of grey meat, tried to chew, gave up and swallowed anyway.

I shuddered. "How can you eat that?"

"I've spent the last two weeks at the Valley Forge. They're eating grass up there, Miss Shippen. Anything looks good after that. We got a drill master, a General von Steuben, over from Europe. Keeps the troops busy marching and presenting arms, and that on no food. Turning us into a regular army. Maybe someday he'll get us provisions, too." He eyed my plate. "You gonna eat that?"

I passed it to him.

"Miss Shippen, it'll be a pleasure, working with you. There's a pretty good network of spies in Philadelphia, but none as high as you. How often were you meeting your last contact, and where?"

I gave the particulars while he crumbled the mold off his bread and mopped gravy from his plate. He said, "There's a big party for Howe next week—"

"The Meschianza." I nodded as I spoke Andre's fancy name for it. "Means 'mixture' in Italian, or so they say, because it'll have a mixture of entertainments, see." I was still smarting at Andre's ordering me about, still humiliated that I hadn't defied him, so I muttered the next words with shame. "I'm cooking for it."

He sat motionless, bread halfway to his mouth. "You're joking."

"No. By order of Captain John Andre."

"Andre?"

"He's in Grey's family. He's pretty accomplished—draws and paints. I think he does maps for Howe. But this party, it's not as though I'll be able to learn anything. I'll be cooking back in the kitchen, not serving where I can hear."

"Wasn't thinking you'd learn anything." He essayed the callibogus again. "We been trying to figure how to get someone in there, and you—well, that settles that. Now we need to decide what to do. See, this party's a chance for us to do something. Something big."

"Bring the troops down from the Forge and invade it. There'll be plenty of food."

"His Excellency wants us to snatch Clinton. Howe too, if we can."

The breath left me.

"'Course, speaking strategically," he continued calmly, "it's useless, grabbing Howe. He's over and done with here. It's Clinton makes the most sense to go after. But what a stroke if we can get them both!"

"Indeed." I could barely whisper for elation.

"Washington'd settle for either one, though, he assured me. But we're stuck on how to get them out of the hall so's we have a chance at them. We could grab them as they're going in at the beginning of the party or coming out afterwards, but that's dangerous because there'll be such a crowd around them."

"Why don't we poison them? I could slip something into their food—"

He shook his head. "Admire your enthusiasm, Miss Shippen, but we don't want to murder anyone. We just want—"

"Why not? They murdered Nathan Hale."

He finished the stew on my plate and stacked it atop of his. Then he wiped his sleeve across his eyes.

"Point of kidnapping them," he said quietly, "is to have something to bargain with, so we can tell king and Ministry to recall their troops. If we nab the commanders on top of the French alli—"

The tavern's door banged open so suddenly we both jumped, and the serving girl, who'd reappeared with more callibogus, ran for the kitchen. A man burst into the room, shouting, "Redcoats, Major, half a mile off."

We were instantly on our feet. 'Twas like our fright at the Bronx River, with Tallmadge grabbing my hand and pulling me after him out of the tavern. "Where's Mumford?" he shouted at his picket.

"Fell behind me, Major, and they got him, damn their scarlet souls."

The picket reached his horse and thwacked its rump, which sent it careering out of the yard while he scrabbled alongside trying to mount. Tallmadge vaulted onto a dappled stallion and hauled me up behind. I nigh tumbled off when the horse wheeled and leaped forward.

We heard shouted commands and drumming hooves, and if they'd been half a mile off, they were a lot closer now.

"Go!" Tallmadge spurred the stallion, though the ground beneath was already a blur.

I looked back and wished I hadn't. A hundred yards away were cavalry, brass helmets gleaming, some of them pointing things that glinted in the sun. There was a puff of smoke, and the dirt to my left spurted.

"Damnation!" Tallmadge cried.

We heard more pops, and something whistled past to knock the major's plumed helmet from his head.

"Damn!" he cried again. "Look, Miss Shippen, can you shoot? I'll hand you back my sidearms."

He took a pistol from its holster on his saddle. I snatched it and fired blindly, the only way you can atop a galloping horse.

A dozen bullets answered me.

"The other one!" he shouted. "Here's the other one!"

We'd reached some trees. I fired the second pistol.

Miraculously, the Redcoats veered aside. I was congratulating myself as a pretty good shot when Tallmadge said, "They won't follow us in here. Our lines are just ahead."

He halted the horse so's we could dismount. My knees shook so bad I leaned against the stallion, foamy though he was, and hooked my fingers in the bearskin flap covering the holster.

The major smiled as he had at the farmhouse well two years before. "Seems we have an adventure every time we run into each other."

I was still breathless and could only nod as I handed him his pistols.

"Scared?" he asked.

I was as terrified as I'd been then, but seeing his courage, I shrugged.

"Good." His smile widened. He took a cartridge box from one of his saddle-bags. "Best sit here a while, let them get back to their outpost. Then I'll ride you to the tavern."

Maybe there's a lady somewhere objects to dallying with a likely man on a spring day, but it isn't me. I sank down under an oak and watched him reload.

Finished, he came over to drop aside me. "No wonder they were chasing us so hard. Most days I don't have a pretty girl with me."

'Twas the first time any man had called me pretty, and it was like kill-devil to the town drunk. A little taste made me want a lot more. Soon I'd be as vain as Peggy, so I hurried to change the subject. "Last time we ran from them, you told me about Captain Hale. I'd sure like to hear another story, if you'd oblige."

He did, making me laugh with tales of their escapades at Yale. Then he asked why I'd removed from New York to Philadelphia. The shadows were lengthening towards twilight when we again mounted the stallion. While we plodded towards the tavern, the major told me to contact him when I had more particulars about Andre's extravaganza and promised to let me know my role that night. "It may be we have nothing for you beyond getting us the plans for the party. Or we may want you to break a tureen over Clinton's head."

We entered the tavern's yard. He handed me down, then reached a hand to my cheek. "Good to meet up with you again, Miss Shippen."

My eyes prickled. Suddenly, I was lonelier than I'd been for months, as lonely as when I first left the army.

Over the next week, Tallmadge sent me instructions through a messenger, a red-headed soldier named Jed, brought to skin and bones at the Valley Forge who hated government more with every missed meal. I had all sorts of details to give him, knew more about the Meschianza than anyone but Andre, I'd wager, for I was spending my days at Walnut Grove, overseeing the purchase of vast amounts of provisions, the grinding and chopping of ingredients for sauces, the preserving of the meats. Jed and I whispered over my uncle's back fence late each night until Peggy caught us and teased me about my suitor.

Andre planned elaborate toasts in honor of Howe and Clinton. The two would receive these after ascending the mansion's mahogany staircase, where the landing overlooked the enormous front parlor, or did once Andre's carpenters knocked down a wall. Not only would that be the perfect time to grab them, but Andre had created a perfect spot for it, too. In demolishing the wall, he'd left a niche all around that could hide four or five men, enough to overpower Howe and Clinton. Once subdued, we'd cart them down the servant's staircase to the back door and a wagon. My job was to admit the kidnappers to the house, lead them upstairs, and then signal the wagon, waiting down the street.

Our plans were well laid and, with a little luck, would succeed. Still, when I arrived at Walnut Grove early on the morning of the Meschianza and set to on some sauce, I was shaking so that I near cracked the eggs against each other before I could break them into the bowl.

My nerves tightened as the day wore on. At noon, when a heavy hand fell on my shoulder, I jumped.

"Lordy, Miss Clem." It was Daisy, one of the Africans conscripted to help in the kitchen. Philadelphia has hardly any slaves, for the Quakers frown on such wickedness, but Andre had rounded up what there was. Which explained why Daisy, a laundress, was cooking this week. Seeing her, and not a British officer ready to gaol me, I nigh wept with relief. "Miss Clem, you's nervous as a cat."

"'Tisn't every day I cook for a thousand people," I said. "What is it?"

"I gots enough onions chopped to suit you? I surely hopes so. I haven't cried so much since they sold my mama off."

I started across the kitchen with her, Daisy muttering she'd be glad to get back to her wash kettles after all this foolery, only for Daisy's husband, Sam, to stop me again.

"Miss Clem, gentman here to see you, says he gots the greens you bought offa him yesterday."

It was Jed, skinny as ever. I slipped a couple of the cookies cooling on the windowsill into my skirts and went to where he waited just inside the door.

"How do, lady," he said as would the farmers thereabouts.

I sniffed and said loud enough for those carving ham to hear, "You come with me out to the wagon, if you please. Your dad tried to cheat me once before."

"That wasn't no cheating, ma'am," he said, following me. "That was a honest mis—"

I shut the door after us, and he left off whining to whisper, "Major says we're set. Remember, soon as Clinton and Howe get up and start for the balcony for the toasting, you run out here to the back with a torch, make like you're looking for something in the garden. That'll signal them to pull the wagon up to the gate there and be ready when Cully and Jeff and the rest bring them down."

I handed him the cookies.

He bit into one, scarce chewing afore he swallowed. "Major wanted me to tell you, he's arranged for a diversion long about the time them toasts start. You'll hear some explosions down towards the outposts. It'll be quite a rumpus, but pay it no heed. We want the Redcoats to think we're attacking, draw a good number of them out of the house so's it's easier grabbing the chiefs. And we're hoping in all the confusion some of our boys down there at the gaol can escape."

The afternoon passed in a blur. As I hurried with a jar of cream or a basket of fruit from one end of the kitchen to the other, I wondered if we'd be prisoners ourselves this time tomorrow. Then we heard a fanfare out on the lawn, and I stationed servants with punch and sangaree, wine and cakes in the mansion's front hall.

We toiled all evening, laying places with china as fine as my uncle's (indeed, some of it had come from him), stacking glasses filled with jellies and other sweetmeats into pyramids down the center of the tables, mixing punch, lemonade, and syllabub. Now and then, I caught the sounds of revelry from outside. There was the cannon that boomed just as a clock somewhere chimed six, in honor of Howe's arrival. Sometime later, officers jousted in knights' dress so that we heard hoofbeats, pistols popping in mock combat, and cheers. When fireworks exploded to "oohs" and "ahhs," I knew 'twas ten o'clock. Supper was to be served at midnight, and we had half the meat yet to carve. But another concern was pressing me.

"I'll be back," I told Daisy and scurried outside. There, sauntering in the moonlit garden, were five men in the rags of wartime's laborers or the Valley Forge. They gathered about me soon as I appeared, and I led them to a door on another side of the house and up to the second floor.

"I'd best get back downstairs," I whispered after pointing out the niche. 'Twas then things begun to go wrong.

I backed into the hall from the landing and bumped into a British officer. He dropped his candle, leaving us only the moonlight coming through the Palladian window.

I gasped. "Your pardon, sir."

He nodded, but I felt his eyes measuring me. I'd glimpsed him passing to and fro this last week, which meant he's familiar with the goings-on and harder to cozen if he'd spied us entering the niche. "Not at all, my fault. But aren't you required in the kitchen?"

"Yes, I—I am, absolutely." I turned to leave, but he caught my wrist.

"Then what are you doing up here?"

I almost said, "The workmen, you see, I showed them the spot needs repairing," but without knowing whether he'd seen us, I hated bringing them into it.

Then footsteps sounded, and another officer and candle appeared. "Ah, I thought I heard voices," this one said pleasantly. "Lieutenant, how are you? And you, Miss Shippen?"

"Well, thank you, sir." I spoke hearty in my relief. 'Twas Captain Montresor, an engineer who'd dined at my uncle's house some weeks ago. I'd found out later he'd seen Nathan Hale hang, same as me. He'd even talked with him whilst they made the preparations, offering him paper and ink for to write his family. I'd nigh swooned when I learned that Montresor was one of the Meschianza's hosts, in charge of the fireworks, thinking I'd have the tale of Nathan's last hour from him. But though I often saw him, he was ever hurrying from one duty to the next. Once or twice I slipped him a morsel when Andre wasn't watching, but even that didn't slow him enough to chat. Still, those bits would save me now, for he was smiling and ordering the lieutenant to let me go. "I was just looking for you, Captain Montresor," I said.

"I'm honored." He bowed. "How may I be of service?"

It didn't seem the time to ask about a rebel spy. The moments fled until I finally gulped, "Well, sir, I, uh—"

Providentially, a crash sounded from below, followed by an awful silence. Then the screams began. I gasped again and raced for the stairs, the officers behind me.

I found the largest pot of boiling water overturned, the two ser-vants who'd been carrying it across the kitchen holding their scalded arms and legs and screaming, with everybody else clustered about and screaming too.

"Get back to work!" I shouted for the lieutenant's benefit as Captain Montresor excused himself and hurried to the party. I wished he'd take the lieutenant with him, set as he was on mischief. "Sam, Ephie, I'll bandage you. Daisy, fetch some rags to clean this up. You, sir." I turned to the officer in his scarlet coat and dressed wig. "Can you right that pot? 'Tis a heavy one."

His brows rushed together. "What do I look like, one of your blackamoors?"

"Anyone standing about here I put to use." Such boldness shocked even me, but it worked. He went all indignant, which was better than suspicious.

"I've duties to attend," he said, "and I'll thank you to remember who your betters are." He raised his hand for to slap me. I skipped backwards, wishing mightily for Captain Montresor. "I'm an officer of the king, entitled to respect from the likes of you." He turned on his heel, stalked to the door. From there he called, "And keep to your kitchen, wench. Next time I'll search you myself, see what you've been stealing abovestairs."

I prayed he wouldn't return abovestairs himself as I pulled the last of the Yorkshire pies from the oven. It seemed but a moment later that

Daisy was telling me the guests were inside and seated. She nodded at the pies. "Want me to start sending them out?"

"Not yet, Daisy, that goes after they drink Their Excellencies' health."

"I dunno, Miss Clem. Looks like they's pretty hungry, you ask me."

"Finish slicing this roast, then, will you?" I wiped my hands and darted from the kitchen to the canvas-roofed hall. Murmuring voices, rustling silk skirts, and clinking goblets drowned the music, though the fiddlers sat not twenty feet from me.

Surely whatever noise our boys made grabbing Clinton and Howe would pass unnoticed.

I craned to see the two generals at the far end of the room, on a platform built for their table. They should be rising any moment and making for the niche. My heart pounded as I thought how this might be the last evening of the war. So intent was I that I didn't notice Andre descending on me until it was too late.

He looked as though he belonged on a crusade instead of strutting round a Pennsylvania mansion. The plume on his hat nodded with his words as he hissed, "We're awaiting our dinner."

"But—but you said—aren't you drinking their health first?"

"No. General Clinton suffered an attack of the gout yesterday, so we thought better about having him climb stairs. We'll salute them, but as they stand at their places. Now the Yorkshire pie, if you please."

Gout! Some of the pies as I carried them steaming from the hearth were flavored with my tears.

The knights' heralds and trumpeters were proclaiming the toasts when we heard Tallmadge's diversion, bombs exploding and men shouting. The healths continued as a major led some captains to investigate.

Between the collation of meats and dessert, I ran outside and waved my torch about. The wagon rattled up instantly. A man crouched inside, face so dark with soot I could hardly see him.

"What door they coming through?" he whispered.

My voice trembled with disappointment. "They changed the plans. Clinton and Howe didn't go up to the balcony."

He turned away and spat. "Where's the others?"

I ran to the house and upstairs. This time, I encountered no Redcoats as I led the five agents to the garden. They climbed into the wagon and were gone as suddenly as they'd appeared.

Back in the kitchen, I found Andre awaiting me. My heart might have failed but for his smile. The help was grinning and laughing both, so I knew he'd been handing money about.

"Ah, Miss Shippen, a lovely dinner, a great success, and we have you to thank for it. Please, accept this as a token of His Majesty's appreciation."

I forced myself to take it, but I never opened the little bag to count the gold inside. Instead, I gave it to Tallmadge when next we met, bid him buy food for the Valley Forge. It fetched two sheep, five dozen chickens, and some wheat from a farmer the next valley over.

The Meschianza's guests had hardly slept off their excesses before the criticism began, and this from Loyalists. They'd had enough of sending their children to bed hungry while General Howe dined in style and refused to attack. Even Becky Franks, as friendly to government as anyone, chuckled when a Redcoat described the teams of officers who jousted at the Meschianza: "The Knights of the Burning Mountain are tom-fools and the Knights of the Blended Rose are damned fools! I know of no other distinction between 'em."

Joseph Galloway, my uncle's kinsman and friend who'd supplied us with salt this winter, sat in our parlor and pounded his cane on the floor. "'Tis a farce of knight errantry," he thundered, and if he hadn't been so angry, I'd have laughed. "How insensible do these people appear, while our land is so greatly desolated!"

"What will Washington think of this?" My uncle sighed. "We must appear as blockheads to him."

Mr. Galloway gave a "tch." "It is really surprising that men of sense could be regaled with such nonsense. Unless—I mean, do you suppose that Sir William Howe is—is not as sensible—but no, after all, he's an officer of the king. Still, sir, I've heard rumors—" He stopped, shook his head.

"Rumors, sir?"

"After the army abandons Philadelphia—" Again, he shook his head.

"Go on, sir."

Mr. Galloway said with effort, "'Tis bad enough they're abandoning us, but you haven't heard the worst. Sir William's advising us, since he won't be here to protect us any more, he's advising us to make our peace with the—the states."

My uncle went limp, as anyone will after a great shock.

"He says," Mr. Galloway continued in a voice sour as yesterday's milk, "he says he supposes they won't treat us harshly."

"The rebels won't?" My uncle nearly came out of his chair. "That's a deal of skimble-skamble stuff. Rebels who lost their homes and—and suffered and starved and died all winter, now that the army's not here to protect us anymore, those rebels won't be bent on revenge?"

"Not according to Sir William, they won't."

"But—but they've already voted. The Pennsylvania Council's voted to confiscate everyone's property who won't swear allegiance to their damned Congress."

"I know. I'm at the top of their list." Mr. Galloway looked as though he'd swallowed that milk and found it harder coming up than going down. "We'll need to make terms with Washington, that's all."

Over the next week, the army withdrew from Philadelphia. "Withdraw" to Redcoats meant "steal everything afore you go." Even the officers helped themselves to whatever they fancied, and wagons making for the wharves jammed the streets. Problem was, there weren't enough ships for so much plunder. There weren't even enough wagons.

Loyalists, too, were packing their belongings, but they had none of the army's vehicles at their command, and the troops had impressed all else with wheels. If I were setting up house, I could have furnished it with the best, and for mere shillings, as folks tried to sell what they couldn't carry. But I owned no house nor money, and most others staying behind didn't neither.

Philadelphia looked like a fair on the last day of business, bedraggled, broken, sad. Desperate refugees drove their mules through the mud and flies as pestilential as those that plagued Pharaoh, now that spring was here with dead horses at every corner and the corpses of prisoners buried shallow during the winter surfacing. Fires blazed along the Delaware, where the Redcoats were burning shipyards, and the air stank of smoke. 'Twas easy to tell a man's sympathies. Joy sparkled in the countenance of the Whigs, and consternation painted those of the Tories.

Andre called to say farewell the evening before he departed. He bowed over all our hands, even mine, thanked us again for our hospitality and help with his party.

"Do take care, sir," my uncle said.

A sob escaped Peggy. 'Twould be parlous for Andre, marching with the troops to New York. Rumor had it that their route through the Jerseys had already been "Arnolded" as the country up around Saratoga had been last fall: wells filled, bridges and food burned, trees chopped across the road and signs tacked to those trunks warning General Clinton he'd be "Burgoyned" if he continued.

Andre gave a patient smile before leading Peggy aside.

"Peggy, dear, don't cry so and ruin those beautiful eyes—"

"But—but—I—you, oh—" She wept harder.

"We'll see each other again, don't worry, once this war's over." He spoke as though she were two years old, mourning a ruined toy, while he, caring nothing for her grief, only wanted her to hush.

But she hid her face in her hands and continued crying.

"Here now, remember you have a job to do," he said. "You must bewitch the rebel leaders as you have us. Get them to lay down their arms, end this matter. All right? Can you do that for me?"

He pulled her hands from her face and squeezed them. She quit sobbing to squint at him. "And then you'll come back? And we'll—we'll—"

"Absolutely. Count on it." He squeezed her hands again, and you could tell how relieved he was that her tears had stopped. He turned to us. "This war can't last much longer, especially if Peggy does her part." He grinned at her and waved away a veil of flies. "I'll look forward to pleasant times with you again after we win…"

"No wonder the Meschianza was such a success if he had you cooking for it," Arnold says. 'Course, I've mentioned naught of our scheme to him, only the herculean task of victualing a thousand. "That supper tonight, well, that's what beef oughta taste like."

"You're very kind, sir." He really is. I'd taken pains with the beef in view of this evening's insult. Long about six weeks ago, the Congress declared today, December 7, 1780, as one of thanksgiving for deliverance from Arnold's plot to sell the enemy our most valuable fort and its 3000 troops. I imagine there are services going on and prayers going up all over New England and Pennsylvania right now, though there's none that I know of here in New York, what with government in control. Still,

I'm sure Arnold must know of the proclamation and grieve, even if he gives no hint of it. So I labored long over the beef, hoping to comfort him somewhat, until the turnips, though not burnt, weren't far from it. Peggy left hers untouched on her plate. But Arnold never mentions my failure, only praises the meat.

In a rush of gratitude, I say, "You went up to the Valley Forge that spring, didn't you, once your wound healed? They must have been glad to see you."

"Oh, you know His Excel—ah, Gen—I mean, Mr. Washington, always courteous and hospitable. He welcomed me…"

…and so did the soldiers, survivors of a winter that starved every fourth man to his grave—an unmarked grave at that, lest spies report how diminished were the Continental forces. Some of these troops had marched with Arnold to Quebec; others had fought at Valcour Island or Danbury. Ragged and cadaverous, they stood before dilapidated huts in the grassless, muddy streets of the Forge to cheer their hero's careening carriage.

Arnold waved from the window, longing to sit his horse as a general should rather than ride inside like a cosseted lady. But his leg would not tolerate it.

More cadavers raised their muskets to him as he passed a redoubt and the breastworks of the inner defenses. Those fortifications should have been alive with soldiers, bristling with guns. Instead, a handful of tattered men huzzahed before turning back to their lone cannon.

Finally, his carriage bumped into a yard as muddy and grassless as the streets to stop before the stone farmhouse Washington had appointed his headquarters. Two of the life guard stood at the door, with more marching a line around the place. Officers clustered everywhere, talking, gesturing, waiting their turn with the commander or his aides, while a messenger dashing out the front door nearly collided with another going in. A horseman galloped into the yard behind Arnold, yelling "Express!", and tumbled from his saddle to run for the house. Following close came another who repeated the performance exactly, even to emphasizing the "Ex" in "Express."

An aide opened the carriage's door. Two more helped Arnold to the ground and then up the building's stoop. His eyes had barely adjusted to the dim interior before a voice was saying, "General Arnold, what an honor! Here, sir, why don't you have a seat there in that parlor while I announce you?"

They half-carried him to a chair, pulled another close for his leg. He sat with eyes closed, willing the pain to stop, until someone said, "General Arnold, sir, this way, if you please. His Excellency requests an audience with you." He heaved himself to his feet and, leaning heavily on the aide, stumped to Washington's office.

He had not seen the Commander-in-Chief since last year. Once again, he was shocked at what the months had done to him. Washington still stood tall and unbowed, but his face was creased with worry. That face had been serene at the start of the war, its smile fresh and eager when commissioning Arnold to liberate Quebec. It had also been dark from the sun, and, though too strong to be handsome, aglow with confidence and vitality. Now it was pasty, with furrows crowding the eyes and a grooved forehead. Washington's smile was tired and old, however encouraging his words.

"General Arnold, welcome, sir! Let me congratulate you on your fine work up north."

"Thank you, Excellency. And you, sir, you're driving the government back to New York, I understand."

"No, General, that, too, is due to your efforts. They'll need to amass their power there now that France is our ally, prepare to meet the French fleet, and all thanks to you." He gestured at Arnold's leg, propped on a chair. "You've suffered much on our behalf."

"Thank you, sir."

"I'm asking Congress for a full pension for you, General. It's the least—"

"A—a pension, sir?" He swallowed, sat bolt upright. "But I thought—I don't want a pension, sir, especially when the country can't even feed men in the field. I want a command, Excellency."

"A command?" Washington stared as though he had requested the moon and a few stars, too. "There's a job I've got for you, General, but it doesn't involve—you're not ready for another command."

"I'll be the judge of that." He spoke more brusquely than he intended, and Washington stiffened. "Please, Excellency, forgive me, it's just—I want to serve, sir, in the field."

Washington shook his head. "I need commanders who can take troops into battle, not—. Let's wait until you've healed, sir. But until then, there's something else of grave importance I've been wanting to ask—"

A knock sounded at the door. An aide opened it and stuck his head in. "Excellency? I've a matter here requires your attention."

Washington excused himself, leaving Arnold to sit crushed and fuming.

His wound had nearly drowned him in despair at first, until he convinced himself he could still command, at least a regiment or two, perhaps a whole wing of the army. And after his victory at Saratoga, they would surely reward him with another assignment. Instead, they were pushing him aside like a beggar, an importunate acquaintance, a cripple—

"Pardon the interruption, General." Washington had returned to stand behind his desk.

"Would you—would you ask them to call my coachman, sir?" His tongue, indeed his whole body, felt unbearably heavy. "I'd best be on my way."

Washington's eyes flashed. "I've not dismissed you."

Arnold settled back with a sigh.

Washington busied himself with the maps on his desk. When he spoke, his voice was courteous again, the rage gone. "There's that matter I mentioned, sir, and you're the perfect man for it. I need a military governor for this whole area, Philadelphia, southern New Jersey across the Delaware, and eastern Pennsylvania."

"A—a governor?" Arnold couldn't keep the frustration from his voice. "But the enemy's retreating. I don't see how—"

"They're retreating, true, but they're leaving behind a goodly number of Loyalists. Quakers, too. As governor, you'll prevent the disorders which are expected upon the return of the Whigs, protect the Quakers and Loyalists. I don't want these people persecuted and turned against us. Heaven knows government's given us thousands of supporters in just that way."

"But, sir, I'm a soldier—"

"That's precisely what I need here, General, a soldier who'll raise more recruits for Congress' army and defend our capital. I want to attack the enemy without worry that I'll be counterattacked in my rear by Loyalist militia, and that would worry me, sir, were anyone else in control."

"But, Excellency—"

Washington raised a hand. "You haven't heard the worst. Congress has already passed resolutions for Philadelphia, once it's ours again, and they're none of them going to win us friends. Seems there's Tory merchants who are hoarding their goods to drive the prices higher."

"'Tis bad business, hoarding."

"My opinion, too. Takes too much trust."

"Ah-yuh, you must trust your competitors, that they aren't selling while you're not. Sooner or later, someone does, and then prices fall, and you're left with near worthless goods. Meanwhile, you've angered your customers, and for what?"

"Well, as a consequence of this hoarding, Congress wants all trade suspended in the city."

"Sus—what?" The breath left him. "Suspend trade? Are they outa their minds?"

"Sir, they—"

"How? How we gonna 'suspend trade'? Imprison folks for buying their dinners? Arrest them for going to the bookseller's or tailor's? That's tyranny!"

"Congress wants the army to have first pick of these goods—"

"Oh, I'll wager they do. We paying for things, or just helping ourselves?"

"And you'll need to keep peace with the government in Philadelphia, too. It's an explosive situation. Joseph Reed's on the Executive Council there. He's convinced we're plotting to overthrow the Council in favor of a military dictatorship."

"Well, mayhap he's right, we go in there stealing and suspending trade."

"'Twas ordered by Congress, sir, let me remind you. And no one's setting up a military dictatorship, not while I'm in command." Washington's voice sank low. "Reed should know better. He was my aide early on."

"But, sir, I was a merchant before the war, and this is what started the whole thing in the first place, the Ministry telling men how to run their business or shutting them down entirely."

"Another reason I want you for this job, sir. You're a merchant. You speak the language of business."

"Well, my advice, then, is to let the market take care of the hoarders. It always does. They'll learn their lesson once one of them starts to sell and the rest are left with warehouses full of stock they can't even give away."

Washington turned to the window behind his desk and stood looking out.

"Excellency?"

Washington sighed. "Now you see, General, this task I'm setting you, 'tis harder than a victory in the field. I need a man who's versed in business and in military matters and, withal, he loves liberty and won't enforce these Congressional edicts more than he has to." Washington faced him. "That's why I want you. You have the best knack I've seen for doing the impossible. And then, sir, once you've calmed this situation here and your leg mends, we'll make use of you again in the army."

Put like that, Arnold saw the sense: he could not yet sit his horse, let alone lead troops to battle. Still, this governorship was utter despotism, and he rebelled at becoming the very thing he warred against. But if he declined, the man appointed might glory in the power Congress handed him, drag freedom low and forget the reasons they were fighting, so long as he could order folks about and gaol those who crossed him.

Arnold felt Washington's eyes on him and glanced up. "All right, Excellency, I'll do it."

"Fine, sir, thank you." For a moment, the young face of three years ago grinned at him. Then the care descended again. "Just one other thing. You'll need to take the Loyalty Oath."

"Loyalty Oath?"

Washington nodded wearily. "The Congress wants all officers to swear allegiance—"

Arnold's outrage would have brought him to his feet had his leg cooperated. As it was, he fell back into his chair after trying to stand, groaning with pain. "God in Heaven, sir," he croaked at last, "doesn't my leg speak for me?"

"As far as I'm concerned, yes, General, it does. But—"

"'Tisn't right, sir. This isn't what we're fighting for! We're fighting to live free, without anyone telling us what to think or believe or how to act, not so we're forced to prove our loyalty when the Congress snaps its fingers."

Washington's silence told Arnold he agreed. But His Excellency rarely criticized the citizens to which he subordinated his army. When at last he spoke, his tone was gentle. "You'll find it's painless, sir, the oath. I speak from experience."

Before Arnold could explode at the Congress' requiring George Washington, of all people, to pledge their vow, His Excellency continued, "Anyway, it'll be a thankless job, keeping Reed's Council happy while you protect folks' liberty. But then you're used to thankless jobs..."

"'Thankless.'" Arnold snorts, and Flash's ears twitch. "That was understating it by a mile. Here I was, ready to like Reed and the way he's protesting tyranny, but from the day I arrived in Philadelphia, Reed and his boys persecuted me."

Arnold's words sound harsh and self-pitying, without you were there, in Philadelphia in 1778. But I was, and "persecuted" don't cover the half of it. The Council hounded and ridiculed Arnold, condemned his every gesture, countermanded or ignored his orders. They criticized his friends, his carriage, his staff, his headquarters. Even his clothes were too fancy, too British, not plain and simple as befit a republican governor.

Petty, you're thinking, and you're right. But that's the way things were going then, in the capital of a country fighting for liberty: its rulers dictated how many ruffles a lady could wear on her dress and whether a gentleman might own silver shoe buckles. See, the "new men" my uncle despised, the ones who pushed him and other royal officers out of posts they wanted for themselves, the stay-at-homes who never ducked a Redcoat's fire while Washington and Arnold and the troops were fighting and dying—well, they'd seen their chance for power and grabbed it. Oh, they cloaked it in nice talk about liberty and Patriotism, even called themselves Radical Patriots, as though the men who'd starved at the Valley Forge weren't Patriot enough. Then they prattled about how they wanted to help us, protect us from the Tories, though by this time, Tories were mighty scarce. Three thousand of them left Philadelphia when the government's troops did, so we was pretty much rid of them.

But that didn't matter to men as hungry for power as the Radicals. They did what tyrants always do when they run scant of real enemies: they invented some. Now you didn't need to support His Majesty to be a Tory. 'Twas enough if you dressed after the British fashion, or you hankered to visit London or admired English art or books or music. Any one of them made you a Tory and fit game for the Radicals. They turned our rebellion against government into a war against the British people, and never mind that most everybody had family in Britain or that our brothers there, many of them, objected just as we did to government's stealing their money for to send troops against us. No, we must despise England and everything British to please the Radicals, especially Joseph Reed.

Reed was a sourpuss who hated to see anyone enjoying life. Later that year, his power spread beyond Philadelphia to the whole state when he become President of Pennsylvania. They say General Washington sent congratulations after the election, even suggested he take vengeance against anyone who'd helped the Redcoats during their occupation. Perhaps some of it's true. Reed served as aide to His Excellency before leaving in a huff, and polite as His Excellency is, he'd congratulate a man, even if he quit and left him short-handed. But I doubt he urged him to revenge. 'Twasn't like General Washington, for one thing, and for another, Reed didn't need urging. He was a vindictive little rat, jealous of every gill of his power.

Reed hated Arnold, not only because Arnold's authority was greater than his but because Arnold didn't flaunt it. Worse, Arnold liked to laugh, sometimes at Reed.

Then there's the whole thing about money. Arnold prized what money could buy, the good times and comfort, while Reed loved gold too well to part with any. Arnold was the kind could sell dirt to a farmer, and get rich in the bargain. But Reed, if you give him a hundred pounds to invest, would lose every shilling, and wouldn't take him long to do it, neither. Still, Reed fancied himself a man of business as Gates thought himself a military genius, and that made him despise the genuine article, when he met it in Arnold, as much as Gates did.

Curious about Arnold. He never had trouble with gentlemen, those bred to wealth and prestige, like General Schuyler or His Excellency or General Montgomery. Maybe they were happy enough in their own good fortune that they didn't envy Arnold his abilities. But the low-born men, the John Browns and Horatio Gateses and Joseph Reeds, loathed him. Reckon they sensed how superior Arnold was, how far above them his genius soared, and they couldn't stand for a man who started off the same place they did to fly past them.

Probably all this together determined Reed to bring Benedict Arnold down.

Chapter Fifteen

The Continentals marched into Philadelphia only hours after the government's troops marched out. 'Twas a Friday in June, with crows cawing over the feasts on every corner and flies thick as ministers in London. Living there, I was used to Philadelphia's devastation. Now I saw it through the troops' eyes.

Whole blocks of houses had gone for firewood, and what was still standing had no lampposts, no shutters nor fences (I misdoubt there's a fence left in Philadelphia), nothing wooden that could warm sentries on winter nights. The Redcoats had robbed the dead, too, using churchyards for cavalry drills and never mind how many headstones they overturned and cracked. They even robbed God, chopping the pews and pulpits from churches for their hearths.

Windows were everywhere missing, in almost all the buildings, for they'd shattered last fall when those warships exploded. Glass was a luxury at any time, but even more so now with necessities like food so scarce. Best we could do was cover the holes with boards.

Smothering everything was a stink so foul it seemed however much vinegar we sprinkled on burning coals, the air'd never be cleansed. Soldiers had cut privies into the homes taken for barracks by chopping holes in the floors. Their filth accumulated all winter, until, with spring's warmth, the stench made them do what decency couldn't. They shovelled out the cellars, piling their dung in the streets.

And so our troops picked their way through dead horses and broken wagons, spiked cannon and abandoned tents, with ruined houses all about and trenches near the State House holding the corpses of 2000 American prisoners. The crows lifted in black mobs as the ranks passed, then scattered with indignant cries when they continued passing. Flies buzzed in my ears until I dropped the handkerchief soaked in cinnamon water I was clutching to my nose and brushed them away with both hands.

The soldiers looked as bad as the city. They were even more ragged than when I marched with them last year. But something was different. Rather than slink along like defeated Continentals, they stepped high and proud as the Regulars that had swung down the street that morning. That drillmaster Tallmadge mentioned had wrought a wonder, for certain sure.

Behind them rode Philadelphia's new military governor, Major General Benedict Arnold. Actually, I couldn't have sworn it was him: 'twas hard to see inside the carriage. Those closest called that it was indeed the fabled warrior, wounded leg propped on cushions.

We cheered ourselves hoarse as the army passed, men who had starved and frozen all winter at the Valley Forge, who refused to go home and eat pie by the fire but instead taught the government such fear it left our city. We cheered even more for the hero of Saratoga, fighting so hard for our Cause.

Arnold and Reed shared a headquarters at first, but soon Arnold took himself to John Penn's mansion on Market Street. 'Twas necessary as governor, for any French bigwig visiting the capital of the new United States would expect Arnold to entertain him—and lavishly, too, as they do in Europe. Withal, Arnold's sister and sons from Connecticut came to live with him, and he needed room for them.

But his grandeur infuriated Joseph Reed. He himself removed to the house of the Reverend Jacob Duche, long since fled to England. It was a little place, and modest, and Duche a traitor who had prayed for Congress until the Redcoats invaded us and arrested him. Rumors flew that they interrogated him worse than usual, and it worked: when they finally freed him, he pleaded with General Washington to submit to Britain. All that let Reed call it "confiscating" when he stole Duche's property.

With the Redcoats gone from our city, you'd think our problems would be, too. You'd think we'd have spent our time cleaning and repairing, which would have more than occupied us. But that didn't suit Reed nor the Council. Better than rebuilding and painting, they thought, was punishing the Loyalists, which of course was nigh impossible since they'd fled. So Reed again minted new ones. Anyone who'd rather plaster his parlor than help the Radicals ferret out Loyalists must be a Loyalist, too. So was anyone who wouldn't tattle on his neighbors, or anyone disagreeing with the Council.

The man who disagreed strongest was Benedict Arnold. But not at first. I think at first it stunned him that the leaders of the new country's capital were tyrants, and bigger ones than ever King George was. Withal, General Arnold was busy, what with his duties as military governor and trying to replace the fortune he'd spent on the war, so mayhap he didn't notice. Or maybe he figured Reed would rein them in, or Congress would, once the delegates returned to Philadelphia and found the Radicals spying on them, too.

Then I went to market, or tried to, and that set me thinking General Arnold was as despotic as Joseph Reed.

I was especially eager to go, for last time I'd overheard two butchers gossiping about a cousin in Connecticut, a rascal if ever there was one who'd jilted his lady some years ago. They'd had too many customers then to interrupt their talk, and I was anxious to find them now.

But a few blocks from the market, I heard a roaring. Drawing nigh, I could see the crowd milling about. Men waved their fists, women shouted and cried.

"What is it?" I asked a woman at the mob's edge.

She carried a baby in one arm and a basket over the other. "They's not selling the beef."

"Is there none again?"

"Oh, no, they's plenty, least enough to keep us from starving like last fall, but that General Arnold, he says can't nobody sell anything."

"*What?*"

She nodded with the satisfaction people take in telling bad news. "You haven't heard? All the shops is closed from now on, and can't nobody sell nothing at all until the army takes what it wants first."

"But they can't—that's just what the Redcoats—how are we supposed to live?"

She looked me up and down. "You come from a rich family, don't you? You got any food on hand you can sell me? I'll pay you good, but I need something for the baby."

I led her through the thrumming streets to my uncle's house and gave her oats and some bread and meat, too. "Save your money," I said as she thrust a handful of Continentals at me. "'Tisn't worth anything."

"I know, but it's all my husband sends me. He's with Wayne somewhere, don't rightly know where since they left the Valley Forge. But I thank you, I truly do, and soon as I get some real money, I'll bring it to you. I don't take charity. It's enough you'll sell me food when I can't get it nowhere else. I aim to pay you for it."

That evening, my uncle talked of inviting Arnold to dinner. "But, Uncle," I said, "what'll we serve? He's closed all the shops. I can't buy anything to feed us, let alone guests."

"Shops can't stay closed forever, Clem. I meant we'd have him once they open again, of course."

"Edward, dear," my aunt said, "he's nothing but a—a shopkeeper, a vulgar man taking advantage of the times to rise above his betters."

"He's an acquaintance, and a powerful one," my uncle said.

"He's no acquaintance of ours."

"He is, my dear. I met him often last summer while you were at the farm. Withal, we dined with the government's officers two or three nights a week. How will it look if we snub General Arnold?"

"The officers at least were civilized." My aunt sniffed, the feathers atop her hair quivering.

"Yes, but you forget, General Arnold's a man of affairs. He's been in town, what, three days now? And already he's got a deal with Willy West where they buy flour here at $5 a barrel and sell it down to Havana for $28. There's profit for any man dealing with Arnold."

"Where are they getting flour for $5 a barrel?" Aunt Shippen asked. And a good question it was, for flour had been scarce all winter at any price.

My uncle shrugged. "Who knows? Most likely 'tis coming from the supplies the Redcoats left. But long as there's a profit like that to be had, who cares?"

That astonished me, for many would care. All the mothers grieving their dead babies from last fall when they couldn't buy food, the

Patriots who watched friends starve and die in prison, the Philadelphians who'd barely kept body and soul together—those people would remember, and care.

The shops opened eight days after they closed, just as I was scraping the bottom of our barrels of food. Before they did, though, Arnold's effigy hanged at either end of town, and the *Journal* and *Ledger* published letters savaging him. So did the *Mercury*.

Those letters hissed that while businesses scrounged for workers, what with Philadelphians too busy with repairs to hire themselves out, Arnold had all the help he needed, though he was but planting the Penn mansion's gardens (not to say they didn't need it, after the king's officers billeted there). Worse, the troops he recruited to weed were supposed to be fighting the enemy. I suppose few soldiers complained, though. Puttering in the shady Penn grove was easier than digging fortifications in the sun, and Arnold poured his rum with a heavier hand than the Continentals' quartermaster.

But the army could have used Arnold's gardeners one blistering Saturday at the end of June near Monmouth, when His Excellency fell on the red line wending its way through the Jerseys to New York. Looked early on like we'd have a victory to match Saratoga's, with Clinton surrendering his Redcoats and suing for peace. And we might have, if Benedict Arnold had been leading men to battle, as he'd wanted, instead of to wheelbarrows. Without him, we barely carried the day.

Then, the next week, 'twas the country's second birthday…

"Seemed a miracle, didn't it?" Arnold grins as he puts out a hand for Flash to shake. Flash lifts a paw, and Arnold says, "Good boy. Couldn't believe we'd survived two whole years."

"Especially with all the defeats. Because other than Saratoga, what had we won?"

But his smile fades, and I wager he's remembering what happened that day in 1778, the ridicule of Philadelphia's radical Council, its damning of him, our worthiest hero…

Arnold woke in a sweat, gut roiling, to a morning that was already hot and steamy. He spent it retching into his chamberpot. By afternoon, weak but recovering, he made his way with most of Philadelphia to the City Tavern.

It was a three-storey brick building with awnings stretched across its front and the windows beneath open to July's breeze. Inside its cavernous Long Room, wine punch was fast disappearing in toasts to liberty, General Washington, the Declaration of Independence, Major General Arnold—he called his compliments while they cheered—the army and officers. Fifers clustered on the stairs, tooting "Yankee Doodle" and "General Washington's March." Patriot soldiers grinned, Patriot ladies laughed through tears of joy. Even those the Radicals had tarred as Loyalists were celebrating. Wigs went askew as their owners threw tattered tricorns in the air. More bodies crowded through the door, and gentlemen removed threadbare coats needing braid and buttons.

His punch slopping over to wet his sleeve, Arnold wormed his way to a window and breathed deeply. Though the day was a scorcher, the breeze was cool after the heat inside.

"General Arnold."

He turned to see the man calling his name.

"Colonel Stewart," he bellowed, "a fine party, sir, a great day."

"Yes, sir, praise God we've lived to see it," Stewart shouted. Even so, Arnold strained to hear him over the din. Beside Stewart stood a young lady with black hair and eyes. "General, let me present Miss Rebecca Franks."

Fighting queasiness, Arnold bowed over her hand. "An honor, Miss Franks."

"I've heard wondrous tales of you, General." A smile softened her sharp features. "I'm just sorry you're on the wrong side."

He chuckled, then leaned close to yell, "Now, Miss Franks, don't tell me a lovely lady like you's cheering for the government."

"Of course, but unfortunately my good sense doesn't extend to my relations. My cousin's in your military family."

"That would be my aide, David Franks, I presume."

Suddenly, Colonel Stewart's eyes widened. He pointed to the window as Miss Franks clapped a hand to her mouth. Arnold turned to look.

The first thing he saw was the wig, the gaudiest, most elaborate ever, a parody of fashionable hairdressing, with curls mounting up and out and a cloud of powder shaking free with every movement. Fruit and beads and even a miniature ship clung to various plateaus, threatening to topple the whole monstrosity. It was nearly as big as the creature under it, an African woman in rags. Her bare legs were thrust into shoes so broken he could see both calloused heels. Bent and toothless, she clutched the cart in which she rode, while Radical Patriots bowed to her from either side of the street.

His stomach cramped until he nearly groaned aloud. Why were they insulting a helpless old hag? What wickedness had Reed invented now?

Drummers beating the "Rogue's March" followed the wagon, and a councilman bellowed to be heard over them. "Here we are, good people! Bow to your mistress, dressed like a British officer's jade and lording it over honest Patriots."

Beginning to understand, Arnold hoped they were paying her well— but doubted it. He swallowed, willing himself not to vomit, as revellers rushed to the windows with cries of "Hush!" and "What'd he say?"

The speaker waited for the drummers to finish before launching his next sally.

"Behold the ruin of Philadelphia." He gestured towards the crone. "While Patriots starved in British prisons and died from British balls, some in this city, your own friends and neighbors, danced with British officers and flirted with British soldiers."

There were a few nervous laughs as the man rolled on.

"Friends, now we got a Yankee governor sent to rule over us, protecting these traitors because he's one of them. He's a Loyalist and Tory. No honest Patriot oughta stand for it!"

This time, the pangs twisted his stomach so fiercely Arnold moaned, but the crowd's murmuring drowned the noise. The councilman smacked the mule pulling the cart, and the animal shambled forward.

Arnold's leg and head throbbed; the urge to retch was overpowering. He turned to shoulder his way to the door, but the throng wedged him in.

Behind him, Colonel Stewart gave a tentative laugh. "Well, the lady's equipped altogether in the English fashion, wouldn't you say?"

Rebecca Franks spoke in cool, amused tones. "Not altogether, Colonel. Though the style of her head is British, her shoes and stockings are in the genuine Continental fashion…"

"Isn't Becky Franks the one who introduced you to Peggy?" I ask.

"Becky Franks?" He gives a keen glance. "What brought her to mind?"

I shrug. I'd had the whole story of the cart and wig from Peggy, who'd had it from Becky the next day, but I won't embarrass him by mentioning the Radicals' mockery.

"Curious," he says, "I was just remembering this joke she made once about barefoot Continentals. But no, 'twas your uncle's invitation to dinner, that's how I met Peggy. I'll never forget the first time I saw her."

He shifts his crippled leg, grimacing, and I say, "Want some hot cloths, sir?"

"That might help, thanks."

His leg's probably ached all day what with the storm, and heat sometimes relieves him. I fetch a kettle of hot water from the kitchen hearth, a basin, and some cloths. Back in the parlor, I pour water over the rags in the bowl. Then I turn to stir up the fire, giving him leave to loosen his breeches at the knee, lower his stocking, and wrap his calf. By his sigh and his "Thank you, Clem," I know he's decent again.

I step over Flash, stretched along the hearth with head on paws, to take my seat. "Your leg was hurting you then, too."

"What? Oh, when I first met Peggy?" He stares into the flames. "That was really the first time I met you, too, I mean, the first time I sat and talked with you."

Actually, I talked with no one that night. I was too busy cooking and waiting table. But he's so grateful for my friendship now—a friendship I'll soon betray as he betrayed our Cause—that I don't correct him. Instead, I listen to his memories…

"Judge Shippen, eh?" Arnold brushed hair powder from his shoulders, then turned from the mirror to face his aide.

"Yes, sir, he's one of the wealthiest Tories—"

"I know, Franks. Remember, I did business here before the war." He swung across the room on two crutches. "Well, send them my thanks and acceptance. Food oughta be good, at least. I hear their cook's the best in the city."

Arnold promptly forgot the engagement, preoccupied with administering the army in Philadelphia, adjudicating disputes between it and the citizens, defending alleged Tories from their neighbors, negotiating deals to restore his fortune. Had Franks not reminded him an hour before he was due at the Shippens, he would have neglected them entirely. As it was, he arrived fifteen minutes late.

"You'll pardon me, sir," Arnold said to his host after introducing him to Franks. "'Tis unwieldy, my leg. It keeps me behind-hand everywhere."

"Of course, General." The judge spoke in the unctuous tones of a man who sat safe while others won the prize but nonetheless expected a share of the profits. "Well, gentlemen, no need to stand here in the hall. Come meet my family."

Either the floor was highly polished or Arnold put his cane down wrong, for the thing flew from him, and he sprawled at the judge's feet. Pain knifed him, so blinding that he bit his lip until he tasted blood to keep from screaming, though even that could not stop his groans.

Through the pounding in his ears, he heard Franks asking, "General, you all right?" Then there were running steps and a woman's voice asking, "Daddy, what happened?"

He opened his eyes but closed them immediately.

There, leaning over him, was Margaret.

The same gold hair, the same grey eyes. And though she was as young as when they'd met, she was also sophisticated, assured. Her hair was upswept instead of flowing down her back, and the miniscule patch beneath her eye marked her a lady of fashion, not the timid girl of his youth. She had been perfected, too. The smallpox scars pitting her cheeks were gone, and the bump on her nose as well, making her face lovelier than was possible on earth. And her hair! The string of gold beads at her throat seemed dull next to that hair, gleaming and shining and beckoning as only an angel's could. Dear God, he'd died and gone to heaven.

"General Arnold?" Margaret's hand lay on his shoulder. He knew it was hers from the way it burned without hurting, and he tingled at her touch. But her voice… It was no longer high and innocent as a child's, but throbbing, even throaty… It made a man wonder things he ought not—

"Peggy," the judge said, "run fetch your brother so we can help him up."

He nearly corrected his host. Her name was Margaret; she hated for anyone to call her "Peggy." But that could wait for later, when she wasn't about to leave. "No, please, I'm all right." He opened his eyes.

Margaret's angelic face twisted with concern, hair abloom with flowers and trinkets, eyes luminous above the patch.

"General, I'm so sorry," the judge was saying.

Arnold nodded, eyes fixed on Margaret, faultless and utterly breathtaking. "Oh, lord, I've missed you."

"Pardon me?" She drew back, puzzled, wary, and he suddenly understood that this was not Margaret at all, only a girl who resembled her.

He lay bereft, heart aching worse than his leg, wishing to die.

"Daddy." She looked up at the judge. "Is he all right?"

"I—I'm fine." Arnold propped himself on his elbow. "May I have the honor?"

Her concern turned to a smile, making her even fairer, if that were possible.

The judge said, "Of course, General. This is my daughter, Margaret Shippen."

"Miss Shippen," he gasped around his agony. "'Tis a delight, absolutely."

"Thank you, General." She curtsied with heavenly grace. "It's an honor to meet you, sir. We've heard much of your heroism."

It was silly, really, to have mistaken the girl for Margaret, though she looked enough like her to have been a sister. Once he recovered from his disappointment, he could enjoy her beauty and youth. He sat across from her at dinner, shared every joke he knew that could be told at table in mixed company, launched one witticism after another, hoping for a grin, not the polite, cosmopolitan half-smile that teased him all evening while she fingered her gold beads…

"She conquered you that first night you came to dinner, didn't she?" I ask, and though I'm not smiling—how could I? It's tragic to see what's happened, thanks to her—he is, bright-eyed as a boy over his first love.

She conquered him, all right, sure as he'd conquered Burgoyne, though, to be fair, Peggy did nothing more than nod at his gallantries. She was still mooning over Andre, still passing most afternoons in her room with a stack of handkerchiefs and whatever preserves I'd concocted. This made her even lovelier, for she'd hardly eaten all winter while the captain squired her about, and she'd lost flesh. Now she was filled out, and rosy, and 'twas clear the general had never seen a woman so beautiful.

Peggy, pining for Andre, didn't return his interest. Then, too, the Continentals seemed prodigiously plain after Cher Jean. But if any of them could match Andre, it was Arnold, with his dash and magnetism, his heroism and fame. And the gifts he brought didn't hurt, neither.

But Peggy only moped after Andre. I don't know what surprised me more: that our foremost hero would woo the daughter of a suspected Loyalist, and that girl fresh from the arms of the enemy, or that Peggy took so long to see the advantages of a military governor as swain.

"Seems ages ago, doesn't it," I say as Arnold settles back, swaddled leg steaming and eyes closed, "that summer you courted Peggy?"

"Only two years, 1778."

"Yes, but such a lot's happened since then."

"I remember the heat, so muggy every day. You made us lemonade most times I called."

The lemonade. I'd forgotten. What a treat, after a starving winter and a summer that saw the Redcoats leave but the hunger stay. Our meals improved with Arnold's courtship, for he never appeared without some delicacy: a ham, bunches of lettuce, a barrel of salt cod, fruit from the Indies. "'Twas kind of you, to keep us in lemons then."

"Well..." He shrugs.

"Especially when you took such criticism for it."

Oh, not just for the lemons. For everything...

Arnold knew he should heed and squelch the rumors the Radicals spread in a city seething over the Congressional edicts he had enforced. But Peggy Shippen obsessed him.

One moist morning in August, he sat in his office with Robert Jones, nodding as Jones droned on about needing partners for the cattle he was driving south but thinking the while of Peggy, her beguiling laugh, her dainty hands and feet, how his whole being hummed at her touch. His longing threatened to smother him.

And so he started when Franks knocked at the door. "Sir? The Shippen ladies are here, say it's urgent they see you."

"What? Miss Shippen, you say?" He leaped to his feet, as excited as when he first courted Margaret, so excited he forgot his mangled leg and nearly shrieked as his weight landed on it. Teeth clenched, he glanced at Jones. "You excuse me, sir, mind waiting outside a moment? Show them in, Captain."

He had eyes for Peggy alone as she and her mother took the chairs before his desk. Though it was early yet, and the heat already stifling, she was as cool and exquisitely dressed as though attending a dance, hair fetchingly coiffed, pearls gleaming at ears and throat.

"What can I do for you ladies?" he asked, though he spoke only to her.

"It's our friend, well, she's our in-law, too," Mrs. Shippen said. "Grace Galloway, General. She needs your help."

"Grace Galloway?" He pulled his eyes from Peggy to catch Mrs. Shippen mopping the sweat from her brow. "Joseph Galloway's wife?"

"Yes, General, but I thought—that is, I'd heard you're protecting Loyalists. And we felt that we were—that we knew you well enough to ask—"

"Absolutely, Madam." But Joseph Galloway? Even Arnold balked at defending the wife of such a traitor, an early member of the Continental Congress who had forsaken the Cause to rule Philadelphia during the government's occupation. Now, with his Redcoated friends gone, Galloway was too, leaving his wife to guard their property.

"General, they are—that Joseph Reed and—and his wicked Council—" Mrs. Shippen bit her lip, motioning for her daughter to continue.

"They're trying to throw her out of her house, have been since His Majesty's troops retreated." Peggy's struggle for control made her voice husky and even more seductive. "Can you imagine, General? They're evicting a lady so they can steal her house from her."

He imagined it too well, felt sick at politicians' assailing a lone woman. Each day increased the Council's audacity. Its latest outrage was to declare folks who owned choice estates Loyalists. Those so attainted must surrender themselves for trial on charges of treason while their homes passed to members of the Council. Still, unlike the Council's other victims, Joseph Galloway actually was a Loyalist.

"But that doesn't give them the right to steal his property." He didn't realize he'd spoken aloud until Peggy beamed at him and her mother lifted hopeful eyes. "You're right, we need to stop them. I'll send some militia over there so Reed can't thieve from her, don't you worry. Franks!"

Gratitude bubbled from them while Franks scribbled the order he dictated. And Mrs. Shippen issued an invitation to supper the next week.

That afternoon, Arnold returned to his office from dinner with Hal clutching his hand. The boy's dog had died yesterday, and Arnold had promised to ask Mr. Lutz, a stonemason and his next appointment, about a cenotaph.

He was wiping Hal's tears and saying, "Come now, son. Let's be brave while we talk to Mr. Lutz" when his door flew open and Reed himself stormed in, past the shouting Franks and Mr. Lutz and a dozen other appointments.

"You've gone too far this time!" Reed lunged forward, black coat flapping, fist raised, so that Hal screamed, "Don't you hit my daddy, you bad man!" and started towards him.

Arnold caught his son, pride in the boy's courage cutting through his anger. "Ah, Reed, always the soul of courtesy—"

"Go to hell, Arnold. I'll see you brought down if it's the last thing I do!"

Beside him, Hal was trembling. "Franks," Arnold said, "take Hal home for me, will you? And then apologize to the gentlemen waiting their turn,"—he spit the words at Reed—"tell them I'll be with them soon as possible."

"You got no call to post militia," Reed yelled, "not when we're evicting a Tory!"

"Right, I shoulda helped you throw the lady out so you can get hold of the property sooner. Look, Reed, we'll all be living together after the war—"

"You calling me a thief, General?" Reed's sneer turned "General" into an obscenity. "I'm a member of lawful government, unlike you. You're just an officer, grabbing power from elected—"

"That oughta comfort folks, to know it's lawful government stealing their prop—"

"It isn't stealing, you damn—"

"I'll remind you of that, case we don't win this thing, when the king comes in here and takes your house away from you." A vein beat in his forehead. "Yes, sir, makes all the difference if it's the king lawfully taking your property instead of a thief."

"Arnold, I'm warning you, stay out of my way. And get those militia off Galloway's land. You got no authority to post them there in the first place."

"Maybe not," he bawled as Reed stalked to the door and slammed it behind him, "but someone needs to protect the good people of Philadelphia from their government."

When Arnold learned that the Council had drafted troops to pry Mrs. Galloway from her home, he sent his housekeeper and coach so that the lady might remove in dignity. Then he pulled a sheet of foolscap to him. He must stop the Radicals. But these personal battles, increasingly bitter, accomplished nothing. However many insults he hurled, however vile the names he called these despots, their crimes went unpunished, encouraging them to new ones. No one man could curb them; Congress alone was that powerful.

He was laboring over his letter's final draft the next day when Franks ushered George Bryan into his office. Bryan was Joseph Reed's loyal shadow, and anything involving him was bound to be contentious.

"Mr. Bryan." Arnold bowed while Bryan remained sourly upright. Objecting to lace and furbelows had not satisfied the Radicals: they denounced bowing as a British custom and decreed that good Patriots would only shake hands. "What can I do for you, sir?"

Bryan flopped into a chair. His coat, though black and shapeless, emphasized the dirt crusting on it and its owner's bulges. His hair was unevenly cropped, as if he had taken shears to his head without benefit of mirror or candle. Bryan was ever an ugly, sloppy man. The Radicals' disdain of fashion had let him grow uglier and sloppier.

Now his eyes roved Arnold's office, flicking from the blue and white tiles surrounding the fireplace to the Chinese porcelain on the man-tel and the mahogany desk covered with papers and polished marble paperweights. Finally, those eyes rested on the man sitting behind the desk in his buff and blue uniform with two silver stars at the shoulder. "Well, General, 'pears the governorship agrees with you. Enjoying your time in Philadelphia, huh?"

"As only the charming and handsome can, Mr. Bryan. Now I asked you before: what do you want?"

Bryan crossed his legs. "See, there's those of us thinks you're enjoying yourself just a little too much. You'd never know there's a war on, that our boys are bleeding and dying, to look at you. How's the people gonna be good republicans when their leaders aren't?"

"You're right, Mr. Bryan." Arnold slapped his desk, and Bryan hitched forward. "I shoulda thought of that myself. I go around in rags and quit visiting the barber,"—he nodded at Bryan—"that oughta stop our boys' dying."

Bryan squinted for a long moment. "You funnin' me, General?"

"Tell me this, Mr. Bryan, because I've been on the battlefield,—" Arnold paused, waiting for Bryan to say that he had, too. But he sat silent, eyes shifting, and Arnold nodded as if to say, "I thought so," before continuing, "—and I can tell you, don't make a damned bit of difference what anyone at home's wearing: those balls come flying at you and hit you, you're gonna bleed. So you tell me, how's it help our boys if I dress like a beggar?"

Bryan flushed.

"Well, Mr. Bryan?"

"Look, General. I'm not here to argue. I'm just telling you what the Council's saying. We're asking you nice to start acting like a republican 'stead of a damned king."

"A republican, sir?"

"You heard me. Stop flaunting yourself. Show some humility. Stop gadding around in a coach and four, and them clothes of yours." Bryan smirked at his uniform. "Every day's not a party, General."

Arnold hauled himself to his feet, face purpling, leg screeching protest. "You're a dog in the manger. You can't enjoy the innocent pleasures of life or let anyone else, either, without grumbling and growling."

"You son of a—"

"Get out, Mr. Bryan."

"Now, General, you—"

"If you think I starved and waded through rivers in the dead of winter and marched without boots and damned near lost my leg and now I'm a cripple—if you think I suffered all that so you and your Council can tell us how to dress and think and live, can dictate to us, sir, as the king never dared—Get out!"

If his leg hadn't collapsed so that he must grab the desk or fall, Arnold would have followed his words with a kick in Bryan's hindquarters. As it was, he could only glare as Bryan waddled to the door.

There he turned to sweep Arnold a look of hate. "We're bringing charges again you, General, mark me. Me and Reed and the boys, we're asking the Congress to bring you down a peg or two."

"It'd be just like the Congress to listen to you, too," he shouted as Bryan stomped from the office.

The Radicals began issuing proclamations, one worse than the next. Surely those who loved Philadelphia's finer things, who paraded in silks and brocades instead of the plain dress that Joseph Reed preferred, must be Tories. And even if they weren't Tories, they were rich, which was just as bad.

Arnold read the handbills in disbelief, then forwarded them to Congress as further proof of Radical insanity. From their detail and venom, Reed must have spied on his neighbors all winter, must have kept lists of who attended British parties or dined with a Redcoat. Had the man nothing better to do? He put the town's gossips to shame with his interest in everybody else's affairs.

Yet enraging as the Radicals were, Arnold was more upset over Peggy's indifference. As summer cooled to fall, he admitted that she cared nothing for him. She was courteous, always hospitable when he visited, and sometimes even accompanied her parents when they returned his calls. But she glanced away each time their eyes met. She sought no opportunities to be alone with him and escaped any he invented.

Then Franks repeated some drivel that explained this. Arnold was signing letters the aide had copied, heedless of Franks' remarks, until Peggy's name caught his ear.

"—Miss Shippen was cozy with them."

"What? What about Miss Shippen?"

"It's causing talk, sir." Franks fidgeted and cleared his throat.

"Franks, who was she cozy with?"

"Some of the king's officers I was telling you about."

A primordial rage swept him, a lust to obliterate anyone Peggy preferred to him. When he could speak, he said, "Tell me again, Captain."

"Miss Shippen went about all winter with the officers, sir, attended their plays and dinners, had them in for tea. Some of them are in Clinton's family now, real ladies' men from what that servant at the Shippens' says. By the way, sir, she's not strictly speaking their servant because she's their niece, too, just so you know."

"And you just happened to be discussing Miss Shippen's habits with her?"

Franks reddened. "I—ah, well, sir, I don't mean to lecture you—"

"Then don't."

"No, sir, but it's causing talk that you're taking up with the sweetheart of the British army. Patriots here don't like it. They say it goes hand in hand with how lenient you treat the Loyalists and—"

"Loyalists gonna be living here same as us after the war, Franks. No point to making them hate us."

"Yes, sir, I agree, but still—. And the way you—you dress, sir, so extravagant."

"What, because I've got a whole uniform? Listen, I wore my share of rags at Valor and Quebec—"

"Yes, sir, but loads of folks, it's not just the Council anymore, everyone's saying you're really a Tory."

The hero of Saratoga sat stunned. "Because I don't want families turned out of their homes who disagree with us, or I won't gaol a man when his neighbors don't like the way he keeps his garden and he happens to support the king, that makes me a Tory?" He glowered. "Those were Washington's orders, anyway, let me remind you. I'm to protect the liberty of *all* Philadelphia's citizens, no matter their politics."

"I'm just telling you what they're saying, sir." Franks took a step backwards.

"That'll be all, Captain," Arnold said at last.

"Sir, I—"

"That'll be all!"

Chapter Sixteen

One crisp morning a month later, Arnold lingered at breakfast answering Hal's questions. The boy never tired of his father's stories. Arnold would wager Hal had asked a thousand times about the march to Quebec alone. Now, toast forgotten, porridge growing cold, his son begged for particulars of the battle at Valcour Island, even following Arnold to his office afterwards.

"Draw me a picture of your ship, Daddy—the one you sailed at Valor Island."

He could never resist Hal's eyes, so like Margaret's, nor his mispronunciation of Valcour. He pulled some paper to him and began sketching, despite the men waiting to see him.

"Sir." It was Franks, no doubt on behalf of those men.

"Five minutes, Franks," he said and bent over the paper again.

When Hal at last scampered from the office, drawing clutched in his fist, Franks reappeared.

"Well, Franks, who's first this morning?"

"Gideon Olmsted, sir."

"Olmsted? Merchant?"

"I wouldn't know, sir." Franks stared past him.

"Something wrong, Franks?"

"No, sir."

"Better pull that nose down, then, or you'll drown next time it rains."

Franks muttered, but Arnold was rifling papers, and all he caught was "stinks."

He set the papers aside. "Beg pardon, Captain?"

"It—it isn't seemly, sir. Folks are talking, criticizing you."

"Again?" He rolled his eyes. "What for now?"

"All these deals, sir. You're using your office to get rich"—Franks flinched at Arnold's scowl—"least that's what everybody says."

"Oh, they do, do they?"

"Yes, sir."

"And 'everybody' never stops to think how much money I've spent on this war, do they? How I paid the troops myself so we could capture Ticonderoga and fight at Valor Island? And 'everybody' doesn't care that I've never yet got a penny of my salary, not one penny, to this day."

"Well, sir, they—"

"'Everybody' was too busy sitting at home, tending to business, whilst we were out there fighting and starving and dying for liberty."

Franks blushed. Coming from a prosperous family, he owned brothers and a father who were making money while he sought honor in the war. Well and good for him to judge those who must scramble for a living.

"Remember, Franks, how 'everybody' sold us rotten beef and barrels of pork with bricks in the middle? But now, when I'm doing deals, honest deals, not selling rotten meat to the army or cheating it, 'everybody' criticizes me?"

"I—I hadn't looked at it that way, sir."

"No, I daresay you hadn't." Arnold gulped air, willed his heart to quit racing. "And it's not 'everybody,' anyway, Franks. It's Reed and his gang. You ask around among men of business, you'll see they back me, not Reed."

"Yes, sir."

"Now, if you'll show Mr. Olmsted in."

Olmsted was an emaciated young man whose skin hung on him as would clothing borrowed from an older, bigger brother. He winced as he bowed and winced some more as he took the chair Arnold indicated. "Thank you for seeing me, sir. I know you're a busy man, but I'm hoping you can help us. My partners and me, we'll make it worth your while."

"What is it you need, son?"

"That Reed fellow, sir, he cheated us. His cousin's the judge on our case, and a course, he decided for Pennsylvan—"

Arnold held up a hand. "Whoa, son, start at the beginning, will you? Take your time."

"Yes, sir." Olmsted eased back in his chair. "Coupla months ago, me and my partners, there's four of us altogether, we're fishing, sir, off the Virginia coast, minding our own business, when all of a sudden, there's nine tars boarding us and telling us we're working for His Majesty's navy now."

"Impressed you, huh?"

"I call it kidnapped, sir."

"So do I." He rested his chin on his hand. "Same as when they draft men for the army, threaten them with gaol or worse if they don't go along and do as they're told. All right, so they kidnapped you. Then what?"

"Well, sir, they forced us aboard their sloop and locked us belowdecks, chained us up like animals, and sailed for Jamaica."

Olmsted shifted, grimacing, so that Arnold asked, "They wound you while they's getting you aboard?"

"No, sir, that come later. See, once we're in Jamaica, they put us aboard the *Active*, bound for New York with arms and supplies for the Redcoats, some coffee and beef and limes and pimientos, and there was chocolate on there, too. Anyway, me and my partners, sir, we determined we're gonna take that ship."

"Take it?" Arnold grinned at such gumption.

"Yes, sir. After all, we're free men, or were till the king's thugs come along, and we wanted our freedom back. And, a course, be nice to have the prize money for bringing in a captured warship. So we waited until we was back in American waters, and then we overpowered them, sir. Captured them, locked them below like the first crew done us, though we didn't chain them up, sir. I wouldn't do that to a dog. Probably should have, though, on account of they got hold of some spoons and melted them down for balls and pried up the hatches and fired on us. That's how I got wounded, sir—took one of them balls in my gut."

Arnold shook his head.

"But the Almighty," Olmsted continued, "He's watching over us. I turned a deck gun on them, got control of the boat again. Damned rascals, though, they cut a hole through the stern and wedged the rudder so's we couldn't steer."

"And you're wounded all this time?"

"Yes, sir, wounded and bleeding."

"How'd you free the rudder?"

"Starved 'em, sir. We didn't give them food or water for the next two days. Well, truth to tell, we couldn't. We were all of us cut up pretty bad and trying to heal. But they thought we was doing it a-purpose, and they turned it loose on their own.

"Finally, we sighted land. My partners and me, we're already planning what we'll do with that prize money, how we're gonna take it easy and rest up from our wounds, when along come two privateers owned by Pennsylvania. Now they board us. Didn't mind at first, we's so close to land and figured they'd come to help. But here they say the *Active's* their prize," Olmsted's voice climbed high with indignation, "and they want the reward. Say they're entitled."

"So you went to court, and—?"

"And a lot of good it done us, sir. That good-for-nothing Reed's got a cousin that's the judge, so the jury went against us. Said the four of us couldn't possibly done what we said we did, overpowering twice our number and taking the ship. Called us liars, sir, and give our money, close to £48,000 that the *Active* brought at auction, to Pennsylvania."

When would the Congress intervene? How many more men would Reed and his Radicals crush before the delegates stirred themselves to action? Arnold sat back in his chair and placed his fingertips together, almost trembling at his helplessness. "And what is it you want me to do, Mr. Olmsted?"

Olmsted stared. "Well, sir, you—you're governor here."

Arnold sat silent, and Olmsted continued uncertainly, "I mean, Reed must needs listen when you—"

Arnold gave a wintry smile. "Ah, but he doesn't."

"He doesn't?" Olmsted's face closed. "But—but you're the *governor*. You saying there's nothing you can do?"

"That's right, sir. I'd suggest you take this to Congress."

Olmsted's jaw dropped. "Congress! But that'll take years! We haven't got—no disrespect or anything, but all the Congress does is talk, and we can't—we're down to our last couple of shillings."

"Mr. Olmsted, believe me, I been fighting Reed for months. Best advice I can give is to take this to Congress."

Olmsted sat bewildered. Finally, he said, "But we—we'd need money, sir. Naught between us but a pound and six. Seeing as how you're—"

"I can lend you some to live on."

"Help us with this appeal, too, sir, and we'll cut you in on whatever Congress awards us."

Arnold dipped his quill and jotted figures as Olmsted offered him an eighth share. They settled on a quarter and no interest on his loan. He handed over all the money at hand and arranged for Olmsted to pick up more in a few days, after he borrowed it.

"God bless you, General." Olmsted rose to leave with another grimace. "You're pretty much our last hope. If you wouldn't help us, well, dunno what we'd do…"

"I'd'a talked with him all day, Clem, a boy with that much spunk," Arnold says, "but for those appointments waiting."

"You'd always rather make deals than be governor, wouldn't you?"

He's nodding before I even finish. "'Course, that wasn't a very profitable deal, that one with Olmsted. I borrowed heavily, and the thing's still dragging along, might go years yet." 'Tisn't likely he'll see a penny of his share, neither, however the Congress rules. "But you're right, Clem. I didn't know anything about governing, none of us did. We were soldiers. We could command a company or regiment, but this governing of free people, ordering them about, managing their lives for them—I hated it."

"It agreed with Joseph Reed, though, governing did."

"For certain sure, and I'll tell you what. Any man enjoys a political office, folks that strive to get themselves into one like Reed, they're all of them tyrants at heart. Because you know what you mostly do as governor?"

"What?"

"Well, most every day, folks came wanting me to do what they oughta do for themselves. They'd complain their baker was charging too much, and couldn't I make him lower his prices? You'd think he's the only baker in town, to hear them, none other around the corner charging a few pence less so's to get their business. Or here they'd bring a petition wanting the city to set up schools for their sons. As though government oughta teach a boy, not his parents. I wanted to ask what we're fighting for, anyway, if it's gonna be me living their lives for them instead of the king. Now Reed, he'd always agree, anything anyone thought government oughta do."

"Gave him more power that way."

"Ah-yuh, folks always traded some freedom for anything Reed and his Council did, every time. But at least it made good farce." He leans back, eyes closed. Can it be? Is he—

"Tired, sir?" I ask.

He opens his eyes, smiles sadly. "No, Clem, just—I dunno, discouraged. Whenever I think about Reed and the Radicals, prattling about liberty but taking it away fast as they could—" He closes his eyes again. "Wickedness," he murmurs. "Must stop 'em."

"But it made good farce, you said."

He nods, eyes still shut. "Ah-yuh, that it did. Our officers weren't gonna be outdone by the Redcoats, no, ma'am. They formed a theatrical company. Kept the old Southwark Theater thumping as much as Howe's Thespians did."

"Scandalized the Quakers, I remember."

"Shouldn't have. They performed Cato, not Shakespeare." He shrugs. "After a day of battling the Radicals, I sure looked forward to an evening at the theater…"

Better yet, Peggy was such a devotee that she eagerly accepted all his invitations, scarcely caring what the play was. And so Arnold would relax in his cushioned carriage, the day's concerns draining from him, as his driver turned from High Street onto Fourth for the Shippens' home. Once they arrived, he must hobble to the door and chat with Peggy's cousin or her sycophantic father. But when Peggy appeared, all soft loveliness and looking like Margaret, his troubles with Reed, the agony in his leg, his worries over money fell away.

With her on his arm, he nearly floated to his carriage, though the trip to the house had tortured his leg. Once they were settled, he knocked the roof with his gold-headed cane, and the carriage lurched forward.

"Well, General." Peggy opened her fan coquettishly. "'Tis kind of you to invite me. I just love theater."

"You've been often, then?"

"Oh, yes, with Cher J—I mean, His Majesty's officers. I really feared we should just turn into cabbages when they left."

"No doubt you'd be the loveliest cabbage ever graced a field, Miss Shippen."

She gave a pleased laugh. "You're very kind, General. And brave, too, when your own Congress tells you this is *verboten*." She lowered her voice to mimic a Hessian.

He made himself chuckle, though he was alarmed by this latest of Congress' requests. It had urged the states to banish "theatrical entertainments, horse racing,"—he'd like to know what Washington thought of that one, eh?—"gaming, and such other diversions as are productive of idleness, dissipation, and a general depravity of principles and manners." He saw Reed's hand in the measure, would wager he'd ordered Pennsylvania's delegation to sponsor it.

Worse was another decree a few days later: "Any person holding an office under the United States who shall act, promote, encourage, or attend such plays shall be deemed unworthy to hold such office and shall be accordingly dismissed." Well, here was one officer attending such plays, and the Radicals be damned.

Peggy asked, "Aren't you worried they'll—they'll—what's that word means they'll throw you out of the army?"

"Cashier me? No." He smiled. "Have you seen any handbills? What's on for tonight?"

"I'm sure you'll enjoy it, sir. It's from Cato."

"And here I was afraid it'd be full of bawdy sentiments indelicate to a modest ear. Though I notice most women can bear a little indelicacy either very publicly or very privately."

"General Arnold!" But the rap her fan administered was playful.

"Cato, eh? I daresay your Redcoated friends wouldn't have staged it."

"Probably not." She fluttered the fan, and they both laughed. "Their tastes ran more to Shakespeare. And farce, of course, there was always a farce. Though I saw from the handbills there'll be one tonight, too."

They stopped before the warehouse of red brick and wood, adorned not only with Palladian windows but a cupola, too, that the Redcoats had transformed into a theater the previous year. Now two Continental lieutenants stood before the door as box-keepers, collecting tickets from bantering officers and ladies. The latter were as colorfully pert as though the country were at peace and the shops filled with velvets and satins. Their hair was powdered and so augmented with wool that their heads looked too heavy for their slender necks to support. Crowning those coiffures were cunning hats, many of them gifts from the government's officers with whom the belles had flirted all winter. Arnold feasted his eyes, though Reed had sniffed, "The young ladies who were in the city with the enemy and wear the present fashionable dresses have purchased them at the expense of their virtue. It is agreed on all hands that the British officers played the devil with the girls."

Peggy seemed to know most of the women, waving as they made their way to the door. "Oh, General, it's just divine," she breathed as he handed over their tickets.

He smiled down at her. "This is what life was meant to be."

He had waited for a cool, rainy day, though it meant missing the first three performances, for the Southwark was poorly ventilated. He had also sent an aide that afternoon to reserve the best seats, ones clear of the warehouse's pillars that offered unobstructed views. Peggy's rapture as they settled into chairs ten feet from the stage was worth the wait and the two dollars the tickets had cost.

Friends and well-wishers, eager to compliment the heroic General Arnold and denounce the Radicals he opposed, thronged him when all he craved was time with Peggy. But at last, with the show about to begin, the crowd surrounding him scattered to their seats. Oil lamps rimmed the proscenium, some with globes, most without, and they shimmered on Peggy's upturned face. He was drinking in the vision when it suddenly contorted. He looked at the stage to see what had upset her.

All he saw was the curtain, lamps shining on the waterfall and forest painted there. The scene was skillfully done, with naught to make a lady bite her lip.

"Reminds me of the Kennebec up to Maine," he said.

She glanced away. "I—I know the gentleman who painted it."

A drum rattled, and the audience hushed as the curtain parted. A man wearing a shapeless black coat and butchered wig stepped from the wings. He was so badly attired and so resembled George Bryan that he had only to scowl for the laughter to start.

When he could be heard, he shouted, "Don't laugh at me and go your way, for I see every slight, sir. I savor them and count them up, before I sleep at night, sir."

Peggy clapped and laughed at more doggerel about the Council's punishing all who offended it by compelling them to dress as shabbily as the speaker. Then a wooden bull chased an actor portraying Reed on stage. Reed lectured the animal, until the man inside lifted the flap beneath the tail and dumped a bucket of manure.

It was delicious by itself. With Peggy beside him, clutching his arm in hilarity, the evening was all Arnold hoped. He laughed loud and long from his prominent seat, enjoying every gibe at the Radicals…

"Reed had his revenge on you, though, didn't he, sir?" I ask.

Flash puts his head on Arnold's good knee, probably so Arnold can scratch his ears, but he looks so sympathetic I want to laugh. Arnold smiles down at him, then says, "The papers, their editors were in Reed's pocket, most of them."

There'd been articles attacking Arnold ever since he arrived in Philadelphia. They reminded us how all winter, we'd watched General Howe and his officers drinking and dining while we struggled to survive. You needn't be a Patriot to resent that your children cried for food while the government's officers and their ladies danced. Patriots had told Tories and Quakers and themselves, "'Twould all be different if our boys were here." Now our boys *were* here, but the lush life in the Penn mansion continued, and the papers carried notice of every party, down to how much wine Arnold served and what kind.

"Don't know what they expected me to do." Arnold rubs his leg, frowning. "Hordes of people trooping through the Penn mansion, merchants, congressmen, leading citizens of Philadelphia, Patriots and Tories both, and for a while there, I was even hosting the new French minister, sent over because of the alliance, you see. And here I'm representing the Continental Army and the United States. I needed a staff, Clem, to entertain all these folks. I wasn't married then, and even though I'd sent for my sister, I couldn't expect her to cook and clean in a great house like the Penn mansion, not when her hands were already full raising my boys. By Heaven, it took three housemaids and a cook and washerwoman, and a steward. Hannah could never handle all that on her own and act as hostess, too.

"You shoulda seen the place, the way Howe left it." He lowers his voice, though General Howe, long since gone to England, isn't likely to overhear. "Man's a pig. Took those housemaids I hired a solid month of cleaning before it was fit to live in. Howe stripped the place bare, just left us his garbage, so I needed to furnish it, too. Cost me over £160 for the dining room alone. But once they finished cleaning, and all that new furniture—" He leans back, smiling. "It was a showplace! First time in three years I slept in a bed or sat at a polished table to eat, regular, every night."

Mayhap 'twas the ease of living in a city again instead of an army camp, even if that city'd been plundered, the thought that after months upon months of starvation and pain, lost sleep and salt meat, he deserved some luxury, that blinded Arnold to what folks thought of his living high while the rest of us scrabbled for breadcrusts.

That's why rumors about Arnold's getting rich off the governor's office fell on eager ears. Such talk was as common in Philadelphia as empty stomachs. And behind those rumors stood Reed and his Radicals.

"Sir." I pause. How *did* he live so well if at least some of Reed's moonshine weren't true? "They said that you, well, that you could afford all those servants and furniture and the rest because you, ah, that you used your office to—"

His face twists with agony, either from my words or his leg. His voice, when he finally speaks, isn't the bellow I expect but a defeated murmur.

"I'm an honorable man, Clem."

"I—I know, it's just—"

"Even my name means 'honor.'"

That silences me, and he nods. "Arnold's an old English name, goes back centuries, but it's always meant 'honor.' Besides, the ones saying I got rich off my office, you ever notice they're all in Reed's camp?"

He's right about that.

"'Tis true I needed money," he continues. "You know, I was a wealthy man five years ago, when the war began, but I spent most

of my capital on marching the troops to Quebec and then building the navy for Valor Island. And I'm still waiting to be reim-
bursed. The Congress has my accounts, least those the enemy didn't
destroy, but all they ever did was talk about them instead of reim-
bursing me. And they've never paid my salary. Now, with my capital
gone and no income, I'm supposed to live in the Penn mansion and
entertain as governor?"

But that didn't stop his generosity to Joseph Warren's orphans after
the Redcoats bayoneted their poor father at Bunker's Hill. Massachusetts
usually voted a pension in such cases, but with their treasury empty and
folks taxed hard for the war, they dared not. Rumor was, Arnold stepped
in and paid to educate all four children. He never breathed a word of it,
so didn't any of us know if 'twas true.

When I ask, he sort of nods and shrugs, too, before saying, "Peggy's
faith in me, that got me through." He unwraps the bandages, now cool,
and tosses them into the basin. Flash watches with tongue lolling, thinking this a new game, I warrant. I poke at the fire again while Arnold
fiddles with his breeches. "Woman like that's worth the world."

I snatch the pot of water from the embers and pour it into the basin,
over Arnold's bandages. Steam hides my face and, I hope, my disgust.
Even now, when Peggy's wickedness has killed one man, corrupted our
most amazing hero, and nigh ruined us, Arnold adores her. Blinded by
her beauty, he never sees her as she is.

I'm not vain; no ugly girl can be. So 'tis fact and not pride when
I say I'm worth ten of Peggy. Yet no man will ever cherish me half as
much as Arnold does her.

And here's another tragedy: Peggy doesn't love him. Never has…

"But, General, I don't love you." Peggy laughed the happy little tinkle that
always set Arnold laughing, too, even when she was shredding his heart.

They were sitting outside her father's house, in a gazebo shaded by
a vine glowing red in the late September sun. Her primly folded hands
and feet crossed at the ankles contrasted with the luscious body straining
her clothes. Arnold nearly reached a hand to her bodice, to unbutton
it and free those curves.

He had sent her a letter three days ago, with a proposal of marriage copied from a gentleman's form-book. He longed to write from the heart for this glorious event rather than rely on the sentiments of a stranger. But fear of rejection dried his thoughts and the ink on the quill before he could scratch a mark.

He waited as long as possible after sending the letter. By the third day, his patience was gone. Withal, a lady of Peggy's breeding was unlikely to respond. He must call on her, receive her answer in person. But he was disappointed. He had dreamt of her running into his arms and limning her devotion, as Margaret would have done—a dream Peggy had blasted as she was now blasting another. He scrambled for cover.

"Ah, my dear." He kept his voice as buoyant as hers. "You needn't love a man to marry him, don't you know that? 'Tis a modern idea, and not necessarily a good one, I'm afraid. True and permanent happiness is seldom the effect of romantic passion—"

Her face lost its gaiety. "Haven't you ever been in love, General? 'Tis most delicious, and nothing I'd want to marry without."

"You might come to love me, Miss Shippen."

The gaiety returned. "I don't think so, General." She fluttered her fan.

"Why not?"

"Well, for starters, you're a rebel. I could never love a ragged, dirty Continental."

"Now, Miss Shippen, I'm hardly ragged. This uniform cost me a month's wages."

"La, sir, I'll admit, it's a handsome coat. But you're still a rebel, though better clothed than most."

"And why else don't you love me?"

She glanced away without answering. But he knew how crippled and old he must seem, especially compared with the boys constantly swarming her.

Then she looked back with another lighthearted laugh. "One day," she said, "when you've lost this war, they'll be hanging you, and I don't care to be a young widow."

Such words were uncomfortably close to his nightmares, but he forced a smile. "Well, I'm disappointed, Miss Shippen. I thought you probably liked a bit of adventure."

"And that's what marriage to you would be, sir? An adventure?"

"Absolutely. I'd want my wife with me on campaigns."

He said it to entice her, knowing how bored she was in her father's home with so many of Philadelphia's beaux gone to war. 'Twas preposterous, really: an army camp was no place for a girl as dainty as Peggy. But she stared, turning white and then red. Finally, she stuttered, "You—you mean—close to—to, we'd be, ah, near the Bri—the enemy?"

"Depends on the distance between the lines. But sure, we'd be near them."

She was still staring with what he took for fear, and he hurried to soothe her. "I was only jesting, my dear, though there's other wives in camp, you know. Mrs. Washington stayed at the Forge last win—"

She muttered something, in French he thought, but when he asked her to repeat it, she only winked flirtatiously. "Well, General, why don't you try to change my mind about—about marrying you? I never object to gentlemen's persuasion…"

My uncle refused the first time Arnold requested her hand. "Too many scandals, Peggy." Uncle Shippen spread his arms. "But that's what happens when you don't know a man's background."

And suddenly, Peggy was on Arnold's side. My jaw dropped as she rushed to the general's defense, for I'd thought 'twas Andre, alone and forever, that moved her. "I know his background, Daddy. He was a merchant before the—"

"That's not what I mean, Peggy. What of his family, hmm? They had no money, nothing to recommend them until this war came along, and all of a sudden, this—this horse-jockey is a general."

"His great-grandfather was a governor of Rhode Island, Daddy." Peggy pursed her scarlet lips. "Or was it his grandfather?"

"His father died a drunk, Peggy. Did you know that? And withal, he's crippled." My uncle pursed *his* lips. "And nearly as old as me, too. I've got only a dozen years or so on him. What'll you do with an old cripple for a husband?"

"But, Daddy, he loves me."

"You're too young to know what love is."

"That's not true. Mama was younger than—"

"Peggy, he'll never be able to support a wife. Good Lord, he can't even walk. How do you expect him to earn a living, once the war's over? And he's making enemies, my dear, powerful enemies, the sort who never forget nor rest. They'll ruin him, mark me."

For a week, we saw naught of the general.

Didn't see much of Peggy, neither. She took to her room, moaning of iron rings and headaches, until the day she asked would I deliver a letter to her suitor. And so I walked streets as thick with fallen leaves as Arnold was with scandal.

Arnold called the next day, while my uncle was gone on business. Peggy and my aunt were embroidering in the back parlor as I read to them from my history of the war. They joked more than they listened, but occasionally they'd remember a detail I'd forgotten.

The general always thumped the doorknocker thrice, and when he did this day, Peggy shot to her feet. "I'll get it." Was she glad to see him—or eager for an excuse to end my reading?

They whispered in the hall, then joined us, Arnold handing smiles around. He was walking without a cane, though his face twisted at every step. He collapsed into a chair and propped his leg on another.

Peggy's laugh trilled. "I heard a story about you, General, that made me think you're quite a rogue."

"Now, Miss Shippen, you can't believe everything you hear." Arnold's eyes fired as they settled on her. I dipped my quill, ready to note whatever she related.

She tossed her head in a way I couldn't copy however I practiced before the mirror. "Becky Franks told me that when Sally Bache showed you her baby daughter—"

Arnold chuckled. "I can't believe she told you this."

"—she said the baby gave you a great big old kiss, and you said—"

"Only in fun, I assure you—"

"You said you'd give a good deal to have her for a schoolmistress to teach us young ladies how to kiss."

Even my aunt laughed.

A few days later, a mob attacked two Quakers the Radicals accused of trading with the Redcoats, threatening them with tar and feathers—or worse. General Arnold rescued the men and remanded them to gaol for trial.

"Oh, isn't he heroic!" Peggy sighed as she'd done three years before, when Benedict Arnold was a legend in the newspapers who conquered the unconquerable and laughed while he did. But the Radicals hissed that once again he'd favored Tories.

The general's visits went scarce the next fortnight as Reed convicted the Quakers of treason and sentenced them to death. Then, second evening of November, I answered the door to find Arnold standing there without his cane, brow slick with sweat despite the cold.

"Evening, Miss Shippen."

"Evening, General. Peggy's in the back parlor, sir. She's expecting you."

Not only Peggy but also my uncle and I were present. These public evenings were the only courtship my uncle allowed.

"Evening, Judge." Arnold settled into his usual chair and propped his leg on a stool, throwing Peggy a grin. Her answering smile lit the room, chased the gloom smothering us, for we'd been discussing Abraham Carlisle and John Roberts, the condemned Quakers.

Mayhap Roberts was a Tory, as Reed charged, but if so, he was pretty lukewarm about it: last winter, when the government occupied Philadelphia, Roberts posted bond for a Continental prisoner of war so that the man might starve at liberty with the rest of Philadelphia instead of doing it in gaol. The soldier broke his parole and rejoined the Continentals, which give the government an excuse to keep Roberts' £100. Roberts had a wife and ten children and a reputation for such charity as persuaded a thousand of his neighbors to brave the Council's wrath and sign a petition for clemency. But clemency wasn't a Radical virtue.

Arnold held his hands to the fire. "Like to invite you folks to a little gathering tomorrow night."

"Tomorrow?" My uncle shook his head. "I'm afraid, General, we'll be too upset in this house to go anywhere then. You know they're hanging those poor men the day after."

"I know, sir." Arnold spoke so low I strained to hear. "That's the reason for my gathering. I'm inviting all the Quakers and Loyalists I know, and Patriots of goodwill, too, to meet at City Tavern. We'll pray for Roberts and Carlisle and then raise a glass in their honor."

My uncle bowed his head. "We'll be there, General, thank you. 'Tis kind of you."

"No more than what any decent person would do, sir. 'Tis tragic that men are dying, and even more tragic that their murderers prattle about liberty."

Uncle Shippen wet his lips. "This war's gone on too long, sir, far too long."

"Ah-yuh, that it has."

"Tell me, why don't you lay down your arms? King's conceded to everything you say you want, but for independency."

"Independency was never the goal, sir—only a means to an end."

"And that is?"

"Liberty, a course." Arnold seemed surprised as he shifted to ease his leg. "'Twas thought that since government's bent on destroying our liberty, we'd best break away, protect our freedom ourselves. 'Tis all there in *Common Sense*, sir."

My uncle colored, perhaps thinking on how he threw my copy to the flames. Then he asked, "And you think liberty isn't important to those who don't favor this rebellion? You'll look long and hard, sir, to find anyone who'll deny the blessings liberty brings. But this hanging tomorrow, it's exactly why we—ah, some people oppose you rebels taking things into your own hands. You want to tear down the old government to protect liberty, you say. But these new men, sir, they're not protecting liberty. They're destroying it."

Arnold sat silent, chewing his lip.

"You doubt that," my uncle continued softly, "just ask those men being hanged, or any of Reed's other victims, poor Grace Gal—"

"They must be stopped, sir, the Radicals!" 'Twas a *cri de coeur*. I'd once heard Andre joke about a crying heart, but here was the real thing in all its anguish. Arnold shook his head despairingly. "I've tried everything, but naught fazes them. And the Congress, why don't they do something? Why don't they stop them?"

"Stop them?" My uncle gaped. "They *encourage* them, sir."

"But they—"

"The king, sir, there's your answer. King George would put them in their place."

"You're joking." Arnold left off shaking his head to roll his eyes. "He'd put us in our place, too, anyone who disagrees with him, wants to trade or manage a business without a minister's say-so, and what about the corruption? Whole government runs on bribes, paying for favors—"

"Well, certainly, I'll be the first to admit the Ministry's corrupt and could use a good sweeping with a clean broom. But reform it, sir. Don't overthrow it."

Arnold moved his leg from the stool, setting it beside the other on the floor. But that emphasized its peculiar angle, and how short 'twas. He tried to hide it behind the other. Then, wincing, he gave up as my uncle continued.

"His Majesty's offered everything but independency, which you say wasn't important on its own anyway. Why not sue for peace? You can work to reform government from inside the Empire, before more good men like Roberts and Carlisle die."

Next evening, when General Arnold led everyone at City Tavern in prayer for Carlisle and Roberts, we were there. It comforted us and, I hope, them too, when they faced the gibbet next day.

December 1778 turned to January 1779, and the general continued to court Peggy—with my uncle's blessing.

"Mayhap I was a bit hasty," Uncle Shippen said. "He's a good man, trying his best to protect us from these rebels. You'd never know he's a rebel himself."

Then, as February howled down our chimneys, Arnold disappeared, gone to New York to see about buying land up there. Much as the Radicals despised the hero of Saratoga, the Yorkers loved him. So much that they wanted him to settle on their frontier with some of his troops, sort of a bulwark lest the Redcoats consider another invasion. They were offering tens of thousands of acres at an unbeatable price, as though a country manor far removed from the strife with Reed wasn't already appealing enough. But if the general hoped my cousin would settle beside him there, away from parties and beaux—well, there's folks think they can teach a cat not to hunt birds.

On the day Arnold rode north, the Council hurled charges after him. They published them just as Arnold left, so's it would seem he fled in a panic, guilty and fearful. But anyone who knows Arnold will tell you he's dauntless, that he faces enemies head-on. 'Tisn't in him to run.

These eight charges, like John Brown's from a couple of years before, covered a peck of ground, everything from the picayune complaint that Arnold didn't treat the Council polite and respectful (Brown whined about his hurt feelings, too) to crimes like defrauding Olmsted over the *Active* and using army wagons to transport Arnold's private wares. The newspapers overflowed with the Radicals' bile. They printed so many letters from Reed and his henchmen—but never signed, you understand, only bearing names like "Tiberius" or "Gracchus" or some such—they hadn't room for much else.

This yanked the general back to Philadelphia in a hurry. There he scribbled his own letters to the *Pennsylvania Packet.*

And then he went to the Congress.

Those rascals did what they do in every crisis: they formed a committee. But its members surprised us with their justice when they found for Olmsted in the case of the *Active* and, what's more, cleared Arnold of most of Reed's charges.

The general celebrated with a ball.

'Twas just the sort would make the Radicals seethe, all joy and feasting and dancing. Candles blazed on every table and windowsill, lighting the Penn mansion bright as day. Ladies rustled in silks and velvets, and most gentlemen wore as much of a uniform as they owned. Food such as we'd only dreamed of last winter crowded the table: roasts and succulent fowl, syllabubs, flummeries, jams and fools, with plenty of cherry bounce to wash it down.

"Congratulations, General." My uncle bowed to our host. "It's good of you to invite us."

Arnold raised my aunt's hand to his lips, though her gaze, like mine, was fixed on the table of sweetmeats.

"Not at all, Judge," Arnold said. "Praise Heaven there's something to celebrate. I must admit, I didn't have much faith in the Congress. But maybe something's new under the sun, after all. Maybe there's a few men of sense over there."

My uncle was chuckling. "Oughta make Reed furious."

"All the more reason to enjoy ourselves." Arnold waved at the room, a swirl of color as his guests stepped to a minuet. "Let him growl all he wants about the imperial Congress and how they're trampling his—er, I mean, the state's prerogatives." His eyes crinkled. "You hear his latest? He's saying Philadelphia isn't big enough for the Congress and him, and one or the other needs to go. What's he gonna do when we win this thing? We're all gonna live together after the war, but way he's going, we whip the Redcoats, Tories'll wanna fight us next."

"Reed's dry as a bull when it comes to the milk of human kindness."

Arnold grinned. "Wait'll he hears I'm asking for a court-martial on the charges they didn't clear me of. He trumped up those charges, so a court-martial'll find me innocent—"

"Sir." My uncle's smile disappeared. "You're not much of a political man, I can tell."

"And proud of it."

"Well, let me give you a word of advice, then, for I've spent a good part of my life in politics."

"I'd be honored," Arnold murmured, but he was watching Peggy and nodding to the music since he couldn't tap his foot, and I misdoubt he heard anything my uncle said.

"Reed's the most powerful of the new men, General. He pretty much arranges Pennsylvania to his liking. And Pennsylvania's a powerful state, what with all the men and food and wagons it supplies the Continental Army. Your Congress remembers that every time it votes. Keeping Pennsylvania happy means keeping Reed happy. So this time Congress threw him a sop by finding you guilty of the lesser charges. My advice, sir, is let it drop. Let Reed have his small victory in the midst of your big one."

Arnold's eyes went to my uncle. "But I'm not guilty, sir."

My uncle sighed. "It's not a question of guilt or inno—"

"I want full exoneration, sir. I've done nothing wrong."

Even I gasped, and I've no more patience for politics than Arnold. My uncle tried again. "Sir, the Congress doesn't care that you're innocent. They—"

"Fact," Arnold's gaze was back on my cousin, "I'm resigning my command here. Never wanted to be governor anyway. I'm gonna insist on a court-martial and clear myself once and for all."

If you listened close the day Congress got that demand, you'd'a heard them groan. All that compromising wasted, and the problem they'd thought gone come back to plague them.

A few days after Arnold's party, I answered the door expecting to admit him. Instead, there's Ben Tallmadge, dashing as ever.

He grinned at my surprise. "Aren't you going to invite me in? I'm hungry, Miss Shippen, and rumor has it you're a good cook."

"Come in, Major, of course." I stood aside, then blushed as he took my hand for to kiss. "What are you doing in Philadelphia?"

"Gonna appear before the Board of War, report on the cavalry unit I've put together." He doffed his tricorn, but my uncle stepped into the hall before I could ask whether he was still an intelligencer.

"Uncle," I said, "this is Major Benjamin Tallmadge of the Continental Army."

They bowed, and my uncle said, "Which part of the army, sir, may I inquire?"

"Second Regiment of the Continental Light Dragoons."

"And how do you and my niece know each other?"

I blushed again at such quizzing. Pray Heaven his next question wasn't, "And are your intentions honorable?"

Tallmadge caught my distress and went all lovelorn. "We met in New York coupla years ago, sir. She saved my life."

"Oh, I did not," I said as my uncle asked, "Did she now? How?"

Tallmadge told of our escape from the Hessians while I fetched a tray with bread and soup, cheese and wine, though why I bothered over a man determined to vex me, I had no idea.

The Board of War kept Tallmadge in Philadelphia for ten days. He called on me each one.

Sometimes I worried that the major and I might be related, for his father hailed from Connecticut, was born and raised there before removing to Long Island. Mayhap he'd known my mother.

But mostly I just enjoyed Ben's courting. 'Twas a novelty, something that hadn't happened since Eli Belks sat in my uncle's parlor and flirted with Peggy. Though, as my suitor pointed out, we talked more about his friend, dead eighteen months, than anything else. We'd been too rushed during the Meschianza to speak of aught besides our schemes for it. Now, with afternoons stretching before us, I asked all the questions gnawing at me, whether Nathan Hale had a sweetheart ("Hundreds of them," Tallmadge said. "Every girl that saw him fell in love with him"), what made him laugh, his favorite books.

"I have letters from him, you know," Ben said. "We wrote each other after we graduated."

"Would you mind—I mean, I'd surely like—"

He held up a hand. "You can read them, Clem. Just promise me you won't swoon." He twined his fingers through mine. "You know, I haven't been able to get you out of my thoughts."

I smiled as Peggy would, even fluttered my lashes. "And why's that?"

When my cousin teased this way, her swains bantered and laughed. But Ben slowly said, "Well, because you're different from any girl I ever knew. You read and care about things that matter, and there isn't a bit of vanity in you."

That's because I'd nothing to be vain about.

"Most girls," he continued, "all they think about is how they look and what the fashions are, and they're buried in the details of their families, and when they've given you the anecdotes of their day's work, and the pretty sayings of the children they know, with a dish of tea, you may go about your business, unless you choose to have the tale over again."

Mayhap he was a bit harsh—for I've known plenty of men who talk only of the weather and crops and there's no dish of tea whilst they bore you to death—but it was so apt I laughed.

"Then there's you!" He shook his head. "I can talk to you the livelong day and not have talked enough." He gave a sidelong glance. "Even if all we talk about is Nathan."

Too soon came Ben's appearance before Congress' Board of War.

"Congress!" he spluttered the next day. "More like an American Sodom, Clem. I consider it as the sink of America in which is huddled and collected villains and vermin from every quarter."

We were taking the air this first balmy day of spring, walking along Third Street. Most folks were outside in the warmth, working. They couldn't replace sheds and shutters gone missing during the government's occupation, for no one had the money. But they were hoeing gardens to plant onions, lettuce, peas.

Ben offered his arm, and I said, "So if—when we win, it'll be despite Congress, huh?"

"In camp, we've got no provisions, no guns, even, but tell the Congress and, well, they respond with all the delay in their power."

He was so grim I hardly dared smile, but when I did, it seemed to lift him somewhat, until he smiled, too.

"So," he continued, "as far as that goes, I'm glad I'll be at a distance from them day after tomorrow—"

Something knotted inside me.

"—but, on the other hand, I wish I could stay longer."

A dozen geese strutted along the street towards us, honking and snapping at garbage. Philadelphia had once been a clean city, nary an apple core or rind of cheese marring its brick roads, but seemed the Regulars took our cleanliness and pride along with our gateposts and hitching rails.

The flock passed us, leaving feathers in its wake, and Ben turned to me.

"Clem, will you marry me?"

My breath left me, and no wonder: when I looked up, I saw adoration shining on his face.

"'Course," he added, "we can't marry till after the war, and God knows when that will be, but I—I love you, Clem. These have been the happiest days of my life, this last week with you. I think about you all day long, when I go to sleep at night, and when I wake up—" He was fingering a pair of gloves more holes than leather. Then he thrust hands and gloves into his pockets. "I love you. Will you marry me?"

"Ben." I hesitated. "There's something, a—a problem, you don't know about me."

I told about my father.

He shrugged. "You're a bastard, then. That what you're trying to say?"

"Well, my mother was married when I was born. It's just—"

"Clem, it's you I want to marry, not your mother. 'Tis a pity she was such a troubled lady, that you grew up in such circumstances, but it only makes me admire you more."

I took a deep breath. "You don't understand. We could be—you see, my father, I don't know who—and—and yours, he's born in Connecticut—"

'Twas a hard thing to say, and offensive too.

He took my hand, bewildered-like, so I closed my eyes against his anger and said, "What if we're brother and sister? Half-brother and half-sister, I mean."

I felt him shaking. When I peeked, I saw 'twas with laughter. "I'm sorry, Clem," he gasped, "but you'd need to know my father to—to—" Guffawing, he dropped my hand.

"Ben—"

"My father's a minister of the Gospel"—he wiped his eyes—"and about as upright as they come. He's no ladies' man and never has been, far as I know."

That was settled then. But there's another problem.

"You're not Nathan," I started to say, until I pictured the years stretching ahead, years I'd thought to live alone. Now here was Ben, loving, witty, handsome. He was a driver, too. Though the war occupied him now, he'd be wealthy one day. He was the sort any woman, even one as beautiful as Peggy, must be proud to claim.

And he loved me. It was enough to set me dancing and singing, right there on the street. Plain and poor, I was still special to someone in this wide world, desirable and worthy enough that a man wanted me to share his life and heart. He would comfort and help me, cherish me, protect and strengthen me. And welcome all that in return.

Almost on its own, my head began nodding. "Yes, Ben, I'll marry you."

He spoke to my uncle that evening for to get his blessing. 'Twas grudgingly given. Betsy, long betrothed to Neddy Burd, had finally married him at Christmas, in a ceremony with twenty-five bridesmaids. Not only had my uncle barely recovered from that, but everyone had watched his daughter wed a Continental officer. He fretted that the next girl should balance things with a Loyalist. Ben's promise to wait until after the war satisfied Uncle Shippen enough that he drank our health.

Next morning, Ben called early to bid us farewell. He bowed over my aunt's hand, listened gravely as my uncle murmured advice, and then led me to the hitching rail where the flies bedeviled his poor horse.

"Wish I didn't need to go," he said, untying his reins. "You've made me tremendously happy, Clem." He kissed my forehead, then grabbed me in a hug. "Maybe we shouldn't wait till the war ends."

"Benjamin!" I squirmed away lest we give my uncle an eyeful.

"I could always resign my commission." He swung into the saddle and smiled down at me.

"And do what? Sit tight someplace while other folks do the fighting?" I shook my head. "Believe me, Ben, 'tis frustrating beyond words."

"Understand it forces some ladies to enlist."

My jaw dropped. "How'd you know about that?"

"I'm an intelligencer, remember?" He leaned out of the saddle to whisper, "We must compare scars one day, my love."

I was blushing too hard to answer and could only wave my farewell.

Chapter Seventeen

"Sir," David Franks said, "letter here for you from Beverley Robinson."
Arnold stared blankly at the packet his aide handed him.
"Robinson, hmmm. Loyalist, isn't he?"

"Yes, sir, from New York, I believe—

"That's right! Has an estate there on Hudson's River, and he's cozy with the enemy, with Clinton himself, as I recall, even raised that regiment of Loyalists for them. Well, what in the world—why would he write *me*?"

Franks shrugged. He returned to copying a stack of correspondence for the file as Arnold broke the seal and glanced over Robinson's lines: "…necessary that a decisive advantage should put Britain in a condition to dictate the terms of reconciliation…no one but General Arnold who can surmount obstacles so great… Render then, brave General, this important service to your country… Let us put an end to so many calamities… United…we will rule the universe…not by arms and violence but by the ties of commerce—the lightest and most gentle bonds that human kind can wear…"

"Good Lord." He set the letter aside, and Franks looked up.
"Sir?"

"Franks, I think he's asking me to—to betray the Cause."

"He can't be serious. *You*, General? Betray us?" Franks roared with mirth.

Arnold picked up the letter and re-read it as Franks, still chuckling, bent over his foolscap. "…important service to your country…an end to so many calamities…" *Nothing's more important than ending the Radicals' calamities. But how?* "The king, sir," Judge Shippen's words echoed in his head. "King would put them in their place."

Abruptly, he stood. "Call my carriage, Franks, will you? I'm going out."

He mulled Robinson's words all the way to the Shippens', kept mulling them until Peggy sat beside him in his carriage. Then, as always, she claimed his full attention.

"I admit, General, when you first came courting, I couldn't see the—the use in it." She pulled her cape tighter and burrowed into the quilt he'd laid across them as they exchanged Philadelphia's hostile streets for the sweet countryside. "But you've changed my mind, sir."

She spoke in the shy, silvery tones that always set his heart thumping, as though he were a boy of sixteen speaking love for the first time rather than a thirty-eight-year-old veteran of battlefield and bedchamber. Peggy snuggled against his arm, and his blood pounded harder at her needing him, wanting him, at her dependence on him even for warmth.

"Well, then, Miss Shippen, you object if I approach your father again?"

She quit snuggling and sat up, away from him, to stare out the window. They were passing fields held lifeless in February's grip. There was nothing to see but an occasional crow, dark and forlorn. At last she said, "He doesn't want me marrying a rebel."

"Why?" Seemed a natural question, but Peggy turned to stare as though he'd uttered nonsense.

"Well," she said at last, "it's—you're on the same side as Joseph Reed and his—that—that Council—"

He shouted a laugh. "Oh, Miss Shippen, I am not! I'm not on their side, you can rest assured of that."

"You're not?"

"Good Lord, no! I'm no Radical. I've opposed them from the day I came here. What do you think all the fighting's about?"

"Well, I—I—'tis true, I guess. Even the newspapers in New York talk about how the Radicals all hate you."

"The papers in New York?"

"You know my father takes the *Royal Gazette*."

"I take it myself, on the theory you want to know what the enemy's thinking."

"Well, then, you see what they wrote about you last month?"

"Haven't read it for a while, press of business and all—"

"They said you're 'more distinguished for valor and perseverance' than any other rebel, even that horrid old Washington you like so much, and that you're another Hannibal. But the rebels don't think you're fit for any further, um, exercise of your—your"—her forehead puckered—"your 'military talents,'" she blurted triumphantly, "not with your leg."

Now it was his turn to peer out the window at a crow flying depressing black loops above rows of snowy stubble.

She giggled. "You shoulda seen what they said about Reed and the Council, how it's a pity after all you've suffered with your wounds that you've fallen into their 'unmerciful fangs.' Can't you just see them, like a set of dogs, snarling at my father or poor old Mrs. Galloway or those two men they hanged at Christmas?"

He took her hand. "I've fought them, Miss Shippen, fought them hard."

"Of course you have, General, but still—" She hesitated.

"Go on."

"They're Patriots, and so are you."

"No, they're not. They're Radicals."

"They say they're Patriots, sir. Perhaps 'tis you who's not, you don't agree with them."

Such insight startled him. Peggy, however alluring and delightful, had never impressed him as a deep thinker. Could she be right? Had the Patriots veered so far from liberty that he and they were no longer fighting for the same thing? He chewed on the problem for a few moments, then cleared his throat. "Miss Shippen, I've bled and starved and near died for our Cause, and you know why?"

"I'm sure I don't, sir." Her brows lifted. "I don't understand why any of you do what you do."

"For liberty, Miss Shippen, freedom."

"Liberty, biberty, that's all you rebels prattle about, morning, noon and night." She widened her exquisite eyes. "All I know is, before this war, I could talk with any gentleman I pleased. Now, I must find out what side he favors first, and if it isn't Reed's, well, then, talking together makes me a Tory, let alone dancing with him."

She had dropped her voice so threateningly on "dancing" that Arnold laughed. But he sobered quickly to say, "Men like Reed, the

Radicals, they're a blot on our Cause, Miss Shippen. They don't care about liberty. They wanna get rid of the king's government, true, but that's only because they don't want His Majesty ordering us around when they can. That's what's wrong, don't you see? You think men fight and die so Joseph Reed can tell you who to talk or dance with?"

She shrugged. "Mayhap you're right, sir."

"Oh, I'm right, Miss Shippen. You can wager your last pound on it. Who's got more right to define our principles, me who's bled for them or Joseph Reed?"

"But he was on Mr. Washington's staff—"

"For a while, in '76. But then he resigned because his personal affairs needed attention." He snorted. "So did mine. So did everybody's. But I stayed and fought and bankrupted myself. My wife died, my boys—"

"General." She laid a hand on his arm, and love displaced his anger.

He covered her hand with his, lost himself in her endless eyes, grey as Margaret's. "Please, Peggy, angel, let me speak to your father..."

The general had persuaded Peggy, but there was still my uncle to convince. Both were men of affairs, so they soon came to an understanding whereby Arnold bid on Mount Pleasant, Philadelphia's finest mansion, as a wedding gift for Peggy. He made sure my uncle knew it carried a mortgage of £70,000. I haven't much of a head for business, so I don't know why that pleased the judge. I'd'a wondered where Arnold would get that kind of money, for neither Continental generals nor military governors could afford such a place. But, as I say, I know little of business, and my uncle, who knows much, gave his leave.

"Just be sure you've thought this through, Peggy," my uncle said. "Remember your general's fighting against the government. When the rebels lose, he'll hang high as Washington and the Adamses, maybe higher. And these charges they're bringing against him, Peggy, the Philadelphia Council, they're serious charges—"

"Oh, Daddy!"

"Marrying such a—a *persona non grata*, your days'll be filled with controversy and trouble, Peggy. That Council's out to destroy every man who won't draw in their harness."

They sure were. While Arnold gazed starry-eyed at his betrothed, Reed sent the Council's charges to the governors of every state.

But we were ignorant of this and supposed our only trouble was giving Peggy the wedding she thought she deserved on what my uncle thought he could afford. Though he'd hosted a grand celebration when Betsy married last Christmas (a point Peggy never tired of recalling, always accidental-like and apologetic), he couldn't now, with his income gone and his capital fast disappearing. So he decreed that Peggy might invite only three or four friends.

Peggy sighed. Then, squaring her shoulders, she resolved to survive the disgrace somehow. They set the date for a Thursday, April 8.

The Monday before, Peggy and I sat in the side parlor going over the food I'd serve, a short list, thanks to the war and regulations and Peggy's niggling.

"Oh, Clem." She studied my notes. "Not beef, do you think? It's so—so *plain*. Now when Susannah Cooper married, they had nuts, and some cheese, too. It was *soooo* elegant."

"Peggy, I haven't seen nuts at market since, well, I don't know when."

"Hmmm. Well, but beef." She tickled her chin with the quill.

"Peggy, I'm not even sure I can get beef. That's why it's underscored. We may need to settle—"

"I know! You can make that sauce for it with the horseradish and chives, and what else did you put in it? Cream or something?"

"Eggs." I groaned. That sauce had been delicious. I'd concocted it during my first month as cook in my uncle's house, when eggs and horseradish and onions and olive oil, though scarce, could still be found. It'd taken hours to prepare, and that with all the ingredients to hand. But what a triumph! I was nigh to drooling just thinking on it.

"Please, Clem, it needs to be special, 'tis for my wedding day." Suddenly, she took my hand. "Oh, Clem, I'm doing the right thing, don't you think?"

She fixed me with those bewitching eyes that said every bit of her awaited my answer. The best I could manage was, "Well, I guess so."

"He's so—so overpowering, I—I—. Sometimes I look at his hands, they're so big, did you ever notice? And I think how he—he's killed men with those hands."

"Peggy, for pity's sake, he uses a pistol or something. He doesn't strangle them with his bare hands."

"But he could," she whispered. Her gaze moved to the window. "Sometimes, he scares me."

"Well, then, don't marry him."

"I must."

I'd been gathering our lists together, but this jerked me to attention.

Her laugh tinkled. "Oh, Clem, I don't mean it that way. It's just—" She sighed. "You'll think I'm wicked."

I already did.

Her face went dreamy, as happens when a lady speaks of her beloved. "You know how—how fond I am of Captain Andre."

So she still fancied Andre, after all. "Then why," I asked, "are you marrying someone else?"

"Oh, Clem, don't you see?"

I shook my head.

"Good! Then likely the general won't have guessed it either. I worry, you know, that he will, and—well, he can get into some violent passions." Peggy's hand dropped to mine. "Clem, don't you ever tell anyone this—"

I scarcely dared breathe.

"Promise me."

I nodded.

"Well, then," Peggy said, "I'm marrying him because Cher Jean thinks I could influence him to—you know, I could be a good influence on him."

I don't know what I expected, but not this paltry, illogical thing. At last I said, "Influence him to *what?*"

"Why, you know, to stop making war."

"Stop making war?" I threw my hands wide. "He can't even walk across a room without help—"

"Oh, but he's healing, and then he'll be back out there, fighting and winning."

I continued staring, and she added, "Don't you want this war to be over?" She shuddered. "I sure do. Cher Jean thinks if they can persuade the rebel generals one by one to stop fighting, and see, I could ask the general to stay home instead of going on campaign—"

"Peggy, come on! You're marrying a man you don't love because the one you do love thinks you could influence him?"

"Well, that's not the only reason."

I waited, and she continued breathlessly, "I'd get to see him again, Cher Jean, you know."

I tried to make sense of it.

But couldn't. "Peggy, look, how does marrying General Arnold—what does that have to do with seeing John Andre? They're enemies, on opposite sides, they—"

"Well, one thing's certain, I'll never see John again, sitting here in horrid old Philadelphia. But if I'm the wife of a Continental general..."

She sat smiling at me. Finally, I said, "What? What does that do?"

"Well, for one thing, it puts me near the army. The Continentals must be near His Majesty's forces if they're going to fight them, right? All I'll need to do is skip across the lines to Cher Jean. You know they let ladies pass back and forth all the time, especially a general's wife. Why, the general's forever issuing passes to ladies who want to go to New York."

"Peggy, you're touched. You can't—"

"There's a better chance that I'll see John again if I'm married to a Continental commander than if I'm not. I've got loads more plans, Clem. There's this one I—"

She stopped suddenly, and I asked, "You mean to say you're marrying a man, and one who scares you, remember, on the chance that you'll see your sweetheart one last time?"

"One last time?" She looked puzzled, then brightened. "No, Clem, you don't understand. I wouldn't—I'd stay there with Cher Jean."

I fell back in my chair.

"See?" She giggled. "Told you you'd think I'm wicked."

Wicked didn't cover the half of it. "Peggy, you know what they call people who go from one side to another during war? They call them traitors."

"They can call me whatever they want, so long as they call me Mrs. Andre." Her eyes shone as they had the winter before last, when the gallant captain squired her about. And I saw that betraying her country was the least of it, for she was planning a greater treason, and smiling while she did.

Then I shook myself. Not even Peggy could be that sinful. Likely I'd misunderstood. And so I tried for a smile myself as I said, "Mrs. Andre? But you'll already be Mrs. Arnold."

"I know, and I feel bad about that, I truly do. I hope he won't be too hurt when I ask for a divorce. I'm not trying to hurt him."

'Twas as I'd feared but still so shocking I couldn't credit it. "Peggy, that's—well, it's—once you're married, you can't undo it. It's not Christian."

"Oh, Clem, you don't under—"

"Besides, what if John Andre doesn't want to marry you?"

"Not want to marry me?" She shook her head and added what was boasting for anyone else but truth for her. "Every man wants to marry me."

"If he wanted to marry you, why didn't he that winter the army was here?"

That stopped her. The brilliant eyes clouded as she sat considering. "Well, because, Daddy wouldn't have allowed it. You're right, I probably should have insisted. John and I've been so miserable since he left. But I was only fifteen then." Her smile was as dreamy and blissful as a seraph's. "Besides, he'll be so grateful for all I've done, you know, all the infor—ah, how I've kept General Arnold from fighting them, of course he'll want to marry me. Do you know, he'll probably be advanced soon, he'll be *Major* Andre!"

My head swam with a new and horrible thought. "How do you know what John Andre—Peggy, have you been—oh, dear God, are you *writing* each other?"

Her gaze roamed the room instead of meeting mine.

"Peggy," I said through clenched teeth. No telling what the unsuspecting General Arnold or his aides might have said in her hearing. "Are you writing to an enemy officer?"

"He's no enemy! Least, he's not my enemy." She jumped to her feet. "No, of course I'm not writing him. How could I?"

But I knew it for a lie, especially when she took to smiling again and hugging herself.

"Oh, Clem, I'm so happy! I just wish this stupid war would end so Cher Jean and I could marry."

"Peggy, it'll never work. Don't be silly. Peggy!"

But she flitted from the room as though I hadn't spoken.

She wed General Arnold of an evening at my uncle's home, with a soldier supporting the groom and a bride as beautiful as anyone had seen. Though I was her cousin, and a woman, I could understand the spell she cast over men. I forgot her selfishness for her gold hair against her red bodice, her flawless skin under the veil, her huge eyes sparkling grey as the ocean.

"Ah, Margaret," the general breathed, though folks seldom called Peggy by her given name.

They pledged their vows, and the veteran of Quebec and Saratoga wiped his tears. I misdoubt he ever once took his eyes from her.

Afterwards, I served beef without any sauce, not even onions, punch, and cake. The general thanked me for it, pitiful as it was.

"And now we're cousins," he said with that twinkle that set a lady's heart fluttering. "You must let me care for you, too, Clem, until that lucky major claims you."

"You're very kind, sir, worrying about me on your special day."

"Bah, Clem, 'tis no kindness. We're family now."

The newlyweds barely tasted the punch before Arnold called for his carriage. I stood with my aunt and uncle at the door, waving farewell. Peggy looked nervous, likely wondering how she'd manage the hero who besieged her until she crumbled and then attacked her father until he did too…

"A veritable Helen of Troy!" Arnold whispers. "Just like my first wife."

We sit silent but for the fire's snapping. Flash yawns, stretches, ambles out of the parlor for the back door.

Arnold heaves himself to his feet, crippled leg held before him. The hall clock strikes midnight as he says, "Well, my dear, you should tell an old soldier to hush instead of boring a lady to death."

"General, you know I love talking with you. And there's my book, too. I need to know whatever you'll tell me for it."

"'Tis kind of you, Clem. I appreciate it."

I stare at the dying fire, unable to meet his eyes.

He begins hobbling towards the garden, and though no agents wait there to bundle him off to Washington, I sit wretched with the knowledge that they soon will. Why did I ever agree when His Excellency asked me to spy on this man? "Oh, by the way," he says, "I won't be needing breakfast tomorrow. I'm leaving early. Be gone 'til dinnertime."

He waits as though I'll ask where he's going, but after all, I'm only his cook.

Finally, he adds, "Have some things to discuss with Sir Harry, about the invasion down South."

I keep my voice light as I say, "You'll be sailing for Virginia soon, then."

"Any day now."

But that's not what he hoped I'd notice. He wants me to see that General Sir Henry Clinton is seeking his advice.

"Well, sir, if anyone can tell Sir Harry how to conquer u—um, the rebels, it's you."

I wake early next morning, but the general's already gone, and Peggy with him. Good. I can search his papers again. The leather notebook I found last time has tantalized me since. Likely it reveals Peggy's part in everything.

I pull on my quilted petticoat and skirt, mobcap, and then a bodice over my chemise, buttoning it as I run to the kitchen. I take no time for breakfast other than a cup of tea, cold as ice and strong from steeping in the pot overnight. Then, shivering, wrapping my cloak about me, I hurry to Arnold's office and slip the key from its new home under the rug.

The book isn't atop the chest anymore. I waste a quarter hour hunting it before I find it behind some ledgers on a shelf. I wriggle it free, hands shaking, then go to the door to listen. All I hear is a carriage rattling past.

Hugging the book to me, I lock the door and fly to my room. If Arnold comes home early, he'll not find me in his office.

I flop onto my bed and untie the book's ribbon. It is indeed a journal—with papers tucked between the pages. I burrow under the blankets and unfold the first sheet I find. My face burns: it's the "wife's letter to her husband" Arnold mentioned when he caught me rummaging his office Tuesday. More correspondence flutters from the journal as I leaf through it, some from Peggy, some in Arnold's hand.

Mortified, despising myself and all spies, I return to the journal. I read its raw notes, really just jots and scribblings. If I didn't know my cousin and General Arnold so well, I'd hardly make sense of it.

But piecing things together with the help of the letters, I see how Peggy traduced the general and understand as much as anyone can how she caught and fooled a hero like Benedict Arnold...

Remembering that his passion had frightened Margaret on their wedding night, Arnold made himself go easy now, though he shook at the thought that this magnificent girl was his. He took her in his arms and kissed her, longingly, lingeringly. She did not protest, but she did not respond, either. Finally, he gently turned her around and put his hands to her dress. "Let me help you," he whispered and set about unfastening the buttons, as he had so often longed to do.

She submitted and kept on submitting until at last he lay gasping in bed beside her. Then he turned to her, expecting to cuddle, but she sat up and swung her legs over the edge.

He reached to caress her back. "I—I didn't hurt you, did I?"

"No." She stood, leaving his hand patting air. Nothing could have shouted more clearly how little she cared. She crossed the room to the screen and the chamberpot behind it.

He lay thinking, stricken, longing for Margaret, her adoration and comfort. Yet Peggy knew what love was: he remembered her paean to it in her father's garden that day. But he also recalled Franks' gossip about British officers.

"There's someone else, isn't there?" he asked at last.

She had reappeared from behind the screen long moments ago, had almost finished dressing. Now she turned to look at him, hairbrush in hand. "What? Someone else? I—I—what are you talking about?"

He said nothing, only stared. He hadn't met the liar yet who could abide silence, especially one as young as Peggy. They convinced themselves that if only they insisted on their falsehood at length and loudly enough, their victims would believe them.

Sure enough, Peggy shook her head. "Really, I don't know what you mean. Why would I—I wouldn't marry unless I—I—remember that day, we were outside, I told you how delicious love is—"

But he turned away, sickened.

Still, he had little time to brood, for the next evening he came home to a house full of well-wishers and a table hidden under food and wine. Peggy presided with glowing face, smiling coyly when speaking the words "my husband" to their guests. His spirits lifted until he, too, was smiling, proud that such a woman was his.

The parties continued all week. One evening, Peggy added a brace of fiddlers, with dancing far into the night. She wheedled until he stepped onto the floor with her, however he protested that his leg wouldn't permit—he had danced often, before he was wounded, though now—

Then the first notes of "Over the Hills and Far Away" swept the room. Eyes locked on Peggy, he hopped forward and would have lost his balance but for her steadying arm. "You can do it, General," she murmured.

And in truth he did. By the time "Over the Hills" gave way to the "Anacreontic Song," his right leg was compensating somewhat for the left. His motions were the most awkward in the room, but he was dancing, moving as he had never thought to again. He dipped and swirled, Peggy's shining eyes cheering him, her laughter making him forget his clumsiness. The longer they danced, the more alive he felt, the years and pain dropping away.

"I wish tonight would never end," he said as they came together in a minuet.

"Don't worry." She smoothed an errant strand of hair. "We'll do it again tomorrow. I've got Becky Franks and the Chew sisters coming, and a few of my other friends, too. Why don't you invite some of your officers, but find some that at least have a whole uniform, won't you?"

He was enjoying himself as he had not for months, whatever Joseph Reed said about it.

Then the bills from the butcher and seamstress and milliner arrived, and by week's end, he was broke.

"Peggy, my love." He looked up from the invoices to see her pirouetting before the mirror in yet another new gown.

"Look, General, isn't it beautiful?" She turned to him, hands smoothing the fabric over her stomach, emphasizing the curves above and below. "Now all I need are some jet earrings and a necklace to go with—"

"Peggy, I, ah, I'm sorry. We need to be frugal, cut our—"

"Oh, but I am, General. I told the musicians we'd only want one of them tonight. We've got just, let's see, fourteen, no, sixteen guests coming, and I think one fiddle—"

"No, Peggy, I mean there can't be any more parties. I can't even afford that gown there."

"No more parties?" She stood with hands outstretched, tragic and bereft.

He flushed with shame.

"But—but, General, don't you want to have fun?"

"Sure I do." He tried to smile through his humiliation. "Wanna have some right now that won't cost us a shilling?"

She only stared before going to the window to stand with her back to him.

"Peggy, I'm sorry. I was enjoying the parties as much as you."

"It's all right, General, it's just—well, we were so careful in my father's house, you know. I'm heartily sick of pinching and scraping." She turned with a smile as bitterly heroic as though she had stormed Quebec. "I thought things would be different with you, but—" She shrugged. "I guess it can't be helped."

His shoulders slumped. Not since he lay shivering at the *Hopital General* with his army defeated in the Canadian snow had he felt such a failure.

"—make some money," Peggy was saying.

"What?"

She glided towards him, turned her back to him again. "Can you unbutton me, please?"

They had not made love since their wedding night, a week gone. He had been tired after the parties, almost sick from the rich food and angry at Peggy's indifference. But now desire surged. He raised trembling hands to her brocaded dress, her scent intoxicating him.

"I know how you can make some money." Her voice was husky, enticing.

He slipped buttons from their loops, thrilling at the sight of silky skin. "How?" he whispered.

"Tell General Sir Henry Clinton you'll join him for the right price."

He started as though burned, and Peggy glanced over her shoulder with a laugh. "'Twas only a joke."

He nodded, tried to smile, then took her hand. "Come to bed."

But it was no better than their first time. Peggy lay limp and compliant, rolling away with a sigh when he had finished...

I throw the letter from me, blushing so furiously I fear the red will ever stain my face. How can I continue nosing through such intimate paragraphs? But if my cousin and her husband are this forthcoming about the most private part of life, surely they wrote of betraying us to the enemy—nor jokingly, neither.

I forsake the bed's warm nest to retrieve the paper I tossed on the floor. Shivering, I plunge back under the covers and resume reading…

He spent the next few days meeting with business associates, coming home late, leaving early. His love had not soured. But it hurt to look at her, to know that another man owned what he wanted most in the world. Only when discussing deals—how many cattle he and his partners could purchase in Delaware for sale in Philadelphia, or what goods the Council was likely to prohibit next, thus increasing their value, and where to buy large amounts of them—could he forget his heartbreak.

"Can you come home for dinner this afternoon?" she asked their tenth morning together. It was not yet light, but he had risen and dressed and was leaning over to kiss her goodbye when she startled him with her question.

"I, ah—absolutely, Peggy. Of course."

He left the house whistling and passed the morning in a hopeful daze. At two o'clock, with Isaiah Brooks still describing the profitability of New York's market, he made his apologies and started home.

She had donned a simple gown, so sheer it could not be worn even before the servants. But she'd dismissed them all anyway, as he discovered when she herself fetched the wine and two goblets.

"To us," he said, raising his.

She giggled and lifted hers. Through the gown he traced her curves. "To us," she said. "Don't you want to take that coat off?"…

I glance heavenward, praying for patience. Will we ever get beyond these *affaires d'amour?*…

He shrugged out of his coat and waistcoat and his boots and breeches as well, and then she was in his arms. He kissed her, and though she endured it without responding, he thought, 'Tis all right. It will take time, but she'll learn to love me, she will. Why else would she seduce me like this? She's trying, Lord bless her.

She even lay with him afterwards, hand in hand as he and Margaret used to lie, his leg thrown over her thighs, her hair tickling his nose.

"General," she whispered, "you asleep?"

He sighed. "Peggy, would you—my name is Benedict. Is it so awful?"

She twisted to look at him. "No. Why?"

"You haven't called me by name since we met. It's always 'General' or 'sir.'"

"What did your wife used to call you?"

Suddenly, it was Margaret's hair he was smelling and Margaret's breath on his chest. He heard her laugh, so loving, so sweet, heard her calling, "Oh, Benny! Oh, my darling, my angel, my love, oh, Benny, my beautiful Benny, I adore you!"

He blinked back tears. "Benny," he said, squeezing fingers he wished were hers. "She called me Benny."

"Well, then, Benny, would you like some dinner?"

And so they sat at the mahogany table, without guests or servants, and ate cold mush and potatoes roasted that morning.

"I'm no cook, Gen—Benny." She blushed and glanced away. "'Twasn't food I was thinking of when I asked you to come home."

He poured more wine. "'Twasn't food I was thinking of when I came home."

She questioned him about his days in the Continental command and laughed as he spoke of Ethan Allen's buffoonery at Ticonderoga and Gates' at Saratoga. "Stop, Benny!" she said at last. "It hurts, I'm laughing so hard."

"Ah-yuh, they have that effect."

"I don't know how you put up with them. You're so much better than they are."

He shrugged.

"Do you know," she continued, "I once heard General Grey say you were the best commander on either side?"

"Grey said that? Nice to have the enemy's endorsement."

"He was dining with us, you know, and he said you were the best."

"Best, how? Easiest to beat?"

"No, silly." She slapped at his arm, then, laughter fading, mused, "You ever wish you were in a, I don't know, a *professional* army?…"

My eyes widen. At last! We've finally reached something worthwhile…

"One that deserved you more?" she added.

He looked at her quickly, but the grey gaze admiring him was wide and innocent.

"No." He struggled to his feet. "Any more of that mush in the pantry?"

She mentioned it again the next morning as he was dressing, rolling over and blinking at the lamp he had lighted. "Morning, Benny."

"Good morning, my love." He limped to the bed to kiss her, then lumbered across the rug for his blue uniform. Aware of Peggy's eyes on him, desperate to seem young and vibrant instead of old and crippled, he tried to walk without limping, putting his full weight on the bad leg. He gritted his teeth against a howl. The blood pounded in his ears as he reached the uniform so that he heard only Peggy's voice, not her words.

He balanced on his right leg, waited until his breath returned so that he could say, not gasp, "What was that, my love?"

"I said, I just love the British Army's uniforms. Don't you?"

He turned to stare, jaw slack. "Their—their uniforms? They're here making war, killing us, and you love their uniforms?"

"Oh, Benny, don't be such a horrid old stick in the mud, for pity's sake. You're as bad as Joseph Reed. I just meant they're a nice, bright color. They make a man look so young and handsome, don't you think?"

He stared a moment longer. Then, as Peggy pulled a face to mock him, he laughed. "See you tonight, my love."

His leg agonized him all day, until he rued the vanity that had made him stride across the bedroom. That afternoon, as well, he left mid-meeting to hobble to his carriage and home.

When he arrived, a manservant opened the door and took his great-coat. "Can you bring me some wine?" he asked, wiping the sweat from his forehead. "And where's Mrs. Arnold?"

"She be upstairs, sir."

He found Peggy at her desk when he gained their room, a fire on the hearth taking the chill from the April day. He leaned against the doorjamb, panting, blinking, so that Peggy turned on her chair and exclaimed, and even in his pain, he thought, See, she's beginning to care. But instead of running to him, she opened the desk's drawer and jammed her papers inside. Only then did she rush to help him.

When at last he was seated, head back, eyes closed, foot propped on a stool, he asked, "What were you writing?"

"Nothing, Benny. The pain any better?"

A knock sounded at the door. Peggy swished to it and returned with a glass and a bottle of wine.

She poured some, handed it to him.

"Thanks." He downed it in one gulp, and she refilled the glass.

When the pain eased, he asked again, "So what were you writing?"

"Nothing. I told you. A—a shopping list."

"Shopping list?" He smiled and offered the glass to her. "Thought it might be a note to a secret lover, arrangements for an assigna—"

"No, Benny." She sipped some wine. "My aunt sent me money for a wedding present, and I—I—there's some things I need that can't be bought here."

"Ah, so you want someone in New York to get them for you."

She gaped. "How'd you know?"

"Half the men I see every day ask me the same thing for their wives. Could I send a letter for them through the lines, just a note to the merchants there, asking to buy some of the goods they're importing from England."

"Yes, well—" She bit her lip, then smiled. "You must admit, English fashions are so much finer than anything we can get here." Her smile changed to a frown. "I can't believe that stupid Council—what business is it of theirs if I want English velvet instead of scratchy old linsey-woolsey some farmwife spins in her barnyard? How dare they call me a criminal just because I like good clothes!"

"And expensive ones." He motioned for the glass and swallowed more wine. "Give me your letter. I'll send it tomorrow."

"Thank you, Benny." She kissed him as though she meant it and skipped to the desk. She fumbled in the drawer, then stepped to the hearth with letter and wax.

"No need to seal it, Peggy. I read anything I send through the lines."

She turned to stare, brows raised. "From your own wife?"

"Actually, my secretary reads them, my love. I haven't the time. But it wouldn't look right for me to exempt you, now, would it? After all, where's the harm? 'Tis only a list."

For a moment she looked like a child whose hopes for a pony-ride have been dashed. "You must be so *proud*, fighting for liberty," she said. Then she got herself in hand. "I'll give it to you tomorrow, Benny. There's a few things I want to add."

He leaned back and closed his eyes again, weak and weary as an old man. He heard her lock the drawer and walk from the room.

After she descended the stairs, he hobbled to the desk. It was built for a lady, and delicate, as was its lock, and he scarcely twisted his penknife in the mechanism before it sprung.

He returned to his chair with the note and poured another glass of wine before unfolding it. 'Twas only a list, as she had said, addressed to a Cher Jean, but it began and ended with more endearments than the wife of one man should decently write another. He frowned at the "Jean." What French officer had enlisted with the Redcoats instead of the Continentals? He studied the note, hatred for the Papist who owned Peggy's heart choking him.

Chapter Eighteen

Peggy didn't refer to it again until a few days later, when they were in the carriage on their way to the theater. Once they were settled, a blanket shielding them from the breeze, he reached for her hand.

"We'll have been married a fortnight tomorrow, my love."

She turned those brilliant eyes on him. "Benny, tell me something."

"Anything, my love."

"Have the rebels, I mean, the Continentals, have they won a battle since you were wounded?"

"Have—what? Why?"

"I don't know. Just wondering, I guess. Have they won any battles?"

"Well, sure, they, ah—"

"When?"

He chewed his lip. There had been the business at Monmouth last summer, when the government's troops abandoned Philadelphia and Washington attacked them on their march to New York. But the Continental command had been confused and inept. The victory would have gone to the Redcoats, had they not been busy making their own mistakes. As it was, both sides claimed the honor, and both knew it for a lie.

Later that year, an allied French and American attack on Newport, Rhode Island, failed too. And in December, Savannah, Georgia, not only the state's capital but a strategic port as well, had fallen to the enemy, affording a toehold for a southern campaign. The Redcoats swept north and took Augusta a month later.

But out west on the Mississippi River, there was a young Virginian, a man with three names, though Arnold was damned if he could remember one, and the ginger to match, who had captured some forts. Virginia annexed the territory, and the state now stretched far and wide—

"Clark!" he blurted. "That's his name, George Rogers Clark. He's taken those forts out on the Mississippi, Vincennes and Kaskaskia—"

"Those don't matter, Benny, so far out in the wilderness. What's it signify to us here?"

"You've been listening to your father again. What are you driving at, Peggy?"

"Oh, nothing." She waved dismissively as the carriage stopped before the theater. "Just that the rebels haven't won a battle since you were laid up with your leg, have they? They can't seem to win without you."

As always, her gaze was innocent, admiring. But her words echoed in his head until he heard nothing of the play, only laughed when Peggy did and could not have said over what.

The Continentals hadn't won without him, true, though he hadn't counted their losses until now. 'Twas no boast that he was the best among them, as General Grey admitted. His strategies were clever; men followed him eagerly; he won against impossible odds.

Then why did the Congress scorn him? Why were they siding with Reed and the Radicals, turning a blind eye, nay, *encouraging* them, as they betrayed freedom for power? And it was worsening: no longer content with Pennsylvania, the Radicals were after the whole country now—and getting it, too, if the laws against theater and horse-racing were any measure. The only hindrance to their authority, distracting Congress and preventing the Radicals' dictating to all thirteen states, was the war. But once the Continentals triumphed, once the fighting was over and the Redcoats were gone—

"Oh, but they can't win without you, Benny." He would have sworn Peggy whispered those words. Yet when he glanced at her, startled, she was staring at the stage with parted lips. He, too, watched the actors, as the voice in his head resumed. "You keep on fighting, though, and the Continentals'll win. Might take months yet, but eventually—" He sensed a shrug. "Then Reed and his boys'll have a clear shot. Meanwhile, you're just a tool in their hands. You gonna let them use you like that? Mock you, torment you, hang your friends, steal from folks—and all the while you're winning battles for them, increasing their control over us? Don't be a fool! Now, on the other hand, you stop fighting or, better yet, join the Brit—"

"Peggy," he whispered.

"Shhh, Benny," she said and laughed with the rest of the audience.

"Peggy, I'm stepping out for a breath of air." He limped to the door, applause sounding behind.

At breakfast the next morning, he asked, "Why'd you wanna know how many battles they've won without me?"

"What? You mean yesterday?" She buttered her toast before answering. "Oh, I dunno." She licked crumbs from her fingers. He had never seen a more seductive gesture. "I guess I was thinking you're their best general, but they sure don't treat you that way."

True.

She pushed her hair over her shoulder. "Such a pity you're not with an army that would appreciate you."

"The British Army, for instance?"

She shrugged, and her robe fell away from her bosom. She nibbled some bread, chewed and swallowed, before pulling the bodice closed. When she spoke, her voice held such sympathy it trembled. "Don't you ever tire of it, Benny, the way they abuse you?"

"Sure," he said, and it was as if the dam inside him broke. The hurts and shame of four years came spilling out to be absorbed by Peggy's bottomless, understanding eyes. "I've nigh died for the Cause, and do I get any thanks? No, I get harassed by the likes of Joseph Reed. It's him and his kind controlling things now, and they don't care a fig about freedom, hate it, in fact—"

"You oughta write Captain Andre," she said softly.

"Who?"

"John Andre. He's on General Clinton's staff. He could help you."

She tossed it off as though it were the most natural thing in the world, and his brows rose to his hairline. "Me, a British officer could help *me*? Help me *what*?"

"Well, he could—you know, he—tell him what you've just told me. Tell him you're tired of this horrid old war and you want to fight with a real army for a change, one that doesn't read people's mail and set men like Joseph Reed over us."

Two weeks ago, her suggestion would have shocked him to silence. Now he said wearily, "Government reads letters going behind an enemy's lines just as we do, Peggy, I assure you, and—"

"Oh, Benny, you don't belong with the rebels, don't you see? Maybe they were fighting for liberty once, but they aren't anymore. All they care about is grabbing more power."

He sighed. She made more sense than he cared to admit.

"Just think, Benny, what a hero you'd be! 'General Benedict Arnold Joins His Majesty's Forces.'" She pantomimed reading the words off a newspaper. "That'd be the end of the war, Benny. Why, half the Continentals'd follow you across the lines. They'd give you your own regiment. King'd probably give you a title and lands."

"Peggy, it's—I'd—"

"You'd be such a hero. Just think, all the history books would write you down as the man who stopped the Radicals!"

"Peggy." He spoke loudly, slowly, emphasizing her name, trying to recall her to sense. "I—I can't. 'Twould be unspeakable. I'd be deserting my friends, men who starved with me at Quebec. I'd be a traitor. They'd—"

"Traitor." Peggy's laugh shimmered. "They used to call Daddy that, my whole family, too. My poor, worried little father, they said he's a spy and a traitor because we removed to New Jersey when their ragamuffins invaded Philadelphia. Daddy thought we'd be safer there. Terrible crime, wouldn't you say?" She was as angry as he had seen her. "They wanted to arrest him for that. My poor dad, just shaking in his boots for fear they'd send him to Connecticut. They sent loads of his friends there, you know, to Simsbury, to the copper mines. Can you imagine, imprisoning men underground, in old mines? You know how many of them have died?"

He sat silent.

When she spoke again, gently, reasonably, her anger was gone. "What do you care if they call you a traitor? What's it signify? They call anyone a traitor who disagrees with them, just like the king does."

"Peggy, I can't do this. I'm fighting for liberty—"

"Well, of course, Benny, I know. That's why I'm suggesting this. For liberty."

He stared, so astonished he dropped his fork with a clatter. "For liberty? How?"

"Well, um—" She took another bite of bread, swallowed, sipped some coffee. "Well, don't you see?"

"No." He waited intently. 'Twas liberty he fought for, not the United States or Connecticut or independency or George Washington or anything but liberty, sweet liberty, a man's right to live and think and speak as he chose, to decide for himself, to be free of government, of all its meddling and its brutal punishment of anyone disagreeing with its edicts. He had offered his services to the Patriots because they loved liberty as he did. Or so he thought until he collided with the Radicals. They didn't fight for liberty. No, Reed himself said morality and religion ought to be the goal. As though either morality or religion could flourish at bayonet-point.

He snorted. "You mean because of the Radicals, that I've tried everything and nothing works, they're even taking over the Congress? You think your father's right, that only the king's strong enough to stop them? That's why I oughta—oughta desert—um, join the Redcoats?"

"Absolutely, Benny."

He remembered Beverley Robinson's letter, his praise of commerce and condemnation of the war disrupting it. Robinson had urged him to work at restoring peace and even implied that friends in the British command would welcome an overture from him.

He stared past Peggy, picturing himself at the head of cheering troops as they galloped for British lines. The huzzahs grew louder as Redcoats turned out by regiments. Harry Clinton stepped towards him, round face aglow. "General Arnold, sir, an honor. I've long admired your tactics. Come, help me plan our next assault. We must stop these Radicals. They're destroying the king's peace." Arnold saw the relief on Patriot faces at their salvation from tyranny, heard Reed's cursing. He would be The Man Who Defeated the Radicals, loved and admired everywhere he went. No more fighting his own side as hard as the enemy. No more criticism, nor scandals, either. No more Reed.

He tried to write John Andre that evening while Peggy lounged on the bed and spoke encouragement to him. In the end, though he sweated and fidgeted for an hour, he crumpled the paper into a ball.

She padded over to him. "What's wrong?"

"I—I can't do it, Peggy. I just can't."

In a moment, her hands were on his slumped shoulders as she pressed her body to his. He nearly shook with desire.

"Sure you can," she said softly. "But it's hard to write it, isn't it? Why don't we just send a messenger? That's easier all the way around."

"There's no one I'd trust to do that." He reached to fondle her, but she stepped back, though her hands remained on his shoulders. "I just can't do this, Peggy. I can't turn traitor—"

"What about me?" Her fingers tightened. "Send me."

"*You?* Peggy, have you lost your mind?" He twisted to stare at her. "Reed and the Congress, they'd never suspect a thing if my wife suddenly took off for enemy lines, now, would they? Let's forget it. I—"

"All right, then, what about Mr. Stansbury?"

"Stansbury? The merchant?" He recalled the name from last summer, when he paid the man £160 to furnish his dining room. No sooner had he settled with him than he saw "Stansbury, Joseph" on a list of victims Reed wanted gaoled. "Tory, isn't he, and a traitor? At least, according to Reed."

"Everybody's a traitor according to Reed. This is Joseph Stansbury. He goes to New York all the time on business—"

"Peggy, I can't, all right? Never should have—"

"You bought the table and chairs from him, remember? Truth is, he, ah—promise you won't be angry at me?"

Something in her tone stole his breath. "What?"

"Well, sometimes I've given him orders for things to bring me. That's how I was going to get that list to New York if you hadn't—" She broke off at the horror on his face. "What? Why are you looking at me like that?"

He could not answer for several moments. Finally, when the whirlwind inside him permitted, he said, "How—how often have you, ah, correspond—given Stansbury, um, orders?"

"Only a few times, Benny. I wanted a few trifles, you know. Nothing outrageous, for goodness' sake."

He sat drowning in the knowledge that his wife was secretly corresponding with the enemy. If Stansbury were ever indiscreet, if Reed or any of the Congress should discover that the wife of General Benedict Arnold was sending clandestine letters, however innocent, through the lines—

"It'd all be over," he whispered. "Nothing I could say or do would save you."

"What?"

He looked up to see Peggy gliding to the bed for her hairbrush. "Oh, my love." He fought to steady his voice. "Don't you see what you've done?"

"Done? What have I done?"

She pulled the brush through her glorious hair, languorously, seductively, until the thought of losing her, and over a few baubles, too, sucked the life from him.

"I ordered a couple of nice bonnets," she said, "and that shawl with the grey satin ribbon through it that you like so much. Oh, and gloves, Mr. Stansbury gets the nicest gl—"

"Peggy, for God's sake, you're corresponding with the *British*! If my enemies find out, they'll crucify you. Oh, God." He leaned forward, clutching his stomach, his despair so overwhelming it nauseated him. "They'd hang you, Peggy, like those poor Quakers at Christmas. There wouldn't be a thing I could do, not a thing."

"Well, maybe you should leave an army that would hang a lady for buying a shawl."

She tossed it off flippantly, never realizing how it pinioned him, nor the choice suddenly, starkly confronting him.

Other folks had faced this same agony. Most famous were Ben Franklin and his son, William, Royal Governor of New Jersey. The old man had washed his hands of Will, left him to the Patriots' mercies, raised no word of protest nor hand to help when they gaoled Will for his Loyalism. Rumor said the two never spoke, that no one so much as mentioned Will's name in his father's presence. And it worked: despite a tainted son, Franklin remained a leading Patriot. But at what cost, dear Lord. At what cost!

Nor were the Franklins alone. As their power grew, the Radicals were tearing more and more families apart, forcing decisions on them no one should ever endure. A lady Arnold vaguely knew had lost her Scottish husband last year when they exiled him for nothing more than the crime of his origin. She pled for him, arguing her own Patriotism, but the Radicals ordered him behind the enemy's lines just the same. In the end, she bowed her head and accepted their verdict, even murmured this was what their Cause required.

But not from him, Heaven help him. Peggy, his boys, Hannah—they came first. No government, no law could change that.

Peggy tossed the brush aside to stand with hands on hips, robe open and framing her curves. "Shall I send for Mr. Stansbury?"

He hesitated, thinking it through once more. Then he nodded. "You leave me no choice."

Stansbury was not the sort Arnold trusted, nor would he have chosen him as messenger. The merchant's reactions were never those of other men. During their first meeting the next morning, with Peggy hovering nervously and Arnold's insides cramped from a flux such as had not afflicted him since the march to Quebec, Stansbury bubbled with admiration for a brooch Peggy wore. The two of them discussed its jewels and cunning workmanship until Arnold thought he must explode.

But then, when he announced that he, Major General Benedict Arnold, victor of Ticonderoga and Saratoga and the man who had almost won Canada, was sick of Joseph Reed's tyranny and his Council as well as the dictators in Congress, and had concluded he could best serve liberty by working with the British, Stansbury only nodded. Finally, he said, "Go on, General. I'm listening."

"Go on?" Arnold bellowed, so loudly Peggy started. "Isn't that enough?"

"Oh." Stansbury rubbed his chin. "Well, sir, I agree with you. Been my sentiments for years, actually, that Philadelphia's Council, and the Congress, too, they're both full of fools that don't give tuppence for liberty. But I don't see why you're telling *me* all this."

Arnold gave Peggy a look that shouted his opinion of her messenger and clumped to the window.

"You see, Mr. Stansbury," Peggy said, "we thought, that is, we're hoping you'll carry word to Captain Andre. He's been put in charge of intelligence—"

How the word grated, even when Peggy's alluring voice spoke it!

"—on General Clinton's staff. My husband's prepared to join the British Army, or, if they'd rather, he'll work for their interests from this side—"

Startled, he turned from the window. They had never discussed his working secretly, dishonorably. "No," he started to say. "No, wait, I'm going over to them, plain and simple."

But Peggy rolled on. "Now, I know you're in New York all the time. Would you, on your next trip, do you think you could see Captain Andre for us?"

"Absolutely." Stansbury's words oozed like oil. "'Course, Mrs. Arnold, there's a lot of risk in something like this, enough risk, maybe, to make that brooch my payment, do you think?"

Within a week, Stansbury was spending more time in the Arnolds' parlor than his own, head bent close to Peggy's, whispering. Arnold was too repulsed by the dishonor of spying, too sickened at the words "traitor" and "betrayal," to play at intelligencing. But Peggy and Stansbury delighted in it. They discussed various schemes and concocted elaborate messages in cipher, Stansbury thumbing the dictionary Andre, recently promoted to major, had specified as their key, calling out the page and line numbers of the words for Peggy to note.

Stansbury was there when the Congress published insults of Arnold disguised as a resolution, and but a month after the wedding, too.

Arnold burst into the house that day to find Stansbury with dictionary in hand and Peggy hunched over a paper writing numbers, tongue clamped between her teeth. Before her stood a decanter of wine and two half-empty glasses.

"General." Stansbury bowed. "We were just drinking Major Andre's health. Will you join us?" He faltered as Peggy looked up from her ciphering with a frown. "It's, ah, h-h-his birthday—"

Arnold heeded neither Stansbury's chatter nor Peggy's discomfiture. "Look at this!" he roared, so commandingly that Stansbury dropped his book, though Peggy, returned to her numbers, spared him no interest. He threw his newspaper onto the table beside her, and she frowned again. "Damn the Congress! Look!" he tapped the paper. "They voted they have the greatest confidence in Pennsylvania's authorities, meaning, of course, Joseph Reed."

"Oh, Benny, for pity's sake." She stifled a yawn. "You know what blockheads they are. Why do you let them upset—"

"Wait. That's not all. They say those authorities got every right to object when someone, say a military officer, meaning me, of course, treats them with less respect or decency than they think they deserve. The Congress, Peggy, of the whole continent. It's not just Pennsylvania Reed's got under his thumb now."

He was still stabbing the paper. Peggy leaned to read it.

Stansbury cleared his throat. "One of the Congressmen was in my shop couple of days ago, General. From what he said, I'd wager that resolution's just the beginning of Reed's revenge on you"—he hesitated as Arnold's glare fastened on him—"for, ah, for the Congress, um, voting in your favor last winter."

"They're talking about bringing me to trial again." He spoke to Peggy's bowed figure more than Stansbury.

"And not just for those charges you wanted a hearing on," Stansbury said. "They're gonna try you for all of them, even the ones their Committee already cleared you of."

Peggy lifted her head. "Well, but they can't do that. It's not fair."

"Once a man's declared innocent," Arnold growled, "you leave him be."

"Unless you're Joseph Reed," Stansbury said, voice sinking theatrically, "bound and determined to ruin Benedict Arnold, even if that means threatening the Continental Congress. You hear about that, General? Reed's gonna withdraw Pennsylvania from the confederation unless they see things his way. Which means the Congress'll give in to Reed, all the men and provisions for the Continental Army that come from here."

He nodded wearily. "There's a piece in the paper about it."

"Well, General," Stansbury clapped him on the shoulder, "good thing you're getting out, what with this war the rebels got going inside the war."

Arnold peered at Stansbury with interest instead of the usual irritation. "How do you mean?"

Stansbury seemed surprised. "What do I mean? Why, 'tis clear as glass. You got two groups of rebels, General. Two factions fighting each other tooth and nail, harder than they're fighting His Majesty."

He nodded, near breathless as Stansbury, Loyalist and a fop to boot, confirmed what he had long suspected. "Go on."

"Well, sir, on the one side, you've got Joseph Reed, and all the sorry folks like him. They don't have much of this world's goods except what they can get through government, through offices and pensions and posts. They're jealous as can be of anyone like you, General, anyone with more than what they've got. Doesn't matter whether it's money or—or power, or ability, even."

"It's not just men." Peggy squared her shoulders. "Ladies don't like anyone who's more beautiful than they are, either. You can't believe the nasty lies they'll tell about me."

Stansbury bowed. "A pity, Mrs. Arnold. Let us pray they never pass a law saying you must make yourself ugly. Because that's what they do, see.

They want a strong government that'll make everything equal—notice the Radicals're always whining about equality, not liberty. But what they mean is, they want laws passed to keep everyone as poor and miserable as they are."

"That's right," Peggy said. "Why, just yesterday, I—"

"Wait, Peggy," Arnold said. "Let him finish. Now, sir, the other side, how do you define them?"

"Oh, that's easy, General, that's our side." Stansbury smiled expansively. "You and me and anyone else that wants to manage his own life. We're men of ability and we know it."

He would have laughed at such presumption, at this peacock's supposing they were alike, if Stansbury had not been articulating his own thoughts exactly.

"No such thing as equality for us," Stansbury continued. "Plain as night and day that folks are different."

Arnold nodded. "Ah-yuh, some men are good in the countinghouse. Others do best aboard ship or planting crops."

"Some ladies are beautiful," Peggy said, "and others are like my cousin. She's a very good cook, and smart, too, smarter than most men, though you wouldn't know it to look at her, she's so homely."

Stansbury smiled. "You see, Mrs. Arnold, able folks don't need government to make everyone equal. Fact, we never need government at all. All it does is hinder us, especially when men who hate us are in office, not us personally, you understand—"

"Oh, they hate my husband personally, I assure you, Mr. Stansbury."

"Well, mayhap they do. But generally they hate anyone that's got enough ability and spunk to challenge them."

Arnold crossed his arms. "This isn't peculiar to our times, Mr. Stansbury."

"What, this war I'm talking about? No, sir, you're right. 'Tis a war's been raging since the Creation, I reckon, soon as Abel had a few more toys than Cain. And one of the first casualties is always justice."

Arnold stared, amazed anew. Who would have guessed Stansbury's fastidious ways and satin waistcoats hid such deep thoughts?

"See," Stansbury said, "soon as Reed started threatening the Congress, telling them Pennsylvania's gonna withdraw from their union, they knuckled under. Got no choice. That's why they're court-martialling you. Now, might be some of them care how unjust it is, but I wager they're too busy bowing and scraping to Joseph Reed to mention it—"

I glance up as Flash barks, scrambling for the front door. Then the knocker thumps. I thrust the journal and letters under my pillows and, smoothing my skirts, hurry downstairs.

It's an aide from Headquarters next door with dispatches for the general. He's delivered about a dozen of these packets since I've been here, but he's some nobleman's younger son, and so not obliged to even bow before he turns on his heel. Used to be, I'd call our thanks after him. Now I don't bother.

I shut the door, then hold the sealed packet to the sunbeam falling through the fanlight. I can't make out much, only Clinton's signature and "December 9th, 1780" on the last page. Champe and I decided long ago we wouldn't get too fancy, trying to ferret out what's in these dispatches.

"Nothing'll itch Arnold more than if he thinks somebody's tampering with military papers," Champe had said. "'Sides, they got the Culpers working on that stuff."

I nodded, thinking on the Culpers, Junior and Senior. Like Mr. Baldwin, they're shadowy men, maybe only one person, maybe ten or twelve. I tend to believe they're father and son from the Junior and Senior, but no one knows, not even His Excellency, and the Culpers like it that way—especially after the terror a few months ago, when Arnold went over. How many agents could he name, how many folks might hang when he's done chatting with his new friends? Most intelligencers, figuring their lives weren't worth beggar's spit, quit spying and sat waiting for Redcoats to come haul them off to gaol. Then, bit by bit, their nerve resurrected. Now the Culpers are back to telling Washington what goes on here in New York, which regiments are arriving and departing, how much forage the Redcoats are stealing out on Long Island, what effect the latest news from London's had on Clinton and the Loyalists. From the quality of what they send, some say there's a Culper next door at British headquarters.

So whatever's in this packet, a Culper's probably already enciphered it for Washington. Still, I tingle to read the pages myself, to discover some bit of information that will give us the victory.

Instead, I put the papers on the mantel. Then I climb the stairs to my chamber and the journal.

I nestle into my bed, still warm from before, and pull a blanket tight about my shoulders. I thumb through the book to find my place: "May 31st, 1779." There follows a list of household accounts, debts collected and provisions bought, noted in dollars. Hundreds of dollars. And all of them worthless.

Congress took to printing money early on, and what that said about their estimate of our wit—and their own—isn't flattering. What farmer exchanges wheat he's harvested with his sweat for bits of paper, even if they're gussied up with scrolls and flourishes? Where's the merchant risks his life and ship to fetch sugar from the Indies so's he can wind up with a pile of those scraps? No one wanted those Continental dollars, and that set the Congress awry. Without that paper, they had nothing to hand their army come payday, nothing to swap for uniforms or supplies or ammunition.

So Pennsylvania's Council forced that paper on us. They made it a crime same as murder or thievery to use gold and silver. A man could be gaoled for offering a merchant real money, and the merchant for accepting it.

And that wasn't the end of their tyranny. They also set prices and wages.

They'd been setting them right along, anytime someone complained that salt was too high or that the poorest among us couldn't buy meat. There was that time early on, when the Redcoats were seizing our ships so that goods from the Indies got scarce, and the merchants charged twice or thrice more than usual for their trouble. From the ruckus some Radical committee raised, you'd'a thought the merchants were slaughtering folks instead of selling us what we wanted to buy. That committee come down hard on them, trying to stir us to hate them as much as the Radicals did, and then they said, "Here's what you can charge for your goods, and no more."

You know what that done. Merchants just packed up whatever they had from the Indies, the fruit and sugar and all those cunning little mahogany boxes, and shipped them out to other places, where a committee wasn't managing their shops for them.

Then the Council spawned yet another committee, until we wondered if the country wouldn't be overrun by them. Those politicians fixed the prices of everything from bread to nails. A couple of Committeemen, foolhardy souls, asked General Arnold for his support. Arnold near kicked them in the hindquarters, hollering that common sense said a man always sells goods for the most he can get while still undercutting competitors and he for one wasn't against common sense, just all these damned committees...

It's lamplighting time, too dark to read without I light one. I take my crusie lamp downstairs to the banked fire in the parlor. Then I return to the journal. Nothing I've seen so far is strong enough to convict Peggy. But mayhap I'll come across something soon...

Spring passed with Stansbury delivering notes from the British command, deciphering them with Peggy, assuring Arnold of Major Andre's delight, and General Clinton's, too, in welcoming him back to his true allegiance.

"You're doing the right thing, General, the only sensible thing, what with the way affairs are headed," Stansbury said.

At first, Arnold heeded him, still awed by Stansbury's analysis of the struggle convulsing the Patriots. But as weeks passed without further profundities, Stansbury chafed him like a pair of wet breeches.

In his fairer moments, Arnold admitted it was the delay, more than Stansbury, irritating him. He had thought to make a grand transition, had imagined himself at the head of a British regiment pursuing Reed and his tyrannical fellows. He had not reckoned on weeks or even months of dickering and correspondence, of heart-stopping anxiety lest someone discover them, of haunted days and sleepless nights.

Peggy tried to make him see reason. "But, Benny, we need to get ready. Good Heavens, we can't just leave our house and—and carriage, and there's your estate in Connecticut that you had with your wife. You'll need to sell that. We need to sell everything, and that takes time. Anyway, we don't want General Clinton to think we're too eager. We want to get the best offer we can from him."

Not only wanted but needed to. Arnold had added the figures time
and again, the years of salary Congress owed him, Mount Pleasant and
the house in Connecticut, even his coach and four—all forfeit once the
rebels learned of his changed allegiance. Unless the king, already quell-
ing riots over the high taxes the war consumed, compensated him with
tens of thousands of pounds, he would be ruined. Yet they had requested
a mere £10,000 lest a higher figure repel His Majesty and leave Reed in
power. Studying the columns in his ledger, seeing what his principles
would cost, he wondered whether a rich man under the Radicals would
fare better than a beggar under the king.

"Our price is too high," he told Peggy after another letter from Andre
spoke only of the king's gratitude and vaguely promised rewards beyond
Arnold's expectations.

"Stuff and nonsense. You're worth twice, no, three or four times,
what we're asking."

"Well, clearly the customer doesn't think so." Bitterness twisted
his voice.

"Customers always want a lower price." Peggy ran a graceful hand
through her hair. "But you're the best officer on either side. You've done
so much for the rebels, been so—so *devoted* to their horrid old Cause, why,
think what it means to have a man like that say, 'I was wrong. I've changed
my mind.' Everyone else'll think he's wrong, too, Benny. Don't you see?"

"Sure I do, but your British friends don't. That's the troub—"

"We're leaving everything behind. We'll need new clothes and shoes,
too. Probably won't be able to pack much when the time comes—how'll
we live if we don't get payment from them up front?" She toyed with a
strand of hair. "Course, if you're commissioned a general in the king's
army, that'll pay something."

"It'll pay barely enough to live on."

"We'll still need to buy a house and a carriage."

"Besides, just because I ask for a general's commission doesn't mean
I'll get one. I—I'm damaged goods." He tried to laugh, but there was no
humor in it. "The Continental Army isn't the only one that don't see
much advantage to paying a cripple."

She twisted the hair around her finger, a golden ring. "I know! Let's
sweeten the pot. But what could you give them? They don't seem to
want secrets and intelligence, do they?"

"They've got so many spies, Peggy, they probably already know every-thing I've sent them."

Andre's next letter held the answer: "'Permit me to prescribe a little exertion,'" Peggy read two evenings later as they lay in bed.

"Oh, for God's sake," he cried, and she clapped a hand over his mouth.

"Benny, hush, somebody'll hear and—"

"I marched in the French War before that coxcomb was out of diapers, and he's *lecturing* me?"

"He's not lecturing, he's—he's—what does he mean, 'exertion'?"

"He means he wants me to *do* something, deliver troops or whatever, to them, not just pass along intelligence. Keep reading. You'll see."

But he need not have urged her, for Peggy's attention had already returned to the ciphered letter. Her eyes darted between it and Bailey's Dictionary, the key, as he watched, drinking in her beauty. Her lips curved tenderly, her cheeks blazed red, and though she was the most exquisite woman he had seen, she was especially vital tonight. He attrib-uted it to the excitement of spying, for the same flame burned in her whenever a letter came from Andre. She insisted on reading them her-self, clutching the paper in white-knuckled hands and caressing the sentences with her eyes, though they were nothing more than strings of numbers naming the page and line where the words could be found. Sometimes he pitied her for having been so sheltered that a dishonorable thing like this moved her. But when at long last she put the letter aside and douted the candle, she would make love to him as passionately as Margaret once had.

Now she said, "They want you to press for a new command. Jo—Major Andre says then you can be surrounded in the next battle and surrender a large part of the army to them."

He groaned. It was as he'd feared. His changed allegiance alone didn't entice them; they wanted much more than that. They sought something tangible, something that would damage the Patriots far more seriously than a wounded officer's desertion—to wit, thousands of troops subtracted from the Continentals' already diminished numbers. Perhaps, he thought despairingly, they considered it a bonus that relinquishing his regiments to them would impugn his honor and martial skill before the world.

"And they want a meeting, Benny!" She turned to him, beaming as though Andre had agreed to their demands for £10,000. "Says here that General Clinton wants you to meet with one of his officers about exchanging prisoners-of-war. That'll be your cover to get you through the lines with a flag."

"Dear God." His voice broke, and he covered his eyes with his arm.

She patted his shoulder. "Benny, it's all right."

"No, it's not." He turned his head to see her staring at the letter, paying him no heed. He snatched the page from her, and her brows rushed together.

"Benny—"

"What do they want to meet for?"

"I don't know. Give me the letter back so I can finish it."

He handed it to her, muttering, "Too risky. If anyone overhears us, or I'm caught, or—or—it's an abuse of a flag of truce. Washington'd hang me. Hell, I'd hang myself."

She glanced up from letter and dictionary. "They don't say why."

"That's all right. I know why. They need to confirm it's me they're dealing with. Look at it from their side. This could all be an elaborate hoax of some sort."

"Oh. Well, it says here they want more than general intelligence at a time when so much greater things may be done."

"Told you. Like what?"

"Wait a minute." Peggy leafed through the dictionary again. Outside, a dog barked, and a horse's hooves clattered over the cobblestones. "It's something about West Point, I think they want to meet you near there."

He groaned again. Not near West Point, not when it had taken three years of labor by homesick, hungry, unpaid boys, shoveling until their hands bled. Their suffering and sweat had sanctified that ground. Then there was the money West Point had cost, three millions of scarce dollars, a fortune that could have bought food at Quebec and the Valley Forge, medicine, ammunition—

He could not, would not, negotiate with the enemy anywhere near there.

Peggy settled back against her pillows. "I was wrong, Benny. They don't want to meet you near West Point."

He sighed his relief. "Thank God, I—"

"They want you to get them West Point."

Chapter Nineteen

The hall clock chimes, and I blink. 'Tis dusk, almost too dark to read, which means the clock rung five times, though I was too far gone in the letters and journal to count. This nigh suppertime, I'd best bustle to the kitchen.

The meal's a quiet affair, with neither Arnold saying much. Peggy's lost in dreams of John Andre, to judge by her sad, longing eyes, and Arnold in dreams of other, more glorious days, judging by his.

Afterwards, he lays a fire in the front parlor while I clean dishes. Then I join him. Flash is already sprawled on the floor, between Arnold's feet and the hearth. As I step over him to my chair, his tail thumps.

"Good supper, Clem, thank you." Arnold says while I settle myself with my needlework. "Apple pie's one of my favorites."

"Mine, too, sir." I take a few stitches, thinking back to last winter when apple pie was a scarce pleasure, for there hadn't been much fruit that fall, and what there was fit only for cider...

'Twas a rainy day in October that I saw apples at market. They were the first in a long time, and not too wormy nor bruised, so I traded some linen my aunt found in the back of a closet for three bushels. I'd slice half for drying and set the rest down cellar.

At home, one of Benjamin's letters awaited me. I ripped into it, hoping for tidbits about Nathan Hale, then tackled the apples. That kept me busy the rest of the day, until lamps were lit and my uncle came home.

"Have you seen this?" Uncle Shippen shook the rain from his hat and greatcoat, then handed them to me and a paper to my aunt. We went to the side parlor, where I spread his things before the fire.

Aunt Shippen sat, slanting the paper towards the hearth. She wore a perpetual smile lately, ever since Peggy had confided that she was with child, but her happiness became a frown as she read: "'All good men who love their homes and country, hear ye, assemble at Byrne's on the Commons, each man with his weapon, this Monday, the 4th instant, to take arms against the Enemy among us.' Oh, Edward, now what?"

"They're saying down at City Tavern that Reed wants all the families of men that've already left the city and gone to the British, he wants all their women and children put aboard ship for New York."

Seemed charitable, the Provincial Council reuniting families. But charity was far from the Radicals, especially Joseph Reed.

My aunt knew it, too. "Why?"

"'Tis plain enough," my uncle said. "All that property abandoned, all those homes and buildings left vacant, no wives or sons guarding them anymore... They say Reed's already drawing up the bills of sale, just leaving a blank to fill in the name later."

Bad as this was, the mob came up with a worse idea when it met. Why not drive all the men who opposed Joseph Reed, men like Benedict Arnold, out of town, too?

Their scheme might have worked—if Arnold hadn't learned of it. Like Johnny Burgoyne two years before, Reed's Radicals were doomed soon as Arnold signed on against them.

I was making soup Monday morning when I heard drums beating and men shouting. Before the war, I'd have run to see the excitement. Now, though my hands shook, I stayed where I was, chopping carrots...

꘎

"We were at James Wilson's," Arnold says, "called it Fort Wilson, and thought we were funny."

"We could hear the shooting at my uncle's," I say, taking a stitch.

"I'd think so, you were, what, a block away? Did it scare you?"

I hesitate. Hard to tell a man who's braved bayonets and cannon that yes, the firing scared us...

"Come on, Clem." My uncle hurtled into the kitchen, Aunt Shippen in tow. "We're going down cellar."

More shots sounded, and glass tinkled. I rushed to the window while my uncle yelled, "Get back, Clem! Get down!"

I heard screams and saw a lady holding a bloody hand to her face before Uncle Shippen pulled me after him.

"Dammit, Clem! Come on!"

"Now, Edward," my aunt said as we tumbled downstairs, "don't talk like that. You're going to be a grandfather. You must set an example."

We huddled amidst the barrels and trunks, my uncle and aunt clutching each other. I fished in my pocket for Ben's letter. It hadn't mentioned Nathan, told instead of Ben's troops attacking Loyalist raiders on Long Island. But it was comforting for all that, as though his easy smile and courage were with me.

Pistols and muskets popped. My aunt sobbed in my uncle's arms as he tried to distract her with talk of Peggy's baby while I ran my eyes over Ben's swirls and flourishes...

"Couldn't see much from the cellar," I say. "What happened?"

Arnold shrugs. "'Twas a boring battle as battles go. Radicals couldn't find enough men at first to fight us. After all, there's me and James Wilson, of course, 'twas his house we were using, and Robert Morris and George Clymer—they'd all signed the Declaration, by the way, but that didn't keep Reed from claiming they're Tories. And there's a coupla dozen reinforcements Wilson brought along, too, that he'd been drilling over in front of the courthouse. And the City Troopers stopped by, and General Mifflin, he fetched muskets from the city's arsenal. So all morning long, while the Radicals were beating their fool drum for recruits, we had a party, kind of like, going in that house."

I remember the feeling from the Brandywine, the confusion and terror, but the excitement, too, the hollowness inside that says something important's happening.

"Come the afternoon," Arnold continues, "there's about 200 Radicals against forty of us, and they had field pieces, too, if you can believe it, several of 'em, but still, 'tis hard, rushing a brick house like that."

That's what the Radicals did to our Cause: turned it from a war on politicians, taxes, and government into a fight against each other.

"I took command on the top floor," Arnold continues, "and Mifflin's down below. We kept firing, hit a few Radicals, too, till they stove the front door in and rushed the stairs. Good man by the name of Colonel Stevens was defending the stairs, and they run him through with a bayonet."

Same as if he was a Redcoat, not a Patriot.

"Then some Continentals arrived, coupla detachments of horse, and Reed had us all arrested. But we mostly posted bail."

I set the pocketbook aside because my hands are trembling too much to sew. For a moment, I understand his treason. Who wouldn't desert a Cause that sent armed men against its greatest hero? A Cause trying to topple tyrants so worse tyrants can oppress us?

"Day or so later," the general says, "I'm on my way home, and another mob starts following me, shouting, you know. I pulled my pistols, and they scattered." He shakes his head. "Peggy wasn't with me, but what if she had been? She was carrying little Neddy, just a few months along with him. I didn't want her alarmed or upset. What if we'd been coming home from supper somewhere and they'd tried that? Nowadays, there's men so lost to honor they'd attack an expectant mother and her crippled husband." His lip curls. "So I fortified my house, armed the servants, moved Peggy and Hannah and my boys down cellar for safekeeping. Then I tried the Congress again. I asked for twenty Continentals to protect us, seeing as how our state authorities wouldn't."

I catch his acrid smile. "And?"

"Congress told me to quit criticizing the state officials, said I oughta ask *Reed* for protection, not them."

How far can you push a man? Can you ask him to starve and bleed while he watches his friends die, can you shrug when he exhausts his fortune and call him a thief because he wants repayment, then damn him when he earns money some other way? Can you change what he's fighting for midstream, tell him it's no longer liberty but power for the Radicals? Can you hold up a cur like Joseph Reed, who's hounded families from their homes and hanged defenseless Quakers and hungers for even more power, can you say, "This fellow and his cronies, they're the ones deciding things for us now, and you don't like it, we'll let him come after you, too"? How long can you do that before a man explodes?

Arnold finally received his court-martial that December, though he must travel to the army's camp at Morristown for it. "I'll be cleared," he told us before he left, "you wait and see. These are army officers who'll be judging me, not Congressmen. They know Reed and the Council are set against me or any man of rank. They'll see justice done."

Peggy was large with child at the beginning of February when she took a chill, and my aunt asked me to fetch her some soup. So I was there when the general's party returned. Watching out the window as he swung off his horse, I knew matters hadn't gone well. He hobbled like a man twice his age, and his shoulders drooped.

"Your husband's home," I told Peggy.

She set aside her soup to heave herself to her feet. When I went to help, she muttered, "Don't ever have a baby, Clem. 'Tis misery, being pregnant. So big and fat and disgorging all the time."

Seemed it took the general forever to pull himself up the stairs. I gathered my things to leave, but Peggy said, "You needn't go, Clem. Please, sit down."

"But he'll want time with you, Peggy. He's been gone six weeks—"

Then the door opened, and General Arnold stood framed there.

He had eyes for Peggy alone. Stumping to her, he hugged her close as the baby allowed and kissed her until I wished myself anywhere else.

"Benny." Peggy struggled to free herself. "Benny, Clem's here."

"I was just leaving," I said as Arnold raised a face I'd swear was wet with tears.

"They convicted me."

"Convicted you?" I stared.

"It'll be in all the papers, the—the insult, the dishonor. I'm ruined. No one'll serve under me after this." Mayhap trying for control was what shook his voice. I'd never heard him sound like that.

Peggy shrugged. "Oh, Benny, 'tis obvious they don't know what they're about. Anyone can see that."

"No, these were officers, Sweetheart, from the army. Men like me. Henry Knox was there, for God's sake. He's led men and starved alongside them as I have. No, when it was Congress, or Reed's damned Council, I knew they were out to ruin me. But this! This was the *army*." His voice broke. "Reed musta got to them, somehow."

Arnold was right: all the papers published the court-martial's verdict. We read how the judges had convicted him of the charges involving abuse of power (an irony through and through, seeing as how 'twas Reed, not Arnold, misusing his authority), while all those regarding money and his deals were dropped. The court-martial voted that His Excellency reprimand General Arnold.

Peggy had birthed and baptized her baby, and Benedict Arnold was a proud new father showing off his son when Washington carried out the court's sentence in his General Orders for the day. That meant the whole army heard it, even the drummer boys.

Newspapers printed it, too, especially those friendly with Reed: "The Commander-in-chief would have been much happier in an occasion of bestowing commendations on an officer who has rendered such distinguished services to his country as Major General Arnold; but in the present case a sense of duty and a regard to candour oblige him to declare that he considers his conduct … peculiarly reprehensible, both in a civil and military view, … imprudent and improper." That day the whole city was staring at General Arnold and pointing, and the mortification must have been crushing.

'Twas barely a fortnight afore the next blow fell.

April had opened warm as milk, with trees and flowers bursting out in color to match any British officer and his lady. I was washing the mud off the front steps when the general's carriage pulled up.

"Morning, Miss Shippen," he called as he limped towards me.

"Morning, sir, how are you?"

I expected one of his witty replies, but all he said was, "Your uncle to home?"

"I think so. You come in and have some coffee, and I'll see."

"Thanks. I need to talk with him privately, if he'd be so kind."

His gloom silenced me as we stepped inside. Something was wrong, and no mistake.

I found my uncle at his ledgers. "General Arnold's here, sir, in the side parlor."

He capped his ink. "Bring us something sweet, will you, my dear?"

I put together a tray of cake and raspberry shrub, then carried it to the parlor. Even from the hall, I could hear Arnold's voice, trembling, desperate. I stood listening, not meaning to eavesdrop but rooted by his passion.

"—not my intention, sir. When I married your daughter, I never thought I—I'd be penniless—"

"General, you've had some reverses, 'tis true, but—"

"Country owes me, Judge, they owe me £7000 sterling."

'Twas a staggering sum, enough to buy a mansion and some ships and set a man up in business, too. It was probably what Arnold had been worth before the war.

The general continued wearily. "I'd been thinking all along they'd pay up, restore the fortune I've spent on the country's behalf. Didn't expect interest, sir—that'd be greedy when they can't even feed an army in the field—but you know, I thought they'd discharge the debt to me. So I submitted my accounts."

"And instead, they're saying you owe them?"

"Yes, sir, payable in gold and silver, not their worthless rags. They want *us* to take their paper, but when it comes to paying *them*, they want the real thing. Even if they were right, and I did owe it, where would I get that kind of money? Only property I've got left I've had for sale for months now, but no one's buying, not with the war on. I—I've got a family to support—"

He fell silent, and I shook myself. 'Twas a bad habit, eavesdropping, left over from my days as an intelligencer. I entered the parlor.

Arnold was as distressed as any man who must beg his in-laws for money, and that when they hadn't approved of him. He hardly noticed my interruption. "We'll need to remove from the Penn mansion, Judge. Can't afford it any longer. And Mount Pleasant, mortgage is due—" He looked away to murmur, "I thought we'd be so happy there."

"You can live in that house I own couple of streets over, long as you need it, General. I'm not collecting rent on it, anyways, with the war and all. Besides," my uncle nodded as he accepted some cake from me, "be nice having you so close."

I left them with my uncle saying 'twas hard, this coming on the heels of the reprimand, and Arnold rising, crippled leg and all, to pace to the window. Upset as he was, I wondered about his wife's reaction...

Worse than having to throw himself on the judge's goodwill was the hurt in Peggy's eyes. Not that she voiced that hurt: she often assured Arnold it wasn't his fault. But the words rang hollow. He knew as well as she why they must remove to a smaller house on her father's charity. He had shamed her and her family.

"Just not fair!" He pounded the table harder than he intended, so that the china rattled and Peggy jumped. The afternoon's wine must be affecting him. He was not drunk. He never got drunk. Remembering his father's humiliation and death, he seldom had more than a glass or two in a day.

But despair was claiming him, such despair that he must dull it or lose his mind. 'Twas hard, to have courted and married Margaret's twin, only to find that her heart belonged to a French Papist. Atop that, Congress refused to acknowledge its debt to him, let alone pay it, outrageously claiming instead that *he* owed *Congress*! And he was crippled for life, with a leg that would ever torture him.

He had received nothing for these sacrifices, certainly not a free country, nor even personal glory. Congress struck him no medals; rather, the army convicted him of Reed's nonsense.

Worst of all, the Cause to which he had dedicated himself, the revolution for liberty, had turned bitter as wormwood. Men scrambled for power like apes for nuts, mocking the troops' bleeding and suffering and dying.

Peggy raised velvety eyes to him. "What's not fair?"

"You—you don't—" But her beauty stopped him. Instead, he cried, "I've bled for liberty, spent my fortune, and what thanks do I get? I starved, all my boys did, we—we—" Tears clogged his throat.

"I told you long ago the rebels don't appreciate you." Peggy shrugged an exquisite shoulder. "They're rascals, Benny, trash. They have no more sense than to throw off the king for Reed, you think they'll be sensible when it comes to you?" She signalled for more roasted beef, then dismissed the servant. When they were alone, she said, "Why don't we write Major Andre again?"

He flinched. Since Andre's mention of West Point, Arnold had neither written him nor discussed the plot with Peggy—though that hadn't discouraged his wife. She'd broached the topic dozens of times despite his responding with naught beyond a grunt or a muttered, "Leave it, Peggy."

Still, he mused constantly about Andre's interest in the Point. How could Arnold hand the tyrants in London a fortress built to defy them, one whose main work bore his own name? How could he cooperate with an empire quashing men's freedom worldwide, with politicians who had plundered an entire continent to enrich themselves and their cronies in the East India Company, who were subduing the Irish and had foisted feudal law on the Quebecois while planning the same fate, the same abject domination, for the American colonies? All so that wealthy, powerful Englishmen might wax even more so.

But the Radicals were also growing wealthier and more powerful, and bolder, too, as their depredations increased. And they executed their evil from a few streets rather than an entire ocean away, making them far more dangerous than the government in London. Only that government was strong enough to stop them; only the British Army and His Majesty could restore what the Radicals had stolen. People afraid to speak to their neighbors lest one day, that neighbor condemn them as a Tory—or be condemned, with their acquaintances suspected, too; widows forced into the streets because their husbands had died of illness at home rather than of wounds in camp; merchants impoverished and children starving because the Radicals controlled business… For too long, Reed and his minions had reigned while Congress twiddled its thumbs or, worse, applauded.

Yet defeating the Radicals meant handing their enemy and his what it demanded, even West Point; Arnold was too good a merchant to fob customers off with less than they expected. There were personal advantages as well. West Point was a solid, satisfying piece of ground to deliver, something substantial that he could point to, should the administration prove slow at indemnifying him, something to remind politicians what they owed him.

A tear spilled over to scald his cheek. Couldn't the Congress see what they were driving him to? Couldn't they see how they were destroying liberty, turning the ideals for which he had bled to ashes in his mouth?

"You oughta write again, Benny." Peggy's voice was as soft as the hand she rubbed against his cheek. "King George wouldn't side with Joseph Reed. Why, he'd hang him and all his set. And he'd pay you, too, Benny, in gold. Think how grand we'd live then, no worries about money at all."

Traitors don't live grand, he wanted to say, but his misery blocked the words.

"You think about it." She was no longer caressing his cheek. He heard the clink of fork and knife, and a mouthful muffled her next words. "Think about all the clothes we'd buy, and the carriages, and the trips and dinners and theater. You promised you'd take me to London sometime, Benny. I've never been and you know how much I want to go." She sipped some wine. "And, Benny, you'd look stunning in scarlet. I wouldn't be—be able to, ah, to resist, um, you know."

He did know and glanced up hopefully. He reached for her hand, but she pulled away and got to her feet. "Let's write Major Andre, Benny, please. Come upstairs and write, and then later—"

He wrote Andre that evening and several times thereafter, Peggy aglow and especially accommodating the while. And while he wasn't ready to relinquish either troops or West Point to the Redcoats, he did report that Washington was marching 4000 Americans to Rhode Island, where they would meet a French army of 6000 for an invasion to the north. He extracted this news—he did not call it intelligence, even to himself, and the one time Peggy did, he corrected her—directly from reports Washington sent him. He felt dirty as he enciphered it, however necessary stopping the Radicals was, and even dirtier sending the message on its way. Praise Heaven, the whole thing proved to be a ruse: the allies had hoped thereby to lure Clinton from their real target, New York City. In fact, he'd done Washington a favor, passing his lie to the British.

But Peggy sighed. "Major Andre'll never believe you're in earnest, and even if he wanted to, Sir Harry Clinton won't. Try again, Benny."

"Aw, I'm not even sure it's Andre I'm writing to."

"What do you mean? Of course it's him."

"How do I know? Answers I get are so vague—'course, they need to be, case they'd fall into anyone else's hands, but don't you see? Who knows who's writing us? It needn't be Andre. There's nothing in those letters only he would know. Could be someone's intercepting my letters to him. Could be Stansbury never takes them to New York at all. Maybe he's running them straight to Washington."

"But Benny, I know Major Andre's handwriting, and those letters he's written, well, they're from him."

"Ever hear of forgery, darling? Andre's Adjutant General now, he's signing letters and proclamations every day. You think any of those might have found their way to Continental headquarters, hmmm? Think this might be a trap someone's laying?"

He was nearly hissing, and tears quivered in her lashes. Then, suddenly, brilliantly, she smiled. "I guess the only way around it, Benny, is for us to meet with him—"

"*Meet* him?" He slapped a hand to his forehead. "God Almighty, why don't you just knot the noose now? They'd hang one of us for spying, no matter where we meet, our lines or theirs."

She continued doggedly. "You need to talk with him face-to-face, Benny. It's the only way." When his answer was to launch himself from chair to window, she said, "What about your trip next week, when you go see Mr. Washington?"

"Peggy, come on. I'll be in the middle of the Continental Army. That's the point of the trip, you know, so I can get a command now that the campaign's begun."

"But, Benny, they have agents in the Continental camp, don't they? Goodness, they've even got them in Mr. Washington's headquarters."

Deep in thought, he said nothing, only glanced at her.

"Why don't you tell Major Andre about your trip?" She continued softly, "He could have an agent meet you."

He turned from her to the window, still musing.

She was right, of course. Someday soon, he must meet with them, to certify their identity and good faith. And they, in turn, must be anxious to confirm both those things in him, especially given his subterfuge during their correspondence, the precautions necessary should his letters fall into the wrong hands: he never used his real name; he dictated most of the notes lest his handwriting betray him; when he did put pen to paper, he disguised his script. Then, too, they needed to settle the scores of details too cumbersome to write, especially in cipher.

But the logistics of a face-to-face meeting, where and when it could be held, keeping their plans secret, made his head ache. And that was saying nothing of the huge risk inherent in meeting, risk that could end at the gibbet for one or all. He tried to imagine sitting across from British uniforms, talking with men in scarlet as confederates rather than enemies subjugating a world to their empire, and his soul shrivelled. They'll save us from the Radicals, he reminded himself, but a sour taste fouled his mouth.

He limped from the window to his desk. He picked up a quill, dipped it, set down the itinerary for his trip. But he paused several times to blink his eyes, and sweat drenched him as he wrote.

When the answer arrived, Peggy's cheeks flushed as always. Arnold reached for a knife to break the seal, but she snatched the packet from him. "Here, Benny, let me."

Her hands were shaking, and she tore at the seal until he said, "Peggy, be careful. You're ripping it." Then the letter lay open before them, Peggy bowed above it.

He scanned it over her shoulder. It was not even enciphered this time, so cocksure had the British grown with their continuing victories over the Continentals, and Andre again harped on West Point. His sentences about the fort leaped from the page.

> ...the having the Command of W. Point would afford the best opportunities...you shall experience the full measure of the national obligation...

Peggy looked up with shining eyes. "Oh, Benny, look! All you need to do is get them West Point, and—"

"And what? And I'll experience the—what's he say?—the 'national obligation'? Come on!" He stumped to the bureau, leaning against it to ease his leg. "Nothing about restoring our freedom and stopping the Radicals, only the same nonsense as always, Peggy. 'Tis a trap. I'm sure of it."

They were in the bedroom, with the door shut and bolted. Still, they heard the doorknocker thump downstairs.

"Now who can that be?" he growled.

Peggy clutched the letter to her. "'Tis no trap, Benny. This is Cher Je—"
He whirled to face her.

"—I mean, Major Andre's handwriting. I'd know it anywhere—"

"What'd you say?"

"I said, I'd know Major An—"

"No." He shook his head, and she stared, puzzled. "No, you said 'Cher Jean.'"

"Did I?" She shrugged. "Some of us girls used to call him that the winter they occupied—"

"Andre? You called Andre 'Cher Jean'?" He grasped her wrist, crushing it, so that her face crumpled, and she whimpered.

"Benny, owww, you're hurting me—"

A knock sounded at the bedroom door. He dropped her arm, and Peggy rushed to answer it.

A servant stood on the threshold. "Miss Peggy, Mr. Stansbury be here. He wanna know can he see you folks a minute."

"Show him to the rear parlor, Billy, and fetch some punch and biscuits for us."

When Billy was gone and she had shut the door, she whispered, "Benny, please, I don't know what you're thinking, but—"

He had himself in hand, now, could keep both face and voice bland as he said, "He's the one, isn't he?"

"Benny, I told you there's no one but you, remember? I told you on our wedding day. Please—"

"That's what's got you so excited every time a letter comes. It's not what I thought, that it's the spying doing it, it's because *he*"—he could not bear to say the major's name, putting all his fury into the pronoun instead—"wrote it. Love letters, passing between the two of you—"

"Benny, please, it's not that at all—"

"Dear God, what a fool I've been."

"Benny." She glided to him, laid a hand on his arm. "Please believe me, you're wrong about this, all right? I—I love you—"

Again, his head jerked up. She had never before said that, however many times he did. But her eyes did not caress him as she spoke, as a lover's would, as Margaret's had. Instead, like a liar's, they stared past him.

"—only you, Benny, it's always been you, you know that. Now, please, come on. Let's go see if Mr. Stansbury's got another message for us."

Stansbury stood near the open window in the parlor. He was wilting in July's heat, his coat black with sweat under the arms and across the back. He accepted some punch from Sam but waited until the servant had left them, with Peggy closing the door, to whisper that he brought word from Andre and Clinton.

"They want to meet with you, get everything set." Stansbury took a draught of punch.

Peggy stepped forward. "When?"

"Soon as you can arrange. They want to end the war with this campaign. No reason to drag it out another winter, they said. Major Andre says he's, let's see, he's 'willing himself to effect the meeting, either in the way proposed or in whatever manner may at the time appear most eligible.'"

Peggy stood speechless, hands clasped to her bosom, while Arnold croaked, "Andre?"

Stansbury nodded. "He says maybe you'd want to fake illness while you're travelling to the Continentals' camp, you know, someplace close to New York, where a flag of truce could reach."

Arnold shook his head as though a fly buzzed at his ear. "Good Lord." He turned from them to stare into the hearth. Of all the officers to meet! He could not, would not, negotiate with the fop who stole Peggy from him. Not unless he had a horsewhip nigh. By Heaven, he'd sit down with him fast enough then.

He whirled to fix Stansbury with a glare, stopping the merchant with a bit of biscuit halfway to his mouth.

"No Andre," he said, and Peggy gasped. "You tell them I—it's too risky. He's the Adjutant General of the Army, for God's sake. If we're caught—"

"I don't know." Stansbury popped the biscuit into his mouth. "He's very much set on meeting you himself. Kept impressing on me that he'd be there to talk with you in person."

"He's a fool. Tell them I want someone else, maybe Colonel Robinson. You know him?"

Stansbury shook his head.

"He's a Loyalist, got an estate up near West Point. He wrote me a while ago. I think Clinton trusts him, and I do too. They're right—we need to meet. Tell them I want a meeting, but I want it with Robinson."

Arnold stumbled to the window, balancing before it on his good leg while Stansbury murmured with Peggy. He fancied he heard the name

Andre, though when he heeded their talk, Stansbury was describing how the ladies of New York were dressing their hair.

Andre! Someday, after the war, he'd confront the rascal, alone, man to man.

Better yet, he'd challenge him, show him for a coward. He pictured a sunny morning, birds singing and the earth still wet with dew. Andre would have the first shot, naturally, though his hand shook and face contorted as he raised his pistol. The ball went wild, showering leaves from the boughs overhead and startling birds.

Then it was Arnold's turn.

Andre fell to his knees, begging, sobbing, while a disgusted Peggy stood with their seconds.

"Really," she said, voice carrying clearly though, figuring the major for a nervous marksman, Arnold had insisted she stand far from them, "I had no idea—he's just not the man Benny is, is he? Benny! Benny?"

He came back to the room with a start to see Peggy beside him and Stansbury waiting awkwardly.

"I heard you," he said. "What is it?"

"Mr. Stansbury's leaving now."

He bowed to the merchant, then said, "I been thinking, Stansbury. It's not such a bad plan they've come up with after all. Tell Andre we'll talk at his convenience. He should write me with the time and place."

Chapter Twenty

When last he visited, Champe said, "I'll meet you outside your church on Sunday, after services, with the rope. Bring something along you can hide it in."

So this morning once I've greeted the preacher, I wait for Champe. He worships with the Anglicans a few streets over, along with Peggy, when she hasn't a headache, and Arnold, and a handful of Redcoats—the only pious ones there are, I'd wager. Their church still stands, at least. Ours is a printer's shop the rest of the week. The Great Fire burned our meetinghouse four years ago, and can't any of us see sense in building a new one so's the enemy can confiscate it for barracks or a riding school.

I stamp my numb feet. Usually, the coals in my foot warmer last through the service, but I left it empty this morning. 'Tis there I'll hide the rope.

I spy Champe coming down the street a few minutes later, tapping the hitching posts along the way. He bows, then stuffs his bundle into my foot warmer while I shield us with my cloak. I try not to think what these coils are for, how they'll bind the hero of Valcour and Saratoga for delivery to the hangman. I'll hide them near the necessary for tomorrow night.

Then, with a nod, Champe's off. I take the long way home, reluctant to get there. Seems the closer this kidnapping comes, the queasier my stomach goes. 'Tis silly, I know. 'Twill be five or six stout fellows, and all of them vouchsafed by Champe, against a crippled man turning forty next month. They'll have the surprise of it working for them, too. We've got our plans laid so tight and provided so well against anything going wrong, we can't help but succeed.

Sometimes, I think 'tis that has me worried. Arnold doesn't stand a chance against us.

I finally reach Broadway, where a familiar figure's stumping along the sidewalk. I'm glad I spotted him first, afore he hailed me or grabbed my arm. Otherwise, I'd have jumped so high on account of what I'm carrying he'd know something's up. He's meandering along, enjoying the bright winter day, and I overtake him easily. "General."

He turns with a smile, the sun showing the grey hair and crow's feet I never see during our nights around the hearth. "Clem, an unexpected pleasure. How's the sermon this morning?" He doesn't even glance at my foot warmer.

"Fine, sir. He preached on Galatians 5:1."

"'Stand fast therefore in the liberty wherewith Christ hath made us free,'" Arnold quotes softly. "One of my favorites."

"Mine too, sir. Lovely weather, isn't it?"

"Especially for December."

He offers his arm, but I hesitate. I am, after all, his cook. He gives a look that shows he understands and says, "We're cousins, Clem. Besides, I like to walk arm-in-arm with a lovely lady whenever I can."

'Tis only more of his kindness, but I blush, especially when he says with a wink, "Now, don't tell my wife, will you?"

So we stroll down Broadway. We pass squads of gawking Redcoats and knots of officers. A few captains and majors coldly nod, but the colonels mostly ignore him. Arnold jokes about the officers, mocking their snobbery and their records, which can't touch his. He laughs and flirts, as though we're partners at a dance instead of cousins-in-law, and one employing the other.

We're having too good a time to realize someone's blocking our path until a voice snarls, "Arnold, isn't it?"

The speaker's wearing the rags of a Continental officer. The faded ribbon across his chest declares him a major. He must be a prisoner of war, allowed to wander the city on his word that he'll not run for American lines. He's an ugly man, made uglier by the hate twisting his face, until I wonder whether he's from Connecticut and almost ask did he ever know my mother. The hate poisons his voice, too, and snags

Arnold's attention. It even stops three British captains and a lieutenant crossing the street.

Arnold sweeps the man a bow. "That's right, friend, General Benedict Arnold. But I don't believe I've had the pleasure."

"I'm no friend of yours, nor of any man sells out his country."

Arnold stares, then says, mildly for him, "The world seldom judges right of any man's intentions, sir. I don't look for it to make an exception in my case."

"Tell you what, General, we ever meet again, when I'm armed and not a prisoner, you just look sharp, that's what. Loads of us'd like to cut off that leg of yourn"—he nods at Arnold's left foot, sticking out useless before him—"bury it with full honors for what it suffered up to Quebec and Saratoga. But the rest of you, sir, the rest I'd hang higher 'n Haman."

He pushes past us, limping, and Arnold squints after him. Then, turning to me and offering his arm again, he says, "Sorry about that, Clem."

"'Tis fine," I say, "don't trouble yourself about it," for he's trembling. "It's just someone out to insult you, General."

"No, Clem, 'twas more than that. Didn't recognize him there at first, but he was with me on the march to Quebec. I gave him my boots when his own wore out."

We say nothing more the rest of our walk, and we're pretty quiet once we're home, too. That man's bile cast gloom over us deep as last winter's, when our Cause was going from bad to worse...

Seemed that whole year we couldn't win even a skirmish, let alone a battle. Meantime, the government took the war south, convinced that folks down there were mostly Loyalist. They weren't, any more than us, but the politicians back in London never would admit how few friends their empire had.

Our troops spent the winter of 1779-1780 at Morristown, in New Jersey. They'd suffered at the Valley Forge, no question, but Morristown beat that. For starters, it was colder, clear down to 16 below. First snow fell in November, and it kept falling until there was four feet of it on the ground. The wind blew closed any paths cut through the drifts.

Ice in New York's harbor was so thick the Redcoats rode their horses over it and, believe it or not, hauled their cannon, too, 'twixt York and Staten Islands.

That kind of weather's hard enough when you're bundled up in your wool surtout on the hearth of the snug house your dad built. Now imagine you're naked as Lazarus, or at best you're wearing rags with no surtout over them, and you're huddled without a blanket in the lean-to you and the boys threw together last month.

Food was even scarcer than at the Forge, though there hadn't been any to speak of then, neither. Between the cold and the snow and the starving, more men than ever took sick.

My heart broke as reports of such torments reached Philadelphia. Shouldn't have surprised any of us, though it did and broke our hearts again, when some of the Connecticut troops mutinied that spring. They paraded under arms around camp, called for food and back pay, even fired on a couple of officers, if you can believe the paper's account. I wondered what Nathan Hale would have done, wondered if his friends were involved. For certain, he'd'a grieved when Washington called out Pennsylvania's troops to put their Connecticut brothers in their place. Then His Excellency hanged two of the mutiny's leaders. I know he could do aught else and must have wept when he did. Still, if I'd been in his place, I'd have fed them, not hanged them.

About the time we learned of the mutiny, we had news from South Carolina. The Redcoats had besieged Charles Town, and taken it, with 5000 of our troops, four ships (those four was pretty much South Carolina's whole navy), and 300 cannon. Our entire southern army gone, just like that, and how we'd ever replace it didn't bear thinking on.

Redcoats seized tons of our supplies in Charles Town, too. Those barrels of flour and meat could have fed our mutineers, might have kept the leaders from the gibbet.

We were all of us pretty low by now. Many times in the last five years defeat had seemed certain. Nathan Hale hanged during one of the blackest times, after our trouncing on Long Island. But the war was younger then, and we hadn't used up our energy and hope. Now we were weary to the bone, and discouraged.

Things grew no better as the summer wore on and the campaign down South became a chase of our troops through heat and despair.

Those regiments had been detached from Washington's handful to replace the ones collared at Charles Town. For sure, we couldn't lose them, too. Yet every day brought the enemy closer to capturing that army as well, forcing Congress to ask for terms.

Then, in August, came another blow. The Congress sent General Horatio Gates south after Charles Town's defeat. For some reason, they figured the commander who'd pretended to the victory at Saratoga would salvage things for us. Instead, the Redcoats thrashed him at a place called Camden. I didn't hear whether he fought or cowered in his headquarters as he done at Saratoga. All anyone talked about was how fast he ran when the enemy routed his troops. Granny's old to be campaigning, somewhere in his fifties. But, as Alex Hamilton sniffed, he fled Camden so fast, his speed did credit to a man half his age.

We were reeling under all these disasters. I woke each day with my heart jumping, sure the newspapers would shout our surrender. Marketing was a chore to put off lest I see defeat in the shopkeepers' faces or hear folks sob over our army's capture.

General Arnold must have been scared, or scared as a lion can be. He knew what happens to warriors of failed rebellions. But no matter: around then, he left Philadelphia to confer with Washington. "The general wants to be active again," Peggy told us. "He's hoping for a post at West Point."

My uncle looked as befuddled as me. It made no sense that Arnold the lionhearted would be content on Hudson's River with the war gone south. 'Twas like Peggy dining with old Widow Sterne when half of Philadelphia was dancing at a ball across town. Though soon enough I fell to musing that Ben Tallmadge was stationed near West Point. If Peggy visited her husband, I'd ask could I ride along and see Ben.

But before I could, Peggy added that the general had already made his headquarters at a house confiscated from a Loyalist, a Colonel Beverley Robinson, across the river and two miles south of the Point. "I had a letter from him," Peggy said. More likely she'd had three or four. "He says I can join him there. He's sending one of his aides for me. Oh, and he mentioned Clem. The cook up there's no good at all, so he wants Clem to come show her a thing or two."

"Let her go, Edward," my aunt said. "With the baby and all, Peggy needs to eat well."

"And Lord knows I can't eat soldiers' grub." Peggy shuddered.

"We'll manage here," my aunt said to me. "Please, Clem, it'd ease my mind, having Peggy so far away."

So it was that I wrote Benjamin, telling him when we would arrive, and then rode north with Peggy and Arnold's aide, David Franks.

West Point straddles an outcropping in Hudson's River, with views stretching for miles north and south and cannon pointed in both directions. The summer'd been a dry one, so the river was low, and the trees alongside were already dropping dusty dead leaves. Still, I not only saw but felt the Point's importance: whoever owned the fort and its cannon controlled the river there as well as access to New York and New England.

We crossed that river, sunk far between its banks, on Arnold's black and gold barge and arrived at his headquarters on the eastern shore, Robinson's Farms. 'Twas a long house of white clapboard, with sections added, I suppose, as the owner waxed richer. The oldest part and one of the additions were two stories tall, with porches running part-way along the front. Wilted orchards and fields covered its plateau high above the river.

Arnold's official family stood waiting to greet us, among them Major Varick and Colonel John Lamb, his half-face beaming.

"Welcome, Mrs. Arnold!" Lamb cried, and for having but one jaw and a sliver of tongue left, he spoke clear. "'Tis good to meet you, and my congratulations on marrying such a hero!"

Peggy curtseyed, but 'twas done, I warrant, to avoid Lamb's eye. She much preferred the dashing Major Varick, who stood as though turned to stone when Peggy gave him her hand.

"You didn't exaggerate, sir," he said to Arnold. "She's breathtaking, motherhood and all."

Peggy twinkled a laugh, and from that moment, Varick was hers. He was only seven or eight years older, with no wife nor sweetheart, so 'twas an easy conquest.

While I spent my time in the kitchen with the cook, a servant named Talia, Arnold either closeted himself with Peggy or ferried her across the river to the Point. I'd pack them a basket of food in the morning and wouldn't see them again until supper.

They were gone the day Benjamin appeared. I looked up from the beans I was snapping to see him dismounting in the yard. For the first time, he wore a whole uniform, blue coat faced with buff, smallclothes to match, and crossed belts that had once been white. A helmet with yellow tassels and a blue turban protected his head. 'Twas as dapper as I'd seen him, though the coat bore the usual patches, and the smallclothes were stained and torn.

I ran outside. "Ben!"

He looped his reins over the hitching rail and rushed to me, sweeping me up in a hug such as husbands give their wives. I squirmed away with a laugh. "Stop it, Benjamin. We're not married yet."

He grinned down at me, his helmet askew. "We'll go hunt a magistrate this minute, just say the word."

"No, we—we can't. Remember, we, ah, we've told everyone it'll be after the war." But that sounded lame even to me.

"Sorry I wasn't here sooner. I'm inspecting the outposts this fortnight, and your letter just caught up with me. Wanna walk by the river? Might be cooler down there."

It was, so we walked and talked the morning away. Ben told me about the new Secret Service and his duties in it with one exciting story after another. "And what of you?" he asked. "You keeping busy?"

I shrugged. "I miss working with you, Ben. I feel so useless, everyone fighting for liberty whilst I pluck chickens and snap beans."

He gazed out over the river, one foot atop a rock, arms crossed on his knee. "Well, but things aren't going our way. We lose, and—"

Though he fell silent, I could finish the thought. When we lost, when the government took to hanging rebels, no telling what rank they'd stop at.

"You'll make a young widow." He was trying to joke, but 'twas too close to the truth. "Anyway, I'm glad you miss working with us because I have it in mind to ask you for a favor."

"Really? What?"

"Been getting reports for months from my spies on Long Island that one of our officers is gonna defect."

"I'm surprised it's only one, bad as things are."

He smiled, but bitterly. "Last time I saw His Excellency, he said the same thing, that 'tis a wonder so many remain faithful, not that here and there a few desert. Anyway, rumor has it this deserter's pretty high up, maybe even a general."

I sat silent, overwhelmed.

"Spies tell me Clinton's been writing this officer over a year now, offering him earldoms and money and I don't know what all to throw us over."

"None of our generals would do that." But uncertainty shook my voice.

"May not be a general." He shrugged. "I don't know how much reliance to put on all these reports. One says one thing, and the next contradicts it, and, like I say, I been hearing this for months but no high-ranking officer's deserted yet."

"You don't suppose that—that His Excellency—" I could not finish from horror but Ben was shaking his head.

"Naw. That was my first thought, too, just because everything's been going against us, not because His Excellency could do something like that. And that's what I come back to, Clem: he just couldn't do something like that. It's not in his character. Washington's the most honorable, most upright, most unshakable man I ever knew."

"Like Nathan," I murmured.

He gave me a look, then said, "And you know what? I decided, if it is him, well, all right then, let the government win and hang us all, because if a man like George Washington can betray us, this isn't a world I want to live in."

I was sitting on a boulder, dangling my feet in the brown river. Ben climbed up beside me and pulled his boots off. "Anyway, here's what I wanted to ask. I want you to come stay with me down at North Castle, be on hand case I need you to check anything or run errands. I need someone there I can trust, Clem. Rumors like this going around, you don't know but what your own colonel might be the one."

I swished my feet in the water. "What do you mean, stay with you?"

"Oh, good Lord." He peeled off what was left of his stockings and plunged his feet into the water. "You'd have your own quarters, Clem. Colonel Sheldon's right there case I try anything."

"I didn't mean—"

"I won't be there this next week, anyway. I haven't finished touring the outposts."

"Ben, please, my cousins are—are paying me. I only meant I must have—"

"Oh. Sorry." He rubbed his chin. "I'll take care of it, don't worry. But it needs to stay between us, all right? Far as anyone knows, you're my betrothed, coming to stay with me because you're alone in the world."

He wanted me to leave for North Castle that day so we could ride together most of the way. I asked Talia could she manage without me, and she said she supposed so and banged a kettle and muttered about how some folks are free as a bird and nigh as dependable, too. Then I left a note for the Arnolds with my apologies.

North Castle had been a grist-mill before the war, built of planks with a single window near the door. Its wheel would probably still turn if the creek that dripped onto it hadn't dried from the drought. Trees and brush traced the banks of that creek. Through their shriveled leaves, I could see outbuildings and gaunt horses grazing sere grass.

Inside I found Colonel Sheldon. He was a pleasant, courteous man and delighted to have a lady to talk to, especially Major Tallmadge's betrothed.

"Heard so much about you, feel like we've already met," he told me. "You know, your major and I are old friends from the first days of the war."

Something was always going on at the North Castle headquarters, so I didn't have time to mope after Ben, away at the outposts. Besides, during our few hours' ride, he'd refused to speak of Nathan. "You're marrying me, not him, Clem," he said. "I don't intend to spend the next forty or fifty years, God willing, talking about my friend with my wife. You want to talk about us, our plans for the future, the wedding, I'm happy to oblige."

Instead, I watched the groups of gunmen that Continentals or farmers thereabouts captured and brought to North Castle. We called them Cowboys if they sympathized with the government and Skinners if they favored us. But other than that they were the same: desperados who used the war as an excuse to rob travellers. They were especially pestiferous near the lines and in the no-man's land between us and the Redcoats to the south in New York City. With Ben gone, Colonel Sheldon questioned the captives and often had a funny tale to tell at dinner. But Sheldon soon departed, too, for other duties. A Lieutenant Colonel Jameson replaced him. He was plodding but genial, with an accent that reminded me of His Excellency's.

Then it was September 22nd, the anniversary of Nathan Hale's death. I rambled along the creek and thought of that day four years ago, and what he might have been about had he lived, and all the sorrow he'd been spared, now that defeat looked certain. I cried some, too, but I scrubbed my face good before I went to dinner. Ben was due back soon, and I didn't want him to hear I'd been weeping.

I'd noticed some berries, withered nigh to specks from the drought, on the creek up the hill behind headquarters where the water once bubbled from the ground. Next day, I set off with a basket after them. Ben loved berry pie, and North Castle's cook had agreed I could borrow her kitchen to make him one.

Getting enough fruit off those poor, thirsty bushes took a while. I'd picked a quart or so and stood easing my back, looking down on headquarters, when a group of horsemen with a prisoner turned into the lane. I'd have said they were Continentals bringing in another Cowboy or Skinner, except that only the captive bore himself like a soldier despite his garish purple coat. I watched them draw rein in front of the mill and pull their victim, arms bound behind him, off his mount and into headquarters.

'Twas too far to see faces, but there was something familiar about that prisoner. I would swear I knew him.

I puzzled over it in the henhouse as I gathered eggs on my way to the kitchen. He was a soldier, more likely an officer, of that I was sure. Had I fought with him at the Brandywine? Had he been in my company?

I fashioned the pie, put it to bake, asked the cook if she'd like me to lay the table for supper.

That done, I settled down with my notes on the war. I was writing about Charles Town's defeat when the colonel stuck his head in the parlor door. "Ma'am, looks like Major Tallmadge is back."

When I stepped outside, Ben was handing his reins to a stableboy. Either his joy at our reunion or the setting sun lent a glow to his face. Mindful of the boy, he didn't hug me but only bowed over my hand before walking me to the house.

I cast about for something to say, something with no Nathan in it, something romantic. "I missed you. Seemed you were gone a fearful long time."

"Seemed like it to me, too, but no more than usual when I check the outposts. Just that this time you were waiting for me." He squeezed my arm. "Though I admit, what with those Skinners and Cowboys running through there, 'tis the most rascally part of the country I was ever in."

"Supper's nigh ready. You hungry?"

"Dear heart, you know a soldier's always starving."

Colonel Jameson was already at table and directing the filling of his plate, though when we entered, he dismissed the servants. He stood for grace, then, as we seated ourselves, said, "Eat up, Major. I daresay you haven't had a decent meal since you left. We'd thought His Excellency might stop here, he'd written he'd like to inspect the troops on his way over to Hartford, so the victuals are heartier than usual."

I tucked into the beans with salt pork as the talk between Ben and Jameson swirled around me. At the first pause, I asked the question that had teased me all afternoon.

'Tis odd how little things make all the difference, how the right word here or the wrong look there can change things forever, can get a man hanged. Had I not taken supper that day, or gone berrying a little later and missed seeing the captive brought in, or not reminded the colonel to tell Ben, the fate of West Point and the war might have been very different.

"Well, Colonel," I said, "who was our visitor this afternoon?"

He smiled gallantly. "Ah, Major, you best watch your sweetheart. She has an eye for a handsome lad." Actually, seeing the prisoner from afar, I had no notion as to his looks. But the colonel rolled on. "I'm glad you mentioned him, Miss Shippen, I meant to tell the major. Very peculiar, Major, *very* peculiar, and I flatter myself I did the right thing. General Arnold has a lot of explaining to do, you ask me. 'Course, you can't say a word against him to His Excellency, way he admires—"

"Colonel," Ben said, "pardon me, but if you'd start at the beginning..."

"Oh, of course. Well, this afternoon, a party of Skinners brought in a gentleman going down to New York whom they supposed a spy."

That was the usual way of it, with the Skinners robbing anyone who looked to have a few dollars about him or had dared cross one of them. Then they'd disguise their theft as a search for incriminating papers. Some weeks these roughnecks marched in two or three "spies." Usually, the victims told the same story of insult and robbery, and usually they were released, though Ben or the colonel examined as many as they could. So far, this account followed the pattern, and I reached for some applesauce as the colonel continued.

"They'd found some papers in his boot, Major, papers on West Point, its garrisons and armaments, that looked like they come straight from General Arnold's files. Fact, he had a pass from General Ar—"

"A pass?" Ben set down his fork to stare at the colonel. He suddenly looked so stricken I was minded of my mother, when she first coughed blood and knew it meant her death. "From *Arnold*? You're sure 'twas in the same handwriting as the papers?"

The colonel frowned. "I didn't notice, Major, but 'twas made out to a Mr. Anderson. That's the fellow General Arnold asked us to watch out for couple of days ago, isn't it? The one coming from New York we're supposed to send through to him?"

"But he didn't come *from* New York, did he? Didn't you say he was going *to* New York with information on West Point?" Ben crumpled his napkin as I tried to think had I ever known a Mr. Anderson.

"Major, wait, you haven't heard the peculiar part of it yet. Here's the thing: when the Skinners first took him, he claimed he's from the king's forces and tried to bribe them to let him go."

"Of course he did, Colonel. Man'll say or do anything to get away from those thieves and their dirty traffic. Where is he now? And his papers, I'd like to see his papers."

"Oh, don't trouble yourself, Major. I sent the papers on to General Washington already. Thought they were of such a dangerous tendency, he'd wanna see them."

Ben nodded, then got to his feet. "I'm gonna talk to Anderson, now, if you'll excuse me. Got some questions for him."

"No need, Major. I already examined him. Withal, you'd have a long ride." The colonel chuckled. "I sent him along to General Arnold."

Ben had been speaking respectful, as you do to superior officers. But now he was all disbelieving and scornful. "*What?* You sent him to *Arnold?*"

"Sure I did. General Arnold give us orders to that effect, remember? I sent him a note, too, about those papers. He oughta be informed, don't you think? Man riding about the countryside with his papers like that—"

"Colonel!" Ben stopped, stood speechless. At last he said, "Sir, you need to *arrest* Arnold, not warn him."

"You mean Anderson. I already did, I told you."

"No, sir, I mean Arnold, he—"

"Arrest General *Arnold?*" The colonel stared as if Ben had sprouted another head. "Whatever for?"

"Colonel." Ben leaned over the table on his hands. "'Tis clear General Arnold has turned traitor and that this Anderson is his intermediary with the Redcoats."

I sat stunned. Not Arnold, please God, not Washington, and not Arnold, no, no, *no!*

The colonel looked as flummoxed as me. "General *Arnold?*"

"Colonel, we must bring Anderson back here. He reaches General Arnold first, before I can put together a detach—"

"General *Arnold?*" the colonel whispered. "You—you're wrong, must be—"

"Arnold finds out we know before my detachment gets there to arrest him, he'll run." Ben leaped to the door and opened it to bellow, "Lieutenant!"

"Now hold on, Major." The colonel adjusted his wig with a shaking hand. "You can't go arresting major generals, especially General Arnold, just because you think—"

He snapped his mouth closed as a boy with crumbs littering his chest appeared in the doorway.

"Lieutenant, run tell Captain Shaw—" Ben began.

"Lieutenant, you're dismissed," Jameson roared. "Major, that's enough. Now sit down!"

I looked from one to the other. The colonel'd jumped to his feet, upsetting his wine, while Ben stood with a face so set and white seemed all the blood had drained from it, maybe even from his whole body. He stood a moment longer, defying the colonel, until Jameson said between his teeth, "That's an order, Major."

Ben pulled out a chair and sat.

'Twas maddening, the colonel's deliberation, as he seated himself and righted his wine glass. "Now, sir, perhaps you'll be so good as to tell me how you decided General Arnold's the traitor, *General Arnold*, mind you, and not this Anderson."

Ben stared at the floor. When at last he spoke, he didn't raise his eyes but kept them fixed on those wide planks.

"Been rumors coming up from my spies around New York the last few months, actually almost a year now, that one of our highest officers was talking to the government. We didn't know who. Now, almost as soon as Arnold becomes commander at West Point, he goes to the trouble of telling us that he's expecting Mr. Anderson from New York. But Anderson's going *to* New York and the enemy."

Jameson considered for a few moments. "You're right, Major," he said at last. "That's suspicious. That's why I detained Anderson. But how you get from that to General Arnold's a traitor—"

"Proves it, sir, because Arnold's protecting him both ways. See, Anderson's the messenger, the courier, and Arnold had no foolproof way to get him a pass unless they met face to face. He couldn't risk sending it to him—if it fell into our hands, their whole scheme's undone. Instead, he gives him a *verbal* pass by telling us to watch for him. That way, if Anderson's picked up by one of our patrols or the Skinners, we'll send him to Arnold. But they've already met, you can see that from the papers and the pass Anderson's carrying. So now, when Anderson must return to the government's lines, Arnold gives him the pass to protect him case he gets picked up on his way home."

I sat crushed and despairing, almost hating Ben for spinning such a tale. Surely he was wrong. If not, how could our Cause endure?

The colonel stared, as distraught as me, then slowly shook his head. "Could be, Major, but more likely you're mistaken, completely mistaken, and I'm damned if I'll take responsibility for arresting an officer like General Arnold."

"I'll take it, Colonel. Just give me authorization for a detachment. I'll—"

"You'll take responsibility for arresting your superior officer?" Jameson was nearly shouting again. "I never heard of such a thing, Major! Are you mad?"

"Sir, if West Point falls, if Arnold's sold us out, the war's over."

I'd never heard Ben plead before, not even when he proposed marriage, but he was pleading now. And still the colonel shook his head.

"All right, sir," Ben finally said, voice cracking. "Then if you won't arrest Arnold, at least don't send Anderson to him. Good Lord, they'll both skip to the government and next thing you know, there'll be a full attack on West Point."

They wrangled for another quarter hour, with Ben finally persuading Jameson to send a messenger after Anderson and bring him back. They'd excuse this to Arnold by claiming that they feared for Anderson's safety due to the Cowboys on the road. So far, Jameson could justify this according to Arnold's orders. But when Ben begged that Jameson's note come back as well so that Arnold wouldn't know of Anderson's capture, nor of the papers on their way to His Excellency, the colonel balked once more.

"Major, that's insolence, and I won't be accused of it. Probably Anderson stole those papers while the general's back was turned. He's a hero, tried and true, remember that."

"Too unlikely, sir, it's plain—"

The colonel held up a hand. "We'll bring Anderson back, Major. I can go that far for you, but that's all. 'Tis only proper to tell General Arnold what's happened here."

"But that lets Arnold escape—"

"Haven't established that he's guilty of anything to escape from, Major." Jameson glared. "We're talking about General *Arnold*, remember. *Major General Benedict Arnold*," he repeated, shaking his head.

Chapter Twenty-one

I woke early the next morning, well before first light. Let Ben be wrong, I prayed this Sabbath day. Please, let Arnold be innocent of this, dear God. We've got so few men that know which end of the cannon to light, let alone how to lead troops, or who'll charge a redoubt at Bemis Heights and win such a victory for us that a whole Regular army winds up our prisoners.

My thoughts moved to Mr. Anderson. However familiar he'd seemed, I recalled no one by that name. I opened my window wide, sat yawning and remembering the officers I'd known. So many dead, so many others wounded and captured. But only one a traitor—dear Lord, don't let it be so.

I dressed and stepped onto the landing to find Ben there, staring out the window. It faced north and West Point.

He turned with a tight smile.

"You look tired," I said.

"I am." He took my hand and squeezed it. "Didn't sleep a wink, but I think I've come up with a way to salvage things." We passed singly down the narrow stairs, Ben whispering behind me. "Gonna try one more time at breakfast to persuade Jameson, and if I can't, there's something I want you to do. When I signal you, say that we're calling off our engagement and you're leaving here, all right? Tell you the rest later," he murmured and held the parlor's door for me.

The colonel looked as though he'd slept no better than Ben or me. We stood for grace, then took our seats as he said, "Major, they brought Anderson back last night. He's in the guardhouse."

"Good."

"'Good,' Major? That's all you got to say? I thought you'd be overjoyed."

"But you're still sending word to General Arnold, sir, which—well, I hate to bring it up again—"

"Then don't."

"Sir, please, sending word to Arnold is the wrong step entirely. It—"

"Major, I thought I'd spoke pretty clear on that."

"Yes, sir." Ben slurped his coffee, then glanced at me sorrowfully. "Beg your pardon, sir, I—I have a—something on my mind."

The colonel looked from Ben to me. I bit my lip. "I'm afraid Benjamin and I have broken our betrothal."

"I'm so sorry," Jameson murmured.

"Thank you, sir." I cast Ben an injured look. "I, ah, I'll be leaving directly, under the circumstances. You understand."

"Of course."

I dabbed at my eyes, then stumbled from the table, though I was still hungry and the bread steamed deliciously.

I went to my chamber, where Ben soon joined me. "I told the colonel I was going to try once more to persuade you." He grinned. "That was wonderful, Clem."

I curtsied. "You're too kind. Now, am I really leaving?"

"I want you to go to West Point, to Arnold's headquarters."

I stared, thunderstruck.

"I can't go," he continued. "Soon as he found me missing, colonel'd have a detachment after me. But you can leave—he's expecting you to. Withal, he doesn't know how you've helped us before. I want you to go to the Point and see what happens. Take my horse. He's fast, and you need to get there quick as you can."

"But—but the messenger—"

Ben nodded. "Lieutenant that was in charge of Anderson is downstairs now with Jameson. He'll maybe eat some breakfast, but he's leaving soon with that fool report for Arnold. So you've got time, but not much. I'll try to hold him here long as I can, see if I can slip him a few dollars so's he refreshes himself along the way."

"But what am I gonna do at West Point?"

"I'm hoping you'll find a way to have Arnold arrested. Might be you can alert His Excellency's family. He's supposed to be stopping there—Oh, good God!" Ben put a hand on either side of his head and tugged at his hair. "Didn't think of it before, but what if Arnold's gonna deliver him to the government?"

"His Excellency?" I've seldom been as staggered. Victory without Washington was impossible. Indeed, the war without Washington was impossible. And he was too good a man for the gibbet. But then, so was Nathan.

"Maybe it's not West Point they're after," Ben said. "Maybe it's His Excellency." Then he brightened. "'Course, Jameson sent Anderson's papers to the general, so he'll know something's up if the courier's reached him. Listen, Clem, you need to get there fast. But whatever you do, don't confront Arnold. He'll be dangerous if he thinks we're onto him. Just watch him, and if he tries to run, find out where."

"I daren't trust anyone around him, either," I said, thinking aloud.

Ben nodded vigorously. "Don't ask 'em for help. No telling how many of his aides are in on this."

We faked a stormy parting, with me pushing my belongings into saddlebags while Ben pled with me in a loud voice sure to carry downstairs.

Then we ran for the stables.

He got the saddle onto his stallion and me into the saddle in two minutes flat, arguing the while that I should give him another chance and I was the hard-heartedest woman ever. I shouted as I galloped from the yard that it might be a hard heart, but he'd shattered it regardless, which should please his little doxy.

'Twas an oppressive day, hot and steamy with black clouds piling high, threatening to make up at long last for the drought. I nigh melted atop my sweaty mount, even if he moved a whole lot brisker than I could in such heat. We covered the thirty miles to Arnold's headquarters across from West Point by four that afternoon, the clouds still low and simmering, however strange it was to be in the saddle instead of a pew at worship.

'Twas a relief to see no flurry of activity, no gouges in the garden from a horse someone had viciously spurred. Instead, Robinson's Farms lay somnolent in the heat of late September.

I found Talia in the buttery. She gave a shriek the Redcoats must have heard down to York Island.

"La, Miss Clem, I's sure glad to see you. Been so tetchy around here, even the crickets afeared to chirp. Maybe Miss Peggy, she sees you, 'll stop getting her headaches. They hurts the rest of us more than they do her, and that's the fact."

"And how's the general?" I asked.

Talia was rolling an empty crock out from under a shelf to replace it with one full of pickles. She plopped down atop the new one and fanned herself with her apron. "He's upstairs now with Miss Peggy and the child, resting, and I don't know who enjoys their nap more, them or me." She got to her feet, and we wrestled the crock into place. "Now, how's about you? You back to stay?"

When I nodded, she threw damp arms around me. "Oh, praise the Lord. I's in need of help, Miss Clem. That old kitchen about to do me in."

A thumping sounded overhead, and Talia sighed. "That be the general, wanting his rum."

"I'll fetch it, Talia."

I climbed the stairs to stand outside their chamber and call, "General Arnold, sir?"

The door opened, and there he stood. I don't know what I expected: a man broken by guilt, cowering and begging mercy? But all he seemed was surprised at seeing me.

"Clem," he said, "you're back. Glad to have you, my dear. We missed you. Peggy," he called over his shoulder, "look who's here! You, ah, staying this time?"

"If you'll have me, General. I—I broke things off with Major Tallmadge."

I heard a smothered laugh from Peggy, but Arnold patted my arm so tenderly my eyes misted. "I'm sorry, Clem, and even sorrier for him, losing a girl like you. But you always have a home with us." He squeezed my elbow. "Especially if you wanna cook. We're about to die on Talia's efforts. And His Excellency's due tomorrow, Clem."

I started violently at that, or thought I did.

But Arnold didn't notice and rolled gently, softly on. "We need someone knows her way around the kitchen with him dining here. Can't feed him Talia's burnt offerings now, can I?"

He chuckled, trying to cheer me. How could a traitor be so kind?

Though I looked the rest of that day for the messenger with Jameson's note, he didn't come. He hadn't arrived before me, neither, or the Arnolds would have been fleeing for their lives, not sitting at table that evening, laughing at their son's antics, Peggy asking for more of my chowder and Arnold ticking off the menu for tomorrow's breakfast with His Excellency. But Peggy's laugh trilled sharper, and Arnold seemed so distracted that by evening I was sure they were guilty. There was no hope of Ben's being mistaken or Mr. Anderson's having helped himself to Arnold's files.

Next morning, I hurried to the kitchen and was mixing the corn-cakes His Excellency favors when I heard horses in the yard.

I dashed outside, but Arnold was already there, greeting his guests nor expecting his kitchen help to accost them. Those guests were smiling instead of drawing pistols, so I knew no courier had reached General Washington. On he'd ride into the danger here, all innocent and unawares. A streak of lightning blinded me, and then the rain started, drops so big two'd fill a dipper. I scuttled back to my corncakes as Talia waddled into the kitchen, full of herself and tidings.

"They says General Worshinton can't come for a while yet. He's stopped to lookit forti—forfications, and we's supposed to go ahead without him." She grinned. "Actually, we's supposed to tell Mrs. Arnold to go ahead. He don't know she don't get up afore noon."

I nodded, so preoccupied with greater worries than breakfast I could scarce think on what yet needed doing. "Um, take in the stewed apples and the ham, then, Talia, and I'll get the coffee."

Through the parlor's windows, I saw that the rain was already quitting, though it'd hardly wet the dust and but teased the thirsty trees. Settling into their chairs around the table were General Arnold and his aides, David Franks and Richard Varick, with their visitors, including Alex Hamilton.

Hamilton dismissed me at a glance, the way men do an ugly woman. As you can judge a lady's character by how she treats a poor man, so you can judge a man's by his courtesies to a homely girl. King Alex ever failed that test. He wouldn't have known whether he'd ever met me before, though I'd quarreled on him after Brandywine. For that I was grateful: this day, 'twas safer to be known as naught but a cook.

I stepped between kitchen, parlor, and buttery, carrying corncakes and syrup and bowls of fruit, keeping an ear cocked to Arnold's talk. It was as calm and cool as though he'd plotted no treason.

Until the sound of hooves carried to us.

Arnold pulled himself to his feet. "You'll excuse me, gentlemen. I have some orders to give," he said, hobbling for the buttery.

I followed him as fast as I decently could to find a muddy lieutenant handing over his pouch. Arnold glanced at it, then me. "Well, Clem?"

"Your pardon, sir," I said, "the—the coffee." But his attention had already gone back to the pouch. He rummaged inside as I reached for the coffee mill behind him.

He withdrew a letter, likely expecting to hear from his new friends among the enemy. But when a sound rose from deep within him, the likes of which I hope never to hear again, I knew 'twas Jameson's note. I had my back to Arnold and could not see his face, and I thank Providence for that, for 'twould have troubled me long afterwards. Then he hurried to the hall and up the stairs.

I waited at the bottom, scarcely breathing. Hard as I listened, I heard naught but flies buzzing at the window, the murmur of the officers in the parlor, a crow squawking outside. Overhead, all was still as death.

"Excuse me."

I leaped near to the ceiling as David Franks brushed past me up the stairs. Then he was knocking at Arnold's door and calling, "General Arnold? His Excellency's nigh at hand."

A door banged open.

Arnold stumbled down the stairs. "My horse!" he cried. "Get my horse!"

"Sir?" I ran after him as he rushed out the door towards the stable. "Sir!"

He turned to me. "Clem, if you please, ask them to get my barge ready." His voice, so calm 'twas dead, contrasted horribly with his anguished face and rooted me to the ground.

We seemed to stand forever there in the sunlight of early morning. Then he bawled, "I'm going to the Point. Please tell His Excellency I'll be back in an hour. Now, would you be so kind?" He jerked his head towards the river.

I ran down the steep path to the dock, planning to say that the Redcoats were coming and Arnold wanted his barge scuttled lest it fall into their hands.

But the crew had heeded his roar. They were loosing the barge's rope and heaving themselves aboard when I reached the riverbank. Short of holding them at gunpoint, and I had no pistol about me, nor even so much as a penknife, there was no way to keep them. I turned to climb the bank as Arnold galloped from the stable, scattering chickens before him. They clucked and flapped their wings as the horse's hooves sprayed dirt.

Four Continental dragoons cantered into the yard—Washington's advanced party!

Arnold's hand dropped to his pistols. I tried to shriek a warning, but 'twas as though I were in a nightmare, where you struggle with all your might to scream but nothing comes out.

"General Arnold, sir," one of the dragoons called, "His Excellency sends his compliments, begs to inform you he'll be here shortly."

Arnold nodded, hands back on his reins. "Fine. You boys stable your mounts and then have yourselves something to eat."

I watched his horse pick its way down the bank to the barge. The wind carried his voice to me as he gave orders to the crew, but I couldn't distinguish the words. I slipped to the riverbank as the boat got underway and saw that it was sailing, not across the river to West Point, but downstream, to the enemy.

General Washington arrived about fifteen minutes later.

With him rode the Marquis de la Fayette and Henry Knox. I'd never met La Fayette, but he intrigued me. He and Washington were as close as father and son, so the rumor went, though the marquis was almost as plain as me. Gangly, with a huge nose overpowering his face and thin hair, he sat his horse superbly. 'Twas clear he shared Washington's passion for riding, just as they were now sharing a laugh over some joke or other.

I served a second breakfast as my thoughts flew. Was Washington in danger? But if Franks and Varick were involved in the treason, they should have fled with Arnold when they saw his frenzy. Yet they seemed unconcerned, however wan Varick was after spending the last few days sick in bed. And Franks had tossed off the lie Arnold had given for his whereabouts as if he believed it; only Washington seemed perturbed—and then for but a moment—that West Point's commander and his good friend was too busy to greet him. Besides, if they were planning to kidnap Washington, wouldn't they have grabbed him when he dismounted and so was off guard? Would they have let him and his aides, who now outnumbered them, into the house where resistance would be easier?

I retreated to the kitchen to set more corncakes frying. Where was the messenger with Anderson's papers? Without them, 'twas up to me to inform General Washington of the plot. But I must catch him alone. I dare not deliver such news in front of everyone, for if Arnold's aides were partners in treason after all, my alarum might get His Excellency killed outright.

I served corncakes, sliced ham, and poured coffee with words of warning whirring in my head but no chance to whisper them. I was frustrated as I'd ever been by the time the general left with his aides for West Point and his meeting with Arnold—or so he thought.

Sometime later, Peggy's bell rang. I climbed the stairs, teacup in hand, to find her at the window in their chamber overlooking the river. The clouds had fled to let the noonday sun lap up every drop of rain, leaving the world even drier than before. The light shining through her gown showed she wore nothing beneath.

I handed her the tea, and she said, "Please tell Major Varick I wish to see him."

"All right." I turned towards the bureau and her smallclothes, figuring she'd dress first. You'd think I'd be immune to shocks by now after all those of the last few days, but here come another.

"Go get him *now*, Clem."

"But—but, Peggy, you're not—you can't—"

"Just get him!" she cried. "And remember you're the cook, not my mother."

Varick still looked a bit green when I knocked at his door. "Mrs. Arnold wishes to see you, sir."

He got that grin men do when a beautiful woman summons them. "Such an amiable lady," he said, voice weak from his fever. "Do you know, sick as I was yesterday, she sat with me for about an hour. She's as good as she is beautiful. The general's very fortun—"

An unearthly shriek interrupted him. It rose before ending in a moan, standing my hair on end. Varick and I looked at each other. When the scream sounded again, we ran into the hall.

Talia waddled from the kitchen. "What on earth—"

Another wail sent Talia and me upstairs. On the landing, we found Peggy lying in a heap. Her sheer silk gown had settled about her like a cloud—and 'twas about as concealing, too, especially with its belt hanging loose. Talia stared at me, horrified. "She done lost her mind, poor child."

"I don't think so—" I clapped my hands over my ears as Peggy unleashed a fourth screech.

I'd had enough. "Peggy, come on. You'll rouse the dead." I pulled her to her feet as Varick's tread sounded on the stairs.

Peggy wrenched free to run towards him, moaning again. That told me for sure Varick was innocent of their plot: Peggy wanted him to see her, wanted him even more in love with her than he already was, so that if anyone accused her, he'd stand by her.

"Peggy!" Talia and I chased after her to pry her off Varick, flabbergasted and blushing but with his arms around her anyhow.

"Oh, help me, sir! Help me!" she pleaded piteously as Talia and I wrestled her back to bed. Lest she give another eyeful to Varick, watching uncertainly from the hall, I slammed the door behind us and fiercely ordered, "Stop it, Peggy!"

Astoundingly, she did. She lay groaning with an arm thrown over her face, but at least no more bellowing troubled us. Indeed, we heard nothing from her for the next few hours.

That was a blessing for, as Talia muttered, things belowstairs were busier than a ant's nest. First, His Excellency's party returned. I breathed a prayer of thanksgiving for their safety while rehearsing the warning I would deliver once the general was settled upstairs.

But he'd barely gained his chamber before there's a pounding at the front door. I started, fearing a contingent of Redcoats with Arnold at its head, though I misdoubted they'd take the time to knock. "I'll get it," I told Talia.

A dusty man stood on the doorstep, alone, no bit of scarlet clothing about him, and his musket holstered on his horse. "Express for General Washington, ma'am."

I sagged with relief. Here was the messenger with Anderson's papers at last. Finally, General Washington would learn the whole mess, and not from my clumsy explanation, would sift the facts and protect either the Cause from Arnold or Arnold from our suspicions.

Then Hamilton sailed into the hall and snatched the precious pouch from me without a single word of thanks. The messenger stared after him, shaking his head. "There's some calls him King Alex, and I can see why," he murmured when His Highness had passed from earshot.

I grinned at his sally, joy at our deliverance making it seem the funniest ever. "Can I get you a sup of something?"

"Be obliged for some kill-devil, you got any."

He'd drained the cup and returned to his horse when a door banged open upstairs and Hamilton shouted for La Fayette. Then, in tones so bitterly heartbroken I hardly knew them for His Excellency's, General Washington cried, "Oh, Father in Heaven, 'tis Arnold, *Arnold* has betrayed us! Whom can we trust now?"

I stood shaken and bereft, head drooping. Soon as His Excellency hears of this, I'd told myself the last few days, he'll fix it. Now he knew, but fixing it was a long ways off.

An hour later, Hamilton came hunting me. His arrogance had deserted him for once, so that he was biting his lip and looking ready to cry.

"Miss Shippen," he quavered, "His Excellency wishes a moment with you."

Upstairs, General Washington gave me a bow and a grimace perhaps intended for a smile. "What do you know of this, Miss Shippen?"

"Sir, forgive me. I kept trying to tell you earlier, but I couldn't find you alone, and I didn't know how far this thing was spread. I thought they might be planning to take you, sir, kidnap you, so I couldn't let them see me talking to you. But now I'm certain-sure 'twas only General Arnold and of course my cou—his wife. I've heard things, you know, that—"

"Pardon me, Miss Shippen, but which direction did Arnold take when he left?"

"He went south, sir."

Hamilton snorted. "Of course he went south, towards the Redcoats."

His Excellency's eyes, grey as rock, flicked towards Hamilton, then returned to me. "How many hours has he got on us?"

"Too many, sir, at least five or six. He left this morning, about half past nine, in his barge."

"By water? He'll have already reached them, then." His voice was flat, lifeless.

"His wife's still upstairs, though, sir. If you arrest her, he'll come back."

He appeared not to hear me. "'Tis bootless, Hamilton, but do your best. Take someone with you and go after him. But bring him back alive. I want the pleasure of hanging him myself."

Hamilton left, and His Excellency went to the window. "Thank you, Miss Shippen."

"Yes, sir." I longed to say more, something that would comfort and encourage and persuade him the thing was not over yet. But what do you say when a man has devoted his life, his honor, his very soul to a Cause, only for his friend to betray him?

I was almost to the door when he spoke again. "How'd it happen you were here, Miss Shippen?"

I told him of Ben's quick thinking and attempts to persuade Colonel Jameson.

"Well," he said, "it seems you and Tallmadge are our only heroes in this."

"You're very kind, sir, but I'm no—a hero would have stopped General Arnold, nor let him get away." I coughed. "Sir, his wife—"

But he turned again to the window.

That evening, His Excellency closeted himself with La Fayette to pour forth orders preparing the army lest the enemy attack West Point. One of those orders also changed the name of the main work at the Point. 'Twould nevermore be known as Fort Arnold.

Clouds again hid the sunset, and thunder boomed as I climbed the stairs for bed. Then the rain began. It poured hard and kept up this time, as though the Lord Himself was weeping over us.

Between the rain and our troubles, I hardly slept. Daybreak was still distant when I stirred the kitchen fire to heat some coffee and fetched me a mug onto the porch. Clouds hung low, spitting their rain now, not pelting it as they done last night. Their blackness was streaked with red towards the east. The dawning world, no longer grey and dusty, had a drowned, gloomy look, and which was sadder, I don't know. I warmed my hands round my coffee.

A rooster crowed, muffled by the rain, as Benjamin entered the yard, dripping and drooping in his saddle. There looked to be near a hundred drenched, tired soldiers following him. They carried their carbines across their saddles, coats or a glove draped over the pan keeping the powder dry, as though expecting attack. Those with muskets had the bayonets fixed.

Ben caught sight of me as he dismounted. He muttered orders to a captain, then, in two strides, was beside me. With the company watching, he gave me no hug but only asked, "His Excellency's here? He's safe?"

I nodded. Ben had barely sighed his relief afore two soldiers pushed a man forward between them. Two more behind kept their muskets in his back.

The prisoner hadn't been barbered lately. His hat was pulled low, but he was wearing the purple coat I'd seen at North Castle, so I knew 'twas John Anderson. The coat was even more garish at close quarters, with tarnished gold lace dripping rain. It hung open to show no waistcoat covering his linen. Yet he was familiar. I was certain I'd known him once, and that he'd been a coxcomb such that his dishabille now would have disgraced him. Then Ben spoke, and I put a hand to my mouth.

"Clem, I believe you know our guest, Major John Andre."

I stood stupefied.

Andre bowed as debonair as possible, what with soldiers gripping his arms. "Miss Shippen, 'tis a pleasure to see you again. It's been far too long."

I was still too staggered to speak, though I don't know why. It made perfect sense. Peggy's interest in the matter had never been political—she cared naught for politics—but personal. She wanted whatever rewards and honors the government would bestow for betraying us, sure. But she also wanted Andre. I saw instantly that he'd been the go-between. He and Peggy had written each other, maybe even met a few times, Peggy happy at any contact with her idol and having an excuse to hand her jealous husband. God in Heaven, what selfishness, what unfathomable evil, to betray us for a flirtation, and that a failure, too, one that Andre, prizing his commission and career, would never take seriously but only use to his advantage.

Fool, I wanted to tell him, don't you see? You thought you could play Peggy like a fiddle, and you did, but you didn't reckon with her husband. Why do you suppose you're under guard now and he's sailed downriver, free as the wind? He couldn't bear for Peggy to love you, and not him, and you walked right into his trap. And all the while, you thought 'twas him being caught, not you.

But I said nothing, only stood with my arms wrapped around me while they brought some kill-devil and bread to Andre and Ben went inside to report. The soldiers nigh Andre levelled their bayonets as one of them loosed his hands.

"You see what a desperate character I am, Miss Shippen." He was trying for nonchalance, but his voice trembled. "Come, gentlemen, I can't escape. Why, that would require vanishing into thin air. 'Tis hard to enjoy one's rum with bayonets crowding close." This earned a few smiles, but not a musket wavered.

Ben returned to say they'd bed down in the barn yonder and get some sleep. "Then, once it quits raining," he told Andre, "we'll be going across the river, to West Point."

"Don't think me importunate, Major," Andre said, corking the canteen of rum. "I know I've asked before, but am I being held as a prisoner of war?"

I gasped, and they both glanced at me. A prisoner of war, captured doing his duty, was entitled to safety and care. Andre had been taken working treachery.

Ben wiped his brow. Gaze locked with mine, he spoke slow and soft. "I had a much loved classmate in Yale College—"

I peeped at Andre to see him baffled, then closed my eyes and swallowed hard.

Ben's voice flowed gently on. "—by the name of Nathan Hale. He entered the Army with me in the year 1776. After the British troops took New York, General Washington wanted information—"

I opened my eyes as Andre shifted his, no longer puzzled. Instead, the color had fled his face, leaving it a sick grey in the wet dawn.

"Captain Hale tendered his services, sir, went into New York, and was taken just as he was passing your outposts." Ben paused until Andre looked at him. "Do you remember the sequel of this story?"

A moment or maybe an eternity passed. Then Andre shuddered and pulled the cork from the canteen. He lifted it for a long drink. "Yes," he finally said. "He was hanged as a spy."

Like a dog, I screamed silently, no trial, all alone—

"But," Andre was almost smiling now, charming, beguiling, a drop of rum glittering in the stubble on his chin, "you surely do not consider his case and mine alike."

He spoke so pleasant that Ben nor I understood at first. Then I took his meaning, that such dishonorable work as spying, such filthy wickedness, was all that anyone expected from Nathan and other rebels, but Andre, an officer of the government and thus superior—

I think Ben saw it that way too, for he stepped towards Andre, face twisting, fist clenched. The soldiers watched impassively. It was for me to grab his arm and whisper, "Ben, don't."

Seemed for a moment he'd punch me, too. Then he shook himself. Opening his hand, he rested it on my shoulder. "Your case and his?" He emphasized every syllable. "Precisely similar. And similar will be your fate."

It was as much as calling him a spy. Andre flushed, started to answer, gulped, stood silent.

Ben turned to give orders about taking Andre to the barn, numbered off the troops that would sleep first while the other half stayed on guard. 'Twas charitable, really, for it gave the prisoner time to compose himself so he could return the canteen with thanks. Then Andre bowed to me, and they led him to his horse.

"I'll be back quick as I can," Ben muttered before he, too, swung into his saddle.

I watched him ride away, trying to collect my thoughts before I stepped into the house. There I almost collided with La Fayette as he clattered down the stairs from His Excellency's quarters. "He would see Mrs. Arnold, yes?" La Fayette asked.

I knocked twice at Peggy's door without an answer before I opened it. She stood at the window overlooking the yard, dressed in yesterday's gown, head hanging, still as death. She must have seen Andre brought in.

"Peggy."

She didn't move.

"Peggy, His Excellency wants to see you."

"What'll they do with him, Clem, do you think?"

Her voice was ragged, and she was shaking from head to foot. I've never pitied my cousin—her beauty, an accident of birth, has kept her loved and coddled all her life and brings her more favors in one day than come to any of us in a year—but in that moment, my heart broke for her. She loved Andre as I had Nathan, and Andre was as doomed as Nathan had been.

"I—I don't know, Peggy. I guess they'll call a court-martial, and, well, 'tis treason he was plotting with you—"

A groan came from her to rival the one I'd heard from her husband with its anguish. Then a keening began. Neddy had been asleep in his cradle, but her sobbing woke him, and he cried.

Peggy moaned again.

"Peggy," I said, "get hold of yourself. General Washington wants to see you."

She and Neddy continued wailing. She stumbled to the cradle and plucked the baby from his blanket.

"Peggy."

She ignored me, rocking the child, though her eyes flicked towards me beneath the hair hiding her face.

"Peggy, General Wash—"

"He's the one!" she wailed.

"The one?"

"The one trying to kill John, my baby! Washington! He wants to kill my baby, my John, but I won't let him! I won't!"

"Stop it!" I said. "Only person General Washington wants to kill is that traitorous husband of yours. Now get some clothes on and come with me."

She ranted some more before sighing that though she'd endured a great shock and was too unwell to leave her bed, she'd receive the general in her apartment. I nigh fainted. Receive a gentleman in her bedchamber, and that gentleman His Excellency?

General Washington's lips tightened when I gave him Peggy's message, though Hamilton, just arrived, murmured, "The poor girl." I could see he knew of Peggy's beauty and, like a fool, would overlook all because of it.

"'Poor girl'?" I glared at him. "She's guiltier than her husband!"

His Excellency silenced us with a look. "You'll come with us, Miss Shippen, if you please." And so I led them down the hall.

We found her nursing her child but looking no more motherly than Aphrodite. She was nigh naked with her gown open down the front.

I started to back out of the room, but Hamilton blocked me. "My God!" he breathed.

I turned, trying to shut the door behind me, but Peggy cried, "Oh, sir, help me, please!" And though my back was to her, I knew from the glint in Hamilton's eye that she'd set Neddy aside to hold out her arms and bare even more.

The general reached us. He was tall enough to stare easily over Hamilton's head, and for sure over mine.

Everyone knows how His Excellency loved the ladies, especially pretty ones. He was gawking his fill now. When he felt my eyes on him, his unfailing dignity failed, and he blushed like a schoolboy caught with dirty pictures.

Hamilton pushed past me to take the hands Peggy was holding out to him. "My dear Mrs. Arnold." He spoke low and intimate. "Hush now. I shall certainly help you, you have nothing to fear." It made my gorge rise.

Washington stepped forward, and Peggy shrank against her pillows, hugging the sheet to her. "'Tis him!" she screeched, as though His Excellency were the Devil himself. Then she flung the sheet aside.

It fell away to reveal dimpled knees and smooth thighs.

I hurried to right the sheet as she brushed hair from her wild, calculating eyes.

His Excellency stood dazed and routed. He put some questions to her hesitantly, then with confidence, until Peggy raised a hand to her brow. Again, the sheet fell from her. Again, I tucked it in. But Washington's voice sank to hoarseness, and his questions were peppered with "if you please" and "so sorry, madam."

They never did get sense from her. She raved about Washington and her baby, though there was no more talk of her John, then cried that iron rings, which only His Excellency could loosen, squeezed her head. Thus did she persuade them she'd had no part in her husband's treason, knew nothing of it, never even suspected. 'Twas a greater shock to her than anybody, so great it unhinged her mind.

Peggy kept to herself the next three days though she was safe, with me alone suspicious. I argued with Ben that she was guilty, as guilty as Andre, guiltier than her husband, but he shook his head.

"Hush, now, Clem. 'Tisn't like you, this—this hatred for your cousin, I mean, the poor girl's suffered such a blow. Her husband's gone—"

"Oh, balderdash, she doesn't care two pins for her husband. 'Tis Andre she loves."

"Well, what if she does? He's a better man than Arnold. Heck, even I like him better than Arnold. Anyone would."

I glanced skyward, praying for patience. Ben had been guarding Andre, which meant they talked away the hours, with Andre's charm on parade, and this was what came of it.

"Look, Ben, she's in this thing. She knew all along, probably put General Arnold up to it. I'd wager my life on it."

But Ben only shook his head.

Peggy never asked to see Andre, likely to avoid the questions that would raise. I doubt they'd have permitted it, anyway.

"Clem," she asked the day after cozening them, "please, will you go to him for me, find out how he is, give him my—my love?"

Though 'twas two in the afternoon of a pleasant fall day, she lay abed, eyes swollen, curtains drawn.

I took the morning's untouched bread from the table beside her to set her dinner there, and Peggy clutched my arm. "Please, Clem, he must know—I need—give him my love."

I pulled away. "You're married, Peggy."

"Clem, please, I beg you." A freshet of tears fell from her. "'Twill mean the world to me, and it costs you nothing."

She was a wickedly selfish person who cared for naught but herself and Andre. Yet if it had been Nathan under guard, and I knew I'd brought about his doom—

"All right, Peggy, I'll try. But if they won't let me see him—"

"Try hard, Clem, please."

I sent twice to His Excellency, but Peggy had already left for her parents' home before he granted my request. General Washington told her she could return to Philadelphia or join her traitorous husband behind the enemy's lines, whichever she liked. Hard as she'd been scheming to reach New York, her reason for doing so now sat a prisoner in our territory. I wasn't the least surprised when she chose her parents.

Meanwhile, the rest of us removed with General Washington thirty miles or so down Hudson's River to Tappan. There they condemned Andre to die for spying.

Tappan is a Dutch village where English is hardly spoke. For all that, it's the county seat. It was also the Continental Army's headquarters, which was why they tried Andre there. 'Tis a pretty place, with houses built of stone, like the ones around Philadelphia, not wood as they are in New England. But it has a green to match any in Massachusetts, and a couple of taverns, too, and a church. They'd even had a courthouse until it burned a few years ago. Streams and brooks flowed all through there, and the bullfrogs at night were a wonder to hear.

They gave Andre a court-martial in the square stone church rather than hanging him from the nearest tree as the government had Nathan. Fourteen officers gathered to hear the charges against him: that they'd caught him behind our lines, out of uniform and with a false name. The greater evil was his scheming with Arnold, but they couldn't try him for that. Everyone in a scarlet uniform wanted to destroy us. That's the nature of war.

He could hang for spying, though.

Naturally, Andre denied being a spy. He claimed he'd only taken the advantage anyone would, of trying to persuade officers to switch their allegiance. 'Twas regrettable that through force of circumstance he'd ridden behind our lines and discarded his uniform. That was indiscreet, certainly, but not criminal. He hadn't done it to spy on us but to meet with Arnold.

Throughout, he was debonair and gentlemanly, until I was sure his charm would fool the judges as Peggy's beauty had His Excellency.

Andre had plenty of help from his commander. General Sir Henry Clinton sent messages near daily, sometimes pleading mercy for Andre, other times warning of revenge on American prisoners for whatever his adjutant general suffered.

Clinton even had his most recent recruit write on Andre's behalf, which shows how panicked Sir Harry was.

I wondered at first how he persuaded Arnold, for 'twas clear the general wanted his rival dead because of Peggy. But when I saw the letter, I understood. There was no begging for Andre's life, not at all. Instead there were threats, and bluster. If anything could determine them to punish Andre for a spy, 'twas hearing such from the man every American now hated. That letter was calculated to provoke Washington and the judges lest Cher Jean had bewitched them.

In the end, they convicted the defendant, charm and all, said he ought to be considered as a spy from the enemy, and that agreeably to the law and usage of nations, he should suffer death. That was on Friday, September 29, four years and a week since Nathan hanged. On Saturday, His Excellency set the execution for the next afternoon, though it was the Sabbath, at five o'clock. They say his hand shook when he signed the order.

But the tries at freeing Andre didn't end. My own betrothed, now itching to pardon the major rather than pummel him, was with those who thought His Excellency too severe, who wanted Andre freed. The first time Ben came out with that, I cried, "How can you say that? He's a spy, an officer of the government, a Redcoat. They hanged Nathan, remember?"

"Nathan, Nathan—everything's Nathan with you. Look, the point I was trying to make was that John is—"

"*John?* You mean Major Andre, don't you?"

"—he's innocent, or nearly so—"

"Innocent? Good Lord!"

"'Tis Arnold we should be after. Hamilton agrees with me—"

"He would." I loaded those two words with all my scorn for King Alex.

"He and I want to ask His Excellency to spare John's life and let us try to catch Arnold."

We'd been arguing a lot recently, so later that afternoon when I came upon Ben leaning against a fence, looking towards the tavern holding Andre, I vowed not to quarrel.

"Did you see His Excellency?" I asked.

He nodded.

"What'd he say?"

He took the straw he'd been chewing from his mouth, tossed it away. "He's already sent a message to Clinton, asking to exchange Arnold for Jo—Major Andre."

"Well," I said, "if Clinton agrees—"

"He won't. It violates every usage of war. He'll send back notice that he can't agree to any exchange, mark my words."

Next day, General Washington granted my requests to see Andre.

His Excellency had taken a farmhouse for his headquarters, a snug little place built of brick and stone nigh eighty years before and called the DeWindt Mansion, which gives you some idea of the housing thereabouts. There were fireplaces at either end, with smoke coming from one as I walked past a well and sweep and a row of pines to the front door.

It was the half kind the Dutch favor, with the top swung open to the breeze. The sentry posted there showed me to the parlor on the right. I stepped up over the threshold to see a fireplace rimmed with the delft tiles you'll find in Dutch homes, the ones with scenes from the Scriptures painted on them so parents can teach their children about the Lord of an evening. Before the sandstone hearth stood a desk, with His Excellency bent over it alongside two aides I didn't know.

"You wanted to see me, sir?" I asked.

"Ah, Miss Shippen." His smile didn't even reach his eyes. "Gentlemen, will you excuse us, please?" They shut the door behind them, and I took the chair he indicated.

General Washington seated himself at the desk and studied me. "Miss Shippen, permit me to ask, why do you want to see Major Andre?"

"'Tis for my cousin, Mrs. Arnold, sir. She was a—a—friendly with him, and she—she asked me to give him a, um, message."

"What message, Miss Shippen?"

I squirmed, hating Peggy for embarrassing me this way. "Her love, sir."

He stared for a moment before murmuring, "Good Lord." I think he even chuckled. Then he went to the window, stood looking out.

"You think Major Andre ought to hang, Miss Shippen?"

"Yes, sir."

He turned that grey gaze on me. "Really? Well, I'll send my critics to you, next time someone tells me how heartless I am, executing him." Whatever test he'd given me, I'd passed, because he sat at his desk and wrote out a pass.

"Here, Miss Shippen. This'll get you in to see him tomorrow."

"Tomorrow? But I thought, that is, isn't the hanging—"

"I've postponed it a day. We're trying to work something out that'll save him. Because I agree with my critics. Andre's more unfortunate than criminal. 'Tis Arnold who's guilty as sin in all this, and he's the one ought to suffer."

I don't know whether I was more bewildered or disappointed. Finally I asked, "But, sir, if that's your thinking, why don't you just free Andre?"

"Can't. We'd look weak, foolish, to the Redcoats and the French, too. Someone must hang for this, and I want it to be Arnold, not Andre." In a softer voice, he added, "I can't even have him shot, poor boy. He's asked if he can be shot as a man of honor, not die like a criminal and spy on the gibbet. But I can't do it. The practice and usage of war is against the indulgence."

I looked away, grieving that no one had fought to save Nathan the way everyone, even our Commander-in-Chief, was battling to spare Andre.

His Excellency continued. "I was hoping to trade Andre for Arnold. General Greene's meeting with the enemy about that now, but I don't expect Clinton to agree. It's against all the rules of war to give up a deserter. Still, I'd like you to suggest to Andre that he write Clinton and plead for an exchange. He's got more reason than any of us to convince Clinton, so maybe he can."

"Me? But—but, sir, surely that's—I mean, wouldn't it be better coming from someone official, mayhap one of your aides?"

He grimaced. "I tried that, Miss Shippen. I asked Colonel Hamilton—"

I rolled my eyes, changing his grimace to a smile.

"—but he told me that as a man of honor, Andre couldn't but reject it. Said he wouldn't for the world propose to him a thing which must place him in the unamiable light of supposing him capable of such meanness—"

"Goodness!"

"—and that he himself felt the impropriety of the measure. Felt it keenly, Miss Shippen." He had slipped into King Alex's self-righteous tones. Then he spoke in his usual voice. "That's why your visit with him, it's my last hope. You're old friends. Mayhap he'll listen to you. And if he won't, if he doesn't agree to write Clinton, he still may tell you things he won't say to any of us, not even Major Tallmadge. Now, there's two guards in the room with him all the time. I want them there while you are. Andre might get suspicious otherwise, and a man doesn't talk when he's suspicious."

"Talk, sir? About what?"

He looked surprised. "Why, where Arnold is."

That baffled me, too. After a moment's musing, I asked, "But don't we know where he is? Isn't he with the enemy in New York City?"

"Yes, but where *exactly*? There's another plan we have, Miss Shippen, but we must know Arnold's exact location. So visit the major, give him your cousin's message, but above all, find out for us where Arnold is."

Sounded simple. But like so many things that do, it wasn't.

Chapter Twenty-two

His eyes were smudged, and he seemed thinner, too. Otherwise, Major Andre was as blithe and gallant as he'd been in my uncle's parlor, never mind his shame as spy and his purple coat. He'd worn that garment since his capture, throughout his trial, and if it had looked ridiculous nine days ago, it looked bedraggled and even more ridiculous now.

He bowed, then, to my surprise, took my hands in his. "Miss Shippen, kind of you to come. Isn't there something in the Good Book about visiting prisoners in their distress?"

"I, um, think so." I glanced at the pair of guards standing this side of the locked door, watching without seeming to watch. They were the only hint that Andre was a captive, for Tappan had no gaol to hold him, just one of the three large rooms in Mabie's Tavern. Mabie's was the only stopping place for miles around, and built substantial to match such importance. Its thick walls made for a stout prison.

Andre followed my eyes to the guards. "They won't bother us, will you, gentlemen?" he said almost gaily.

One gave a slight nod, and the other said, "Don't pay us no heed, ma'am."

Andre said, "I flatter myself I've never been illiberal, but if there were any remains of prejudice in my mind, my present experience must obliterate them. Companionable guards, as you can see, and did you know I receive all my meals direct from Mr. Washington's table?"

I frowned. "General, you mean."

"Your pardon."

I took a breath and lowered my voice. "I'm sorry about all this, Major, even though—" I stopped. No need to say 'twas a heinous thing he'd tried to do. I settled for "'Tis just too tragic."

"It was an honest zeal for my king's service, Miss Shippen." His gaze didn't waver. "I'm no spy."

"My cousin sends her love."

"Ah." This time, too, his eyes were steady. And when he said, "A lovely lady. We shared some good times," I saw she was nothing more than that to him, a lovely lady like so many others, and all of them sharing good times. Once more, I pitied my cousin, that she had sacrificed her husband's devotion—and our freedom—to this flirt.

"Please," he said, "won't you sit down?"

There wasn't much to choose from for seats. A table stood before the room's only window, with a chair before it, but both were buried beneath papers, inkwells, stacks of drawings. That left the bed and windowsill. I chose the bed. Andre sat aside me.

"My cousin requested a—a keepsake from you, sir, perhaps one of those drawings there, or a lock of your hair next time the barber comes." She'd asked for no such thing, had been too distracted even to think of it. But I knew 'twould have comforted me to have something of Nathan's, and, as Peggy said, such kindness cost me nothing.

"She shall have both." He plucked a drawing from the nearest pile. "Now, tell me, Miss Shippen, how—"

"General Arnold betrayed you, didn't he?"

The words seemed to enter the room without my speaking them. Andre sat silent, pulling the drawing back and forth between his fingers. Finally, he said, "Miss Shippen, as a gentleman, I—I hesitate to accuse anyone of such—such perfidy."

I watched the drawing, not his face, as I said quietly, "You know they're trying to come up with a way out of this for you."

The drawing fluttered. "Heard a rumor to that effect."

"You'd help things along if you'd write General Clinton and—and—"

"And what, Miss Shippen?"

I raised my eyes to his. "Ask him to trade Arnold for you."

"Trade us?" He smiled. "What are we, horses?"

He was joking to spare me, but I owed it to His Excellency to press the matter.

When I did, Andre answered as King Alex predicted, saying he was sorry to have given the impression he would ever urge his commander, especially one as respected as Sir Harry, to such ignominious conduct, and while he appreciated our concern, he could not act on it, for he was still a man of honor, however they called him a spy, etc., etc.

Thus did I fail my first assignment. I breathed deep afore plunging into the second. "What happened, then, Major? If you're no spy, how'd you come to be caught out of uniform, behind our lines?"

Again he hesitated, then spoke so soft I strained to hear. "'Twas my own fault, I guess, too eager for—for—to make my mark. If I'd abided by Sir Harry's advice, I'd be back at headquarters now, and all this—" He shook his head. "All this would be just a bad dream."

"What advice? What did he tell you?"

He sat silent for a moment, then glanced up with half a smile. "Just about everything I've done the last few days, he told me to do the opposite. 'Don't go behind their lines, don't take off your uniform...'" He sighed. "I should have listened. But Sir Harry's old and cautious, old enough to be my father, and I—you know how 'tis, you laugh at an old man's caution. And I was eager, Miss Shippen, I wanted a promotion. I'm adjutant general, of course, but that's just temporary. Sir Harry'd said there was nothing he could do as far as promoting me. Not that he hadn't tried, but I was too young. The War Office told him there were dozens of men ahead of me with three or four times as much service. What I needed—we both knew it—I needed a grand stroke, something so stupendous that no one in London could deny me anything."

I itched for the quills and paper sitting to hand on the table so's I might capture every word he spoke. Not only could His Excellency study my notes as to Arnold's whereabouts, but they'd help with my book, too. Yet I knew Andre'd fall silent soon as I started writing. So instead I listened, intent as a body can be...

"I want to go over things one more time, Major." General Sir Henry Clinton had gestured to the chair before his desk and poured two glasses of red port wine. Behind him, through the window of his headquarters on New York's southern tip at No. 1 Broadway, Andre could see mounted officers and soldiers on foot, with ladies of dubious virtue smiling at both this sunny afternoon in September.

Clinton handed one glass to Andre, then sipped at the other. "You're sure you want to go through with this, Major? You know we can send someone else."

"Thank you, sir, but I count it an honor to serve the king." And, more importantly, a sure means of promotion. Andre treasured the power and recognition that the adjutant general's post bestowed, yet his continuance in it depended on Sir Harry's good graces.

And that worried him. The general was notoriously moody. What if the camaraderie they shared today evaporated tomorrow? Then, too, Clinton was as homesick as he was moody. He might resign his command at any moment and sail for England, leaving Andre stranded, a lowly aide dependent on snagging the attentions of another general. No, Andre's high rank must be official: no whim of fate or Clinton should snatch it from him. He needed a *coup manqué*. What better than to present his sovereign with the rebels' ablest warrior and most valuable fort?

Sir Harry stared with bloodshot eyes. Finally, he tossed back his port. "You'll go up Hudson's River tomorrow, then. I've got them holding a boat for you already. It'll take you to the *Vulture* where it's anchored off Teller's Point. Beverley Robinson's on board there; he'll provide a cover for us. It's his house Arnold's taken as headquarters, so Robinson'll request a meeting with him to discuss his property. Now you'll still be about twelve, maybe fifteen miles below West Point, but rebel outposts start another—"

"—another couple of miles north of Teller's Point, sir. I know." He smiled, but Sir Harry stared glumly.

"Remember that you're not to go near those outposts, understand? I don't want you crossing enemy lines. I don't trust Arnold, don't trust any traitor. So you look sharp, Major, make sure he doesn't cut corners, take any chances with you. 'Course, whole thing could be an ambush."

"Unlikely, sir." If Arnold were hoaxing them, spies would have heard of it by now and warned them. "Too much trouble to catch an officer or two."

"Well, make sure you're in uniform, no matter what. You change your dress, and anything goes wrong, you could be charged with—with spying." Sir Harry lowered his voice as if naming a perversion.

"Yes, sir. I'll take care, sir. After all, I intend to come back and enjoy our victory." Though he meant it for wit, Clinton's eyes fixed on him sadly.

"Major, you been like a son to me—" Abruptly, Sir Harry turned his back to fiddle with some papers on his desk. When he finally spoke, his voice was casual. "Thought I'd ride out to Mount Pleasant this afternoon, visit the Riedesels. You want to come, Major?"

"Ride'd be nice, sir. Thank you."

But ambling up the Post Road in the afternoon sun, Andre wished he had refused. Sir Harry roused himself for repartee now and then, but on the whole, he was morose. Andre often found his eyes, fatherly and concerned, on him. Then, too, Andre seldom saw Mount Pleasant and the Beekman mansion crowning its summit without remembering that a young Continental had spent his last night there in '76, an officer who read Latin as well as he did, who was charming, brilliant, beloved. He had no need to be reminded of Nathan Hale this day.

Hudson's River lay silvery and sparkling beneath the moon as Andre paced aboard the *Vulture*. He was sure morning's light would show a groove worn in the planking, for he had been walking the deck all evening, awaiting the messenger that Arnold was sending as a guide to their rendezvous. Colonel Robinson had kept him company the first hour. But with their small talk exhausted, Robinson repaired below. Then Andre's solitary vigil began, a wait that stretched his nerves and churned his stomach. The mission had been dangerous enough when he was busy with other matters. Now that he had time to think, he counted a thousand things could go wrong.

Morning dawned without sign of any messenger. Andre retired to his cabin. He would spend the day there and wait for the man again that night. He fell asleep to the lapping of the river.

"Major?"

It was Colonel Robinson's voice, and Andre jumped from bed to fling open the cabin's door. He squinted in the light of Robinson's lantern. "The messenger here?"

Robinson nodded. "Name's Smith, Joshua Smith. But there's a problem. Pass he brought only covers one of us, not both."

"Only one?"

Robinson nodded. "Reckon I'd better go, sir. After all, I'm the reason for the meeting, and—"

"No!" It was forceful, desperate, and Robinson's brows rose. But Andre's promotion must not slip away. "No, Colonel, I'll go. Arnold's been dealing with me—he'll be expecting me."

Andre buttoned his waistcoat and pulled on his uniform. The evening was warm, but he threw a surtout over his shoulders to cover his regimentals. Relieved that the moment was on him, eager to make his mark on history, he followed Robinson on deck.

There the colonel introduced him to the messenger as John Anderson. Then Andre slipped and slid with Joshua Smith down a rope ladder into a rowboat.

Their trip upriver seemed to take forever, between Andre's nerves and Smith's proclivity for chatter. Tall and too thin, with baggy eyes in a homely face, Smith said nothing and took a long time about it, too. But at last he directed the oarsmen into a cove on the river's western shore.

Andre stumbled after him up a bank littered with shale and pebbles to a copse of pine trees. The twigs beneath his feet snapped loud as cannon fire. His heart hammered at how the fate of the war, not to mention immortal fame, lay before him. This time next year, he might be Sir John, knighthood already conferred and living on the estate the king had granted.

A shadow waited under the trees ahead. "Smith?" a voice rasped over the cracking sticks, and a powerful shape limped forward into moonlight. Andre recognized the determined jaw and long nose from woodcuts in the newspapers, and his worries dropped away. It really was Arnold, ready to sell West Point and with it a rebellion.

"Yes, sir," Smith was saying, "I got Mr. Anderson here."

"All right," Arnold said, "leave us then. Go down and wait with the boat, if you please."

Arnold was too busy peering at Andre to bow, remembering his manners only when Andre coughed and said, "An honor, General Arnold."

"Yes, forgive me, honor's mine. I've heard quite a lot about you, sir. My wife speaks highly of you."

Andre had thought they would get right to business, so this surprised him. Otherwise, he might have noticed the sarcasm. "Well, ah, she—she's very kind, sir."

"You're the only bright spot in the war for her."

"You're very fortunate to have won her, sir. She's a beautiful lady."

Arnold continued to speak of Peggy, repeating her memories of the months Andre had spent in Philadelphia and listening with obvious fascination to his rejoinders. At last, the night fleeing, Andre said, "Perhaps we ought to get to business, sir, much as our present topic pleases me."

"Does it?" Arnold stared as Andre gave an uncertain smile. Then Arnold said brusquely, "You're authorized to speak for General Clinton?"

At Andre's nod, he continued, "I want assurance that your aims and mine are the same here for ending the war. There's to be amnesty for everyone, officers and men; we were only fighting for our freedom, after all. Everyone'll lay down his arms and go home, including your troops. Now His Majesty agreed, what, two years ago, he'd stop taxing us, stop interfering with our commerce, said he'd grant everything we want but independency. I need Sir Harry's word on it that those sentiments are still current. And the Radicals! He must rid us of them before they hang half of Philadelphia."

Andre lost all sense of time as they talked, concerned only with Arnold's demands. He demurred at first, but when Arnold threatened to end the discussion then and there, he relented. Wearily, he remembered that the legendary warrior had been bargaining in the West Indies while he himself was still clinging to mama's skirts. He would never best him in this.

Finally, Arnold said, "All right, let's decide on your plan of battle for taking West Point, Major."

Andre sat silent from astonishment.

"Major?" Arnold repeated.

"By God, sir, I can't do that. That's up to Sir Harry and the field officers."

Arnold hissed, "Major, you're trying my patience. You want the Point or not?"

"But, sir, you ask for things that aren't mine to promise. I can't—"

"How you expect me to surrender if you don't cooperate? Look, you're used to Redcoats. They obey orders without question. But me, I've got Yankees by and large, free men. They don't do anything unless they see why. I start giving them orders that don't make sense, try to march them out of the fort to you in surrender, and they're not gonna obey, you understand?"

They whispered back and forth until Andre capitulated. Only then, with the night half gone, did they discuss the plan of attack. Andre was still reviewing it when the sound of footsteps reached them. Arnold fell silent and held up a hand.

"General Arnold, sir." It was Smith. "'Tis near dawn, sir, and we got a problem."

Andre jumped to his feet. Now that Smith mentioned it, he saw that the trees around them were no longer black but grey. "I must be getting back, General Arnold."

Smith stood with them now, shaking his head. "That's the problem, Mr. Anderson. Can't get you back to the *Vulture*."

"Can't get me—what do you mean?"

"Fellas rowed us here won't take you back no-how. Say the night's too far gone for rowing up to a enemy ship. Our gunners ashore'd see 'em and fire on 'em."

Andre felt the first frisson of fear down his back. This could not be. It would lead to another thing gone wrong, and another, and before long... "Mr. Smith," he said, "perhaps they don't appreciate the urgency. I have important business aboard the *Vulture*. I can't be detained."

"Well," Smith said, "you better go talk to them, then. But hurry: they's paddling out of here for home."

Andre scrambled down the shale so fast he fell. The boat was already half a mile upstream, silhouetted against the streaked eastern sky.

Sweat broke on his forehead. In a frenzy, he looked south, towards the black hulk of the *Vulture*, and took a step into the river, and another. He would swim it. But he had seldom been in water above his knees, would likely drown when the river, low as it was, rose above his head. Scarcely knowing what he was about, he turned to find Arnold's eyes, cool and amused, on him.

"Come, Mr. Anderson, 'tisn't the end of the world." Arnold brushed pine needles from his coat, and Andre realized he was right. As long as the *Vulture* anchored there in the river, waiting for him, he was safe.

Arnold continued. "We'll get you back to the *Vulture* somehow or other, just need to get us another boat. Meantime, why don't we go to Smith's house, have some breakfast?"

Smith was crowing assent as Andre asked, "But—but what about Mrs. Smith and—and your children, sir, I—ah, if you have any."

"Oh, got a couple of 'em," Smith said, "but the general there said you might be needing my help, so I packed the family over to Fishkill for a visit. Me and my house're at your service, gentlemen." His bow was as ludicrous as a comic actor's.

"Thanks, Smith," Arnold said. "Why don't you see if you can scout us another boat?"

Smith scampered up the bank to the clearing where the horses were tethered.

Wondering if this were a nightmare, hoping to wake if it were, Andre waded out of the water and started after Smith. Arnold grabbed his arm. "Get hold of yourself," he ordered softly but sternly, "you'll give us away otherwise. Here, take this horse."

He shook loose from Arnold's grip but made no answer, afraid he would gabble incoherently, desperately.

He mounted the dappled bay Arnold indicated as the traitor's freezing stare rested on his exposed regimentals. Wrapping his surtout tightly about him, he nudged his animal after Arnold's in a daze. *'Tis but a temporary setback. Long as the* Vulture *waits for me, everything's all right.*

The road lay empty before them in the sunrise, wilted grass and clover down the middle testifying to the country's emptiness as crows cawed deafeningly from either side. Fields that had once yielded bushels of corn now lay desolate and smothered with dusty weeds. Trees bowed nearly to the ground with fruit, hard little balls craving rain. Birds perched in the branches, pecking at apples and pears, peaches and plums. They passed blackened stones and foundations where houses had once stood. The war had not been kind to this area.

They'd traveled barely a mile when a man wearing a tattered Continental coat and a Hessian helmet stepped into the lane before them.

"Halt!" he cried. But on recognizing Arnold, he waved them along.

Andre's stomach fell away. He was behind enemy lines. "My God," he whispered.

Arnold shot him a look. Andre swore there was malicious glee in it.

They reached Smith's house, situated at the summit of a hill over-looking the river. It was a lovelier place than such a buffoon deserved, two stories tall.

Arnold led Andre up the stairs to a bedroom. The door had not even closed behind them when Andre said, "General, this is unconscionable! I'm behind your lines against my stipulation, my intention, and without my knowledge beforehand—my God, you have any idea the danger we're in? They'll take me for a sp—"

"Don't lecture me, Major." Arnold scowled. "I'll get you back to the *Vulture*, but it'll take some time, understand? Meanwhile, you just look sharp and stop acting like a fella with a guilty secret—"

A cannon boomed from below. Both men leaped for the window and through it onto the balcony outside, startling a crow in the large oak to their right. Smoke drifted from a gun on the opposite shore while a second cannon belched a ball.

The *Vulture* rocked under the impact.

"Hey, now," Arnold said, "I gave orders not to fire on any shipping."

Andre glared. Why hadn't Arnold mentioned that before, when the boatmen were refusing to return to the *Vulture*? Andre might even now be boarding ship, not staring, horrified, as the *Vulture* helplessly with-stood Continental cannon. Nor could she easily turn her guns broadside towards the rebels' artillery, thanks to the slack wind and tide. And if she did swing about, returning fire would bring on an engagement, endangering the whole plan. No, the *Vulture*'s only course was to tack south—stranding him behind enemy lines.

This blow, following so closely on the others, left him speechless. He stood beside Arnold on the balcony until despair overcame him. Then he crawled back inside, stumbled to the bed, and collapsed.

A second explosion rocked the room. Again, both men jumped for the window to see a black cloud rising from the rebel guns, now silent, across the river. The *Vulture* would not go quietly.

"Musta got the magazine," Arnold said.

Andre fixed his eyes on the ship. *Please don't leave me.*

Arnold muttered something about breakfast and left the room. Andre slumped against the window, wishing he were religious, that he could pray. He bowed his head in his hands. His brow was slick with sweat. He shrugged out of his surtout, taking strength at sight of his red uniform. *You're a British officer. Courage! We've conquered the world. A few stupid rebels won't defeat me.*

Someone knocked at the door. Hoping it was Smith with his boat, Andre leaped to answer it. Arnold and Smith both stood there, the latter bearing a tray of food. His eyes rounded at sight of Andre's regimentals. Arnold frowned.

Andre ignored both reactions. "You find a boat, Mr. Smith?"

"Naw." Smith set the tray on the room's only table with a nervous giggle. "I can see why you wanna get back though, wearing that color and all." Catching sight of Arnold's face, he hastily added, "'Course, it isn't none of my business."

Andre was suddenly so tired his legs wobbled. "I, ah—"

Arnold interrupted. "They still cannonading?"

The booming from below plainly said they were, but Andre stepped to the window, content to let Arnold explain his uniform, too fatigued to form his own lie. His head was beginning to throb so that he scarcely noticed what he ate or drank when he joined them for breakfast. After only a few bites, he pushed the food from him. Smith too was yawning and before long excused himself.

When they were alone, Andre ran to the window, Arnold beside him. The *Vulture's* sails had filled with wind, and she was tacking south. "Oh, God, no," Andre whispered, leaning his head against the pane.

"Major," Arnold said, "I must get back to headquarters, but here, here's a pass. It'll take you to the *Vulture*."

Andre accepted the paper but read it twice before it made sense. "Permit Mr. John Anderson to pass the guards to the White Plains, or below, if he chooses; he being on public business by my direction. M Genl B Arnold."

He looked up to find Arnold watching with glittering eyes. "No, sir, this isn't acceptable. I'm going on the river, soon as we get another boat. I need a pass that covers a boat."

Arnold started to argue, then nodded. "Fine, Major, I'll write another pass. Now, listen, there's some papers I want to show you before I leave."

Through his despair and exhaustion, Andre tried to focus on the pages Arnold was smoothing over his knee. The man's crisp voice rasped on, as energetic as when they had first met last night. Did nothing tire nor discourage him? There was a return of the garrison and ordnance, notes from a recent Council of War, an estimate of the troops Arnold would add to West Point's defense who would also be captured. The numbers merged and wavered, however Andre blinked and rubbed his eyes. Then Arnold was folding the sheets, pressing them into his hands. "Major, this is important, what I'm telling you. It'll make it easy, capturing the fort. Here, you hide these in your boots. That way you needn't remember anything."

Papers in his boots—that spy they'd taken three or four years ago, that Hale fellow, had hanged for that. He glanced at the sheets and handed them back.

"No, you keep them," Arnold said.

Andre spoke with difficulty through the fog enveloping him. "Thanks...not necessary...I'll memorize them. I'm no spy. Don't want to carry—"

But Arnold was the sort to brook no disagreement, even if Andre had not been too weary to contend. Eventually, he sat on the bed to pull off his boots and slip the papers into his stockings. He felt himself nodding as Arnold wrote another pass and then he was asleep.

He woke with a start, dreaming that rebel marksmen were shooting at him from the *Vulture*. At first he could not remember where he was. The house was quiet, without sound save for birdcalls to give him a clue. He pulled his watch from a pocket. It was not yet noon. Then he was on his feet at the window, peering south, hoping to discern the *Vulture*. But he saw only a wide brown ribbon curling between high banks lined with roots straining towards the water.

The river was still empty ten minutes later when a floorboard creaked outside his door. "Mr. Anderson?" Smith called.

"Come in."

Smith joined him at the window. "Your ship's not back yet, huh? Well, come on up the attic with me. There's another winda up there gives a better view than this. Maybe we'll see her from there."

At another time, Andre would have enjoyed the panorama from the third floor, would have yearned to sketch the broad river, the highlands beyond, the wheeling birds and majestic trees. But he had eyes for the *Vulture* alone and, missing it, turned despondent from the window.

"Guess we'll be going the long way round tonight," Smith said. "No sleep again."

"No, we'll be going down the river. General Arnold gave me a pass—"

Smith chuckled. "Pass won't do you no good. There's warships out there. They'd fire on us. Now if the general'd give you a flag of truce—. Don't know why he didn't order you one from Stony Point."

Andre was still groggy, his mind working slowly. "What do you mean?"

"Well, he coulda sent you south under a flag, probably catch up with your ship 'fore too long. But with only a pass, see, we're obliged to go overland"—Smith shrugged—"which means crossing the river and hills, and the road follers way over to the east there, 'fore it brings you out near British lines."

"But—but—you mean—didn't he order a flag?"

"Not that I know of, no."

Andre staggered back a step, and Smith continued. "Never seen him forget something like that. He's prodigiously smart, the general is, usually thinks of everything. Well, sir, I'm gonna go get me some more sleep, we gonna be running all over Creation tonight."

I'll kill him, Andre thought. God help me, when this thing's over and we're back behind our lines, I'll shoot him myself.

He dozed fitfully the rest of the day, jumping up every quarter-hour to check for the *Vulture*.

"Mr. Anderson?"

Again, he had no idea where he was, could only gape at the man sticking his head in the door, wondering why he called him by the wrong name and why, despite the heat, he wore a beaver hat.

"I knocked, but I guess you didn't hear me. Sound asleep, huh?"

Then it came to him that this was Smith, that he was in the rebels' territory, that perhaps the *Vulture* had returned. Andre leaped from the bed and was halfway to the window when Smith said, "No sign of your ship, and it's getting dark, anyway. General Arnold wanted me to take you to the government's lines, but you need to leave those clothes here, Major." Smith's eyes went to his epaulettes. "Most folks round here aren't as easygoing as me. They take offense at a red coat."

Andre glanced at Smith to catch a sly smile on his face.

Smith proffered a moth-eaten purple rag trimmed with frayed gold lace. "Here, get that uniform off and put this on."

When he hesitated, Smith whispered fiercely, "Look, Major, I don't know who you are and I don't wanna know. But I'm not gonna get myself kilt riding about with the enemy."

"No, I—but see, that makes me a sp—"

"Shhh!" Smith looked about, eyes bulging. "It's not just the walls got ears nowadays, the floors and ceiling does too. Now, you want me to take you to the lines, it's gonna cost you, and part of the price is you get rid of that." He pointed to Andre's uniform.

"What's the rest?" Andre was prepared for a number in the hundreds, was already trying to figure how the sum could be advanced, so he nearly laughed when Smith said, "I reckon a guinea ought to do it. In gold, mind you."

Andre flipped a coin to him. "Here."

Smith nodded. "Obliged. Now take this hat, too." He lifted the beaver from his head. "You can't wear your own."

The sun was setting as they mounted. Andre's guinea had bought him not only Smith's services as guide but his goodwill as well. He chattered from atop his mare, though Andre, tired and shaken, gave little encouragement.

They had ridden less than a mile when a horseman whose uniform consisted of epaulettes missing most of their bullion hailed them. Smith greeted him enthusiastically, oblivious to Andre's discomfort. "Mr. Anderson, 'tis an honor to present Major John Burroughs of the New Jersey line. So tell me, now, Major, when you gonna visit the missus and me?"

Smith and Burroughs laughed and joked before Burroughs cantered off down another lane. Only then did Andre dare breathe.

His relief lasted until they reached King's Ferry. They found the ferry's crew drinking with some rebel officers and troops. Their informality amazed Andre, though it was also a comfort. What had he to fear from such an unprofessional foe?

Smith nearly fell off his horse, so eager was he to join the drinking. He greeted the men as old friends while Andre nudged his mount towards the river, wondering whether Smith knew everyone in the rebel army and trying to hide his impatience.

Finally, they boarded the day's last ferry and crossed. Smith waved farewell to his friends. Then he and Andre were off, riding south for the king's lines.

He was teaching Smith a drinking song from his days as a schoolboy when a handful of men stepped into the road ahead of them. Moonlight gleamed on their muskets, and Andre's heart failed once more.

"Friends!" Smith cried. "We're friends! Don't shoot, for God's sake!"

"Where you going to?" one of them asked, but they lowered their muskets, and Andre, a freethinker, fervently thanked Heaven.

Smith produced Arnold's passes. Andre counted the minutes as the soldiers scrutinized these by lantern light.

The passes turned the men into allies, concerned and garrulous. "You don't wanna keep going, least not tonight," said their leader, a Captain Boyd. "All kinda Cowboys down the road a piece. They'll kill you soon as look at you, take your money and dump your body at a government post, claim you tried to run when they was making you a prisoner." Boyd spat. "Wickedest men in the world. You'd best bed down round here, set out again in the morning."

Andre could not logically protest that. Besides, the Cowboys would not scruple to kill him even if he announced himself a British major. They knew officers carried gold watches and coin.

So it was that they wound up at a farmhouse belonging to a friend of the captain. "Anyone old Boyd sends us, why, you're more'n welcome," the farmer said, clutching their hands. "But I can't feed ye. Cowboys raided me coupla days ago, and we haven't got enough to keep body and soul together. Got a good bed upstairs, though, and it's all yourn."

Andre thought that he would sleep soon as his head hit the pillows, tired as he was. But his strain prevented that. Smith was no help, complaining when Andre insisted on wearing his boots to bed and calculating that they were still more than twenty miles from British lines.

Andre spent a hard night. He woke himself more than once with his mutterings, then lay with heart pounding, wondering what he had said, whether it was incriminating, whether Smith had heard and understood. How had he ever thought subornation a game, a stage with him the admired player, bowing to a house wild with applause?

Finally, he stumbled from bed to use the chamberpot. He snatched his watch from the chair, its military seals tinkling, and peered at it in the moonlight. Nearly five, time enough that he could rouse Smith. Indeed, he should have been up already, if he weren't a lazy colonial, safe and snug in his own country.

But however Andre shook him, Smith burrowed deeper into the pallet, until the major dribbled some water from the washstand on him. Then Smith bounded upward, fists doubled.

"You pissing on me?" he fairly shouted.

"Hush," Andre hissed, though he shrank before those ham-sized fists. "You'll wake the house. Let's be on our way."

Smith muttered mutinously as he wriggled into his coat and breeches and stumbled downstairs behind Andre. He continued complaining while they saddled their horses and led them into the yard.

They rode some miles through the dusty morning before another sentry stopped them. Again, the passes worked their magic, sent them on their way with the man's Godspeed ringing in their ears.

The sun rose, and Smith's complaints gave way to silence, then whistling and tomfoolery as his grouchiness fled. He cried that there was a militiaman right there, through them trees. Andre's heart threatened to burst as he kicked his bay into a gallop. He bent low over the horse's neck, choking as he imagined a rope around his own. He heard hooves behind him, closing on him. He should have taken a faster horse, should have made Arnold give him his best mount, should never have followed the traitor behind enemy lines. Look what it had bought him, dishonor and a gibbet in a strange land, with farmers chasing him, *him*, the king's adjutant general—

He chanced a glimpse behind and saw only Smith pounding away behind him, mouth open and face red with laughter. "Whoa, there, Major. There's no—"

Instantly, Andre's pistol was in his hand. "Shut your damn mouth." He spoke as ferociously as he could, panting from the ride and his fright. "I'm 'Mr. Anderson' to you, you understand? You stupid, ignorant—" He checked himself. He was ranting, falling victim to anger, to fear, when he must keep a clear head. "Come on. Let's go."

They had not covered a mile before horsemen appeared to the south, coming towards them. There was something familiar about the man in the lead, even this far away. As the distance between them narrowed, Andre's hair stood erect. Under a coating of dust was Sam Webb, a rebel officer who had lived in New York as a prisoner of war. Andre had played cards with Webb a few times, had even gone riding with him once. Webb would surely recognize him despite his own layer of disguising grit. His hand dropped to the pistol in his pocket—

"Morning, gentlemen," Webb called.

"Morning," Smith said.

They were abreast now, Webb's eyes studying him. Andre nodded to him and his handful of cavalry; by superhuman effort, he resisted kicking his horse into a gallop. Sweat drenched him, turned the grime on him to mud, as he waited for Webb's shout, the pop of his pistol. Instead, Andre's bay shambled on through the morning.

They rode in silence the next half hour while he recovered and Smith sulked over Andre's calling him stupid. At last, his guide roused himself to announce, "I'm hungry, Anderson. Seems like we been riding all day."

"We've only come seven miles."

"Well, that don't fill my stomach. There's a farmhouse down there to the right. See it? I'm stopping there. You suit yourself." He galloped ahead, leaving Andre to choke in a cloud of dust and wonder why Smith could not show half the industry for getting him back to his lines that he did about stuffing his gut.

At the house, he found Smith cajoling an old woman to feed them.

"Can't give you nothing but mush," she was saying. "Them Cowboys come through here two, three days ago and went and drove off all my cows but one."

"Mush's fine with me." Smith licked his lips. "And with Anderson, too, I wager. We haven't eat since yesterday morning."

Before Andre could demur, the lady was shuffling to her hearth, where a pot hung over a feeble fire. She spooned some of its contents into a bowl and handed it to him. Andre stared at the yellowish mass, still bubbling, and felt nausea, not hunger. He took it to the back stoop where he swallowed a few mouthfuls while Smith and his hostess gossiped over theirs.

At last, they were outside and ready to ride south.

"Think I'm gonna turn back here, Anderson," Smith said when they were out of earshot of the house.

"Turn back?"

"Fishkill's right over yonder. Time for me to go fetch my family. 'Sides, 'tisn't hard from here. You just foller this road two mile or so to the White Plains. You wanna be careful of them Cowboys, though."

"But you can't—I don't know the country here, I—"

"Just foller the road, Mr. Anderson—you *stupid* or something? 'Sides, you got that map the general give you—"

Andre had forgotten about the map, and his spirits lifted as he saw he could do without Smith after all.

"—and you're just a mile or so from the Neutral Ground. You get to the Neutral Ground, and you're safe as can be, 'less you meet up with some Cowboys."

He did not even watch Smith wheel his horse. Instead he flicked his reins and chewed his lip while his bay continued south.

But as the horse carried him safely, however slowly, towards the lines, his anger at Smith ebbed. What had he to fear, really? If a Loyalist patrol stopped him, all the better: they would conduct him to British lines. And Arnold's pass would vanquish a rebel one—if any were in the area, which seemed doubtful given that Cowboys, not Skinners, were prey-ing on the peasantry. He had endured a day and a night behind enemy lines, had outwitted the silly American militia, had met an enemy officer who should have recognized him. And none of these had beaten him.

Withal, beneath the powder caking everything, the day was beautiful, the sun warm but not oppressive, autumn's tang in the air, goldenrod and asters cheering the way and the birdsong a fair symphony. Each step, each minute brought him closer to survival, to success, for God's sake, such as most men only dreamed of. No one would dare whisper that he was too young, that he had not earned his honors, after this. No, they would be too busy bowing and scraping, begging a moment, just a word or two, with—dare he think it?—General Andre. General Sir John Andre.

He had traveled at least four more miles—the lines were further than Smith thought, that was clear—when he came to a bridge. Was that on his map? He pulled it from his saddlebag and studied it. Ah, this must be Tarrytown. He was in the Neutral Ground, had been for the last ten minutes. Exhilaration coursed through him. Safe, he was safe, and his mission a success! He rolled the map, nudged the horse on, and lost himself in daydreams.

He was imagining himself in full regimentals at Ranelagh Gardens, flirting ever so charmingly with Queen Charlotte, when he passed a spreading tulip tree, each enormous leaf brown with dust.

A man as dusty as the leaves stepped from beneath the branches, so close Andre's horse shied.

At first he felt only annoyance at the interruption—Her Majesty had been bestowing a compliment—but indignation replaced that as the man trained a musket on him. Andre wet his lips and gazed down the barrel, gleaming wickedly in the sun.

The gunman put his tongue between his teeth for an ear-splitting whistle. Two more men shambled out from under the tree, muskets at the ready. Still, Andre felt no fear, knowing them for Cowboys. That skinny one there was even wearing the uniform of a Hessian unit, a green coat faced with red, though both colors showed dull through the grime. They could guide him to British lines below, where he would give them a lesson in the king's discipline.

The race was run, his hours behind enemy lines at an end, and so he gaily called, "I hope, gentlemen, you belong to the lower party."

The muskets never wavered, though one of them nodded and stepped forward to grab his reins. "We do."

You're a disgrace to us, then, he thought, eyeing their tatters and the filth crusted on their hands and faces, but he smiled joyously. "So do I."

Still, they did not lower their muskets. The first doubts entered his mind. Then he realized that they would want proof. Dressed in this preposterous purple instead of his uniform, he could hardly be taken for a royal officer. He pulled his gold watch from his pocket and held it up for inspection. Their eyes gleamed. "I'm on important business for His Majesty that can't wait. You must let me pass—"

Green Coat stepped towards him, caught his arm and, with a strength belying his cadaverous frame, twisted the watch from his grasp. "Get down."

"Down?" He sat stupidly, scarcely believing that ragamuffins presumed to dictate to a man the queen had praised.

"You heard Paulding there, you damned Redcoat," another one said. "Get offen that horse now else'n I'll blow you off."

Act, he told himself. Act. He tried for composure as he slowly dismounted, tried to realize they were Skinners, not Cowboys, rebels who would turn him over to Washington instead of escorting him to the *Vulture*.

"My God," he heard himself saying, and laughed, but it was a stage laugh, without conviction. He had ever been a poor actor. "I must do anything to get along. Here, here's my pass from General Arnold." He fished the paper from his pocket and thrust it at the nearest one, who handed it to Paulding. "Thought you lads were with the Brit—the enemy. Country's thick with Cowboys, or so everyone's been say—"

"Probably gots money on him," one of them said as Paulding peered at the pass.

"For damn sure, he's got pistols," said the third one. "Give 'em here, Johnny Bull, and don't try nothing, neither."

Andre handed over his pistols, certain Paulding would react to the pass as had the other sentries, that he would offer an apology and good wishes once he read about Mr. Anderson's public business and M Genl B Arnold. But Paulding continued to study the pass, darting suspicious looks at him, and Andre's nerves, wound tighter than a Hessian's queue, snapped.

"You'd best let me go." He realized as he spoke that he was rambling, that he was too tired and frightened to win this game of wits. "You're detaining the general's business. I'm going to—to—" he paused, desperate, until a name from the map came to him—"to Dobb's Ferry, meeting somebody there and getting informa—"

"Shut your phiz and lemme read." Paulding did not lift his eyes from Arnold's writing.

"Aw, damn his pass!" Shifting his musket to one hand, the man with his pistols stepped forward to grab the purple coat below Andre's throat. He looked as though he had spent years heaving hay on the farm, and he hoisted Andre effortlessly. "You said you's a gov'ment officer. Now where's your money?"

"I—I spent the last of it. I have none about me." The man's huge hand was choking him, reducing Andre's voice to a terrified squeak.

The farmer dropped him in disgust. "You, a gov'ment officer, and no money." He turned to Paulding. "Let's search him."

Andre rubbed his throat, too relieved as air rushed into his lungs to realize what they had said. Then a musket prodded him.

"Get on there, Johnny Bull, into the trees. We'll see whether you gots any money or not."

With a robber clutching either arm and the third keeping a musket in Andre's back, they pulled him into the gloom under the tree and from thence into a thicket. A deck of cards littered the ground, as did the remains of breakfast, while uncorked canteens scented the air with rum.

"Gimme your coat." Paulding held out a hand.

When Andre hesitated, Paulding said, "Tell you what: you don't wanna take off your clothes your own self, I'll help you out. I hear your boys in the navy like that. I haven't never tried it myself, but there's always a first ti—"

"Here." Andre hastily shrugged out of the coat. More of his clothes followed, until he stood shivering in the deep shade, with only his boots and stockings and breeches left him.

"Puny little thing, isn't he?" the farmer asked.

The other two were wadding his clothes between their hands, pulling pockets inside out, ripping seams in their haste. Paulding handed back his linen.

"Told you I had no money," Andre said.

"Huh." The farmer spat. "Wonder what's in them boots."

They were on him, then, the farmer knocking him to the ground and holding him there while the other two pried his boots and stockings off him, despite his kicks and flailing.

"Sure as hell got something here," Paulding cried. "Hooo-whee, lookit this!"

The farmer was sitting on him, pushing his face into the long, scratchy grass, so he could only hear the papers rattling and Paulding's labored breath.

"What's it say?" the third one asked.

"He's a spy, boys," Paulding crowed. "We caught ourselves a spy."

"I am not! I'm no spy," he insisted, but only the earth heard him.

"Let him up, Van Wart. Don't want to crush him or nothing. They's paying pretty dear for spies this week up on the Continental line." Paulding cackled as Van Wart rolled off Andre and hauled him to his feet.

"Now wait a damn minute, Paulding," the third man said. "They're not paying dear for anything on the Continental line. They got no gold to pay with, don't you see. But him being a Redcoat officer," he nodded at Andre, "he's probably got plenty of money somewhere or 'nother. We just need to let him get it. Sorta like you's paying us to let you go."

"Of course, gentlemen," he said with as much dignity as he could muster while standing coatless, hatless, with bare legs and feet. "You can have my horse and bridle, and my watch"—the watch was gone anyway, into Paulding's pocket to judge by his smirk—"and I'll even throw in another hundred guineas. But I'm no spy. I'm on important business, I may have mentioned. I can't be detained—"

"We heard you," Paulding said. "Gitcher boots on. Let's go."

As Andre donned his stockings, the three stood around him, muskets trailing, and speculated about their share of the hundred guineas.

"It isn't enough," Van Wart said, and the third man agreed. "Hell, they'd hang him, we take him to the Continentals. Seems like an officer's life oughter be worth more than a hundred guineas split up three ways."

Andre was dressed and on his feet, brushing the grass and dirt from his clothes. "I agree, gentlemen," he said. "Perhaps I was too niggardly. Let's make it 500 guineas." What did it matter? He would have them arrested when they presented themselves to collect the money.

"Well—"

"All right, then, a thousand. You drive a hard bargain." He attempted a merchant's smile at a deal well done, but the trio only stared.

Greed at the mention of a thousand guineas—a thousand! Who had ever seen or even imagined that much gold?—battled suspicion on Paulding's face. Suspicion won. "Damned Redcoat, he's setting a trap for us. He'll have a hundred of his mates on us when we show for the money. I'm not a-going back to one of their damned prisons, not when I just got out four days ago. Three months there, and I damned near starved to death."

"Look." Andre tried to keep the panic from his voice as he rushed reinforcements to the aid of Paulding's greed. "I'll give you a draft right now, one or two of you stay here with me while the other goes to get the money."

He negotiated and bargained as he had two days before with Arnold, but in the end, they bound his arms behind him, shoved him atop his horse, and set off north, for Continental lines.

With one man leading Andre's bay and another on either side, they travelled the rest of the day, winding up one parched lane and down another, stopping a few times to refresh themselves. Paulding delighted in his new watch so much that he constantly pulled it from his pocket to announce the time. This set Van Wart to wondering why Paulding should have the watch, and not him. For a while, Andre thought they might come to blows over it and give him a chance to escape, but then Paulding settled the matter by agreeing to take less of whatever reward they received.

"'Tis five by the clock," Paulding announced as they turned into the American outpost at North Castle and rode past gawking sentries.

Far from a proper military site, with fortifications and barracks, North Castle consisted of a barn, grist-mill, and proprietor's house, with shutters at the windows and what had once been a garden shriveling near the door. The mill-wheel squeaked in the wind, flattening his horse's ears, rustic as anything van Ruisdael had painted.

Andre's hopes rose when he met the post's commander, a Colonel Jameson. He had known many such officers in the king's army: professional, unimaginative, slavishly obedient to orders. Jameson would appreciate his pass from Arnold, would likely release him instantly. As it was, the colonel ordered his arms freed and his captors from the room.

"They're trash, sir," the colonel said in the South's lilting accent. "I apologize for the treatment they gave you."

"Thank you, sir." Andre smiled. "Good to be among gentlemen again. Now, Colonel, there's my pass from General Arnold, and, as you can understand, this, ah, detention has set me back in my duties quite a bit. If 'tis all right with you, I'd best be on my way."

But the colonel picked up the pass and examined it as though he had not already read and re-read it. "What's your name, sir?"

"John Anderson." He tried to keep the impatience from his voice. "It's right there on the pass, sir."

"Yes, sir, it is." Jameson raised troubled eyes. "But here's the problem. General Arnold's told us to be watching for you, sir. He said you'd be passing through this way on business for him, and we should send you to his headquarters at West Point."

"Yes." He smiled politely, then, when the colonel remained silent, said, "I'm sorry, sir. I don't see the problem."

"The problem, Mr. Anderson, is this. He never said anything about you carrying papers like these." Jameson lifted the sheets one by one to read their headings. "'Artillery Orders' dated the fifth, instant, as well as a return of ordinance. 'Estimate of the Force at West Point and Its

Dependencies, September 1780.' Estimates of how many men to man the works, with remarks. Oh, and here's a copy of a 'State of Matters Laid Before a Council of War by His Excellency General Washington,' held"—Jameson squinted at the paper—"held the sixth of September, 1780. Now, Mr. Anderson, General Arnold made out that you was a merchant, coming up here on regular business. Why would a merchant be carrying papers like this?" The colonel tapped the stained, ripped sheaf. "And then those boys brought you in, they kept saying you're one of the government's officers. Now they're the lower sort, sir. I don't take the word of such as them against a gentleman, but all the same, makes me wonder where they got an idea like that." Jameson paused for an explanation or excuse or a comment of any kind, but Andre could only sit staring.

Finally, Jameson resumed. "See, Mr. Anderson," he said, stacking the papers, carefully aligning their corners, "you're traveling *to* New York, *to* the enemy, with all this. That don't look quite right to me. Fact, none of this does." Jameson quit tinkering with the notes to lean back in his chair, scrutinizing his prisoner, again awaiting an explanation.

Andre prayed for inspiration, but his mind remained blank. Could he say he was a double agent? Would the colonel buy such a story? But the papers were accurate, detailed, gave far more information than a double agent would.

He was too tired, too scared, to think his way out.

"Well, Colonel," he said at last, voice weak, "I can see how it looks, but all I can tell you is that those papers are what General Arnold gave me to deliver in New York. I'm just acting as a messenger for him."

"Uh-huh."

My God, Andre thought, sweat trickling down his back, he's going to order me hanged on the spot, no court-martial or anything, like we did that Hale fellow.

So the colonel's next words were all the more surprising.

"Tell you what I'm gonna do, Mr. Anderson." The colonel selected a quill from his inkwell and reached for a piece of foolscap. "I'm gonna send you on to General Arnold, accordin' to orders, but you'll go under guard, sir, as a prisoner, until this matter's cleared up."

To Arnold? Andre would have snickered at the colonel's stupidity had he not owed his life to it. He barely restrained himself from gushing his thanks, from saying how unnecessary a guard was, that he would gladly fly to Arnold on his own so they could both escape down the Hudson. This time he would not allow Arnold to fob him off on a fool. This time he would tie Arnold's fate to his.

The quill scratched interminably across the paper. Finally, the colonel raised his head. "I'm writing General Arnold about all this, too, so he can get to the bottom of whatever game it is you're playing."

"That's fine, sir. I understand. I'd probably do the same in your shoes." He tried to sound aggrieved despite his overwhelming relief.

Then the colonel shattered that relief.

"These papers, though—" Jameson glanced over them again, shaking his head. "These I'm sending to General Washington."

Fortunately, the colonel was inexperienced enough to be studying the notes, not Andre's face, when he fired that cannonball, or he would have seen his captive's horror. Several moments passed before Andre realized there was still a chance, that he might reach Arnold before the packet reached Washington. And once it did, Washington must investigate the contents, and immediately, too, not set them aside for a more convenient time, or hand them to an aide. Then he must not only absorb but recover from the unthinkable: the heroic, brilliant, enthusiastic General Benedict Arnold had turned traitor. He must issue orders through couriers who then had miles to gallop before relaying his commands... Yes, there was more than a chance! It was probable that Andre, even under guard, would attain West Point long before the hapless Washington could react.

The horror was gone, replaced with Andre's polite but pained smile, by the time Jameson had finished scrawling his explanation and sealed it into a packet with the papers.

Then the colonel was on his feet. "You carrying any weapons, Mr. Anderson?"

"Not any more, sir. You can ask those three who brought me here. They rifled me pretty thoroughly looking for money."

"All right, then. Whitney!"

An aide appeared in the doorway. "Yes, sir?"

"Tell Lieutenant Allen to get a detachment together for taking a prisoner to General Arnold up at the Point."

The horse Andre rode this time was a weary nag without a gallop left her could he have managed to slip his guards. They bound his arms

behind him again, with one of the four militiamen surrounding him
holding his reins. Their progress was maddeningly slow, given the race
he alone knew was being run. Nevertheless, his spirits lightened with
every mile until he could enjoy the dusk of the late summer evening.
Crickets chirped and lightning bugs flashed while rabbits bounded
through the dust at their approach. So close! He had been so close to
disaster, had dangled over its yawning pit. But now—! His only worry, a
slight one, was that the colonel would realize his error and send someone
after them with different orders.

Night closed around them, the guards' banter lulling their exhausted
prisoner. The day had been long and full of strain. And it was not yet at
an end: Andre had heard the men complain a moment before that ten
miles remained to West Point, to escape and safety. Two more hours of
riding when he was ready to doze off in the saddle—

Andre jerked awake. They had come to a halt while hooves galloped
up from behind. He turned as much as his restraints allowed to see a
horseman with a torch bearing down on them. "You Lieutenant Allen?"
the man shouted into the night. "A-going to West Point?"

"Ah-yuh."

Andre's stomach somersaulted as the newcomer reined in, his torch
throwing monstrous shadows. He handed Allen a packet and said, "Your
orders' countermanded. Colonel says come on back instead."

Andre almost cried aloud, but one of the militia did it for him. "Aw,
hell, we've already rode better'n half the way."

Allen, busy with the packet's seal, made no answer, but the messenger said mildly, "Colonel says bring the prisoner back."

"Like hell we will!" the same man bawled. "We been riding all night.
We only got another coupla hours to the Point—"

Allen glanced up from the note inside the packet. "He's right. Colonel
says there's a party of the enemy above, Cowboys most likely, I'd wager,
and he don't want Anderson taken or getting away." He sighed. "Come
on. It's gonna be morning afore we get there."

"Aw, Lieutenant, now wait a minute—"

"Shut your phiz, Hopping," Allen said, "or you get to turn around
and ride back to West Point with me tomorrow. Colonel says I'm to
continue on and deliver his packet to General Arnold—"

No! Andre's heart stopped. Arnold would run while he—he—

"—and I'm s'posed to pick a man to go with me. That'll be you, Hopping, you keep it up."

"Aw, hell, damned army never knows what it's doing." Hopping spat. "Wish I'd'a known when I 'listed I'd be riding around creation all night. God damn it."

"Quit your cussing," Allen said.

"Aw, you'd cuss too, you had the piles I got, and damned army keeps you in the saddle all night. Hey, boys, now look here. No reason for us to lose sleep just 'cause the colonel can't make up his mind. I say we keep on our way to West Point, fight them damned Cowboys, we come across any of 'em."

"Hopping, the colonel's give us an order—" Allen began.

"The hell with his order!" Hopping shouted, and the others joined him.

Through his despair, Andre listened in shock as they cursed the colonel and lieutenant and the army in general before resuming their argument over the order. He could scarcely believe his ears. Never in his years with His Majesty's forces had he heard any command debated. Underlings obeyed, promptly and without question. But these ignorant farmers and shopkeepers dared call themselves soldiers when so basic a thing as deference eluded them. Arnold's words about the impossibility of controlling Yankees came back to him.

The messenger announced one last time that they were to retrace their route and then disappeared down the road. As the guards continued quarreling with the lieutenant, Andre roused himself. Salvation lay in their impertinence.

When the last man finished bewailing his fate, Andre said, "Surely, Lieutenant, it can't hurt to go to West Point just for tonight. We can start back in the morning." The lieutenant hesitated, and he added, "After all, there's an entire fort there. I can't very well escape, can I? We're all tired. The journey won't seem nearly as onerous in the morning."

The lieutenant's eyes moved from one guard to the next. When he spoke, it was in a quietly firm voice. "We're a-going back. Any man wants to dispute that can do it at a court-martial. Now let's go."

"Aw, hell," Hopping said. But he wheeled his horse to follow the lieutenant...

"They took me back to North Castle, where your betrothed awaited me, Miss Shippen." Andre bowed, slightly, teasingly. I glanced away lest he see the tears suddenly film my eyes. "And that is how you find me here." He tossed off a smile to match the bow, but last I saw of him as the guards shut the door behind me, he was staring out the window, hands in pockets, shoulders slumped.

Then dawned the morning of Andre's execution, with all the attempts to save him in vain and sadness filling the air.

It was awful, more for me than anyone but Andre, I'd wager. For I was seeing not only this hanging but Nathan's too, remembering the agony, feeling the dread.

It had been hot then, but this morning was cool, with honeysuckle strong in the air. It lined the roads along there, where the tangle of wild grapevines would let it. There's a tremendous crowd, not just the handful that witnessed Nathan's death, for yesterday's General Orders commanded that a battalion of eighty files from each wing attend the execution. That meant these, like that handful four years ago, was mostly soldiers. Seemed like many hundreds, if not thousands, covered the hills clear over to Hudson's River. The roar that comes from any large crowd rose from this one, with dogs barking and commands shouted and men talking, coughing, laughing nervously while horses neighed and stomped.

I got there late, just as they were opening the door of Mabie's Tavern. The sun was high overhead, and a captain's escort stood at attention. Andre stepped out and paused to give a small smile. Or maybe 'twas so we could admire him, for the purple coat was gone, and he was most elegantly dressed in his regimentals. His servant had fetched a new set from New York, all aglitter with braid and buttons. They'd barbered him, too, and his hat sat jaunty on his head. After a moment, he linked arms with the guards on either side and pulled them down the steps, as quick and lively as though no execution were taking place. Only his pallor showed he's fearful.

Mounted officers led the way, with the black coffin coming next on a baggage-wagon. More officers, this time afoot, followed. In the rear come Andre and his guards. Ben walked behind, sorrowful as I'd seen him. The drummers and fifers struck up the "Dead March" soon as Andre appeared, and he turned halfway round to say to Ben as they passed me, "I am very much surprised to find your troops under such good discipline, and your music is excellent." His voice, high and with nary a quiver, carried clear. Andre's a freethinker, but still, 'twas a marvel that any man could speak so frivolous walking to his death.

We turned left from Mabie's, up roads sweet with honeysuckle and wild grapes. Andre walked along with as much ease and cheerfulness as if he'd been going to an assembly room—until he caught sight of the gallows atop a hill. Then he stopped dead. There's too many guards around him for me to see this, but I heard it from Ben that night while the bullfrogs croaked. We sat before the fire at the tavern, across the hall from the room where Andre had smiled and bantered and charmed the world these last days, with Ben getting drunk on the peach brandy Mabie's is famous for.

"When he saw the rope dangling there, he turned pale." Ben swigged more brandy. "He'd been easy and, I guess, not happy, but you know, pleasant, like he hadn't a care to trouble him. He'd been bowing to some of the gentleman along the way that he knew, some of the officers that sat on his court-martial. But when we get in sight of the gallows, I heard him swallow pretty hard, and he says, 'I am disappointed. I expected my request would have been granted.' You know he—he's never admitted to being a spy, and he didn't want to die like one."

I nodded.

"He told me, 'I am reconciled to my death, but I detest the mode.' Still, he walked the rest of the way with his head up. His conduct was unparalleled on the occasion. Never seen anyone march so cheerfully to his—the place of execution. I cannot say enough of his fortitude." He took another long pull of brandy.

When they reached the hill, I watched the guard line up three deep around the gallows, with their backs towards it and bayonets fixed. I peered between them as Andre called various men to him, speaking with them as he took their hands. I saw Ben go to him, his fair head bent close to Andre's dark one and Andre's red-clad arm around Ben's waist. He clapped Ben's shoulder once, twice, and then my intended stumbled away, head bowed and a hand to his eyes.

Now was the time for a preacher to say a psalm. The government didn't give Nathan a chaplain or even a Bible, but what was worse was that Andre didn't want either, and that seemed to baffle the attending officers. They buzzed about until finally Colonel Scammell took things in hand and read the sentence.

He gulped a few times and even paused to wipe his eyes. And he wasn't alone. All the spectators seemed to be overwhelmed, and many were suffused in tears. I remembered how the British provost had gulped, too—rum from his flask as he swung Nathan off while only a few of us cried for him.

When the colonel finished reading, he ordered Andre to mount the cart under the gallows. 'Twas a step over to the coffin, and then the condemned was atop that, too, hands on hips, pacing, eyeing the pole above with its rope. He halted, doffed his hat, and laid it at his feet. We saw a long and beautiful head of hair, which, agreeable to the fashion, was wound with a black ribbon and hung down his back.

A hangman, face smeared with tallow and soot, clambered onto the cart. He pulled the rope down to Andre's head, meaning to slide it over his face, but Andre snatched it from him and did it himself, even tightening the knot. I wasn't the only one to gasp. Then Andre drew two silk handkerchiefs from his pocket. He give one to the hangman for his wrists, then tied the other around his own eyes with perfect firmness, which melted the hearts and moistened the cheeks of most everybody.

"Major Andre," the colonel said (they had never once called Nathan "Captain" but only "rebel" and "Yankee"), "speak now, sir, if you please, for the time draws close."

We hushed as always at such occasions and crowded nigh to hear, as we had for Nathan. But this time we weren't rewarded with glorious words that would live forever, that would give us somewhat to think on around the hearth as we strived to live up to them. Instead, we got the self-congratulations of a freethinker and royal officer.

"Gentlemen," he called, jaunty-like, "I have nothing more to say but this: you all bear me witness that I meet my fate as a brave man."

Then they lashed the horses, the cart jerked away, and the charming Adjutant General of the British Army in North America danced in his bright uniform.

Chapter Twenty-three

It was late the next morning before Ben and I met down by the creek that waters the DeWindt property General Washington had borrowed as headquarters. Ben's eyes were bloodshot from the brandy he'd drunk last night, and puffy, too, as if he'd sobbed for Andre after we'd parted.

'Twas that set me off, made me mention Nathan, and never mind how Ben was hurting. "You think Andre's as—as courageous as Nathan, don't you?"

He stared into the stream for a long moment, then sighed. "This is the oddest courtship, Clem. All we do is talk about Nathan. I wonder if you care for me at all. Seems like he's the one you love, not me."

My breath left me, as it will anyone when the truth's spoke. Yes, I thought, 'tis Nathan, and only Nathan, I love, and I always will.

I started to tell him he was right, but I couldn't bear to hurt him more. Besides, without Ben, I was certain to live the rest of my life alone.

But 'twas he who spoke the words in my mind. "Clem." He said it slow, not meeting my eyes. "Been doing a lot of thinking. Nathan was my friend and all, but I'm not sharing my wife with him."

I waited, but he was too fine a gentleman to continue, only stared miserably at the creek.

Finally, I said, "Ben, we aren't—I should never have promised to marry you."

He started to protest, but behind him, I saw King Alex approaching. I put a finger to my lips.

Hamilton reached us to say, "His Excellency requests a word with you two."

"With both of us?" We exchanged a look.

"That's what he said."

We followed him back to the general's office.

"Colonel." As we entered, General Washington did not turn from his post at the window. "Wait outside, if you please. Make sure no one comes near the door."

'Twas obvious King Alex didn't care for drawing guard duty like any sergeant. But I shivered. I'd thought 'twas a social visit when His Excellency asked to see us together. Yet such privacy implied a military purpose, mayhap intelligencing.

The door closed behind Hamilton, and the general bowed to us. "Please, sit down. You attended the hanging?"

"He was a brave man, sir." Ben's voice trembled.

"And amiable." His Excellency sighed. "An accomplished man and gallant officer."

"No more so than Nathan." I blurted, and they looked at me.

"That's right," Washington said. "You knew Captain Hale."

Tears clogged my throat until Ben answered for me.

"She saw him hang, sir. It made quite an impression on her."

His Excellency nodded. "It's been my fortune to know many worthy young men in this war—or maybe it's been my curse, to have seen so many die. But Captain Hale—" His voice sank. "A truly great loss." He turned to the window again, and Ben lent me his handkerchief.

"But you're wondering why I asked to see you." Washington was at his desk now, unrolling a map. "The wrong man hanged yesterday, I'm sure you agree. Arnold caused this mess, and Arnold should have answered for it, not Major Andre."

"I thought as much myself, sir," Ben murmured, full of grief. "When I saw him swinging under the gibbet, it seemed for a time as if I could not support it."

Ben was coming nigh those criticizing Washington for hanging Andre, and ice entered the grey eyes. Yet Washington's next words didn't scold Ben as I expected. Instead, they were a child's fretful cry, demanding something it cannot have, though His Excellency's measured tones spoke them.

"I want Arnold, sir. I want to hang him."

Ben was as shocked as me. "But—but, Excellency," he managed at last, "the, ah, government, sir, he's with them somewhere, with Sir Henry Clinton."

"Yes, Major, that's why I asked for both of you." Washington spoke serene as though we were discussing the weather, uncommonly warm this day. "I thought, Miss Shippen, if we may presume upon you yet again, that if we can get you across the lines and into Arnold's family, you'll be a great help in our plan to seize him."

"Seize him." Ben's echo was faint.

"Yes, Major, I want him brought back, court-martialled, and executed. I'll knot the rope myself." His Excellency uttered those violent words so calm, I reckoned his mind had finally snapped. "He's a traitor, sir, hackneyed in villainy, lost to all sense of honor. He used the country contemptuously, it's more than I can compass, as though all our starving and freezing and—and wounds and suffering meant nothing. Yet I defended him, sir, when the Congress passed him over, or they refused to pay his accounts, I took it as jealousy of a brilliant man, and I defended him. But he would have delivered me too, sir. He would have seen me hang." He wasn't calm now but quivering with a rage such as I'd never known, though Ben told me later he'd seen him that angry once before, back the week Nathan died, when the Redcoats landed on York Island and our troops fled before them.

Hands atremble, Washington shuffled some papers on his desk. Finally, with his usual serenity, he said, "Could Arnold have been suspended on the gibbet erected for Andre, not a tear or a sigh would have been produced, but exultation and joy, sir, would have been visible on every countenance. So I shan't rest till he's in our power. Lee and I've been talking about it, Harry Lee with the Light Horse, you remember him, Major?"

Ben nodded, too dazed to speak.

"Been thinking on it the last week, trying to figure some way of getting Arnold back so we could hang him instead of Andre. But the trial went so quick, there wasn't time to get our man into New York, let alone find Arnold and bring him back here, so—"

"Your pardon, Excellency." Ben held up a hand. "You—I don't understand, you sent Lee into New York after Arnold?"

"Lee? No, Major, I've just talked with him about it, planning it, you see, and we've come up with something, workable, I think. We need you in on it, both of you. But 'tis no ordinary thing I ask, and dangerous, too, so if you refuse me—"

"I'll do it, Excellency."

The grey gaze swung to me.

"Arnold's spit on the memory of Captain Hale," I said, "and every man who's died at their hands. But, General, 'tis his wife, really, put him up to it."

"Your cousin?" Washington's brows climbed his forehead. "You mean Mrs. Arnold?"

"She's guiltier than he is. I'd wager my last pound on it."

"Clem, let it go," Ben whispered.

Washington shook his head. "But she's a—a lady, so very sweet and—and lovely"—he blushed—"I can't believe—"

"No one ever believes it, sir, don't you see? That's what she's counting on."

Washington studied me.

"Please, sir," I said.

"You'd need to prove it, Miss Shippen. These are serious charges. Still, it's Arnold I want now. Is that clear?" He looked from me to Ben. "And I want him alive. No circumstance whatever shall obtain my consent to his being put to death."

I could see Ben's staggered anew at that one. "Make it easier, sir," he finally said, "if we could just put a ball through him and get out of there. Cleaner, too."

I misdoubted Ben was right. No clean nor easy way of killing Benedict Arnold, however you went to do it. He'd fight death vigorous as he'd fought the Redcoats. Fight and probably win.

Didn't matter, though, for Washington was saying, "No. The idea which would accompany such an event would be that ruffians had been hired to assassinate him. My aim is to make a public example of him."

We passed the next hour with the general telling us what plans he'd laid with that Virginian he'd mentioned, Light Horse Harry Lee. Major Lee was gone back to his troops in New Jersey to find a strong man of daring and intelligence who'd actually seize Arnold. His Excellency asked Ben which agents in New York were best suited to help, if help was needed; did he think we could tap Culper Junior? Meanwhile, one of those intelligencers had done what I couldn't during my chat with Andre and confirmed Arnold's presence there in the City; he wasn't yet commanding in the field with his new army. Strange, given how superior his soldiering was to the Redcoats', that they hadn't immediately sent him against us, especially when they'd gone to such trouble to suborn him. But... Washington shrugged. So they'd leave the details of abducting Arnold to me, under a Mr. Baldwin from Newark who'd be our contact.

"You'll be there, Miss Shippen, on the scene," His Excellency said. "Lee says that's crucial, having someone there in the house with Arnold, and I agree. You'll know better than anyone what to do, and how. Withal, you're a lady of sense and courage. I'll speak to Baldwin, tell him Lee's man will report directly to you. Meantime, if you make your way to Arnold's home and offer your services as cook, you think he'll take you in again?"

"I'm sure he will, sir, if only because I might bring news of his wife."

Washington nodded, quick-like, and brushed some lint from the map, perhaps resisting visions of the naked Peggy. "You'll leave tomorrow, Miss Shippen?"

"Yes, sir."

"Good." He handed me a pass. "Major Tallmadge, you stand ready in case you're needed. Thank you both."

We left His Excellency at the window again, fists clenched.

Ben and I passed a bad afternoon, with him trying to persuade me not to break our betrothal, and me insisting we could do aught else, and our upcoming goodbye, the final one this time, hanging over it all. Ben was ever a gentleman, and never more so than now. He tried to make me see the sense that would have cost him the rest of his life if I had, and I came pretty near to loving him then.

There weren't many men would overlook my homeliness, and withal, they usually cared more about who a girl's father was and how big a fortune he had than they did the girl herself. Ben didn't mention either one, but I was thinking them all the same.

His last appeal, and an eloquent one, too, came as I finished tying my bundle. I wasn't like anyone he'd ever known, he said, a treasure, the apple of his eye and he couldn't let me slip away, why, look what I was doing now, a mission no other girl would undertake, nor very few men, neither.

I hoisted my bundle and faced him. "Thank you," I said softly.

He looked into my eyes, kissed my brow, and was gone.

Next morning, I set off for New York City. Should have been excited about my mission, but instead, 'twas Benjamin occupied me and kept me tearful.

Once through our lines, I threw His Excellency's pass into the trees, not wanting to have it about me when I reached the government's pickets. Between thoughts of Ben, I rehearsed my story so that when I reached my first Redcoats, it flowed full and convincing and took me to a sergeant. He glanced at me and asked, "What's your business?"

I could see he's the sort thinks speaking with a plain woman a waste of time. "I'm trying to find General Arnold."

"The traitor? Gor! Whatever for?"

"I was his cook at West Point. I'd like my old post back."

"But he's with us now."

"Good. Maybe you'll pay him better than the rebels. And in gold, too, I'm tired of those Continental rags they call money."

"You just come from West Point, did you?"

"Oh, within the last week." I shrugged. "I stopped to see my sister in White Plains—"

"Wait here a minute."

He returned with an ensign who would escort me to Clinton's headquarters. And so, for the first time in three years, I saw the city of my birth, where the only father I knew had died, near which my mother and I kept tavern and Nathan Hale hanged.

'Twas no longer a city, really, just a set of filthy streets, as ruined from the government's occupation as Philadelphia had been. No one had rebuilt what burned in the Great Fire when Nathan died and another two years later, for the army would only seize them for quarters. Instead, folks stretched sailcloth over blackened foundations as crude tents. Others had scrounged brick and stone to build hovels.

Weren't any trees left, either, none of the ornamental apples and cherries that once swayed along Broadway, no elms, locust, or beech. Where limbs and leaves used to dance in the wind, now only ragged stumps were left, or maybe just a hole filled with roots and mud and trash. What houses still stood had nary a fence or outbuilding. New York's wood hadn't fared any better than Philadelphia's.

We turned onto Broadway, then, and came to Clinton's headquarters in what had been Mr. Kennedy's mansion. There I saw my first shutters in a long time. They were painted green and still hanging only because of the sentries posted there.

I'd never met Sir Henry Clinton, had only glimpsed him from a distance at the Meschianza, so his petulance as he sat behind a desk in one of the high-ceilinged parlors surprised me. Here was none of the amiability that softened Washington's authority.

"So," he said, "you're looking for General Arnold—" His face clouded. "Good God, what a *coup manqué!*"

I gave him my cook's story, though of course 'twas the Continentals' opinion of Arnold's treason that interested him. So I told him what he wanted to hear: that many were ready to follow Arnold's example, trade their tatters for His Majesty's smart uniform, for they'd rather beat the French out of America than fight against British soldiers, our own flesh and blood, really. "'Course," I concluded, "I've not much of a head for politics, sir, but I must say, I thought he did the right thing, coming home to you."

This pleased him, and he nodded. "I'll have one of my lads take you to General Arnold's headquarters. 'Tisn't far, just next door."

It was a substantial house of grey stone with an imposing entry. Clinton's aide led me through the crowd milling before it and banged the door. A dog within set to barking as Arnold himself answered.

"Clem!" He was surprised, for sure, but also happy. "Clem, it's good of you to come. You show more loyalty than any of my family, more than anyone but Peggy, God bless her. How is she? When'd you last see her?"

He drew me inside. The dog, a large brown animal missing fur here and there, left off barking to sniff my skirts. The house around us sagged in disarray.

"Perhaps, sir," I said, offering my hand to the dog for to smell, "I should act as housekeeper."

He laughed. "Still a saucy one, aren't you? It's the war, Clem. All the good servants are gone."

"This your dog?"

"He was here with the house, poor boy. Hungry and sick when I got him, but I've been feeding him, putting salve on his sores, and he's healing, aren't you, fella?" The dog cast Arnold a glance more loving than Peggy ever did and padded over to him. Arnold sank into a chair there in the hall and petted him. "Name's Flash. Friendly as a sailor's—ah, friendly, but not much of a watchdog."

Thank God.

"Now tell me about Peggy."

"She's in Philadelphia, sir. Went there with Major Franks as escort."

"Yes, yes, I know. But have you heard anything else?"

"No-o-o-o, why would I?"

"Well, I thought with Andre there at the Point and all...they were close, you know, before she and I met, old friends...I thought, with his trouble and everything, she'd have written him..."

"No, sir," I said, sorry for a man so obsessed with a woman he'd welcome any word from her, even one meant for her lover.

"Well, still, 'tis good to see you. Now, I'm having a supper tomorrow night for some of the officers, nothing elaborate, just a collation of meats—"

"Then my post's available?"

"Clem, we don't stand on formality, you and I."

I'd been there nigh a week, days filled with thoughts of Ben and nights with dreams of Nathan, when Flash began barking one afternoon. He finally quieted, and I heard Arnold calling me.

I ran from the buttery, wiping my hands on my apron. Arnold stood in the hall beside a man who towered over him, Flash jumping around them in circles.

"Yes, sir?"

"Clem, lay another place for supper. Sergeant-Major John Champe is joining me." Arnold clapped the man on his beefy shoulder. "He's come over from the Patri—ah, the rebels. Just the beginning of a whole exodus, I'd wager."

"Were you at West Point, sir?" I asked Champe.

"No, ma'am, of late I was over in New Jersey, with Light Horse Harry's troop."

Hope rose strong within me. Young, maybe twenty-three or twenty-four, full of bone and muscle, Champe could easily overpower Arnold. And he'd have the surprise of it working for him, too.

"Come on to supper, son, so's you and I can talk particulars." Arnold slapped his shoulder again.

Serving the courses, I heard Champe demur about joining Arnold's American Legion. He was sick of war, he protested, wanted only to retire to some nice little farm somewhere. "Besides," Champe said as I set a tipsy pudding before them, "I daren't be captured. They'd hang me sure, for desertion."

By the time Flash fell asleep on the hearth, Champe had not only joined Arnold's regiment, he was earnestly reciting "intelligence" that had been known for the last week. Arnold soon called me to fetch Champe's hat and cloak.

"You won't regret signing up, son," Arnold said as I handed Champe his surtout. "We'll likely see some vigorous action."

"Hope so, sir." Champe turned to me to take his hat, or so I thought. Instead, he shuffled his feet and muttered, "Might I call on you, ma'am? That is, unless you got a husband or a—a regular fellow."

I bit my lip with longing for Ben.

Arnold's eyes widened with goodwill. He should have excused himself and left us alone, which is what Champe was angling for, but instead he stood awaiting my words eager as Champe seemed to be.

"I'd be honored, sir." I gave him my hand for to kiss and blushed.

Then Champe was gone, and I scampered for the kitchen. I was still blushing when I heard Arnold limp for the garden and the hall clock strike midnight.

During his next visits, Champe kept trying to catch me alone, but Arnold chaperoned us close as though I was his daughter born. He was too much a romantic, as interested in affairs of the heart as any woman, to ignore some under his own roof.

And even if he'd gone out for an afternoon, Peggy was flitting about. She'd arrived along with the first snow, infant son in arms. You'd have thought 'twas by her own will to hear her tell it, and not because folks down to Philadelphia exiled her for marrying a traitor. No matter: her husband was too happy she'd come to worry over why.

But at last Champe struck it right and found me home by myself.

I poured us tea in the side parlor. Champe warmed his hands around his dish.

"You come up with any sort of plan for the kidnapping yet?" he asked. "I'd just as lief do it at night, under cover of darkness, if it's all right with you."

"Yes, I think that would be best. And um, well, he visits the, ah, garden around midnight every night, regular as clockwork."

"'Tis a large garden out back there, runs all the way down to those black rocks on the Hudson's shore, don't it?"

"Whole thing's fenced, too." I stirred sugar into my tea. "I thought we'd take him then."

Champe sat back, jaw agape, to stare at me. "You mean while he—he's pissing?"

I turned as red as when Champe asked could he call on me. "I was thinking, you know, he'd be, um, occupied—"

Champe rubbed his lip. "Aye. And not expecting anything right then. Fence'll hide us from anyone ashore, and anyone out on the river's not likely to see, either, what with the dark and the yard being so big and all." He grinned. "Miss Shippen, that's brilliant."

"Maybe you can slip out there the day before and loosen a couple of palings in the fence. That way, once you truss him, you can just push him through the fence and be in the alley—won't need to take him out the front of the house and risk someone seeing."

"Brilliant!" he repeated. Then he added with a sigh, "I'll run it past Baldwin." Mr. Baldwin was proving difficult, refusing to authorize any of the plans we'd come up with so far. "I'll tell the boys that're gonna help carry him away to stand ready, case we get approval this time. He won't be in any condition to fight us off, anyway, if he's been out drinking with his Redcoat friends that night."

I snorted. "He has no friends, their side or ours. They blame him for Andre's death."

It took three more weeks for Champe to alert his agents, find a boat that would row Arnold and us across Hudson's River to New Jersey, and a place to hide it until we needed it. Meantime, I watched and waited, made sure Arnold's orders didn't change, nor that he didn't grow suspicious.

But I also listened to his stories. We relived the war, and the Radicals' reign, too. Arnold was right: compared to the Radicals, George III was a piker when it come to thirsting after power. What would happen if the Continentals won? Would we finally live free, or only bow to worse masters? More and more I understood General Arnold's reasoning, and I sympathized, too. More and more I wished myself anywhere but here in his house, spying on him and plotting against a hero who was trying to save us from tyrants worse than London's.

At long last, Champe brought word that Mr. Baldwin had approved our scheme and grinned in tired triumph. But I had no answering smile. That night I cried myself to sleep.

Now Arnold and I sit before his fire on our last evening together. By midnight tomorrow, one of us will be wearing chains, him if we're successful, me if we're not.

A log settles on the hearth, spraying sparks, and Arnold says, "Clem, you mind fetching me some pen and paper and ink? Thought I'd try my hand at poetry, a poem, you know, for Peggy."

Peggy, I think as I collect the things, it all comes back to Peggy, so beautiful, so wicked. And I wonder, if I were given a choice, if I could be beautiful but must be wicked too, so that I would destroy the man who loved me better than life and make his name a curse—would I choose to stay ugly? Or would I want the love such beauty bought, the power it gave, that I could commit treason, get a man hanged, and land on my feet?

Arnold's reached the end of his stories. He spends the evening hunched over his paper, grinning like a schoolboy writing his sweetheart. I marvel at such blindness as I take up the pocketbook. I check the legend. "M Genl B Arnold, Hero of the Ti, Quebec, Danb'y, Saratoga," it reads, and this time, though the letters are graceless, they're all there. 'Twill take this whole evening, and more work tomorrow, afore it's finished, and I wonder as I stitch when I can present it to him. When he's bound and gagged in the boat? Awaiting trial? On the way to the gibbet?

I wake the next morning with my insides already quivering, though I lie for a moment without remembering why. Then I leap from bed and rush to the kitchen.

The morning vanishes in a blur. I try to act normal but fail so bad that Arnold eyes me as I set his tea before him.

"Not having trouble with Champe, are you, Clem?"

"No, sir, thank you, sir." I hurry back to the kitchen. Today of all days, I cannot abide his kindness.

Arnold passes the morning in his office. That's where I'd planned to spend it, were I alone in the house. I've not yet found the evidence that'll convict Peggy, and this is my last chance to search.

Instead, I stir up bread and a pie and try to still my nerves.

Dinner is a quiet affair, marred only by a messenger from General Clinton. Then, afterwards, as I take my notes on the war to the desk in the side parlor, Arnold comes thumping downstairs with Peggy on his arm and Flash barking behind.

"We're going next door, Clem," Arnold says. "That message from Sir Harry asked us to call this evening. Shouldn't be too long."

"You keep an ear out for Neddy, will you, Clem?" Peggy shines her smile at me. "I already put him down. He'll probably sleep through. He didn't get much of a nap this afternoon."

I wait half an hour after they leave, one moment rejoicing at this chance to search, the next worried that they won't be back before Champe and his boys get here. Then I take the crusie lamp and make for the stairs. The clock chimes eight. Just four hours until the kidnapping. My stomach's so knotted I'm nauseated. Arnold betrayed us, he deserves to hang, yet somehow all I can think on are his kindnesses to me, our talks by the fire, his hatred of tyranny and the Radicals.

'Tis Peggy who led him into his evil, and Peggy who ought to suffer. I unlock his office with fierce resolve, then march to the shelf where I left off last time. Surely one of these letters will be from her. Surely she'll have condemned herself out of her own mouth.

I thumb through the first stack, holding them towards the lamp. Letter from Dr. Warren and the Committee of Safety...from his sister Hannah...his parents when he was a schoolboy...General Montgomery in Montreal...a Daniel Watkins...

The next one's folded, so that the first thing I see is Arnold's endorsement on the back: "Rec'd May 28 1756 Norwich Town." I smooth the sheet and look for the signature.

There isn't none. But I instantly know who wrote it from the crooked scrawl.

I nearly drop the paper. Why would my mother write Benedict Arnold?

Then I understand, even before I scan the lines. My stomach clenches tighter. "Dear God," I breathe, "no, please, no."

Yet there 'tis, in faded black and white.

"Benedic, Yu knotiss i dont say Dere acuz Yur not dere to Get me in This and leve me. if its a Boye he wont be Name benedic thats shure. i hope yu cume to a Bad End."

I sit dumfounded until the crusie lamp burns the last of its grease, flares, and dies. An hour gone, and I can't say where.

When the front door opens, the letters are put away, the office is locked, and I'm back at the fire, cursing myself for a fool. All these months, when I looked for my father in every man, merchant, mechanic, or soldier, I never thought of the officer right under my nose. The one who took such interest in me, who was always so kind—

Over Flash's barking, I hear Peggy's voice.

"—tired, Benny. I'm going upstairs. 'Tis nigh eleven, for pity's sake."

"But this is the last we'll see of each other for a while. You can sleep later, plenty of time then."

Peggy waves to me as she passes. I nigh laugh to think I'm her step-daughter and not a cousin after all.

But that's hysteria, and I push my words down. In the doorway appears General Benedict Arnold, hero of the assaults on Ticonderoga and Quebec, genius of Valcour Island, Danbury's avenger, victor at Saratoga, archenemy of tyrants everywhere, West Point's traitor, and my father.

"Clem," he says with his usual heartiness, "what's the matter? You look all excited. Those cheeks of yours go any redder, they'll catch fire."

I expect him to limp to his chair, but he only stands there.

"Sir." I wet my lips. "I—I—there's something, ah, must tell you, um, I—I, uh—"

He pulls off his gloves. "Come, Clem, what is it? We don't have much time."

"We—we don't?"

"No. Now what do you want to tell me?"

I gape. 'Tis as if he knows about the kidnapping, else what can he mean?

He shrugs, turns away. "You must excuse me—"

"No, wait." I gasp. "Did you once know a—a lady—" But my thoughts and tongue halt.

He gives a little bow. "I've known many ladies, my dear, though few as charming as you. Now, please—"

"—a lady," I whisper, "named Hepzibah Heyes?"

'Tis a silly name, I know, and shows my grandmother cared as little for her daughter as Mother cared for me. But it's also a name you don't forget. Arnold's smile fades as his eyes fix on mine.

"Once," he says after a few thuds of my heart. "I knew her once, long ago."

He's too shrewd to say more.

"She was my mother," I tell him.

Still he stands silent, watching me.

"She grew up in Norwich Town," I continue.

"Down by the wharves."

"That's right. You remember her, then."

"Very well. Tetchy little thing, a real fighter."

That was Mother, all right. "Before she died, she told me my father—that I—that the man who raised me wasn't really my father, that—that—" But what can I say? No guarantee Mother was telling the truth, as Uncle Shippen pointed out that day in his parlor. And I daren't mention her note upstairs.

He gives me no help, only studies me with those eyes that miss nothing.

I take a deep breath. The world shrinks to the two of us. "Are you my dad?"

For a moment, I think he'll deny it. And I'm glad. We can go ahead; I can deliver him to General Washington without worry that I'm hanging my own father.

Then he smiles. That smile kept starving men marching on Canada, persuaded militia at Danbury they could stand against Regulars, charmed my mother twenty-four years ago.

"I've suspected as much ever since I met you, Clem. Stared at you so hard that first time I was downright rude, I know. But it bothered me. I was thinking how you looked so much like someone I knew. Couldn't place it, though, and then with the press of business, first one thing, then another, well, wasn't any time to worry over it. But this last month by the fire, it come to me, and one night I almost told you, except Champe happened by on some errand or other—Clem, dear, don't cry. Here, here's my handkerchief."

He hobbles across the room to press it into my hand.

"Clem, forgive me. I must hurry. There'll be plenty of time later—"

"Sir, there's something else." But as I think how I'm about to betray liberty and His Excellency and Nathan—Oh, Nathan! What would you say? What would you do?—I sob harder.

And Champe, what will happen to Champe? I must make Arnold promise first that he'll spare Champe, nor turn him over to the government. But will he honor his word, this man who threw Andre to the hangman?

Then again, Peggy's never been in love with Champe.

I need to tell him. Champe will be here in half an hour; Arnold must escape. "Sir, I—there's something else—"

He pats my shoulder. "Whatever it is, Clem, it must wait. I'm sorry. I need to pack. I'm boarding ship soon as I can get to the harbor."

"Boarding ship?"

"For Virginia. Time to end this war, it's got me trembling for the liberties of America. Reed and his boys, they're taking over the Congress, Clem. If the Continentals win this thing, that'll be the end of our freedom, make no mistake. Worse'n the king ever was, far worse." He shakes his head. "We're going south, gonna win this war and stop the Radicals. We'll pin Greene's troops down there between me and Cornwallis, finish this thing. Sir Harry gave the orders tonight. We're leaving immediately—"

"Leaving? For Virginia? But—but—"

"Go on, Clem, upstairs. Help Peggy get my things together. She's all a-flustered. Oh, and you might want to save this for a better time—our little secret, you understand." He gives me another smile and a wink, too. "Don't know how Peggy will take to having a twenty-one—twenty-two? How old are you?—daughter."

"But—but—sir, you see, Sergeant-Major Champe and I—"

"Don't worry about Champe, Clem. He's going with me."

"He is?"

"I already gave orders to board the troops. He's probably asleep in his berth by now. But I must say, I been having second thoughts about him."

"You—you have?"

He nods. "Don't appreciate the way he's leading you on. No daughter of mine oughta be kept waiting by a man doesn't know his own mind. What's he think, Clem—he's going to find someone smarter than you? More sympathetic?"

"I, ah, well, sir—he, ah—"

"Now go on, Clem. Go help Peggy. Plenty of time for us to have a father-daughter talk later, after the war. You'll make your home with us, won't you?"

"Well, I—I—"

"At least think about it, Clem."

Somehow I got to my feet and out of there.

I don't remember how I passed the next half-hour. Maybe I helped Peggy pack, or maybe I went to the kitchen to scrape together a late supper for them. I do remember that on the stroke of midnight, Arnold hobbled to the garden while I leaned against the icy windowpane in the back parlor and shivered and watched. As usual, he opened the door of the necessary and disappeared inside. As usual, no agents ripped that door from its hinges, nor tied nor gagged him. As usual, when he reappeared, he glanced skyward, admiring the stars, before clumping back to the house.

Some moments later, he cajoled Peggy and his bags into the carriage and came to hear my answer to his invitation. I made some excuse about needing time to think things through. 'Twasn't every day a lady found out her father was one of history's greatest heroes, and anyway, unless he settled close by here, I'd be homesick so far from Philadelphia and New York. He pressed some money on me—blood money, I couldn't help thinking, bought with Nathan's life and Andre's and the men he'd tried to sell with West Point—and told me to write him down south.

"War'll be over soon, Clem, you'll see, and you'll be making your home with us then. Count on it." He bent to kiss my forehead. "You got some half-brothers to meet. And my sister, your Aunt Hannah. You'll love each other."

Then he hurried outside to Peggy.

I never saw either of them again.

Epilogue

I never saw Sergeant-Major Champe again, either. He sailed to Virginia with the rest of Arnold's company, just as Arnold said. Once they landed, he deserted and made for Light Horse Harry's regiment, though it took him till May of 1781 to find them, way down in the Carolinas. There he got a hearty welcome before His Excellency himself discharged him, for 'twas too risky for Champe to keep soldiering. Had the Redcoats captured him, they wouldn't hang him for spying, for they never knew about that. But they did think him a soldier in Arnold's American Legion, so he'd have hanged for desertion if they didn't whip him to death first.

As for my father (you ought to see my hand shake as I write that, still disbelieving, still trying to decide whether that kind rascal, that fierce lover of liberty who betrayed his country, was the best or worst of men, still hoping the whole thing's a hoax or a nightmare, that his design in going over to the Redcoats was only to deceive them into giving him a command where he could better serve America by betraying our enemies)—as for my father, he was luckier than a cat with nine lives when it come to his treason.

This man who Fate pummeled all the long way from Cambridge to Quebec, whose fortune throughout the war got worse and worse, of a sudden conquered his curse. Not only did he fly free as the wind, but remember, they schemed for a year and a half, and all sorts of people in on it, yet no one breathed a word. You wouldn't expect Clinton or Andre to, of course, nor Arnold nor Peggy, either. But there was Admiral Sir George Rodney, arrived September 14th in New York Bay from the West

Indies with a fleet bigger than the French one. They must needs tell him
so the ships could be ready to sail up Hudson's River and attack West
Point once Andre and Arnold consummated the deal. Seems incredible that none of our spies got wind of that. And there were messengers
involved here, running the enciphered letters back and forth, three or
four men who might've stopped in a tavern any night and let slip how
important they were, and you don't believe it, why here's a letter, see, in
cipher, it's from General Arnold, that's right, *the* General Arnold, he's
gonna go over—well, never mind, you wouldn't credit it anyway... From
there, would have been a short step to the provost gaol and a talk with
Washington's aides.

But nothing like that happened. My father's luck held even when
His Excellency made another try at seizing him.

Once Arnold landed in Virginia, Washington sent 1200 troops
from his army down there, marching under La Fayette. He ordered the
marquis to execute my father soon as he captured him—if he did.

He didn't, but this started a game where the government sent a
couple of detachments to answer ours, and we sent some more, and all
of them marching towards a peninsula called Yorktown.

Then Major Allan McLane, the same as managed the diversion
during the Meschianza, noticed that Arnold rode out to the shore of
the Chesapeake Bay every morning. 'Twould be easy, catching him, or
so McLane thought. He laid his plans according. He hadn't reckoned
on enemy warships sailing up the Bay and anchoring there while he lay
waiting, and all by mistake, too. Turns out those ships were lost: two
days later, they rejoined their fleet. But by then, McLane was detailed
to other duties.

With a fraction of my father's luck, Nathan might have lived to be
an old man.

I'm old myself now, with these deeds long done and the passions they
roused quiet and rusty, all but my love for Nathan. Him I see bright as
sunlight across the years, shining and young and unconquerable, blue
eyes flashing as he faces down tyranny. Expect I'll be joining him soon,
him and Washington and the others who, for freedom's sake, gave
everything they had, lives and fortunes and sacred honor. I wonder will
we gather round a campfire in that next world, and tell our tales, and
laugh and weep together.

Seems like I was a different person then, when I was living those tales, for the rest of my life's been uneventful. I never did marry and don't regret it, neither; beside Nathan, none could satisfy me. Instead, I made my way cooking in one tavern or another. End of the day, I'd think back on things and sometimes long till the tears came for those days and sometimes just thank the good Lord He put me down here when and where He did. I wouldn't have missed our Revolution for the world.

The war ended at last, and we had us a new country, a free one—or so we thought. But we'd no sooner signed that treaty in Paris than Joseph Reed reared his head. Oh, not the one that devilled my father. Truth to tell, I don't rightly know what happened to that Reed, think he died just before or after the war finished. But there's thousands, maybe millions, of Joseph Reeds, and they all stepped forward now, when we were recovering from eight years of battles and bloodshed. You've seen the kind: think they know best, want to tell the rest of us how to live, and if we don't hearken, they'll bring government's power against us. All those Reeds hated our freedom, and our Articles of Confederation that stripped rulers of their power, on account of Reeds like laws, and plenty of 'em, that make everyone mind them.

So the Reeds clamored for a stronger government until they got it, and a Constitution, too. Reeds were thick at the convention that wrote this Constitution. It provided the most tyrannical power of all, the one we'd fought hardest with our Revolution: taxation.

'Twas a sad day when they ratified that paper, but all I did was stir my stews and roast my meats. The time when I could have made a difference had passed.

And so the years went, and then the century itself, taking General—I mean, President Washington with them. He was born in and fitted perfectly to other times, now gone forever, and though I grieved plenty to think of that stalwart, courageous gentleman in the grave, 'twas a mercy too. Reckon he'd be shamed could he see what the country's about now, how it scorns liberty.

My father died a couple of years later, in England, aged sixty. Likely 'twas his years of campaigning, the demands he'd laid on his body, the starving and wounds and exposure, that done it. But the romantics out there blame his broken heart, for Americans despised him the rest of his life, and never mind all the good he did us. Still do, and it's twenty years since he died. British never liked him much, either.

Peggy soon followed, stricken with the cancer when she was forty-four or thereabouts. 'Twas her female parts it attacked, which seems a justice harsh but pure. Here's a lady proud of her hold over men, brought to the grave by the femininity that was her glory.

To this day, I can't decide whether I should love Arnold for what he did or loathe him for what he tried to do. With Peggy, there's no such problem. She was beautiful, the most beautiful woman ever, I warrant, but she was evil, too.

'Tis one of the mysteries I ponder now, why the Lord suffers the wicked to flourish, why He lets them take the good and the innocent and corrupt them or string them up from the nearest tree. Why should Peggy have suborned my father and escape justice, yet Nathan pay so dear? I suppose I might as well ask why the sun rises in the east or water flows downhill.

Such thoughts have occupied me all day, as happens whenever I see something in *The Evening Post* as I done last night: "Monday, August 13, 1821. The following account of the disinterring the remains of Major Andre was handed us by an eye witness..."

I dropped the paper, for of a sudden, I was back in Philadelphia, a skinny girl of twenty-two, watching a British captain flirt with my breathtaking cousin, seeing the light on his face and his sparkling eyes, the life laughing in him. Another moment and I'm standing in the cool of an October morning, honeysuckle strong in the air, a Continental fife playing, and Ben Tallmadge stumbling past while a clear, high voice compliments the music...

I never did read the report and wouldn't have learned about Andre's remains but for Daisy coming by this morning. You remember her: the servant who cooked with me for the Meschianza. She and her husband used the gold Andre'd paid them towards buying their freedom; the rest of the price come from the laundry they took in. Once freed, they kept taking in laundry to buy their children, and Daisy's sister, and then their cousins, and by now, I reckon they've freed more Africans than the state legislatures that are banning such sin. Daisy and Sam have been washing my laundry for years, not because I can't myself, even now, for at sixty-five I'm still spry, but because I want to help ransom their family, and they won't take money from me outright.

"No charity, huh-uh," Daisy said that first summer that she and Sam removed to New York City, what with it being the new capital and plenty of congressmen needing their linen cleaned. "We's free now, Miss Clem, free as you, and proud, and us proud folks works. We don't take charity. Now, you wanting someone to do your laundry, or isn't you?"

Daisy about worships Andre's memory, figuring it's him as set her free. I gave up trying to make her see sense about this—finally realized I was wasting my breath arguing that she and Sam earned every shilling he give them, all the work they did cooking that week.

"Worked hard all my life," she'd say, "and Massa never give me nothin' but a scoldin' for it."

Anyway, 'twas Daisy as asked this morning whether I'd heard about "our major," as she calls him. "They dug up his grave there. Some men come all the way from England a-purpose, went up that hill where they hanged him and dug him up." She clucked. "Them British is crazy, messing with dead persons that way. Now, our major isn't the kind to haunt a body, but still, seems like asking for trouble, don't it?"

"Why'd they do it?"

"Say they gonna take him over there to their own country, bury him in some big old church with a monu—mona—a big old piece of marble over him. Just imagine! Our major!"

I wonder what a certain intelligencer thinks about it. For sure, he still grieves over Andre. I know because I heard a story couple of years ago about the Honorable Benjamin Tallmadge, Congressman from Connecticut. Seems David Williams, John Paulding, and Isaac Van Wart, Skinners who captured a spy one parched September day, begged Congress for an increase in their pensions. Nothing unusual there—veterans who spent their youth fighting for liberty now besiege the Congress in their old age, urging it to steal our money on their behalf. So the Skinners brought their petition, arguing that they deserved more than $200 per annum because without them, Arnold and Andre might have succeeded. Tallmadge rose to object. He must have done a fine job of it, because Congress, which usually grants such increases, denied these.

Daisy bundles my laundry into her sack: a tablecloth I haven't used since the last time she washed it, a skirt stained with celery sauce, my linen of the last fortnight. I count out her wage from my pocketbook. 'Tis double-sided, this pocketbook, dirty and faded after all this time, its legend missing letters so that "Saratoga" reads "Sa a oga" and "Genl" has lost its curious "G." It caught up with me two years after Arnold died, with a father's loving note tucked inside. There was naught of West Point nor treason in that note, so I'll say no more about it, for 'twould interest none but me. But the pocketbook! Sometimes I shiver to touch it, born as it was during those evenings around the hearth. Fingering its stitches, I hear his stories again, feel the warmth of the fire, the strength of his courage and ideals, see the shadows flickering on his wounded leg. 'Tis my one memento of those anxious, stormy, better days.

I hand Daisy some coins, and she thanks me and says, "'Til next time, then, Miss Clem." We hug before she leaves. She's grown stouter and jollier with freedom and the fleeing years, and her hugs are pure pleasure, all softness and joy.

I fetch the beans that need snapping and repair outside, to the big maple that shades my house. It's a hot day, but tolerable here in the shadows with a breeze rustling the leaves. The memories are strong on me, so strong it almost seems everyone's here, as young and dashing and vibrant as during the war: Nathanael and Caty Greene, and Lif, and Asa whistling Sally's song, and La Fayette, and King Alex, nose high in the air as ever, and His Excellency, and Champe with Flash snarling at him, and Ben, dear Ben, and my father, flourishing his sword, the glory of Saratoga flaming round him while Peggy's an undreamed nightmare.

And Nathan. Always Nathan....

Author's Note

If Major General Benedict Arnold had died of his wounds at Saratoga, he would have been the Revolution's greatest hero after Washington, his treason unthought of and unthinkable. As it is, one of history's most baffling questions concerns his change of allegiance and attempted betrayal of West Point.

Baffling, that is, until we consider something never discussed in the extensive, and usually hostile, oeuvre on Benedict Arnold: his fierce devotion to human liberty. Consistently and constantly, in word and deed, General Arnold proved himself committed to freedom, whatever the labels, forms of government, or propaganda its enemies—and proponents—advanced.

But this satisfactory, obvious and truthful explanation didn't serve the Radical Patriots' agenda. Ergo, they slandered their nemesis with lies and grotesque exaggeration. Their most outrageous falsehood, which historians have echoed ever since, blamed General Arnold's treason on greed.

According to the Radicals, Arnold was the greediest man in America—perhaps even the world and all history. He blithely, callously planned to make his fortune on the Patriots' ruin.

But the facts gainsay such whoppers. First and most tellingly, Arnold lost money—lots of it—by switching sides. And knew he would, too. He paid dearly for his principles.

Second, Arnold was guilty all his life of personal extravagance and even more extravagant generosity. Unless he was campaigning, he lived as high as he could—not exactly a miser's *modus operandi*.

Then there's his liberality to friends and causes. Arnold's financing of various campaigns or parts thereof, the £1000 he gave Colonel John Lamb, the money he pressed on such distressed soldiers as the feverish John Henry, his assistance to Joseph Warren's children, and many more such instances testify to a munificent, humane, and immensely admirable spirit.

Third, all but one of the allegations about Arnold's supposed avarice post-date the treason: before 1780, only the somewhat deranged John Brown in his absurd pamphlet mentioned a trait that everyone should have noticed if it were as outsized as claimed. And all those allegations after the treason originate with the Radical Patriots. Like most propagandists, they insisted on their lie, publishing it over and over, until Americans unquestioningly believed it. We can excuse Arnold's contemporaries for such gullibility: passions were high, the war preoccupied them so that time for analysis was scarce, the Radicals were as influential as they were deceitful, and Arnold's treason couldn't have come at a worse time. But why have later generations swallowed the Radicals' hogwash?

Meanwhile, many people have tacitly admitted their dissatisfaction with the Radicals' nonsense by offering other motives. And at least they grounded these in fact: General Arnold's obsessive love for Peggy Shippen, who was a Loyalist by association (as Judge Shippen's daughter and as the sweetheart of the British Army); his suspicions of the Catholic French, which most Revolutionary Americans shared; and the utterly disgraceful abuse he suffered from the Continental Congress. These probably all played a part. But chiefly responsible was Arnold's enthusiasm for freedom and his growing suspicions that the Revolution had not only abandoned but was actually inimical to that ideal.

The Radical Patriots are a seriously slighted organization. Though historians ignore them, they were a recognized political party of tremendous influence at the time, equivalent to modern Progressives. Yet an exceedingly small number of books even acknowledge their existence, and then usually with lowercase letters ("Some of the more radical patriots in Philadelphia..."). To my knowledge, only one author devotes a monograph to them, and he bluntly confessed himself a Marxist who lauded both the Radicals and their goals.

I began my research on Arnold somewhat ignorant of his heroism and completely ignorant of the Radicals. I was determined to show

Arnold for a traitor and a fool. Within a few months, my opinion of him had changed completely, based on the evidence. Certainly, he was flawed, as are we all. But he also owned such courage, magnanimity, and conviction as bless few people.

Throughout this novel, I have endeavored to adhere to history and fact, where they are known, even to lifting dialogue directly from eighteenth-century letters and diaries. Arnold and Andre, for instance, often speak passages from their respective correspondence. Sometimes, an anonymous or lesser-known writer has graciously lent himself to this technique as well: someone else wrote Tallmadge's words about ladies who relate anecdotes of their day's work and the pretty sayings of the children they know. In a few cases, I borrowed a quote from one character for another. Andre's description of the Continentals' determination—they "fight, get beat, rise and fight again"—was, of course, General Nathanael Greene's well-known prescription for his successful southern campaign.

However, in many instances, I elided or changed details. I had to: the first draft of this novel weighed in at almost thrice the current one's length. This shortening and telescoping have simplified the incredibly complex events in which Arnold participated as well as the sophisticated character of Arnold himself; they also prevented my exploring such issues as the politics that repeatedly snared him, or the enemies who not only never forgot their envy of him but who resurfaced many times in his life. (David Wooster, for example, prohibited Arnold's militia from marching to Massachusetts' aid during the earliest days of the war; Wooster pops up again in Canada and at Danbury, too. I included Wooster in my first draft. He and many other such characters didn't survive the second rewrite.)

To cite another instance of abbreviation, Arnold learned of Margaret's death later than I portray. His men at Ticonderoga mutinied when the Congress dismissed their commander and them without back pay, and they locked Arnold in a cabin aboard ship lest he quell them. Thereafter, he started for home, visiting friends, including General Philip Schuyler, along the way. He was probably *en route* when he learned of Margaret's death.

Nor is there any documentary evidence for Peggy Shippen Arnold's affair with John Andre. The Shippens would have destroyed whatever correspondence the two shared for fear of reprisals in the wake of the treason, and other testimonies to their relationship—except that offered by tradition, which has the ravishing Peggy and gallant Andre deliriously in love—are ambiguous. I accepted some of the tradition for these reasons: John Andre was a known ladies' man; Arnold's abandonment of him, verging on sabotage, after their clandestine meeting is puzzling unless motivated by intense hatred (occasioned by jealousy?) since his treason's success was knit to Andre's fate; and Peggy's children discovered a locket with Andre's hair among her effects at her death (supposedly, she hid it from General Arnold throughout their wedded life).

That marriage may or may not have been empty and bitter. If Peggy loved her husband, it's surpassingly odd that she chose to join her parents rather than Arnold, who was crippled and in desperate need of a wife's care and comfort, after discovery of the plot against West Point. Yet she had no sooner reached Philadelphia than Pennsylvania's Supreme Executive Council began trying to exile her. And once again, Peggy reacted very strangely for a loving wife: when her father pleaded with the Council for mercy, she not only cooperated rather than trying to dissuade him, she even pledged not to write Arnold and to surrender whatever letters she received from him to the authorities. We are blasé about such heartbreaking disloyalty. But in the eighteenth century, Peggy's betrayal would have shocked, and deeply: Americans considered married couples truly one flesh. Peggy's groveling went for naught, anyway, when the Council ordered her to New York. More evidence of the marriage's misery comes from complaints Peggy wrote in later years to her father and siblings.

On the other hand, Peggy and Arnold frequently expressed their love in their correspondence with each other. And she was genuinely distressed whenever Arnold's adventures threatened his life. So perhaps she cared more than even she realized.

The Treaty of Paris in 1783 did not end General Arnold's swashbuckling adventures. He and Peggy moved to England, then back to North America, settling in Canada, and finally to England once more. Money was a constant problem, especially since Arnold received very little reward for his treason, less than $1,000,000 in today's terms. Stacked against the property he thereby forfeited, such as Mount Pleasant, and the debts from Congress he would never collect, that was paltry indeed. Even Ben Franklin testified to the treason's scant recompense with his famous quip: "Judas sold only one man, Arnold 3,000,000. Judas got for his one man 30 pieces of silver, Arnold not a halfpenny a head. A miserable bargainer."

Arnold's family fared better. He secured a commission for each of his sons in the British Army, which meant they received a pension for life, even if they never donned a uniform. And Peggy's beauty so impressed Queen Charlotte when the Arnolds were introduced at Court that Her Majesty established a pension for Peggy from her privy purse (*i.e.*, she compelled British taxpayers to support a woman she found intriguing).

Arnold offered his services to the king during the Napoleonic Wars but received no command. Nevertheless, he bought a ship and traded in the Caribbean, sharing the intelligence he thereby gleaned with the Crown. At one point, he sailed towards an island that had recently, and unbeknownst to him, passed from the British to the French. He discovered the change too late and tried to bluff his way through, representing himself as an American merchant—alias John Anderson, poignantly enough—but rulers there recognized him and imprisoned him as a spy. Condemned to hang, he made his escape the evening before by bribing his guards and slipping into a rowboat they provided. He paddled with his hands to a British frigate in the bay, through shark-infested waters, with a French boat chasing him.

Arnold died June 14, 1801. He left a number of debts, which Peggy repaid "to the last spoon," as she put it, before her death three years later, on August 24. Some people hated her for marrying a traitor; many pitied her. But few thought her guilty of treason: eighteenth-century mores considered well-born ladies of legendary beauty too innocent for such sordidness as espionage. Only the discovery and publication of Sir Henry Clinton's papers in the 1940s established Peggy's complicity. It further testifies to Benedict Arnold's character that he never refuted the notion of his beloved wife's marrying a monster, preferring to bear the public's censure himself.

Benjamin Tallmadge outlived them both. In addition to his stint in Congress, he invested in the Ohio Company of Associates, which settled parts of Connecticut's Western Reserve (there is a Tallmadge, Ohio, to this day). He was married twice, first to Mary Floyd, daughter of William Floyd, one of New York's signers of the Declaration, and, after her death, to a woman much younger than he. Late in life he wrote his memoirs at his children's request. Curiously, he doesn't mention his dear friend Nathan Hale, but he describes Major Andre's capture, imprisonment and death in detail.

Finally, Clem Shippen is fictional. General Arnold did father an illegitimate child, but it was a son, and he was born after the Revolution, in Canada. (Arnold provided for him in his will, more evidence of the general's magnanimity as bastards were seldom acknowledged.)

Clem's wholehearted devotion to liberty, like General Arnold's, was typical of those times.

Acknowledgments

Thanks to Vaughn Kraft, Ginny Schilling, Dalwyn Merck, Vilma Oman and Rick Burner.

Halestorm
Becky Akers

Itching to know more about the dashing young hero whose courageous death inspired Clem Shippen? Then treat yourself to a copy of *Halestorm*—

Handsome, brilliant, memorable: he was the wrong man for the wrong assignment. No wonder Nathan Hale's first mission behind enemy lines was also his last. But from his failure came the hope and determination that birthed a new nation.

Early death ought to be enough disaster for any guy, but Nathan also has a spirited sweetheart, a penchant for puns—and a deadly rival for his lady's hand.

Filled with love and conflict, murder and betrayal, *Halestorm* stirs our deepest emotions as it transports readers to the exotic world of Revolutionary America and asks, "What would you choose: love, honor, or freedom?"

Critics love Halestorm

"...a triumph of literary artistry and historical research..."
— *American Daily Herald*

Better yet, so do readers:

"I have never been so moved by a book in my life. This was so well written and engrossing that I could not put it down. I even cancelled dinner with a dear friend. I will be urging everyone to read Halestorm *... This book will stay with you long after the final page is read. I am sure of that. It was incredible. Heartbreaking, but incredible."*

"The author weaved known facts with likely possibilities to create a masterpiece."

"Wow! Very poignant and moving story. It reads like a mini-series or made-for-TV movie. It is a love story, war story, a tale of a hero..."

"Loved this story!! A wonderful yarn of fiction spun from the life of a barely known American Hero. It was full of wild speculation, forbidden love, vengeful hate & best of all true integrity & honor."

"Even knowing how it had to end I couldn't help but cry when I got there. The stirring moment of his death, the way it was written...it was beautiful & moving. It embodied the best of the American Spirit, the love of liberty & freedom that was our foundation. EVERYONE should read this!!"

98433715R00275

Made in the USA
Middletown, DE
09 November 2018